darkest hour

ALSO BY MARK CHADBOURN

Underground
Nocturne
The Eternal
Scissorman

The Age of Misrule:
Book One: World's End

Non-fiction

Testimony

darkest hour

book two of the age of misrule

MARK
CHADBOURN

VICTOR GOLLANCZ

LONDON

This edition published in Great Britain in 2000 by

Victor Gollancz
An imprint of Orion Books Ltd
Orion House, 5 Upper St Martin's Lane, London WC2H 9EA

To receive information on the Millennium list, e-mail us at:
smy@orionbooks.co.uk

A CIP catalogue record for this book is available
from the British Library

ISBN 0 575 069031

Typeset at The Spartan Press Ltd,
Lymington, Hants
Printed in Great Britain by
Clays Ltd, St Ives plc

Acknowledgements

Roman Camp Country House, Callander;
The Point Hotel, Edinburgh;
Kingsmills Hotel, Inverness;
Warren Ellis

For information about the author and his work:
http://www.markchadbourn.com

contents

chronicles

The wind blows harshly through the cloisters; to my fancy, it brings with it the distant cries of anguish and despair that echo now around our land. These are indeed dark times. Here, beneath the magnificent vaulted roof of Salisbury Cathedral, a few of us struggle to keep the candle of humanity's faith alight; the last outpost of Christianity in a world grown Godless through too many gods. Sometimes even my own faith grows dim, though I joined the church more than thirty years ago. The old certainties have been blown away by that cold wind. Simply to believe in the one, pure thing in a time of everyday wonders and miracles is almost too much. For why should anyone believe in one thing when it is possible to believe in everything? But I struggle and I strive, and I continue the ministry that I have held all my adult life. Now, more than ever, I have a purpose. The Lord, perhaps, will grant me the strength to see Him clearly once more and permit me to spread His word across the land as my antecedents did in the first Dark Age.

It seems that in my blackest moments I draw most comfort not from contemplation of the divine, but through an examination of humanity. And in those times I like to turn my thoughts to the five who set out to be the saviours of our race, not through any desire for glory, but simply to serve the greater good; in their example we see humanity in its most glorious essence, forged through hardship and conflict.

The first of the five was Jack Churchill, an archaeologist, known to his friends as Church. A good man in many ways, but one damaged by life. For two years he had struggled with the blackest of emotions that accompanied the suicide of his girlfriend Marianne: grief, certainly, but mainly guilt that he had somehow been complicit in his inability to recognise whatever internal turmoil she had been experiencing that had driven her to such a

I

terrible act. The second of the five was Ruth Gallagher, a lawyer, introspective and intelligent, given to controlling her emotions. She felt trapped in a career she found soulless, but which had been the wish of her father who had died of a heart attack soon after his brother had been murdered.

The two of them met one misty February morning just before dawn, underneath Albert Bridge on the banks of the Thames in London, where they witnessed an act of terrible ferocity: the murder of Maurice Gibbons, a Ministry of Defence civil servant, by a giant of a man whose face seemed to melt and change. Whatever it became was too awful for their minds to comprehend and they both fell unconscious.

Over the following days, the repressed memory of the sight assailed their subconscious, driving them to the edge of despair, forcing them to join forces to uncover the truth of what they had seen. And what they found when they probed into the hidden areas of their minds was at first too much to believe: it appeared that the figure had transformed into a monstrous, demonic being. Yet when they encountered Kraicow, an elderly, bedridden artist, their worst fears were confirmed, for Kraicow, too, had seen the creature.

During this period of personal upheaval, the world seemed to have been turned on its head. From all over the country came reports of bizarre supernatural acts, spontaneous miracles, wonders and terrors, discounted or jeered at by the cynical media. If only we all could have recognised those first signs then, we might have been able to prepare ourselves for what was to come. The culmination of this outbreak of the unknown, for Church at least, was the manifestation late one night of his dead girlfriend's spirit.

It was a turning point for this young man who was filled with so much darkness: a chance, possibly, to find the answer to all the questions that had tormented him. When he received a message over the Internet with a cryptic comment about 'Marianne' from a woman purporting to have an insight into the strange events, he felt driven to investigate further. And so the external crisis and his own personal troubles converged.

A meeting was arranged with the woman, Laura DuSantiago, in the west of the land, and Ruth accompanied him. Yet they had barely passed beyond London's city limits when the dark forces moved against them. At a service station an attempt was made to kidnap Ruth by another face-changing creature much like the one they had seen that night they came together. With the help of a mysterious, elderly wanderer named Tom, Ruth was rescued, but by then it was impossible to deny that they had become targets, although they knew not of whom – or what.

Tom joined them on their journey. He was a fellow who kept his secrets hard inside him, and although he was not one of the five, his role in the epochal events that were fast approaching was pivotal.

As night fell, the Evil abroad increased its attempt to prevent the five coming together. While heading west along the M4, a Fabulous Beast soared down from the black sky, its scaled body glittering in the headlights, blasting fire from its mouth. The motorway became the scene of a terrible conflagration; many died. It was the first of the great slaughters. There was no Saint George to slay the creature; Church, Ruth and Tom could only flee.

Tom, in his wisdom, took them to Stonehenge, which proved a remarkable sanctuary against the attack; there, Church and Ruth were initiated into the ancient mysteries. Tom told of the lifeblood of the earth, the blue fire, long dormant but slowly awakening after the great change that had overtaken us all. Rejuvenating, powerful, the source of all magic, it seared along the lines of force; the age-old sacred sites marked the areas where it was most intense. The Fabulous Beasts were both its symbols and its guardians; the one that attacked them had been briefly corrupted by the power of the forces raised against them. And there, too, Ruth and Church first began to learn of their true destiny as the Brothers and Sisters of Dragons, the spiritual bond that was linked to that earth energy.

They underwent a night of revelation as Tom told of the return of a race of tremendous power and evil which had terrorised the land in the near-forgotten past. The seasons had turned; dark days had come around again.

Deep in the night while they slumbered among those ancient stones, Church woke to discover the spirit of Marianne hovering in the shadows beyond the henge. Though terrible to look upon, she did not talk and she retreated when he approached, but she left behind a mysterious gift – a black rose, known by its Gaelic name, the *Roisin Dubh*. Church's decision to take it as a *memento mori* would prove devastating.

In the light of their experiences, plans were changed and Laura DuSantiago agreed to meet them here, in Salisbury. While they waited for her arrival the great powers grew closer. In the cloisters of this very cathedral, Church encountered the demonic black dog known as Old Shuck; it heralded the unrelenting onset of the Wild Hunt. At the same time, Ruth was haunted by a figure which seemed to change from hag to middle-aged woman to young girl. Any student of folklore would have recognised the archetypes, the mother-maiden-crone of the old religion, but Ruth was unaware it was her destiny calling. And that night in a local pub they crossed paths with a seemingly harmless wanderer by the name of Callow. Loose lips ensured one of the companions would pay a terrible price for that fateful meeting.

The following day they were introduced to Laura DuSantiago, the third of the five, and a woman both secretive and deeply troubled. Scarred on the inside as much as her body was marked by a mother who used her religion to mask her madness, Laura still exhibited a remarkable tenacity and fire but the death of her mother, which she believed to have occurred by her own hand, was the defining aspect of her character.

Laura led the others to an industrial estate on the outskirts of the city where she had experienced something unbelievable. It was one of the fluid spots, as they have come to be known in these strange times; Church and Laura crossed over to the Watchtower which hung in the space between worlds, while Ruth and Tom were left behind to face an attack by the terrifying shape-shifting creatures. In the Watchtower, Church reeled under the onslaught of premonitions – his own death, a city burning – before he came face-to-face with a beautiful woman who had haunted his dreams since he was very young.

She never told him her name, but she did finally shed light on the mysteries that had wrapped tightly around his life. It was an astounding tale of two fantastic races which first came to earth in the dim and distant past; almost *too* fantastic – their supernatural powers were at odds with every notion we had of rationality and logic, but it is a story which, for our sins, we have all since come to know is true. The Celts knew them as the Tuatha Dé Danann, also called the Golden Ones, and the Fomorii, the misshapen, evil Night Walkers. For a period, they opposed each other while the humans watched these gods with tremendous fear. Then, after one final, brutal battle which saw the Fomorii defeated, they and all other supernatural creatures departed the world for their homeland, the place the Celts called T'ir n'a n'Og. The barriers between here and there were supposedly sealed for all time, but some of them still managed to flit between, giving us our legends of fairies. No fairies from a storybook, these, though; they were so alien and unnknowable we could never see their true shapes, just the simple forms our own minds projected on to them to maintain our sanity. They came from a place where everything was fluid in our terms – physical reality, time and, I would aver, morals. They are so far beyond us we must seem like a bacterium to them. Is this a definition of godhood? That is the question that has troubled so many, and that is where I take refuge in my own Faith, for I cannot accept that power without morals is any justification. There must be some sense of right and wrong, good and evil. There must.

But I digress. Church was told the Fomorii had broken the old pact and returned to earth. The Tuatha Dé Danann, the only ones who could possibly oppose them, had been scattered by something called the Wish-Hex; some were trapped, others were temporarily corrupted by the

Fomorii's power; a handful had escaped. The task bestowed upon Church and the other Brothers and Sisters of Dragons was to locate four long-lost mystical items which once belonged to the Tuatha Dé Danann, and to use them to summon the race back from wherever they had been banished. Four talismans: a stone, a sword, a spear and a cauldron, more archetypes branded on human consciousness. And it all had to be done by the feast of Beltane – May Day – or the Tuatha Dé Danann would be lost for ever.

Reluctantly, Church accepted and, with Laura, returned to earth. In the meantime, Ruth had escaped the attack of the Fomorii shapeshifters, but Tom was missing. The three remaining companions set off following the Wayfinder, another mystical artefact which resembled an old lantern lit by a flame of blue earth energy; the flickering light pointed them in the direction of the talismans.

Their first destination was Avebury and its awe-inspiring stone circle. Here they encountered a man known only as the Bone Inspector, an odd fellow who considered himself a guardian of the old sacred sites and keeper of ancient wisdom. His people had once administered their powerful lore to the Celts from the hawthorn groves before they had been driven under-ground by the invading Romans. The Bone Inspector showed them the secret entrance to the place that lies beneath Avebury, where the blue fire is at its most potent, guarded by the oldest of the Fabulous Beasts. And there Laura retrieved the first of the talismans, what had been known to the Celts as the Stone of Fal which supposedly screamed when touched by the true king of the land; much to his consternation, it cried out when it came into contact with Church.

Leaving the Bone Inspector behind, the three companions continued on their quest. It was at this time that we all became aware of the disruption of what we arrogantly believed were the only true rules of existence; technology began to fail intermittently, inexplicably. It was a sign that things truly had changed; nothing could be relied upon any more.

When their car gave out, they set up camp in the countryside outside Bristol, and it was here that Church met a young girl, also called Marianne. For a man given to a brooding outlook, it was understandable that Church was charmed by her bright, optimistic personality, but for some reason that went beyond the concurrence of their names, he also made a psychological connection between this child and his much-missed girl-friend. She gave him her locket which contained a picture of Diana, the Princess of Wales, a tragic figure in whom Marianne had invested much belief and hope.

That night, Ruth also had an encounter which changed her life. In the dark of the woods, she once more came face to face with the triple goddess, the mother-maiden-crone, who called on her for help and gifted her a *familiar*, an owl which was more than an owl.

Church's plans to return the locket to Marianne the following day were thwarted when he found her on the brink of death from a blood clot which had been with her for many months. Church and the others rushed her to the hospital in Bristol for an emergency life-saving operation, but before it could be completed the technology failed once more. It was night, a storm was raging and the hospital was plunged into darkness. After briefly losing consciousness, Church was drawn through the confusion to mysterious bursts of a pure white light. And there he found the young Marianne, dead; but in her last dying moments she had found some power deep inside her that had cured an entire cancer ward. It was a sign that in those first days when everything seemed to be spiralling down into darkness and terror, there was a place for miracles too.

Taking her locket, Church, Ruth and Laura followed the lantern south, pausing at a service station off the M5. Here they were once again terrorised by Old Shuck, and had their first warning that the Wild Hunt was close behind. Continuing on their way to Dartmoor, they sheltered in an isolated pub, a brief moment of calm when they all got to know each other a little better. But that night, led by the monstrous Erl-King, the Wild Hunt attacked in force, slaughtering many of the pub's customers. In desperation, the companions agreed to split up in the hope that one of them would lead the Hunt away so some could escape the carnage. While Ruth and Laura sped away to the east, Church scrambled across the moor on a motorbike, but it was not long before he hurtled into one of the abandoned mineshafts that littered the area.

On a deserted road, Ruth and Laura encountered the fourth of the five, Shavi, a young Asian man, kind, charming, good-looking, thoughtful and intellectual, the epitome of that to which the five aspired. Like the others, he had been touched by death; a bisexual, he had seen his boyfriend murdered by a mysterious assailant in a London street. Since the change in the world he had discovered within him abilities which in earlier times would have led to him being considered a shaman.

They had barely exchanged greetings before the Wild Hunt was upon them. Through a desperate night flight, they evaded the Hunt's grasp only because dawn arose, the supernatural creatures bound by some unknown rules to retire at first light. And then they found themselves in Glastonbury, a site of such religious significance, both to my own beliefs and whatever spirit manifested itself in the earth energy (perhaps the same?), that it had become a mystical haven where the Fomorii could not exert their influence.

Church, meanwhile, awoke in chains, the prisoner of the Fomorii in an abandoned mine far beneath Dartmoor. With him in his cell was the fifth of the five, Ryan Veitch, a young, physically powerful man from South London who had been dragged into a life of petty crime from an early age. Veitch's body was covered in tattoos, depicting many of the strange dreams which had troubled him all his life. But what distressed him the most was his accidental murder of a man in a building society robbery which went badly wrong, a man who, it later transpired, turned out to be Ruth Gallagher's uncle, thus throwing them into opposition.

Here Church and Veitch were tortured by a sickly, sadistic, half-breed Fomorii by the name of Calatin. Calatin was the leader of the main Fomorii tribe which achieved ascendancy after the long-ago destruction of the supreme, Evil power which had controlled and shaped their race. This power, as we all soon came to learn, had been known by the Celts as Balor, the one-eyed god of death, but even that description does not do justice to a force that epitomised the ultimate darkness, the ultimate evil, the end of everything. Yet Calatin's path was not clear; there was insurgency within the ranks, and another, smaller tribe, led by a Fomorii sorcerer named Mollecht, challenged for authority. Whichsoever of them destroyed the Brothers and Sisters of Dragons and gained the four talismans would have the upper hand.

In the cells, Church was reunited with Tom, who had been taken prisoner by the Fomorii after the events in Salisbury. With the help of the woman from the Watchtower, the three prisoners escaped and continued on their quest.

In Glastonbury, Ruth, Laura and Shavi followed a trail of clues which eventually brought them to my attention and the secret which I and my peers had guarded for so long: the hiding place of the cauldron talisman, which I knew as the Grail, deep within Glastonbury Tor. That brief meeting with them transformed my life and prepared me for the privations which were to lie ahead; it was obvious, even to me, that they were special, that they, perhaps, were our only hope. They left for the tor with my prayers.

Church, Veitch and Tom made their way slowly across Cornwall, where another manifestation of the dead Marianne made Church realise, for the first time, that she had not taken her own life; she had been murdered. That recognition was a turning point. Eventually they arrived at Tintagel, one of the legendary homes of King Arthur, and here Tom finally revealed Arthur was not a real person, but a symbol of something he called the Pendragon Spirit, the force that was encompassed by the blue fire and which bound the five of them together. The myths and legends were the secret history, he said; a code that was written large across the landscape.

From under Tintagel they took the second of the talismans, the sword.

Barely had they held it in their hands than they fell under attack once more, this time from Mollecht, whose dabbling with the blackest magic had transformed him into a nexus of energy which could only be contained by a constantly swirling murder of crows. Cut off on the bleak promontory, they eventually found themselves tumbling into the raging sea.

It should have meant certain death, but they were reborn from the waves, the first of many resurrections which has served only to cement their reputation as their story became widely known. Their saviour on this occasion was Tom, a man who consistently claimed he could tell no lies, but who rarely volunteered the truth.

His reticence masked both his true worth as a person and his abilities; he had shown before that he was a font of wisdom, but they had no idea he had a smattering of what can only be called magic; an ability to control, if only in small ways, the blue fire. As they fell to the waves, he somehow focused his mind enough to move them along the lines of energy to another powerful node of the earth force.

And so, as Ruth, Laura and Shavi sat atop Glastonbury Tor waiting to seek out the third talisman, they were shocked to see Church, Tom and Veitch fall from the sky nearby, their lungs filled with sea water, on the highest point in the surrounding landlocked countryside.

Thus the five Brothers and Sisters of Dragons assembled for the first time and after entering Glastonbury Tor, they made their initial crossing to the other place, T'ir n'a n'Og, the Land of Always Summer, home of the gods. The third talisman was deep inside a temple guarded by a strange hall of mirrors; the reflections cast by the glass tormented the five with their worst fears, but Church battled through and seized the cauldron. If only I could have been there when they returned to Glastonbury to see the Grail, the manifestation of God's love and power, for the first time in an age. Even though it harks back to a time before Christianity, thus disproving many of the apocryphal stories of the crucifixion, something so wonderful could only have come from God.

But the five were not concerned with such matters; to them it was a tool to save our world. From Glastonbury, the six companions travelled into South Wales to reclaim the final talisman, the Spear of Lugh. Part of it was held in a grove of severed heads on Caldey Island near the resort of Tenby, and the spearhead was hidden underneath Manorbier Castle, which lay on a nearby headland. Once the two were joined, the task appeared to be complete; but of course the Fomorii would not cede victory in that way.

That night the Wild Hunt attacked in earnest. The companions fought bravely, but their strength was nothing compared to the terrible super-natural power ranged against them. Finally, in a valiant act of sacrifice, Ruth launched herself at the Erl-King with the Spear of Lugh, ramming the weapon into his chest. When the two of them disappeared down a hillside into the night the others thought her dead, but Ruth had survived to witness an amazing transformation in the Erl-King. The monstrous form he had adopted as part of the Wild Hunt was just one of his aspects; he was a Golden One, one of the senior entities with an affinity for nature, whom the Celts had named Cernunnos, among many other shifting identities. He had been corrupted and controlled by the Fomorii Wish-Hex, but the Spear had freed him. In gratitude, he offered Ruth his patronage and branded her hand with his seal to mark his support.

With the Wild Hunt departed, the storm was over, and the companions were free to continue their mission, or so they thought. The next morning the others sought provisions, leaving Laura to guard the talismans. She was attacked and left for dead by Callow, whom they had not seen since that night in the Salisbury pub. He had accepted the patronage of the Fomorii; become a quisling, a betrayer of his entire race. He took the talismans and gifted Laura a face scarred by his razor.

Of all the players in this great game, Callow still haunts me the most. I often wonder what motivated him to throw in his lot with creatures so alien and powerful they could have crushed him in an instant. His life had been difficult, certainly, but was that justification enough for him to seek personal gratification at the expense of everyone else on the planet? It seems to me now that Callow was the antithesis of the five Brothers and Sisters of Dragons. Faced with hardship, they gave of themselves selflessly. Faced with the same choice, Callow simply did what he could for himself. There we have it, the best and worst of humanity given flesh.

With Laura on the brink of death, the others had no choice but to take her with them in pursuit of Callow. They raced across country and prepared to head him off in the Lake District, where the first of the great betrayals took place. And of all people, the betrayer was Tom, although he was not truly to blame. While a prisoner of the Fomorii, they had inserted a Caraprix into his head; these, as we have all since become horribly aware, are small, shapeshifting creatures with which both the Fomorii and the Tuatha Dé Danann have some strange relationship. In Tom's case, it attached itself to his brain and controlled his actions, forcing him to lead the others into the hands of Calatin; all, that is, except Ruth, who escaped. Encountering a wise woman, she was shown her destiny as a controller of the powerful forces which came from the moonlit realm of the triple goddess. Within hours she had once more proved her remarkable worth by rescuing the others while Mollect and Calatin's tribes foolishly fought over their prisoners. With the talismans once more in their possession, they fled for Scotland.

But they had another problem. Only Tom knew how to use the talismans to summon the Tuatha Dé Danann and he was still under the control of the Caraprix. While Laura grew closer and closer to death, Tom still had enough free will to direct them to another fluid spot where they could cross over to the Far Lands, and there they met Ogma, keeper of wisdom, one of the few Golden Ones to escape the Wish-Hex. Using the medical lore he had learned from the god the Celts called Dian Cecht, he removed the Caraprix from Tom's head and cured Laura. Here the companions also learned of the Fomorii's true aim: to bring back Balor and thereby damn us all. Tom, too, had a revelation which shocked them all: his real identity was Thomas Learmont, a thirteenth-century landowner who became known as that famous figure of Scottish mythology, Thomas the Rhymer, after he fell through into the land of Faerie and was given mystical powers by the Queen of Faerie herself, or so the old legends said. Only the reality had been much harsher than the myth. After finding himself in T'ir n'a n'Og, Thomas had been subjected to the torments and wonders of the Tuatha Dé Danann, a race so far beyond us they barely noticed the suffering they were inflicting. What is understood is that he was significantly changed by his ordeal, both psychologically and physically. He received the gift of prophecy and his long life was attributable to his repeated stays in that other world where time does not flow constantly.

There was a brief time for refreshment and revitalisation which also allowed Church and Laura to consummate their long-simmering affection and then the companions returned for the summoning, which was to take place at Dunvegan Castle on the Isle of Skye.

By the strange warping of time which takes place in the Far Lands, they arrived back on the day of their deadline, the feast of Beltane. As they headed towards the Kyle of Lochalsh for the crossing to Skye, they passed what resembled a mediaeval battlefield, slick with blood where numerous soldiers had been butchered, obviously in final battle with the Fomorii. When they arrived at the Kyle of Lochalsh, the place was in flames, all the inhabitants dead. The Fomorii had massed just across the straits on the shores of Skye, an impenetrable barrier between the companions and Dunvegan.

The only option was to take a boat and attempt to sail around Skye to the castle on the north-west coast, but the waters were guarded by a ferocious sea serpent which could only be controlled by Shavi's shamanistic abilities; the effort, however, scarred his mind.

At Dunvegan, they left him in the boat while Ruth, Laura and Tom went to summon the Tuatha Dé Danann. Church and Veitch were despatched to another fluid place known as the Fairy Bridge to at least try to delay any

Fomorii attack. None of the companions truly realised how devious the enemy were; they had sown the seeds of their plan long in advance. The *Roisin Dubh* given to Church by Marianne's spirit was Fomorii in origin; it was the Kiss of Frost, a subtle force which gradually corrupted the holder, and Marianne, his great love, had had her spirit imprisoned and tormented by the Fomorii and used by them to manipulate him. In a battle with Calatin, Church was slain, as had been foretold in the Watchtower.

But in this terrible new world, death was not the end. The others had succeeded in freeing the Tuatha Dé Danann who rushed to the bridge, driving the Fomorii away. The Cauldron of Dagda, the wondrous Grail, was brought to Church's lips and its tremendous power gave him back his life. Reborn into the world – I shy away from saying *resurrected* although I wonder in years to come how this event will be seen – Church was changed in a fundamental way; some essence of the Tuatha Dé Danann had been instilled in him by the contact with the Grail, but he also still bore the corruption of the Fomorii, the light and the dark fighting within him.

Then came the bitterest blow of all. Because of Church's own weakness in allowing the Fomorii corruption into his life, the Tuatha Dé Danann refused to help. Worse, the companions discovered the ones they had counted on as saviours were as devious and amoral as the foe they faced. The Tuatha Dé Danann revealed their own plans had been put into effect many years ago; the Brothers and Sisters of Dragons had been manipulated throughout their lives, secretly, from beyond the barrier. To bring the Pendragon Spirit to the fore in force enough for the companions to help the Tuatha Dé Danann they all had to experience death. And so the Tuatha Dé Danann had controlled an agent: to murder Marianne; to slay Shavi's boyfriend; to kill Laura's mother; and they manipulated Veitch into killing Ruth's uncle, which led to the death of her father. That their entire lives had been condemned at the whim of a higher power was a revelation of such abject heartlessness, it almost destroyed the five. The fact that they survived is a testament to their enduring spirit which gives me so much comfort and hope in these dark times.

And so the Tuatha Dé Danann were loose in the world, untrammelled by rules, free to torment and destroy creatures they considered less than nothing. And the companions, in their despair, feared they had helped bring about that which they had attempted to stop: the destruction of everything we had built here on Earth.

But life goes on, and hope always burns, and the companions, as we all know, did not give up. Forged by their experiences, they grew closer together, seeking strength in their very frail humanity.

Not even the radio announcement of martial law and the Government's tacit admission of impotence in the face of such unknown power could deter them. The Government, of course, had known all along what was happening; not exactly, I am sure, but certainly enough to convince them to stifle any media reports of the growing crisis. And so the people were left in the dark until the last, worst moment.

But I digress once again. This is not a story about politicians or soldiers, it is about everything that is good about the human soul. About hope, and faith, and a quest for meaning in a world floundering in darkness. Perhaps it will shine a light that illuminates the way ahead. New legends for a new age.

But now my eyes grow weak. Too much writing by flickering candle flame has taken its toll, and I dream of the time when we took for granted a burning light bulb in every home. Yet there is much of the story still to tell: great battles, great loves, terror and wonder, intrigue and betrayal, sacrifice and death. But most of all, about what it means to be human.

James
Watchman
Salisbury Cathedral
Year One NDA (New Dark Age)

a prologue

life during wartime

May 2, 8 a.m.; above the English Channel:

'Somebody must have some idea what's going on.' Justin Fallow fiddled uncomfortably with the miniature spirit bottles on his tray as he watched the dismal expressions sported by the air stewardesses. It was amazing how little fluctuations in the smooth-running of life were more disturbing than the big shocks. Those looks were enough to tell him something fundamental had changed; he had never seen any of them without those perfectly balanced smiles of pearly teeth contained by glossy red lipstick.

'I wouldn't lose any sleep over it. Everything will be back to normal in a few days.' Colin Irvine stared vacuously out of the window at the fluffy white clouds. The reflection showed a craggy face and hollow cheeks that seemed older than his years. The trip to Paris had been better than expected; the business side tied up quickly, then two days of good food and fine wine, and one brisk night at a brothel. His head still felt fuzzy from the over-indulgence and he would be happier if Justin shut up at least once before the plane landed.

'Well, I wish I had your optimism.' Fallow's public school accent was blurred by the alcohol and he was talking too loudly. He flicked back the fringe that kept falling over his eyes and snapped his chubby fingers to attract the attention of one of the stewardesses. 'Over here, please. Another vodka.'

'I like a drink as much as the next man, but I don't know how you can get through that lot at breakfast,' Irvine said, without taking his gaze away from the clouds.

Fallow slapped his belly. 'Constitution of a horse, old chap.' When the vodka arrived, he brushed the plastic glass to one side and gulped it straight from the bottle.

13

'Steady on, eh?' Irvine allowed himself a glance of distaste.

'But what if it isn't going to be sorted out in a few days?' Fallow drummed his fingers anxiously on the tray. 'You know, we have no idea what's going on, so how can we say? A sudden announcement that all air traffic is going to be grounded indefinitely doesn't exactly fill one with confidence, if you know what I mean. Now *that* sounds serious.'

'We were lucky to get the last flight out.'

'I mean, the country could be on its knees in days! How will business survive?' His startled expression suggested he had only just grasped the implications of his train of thought. 'Never mind your bog-standard business traveller who has to get around for meetings – they can muddle through with a few netcasts and conference calls in the short term. But what about import–export? The whole of the global economy relies on—'

'You don't have to tell me, Justin.'

'You can sit there being sniffy about it, but have you thought about what it means—?'

'It means we won't be able to get any bananas in the shops for a while and international mail will be a bastard. Thank God for the Internet.'

'I still think there's more to it than you think. To take such a drastic step . . . Trouble is, you can't trust those bastards in the Government to tell you anything important, whatever political stripe they are. Look at the mad cow thing. It's a wonder we're not all running around goggle-eyed, slavering at the mouth.'

'You obviously didn't look in the mirror last night—'

'This isn't funny. Go on, tell me why you're so calm. What could cause something like this?'

'Let me see, Justin.' Irvine began counting off his fingers. 'An impending strike by all international air traffic control which we haven't been told about for fear it causes a panic. You know how much pressure they've been under recently with the increase in the volume of flights. Or some virus has been loaded into the ATC system software. Or the Global Positioning Satellite has been hit by a meteorite so all the pilots are flying blind. Or all those intermittent power failures we've had recently have made it too risky until they find the cause. Or they've finally discovered that design glitch that's had planes dropping out of the skies like flies over the last few years.'

'I'd rather we didn't talk about this now, Colin.'

'Well, you started it.'

Justin sucked on his lower lip like a petulant schoolboy and then began to line up the miniature bottles in opposing forces. 'I suppose all the trolley dollies are worried they might be out of work,' he mused.

A crackle over the Tannoy heralded an announcement. 'This is your captain speaking. We anticipate arrival in Gatwick on schedule in twenty minutes. There may be a slight delay on the—' There was a sudden pause, a muffled voice in the background, and then the Tannoy snapped off.

Fallow looked up suspiciously. 'Now what's going on?'

'Will you calm down? Just because you're afraid of the worst happening doesn't mean it's going to.'

'And just because you're not afraid doesn't mean it isn't.' Fallow shifted in his seat uncomfortably, then glanced up and down the aisle.

What he saw baffled him at first. It was as if a ripple was moving down the plane towards him. The faces of the passengers looking out of the starboard side were changing, the blank expressions of people watching nothing in particular shedding one after the other as if choreographed. In that first fleeting instant of confusion, Fallow tried to read those countenances: was it shock, dismay, wonder? Was it horror?

And then he abruptly thought he should be searching for the source of whatever emotion it was, but before he had time to look, the plane banked wildly and dropped; his stomach was left behind and for one moment he thought he was going to vomit. But then the fear took over and it was as if his body were locked in stasis as he gripped the armrests until his knuckles were white. He forced his head into his lap. Screams filled the air, but they were distant, as though coming at him through water, and then he was obliquely aware he was screaming himself.

The plane was plummeting down so sharply vibrations were juddering through the whole fuselage; when it banked again at the last minute, the evasive action was so extreme Fallow feared the wings would be torn off. Then, bizarrely, the plane was soaring up at an angle that was just as acute. Fallow was pressed back into his seat until he felt he was on the verge of blacking out.

'It can't take much more of this punishment,' he choked.

Just as he was about to prepare himself for the whole plane coming apart in mid-air, it levelled off. Fallow burst out laughing in hysterical relief, then raged, 'What the *fuck* was that all about?'

Irvine pitched forward and threw up over the back of the seat in front; he tried to get his hand up to his mouth, but that only splattered the vomit over a wider area. Fallow cursed in disgust, but the trembling that racked his body didn't allow him to say any more.

One of the stewardesses bolted from the cabin, leaving the door swinging so Fallow could see the array of instrumentation blinking away. She pushed her way up to a window, then exclaimed, 'My God! He was right!'

The whole planeload turned as one. Fallow looked passed Irvine's white, shaking face into the vast expanse of blue sky. The snowy clouds rolled and fluffed like meringue, but beyond that he could see nothing. Then, out of the corner of his eye, he noticed a shadow moving across the field of white. At first he wondered if they had narrowly avoided a collision with another plane, but the shadow seemed too long and thin; it appeared to have a life of its own. There was a sound like a jet taking off and then the colour of the clouds transformed to red and gold. A belch of black smoke was driven past the window.

Fallow rammed Irvine back in his seat and craned his neck to search the sky. Beside and slightly below the plane, flying fast enough to pass it with apparent ease, was something which conjured images from books he had read in the nursery. Part of it resembled a bird and part a serpent: scales glinted like metal in the morning sun on a body that rippled with both power and sinuous agility, while enormous wings lazily stroked the air. Colours shimmered across its surface as the light danced: reds, golds and greens, so that it resembled some vast, brass robot imagined by a Victorian fantasist. Boned ridges and horns rimmed its skull above red eyes; one swivelled and fixed on Fallow. A second later the creature roared, its mouth wide, and belched fire; it seemed more a natural display, like a peacock's plumage, than an attack, but all the passengers drew back from the window as one. Then, with a twist that defied its size, it snaked up and over the top of the fuselage and down the other side.

Shock and fear swept through the plane, but it dissipated at speed. Instead, everyone seemed to be holding their breath. Fallow looked around and was astonished to see that faces that had earlier been scarred with cynicism or bland with dull routine were suddenly alight; to a man or woman, they all looked like children. Even the stewardesses were smiling.

Then the atmosphere was broken by a cry from the aft: 'Look! There's another one!'

In the distance, Fallow saw a second creature dipping in and out of the clouds as if it were skimming the surface of the sea.

Fallow slumped back in his seat and looked at Irvine coldly. 'Everything will be back to normal in a few days,' he mocked in a singsong, playground voice.

May 2, 11 a.m.; Dounreay Nuclear Power Station, Scotland:
'I just don't know what they expect of us!' Dick McShay said frustratedly. He threw his pen at the desk, then realised how pathetic that was. At 41, he had expected a nice, easy career with BNFL, overseeing the decommissioning of the plant that would stretch long beyond his life span; a holding job, no pressures apart from preventing the media discovering information about the decades of contamination, leaks and near-disasters. Definitely no

crises. He fixed his grey eyes on his 2-I-C, Nelson, who looked distinctly uncomfortable. 'I have no desire to shoot the messenger, William, but really, give me an answer.'

Nelson, who was four years McShay's junior, a little more stylish, but without any of his charisma, sucked on his bottom lip for a second; an irritating habit. 'What they want to do,' he began cautiously, 'is make sure most of Scotland isn't irradiated in the next few weeks. I don't mean to sound glib,' he added hastily, 'but that's the bottom line. It's these power failures—'

McShay sighed, shook his head. 'Not just power, William, technology. There's no point denying it. Mechanical processes have been hit just as much. I mean, who can explain something like that? If I were super-stitious . . .' He paused. '. . . I'd still have a hard time explaining it. The near-misses we've had over the last few weeks . . .' He didn't need to go into detail; Nelson had been there too during the crazed panics when they all thought they were going to die, the cooling system shut-downs, the fail-safe failures that were beyond anyone's comprehension; yet every time it had stopped just before the whole place had gone sky-high. He couldn't tell if they were jinxed or lucky, but it was making an old man of him.

'So we shut down—'

'Yes, but don't they realise it's not like flicking off a switch? That schedule is just crazy. Even cutting corners, we couldn't do it.'

'They're desperate.'

'And I don't like *them* being around either.' He glanced aggressively through the glass walls that surrounded his office. Positioned around the room beyond were Special Forces operatives, faces masked by smoked Plexiglas visors, guns held at the ready across their chests; their immobility and impersonality made them seem inhuman, mystical statues waiting to be brought to life by sorcery. They had arrived with the dawn, slipping into the vital areas as if they knew the station intimately – which, of course, they did, although they had never been there before. *For support*, they said. Not, *To guard*. Not, *To enforce*.

'All vital installations are under guard, Dick. So they say. It's all supposed to be hush-hush—'

'Then how do you know?'

Nelson smirked in reply. Then: 'We might as well just ignore them. It's their job, all that Defence of the Realm stuff.'

'What are they going to do if we don't meet the deadline? Shoot us?'

Nelson's expression suggested he thought this wasn't beyond the bounds of possibility.

'I just never expected to be doing my job at gunpoint. If the powers that be don't trust us, why should we trust them?'

'Desperate times, Dick.'

McShay looked at Nelson suspiciously. 'I hope you're on our side, William.'

'There aren't any sides, are there?'

A rotating red light suddenly began whirling in the room outside, intermittently bathing them in a hellish glow. A droning alarm pitched at an irritating level filled the complex. The Special Forces troops were instantly on the move.

'Shit!' McShay closed his eyes in irritation; it was a breach of a security zone. 'What the fuck is it now?'

Nelson was already on the phone. As he listened, McShay watched incomprehension flicker across his face.

'Give me the damage,' McShay said wearily when Nelson replaced the phone.

Nelson stared at him blankly for a moment before he said, 'There's an intruder—'

'I know! It's the fucking intruder alarm!'

'—in the reactor core.'

McShay returned the blank stare and then replied, 'You're insane.' He picked up the phone and listened to the stuttering report before running out of the room, Nelson close behind him.

The inherent farcical nature of a group of over-armed troops pointing their guns at the door to an area where no human could possibly survive wasn't lost on McShay, but the techies remained convinced someone was inside. He pushed his way past the troops on the perimeter to the control array where Rex Moulding looked about as uncomfortable as any man could get.

Moulding motioned to the soldiers as McShay approached. 'What are this lot doing here? This isn't a military establishment.'

McShay brushed his question aside with an irritated flap of his hand. 'You're a month late for practical jokes, Rex.'

'It's no joke. Look here.' Moulding pointed to the bank of monitors.

McShay examined each screen in turn. They showed various views of the most secure and dangerous areas around the reactor. 'There's nothing there,' he said eventually.

'Keep watching.'

McShay sighed and attempted to maintain his vigilance. A second later a blur flashed across one of the screens. 'What's that?'

The fogginess flickered on one of the other screens. 'It's almost like the cameras can't get a lock on it,' Moulding noted.

'What do you mean?'

There was a long pause. 'I don't know what I mean.'

'Is it a glitch?'

'No, there's definitely someone in there. You can hear the noises it makes through the walls.'

McShay's expression dared Moulding not to say the wrong thing. 'It?'

Moulding winced. 'Bob Pruett claims to have seen it before it went in there—'

'Where is he?' McShay snapped.

As he glanced around, a thickset man in his fifties wearing a sheepish expression pushed his way through the military.

'Well?' McShay said uncompromisingly.

'I saw it,' Pruett replied in a thick Scots drawl. He looked at Moulding for support.

'You better tell him,' Moulding said.

'Look, I know this sounds bloody ridiculous, but it's what I saw. It had antlers coming out like this.' He spread his fingers on either side of his head; McShay looked at him as if he had gone insane. 'But it was a man. I mean, it walked like a man. It looked like a man – two arms, two legs. But its face didn't look human, know what I mean? It had red eyes. And fur, or leaves—'

'Which one?'

'What do you mean?'

'Fur, or leaves. Which one?'

'Well, both. They looked like they were growing out of each other, all over its body.'

McShay searched Pruett's face, feeling uncomfortable when he saw no sign of contrition; in fact, there was shock and disbelief there, and that made him feel worse. Moulding suddenly grew tense, his gaze fixed on the monitors. 'It's coming this way,' he said quietly.

Unconsciously, McShay turned towards the security door. Through it he could hear a distant sound, growing louder, like the roaring of a beast, like a wind in the high trees.

'The temperature's rising in the reactor core,' Nelson called out from the other side of the room. The second tonal emergency warning began, intermingling discordantly with the intruder alarm; McShay's head began to hurt. 'The fail-safes haven't kicked in,' Nelson continued. He pulled out his mobile phone and punched in a number; McShay wondered obliquely who he could be calling.

'It's nearly here,' Moulding said. McShay couldn't take his eyes off the security door; he was paralysed by incomprehension. That horrible noise was louder now, reverberating even through the shielding. He couldn't understand how the troops could remain immobile with all the confusion raging around them; their guns were still raised to the door, barrels unwavering.

The one in charge glanced briefly at McShay, then said, 'If it comes through, fire the moment you see it.'

What's the point? McShay thought. *It's been in the reactor core and it's still alive!* He was overcome with a terrible feeling of foreboding.

There was a sudden thundering at the door and it began to buckle like tinfoil; McShay thought he could see the imprints of hands in it. Despite their training, some of the troops took a step back. The roaring which sounded like nothing he had ever heard before was now drowning out the alarms.

'I don't wish to state the obvious, but if that door comes down, it will take more than a shower to decontaminate us,' Moulding said in a quiet voice that crackled with tension.

McShay came out of his stupor in a flash; the thought that a security door designed to survive a direct nuclear strike might ever be breached was so impossible, his mind hadn't leapt to consider the consequences of what was happening.

'Everybody fall back!' he yelled. 'We need to seal this area off—'

The next second the door exploded outwards. McShay had one brief instant when he glimpsed the shape that surged through and then the gunfire erupted in a storm of light and noise, and a second after that a wave of soft white light came rushing from the reactor core towards them all.

The first person to see what had happened to Dounreay Nuclear Power Station was a farmer trundling along the coast road in his tractor. The sight was so bizarre he had to pull over to the side to check it wasn't some illusion caused by the sea haze. The familiar modernist buildings had been lost behind an impenetrable wall of vegetation; mature trees sprouted through the concrete and tarmac, ivy swathed the perimeter fences and buildings, dog roses and clematis clambered up the side of the administration block, cars were lost beneath creepers; all around squirrels, rabbits and birds skittered through the greenery. And if anyone had decided, for whatever reason, to check for radiation, they would have found none, not even in what had been the reactor core. Nor would they have found any sign of human life.

May 2, 8 p.m.; News International: Wapping, London:

'There's no point in us being here.' The accent was pure Mockney, hiding something from the Home Counties. Lucy Manning repeatedly punched the lift button, then shifted from foot to foot with irritation as she watched the lighted numbers' soporific descent. She was in her twenties, dyed-blonde hair framing a face that had the cold hardness of a frontline soldier.

Beside her, Kay Bliss could have been a mirror image or a copycat sister, but the look and the accent were all part of the office politics; a game they both knew how to play. 'Oh, fuck it, Lucy, we're getting paid, aren't we? It's nice not to be out doorstepping some twat until the early hours for a change.' Her voice had the hard vowels of a Geordie, though she could hide it when she had to.

'There's some idiot from Downing Street permanently in the newsroom,' Lucy continued, 'going over every piece of copy with a fine-tooth comb. D-Notice on this, D-Notice on that. We'll be like some fucking cheap local rag soon. Golden wedding stories and photos from the Rotary lunch.' Lucy strode into the lift the second the doors opened, then rattled her nails anxiously on the metal wall. 'Come on. Why are these things so fucking slow? All the technology we've got in this place, you'd think they'd be able to get lifts that worked quickly.'

'We're not even supposed to be using them. All those technology crashes—'

'Like we've got time to walk up and down flights of stairs all day.'

Kay held her breath until the doors opened on the newsroom floor. She'd spent an hour stuck in it with three monkeys from the loading bay and it wasn't an episode she wanted to repeat.

Lucy was still talking as she dodged out between the opening doors, 'It started with that terrorist strike on the M4—'

'Damon covered that.' Kay looked puzzled for a second. 'Terrorists?'

'It had to be terrorists. It wasn't that long before the Martial Law announcement.'

'Someone said a Yank plane had gone down carrying nukes.'

Lucy shrugged. 'And there were all those phone calls from the great unwashed claiming they'd seen some fire-breathing monster.' She flung open the swing doors. 'Sometimes I wish I worked for the *FT*.'

The newsroom was quiet now that all the dayshift had departed. The night news editor stared at the slowly scrolling Press Association newsfeed on his computer while lazily chewing on a cheese roll. One of the sports reporters whistled loudly.

''ello, darlin',' Kay shouted back with a cheery wave.

'It's all right for them,' Lucy muttered moodily, 'their Ludo tournaments never get censored.'

'You're in a right mood, aren't you?'

They'd walked on a few paces before Lucy said, 'I had the splash today and they pulled it.'

'Oh, that explains it. Bitter and twisted at not getting any front page glory. What was the story?'

'A whole unit of Royal Marines slaughtered up in the Highlands. A hot tip from my man at Command Headquarters.' She stuck out her bottom lip like a sulky child.

'Wow. A *proper* story. No *EastEnders* stud getting bladdered in that one,' Kay said with what Lucy thought was an unreasonable amount of glee. 'But you didn't really expect to get it through, did you?' Lucy shrugged. Kay's expression gradually became troubled. 'Slaughtered? In Scotland?'

'Hey, it's the Barbie twins!' Kevin Smith, one of the sales managers, had been lurking around the news desk. The hacks hated him for his retro-yuppie look and his aftershave stink, but he insisted on pretending he was one of the boys.

'Fuck off, Kevin,' Kay said with a mock-sweet smile.

'Careful you don't cut yourself with that.' He patted the desk so they could both sit next to him, but they studiously went round to the other side where they could talk to the handful of freelancers doing the night shift.

'What's up?' Lucy perched on the edge of the desk so she could tease the newbies with a flash of her thigh.

'Don't bother the fresh meat!' the news editor barked. 'Get over here!'

Kay was first over. 'What is it, chief?'

He tapped the screen as he spoke through a mouthful of cheese roll. 'PA says the PM's making an announcement at nine. Half the cabinet is getting the boot and they're setting up a coalition with the other parties. Government of National Unity or something.'

'Good policy. Get all the losers in one place. It'll probably be as successful as their Martial Law that they haven't got enough manpower to enforce.' Kevin had wandered over and was reading the newsfeed over the night news editor's shoulder.

'I'll take that one,' Lucy called out.

'You're both working on it.' The night news editor rammed his chair backwards into the sales manager's groin. Kevin exhaled sharply, but continued to force a smile.

Kay tore off a sheet of printer paper to make notes. 'Blimey. Two proper stories in one day. It's a sign – the world really is coming to an end!'

They all stopped what they were doing as the night news editor leaned forward to peer at the screen, swearing under his breath. 'Somebody must have rattled Downing Street's cage. There's a whole load of stuff coming up here. Flights grounded earlier, now we get "train services limited . . . No international calls . . . maybe extended disruption of the phone network . . . orders to shoot looters on sight . . ." What the fuck is going on?'

A middle-aged man in a smart dark suit moved slowly from the editor's office towards the news desk. He had a nondescript haircut and bland features and he carried himself with the stiff demeanour of a civil servant.

'When are you going to tell us what the fuck's going on?' the night news editor bellowed. 'It's a fucking outrage! The people have a right to know—'

The dark-suited man dropped a sheet of paper on the desk. 'This is tomorrow's page one story. "PM Launches Battle of Britain".'

They all looked at it, dumbfounded. 'You can't do that!' Lucy could see another byline disappearing before her eyes.

The night news editor scanned the paper, then hammered it beneath the flat of his hand. 'We can't print this! It doesn't fucking say anything! Just fucking PR guff! Nobody has any idea what's going on, they don't know who the fucking enemy is! It could be a fucking coup for all anyone knows! There'll be panic in the streets—'

'This has been carefully designed to *prevent* panic,' the man said calmly. 'The problem is internal, but not a coup. That is for your information only. The Government needs to act quickly and efficiently and that means the public must not get in the way—'

'It's like *1984*!' The night news editor's face was flushed bright red.

The civil servant held up a hand to quieten him, which served only to irritate him more. 'This is being done with the full approval of your editor—'

'Does *he* know what's happening?'

'He's been briefed by the PM personally, as have all media editors—'

'What's it got to do with all the technology blackouts?' Kevin interjected. 'There's stuff happening there that makes no sense at all. And all those freak calls we've been flooded with . . . people claiming they've seen UFOs and God knows what. I mean, someone said their dead uncle had come back to haunt them. And some farmer said his cows were giving up vinegar instead of milk. I mean, what's that all about?' He looked from face to face; everyone was staring back at him as if they had a bad smell under their nose. 'The switchboard keep putting them through to my office.'

'I wonder who arranged that?' Kay eyed the night news editor, who gave nothing away.

'We will be making a full and clear statement as soon as the situation demands it,' the civil servant said blandly. 'We have no intention of a cover-up. There is a state of emergency for a very good reason and our primary directive has to be to deal with that. It is taking all our resources. You have to believe me on this. Keeping everyone informed comes a very distant second.'

The night news editor read the replacement story one more time, then lounged back in his chair with his hands over his face. 'I don't know why I'm even bothering. We might as well all go down the pub—'

'You can't go out,' the civil servant said. 'There's a curfew once the sun goes down.'

'And you're going to stop me personally, are you, you cunt?' The night news editor glared at him venomously. Kay noticed a strange note in her boss's voice, something that was a little afraid; a suspicion of how bad things really were.

She glanced back to the civil servant who sported a curious expression; it reminded Kay of the look some older people, burdened by life's problems, gave to teenagers acting stupid and frivolous; a *one day you're going to have a rude awakening* look. He masked it quickly with expert precision, shrugged as if everything were beneath his notice, then sauntered slowly back to the editor's office.

Kay shrugged too. What did he know? Boring, jumped-up twat.

Once the office door had been closed the night news editor said, 'I think I might have to kill the bastard.'

'I'm getting a bit worried about this.' Kevin chewed his lip, his gaze still fixed on the office door. 'It seems really bad.'

'If it's a war I could be a war correspondent.' Lucy made a paper aeroplane, but it died mid-flight.

'Aren't you worried?' Kevin asked.

She eyed him contemptuously. 'What's to worry about? You want to try getting a drink up the road when all the circulation twats are in trying to pinch your arse. That's dangerous.'

'Hang on.' The night news editor was staring intently at his terminal.

'Not more bad news,' Kevin said.

The PA newsfeed seemed to be melting, the letters sliding down the screen into a mass at the bottom. Eventually the whole screen was clear. A second later a single word appeared in the top lefthand corner: WARE.

'What does that mean?' Kay asked. 'Software?'

The word began to repeat until it filled the whole screen.

'It might mean Be-WARE,' Kevin said. 'Some kind of warn—'

'Lucy, get on to Systems.' The night news editor threw the phone across the desk. 'This fucking thing isn't much use to us at the moment, but at least I can see what PA are doing.'

Lucy picked up the phone and instantly dropped it as ear-piercing laughter shrieked from the receiver. 'Fuck! What was that!' She stared at the phone as if it were alive.

'Interference,' Kay said wearily. 'Try the other one.'

The same inhuman laughter burst from that one too. They had an instant to look at each other in puzzlement and then all the lights and the computer screens winked out, plunging the entire windowless office into total darkness.

There was a long period of deep, worrying silence until everyone heard Kay say, 'Fuck off, Kevin.'

May 2, 11 p.m.; Balsall Heath, Birmingham:

'What did your dad say?' Sunita chewed on a strand of her long, black hair while she watched Lee's face. The night was uncomfortably muggy against the background stink of traffic fumes drifting in from the city centre.

Lee shifted uncomfortably as he scrubbed a hand across his skinhead crop. 'What do you think he said?'

The glare from the streetlamp over their heads seemed to draw out the sadness in her delicate features; her large eyes became dark, reflecting pools. 'That he doesn't want his son going out with some Paki.'

'He's not my dad anyway,' Lee said defensively. 'Stepdad.'

They both subconsciously bowed their heads as across the road a crowd of youths making their way back from the pub made loud kissing noises. Once they'd passed, Lee slipped his arms around her back; she felt so fragile against the hardness of his worked-out muscles that he just wanted to protect her.

'Why do we get all this shit?' She rested her head on his chest. 'I'm not even twenty yet! We should be having a good time, enjoying it all. Sometimes I feel like an old woman.'

He knew how she felt. When they'd first started seeing each other a year ago he had been almost overwhelmed by the *frisson* of doing something wrong, at turns both exciting and deeply disconcerting. And the fact that he did feel that way made him queasy because he knew how much his stepfather had corrupted his thought processes. There *was* nothing wrong with their relationship, but he'd had to keep it secret from his stepfather through what seemed like a million minor deceptions and big lies. It had cast a shadow over everything, when they should have been revelling in the feeling of falling in love; that pure sensation had been lost to them and he hated his stepfather for that loss. There was relief when he finally discovered who Lee was seeing after spotting them holding hands on New Street, but that had brought with it a whole different set of problems, the most worrying of which was that Sunita might no longer be safe. His stepfather's *associates* from his weekly meetings were brutal men with a harsh view of life that didn't allow such weak concepts as love the slightest foothold, and they were relentlessly unforgiving.

Sunita knew all this, and she knew it would be safer for her to leave Lee well alone, but how could she? The choices had been made and imprinted on their souls; they had to live with the consequences. 'What are we going to do? Carry on as normal, just . . . going to different places?'

'You know we can't do that. They know where you live.' He took a deep breath. 'We're getting out of Birmingham.' He paused while he watched her expression. 'Least, that's what I think. I know it'll be hard with your family—'

'It'll be a nightmare! My dad'll go crazy, my mum . . . all that wailing!'

'You're old enough—'

'That's not the point.'

He winced at being so insensitive, but he found it hard to see anything from the perspective of a loving, caring family. 'I'm sorry, Sunny, but, you know, we've got to do something—'

'Where were you thinking of going?'

'Down south somewhere. Just hit the motorway and see where we end up. They'll never be able to track us.'

She sighed. 'It's not just your dad. It'll be good to get out of this city. Sometimes it seems like it's choking the life out of me. There's something . . . a meanness . . . it just gets me down.'

'I know what you mean.' He listened to the drone of city centre traffic drifting over the wasteland and abandoned houses waiting for demolition. 'It'll be good, a fresh start.'

'Do you think it will work out?'

'I know it will.' He wondered if he could tell her why he was so sure; saying it out loud made even him feel like he was crazy; and he'd been through it. 'Come on, let's walk.' He took her hand and began to lead her in the direction of the house.

She looked uncomfortable. 'Your dad—'

'He's at one of his meetings, wishing we still had an empire.'

The familiar streets were thankfully empty, adding to the wonderful illusion that they were the only people left in the world. Away from the wasteland the air was a little fresher. They turned down the hill from the imposing big houses towards the line of pokey semis where Lee had lived all his life. It felt odd to think he might not walk down there again. He'd miss his mum, and Kelly, but not Mick; he'd be happy if he never heard Mick's voice again.

'When are you thinking of going?' Sunita asked.

'Now. Tonight.'

'Oh.'

He couldn't tell her that his stepdad's beetle-browed cronies might act after they'd finished their rebel-rousing for the night. They had to be as far away as possible from Brum before everything blew up. But even though he didn't say anything, he could tell from Sunita's response to the tight deadline that she understood the dangers.

'Mum and Dad will understand,' she said confidently. 'I'll call them once we're on the road. They'll be asleep when I get back to pack. Though you know, things aren't so different between us. They both wish I was with a boy who knew the Koran back to front.'

He shrugged, said nothing. There were always too many people wanting to interfere in everybody's life.

Sunita slipped her arm through his and gave it a squeeze. 'We'll never be able to agree on the music for the car, you know. There'll be me with my Groove Armada and Basement Jaxx and you with some ancient old toss like The Redskins or one of those other old fogey bands you like. I don't know how you got into all that stuff. Most of them were playing before you were born.'

'You've got to appreciate the past to know where you're going.'

'You've been reading books again, haven't you? I told you it was bad for you.' She smiled, but it drained away once she realised they were standing outside his home. Over the year her imagination had turned it into some kind of nightmarish haunted house, the place where all bad things originated. Even on the few times she'd been into the empty place there'd been an unpleasant atmosphere mingled in with the cheap cigarette smoke and smell of fried food. 'Are you sure he's not in?'

'He never misses a meeting.' Lee led her round the side of the house. The small back garden was in darkness; a few items of clothing still fluttered on the washing line.

'What about your mum and Kelly?'

'They'll have stopped off for a drink after the bingo.'

'Lee, why are you bringing me here?'

'There's something I want to show you. To put your mind at rest.'

'About what?'

'That everything'll be all right.' She still seemed unsure, so he took her hand and tugged her towards the shed in the shadows near the rear fence. It was much larger than average. Mick had put it up when he was thinking about breeding racing pigeons, but he'd never got round to that, like so many other things in his life.

'You don't want to get down to it here one more time, do you?' she said with a sly smile.

'Wait and see.' They stepped into the darkness of the shed and its familiar smell of turps and engine oil. He took her hand and waited a couple of seconds before saying in a clear voice, 'Come out. It's me.'

In the dark Sunita looked at him in puzzlement; she could feel his hand growing clammy. 'Who are you talking to?'

He hushed her anxiously. He kept his gaze fixed firmly on the back of the shed and when he didn't get whatever response he had been expecting, he tried again, a little more insistently. Still nothing. 'Please,' he said finally. 'This is Sunita. I told you about her. She's okay, you know that.'

He waited for another moment and then sighed. 'We better go,' he said reluctantly.

Outside, she gave him a peck on the cheek. 'It's a good job I love mad people. Now are you going to tell me—'

'You better not laugh!'

'Of course not.'

'Promise?'

'I promise, idiot. Now get on with it.'

He bowed his head with the odd, wincing expression which she knew signalled deep embarrassment. 'It started a couple of weeks ago. I kept hearing noises in the shed.'

'Noises?'

'Yes, you know . . . voices. They kept chattering in there. I thought some smackheads had broken in, but every time I went to check there was no one in there.'

'Ooh, spooky!'

'Yeah, that's what I thought. But then last week there *was* someone there.'

Sunita eyed him askance, trying to predict the punchline. 'Who was it?'

He rubbed his chin, obviously not wanting to continue. Finally he said, 'Do you believe in fairies?'

'Fairies?' She burst out laughing.

'You said you weren't going to laugh!'

'Sorry, but . . . You can't be serious!'

He looked away grumpily.

'Okay, go on!' she said, tugging at his sleeve. 'What did they look like?'

'They looked like fairies! Well, *a* fairy. Small, pointed ears, green clothes. It was just like one I'd seen on a book I had when I was a lad.'

It took him another ten minutes to get her to take him seriously, but eventually she accepted it. 'Okay, there's been a lot of strange stuff going on all over. If you say fairies, I believe fairies,' she said, bemused. 'So there are, really and truly, fairies at the bottom of the garden.'

'I don't know why I even bother with you,' he sighed. 'Just listen then, if you're not going to believe me. I tell you, I thought I was going loopy to start with, but every time I went in, there he was, so I *had* to accept it. And we started talking.' He snorted with laughter at the ridiculousness of the idea. 'I told him all about you, about my dad, about . . . well, everything.'

'I bet he had a good fairy laugh at all that,' she said bitterly.

'No, actually. He said his people always looked after young lovers. "Simpletons and those in love", that's what he said.' He laughed. 'Same thing, I suppose. Anyway, I told him I was going to leave town and he said not to worry, everything was going to be all right for us.'

'So where was he just?'

Lee looked troubled. 'I don't know. He's been in there every time I've been in recently. Maybe he doesn't appear if there's more than one person . . .' His voice faded away as he recognised how stupid he sounded. 'Or maybe all the stuff with Mick really has turned my brain to jelly.'

'Jelly boy!' She danced a few steps ahead before he could pinch her; instead he swore forcefully. 'Okay, okay!' she laughed. 'But there's one thing I never could quite work out as a girl. Can you really trust fairies?'

From the darkened lounge Mick Jonas watched his stepson and the Paki bitch step into the shed, obviously for a quick touch-up, and he was still watching when they headed back towards the road. He quickly switched on his mobile phone and hit the speed dial. 'They're on their way now,' he said in his thick Birmingham accent. 'Follow 'em till they're outside Brum then get 'em off the road. You can do what you like to the cunt, but just give our Lee a good fucking hiding. Teach him a lesson.' He listened to the voice on the other end for a second, then added, 'If you want to use a can of fucking petrol on her, pal, you do it. Just make sure Lee doesn't get burned up. The old woman would kill me.'

He switched off the phone and lit a cigarette before lowering his overweight frame into the frayed armchair he had made his own. He felt a triumphant burst, that he'd got one over on his lefty, Paki-loving stepson who thought he was so fucking superior. But Mick had seen him sneak the suitcase out and store it in the boot of his old banger. He knew what the little shit was planning.

He closed his eyes and sucked deeply on the cigarette, enjoying the moment and the certain knowledge that a blow had been struck against the fucking multi-cultural society. But when he opened his eyes a moment later he was almost paralysed by shock. Through the window he could see something moving rapidly across the lawn from the bottom of the garden. He couldn't tell what it was – its shape seemed to be changing continuously and his eyes hurt from trying to pin it down – but it was horrible. The scream started deep in his throat, but it hadn't reached his mouth before the window had imploded, showering glass all around him. And then it was on him.

Maureen and Kelly returned from the local five minutes later. They tiptoed through the front door, just in case Mick was dozing after a few pints. They'd both pay the price if they woke him. But the moment she was across the threshold, Maureen had the odd feeling something was wrong. There was a strained atmosphere, like just before a storm, and an odd smell was drifting in the air. While Kelly went to the bathroom she crept into the lounge to investigate.

The first thing she saw was the broken window and felt the glass crunching underfoot. Her mind started to roll: burglars; some of those shabby youths who didn't like Mick's little club.

And then she looked into Mick's armchair and at first didn't recognise what she was seeing. It was black and smoking and resembled nothing more than a sculpture made out of charcoal. A sculpture of a man. And then she looked closer and saw what it really was, and wondered why the armchair hadn't burst into flames as well, and wondered a million and one other things all at once.

And then she screamed.

'I don't believe we did it!' Lee was bouncing up and down with excitement in his seat as the car pulled on to the M6 heading south.

'Well, your fairy told us, didn't he?' Sunita said with a giggle.

He gave her thigh a tight squeeze. 'This is about us now. We can do anything we want. We can really enjoy ourselves, just the two of us. God, I love you!'

She smiled and blew him a kiss. 'Things are strange right now, aren't they?' she said dreamily as she stared out of the passenger window into the night. 'People seeing all those weird things. You and the fairies. Uncle Mohammed having those dreams that came true.'

'Maybe it's a sign.'

'Of what?'

'I don't know. Of hope. That things are going to get better.'

She shook her head, her smile not even touching on the endless happiness she felt. 'You're a hopeless romantic.'

And the road opened up before them.

chapter one

what now my love

Smoke still billowed up from the ruins of the Kyle of Lochalsh across the water, sweeping a curtain of grey across the bright moon. Here and there small fires continued to burn like Will-o'-the-Wisps. The night was thick with the reek of devastation and despair, the smell of a world winding down.

Jack Churchill, known to his friends as Church, sat on the sea wall at Kyleakin next to Laura DuSantiago, and together they surveyed what little of the carnage they could make out on the mainland. It provided an odd counterpoint to the tranquillity that came from the gently lapping waves and the wind which blew through the deserted village. They were both exhausted after the nerve-racking journey across Skye in an abandoned car they had found in Kilmuir. The oppressively claustrophobic atmosphere was brought down by their fears of an ambush at every bend in the road, and magnified by the eerie stillness of the surrounding countryside, devoid of any sign of human life; it had been eradicated as easily and completely as a germ culture on a microscope slide. Nor were there any bodies; whatever the Fomorii had done with the former inhabitants did not bear considering. By the time they reached Kyleakin they had to accept that the Fomorii had deemed them too small a threat to pursue them any longer, and somehow that was even more jarring than the constant fear of attack. They were worthless.

'Well, it could be worse.' Laura brushed a stray strand of dyed-blonde hair out of her eyes as she shuffled into a more comfortable position on the wall.

Church, his dark hair emphasising the paleness of his wearied face, looked at her askance. 'How could it possibly be worse?'

'We could be going to work tomorrow.'

She kept her gaze fixed firmly across the water, but Church had learned to read the humour in her deadpan expression. Their relationship, if that was what it was, still surprised him. He wasn't quite sure how he felt about her. On the surface they had nothing in common, but deep down it seemed that something had clicked; after so long in the emotional ice-field following Marianne's death it felt good to reconnect with another human being, and the sex had been great. He hoped it was more than a simple alliance forged through the desperation of terrifying times, but there was no point losing sleep analysing it; it would find its own level soon enough, he was sure of it. Cautiously he reached out and took her hand. She was so unpredictable he half-expected her to snatch it away and accuse him of being a romantic idiot, but her fingers closed around his, cool and comforting.

'Do you think the others have forgiven me for screwing up so badly?' he asked. The notion drove a pang of guilt through him.

'They didn't give it a second thought. They might look like morons, but they can see you're all right. For a dickhead. And let's face it, you only acted like a human being. One who doesn't tell his friends anything, but a human being nonetheless. Who's going to fault you for that?'

Despite her words, Church couldn't stop the guilt growing stronger. The Tuatha Dé Danann had been right in their brutal assessment of his worth; it was his own weaknesses that had dragged them down. If he had told the others about the visitations of Marianne's spirit, about the Kiss of Frost that had corrupted him and brought about the Danann's contempt, the world might have been saved.

'Did you ever hear *Beyond the Sea*?' he asked, staring into the chopping black waves.

'Is that by one of those dead, old white guys you enjoy so much? Some Sinatra shit?'

'Bobby Darin.' He didn't rise to the bait. 'It's the best metaphor for death I've ever heard. Just a simple little song, but when you think about it in those terms it becomes almost profound.' He sang a few bars: '*Somewhere beyond the sea, somewhere waiting for me, my lover stands on golden sands*. So sad, but so optimistic. I'd never really thought about it like that until just now, you know, about it talking about what lies beyond death—'

'Or it could just be a simple little song.' The comment would normally have been concluded with some note of mockery or contempt, but when none came he turned to look at her. Laura's face was still and thoughtful, and when she spoke again her voice was uncommonly hesitant. 'How do you feel?'

'What do you mean?'

'All that stuff floating around inside . . .' She was skating around the edge

33

of an issue that was so monumental it was almost impossible to put it into perspective.

'I feel okay, under the circumstances. Different, though I'm not sure how. Sometimes I get a wave of cold when the Fomorii corruption seems to get the upper hand. Sometimes I feel like I've got liquid gold in my veins, thanks to whatever the Danann did to me. The rest of the time I just feel like me.'

'Must be a real head-fuck to die and get reborn.'

'Yes.' In his darker moments he wondered if it meant he was still human, still alive, even, in any sense that people understood. How could you die and then come back? What scars did that leave on the soul, if such a thing existed? And what did it mean for the rules that were supposed to give a structure to existence? He combatted such black thoughts by trying to consider his rebirth an opportunity to leave the past and all his weaknesses behind, to become something much more valuable. It was the only way to stop himself cracking up.

'When you died, you know, what was it like? Inside?' It was obvious Laura wasn't about to let the subject drop. Though her face remained impassive, there was a deep gravitas at the back of her eyes that showed how much the issue meant to her.

He threw his mind back to when he was lying half in the stream, his blood mingling with the water, his body racked with pain. 'Like slipping into a hot bath and just carrying on down and down.'

She nodded thoughtfully. 'And after that?'

He winced. 'I don't remember.'

'Nothing at all?'

His sigh was uncomfortable. 'Just fragments . . . nothing that makes sense. And it's all breaking up like a dream after you wake.'

'But you remember something?'

'Just something that looked like a big church.' There was a sharpness to his voice that he regretted, but couldn't control. 'Or a cathedral. Massive, going right up past the clouds. That's it.'

'Okay, I won't bug you about it any more.' She made to leave, but he caught her arm and pulled her back. She gave a wry smile. 'Getting frisky?' Before he could answer, she pushed him back off the wall and followed him down.

'You ever wonder why there aren't any bodies?' Ryan Veitch put his street-hard shoulder muscles to the rear door of the grocery shop and heaved one final time; it burst open with a crack.

'I don't want to think about that.' Ruth Gallagher looked around uncomfortably. Even though she knew they were the only ones in the area and that the laws of the land probably didn't hold much sway any longer, she still didn't feel right breaking and entering.

Veitch didn't have any such qualms. His increasingly long hair hid his expression from her as he headed through the doorway, but she could have sworn he was actually enjoying it. Inside the store her fears were confirmed when the makeshift torch illuminated his hard, handsome features; he was grinning. 'I'll be happier when the power comes back on,' he said.

'Maybe it's gone for good this time,' Ruth said morosely, as she reluctantly followed him in. Cartons of tins and breakfast cereals were piled around and it smelled warmly of fruit and bread. 'Enough of the talk. Just get the provisions we need and let's get out of here.'

'I like to talk. Anyway, who's going to rumble us here?'

Ruth pushed past him with a flick of her head that sent her long, brown hair flying. She began to fill a dustbin bag with packets of muesli. 'Perhaps we should leave a note for the owner. Tell him why we took the stuff. Offer to pay him back—'

Veitch gave a derisory snort. 'You're living in cloud cuckoo land, you. Get real. He's not coming back. None of the poor bastards are. The Fomorii have hauled them off to their larder.'

Ruth glared at him, but his words made her feel numb and she quickly returned to her petty pilfering.

Veitch helped her halfheartedly and then said out of the blue, 'Are we going to start getting on?'

'We're stuck in this together. We don't have any option.'

'That's not good enough.'

Her eyes flashed. 'Well—'

'No, listen to me. I know I've done some bad things in my life, but you can't keep on blaming me for what happened to your old man—'

'How can you say that! You shot my uncle!' As she turned to face him her elbow clipped a box of *Special K* and sent it flying across the storeroom; all the emotions which she had bottled up for so long rumbled to the surface. She fought to hold back tears that seemed to come too easily, then said, 'I'm sorry. I heard what the Danann said—'

'That's right! It wasn't my fault. They made me do it, like they made all of us suffer.'

Ruth remembered the horror she felt when the Danann explained how all five of them had been forced to experience death as some sort of preparation for the destiny that had been mapped out for them.

'I might be a stupid little two-bit crook, but I've never killed anybody in my life before!' Veitch continued. 'I'm not that kind of bloke. I wish you could know how much it screwed me up when I saw I'd shot your uncle . . .'

35

He winced at the memory. 'Listen, all I want to do, all I've *ever* wanted to do in my life, is do something that's right, you know what I mean? Be a good guy for a change. But even when I try, it seems to go wrong. I just want a chance to show what I can do.'

His pleading was so heartfelt, Ruth couldn't help feeling sympathy.

'Because I like you,' he continued. 'I like all of you. You're all trying to do the right thing, whatever it might mean to you, and I've never been around people like that before. I don't want you all thinking bad of me all the time.'

Ruth read the emotions on his face for a long moment, then returned to her packing. 'Okay,' she said. 'I forgive you. But it's not going to be forgotten just like that—'

'I know. I just want a chance.'

'You've got it.'

She could feel him staring at her like he couldn't believe what she had said, and then he started loading up his bag with gusto. Once they'd got everything they might need for a few days, they headed back out. As they slipped away from the shadows at the back of the shop, a dark shape flashed out of the sky and circled them, drawing closer. Veitch was instantly alert, ready for defence.

'It's okay,' Ruth said. The owl, her gifted companion, glided down and landed on her shoulder; she winced as its talons bit into her flesh, then pushed her head to one side for fear it would start flapping its wings. It was the first time it had come close enough for her to touch. The owl turned its eerie, blinking eyes on Veitch, who was grinning broadly.

'What's his name?' He reached out a hand, but the owl snapped its beak in the direction of his fingers and he withdrew sharply.

'Who says it's a he?'

'Well what's *its* fucking name then?'

'It hasn't got a name.' She paused. 'Not one that I know, anyway.'

'Well, don't you think you should give him one? Or her. It. If it's going to be on the team—'

'Maybe I'll ask it later.' Her eyes sparkled.

Veitch looked at her for a second or two, but he couldn't tell if she was serious or teasing him. He decided to opt for the latter and responded in kind with a faint smirk. 'Witch.'

'Fuckhead.'

Their eyes locked for a long moment, then they burst out laughing. Turning, they threw the bags over their shoulders and marched towards the seafront.

'So what exactly can you do?' Veitch said.

Ruth shrugged. 'I don't know yet. It's like spending all your life as a man and then someone coming up to you and telling you you're actually a woman. How do you get your head round something as monumental as that? How can you comprehend you've been chosen by the gods for some task?'

'Sounds pretty cool to me. I wouldn't mind.'

'You might think differently if it actually happened to you. It's hard enough understanding that the world's changed. That different rules operate now, fundamental rules, about the way everything works. The woman I met in the Lake District—'

'The old magic-biddy?'

'The Wiccan. She'd spent years practising certain rites and not getting anywhere. Then, earlier this year, she woke up and suddenly found out things *happened*. At her command.'

'What kind of things?'

'Altering the weather. Controlling animals . . .' Ruth had a sudden flashback to the spirit-flight she experienced and was surprised at the depth of her yearning to savour it again. 'I don't think it's a matter of having any kind of power. It's just an aptitude for controlling things. Like physicists bending nuclear power to their will. You have to learn how to access it.'

'Any luck so far?'

'I haven't really tried. I'm a little nervous.'

'I read sex helps with magic.' He didn't look at her, but she could sense his grin.

'Don't go down that road. You're still on probation.'

'Okay. Just offering my services if you need me.'

'Thanks, but I'd rather put my eyes out.'

For a brief moment the wind shifted and the omnipresent stink of burning was replaced by the salty aroma of the sea and the heady tang of green hills. They both stopped and breathed deeply.

The fire roared as Tom threw on another broken dining chair, the glow painting a dull red over his wire-rimmed spectacles. Shavi sat cross-legged in front of his tent, staring deep into the flames. His long hair hung limp around his face, his perfect Asian features so still he could have been a mannequin. Wiping the sweat from his brow, Tom eyed him surreptitiously as he turned from the blaze.

'It was a terrible experience, but you gained wisdom from it.' He adjusted the elastic band holding his grey ponytail in place.

Shavi's eyes flickered, as if he were waking from a dream. 'At the moment that seems little consolation.'

'There's always a price to pay for knowledge. What you did was a great leap forward in your abilities.' Tom sat next to him, but far enough away so as not to encroach on the invisible barrier Shavi had placed around himself.

'I feel something has broken inside, deep in my head. Only I cannot tell exactly what. I simply feel different, damaged.'

'You projected your consciousness, your very self, out of your body and into an unthinking beast. It was a triumph of your shamanistic abilities. Unfortunately there will be short-term repercussions—'

'I have no wish to talk about it further.' Shavi fell silent for a few minutes, then said, 'I am sorry. I am being very insensitive. What I have experienced is nothing compared to your suffering over the centuries in Otherworld.'

'It wasn't centuries when I was there.' Tom paused. 'Although it felt like it.'

'And was the wisdom you gained from your experience worthwhile?'

Tom looked away into the night.

'What does your power of prophecy say for us, True Thomas?' Shavi lay back so he could watch the stars twinkling through the gaps in the smoke. He felt a twinge of deep regret that his experience with the serpent on the crossing to Skye had left him with such a black depression that he could no longer truly appreciate them.

'There are hard times ahead.'

'Even Ryan could have predicted that.'

'It's not as if I see the future rolled out before me like a map. There are flashes, glimpses through different windows on a winding staircase. I prefer not to say too much. Guessing at the meaning of a future image can alter the way one would react in the present.'

'Do you know who will live and who will die?' Shavi's voice floated up hollowly.

Tom remained silent.

A second later they heard the sound of the others approaching up the road from Kyleakin. Church had his arm around Laura's shoulders, while Ruth and Veitch carried the bags of provisions. They were all laughing at a joke.

'Come on, you old git. It won't ruin your image if you smile. It's not as if you're going to get any more wrinkles,' Laura shouted to Tom. He looked away haughtily.

Shavi forced a smile. 'Any fine food for dinner?'

Ruth upended her bin bag. 'Beans, fruit salad, muesli, pasta or any combination of the above.'

'Better get your cauldron on then,' Laura said to her tartly.

'There's meat for those who eat it.' Tom motioned to a brace of pheasants that lay on the outskirts of the camp.

'How the hell did you get those?' Veitch asked in amazement. He picked up one by the claws and searched for any kind of injury.

'Don't ask him that,' Church said. 'It'll just give him a chance to put on his mysterious-but-wise Yoda routine.'

'Well, meat for me.' Veitch threw the bird down. Laura wrinkled her nose in distaste.

While Tom set about preparing the birds, Ruth got out the cooking utensils they had picked up from the camping shop where they'd also, in Laura's words, *liberated* the tents. Tom jointed the pheasants with his Swiss Army Knife and they cooked quickly over the campfire, while Veitch prepared pasta and beans to accompany them.

After they'd eaten, they all sat back listening to the crackle of the fire. It was Church who spoke first, and from the way they turned to him as one he realised they had been waiting for him. 'I think,' he began, 'it's time to decide what we're going to do next.'

'Let's weigh up the options.' Church watched Ruth's face grow serious as she turned her sharp lawyer's mind to the mountainous problems that faced them.

'Rolling over and doing nothing, always a popular favourite. That's my number one.' Laura began to count off on her fingers. 'Driving off until we find a nice, secluded beach somewhere. Taking a boat and getting away across the Channel. Taking a shedload of drugs and spending whatever time we've got left blissed out.' She paused thoughtfully. 'Um. Burying our heads in the sand—'

'Or,' Veitch interrupted, 'we could do the right thing.'

'And what's that?' Laura sneered. 'Rob a building society?'

Shavi leaned forward, his eyes pools of darkness despite the firelight. 'We are Brothers and Sisters of Dragons. After all that has happened, there is no denying it. For better or worse, we, of all the people in the world, have had responsibility thrust upon us. We can no more turn our back on what is expected of us than we could on life itself.'

'Speak for yourself,' Laura sulked.

'And what *is* expected of us?' Church said, although the answer was obvious.

Shavi moistened his lips. 'To oppose the powers that threaten to drive humanity into the shadows. To shine a beacon of hope in the night. Whatever the cost.'

'Plain English,' Veitch interjected. 'To overthrow the bastards or die trying.'

Ruth raised her eyes and muttered, 'Thank you, John Wayne.'

They all fell silent for a long moment, and it was Laura who gave voice to the thought on all their minds. 'Look at us. What can *we* do?'

39

'I can give you all the clichés,' Church began. 'David and Goliath. The ant that moved several times its own weight—'

'Okay.' Laura smiled falsely. 'Now let's talk about the real world.'

'There's some way out there,' Veitch said adamantly. 'We don't have to go out in a blaze of glory like the Wild Bunch. There's guerrilla warfare. There's—'

'—different rules now,' Church said. 'Powers out there we can use. Like the artefacts we uncovered.' He still felt troubled that objects of such great power were in the hands of such an unpredictable race as the Tuatha Dé Danann.

'Guerrilla warfare,' Ruth said. 'I like that. We turn our weakness into a strength. Move fast, strike hard and be away before they can respond.'

'Excuse me? Are we living in the same world?' Laura said. 'These are things that can crush us faster than you can get on a high horse.'

'Get a spine.' Ruth turned to the others. 'We all know what's going to happen next.'

Every head dropped as one.

'Somebody's got to say it—'

'Let's not, and say we did.' Laura tried to make out it was more sour humour, but they all heard the faint undertone in her voice: fear.

Ruth looked around the circle slowly. 'They're going to try to bring Balor back. If we don't try to stop them—'

'Why us?' Laura no longer made any pretence of humour.

'But that is why we have been brought together,' Shavi said quietly. 'That is the reason why we contain this nebulous thing called the Pendragon Spirit, this thing that none of us truly understands. But it has been gifted to us so we can defend the land against this overwhelming threat.'

Laura winced. 'If you can believe all that—'

'You don't believe it?' Veitch asked sharply.

'You know what? I don't feel any different to before I met all you. You're just fooling yourselves, playing at being heroes. We're normal. Some of us, worse than normal. Weak, pathetic little shits. And the only time you're going to realise what a fantasy it is, is that second before you die in a gutter.' Her features were flinty; it was obvious she wasn't going to back down.

There was a long period of silence filled only with the crackle of the fire. Then Tom began slowly, 'It is all right to be scared of Balor. This is not some Fomorii like Calatin or Mollecht, who are frightening, but within our power to beat. As the Fomorii are to us, so Balor is to the Fomorii. He is their god, the embodiment of darkness, evil, death, chaos . . .' He shook his head slowly. 'He is more than a force of nature, he is an abstract given form: destruction. You only have my word for this, but I can see from your faces your fear goes beyond what I say. Because you know. In the furthest reaches of your worst nightmare, in the dimmest purview of your race memory, in your primal fear of the night, he lives. If Balor returns, it truly will be the end of everything.'

No one spoke. They listened to the wind whistling across the hills of Skye and somehow it seemed harsher, colder, the night too dark.

'Then we really do have no choice,' Church said.

Laura turned away so the fire didn't light her face.

'How are they going to bring him back?' Ruth asked finally.

'None of those ancient races truly die,' Tom said. 'They flitter out of this existence for a while. Time is meaningless, space insignificant. They simply need to be anchored and dragged back.' He shrugged. 'How? I have no idea. Some ritual using the powerful distillation they have been amassing which we saw in Salisbury and under Dartmoor.'

'Then we've got to stop the bastards before they start the ritual.' There was an innocent optimism in Veitch's voice that raised all their spirits slightly.

'But where will they be doing it? And when?' Ruth asked.

'The when I can answer,' Tom said. 'The ritual of birthing will not be conducted until the next auspicious date when there is a conjunction of power and intent. What the Celts named the feast of Lughnasadh, the Harvest Festival. August 1.'

'Three months.' Church mulled over this for a second or two. 'Doesn't seem very long. But we managed the unthinkable by our last deadline—'

'With no time to spare,' Tom cautioned. 'This task is far, far harder. The essence of Balor will already be contained in the birthing medium, ready for the ritual, and the Fomorii will have it hidden in their deepest, most inaccessible stronghold. To them, this thing is more valuable than anything in existence. Imagine if you held the spirit of your God? How much would you fight to protect it?'

'Do you think they've got it at that fortress we saw them building in the Lake District?' Ruth asked.

Tom shook his head. 'It will be somewhere none of their enemies will have seen, beneath ground, certainly, and protected against all eventuality.'

The wind came howling down from Sgurr Alasdair high in the Cuillin Hills, whipping up the fire so the sparks roared skywards like shooting stars. Looking up into the vast arc of the heavens, they felt suddenly insignificant, all their plans hopeless.

'Then how are we going to find it?' Ruth asked. 'If they've gone to such great pains to make it safe for them, we're not just going to stumble across it.'

41

Tom nodded in agreement; slowly, thoughtfully. 'We need guidance. There is a place we could go, a ritual I could conduct—'

'Then let's do it as soon as possible.' Church looked around at their faces; they were watching him with such intensity it made him feel uncomfortable. He didn't want the responsibility they were forcing on his shoulders.

'So you've decided, then.' Laura's expression hid whatever she was thinking. 'We've been lucky so far.' Her hand went unconsciously to the scars on her face. 'If you can call barely surviving luck. But sooner or later someone's going to die, and I don't intend it to be me.'

'No one wants—' But she had risen and marched off into the night before Church had a chance to finish. He sighed and waved his hand dismissively. 'We better get some sleep. We can start at first light.'

Veitch and Shavi headed off to their tents while Tom lit a joint from his rapidly diminishing block of hash and wandered off beyond the light of the campfire.

Ruth sat down next to Church, slipping a tentative arm around his shoulders to give him a comforting squeeze. 'No rest for the wicked.'

'No rest for anyone.' Church sighed. 'I wish I had some Sinatra to play. He always makes me feel good at a time like this.' Overhead a meteor shower set pinpricks of light flashing in the black gulf. 'You remember when we sat in that café after we first got dragged into all this under Albert Bridge? You asked me if I was scared. I didn't even know what the word meant then. Now every morning when I wake up, it hits me from a hundred different directions: fear of screwing up again, fear of dying, fear that the world doesn't make sense any more, that there's no secure place anywhere.' He paused a second before continuing, 'Fear of what this nightmare means on some kind of spiritual level. That there is no meaning. That we're just here as prey for whatever things are higher up the food chain than us. Fear that the whole mess doesn't even end with death.'

'You think too much.' Ruth gave him another squeeze before removing her arm. 'That morning in the café? It seems like a lifetime ago, doesn't it? I barely knew you then.'

Church looked up, unable to pinpoint the tone in her voice. She was smiling, her eyes bright in the dying firelight.

'I think you should look for meaning in the small picture, not the big one,' she continued. 'It seems stupid with all the upset and suffering, but on that micro level my life is better now than it ever was before. I was in a job I hated, just going through the motions because I knew it would have made my dad happy, not really having any idea who I was at all. Now everything in my life seems heightened, somehow. Even the smallest thing has passion

42

in it. You know I'm not one to get poetic, but compared to how I live my life now, I was dead before. Maybe that's where the meaning lies.'

'Maybe,' he answered noncommittally, but he knew what she meant.

'And I feel like my life's been enriched for knowing you and the others. I feel closer even to the ones I don't particularly like than anyone I knew before. Maybe when the rulebook was redrawn, the dictionary was too.' She laughed at her metaphor.

'What do you mean?'

'I know what friendship means now.' Her smile slowly faded until her features were sadly introspective. 'I don't know how to say this, but at this point, with all that shit lying ahead, it seems important.'

'So what does friendship mean?' He tried to raise the mood with a smile.

'It means being prepared to lay down your life for someone.'

'If we're careful, that's something we won't even have to think—'

'Church, be realistic. If we go into this, we're not all, maybe not any of us, going to come out of it alive. You know that. Don't insult me by pretending it's not true.'

He was hypnotised by what he saw in her eyes.

'You've changed too,' she continued. 'You've grown in a lot of ways, in just a few short weeks.'

'Yeah, well, you know how it is. Pressure is the catalyst for change.'

'It's a shame we have to lose our innocence.' Although she said *we*, Church felt she was talking about him.

'You can't stay innocent and face up to sacrifice and death and war. Those bastards killed my innocence when they arranged for Marianne to die. *To forge my character,*' he added with a sneer.

'You mustn't let it eat you up.'

'I won't. I let that happen before, when I thought I was somehow complicit in Marianne's *suicide.* It's not going to happen again. I'm going to find whoever killed Marianne and I'm going to get my revenge, but I won't be *consumed* by it. This is different. It's colder, harder.' He could tell she wasn't happy about what his words implied about the change in his character, but on this subject he didn't care. 'I'm not stupid. I've read the classics and I know how revenge destroys people. But for the kind of suffering that's been caused to all of us, there has to be some kind of payback.'

The fire was starting to die down and a chill crept across the campsite, belying the summer that was just around the corner.

'What's to become of us all?' Ruth said with a troubled smile.

It was a rhetorical question, but Church felt the need to answer it nonetheless. 'We'll do the best we can and damn the consequences.'

The morning was clear and fresh. The fires on the mainland had mostly burned themselves out, but there was still the occasional tendril of smoke snaking up into the blue sky. Shavi was the first to rise and he immediately went to the sea wall to survey the stretch of water that separated Skye from the blackened ruins that remained of the Kyle of Lochalsh. Returning to the camp as the others prepared breakfast, he announced that the serpent which had patrolled the waters seemed to have departed with the Fomorii presence. Only Ruth caught the glimmer of relief in his face.

After they had eaten an unappetising breakfast of muesli and water, they found a boat on the sea front and Tom steered it across the strait to where they had abandoned their van the previous day. By 10 a.m., they were on their way north along deserted main roads. Ten miles outside of the Kyle of Lochalsh, they saw a farmer attending to hedges away on a hillside, and the further they progressed the more signs of life they encountered, until it seemed the devastation they had encountered was just an aberration.

When they stopped at a pub in Achnasheen for lunch, they were chased away by the landlord and some irate locals. The explanation came at an old-fashioned garage further along the road. When the owner shuffled out to fill their tank, checked cap raised over a ruddy face, he told them of a rumour circulating in the area that the Government's imposition of martial law and the censorship of the media was to prevent panic because a plague was loose in the country; what kind of plague, no one was quite sure. He didn't believe it himself. The view among his own particular group was that the 'bastard politicians' had finally been overcome by their innate corruption and were using a manufactured crisis as a smokescreen to get rid of the democratic process. It had all started with the gun laws, he said. The tragedy at Dunblane was the excuse, but the weapons had really been controlled to prevent an armed uprising. But, he said conspiratorially, a few landowners had held on to their shotguns and were stockpiling them for use 'when the soldiers come'. At this, he decided he had said too much and took their money in silence before retreating to his dusty shack.

The further north they travelled, the more the people seemed to be untroubled by everything that was happening. They stopped at one farm for supplies of milk, bacon and eggs, only to discover the farmer's wife who served them knew nothing of the martial law. 'We don't have a telly,' she said in her thick Highlands accent, 'and we're too busy to listen to the radio.'

The final leg of the journey took them on a road that was straight as a die through the Beinn Eighe nature reserve, where pine trees and gorse clustered hard against the road. The wildness of this no man's land made them all uncomfortable; they felt as if humanity had been driven out by an angry, hateful nature for all the crimes it had committed; the new occupants were more respectful of nature's rules, and unforgiving of anyone who dared venture back into that dark, green domain. Sometimes strange movements could be glimpsed among the shadows beneath the trees; occasionally the quietness was disturbed by cries that came from no bird or animal they could recognise.

The oppressiveness eased slightly when the road took them along the banks of Loch Maree, which was so clear and still it looked like the sky had been brought down to earth. The scenery all around was breathtaking. Across the loch, the banks rose up sharply to soaring, rocky hillsides which were dappled by purple cloud shadows interspersed with brilliant patches of sunlight. From the top, white waterfalls cascaded down gloriously.

Soon after they arrived at Gairloch, a small fishing village perched on the edge of a sheltered sea loch. It was a balmy late afternoon with the seagulls screeching overhead and the smell of the day's catch mingling with the salty aroma of seaweed all along the harbour front. Boats sat up on trailers everywhere, but only the gentle lapping of the waves disturbed the lazy atmosphere.

After parking the van overlooking a tiny jetty, Veitch clambered out and stretched his muscles before turning to survey the thickly wooded slopes all around. 'I thought we were driving up to the bloody top of the world. Who the hell are we supposed to be seeing up here?'

Ruth turned her face to the warmth of the sun. 'Come on, Tom. You've kept us in suspense all day.'

'You know, the old git only does it because he knows if he tells us everything we'll dump him in the nearest rest home.' Laura adjusted her sunglasses, studiously avoiding Tom's fierce glare.

'You'll wait until the time's right,' he said icily. 'If you had a little patience and started listening a little more, you might actually gain a little wisdom. We won't be doing anything until sunset so you may as well make yourself busy.'

They unloaded the camping equipment and split it between them before setting off on foot along a valley that ran up into the hills. They walked for two hours until they were exhausted, continually scanning among the trees for any sign of danger. When they broke above the treeline they pitched camp on the sunlit, grassy slopes, admiring the amazing views across the wildly beautiful countryside. After lighting a fire Shavi cooked the bacon and eggs and prepared beans on toast for Laura, which they devoured hungrily after their exertion.

Tom avoided all their questions in his usual irritatingly brusque manner until the sun started to ease towards the horizon, and then he marshalled them and led them across the slopes and around rocky outcroppings where the only sound was the whistle of the wind. Finally they mounted a bank and looked down on the remnants of a stone circle.

It was only identifiable as a henge at close inspection; to the cursory observer the arrangement of rocks looked almost natural, an illusion that was added to by the few recumbent stones which had not survived the passing of the centuries. Set on the grassy plain, with a vista across the forested landscape towards the setting sun, they could fully understand why their ancestors had located it in that spot; there was a sense of awe from simply being there with only nature all around. A respectful silence came over them the instant they laid eyes on it and, automatically, they all bowed their heads in respect. When they were just a few feet away, Church dipped down and stretched out his fingers to the short grass. A blue spark leapt up from the earth to his fingertips and disappeared up his arm.

'It's true,' Ruth said. 'Can you feel it?'

Shavi closed his eyes and put his head back beatifically. 'Yes. The earth power.'

'A few weeks ago I didn't feel a thing in any of these old sites. Now I've got a tingling in my legs, my hands.' Ruth looked round curiously. 'A feeling of—'

'Well-being,' Tom interrupted. 'The Pendragon Spirit within you has grown stronger through your experiences. The spirit and the earth power come from the same source. Naturally, you sense an affinity.'

'If the spirit inside us grows stronger, where will it end?' Shavi asked with an expression of wonder.

Tom smiled enigmatically. 'Millennia ago, when the blue fire pulsed through the arteries of the earth, all men experienced what you feel now. And perhaps they will again. Once you have awakened the sleeping king.'

They processed into the centre of the circle and looked around. All was silent apart from the breeze humming in their ears. The sun was fat and scarlet on the horizon, about to tip below the distant hills, the sky red at the lowest point, merging through purple to dark blue.

'There's no one anywhere near here,' Veitch protested. 'We just going to sit around till somebody turns up?'

'No,' Tom replied. 'We are going to summon the *Gruagaich* and petition them for aid.'

There was suspicion in all their faces, to which Church gave voice. 'We've had enough of being manipulated by any supernatural force that happens to cross our path—'

'Don't worry,' Tom interjected sharply. 'This time we turn to our own.'

'What do you mean?'

Tom motioned to the stones. 'This has been a place of summoning for as long as people have settled in the area. You see that stone over there? It is the *clach na Gruagaich*, one of several by that name scattered around Scotland. This site is hardly known by anyone outside the locals, who would leave an offering in its hollow for the spirits they knew could be contacted here – mainly milk, for protection of the cattle. They believed the spirits were brownies or some other *daoine-sith*.' He smiled contemptuously. 'The *good neighbours*, their euphemistic term for the beings of Otherworld, or Elfame as they called it. Faerie.'

'But they weren't?'

'No. The clue is in the name. *Gruagaich. Long-haired ones.*' He watched the sun for a long moment. Only a thin arc was visible now above the silhouetted hills. 'The first among the old tribes. The people who took up the mantle of the power discovered by the ones who put up these stones. The Celts.'

After a long pause, Veitch said doubtfully, 'You're going to talk to ghosts?'

'We will summon the Celtic dead,' Tom stated emphatically.

Ruth's brow knit. 'What can they know that could help us?'

'In the spirit world, all vistas are open. And these are not just any spirits. They are linked to you through time, the first Brothers and Sisters of Dragons.'

Tom's words sent a shiver running through all of them just as the sun slipped completely below the horizon and darkness swept across the land. But a second later, a cloud drifted away and the moon cast its silver light on the circle, limning every stone, throwing long shadows across the grass.

'It's time,' Tom said.

From his left pocket, he took a plastic bag which appeared to contain pieces of twig and dried vegetable matter. 'The sacred mushroom,' he said.

'You're a regular drugstore.' Laura's normally confident tones were softened by apprehension. 'I know where to come when I want to get blasted.'

Tom ignored her. He took a handful of the psychoactive mushrooms from the bag and moved among them, placing small quantities in their mouths. They chewed the rubbery, metallic-tasting pieces and swallowed with distaste.

Tom ingested several himself, then took out the battered tin in which he kept his hash and meticulously constructed a joint. When he was done, he lit it and inhaled before walking over to the altar stone. There, he blew out the smoke gently. It rose like a ghost in the moonlight. Using his lighter, he charred the edge of the remaining hash and crumbled some of it into the hollow on the stone. Then, head bowed, he took a few paces back and sat cross-legged, drawing the pungent smoke deep inside him.

Veitch and Laura shifted uneasily, but Shavi, Church and Ruth were overcome by an atmosphere of sanctity. On some level they couldn't quite comprehend, they sensed a change begin to take place around them, as if the air itself were growing heavier, filled with the weight of what was to come. Church swallowed and tasted iron filings in his mouth; his heart began to beat faster as a tingling sensation ran from his groin along his spine to his head. He wondered how much was the drugs and how much was actually happening.

It felt like they waited for an age, feeling the wind gently brush their skin, filled with the summery scent of the warm pine forests. But then they noticed a distant movement away in the night. Initially it seemed to be only moonshadows on the rolling terrain, except it became too insistent; the blurred edges of the shadows hardened, the undulating movement became more defined into smaller units. Slowly, Church scanned the area, squinting to draw form from the gloom. Another shiver ran through him when the images finally took shape.

Figures were separating themselves from the landscape in a wide arc, advancing slowly on the stone; he estimated there must have been about a hundred of them, mostly men, but some women. At first they were just silhouettes against a lighter dark, but in their eerie, silent advance, details began to emerge. Long, dark hair; skin that was swarthy where visible but in the main covered by what appeared to be mud, as if they had camouflaged themselves for guerrilla warfare; with the furs and hides that kept them warm and the way they moved, in a low, loping way, they resembled some odd half-beast creatures.

Finally they came to a halt thirty feet from the stone. The breeze blew among them, rustling hair and furs, but they were so unmoving in the gloom they merged with the stones and the outcropping rocks. It was impossible to discern their faces; pools of shadows filled their eye sockets, leaving Church and the others with the horrible sensation that if the shadows cleared, there would be no eyes there at all. The night was suddenly alive with anxiety and danger; Church knew in some instinctive way that however insubstantial the revenants appeared, they were not passive creatures; he couldn't shake the feeling that, with the wrong word or movement, they would attack. From the corner of his eye he could see the others staring at Tom, silently urging him to break the oppressive mood.

After what felt like an age, Tom rose to address the dark assembly; he held out his hands in the universal sign of friendly greeting.

'What do you want, teacher?'

The voice seemed to be in Church's head. The words rumbled with a strange accent, but they were clearly modern English, although he couldn't begin to understand how the communication was taking place. One of the figures moved out of the mass. He didn't appear to walk; it was almost as if, in the blink of Church's eyelid, the figure had shifted forwards several feet. There was nothing about him that signified he was a leader or spokesman.

'We come in this time of crisis to call upon your great wisdom, revered ancestor.' Tom's head was slightly bowed in respect.

'It must be a matter of import to summon us back from the Grim Lands.' There was a worrying note in the words, but then the speaker inclined his head slightly towards Church and the others and his tone became more respectful. 'I sense in these the shimmering blue fire of the Great Mother Bridgit.'

'They are Brothers and Sisters of Dragons.'

The Celt bowed his head. 'The fire of life has found a good home.'

Church felt a sudden surge in his heart. In the Celt's words was a regard and acceptance that cut through his own fears about his abilities.

'In our hearts and spirits, we make our offerings,' Tom continued. 'Will you hear me?'

'We know you too, brother. Your kind administered to us from the sacred groves. It is good to know the lore survives the years. We will hear you.'

Church saw the tension go out of Tom's shoulders. 'You will be aware, as in the first days, that there is darkness on the land and blood in the wind. The Fomorii have returned.' A tremor seemed to run through the throng; Church's heightened senses felt a wave of threat. 'They wish to trap the people in the Eternal Night. That must never happen again. We can no longer rely on the comfort of the Children of Danu. But, as in your days, though the arm is weak, the heart is strong. Yet, still, we need something more to aid us in our struggle. Guide us with your wisdom.'

There was a moment of hanging tension when Church thought the spirits weren't going to answer. Then: 'You must find the Luck of the Land if you are ever to unleash the true power of the people.'

'What is the Luck of the Land?'

Silence; just the soughing of the wind. Tom chewed on his lip. 'Then tell me this, I beseech you: in the Grim Lands, all existence is laid out before you. Where is the Fomorii nest where Balor will be reborn?'

'The Heart of Shadows will rejoin this world betwixt here and there, but he will find his home where the Luck of the Land is kept.'

Church could sense Tom fighting with his normally irritable nature at their opaque answers, but the Rhymer knew a word out of line would not only ruin their opportunity to discover more information, it could prove fatal to them. The spirits may once have been kin, Church thought, but their time in what they called the Grim Lands had changed them immeasureably; he didn't want to antagonise them at all. Cautiously scanning the massed ranks for any sign of attack, he saw a shape that seemed familiar. It was only a fleeting glimpse of a profile against the starlit sky, but it struck a chord with him. He lost it almost instantly and before he had chance to seek it out again, Tom's measured tones distracted him.

'Revered ancestors, is there any guidance you can give us which will aid us in our great task? Anything at all?'

'Wise teacher, in my words lies your salvation. You require more? Then heed this: for the source of threat, look within as well as without. For direction, follow your hearts south to the city of the Well of Fire. For success in battle, cleanse the darkness from the spirit of your chieftain. And remember this: an ally already stands tall among the Children of Danu. Treat him with respect to keep his comfort close. Now, your offering was gratefully received, but it will buy no more of my patience. If you require anything else, you must pay for it with a life. Do you wish to proceed?'

Suddenly, the arc of Celts seemed too close, ready to cut off any retreat. As Church looked round, they seemed to waver like an image in a heat haze and for a moment he sensed something very like hunger; anxiety began to turn to fear deep in the pit of his stomach.

'Revered ancestor, we have been enlightened by your wisdom,' Tom began. 'And we offer our gracious thanks for your time. We shall delay you no more. We wish you well on your return to the Grim Lands.'

The Celt who had addressed them lowered his head slightly in parting and, for the briefest instant, the shadows that covered his eyes seemed to clear; what Church glimpsed there made his mind squirm and he had to stop himself fleeing back to the campfire.

It was several minutes after the Celts had melted back into the landscape before anyone spoke. It was as if they were coming out of a dream, one tinged with incipient menace where strange truths had been made known, so strange that they could barely be comprehended upon awakening. The feeling was heightened when they realised they could only hazily remember what they had seen, although the words still rang out in their minds.

'Did we actually experience that, or was it the mushrooms?' Ruth asked. Church saw she was gripping her hands together to prevent them shaking.

'A little of both,' Tom replied.

Shavi nodded in agreement. 'The mushrooms are the key to opening the doors of perception.'

Tom smiled suddenly. 'I remember seeing Jim Morrison perform in Florida—'

'Most old gits talk about the war,' Laura interrupted. 'We get reminiscences of the happy hippie trail. Now can we get back to the fire – it's freezing out here.'

Veitch pulled out a bottle of single malt he'd found in the grocery store on Kyleakin and they drank it from plastic cups around the fire.

'So, correct me if I'm wrong, but that was just a load of cryptic bollocks that wasted our time, right?' Although Laura sat next to Church, she was careful not to make the others feel uncomfortable by showing any sign of her affection for him, though Church had sensed an obvious proprietary instinct in the way she had taken her seat just as Ruth was walking up.

Tom shook his head. 'They didn't make it easy for us, but all the information they offered is vital.'

'Except we probably won't crack the code until it's too late,' Church noted. 'What's the Luck of the Land?'

'I have no idea. The Celts believed it was dangerous to name a sacred thing by its true name, which is why these exercises end up in irritating circumlocution.' Tom took a deep swig of the whisky and then said tartly, 'But we can pull some pearls from the verbal ordure. The city of the Well of Fire is Edinburgh. There's an extinct volcanic feature in the city called Arthur's Seat.'

'More Arthurian code for a site linked to the earth power?' Church mused.

'It's a very powerful source, the most powerful in Scotland. The Well lies under Arthur's Seat.'

'Then that's where we've got to go. Shouldn't take too long from here.' Veitch lay back with his hands behind his head.

'The ally is obviously Cernunnos.' Ruth examined the mark that had been burned into the flesh of her hand by the nature god. She had a sudden flashback to the rainswept night in Manorbier, the terrifying power she had seen in the being as its body melted and changed like oil on water.

'Your ally,' Veitch noted. 'You're his big pal.'

'As long as I'm with you, he's with you. But how are we supposed to show him *respect*?'

'These beings,' Shavi mused, 'seem to expect deference from those beneath them in the hierarchy of power.'

'I'll just tug my forelock in front of the toffs,' Veitch sneered. 'Blimey, talk about things being the same all over.'

'The Celts rightly believed islands were prime places for carrying out rituals,' Tom stated. 'Not far from here, in Loch Maree, there's an island called Eilean Maree, with a sacred grove dedicated to the Tuatha Dé Danann, where we can make an offering to—'

'How do you know all these things, *wise teacher*?' Laura asked pointedly.

Shavi eyed Tom incisively. 'Tom knows all of the lore of the Celts, is that not right? You told us you were tutored by the people of the Bone Inspector—'

'And so the knowledge of being a freak is passed down,' Laura sniffed.

'And the Bone Inspector spoke of his people, an unbroken line of guardians of the *old places* stretching back through history,' Shavi continued.

Church threw another branch on the fire. 'Well, we all know what cleansing the darkness from the chieftain means,' he added sombrely, 'though a little guidance on how to go about it wouldn't have gone amiss.'

'There was one other thing,' Ruth said. 'What did *for the source of the threat, look within as well as without* mean?'

'As if you don't know.' Laura stared deep into the heart of the fire. 'It means one of us is looking to earn thirty pieces of silver.'

After the others had retired to their tents, Church and Laura sat warming themselves by the dying embers. In the midst of all the chaos and tension, Church felt remarkably comforted to have Laura curled up next to him. With his arm around her and her head on his shoulder, the emotional closeness to another human filled him with a sense of well-being.

'This is what it's all about,' he muttered to himself.

'You're talking to yourself again.'

Although they were entwined, Laura still seemed a little stiff and distant. He had started to strip away the many defences she had erected to protect herself, but he knew it would be a long time before she gave her inner self up freely. In fact, the more he got to know her, the more he felt the acid-tongued, confident, aggressive Laura was a character that had been completely constructed, and whatever lay within was something he might not recognise at all. But that sense of protecting the vulnerable heart of their being was something they shared, and possibly what had attracted them in the first place.

'So this Marianne must have been a big thing in your life,' she said after a long period of introspection.

'We'd been together a long time. We were going to get married. So, yes, she was a big thing.'

'I suppose that explains why you were knocked so out of whack when she died. Do you think you'll ever get over it?'

'I don't think anybody ever gets over something like that. You just learn to accommodate it.'

She thought about this for a moment, then said, 'What was she like?'

'Oh, I don't know—'

'Go on, I want to know. Was she a good person?'

'I suppose. I never really thought of her like that. She was pretty much a malice-free zone. But she had her bad qualities – who doesn't?'

'Yeah, right. But it's a balancing act, isn't it? There aren't any real goodies or baddies. Most people manage to keep that scale just right, a little bit up, a little bit down, over the course of a life. And just a few go up one side or the other.' She dug him sharply in the ribs with her elbow. 'Christ, it's like getting blood out of a stone with you.'

'I think that's a black kettle and pot situation.' He sighed. 'She was smart. She read a lot. She liked to talk about ideas, about things that mattered. She made me laugh. She took the piss out of me when I was being pompous. She didn't take the piss out of me when I was talking about a list of dreary finds from some boring dig in Somerset. She could argue the case for northern soul when I was banging on about guitar music. She'd watch *Star Wars* with me and wouldn't beg me to watch *Jean de Florette* with her. And she allowed me to be weak.' He paused, feeling the rawness of some of the emotions that were surfacing. '*Life's good as long as you don't weaken* – that's a pretty good rule of thumb. We all have to keep up a resilient front, but you know you've found someone good when you can let the barriers down to show that weak, pathetic, character-destroying side of you, that part that you have to let out every now and then or go mad, but you normally have to do in the privacy of your room.' He took a deep breath and let it out slowly. 'Is that good enough for you?'

'It'll do. For now.'

'Why did you want to know? For the sake of comparison?'

'No. What's gone is gone. That doesn't bother me. But you can find out a lot about someone from the way they view the love of their life.'

Her words made him give pause. 'Very lateral thinking. So what did you find out?'

'You don't think I'm going to tell you, do you?'

'Okay. Tell me about the love of your life.'

She laughed. 'You must think I'm a real sucker. Sorry, pal, my past is a closed book.'

He pulled her in tight and gave her scalp a monkey scrub.

'Ow! Just because you can't compete with my intellect.' She pinched him hard until Veitch hollered from the depths of his tent for them to be quiet. Then they giggled like schoolchildren and continued their conversation in hushed tones.

'So,' Church said eventually, 'do you and I get a happy ending, do you think?'

There was a long pause that surprised him, and when he looked up at her face he saw the humour had drained from it. 'Come on, Church, you're a big boy now. Look around you. There aren't going to be any happy endings.'

Church sighed. 'Why's everyone so pessimistic? Ruth said something similar.'

'Yeah, I knew she'd been talking to you. Well . . . maybe it's a chick thing. You boys have no perception. No happy endings. We just have to make the most of what we've got for as long as we've got it.' There was a note of deep sadness in her voice, but a second later she had forced herself to brighten and was tugging him towards the tent. 'Come on. I want my brains removing and you've got just the tool to do it.'

chapter two

turn off your mind, relax, and float downstream

'It's beautiful.' Pressing her face against the window, Ruth looked out at the tranquil expanse of Loch Maree. The water was as glassy as it had been the previous day, reflecting the overcast sky punctured by bursts of blue and the hillsides that soared up steeply in a breathtaking wall of brown, purple and green. In the centre of the water lay Eilean Maree, serene and secret among its thick trees.

It had taken them only twenty-five minutes from Gairloch after a hearty breakfast of farmhouse bacon and eggs. They were all eager to continue on to Edinburgh and civilisation, but Tom had convinced them that a brief pause to make an offering to Cernunnos would pay dividends in the long run.

'I've got some reservations about this,' Church said as they parked up on the water's edge. 'Making an offering is a tacit admission that we accept they're our gods rather than simply beings that are more powerful than us. I have no intention of doffing my cap and being fawning—'

'Even if it means saving your life?' Tom interrupted.

Church radiated defiance. 'Even then. I'm not bowing down. I'm not folding up and showing my throat—'

'Then don't see it as an offering. See it as a bribe.' Tom marched off across the pebbles to a small boat that had been pulled up on the bank.

Veitch rowed Laura, Ruth and Tom over first, then came back for Shavi and Church. The island was small and rocky along the shoreline, but heavily wooded with a thick undergrowth. They moved cautiously away from the light at the banks to the shadows that lay beneath the leafy covering. There was a tangible atmosphere of peace which put them at ease; it reminded

Shavi of the aura of calm that hung over the grounds of Glastonbury Abbey. Yet despite the idyllic setting, no birds sang at all.

Tom led them through the trees to the tip of the island. In a grove, out of sight of the road, an obvious altar had been created from a tree stump. Wild flowers lay on it, along with a cup of milk and the remnants of a loaf of bread. The air of sanctity was at its most concentrated in the altar's vicinity.

'Looks like someone's been here before us,' Church noted.

'The power that Cernunnos represents didn't die away when the old gods left,' Tom replied. 'In places away from the cities there's been an unbroken chain of worship. Some people are still close to the land. Some refuse to forget.'

'Fuckin' nutters,' Veitch muttered.

'And there's the arrogance of the urban dweller.' Tom pressed his spectacles back on to the bridge of his nose, a mannerism which Church recognised as a sign of irritation. 'I thought you would have learned by now not to judge by surface. Whales move in deep water and leave no mark of their passing.'

'Whales?' Veitch said distractedly. 'What the fuck are you talking about?'

They stood in front of the altar for a moment, deep in thought. Then Ruth said, 'I want to make an offering too.'

Church looked at her in surprise, but Tom said, 'As you choose. You must respond to your feelings.'

High in the branches above them echoed a long, mournful hoot which seemed to come in response. Church picked out Ruth's owl looking down at them. 'Your familiar seems to be happy about that.' He had a sudden twinge of uneasiness when he glanced back at Ruth; he couldn't shake the feeling she was being sucked into something she couldn't control.

'What would make a good oblation, I wonder?' Shavi asked.

'Something important to us,' Tom replied.

Shavi searched in his pocket for the few remaining magic mushrooms which he used to induce his shamanistic trances. Church thought he laid them on the altar with undue gratitude.

While the others discussed the offering, Laura drifted away. She had little interest in what they were doing, certainly little belief, and sometimes she was overcome by an abiding need to be on her own, alone with her thoughts; since they had joined forces there had been little opportunity for that.

She leaned on one of the trunks and looked through the trees, watching the rippling waves sparkle in the scant sunlight. The place made her feel good in a way she hadn't really experienced before; it was so peaceful she wouldn't have complained if they'd decided to pitch camp there for a few days, maybe even longer.

It was only when the tranquility blanketed her that she realised how anxious she always felt, a constant buzz that set her teeth on edge and locked her shoulder muscles. Gradually, though, the stress began to ease away, and the droning voices of the others slipped into dim awareness. It stayed that way for long enough that she felt a wash of damp emotion when she realised something had changed. It took her a second or two to grasp what it was: no one was speaking in the background. An unsettling tingle started at the base of her spine. Her first thought was that they had all stopped talking to stare at her. She prepared an acid response and turned to confront them.

She was surprised and unsettled to see they were still standing in the same position, unmoving; a deep unnatural silence lay over them. They weren't holding their breath, or listening for something. Everyone was frozen, hands mid-gesture, mouths poised in question or response, as if time had stopped in that one small spot.

Laura felt a chill creep over her. A change had come to the soothing atmosphere on the island too; it was now heavy with anticipation.

Something's coming, she thought, without quite knowing how she had recognised that.

Her eyes darted among the trees. The island wasn't so big that someone could creep up on them unannounced; they would have heard *something*. As if in answer to her thought, she *did* hear a sound. Branches cracked, leaves rustled suddenly. She spun round quickly, her heart hammering.

Light and shadow changed on the periphery of her vision. It could have been an illusion caused by her blinking, but, coupled with the sound, she was sure: something big was lumbering around in the trees. But whenever she tried to pin it down among the undergrowth it had already moved on to somewhere else. She caught a flicker of a silhouette, then gone. A heavy footstep that sounded only feet away, then another one near the water's edge.

She backed up hastily to the others, tugged at Church's arm in the hope of somehow waking him, but when her fingers brushed his skin, it felt as cold as marble. Something like a stone seemed to grow in her throat. She crouched down to lower herself below the line of sight, then moved forward through the vegetation. If she could get to the boat, she could row out on to the water and reassess the situation, possibly go around the island until she could get a good view of what she was up against. Either that, or she could just run back to the van and drive off.

But the moment she was away from the tiny clearing surrounding the altar, things became even more confusing. Sounds were distorted by the undergrowth, the shape began to move faster, its thrashing becoming more animal-like. Anxiety knotted in her chest. She put her head down and dashed, but she hadn't gone far when her foot caught on a branch which she was convinced hadn't been there before. She went sprawling; the impact knocked the wind out of her. As she attempted to scramble back to her feet, a dark shape loomed above her like a cloud moving across the sun. Cold, unforgiving. She glanced up into a face which registered for only the merest instant before her consciousness winked out under the protest of an incomprehensible, alien sight.

When she came round, Church was crouching next to her. The others had gathered a few feet away, watching her with concern.

'Stop looking at me,' she snapped.

'What happened?' Church asked.

'There was something here, in the trees.' As her thoughts whizzed, she became aware of a dull ache on the back of her right hand. She raised it slowly, turning it until she located the right spot. Burned into the flesh was a familiar design: interlocking leaves in a circle.

Laura's attention snapped on to Ruth who was staring in shock at the tattoo. It matched the one she carried: the mark of Cernunnos delivered to her after the confrontation in Wales.

'Get a grip. It doesn't make us sisters.' Laura rubbed her hand, obscuring the sign.

'It looks as if our great nature god has decided to honour two of our number,' Shavi said thoughtfully.

'He told me there were two of us.' Ruth looked at Laura curiously.

'What's the matter? Can't believe you're not *special* any more?' Laura let Church haul her to her feet, then quickly thrust her hand into her trouser pocket. 'So does this mean I'm going to be a witch-bitch too?'

'It simply means,' Tom said, 'that Cernunnos has some plan for you.'

'That's a relief,' Laura said sourly. 'I thought it was something bad.'

They rowed back across the water in silence. Laura seemed even more locked-off than normal, ignoring all their attempts to get her to talk about her experience, but they could see it lay on her shoulders like a rock. Church, who probably understood her the best – and even then, not very well at all – saw something in her eyes that made him want to take her on one side and hold her; it was a look that suggested she was ready to run from something with which she could no longer cope.

As they gathered at the water's edge, mulling over what the encounter meant, Shavi glanced towards the van and raised the alarm. They all scrambled over the rocks as one, but Church was the first one to reach it, not quite believing what he was seeing. On the bonnet was a dead rabbit, its blood trickling down towards the radiator grille. It had been gutted, the stomach cavity splayed to the air, its internal organs carefully laid out beside it.

'What the fuck's this?' Veitch said in disgust.

Shavi stepped forward and examined the carcass without touching it. 'It was left for us particularly,' he said after a brief moment. 'You can see the precise nature of the cuts. Someone took the time to do this.'

'Is it linked to what happened on the island?' Ruth asked.

Tom shook his head. 'I wouldn't think—'

'Wait!' Shavi leaned forward to peer into the stomach cavity. 'There is something in here.'

'Don't touch it,' Ruth pleaded.

Church watched her from the corner of his eye; she seemed unnaturally fearful, as if she were sensing something without being aware of it. 'Be careful,' he cautioned.

Shavi looked around until he located two twigs which he held like chopsticks. Cautiously he used them to investigate the rabbit's interior. A second later he retracted what at first appeared to be a small pink slug smeared in blood.

'That is gross!' Laura screwed up her face, but couldn't tear her eyes away.

It was a finger, severed at the knuckle.

Shavi laid it on the bonnet and they all gathered round, as if they expected it to move. 'Who could it belong to?' Shavi mused. 'And why was it left here for us?'

Veitch scanned the deserted hillsides, which were suddenly unwelcoming and lonely. 'We should be getting out of here.'

The grisly discovery cast a pall over their journey south. For the first few miles they travelled without speaking, struggling to make sense of it all, feeling a deep dread creeping out of the mystery. There was something about the image that was inherently evil, ritualistic, beyond mere threat. Yet it made no sense, and it was that which wormed its way into their subconscious and lay there, gnawing silently.

They picked up the A9 just north of Inverness and followed it south through the rugged, desolate landscape of the Cairngorms. Two technology crashes slowed them up and it soon became apparent they would be searching for somewhere to stay in Edinburgh by the time the curfew came around. The best option seemed to be to break their journey and set off for the city fresh and early the next day. So, hungry and bored with the road, they arrived in the small town of Callander at the foot of the Highlands in the late afternoon.

The jumbled collection of stone buildings nestled so hard against the thickly wooded foothills that, with the mountains soaring up in the background all around, they felt instantly enveloped and protected; it was a pleasant sensation after all the wide open spaces. The town smelled of fish and chips and pine, but that too was oddly soothing. A lot more people were wandering around than they had seen for days, their faces free of the taint of fear. It gave hope that the major centres of population still hadn't been too affected.

It was a long time since they had experienced the comfort of a soft bed so they opted to spend the night in a hotel. The Excelsior lay at the end of the main street, a Gothic-styled pile of stone that resembled a fortress with its turrets on four corners and enormous windows looking out on all sides. The thick, wild forest swept down almost to the very back of it, but it still seemed a place that could be secure.

While the others rested or abluted, Church and Veitch went down to the hotel bar. It was comfortingly cool and dark away from the bright afternoon sun and had the cosy feel of a place which had grown organically rather than been designed to fit the frenzied drive for increased profits. Veitch had a Stella, Church a Guinness, and they took their drinks to a table in a window bay where they could look out on to the sun-drenched main street.

'It's the little things I'm going to miss,' Veitch said introspectively.

'What do you mean?'

'Like this.' He held up the pint so it glowed golden in a sunbeam. 'If things carry on falling apart, we're not going to keep getting things like this, are we? It won't be important. All the bigshots will be making sure everyone just has enough food, trying to keep the riots to a minimum.'

Church laughed quietly. 'So that's your motivation, is it? Fight for the pint?'

'No,' Veitch replied indignantly, missing the humour. 'It's just the little things that bring all this shit home. You look out there and you can almost believe everything's the same as it always was. But it's right on the brink of going belly-up. How long do you think it's got?'

Church shrugged. 'Depends how soon the Fomorii and the Tuatha Dé Danann start flexing their muscles and really screwing things up. Maybe they'll leave us alone enough to carry on with some kind of normality.' Even to himself, he didn't sound very convincing.

There was a long pause while they both sipped their beer and then Veitch said, 'You know what those spooks said. About one of us being a snake in the grass. It isn't me, you know.' He looked at Church uncomfortably. 'Because with my past record, I know that's what everyone's going to be thinking.'

'I don't think that's true, Ryan.'

'Don't get me wrong, I don't blame them. Everything I've ever done points in that direction. I'm just saying. It's not me.' His gaze shifted away as he asked, 'Do you believe me? It's important that you believe me. The others, I don't—' He held back from whatever he was about to say.

Church thought for a moment, then replied, 'I believe you.'

Veitch's shoulders relaxed and he couldn't restrain a small, relieved smile which crept around the lip of his glass. He finished the lager with a long draught. 'All right, then. Who do you think it is?'

'It's hard to believe any of us could be some kind of traitor. I think I'm a pretty good judge of human nature and I don't see anything that makes me even slightly suspicious.'

'The old hippie sold us down the river once.'

'But that wasn't his doing. Anyway, that's been sorted out. Once the parasite was removed from his head he was back to normal.'

Veitch leaned back in his seat and rested one foot on a stool. 'You reckon they were making it up then?'

'Not making it up exactly. It seems to me that whenever any information comes over from some supernatural source, it's never quite how you think it is. They're saying one thing, you hear another. I think they do it on purpose, another power thing,' he added with weary exasperation.

'Well, I'm going to be watching everyone very carefully.'

'That's what I'm worried about. I don't want paranoia screwing things up from within. There's enough of a threat outside.'

An old man with a spine curved by the years and a face that was little more than skin on bone shuffled in and cast a curious glance in their direction before making his way to the bar. He was wearing a checked, flat cap and a long brown overcoat, despite the warmth of the day. Pint in hand, he headed towards a seat in a shadowy corner, then seemed to think twice and moved over to the table next to them.

'Mind if I sit here?' His accent had the gentle, lilting quality of the Highlands, his voice steady, despite his appearance. Once he'd settled, he glanced at them with jovial slyness. 'Out-of-towners?'

'We're travelling down to Edinburgh,' Church said noncommittally.

'On holiday?'

'Something like that.'

The old man sipped his beer thoughtfully. 'You wouldn't happen to know what's going on in the world, would you?'

'What do you mean?'

'With the papers all printing junk and the TV and the radio playing the same old rubbish from the Government, you can't get any news worth hearing. It's got to be something bad to shut down the TV. We always get lots of tourists travelling through here from the cities, but there's been nary a soul over the last few days. So what have you seen?'

Church wondered how he could begin to explain to the man what was happening; wondered if he should. Veitch interjected before he could reply, 'All seems pretty normal to me, mate.'

'Aye, that's what everyone round here is saying. Oh, there was a bit of panic when those Government messages started repeating, but once the police went round calming everyone down and we all saw it wasn't the end of the world, everyone carried on as normal.' He chuckled. 'What are we going to do with us, eh?'

'So what do you think's happening?' Church asked.

'Aye, well,' the old man rubbed his chin, 'that's the question. Like I say, at the moment it doesn't seem too bad. Oh, there's a few things you can't seem to get in the shops, but there's talk they might be rationing petrol—'

'Oh?' Church glanced at Veitch, both aware of the problems that might arise if their ability to travel was hampered.

'Aye. So they say. Could be shortages. And the phone's off more than it's on. It's awful hard trying to find out what's happening in the next village, never mind in the cities.' He looked at Church and Veitch with a tight smile. 'Reminds me of the war.'

Church glanced out into the main street at a boy cycling by lazily. 'I bet you get a lot of your income round here from tourism. What's going to happen if that dries up?'

'People will find a way to get by.' The old man took out a pipe that looked as ancient as he appeared and began to feed it with tobacco from a leather pouch. 'They always do, don't they? The Blitz spirit. People find a way.'

They all gathered in the bar at 6 p.m. to eat. The food was plain but filling and it was even more comforting to feed on something they hadn't prepared themselves on a Calor Gaz stove. The atmosphere in the place seemed so secure and easy-going after their nights on the road that even Laura's usual complaining seemed half-hearted.

After they ordered drinks, they assessed their situation and considered their plans for the future. Ruth and Shavi were bank-rolling them as the others had all run out of funds, but the two of them still had enough savings to keep them going. They discussed the possibility of fuel rationing and agreed to top up the tank first thing and, if possible, get some large diesel containers they could keep in the back. None of them discussed their prospects for success, nor did they mention Balor by name, although his presence hung oppressively on the edge of the conversation.

Apart from a few minor points, it was the severed finger that concerned them the most. During the day its obscure symbolism had set unpleasant resonances deep in their minds, triggering images which they couldn't recognise; the lack of obvious meaning made them feel hunted and insecure.

'The Fomorii wouldn't have resorted to such a subtle tactic,' Tom noted. 'They would have been upon us in an instant. But they don't care about us any longer. We're no longer a threat. In their eyes, we have failed in our primary mission.'

'Losers,' Veitch said with obvious irritation. 'At least if they're not watching us we can come up on their blind side.'

Church was heartened to see the fatalism which had infected them ever since they came together was slowly dissipating; now there seemed no doubt that they could do *something*, however little that might be. Against the all-powerful forces lined against them, that was a great victory in itself.

'It has the hallmark of someone working alone,' Shavi noted. 'In this new world, perhaps we inadvertently antagonised something. Trespassed on land it presumed was its own.'

'But who did the finger belong to?' Ruth asked.

'Some poor bastard,' Church muttered.

'Let us hope it was a warning not to go back there,' Shavi said, 'and that it has not decided to pursue us for recompense.'

The hotel was holding its weekly ceilidh that night and by 7.30 p.m. the regulars began to drift in to the large lounge next to the bar. The band had already started to set up; it was the fiddle player's intense warm-up which had attracted Church and the others. They wandered in with their drinks and were welcomed with surprising warmth. The old man Church and Veitch had met in the bar earlier was there and gave them a wink as they took a beer from the barrels lined up on a table at one end of the room.

At 8 p.m. the dancing began. The moment the fiddle player launched into his reel the lounge turned into a maelstrom of whirling men and women of all ages, skirts flying, heels flicking, grins firmly set on faces. A girl of around seventeen grabbed Shavi's arm and dragged him into the throng. He took to the dance with gusto.

Veitch backed off in case anyone pulled him in. 'Bleedin' Scottish dancing. Not my scene, mate,' he muttered.

The drink was flowing as fast as the music, with every glass of beer followed by a chaser of malt. In that atmosphere of wild abandon and life celebration it was impossible not to become involved, and soon Church and the others had lost all thought of the stresses and tensions that assailed them.

As the night drew on, they made new friends and drifted from conversation to conversation. Shavi seemed particularly popular with the young women and Ruth with the men; she surprised herself by revelling in the attention she was getting, a liberating experience after the oppression of the previous few weeks.

Sweating after a vigorous dance, she adjourned to the bar area where she found Laura lounging against the wall, sipping on a glass of neat vodka.

'Keeping all the boys happy,' Laura said coolly.

Over the weeks, Ruth had learned to ignore Laura's baiting, but with the drink rushing round her system, she found herself bristling. 'I can understand how you'd be jealous of someone who's popular.'

'Jealous? Look in the mirror, Frosty.'

'What do you mean?'

'You know what I mean.'

Ruth did, and that irritated her even more. 'If you think I'm bothered about you and Church—'

'It's pretty obvious you've been trying to wrestle him to the ground since you met him. But he's got about as much in common with you as he has with Shavi. Face it, the best woman won.' Laura smiled tightly, but her eyes were cold and hard.

Ruth could feel her anger growing, which made her even more angry. She hated to lose control, but somehow Laura knew how to punch all the right buttons. 'Do I hear desperation in your voice? Now you've got him, you're afraid of losing him, aren't you?'

Laura thought about this for a moment. 'We're right for each other.'

'What you mean is, he's right for you. You've finally found someone strong enough to carry the weight of all your emotional baggage.' Ruth caught herself before she said anything more hurtful.

'What do you know about emotions? You're an ice queen.' Laura tried to maintain her cool, but she knocked back her vodka in one go.

'That shows how much you know.'

'All I'm saying is, stay away from him. I saw you talking to him the other night, trying to wheedle your way into his affections—'

'I wouldn't dream—' Ruth caught herself as her defiance suddenly surfaced. In the background the music was raging and she had to raise her voice. 'And what would you do if I did?'

Laura turned and stared at her for a long moment with eyes impossible to read and then walked away through the crowd.

Veitch and Shavi had got into a drinking competition, knocking down shots while they were egged on by a cheering crowd. But all paused as Tom stepped onto the small, makeshift stage and whispered something to the fiddle player. A second later the musician handed over his instrument which Tom shouldered before beginning to tap out a rhythm with his right foot. And then he started to play, a low, mournful sound that made everyone in the room stop what they were doing and stare. The tune was mediaeval in construction, the melody filled with the ache of loneliness, of love never-to-be-found, of yearning and failed desire; Church felt a cold knot develop in his chest, but Tom's face was impassive, his eyes icy. And then, as if he had suddenly awoken to the fact that he had dampened the mood, Tom began to pick up the beat, slowly at first, but then quicker and quicker, until he had developed the melody into a rampant jig. A couple down the front began to clap, and the sound ripped back through the crowd until everyone was joining in, physically driving the mood back up. Within a couple of minutes, everyone was dancing again and Tom seemed to be having the time of his life.

As Church sipped on his glass of malt, his head woozy from drink, feeling uncommonly happy for the first time in days, he felt a strange sensation prickling along his spine, as if someone was watching him. In the days since he had first encountered the unknown under Albert Bridge he had learned to be attentive to his instincts. He turned quickly. There was no one behind him, but the door to the corridor which ran down to the hotel entrance was open. For a second or two, he weighed his options, then crept over to the doorway and peered out. The corridor was empty.

He had just about convinced himself it was nothing but his imagination at work when the door out on to the street swung open slightly, as if it had been buffeted by a breeze; as it did, he thought he heard a faint, melodic voice calling his name.

His heart picked up a beat, but after all he had been through, he still didn't feel wary. There was something . . . a feeling, perhaps . . . which seemed to be floating in the air from the direction of the door and it was over-whelmingly comforting. His first reaction was that he was being summoned by the spirit of Marianne, as he had been twice before, but it felt different this time. He finished his whisky, left his glass on an ornamental table in the corridor and walked towards the door.

The main street was completely still, although it wasn't late in the evening. The streetlights were bright, but not so much that they obscured

65

the glittering array of stars in the clear sky. The night itself was balmy with the promise of summer just around the corner. He looked up and down the deserted street until he saw something which caught his eye.

Across the road was the park that rolled down to the river. During the day it had been filled with the whoops of children racing around the adventure playground and the jeers of teenagers hanging out next to the log cabin where the refreshments were served, but at that time it was deserted and unnervingly quiet. He crossed the road and leant on the wall, searching the paths that wound among the waving, fluffy-tipped pampas grass. Something moved. His rational mind told him it would be ridiculous to venture down into those wide open spaces, but his instincts didn't register anything that worried him. He steeled himself, then opened the gate.

Away from the streetlights, he was uncomfortably aware of the wild presence of nature looming away in the dark, but the splashing of the river prevented the silence becoming too oppressive. Whatever had brought him down there seemed to be leading him. Every now and then he would catch sight of a movement ahead, steering him down the paths until he was following the course of the river back towards the heart of the town. Eventually he came up to a brick bridge with an old churchyard next to it. It was an odd, triangular shape, the jumbled mass of markers mildewed, with some so timeworn they resembled the ancient standing stones of Gairloch. The grass among them was thick and along the walls age-old trees were so gnarled and wind-blasted they looked like menacing figures daring him to enter. It was so eerily atmospheric in the quiet that he almost did turn back, but after another movement on the far side, he took a deep breath and swung open the green, iron gate that hung ajar.

Cautiously, he moved among the white and grey stones muttering, 'Stupid, stupid, stupid,' under his breath, but the truth was, he still didn't feel any sense of threat. And then he reached the far side and the shape that had been luring him was no longer insubstantial.

Before him stood the woman he had encountered in the Watchtower floating between the worlds, the one who had visited him on the edge of dreams as a child, and freed him from the Fomorii cells, claiming to be his patron. She was one of the Tuatha Dé Danann, infused with the beauty which permeated that race. It was almost as if her skin was glowing with a faint golden light. Her eyes, too, were flecked with gold, and her hair tumbled lustrously about her shoulders. She was wearing the same dress of dark green he remembered from before; its material was indeterminate, but it clung to her form in a way that was powerfully appealing.

She was smiling seductively, her eyes sparkling. At first Church felt as

66

entranced as he had the first time they met as adults, but gradually a mix of other emotions surfaced: suspicion, sadness and then anger.

'You tricked me,' he said. The anger took shape, hardened. 'You and all your people. You had Marianne killed. So I could be shaped into your slave to set your people free in your hour of need. You discarded a human life—' he snapped his fingers '—just like that.'

There was no sign in her face that she had been offended by his words. 'There is little I can say to put right the hurt you feel.' Her voice remained gentle. 'There is tragedy stitched into the fabric of the lives of all Frail Creatures and sometimes my people, in their endless, timeless existence, forget the suffering that comes from a simple passing.' For a surprising second, he thought he saw real tenderness in her eyes. 'I have been close to you all your life, Jack Churchill. I watched when you were born, when you played and learned. And when you were old enough, I came to you on the edge of sleep to see if you were the one who fitted the eternal pattern. The true hero infused with the glorious essence of this land. I saw in you . . .' She paused and, for the first time, seemed to have trouble finding the correct words. '. . . a nobility and passion which transcended the nature of most Frail Creatures. The Filid will one day sing tales of the great Jack Churchill.'

'That's not—'

She held up her hand to silence him. 'My part in this was small. I guided the destinies of the Brothers and Sisters of Dragons, but the decision to shape you in the crucible of death was taken elsewhere. It was never my intention to see you hurt, Jack.'

There was something in her words, in the turn of her head and the shimmer of emotion across her features, that made him think she was saying something else beyond the obvious. Her eyes were so deep and numinous he felt swallowed up by them; he couldn't maintain his anger towards her.

'If not you, then someone else is responsible. They'll have to pay. I can't forgive and forget what's been done to me, to all of us.'

'Nor would I expect you to.'

'Then who arranged it? And who carried out the act? Who killed Marianne and the others?'

'I cannot say.'

'You can't or you won't?' He tried to keep his voice stable in case he offended her. Despite her demeanour, he sensed great power and unpredictability just beneath the surface.

She pressed her hands together, almost as if she was praying. 'From your perspective, we may seem untrammelled by responsibility, as fluid in our actions as our natures. But we are bound by laws in the same way that you are, in the same way as the mountains, the seas and the wind. No one is truly free. I cannot tell you what you wish to know.'

'I'll find out.'

She nodded, said nothing.

Once he had got that out of his system, he became more aware of the situation. 'Why've you come to me?'

'To renew our acquaintance. To show you that I have no desire to abandon you, even though my people have achieved their desire.'

Church was troubled by the complexity of the emotions running through him. He felt drawn to the woman, but he couldn't tell if that was an honest feeling or simply a by-product of her manipulation of him over the years. 'What are you saying? That you want to be an ally?'

'That, and more.'

'How, more? A friend, then?'

She didn't reply. Her smile remained seductive.

Church felt a shiver of attraction run through him, fought it. 'If we're going to be friends, then you ought to tell me your name.'

'I have many names, like all my brethren.'

He waited, refusing to be drawn by her game-playing.

Her smile grew wider. 'I have been known as the Queen of the Waste Lands.'

This raised a spark of recognition in Church, but he couldn't remember where he had heard it before.

'Of the many names I have been called when I last freely walked your world, the one most used by your people was Niamh.'

'Niamh,' he repeated softly. A gentle dreaminess seemed to encircle them both; when he looked away from her, the surroundings shimmered and sparkled. 'So you're royalty?'

'In the hierarchy of the Golden Ones, I hold a position of privilege.' She held out a hand to him, and he didn't think he could resist it even if he had wanted to.

Her fingers were long and cool. They closed around his and gently pulled him towards her. As he moved in, the scent of her filled his nostrils, like lime and mint. For a moment they seemed to hang in stasis, their eyes locked; Church felt he was being pulled beneath green waves, deep, deep down to the darkness where miracles and wonders lived. And then, slowly, she moved her face closer. He felt the bloom of her breath on his lips; a tremor of anticipation ran through him down to his groin. When her lips touched his, he almost jolted from a burst of energy that could have been physical, emotional or psychological, but it left his head spinning. Her lips were as soft as peach-skin and tasted of some fruit he couldn't quite place. Her tongue flicked out and delicately caressed the tip of his own. And then the passion rushed through him, driving out all conscious thought, filling him up with insanity, and he was kissing her harder and feeling his hands slide around her slim waist to her back. And the sensation was so beyond anything he had experienced before he was suddenly tumbling through a haze into blackness.

There was darkness and then awareness that someone was summoning him. Church thought instantly: *I'm dreaming*, although he knew in the same instant that it wasn't a dream. From his vantage point at the centre of an inky cloud he saw Ruth's owl circling and at first he wondered obliquely if it was hunting. Then he realised its movements were frantic, as if it was disturbed by something attacking it.

'What's wrong,' he called out; his voice sounded like it had come from the bottom of a well.

The owl drew nearer, and then, suddenly, it was not an owl, although he wasn't quite sure what it was. It had the shape of a man, yet certain characteristics of an owl around its face, and batlike wings sprouting from its back which flapped powerfully. There was something so terrible about it that he couldn't bring himself to look it full in the face.

You must go to her. The creature's voice sounded like a metal crate being dragged over concrete. *She is in great danger. I can do nothing.*

'Who?' Church asked.

Blood. Its voice was almost threatening. *Blood everywhere.*

Church woke on the ground so disturbed he instantly jumped to his feet, as if he were under attack. An overwhelming sense of dread flooded his system. At first he couldn't fathom what was happening to him, but as he frantically looked around the deserted churchyard it started to come back. There was no sign of Niamh. And with his next thought he recalled the odd dream of the owl-thing and suddenly he understood his feelings.

'Ruth,' he murmured fearfully.

Shavi, Veitch and Tom were gathered together around a table in the hotel lounge. Church had no idea how much time had passed, but everyone else in the room had gone. They all looked up in surprise as he burst in.

'Where's Ruth?' he barked.

'Went upstairs,' Veitch slurred. 'Ages ago. Couldn't stand the—'

But Church was already sprinting back out into the corridor to the stairs. As he reached the foot, he was brought up sharp by Laura, who was just making her way down. She was staring at her hands in a daze, leaning heavily against the bannister. In horror Church saw she was splattered with blood.

'My God.' His voice seemed to be coming from somewhere else. Desperately, his eyes ranged from Laura's hands, to her face, to the blood. 'What's happened to her?'

Laura shook her head blankly, struggled to find any words that made sense. But all the backed-up tension had suddenly burst out and Church was taking the steps two at a time, pushing past her. At the top he bolted down the landing until he came to Ruth's room. The door was ominously open. He kicked it wide and barged in.

There was blood splattered across the quilt, droplets thrown up the wall like a Jackson Pollock painting, a small pool already soaking into the thick carpet. Church glanced around frantically. Ruth was nowhere to be seen.

He was halfway back to the door when his eyes lighted on the small table under the window and he was brought up sharp. Laura appeared in the door, still looking like she was somewhere else. But when her gaze followed Church's it was like she had been slapped across the face.

'Jesus!' Her hand involuntarily went to her mouth.

On the table was another finger in a little puddle of blood with other droplets spattered around. And from its long delicate shape they could tell it was Ruth's.

A few seconds later the others shambled in. Although they were worse for wear from the alcohol they soon sobered up when they glanced from Laura's tear-streaked face to Church's bloodless expression of horror and despair.

Before any of them could speak, Church shrugged off the paralysis and ran out onto the landing. For the first time he noticed tiny splatters of blood leading away from Ruth's room down the stairs. Frantically he threw himself down them, following the stains out to the street. But there the trail ended and he found himself running backwards and forwards along the deserted road searching futilely for any sign of what had happened to her.

Back in the bedroom, the others could read what he had found in his dejected face.

Veitch suddenly noticed Laura standing apart, still in shock. 'What did you do?' His voice rumbled out infused with so much threat, Church felt his blood run cold.

Laura shook her head dumbly. 'I don't know—'

Veitch moved quickly. He was already gripping Laura's shoulders roughly before the others realised. 'You better tell us, you bitch. You're the one! Look at all the blood—'

'Ryan!' Church and Shavi grabbed him by the arms and hauled him off her roughly. His face was filled with rage.

'Look at the blood!' Veitch spat accusingly.

Laura held out her hands which were stained red. 'It's not like that—'

'What is it, then?' Veitch struggled briefly, than allowed the others to restrain him.

'I was asleep on my bed,' Laura began hesitantly. 'I woke up . . . some kind of noise. My head was fuzzy . . . you know, the drink.' She looked around the room, didn't seem to see any of them. 'I got up to find out what it was . . . thought it might have been Church. When I was out on the landing there was another noise. I saw Ruth's door was open.'

'Who was there, Laura?' Shavi asked calmly.

Her eyes widened and filled with tears as she looked past him into the shadows in the corners of the room. 'I don't know . . . I can't remember!'

Veitch searched her face. 'You're lying,' he said coldly.

She shook her head, held out her hands pleadingly, but all anyone could see was the blood.

'You don't remember anything?' Church asked.

There was a flicker of pain in her eyes. 'Don't *you* believe me?' She started to back towards the corner.

'Stay calm, Laura.' Shavi's voice was warm and reassuring. 'We are simply trying to find out what has happened to Ruth—'

'We haven't got time for this!' Veitch snapped. His clipped movements and roving eyes reminded Church of an animal; he was surprised how concerned Veitch seemed to be for someone who had hated him only a few days before; it suggested feelings beyond friendship. Church laid a calming hand on Veitch's upper arm. He half-expected Veitch to throw it off instantly, but the Londoner responded almost deferentially.

Laura slumped on to a chair in the corner and rested her head in her hands before realising she was smearing the blood over her face. She jumped up in a fury and stormed into the bathroom to wash herself.

Her departure seemed to break the dam of disbelief that constrained the others. 'Why weren't we more careful? Christ, we should have known by now.' Church's voice hummed with repressed emotion.

Veitch glanced from one to the other. 'Do you think she did it?' he whispered, jerking his head towards the bathroom. 'All that blood on her—'

Church gnawed on a knuckle. The others looked away, unsure what to say.

Veitch scrubbed his face, suddenly sober, then walked over to the window and threw back the curtains. 'Where is she?' Then, fearfully: 'Do you think she's dead?'

'They'd have left a body,' Church replied. 'Wouldn't they?'

'Unless they needed it for ritual purposes,' Tom noted. Church glared at him for his unfeeling bluntness.

Veitch finally found it within himself to look at the finger on the table. 'What kind of a sick bastard would do a thing like that? Christ, what must she have felt—' His voice choked off.

Shavi dropped to his haunches to scrutinise the stains on the carpet. 'The amount of blood is commensurate with the removal of a finger. There is a chance—'

'Don't touch it!' Tom yelled as Veitch stretched out a trembling hand towards the finger. Veitch snatched his arm back as if he'd been burned.

Tom marched over and bent down to examine the finger at table height. 'I think it's a sign.' He removed his cracked glasses and said, 'Which direction do you think it's pointing?'

Shavi glanced out of the window. 'The sun set over there,' he said with a chopping motion of his hand, 'so I would say, maybe, south-east.'

Tom replaced his glasses and stood up. 'Exactly south-east, I would guess. Towards Edinburgh.'

Church broke the long silence that followed Tom's comment. 'What does it mean?'

'Whoever did it is showing us the way. They want us to follow.' He stared out to the shrouded countryside that lay beyond the feeble lights of the town. 'In all this there is the pathology of evil, of ritual. Somebody is trying to bend the power that is loose in the land towards darkness.'

'Calatin?' Church suggested. 'Mollecht? Some other Fomor?'

Tom shook his head. 'This is not their way. It is the first play in a new game.'

chapter three

new words for an auld sang

The night dragged on interminably. They sat in a state of near-paralysis, fearing the worst, afraid to discuss what had happened, unable to decide what they should do next. The finger remained on the small table, the blood rapidly congealing. Their gaze kept returning to it, as if its unchanging pointing were a Poe-esque accusation.

Laura sat apart, staring out of the window blankly. Church found it impossible to read her; the impassive expression could have been hiding a sense of deep betrayal, or something he didn't want to consider, but which was nonetheless licking at the back of his mind. He hated himself for thinking it, though when he looked around he could tell the others felt the same. The thing he had dreaded had come to pass: a cancerous suspicion was eating away at them all.

Beyond that he found it almost impossible to cope with the raw emotion searing his heart. At times, if he allowed himself to inspect it too closely, it reminded him of those terrible feelings that had consumed him after Marianne had died, and that surprised him; had he grown so close to Ruth so quickly? So much had changed over the past few weeks, bonds materialising on a spiritual level, others being forged through hardship: he hadn't even begun to get a handle on what was happening inside him.

As the first rays of dawn licked the rooftops across the street, the intermittent, stuttering conversation told him what he feared: that the others were looking to him to make a decision. Before Beltane, he would have wanted to tell them he wasn't up to it, he didn't have the resilience or tenacity of leadership within him. But his failure had made him face his responsibilities, and he would take the difficult decisions however much they might corrupt his essential character and beliefs. *That*, he told himself, *is what it's all about.* He had to make sacrifices for the greater good. He just

73

hoped the sacrifices wouldn't be so great that there would be nothing left of him by the end of it.

'We need to move on to Edinburgh rapidly,' he said eventually.

'We are going to look for Ruth, right?' Veitch asked.

'Of course.'

Veitch eyed him suspiciously. 'What would you have done if she'd been taken in the opposite direction?'

Church didn't answer.

None of them could decide how they should dispose of the finger so they wrapped it in a handkerchief and buried it in the depths of Church's bag. They packed quickly and checked out, despite the obvious concern of the hotel manager who wondered why they were leaving so early, without breakfast and one travelling companion short.

The last building of the town was barely behind them when a police car came screaming by, lights flashing, forcing them to pull over. The driver was a man in his mid-forties with greying hair and the wearied expression of someone who had been pushed to the limit, while his eyes suggested he'd been dragged out of bed to catch them. Veitch wound down the driver's window as he approached.

'You're going to have to accompany me back into town, sir.' His eyes were piercing, but Veitch didn't flinch from the stare.

'No can do, mate. We've got business down south.'

'I don't want to have to ask you again, lad. Since the martial law was brought in, I've been run ragged. They don't think it's the rural areas that need the help, so we have to fend for ourselves. So don't push me around because I'll push back harder if it makes my life easier.'

As Veitch bristled, Church hastily leaned across him. 'What's the problem, officer? We were driving okay—'

'You know what the problem is.' There was a snap of irritation in his voice. 'A certain matter of blood on the carpet.'

'Oh, that. A bit of horseplay that got out of control. If the manager wants us to pay for cleaning—'

'Get out of the van. Now.' The policeman's body grew rigid with tension.

Shavi tugged at Church's jacket from the back. 'He thinks we killed Ruth,' he whispered, too low for the policeman to hear. There was something in his voice that suggested he wasn't simply reading the policeman's mannerisms.

Everything seemed to hang for a second. Church saw Veitch's eyes narrow, his forearm muscles tense, and an instant later he had snapped on the ignition and popped the clutch. The van roared away, leaving the policeman yelling furiously behind them. Veitch drove wildly until the police car was out of sight, then he slammed on the brakes and reversed up a rough foresters' track which wound through ranks of pine. When the trees obscured the road he killed the engine.

'Big macho idiot,' Laura said coldly from the back. 'Now we'll be on everyone's most wanted list. We won't be able to travel anywhere.'

Veitch glared at her. 'You haven't got any right to talk. We wouldn't be here if not for—'

'Leave it out,' Church ordered.

Veitch grew sullen. 'The moment he got a look at my record we wouldn't stand a chance of getting out of the area for days,' he continued. 'We can't afford to waste that time.'

'You did the right thing, Ryan.' Church put his head back and closed his eyes wearily. 'If things are as bad as they seem . . . if things are going to get as bad as we expect . . . the cops will have too much on their plate to worry about us. It might make things a little more difficult, but if they're not putting a dragnet out, I reckon we'll be okay.'

'You better be right,' Laura said gloomily.

Church recalled Shavi's apparent knowledge of the policeman's thoughts and turned to him. 'You can read minds now?'

Shavi shrugged. 'It was empathic.'

'But you can get into heads, you've shown us that.' Shavi wouldn't meet Church's gaze.

'What are you getting at?' Laura asked.

'I think Shavi should try peeling back the layers of your memory so we can find out what you really did see last night.'

Even Laura's sunglasses couldn't mask her concern. 'Not in my head.'

'What have you got to hide?' Veitch asked coldly.

Laura's face froze.

'Ruth and I went through something similar when all this mess started.' Church tried to be as reassuring as he could, for Shavi's sake as much as Laura's. 'It wasn't so bad. And it really helped us to get all those trapped thoughts out in the open.'

Laura moved her head slightly and Church guessed that behind her sunglasses she was looking at Veitch, weighing up his words and her options; his barely veiled accusations made it impossible for her to back out.

'Okay, Mister Shaman. You get to venture where no man has been before.' Her voice was emotionless.

Church clapped a hand on Shavi's shoulder. 'It'll be okay.'

Shavi smiled at him tightly.

★

They locked up the van and ventured into the pines until they found a spot where the sun broke through the canopy of vegetation, casting a circle of light. Laura and Shavi sat cross-legged in the centre, facing each other, while Church, Veitch and Tom leaned on tree trunks and watched quietly. Shavi had already eaten some of Tom's hash to attune his mood. He spent a few moments whispering gently to Laura; after a while her eyes were half-lidded, her movements lazy.

The atmosphere changed perceptibly the moment Shavi leaned forward to take Laura's hands; the birdsong died as if a switch had been thrown, even the breeze seemed to drop. There was a stillness like glass over everything.

When Shavi spoke, the world held its breath. 'We are going back to last night, Laura. To the hotel, after the dance. You and Ruth had gone to bed early.'

'I wasn't in the mood. I'd had enough of Miss Prissy. And too many people were looking at my scars.'

'You both went into your rooms. And went to sleep?'

'I lay down on the top of the bed. I was tired, the booze was knocking me out.' Her voice was soporific. 'I don't know how long I was asleep. Couldn't have been long. I heard a noise—'

'What was it?'

'I can't remember.'

'Try.'

She thought for a moment. 'It was Ruth. She cried out.'

'What did you do then? Tell me, step by step.'

'I got up. I felt like someone had beaten me around the head with a baseball bat. I walked to the door . . . Actually, it was more of a stagger. I thought, "I'm glad Church isn't here to see this. I'd never live it down." There was another noise. Sounded like a lamp going over. I thought I could hear voices through the wall. I stepped out on to the landing . . .' Her breath caught suddenly in her throat.

'What was it?'

Tears sprang to her eyes and trickled down her cheeks. 'I . . .' She shook her head, screwed her eyes up as if that would prevent the images forming.

Shavi's reassuring voice grew so low the others could barely hear it. 'Concentrate, Laura. Focus on the interloper.'

'It was . . .' A shiver ran through her. 'No, no. I see a large wolf. It reaches right up to the ceiling. Bigger. Passing through. It's growing to fill the whole hotel. It has sickly yellow eyes and it turns them on me. And it smiles . . . it smiles like a man.'

She started to hyperventilate. Shavi let go of her hands and put his arms

76

around her shoulders, gently pulling her towards him until she was resting against his chest, where her breathing gradually subsided.

'A giant wolf? She's making it up,' Veitch hissed.

They moved into the circle of light and squatted down, waiting for Laura to recover. She wouldn't meet any of their eyes. 'That's what you get delving around in the depths of my mind. I told you I'd done too many drugs.'

'What do you think? A shapeshifter?' Shavi seemed to have gained renewed confidence from the success of the exercise; the faint, enigmatic smile Church remembered from the first time they met had returned to his face.

'I don't think so.' Tom's expression was troubled. 'The wolf could be representational of whatever she saw. She might be converting her memory into symbols to help her deal with it.'

Church remembered his own experience of regression therapy to try to unlock the memories of the terrible sight beneath Albert Bridge, images so horrible his mind had locked them away. Although what eventually surfaced had proved to be the truth, the therapist had talked about false *screen* memories designed to protect the mind's integrity from something too awful to bear.

'This is doing my head in,' Veitch said. 'It's like you can't believe anything you see or remember or think!'

'That's how it always was,' Tom replied curtly.

'So how do we break through the symbolism to get to what Laura really saw?' Church asked.

Shavi rubbed his chin uncomfortably. 'I would not like to try again so soon after this attempt. I think Laura . . . both of us . . . need time to recover. The mind is too sensitive.'

'Yeah, and it's the only one I've got.' With an expression of faint distaste, Laura rubbed her hands together as if wiping away the stain of the memory.

'At least we know Laura saw something . . . someone,' Shavi continued.

'So do you believe me now, musclehead?' With her sunglasses on, Church couldn't tell if she was talking to him or Veitch.

'I still think she could be making it up,' Veitch said suspiciously. 'None of you know what's going on here, what her mind can do, what's real and what's not. She might have dreamed it up this way. Some kind of self-hypnosis, I don't know.' He turned to Laura. 'You didn't say anything about how you got the blood on you.'

'I remember that now. Whatever I saw turned my head upside down. I wandered into Ruth's room like some kind of mental patient and I just, sort of, touched the blood because I couldn't believe what I was seeing.'

'Fits together perfectly, don't it?' Veitch sneered.

As Laura bristled Church jumped in to prevent further confrontation. 'We can't stay here any longer with that cop driving around.' He glanced among the trees. 'Who knows what's in these woods anyway? We need to get to Edinburgh.'

'That cop will at least have put out the van's description and number,' Laura said. 'Face it, we're not going to get far in that.'

'Then we dump it, find another form of transport,' Church said. 'Time to use our initiative.'

Before they left, they took Ruth's finger and buried it in the leaf mould. It made them sick to leave it there, but there was nothing else for it. Then they took the A84 to Stirling where they found a dealer who took the van off their hands for two hundred pounds. It was an effort to lug their bags, camping equipment and remaining provisions to the station, but they didn't have long to wait to pick up a train to Edinburgh Waverley. There were only two carriages but apart from a trio of people at the far end of their carriage, the train was empty.

'I thought they would have shut the trains down by now,' Church said to the conductor as they boarded.

'Make the most of it,' he replied gruffly. 'The last service is tonight. Indefinite suspension of the entire network.' He shrugged. 'I still get kept on at full pay, at least for the moment. Not many people travelling anyways.'

They settled into their seats, lulled by the sun-heated, dusty interior, and once the train gently rocked out of the station they found themselves drifting off after their night without sleep. The journey to Edinburgh would be under an hour, but they had barely got out into open countryside when they were disturbed by the loud voices of two of their fellow travellers. It appeared to be a father and daughter conversing in a heated manner. His greying hair was slicked back in a manner popular during the war, and he had on an old-fashioned suit that seemed brand-new. A cracked briefcase was tucked under one arm. The daughter, who was in her early thirties, wore clothes that were smart, if unstylish. She was quite plain, with a complexion tempered by an outdoor life.

Drifting in and out of half-sleep, Church made out they had a farm somewhere outside Stirling which was experiencing financial problems and they were heading into Edinburgh to attempt to secure some kind of grant. But there was an edgy undercurrent to their talk which suggested some other issue was concerning them and they couldn't agree about how to deal with it.

Veitch shifted irritably in his seat and plumped up his jacket as a pillow. 'Just shut up,' he said under his breath as their voices rose again.

They all managed to get some sleep for the next ten minutes, but then they were jolted sharply awake by the farmer snarling, 'There's no bloody fairies in the fields! No bloody God either! It's not about luck! It's about those bastards in the Government, and in Europe!'

Church glanced around the edge of the seat ahead. The woman was pink with embarrassment at her father's outburst and trying to calm him with frantic hand movements. But there was something else concerning her too.

'What are you talking about, girl? Words can't hurt anyone! Who's listening?' The farmer's face was flushed with anger. 'This is what's important: the farm's going broke and we'll all be in the poorhouse by the end of summer if something's not done!'

His rage was born of desperation and tension bottled up for too long, and he probably would have carried on for several more minutes if the woman hadn't suddenly jumped to her feet and marched to the toilet.

The strained atmosphere ebbed over the next few minutes as Church drifted again. In that dreamy state, he found himself faced with an image of Ruth pleading with him for help in a scene disturbingly reminiscent of when the spirit of Marianne had begged him to avenge her death. His anxiety knotted: so much pressure being heaped on his shoulders, so much expectation he was afraid he couldn't live up to. And then he looked into Ruth's face and all the emotions he had tried to repress came rushing to the surface. He had tried to pretend she hadn't suffered, wasn't dead, but—

A piercing scream echoed through the carriage. All five of them jumped to their feet as one, ready for any threat, hearts pounding, bodies poised for fight or flight. The woman had returned from the toilets and was standing opposite her father, who had his back to them; her face was frozen in an expression of extreme shock.

Shavi was the first to her, grabbing her shoulders to calm her. She was shaking her head from side-to-side, oblivious to him, her eyes fixed so firmly on her father Shavi was forced to turn to follow her gaze. The old man was no longer there; or rather, his clothes and his briefcase were there, but his body had been replaced by straw; it tufted from the sleeves, dropped from the trouser legs to fill the shoes, and sprouted from his collar into a hideous parody of a human head, like an enormous corn dolly.

'Dad!' the woman croaked.

Veitch reached out to prod the shoulder curiously and the mannequin crumpled into a pile of clothes and a heap of straw. This set the woman off in another bout of screaming.

'What happened?' Laura asked with a horrible fascination.

While Shavi led the woman to the other end of the carriage where he attempted to calm her, Tom knelt down to examine the remains. 'You heard the things he was saying,' he said.

'I don't get it,' Laura replied. 'So he was a crotchety old git like you—'

'In the old days, the people who worked the land were terrified of saying anything which might offend the *fairies*, the nature spirits, whatever,' Tom snapped. 'They even had a host of euphemisms like the Little Folk or the Fair Folk in case the powers took offence at their name.'

'And now they're back . . .' Veitch began without continuing.

'They always were a prideful race,' Tom said. 'They demanded respect from all those they considered as lesser.'

'But all he said was . . .' Laura caught herself before she repeated the farmer's words. She glanced back at the sobbing daughter. 'Poor bitch. At least the old man will be able to keep the crows off the fields.'

'Oh, stop it!' Church said sharply. He looked at the broken expression on the daughter's face and read her future in an instant; he felt a deep pang of pity.

'It simply shows the contempt in which they hold us,' Tom noted. 'We need to be kept in our place.'

Veitch looked round suddenly. 'Wasn't there someone else in here?'

'That's right. There were three other passengers.' Church looked to the seats where the third traveller had been. 'I don't remember him getting up. No one got off.'

'That might have been one of them.' Tom hurried to the adjoining door to peer into the next carriage. It was empty. 'Now they are back, I presume they will be moving among us, seeing how things have changed.'

As if in answer to his words they heard a sudden scrabbling on the roof of the carriage, then a sound like laughter and footsteps disappearing to the far end. Veitch ran after it and pressed his face up close to the window in an attempt to peer behind, but all he saw was a large, oddly shaped shadow cast on the cutting. It separated from the train, rose up and, a second later, was gone.

Soon after, the train trundled slowly through the regimented green lawns and blooming flowers of Princes Street Gardens into Waverley Station, the volcanic ridge topped by the imposing stone bulk of Edinburgh Castle rising high above them. The daughter was bordering on hysteria by the time Shavi led her out on to the platform in search of a guard, who promptly took her off to the medical centre for treatment. There were few travellers around for such a large station, but that only made the small pockets of police more obvious; at the furthest reaches of the platforms where they would be unobtrusive to the majority of travellers, armed troops patrolled.

'This is creepy,' Laura hissed. 'It's like Istanbul or something.'

Paranoia crept over them when some of the police started looking intently in their direction, and they hastily collected up their bags and moved off. 'Do you think that bastard in Callander radioed through our descriptions?' Veitch said under his breath.

'Just another worry to add to the list,' Church replied darkly.

They argued briefly about conserving their cash – a policy favoured by Church and Shavi – but eventually agreed credit cards would probably be useless within a short time and so opted to live in style while they stayed in the city. It was Laura who won the argument when she said, 'Might as well make the most of it. We may not get the chance again.'

For accommodation, they selected the Balmoral, an opulent Edwardian pile that loomed over Waverley Station at the eastern end of the bustling main drag of Princes Street. They all laughed at the comically shocked expression on Veitch's face when he first walked into the palatial marble reception, but although he slipped to the back, where he furtively eyed the smartly uniformed staff as if they were about to throw him out, he was soon making the most of the luxurious surroundings when they were shown to their rooms with views of the castle and the Old Town.

Despite all that was happening, at first glance the city seemed virtually unaffected; cars still chugged bumper-to-bumper through the centre, people took their lunch in the sun in Princes Street Gardens and the shops and bars of the New Town seemed to be doing a brisk trade.

But as they took a stroll towards the Old Town, they could see it was different. It was almost as if the people had taken a conscious decision to avoid its long shadows and gloomy stone buildings, driven out by an oppressive sense of old times. The pubs, restaurants and shops still remained open, but the crowds that moved among them were thin; they always kept to the sunny side of the street, expressions furtive, shoulders bowed by invisible weights.

It was Shavi who characterised it the best as he stood on the Esplanade and looked from the jumbled rooftops of the Old Town to the clean lines and Georgian crescents of the new: it was a city split in two, Jekyll and Hyde, light and dark, night and day.

'Another sign of the duality that seems to be infusing everything in this new age of metaphor and symbolism.' The wind whipped Shavi's long hair around his face as he scanned the area.

81

Laura pressed her sunglasses up the bridge of her nose. 'At least we know which side we'll be drinking in tonight.'

Tom shook his head. 'Look at the New Town – it hasn't been affected yet. This seems to be the centre of change. If we want to learn anything, we have to come here.'

Laura scowled at him. 'You always know how to bring things down, you old git.'

They ate dinner in the hotel's elegant dining room at a table far from the few other residents. But despite the high quality of the food, they only picked at their meal; after Ruth's disappearance, an air of hopelessness had started to congeal around them, growing stronger with each passing hour.

It was Veitch who finally gave voice to the questions that troubled them all. 'What's the plan? Try to find Ruth or work out why we're supposed to be here?'

All eyes turned to Church, but he kept his gaze fixed on the remnants of his venison. 'We can't waste time looking for Ruth.' His words sounded harsher than he intended, but it was impossible to soften them. 'We don't know if she's still alive. And if she is, we can't even be sure she's here in the city. A hunch about the direction of the city just isn't enough.'

'What are you saying? That we just forget about her?' Veitch's face grew colder.

'Of course I don't want to forget about her, but we've only got a few short weeks to prevent the Fomorii bringing Balor back and that time will go quickly, believe me. Christ, we've got no idea how we're going to start. The way I see it, it's our responsibility. We're the only people who might stand a chance of succeeding, and a slim one at that. If we get distracted, the whole of the world goes to hell. Could you live with that?'

'You know what? Right now I don't really care about that.' For a second Veitch looked like he was going to cry.

'It's heartless, but those are the kind of choices we're being forced to make.' Church kept his face impassive because he knew if he allowed vent to even the slightest fraction of the emotion he was feeling, he wouldn't be able to maintain the strength they expected of him. Ever since Ruth had disappeared he'd been tearing himself apart about what they should do, but on cold reflection he knew where his responsibilities lay, whatever that did to him, however much the others grew to hate him for it.

'So that's it? She's gone? Just like that?' Veitch looked around the others for support. They said nothing, but the conflicting emotions struggled just behind their features. Veitch shook his head slowly. 'Fuck it.'

'Ryan—' Church began.

'What is it? She means nothing—'

'Of course she doesn't mean nothing.' The steel in Church's voice brought Veitch up sharp. 'And I don't believe this is the end of it. Whatever got to her isn't going to leave us alone. And when he or it or whatever it is comes back we're going to find out what happened to her before we gut the bastard.'

The unrestrained venom took the others aback. Laura pushed the vegetables around her plate with her fork while Tom tapped out a beat with his spoon.

Shavi leaned forward and broke the silence diplomatically. 'Then what is our next step?'

Tom answered. 'The guidance offered to us specifically mentioned the Well of Fire. Historically it was the most abundant and powerful source of the earth energy. Some say it even provides a direct channel with the source of the energy, whatever or wherever that might be. But with the gradual break between land and people it has lain dormant for a long time.'

Church nodded. 'We're supposed to be waking the sleeping king . . . arousing the wounded land . . . whichever metaphor you want. This fits the pattern. How do we get to it?'

Tom shrugged. 'The entrance lies somewhere on Arthur's Seat, that big pile of rock at the bottom of the Royal Mile, in the middle of Holyrood Park—'

'But the guidebook says the name has nothing to do with Arthur,' Church interjected. 'Not like all the other places where the blue fire is strong. Historians think it's just a corruption of Archer's Seat.'

'Which shows how much they know.' Tom removed his spectacles and polished them with the tablecloth.

'Then we head up there.' Church glanced through the window at the late afternoon sun. 'Tomorrow, now. And tonight—'

'Tonight,' Tom continued, 'we visit the Old Town.'

The warm evening was filled with the oddly comforting aromas of the modern age: heated traffic fumes, food cooking in restaurants downwind, burnt iron and hot grease rising from the train tracks that cut through the city. Girls in skimpy summer clothes and young men in T-shirts and jeans lounged in the late sunlight outside the Royal Scottish Academy on the Mound. There was an air of spring optimism that made it almost impossible to believe that anything had changed.

But as the companions wound their way up Ramsay Lane into the Old Town, the shadows grew longer and an unseasonal chill hung in the air despite the heat of the day. The area centred on the Royal Mile was the oldest part of the city. In the Middle Ages it had been hemmed in by city walls, forcing the housing to be built higher and higher; they were crammed too close together, blocking out the sky, so that a claustrophobic anxiety seemed to gather among them. Tom, who had obviously been in the city before, led them down Lawnmarket to one of the numerous, shadowy closes that lined the Royal Mile. At the end was an eighteenth-century courtyard and the Jolly Judge pub. They decided it was as good a place as any to discuss their plans.

It was small and cellar-like, with a low, beamed ceiling painted with flowers and fruit. A fire glowed nicely in the grate and the comfortable atmosphere was complemented by the hubbub of conversation coming from numerous drinkers gathered at the tables or leaning on the bar.

As they bought their drinks, Veitch said, 'It doesn't seem right sitting here getting pissed.'

'We could be roaming the streets like some moron tourists.' Laura took a gulp of her vodka as if she hadn't drunk for weeks.

'She's right,' Tom said as he led them over to the only free table. 'Inns are still the centres of community, even as they were in my day. Sooner or later all information passes through them. We simply have to keep our ears and eyes open.'

'That's good,' Church said, recalling all the pubs he'd passed through with Ruth, 'because I don't feel much like drinking.'

He changed his mind quickly. There was a desperation to all their drinking, as if they wanted to forget, or pretend the blight that was infecting reality was not really happening. The rounds came quickly, their mood lifted as they settled into the homely ambience of the pub. And once again Tom was proven right. They overheard snippets of conversation which added to their knowledge of the situation in the city, and Laura and Shavi engaged in brief chats with people they met on their way to the bar or the toilet.

As they had found elsewhere, after the announcement of martial law there had been an initial flurry of panic, but when no hard evidence of anything presented itself, people slipped back into old routines, cynically blaming the Government for some kind of cover-up or coming up with numerous wild hypotheses in the manner of old-fashioned campfire storytellers. It quickly became apparent to everyone that martial law wasn't enforced anyway; the police and armed forces appeared to have more important things on their minds, so everyone quietly ignored it. That resilience gave Church some encouragement, but he wondered how they would fare once the true situation become known.

Certainly everyone seemed to accept that some kind of change had come over the Old Town, although this was a topic few were prepared to discuss. When Church raised the matter, conversations were quickly changed or eyes averted. All that could be discerned was that the ancient part of the city had somehow become more dangerous and that after the pub closed the drinkers would 'hurry home to wifey'. But Church could tell from their faces that some of them had seen or experienced things which they couldn't bring themselves to discuss with their fellows.

Sometime after 10.30 p.m. another technology failure took out all the lights, but the drinkers dealt with it as they did any of the other minor changes which had come into their lives. A loud cheer went up, a few shouted comments about raiding the pumps while the landlord couldn't see, and then lots of laughter. The blazing fire provided enough light while the bar staff scrambled round for candles which they quickly stuffed into empty wine bottles and placed on every table and the bar.

'Nice ambience.'

Church started at the voice which came from the previously empty seat beside him. A large-boned man carrying a little too much weight inside an expensive, but tie-less, suit was smiling knowingly, a pint of bitter half-raised to his mouth. His hair was collar-length and he had a badly trimmed beard, but the heaviness of his jowls took away any of the rakishness he was attempting. Church placed him in his early to mid-thirties and from the perfectly formed English vowels of his public school accent it was obvious he wasn't a local.

'Pleasant enough,' Church replied noncommittally.

'And how are you finding this new world you're in? A little destabilising, I would think.' He smiled slyly.

Church eyed him suspiciously. There was an awareness about the stranger that instantly set him apart. 'Who are you?'

'A cop,' Veitch said threateningly.

'Good Lord, no,' he replied, bemused. 'How insulting.'

Church inspected the cut of his suit, the arrogance in his posture. 'Security services.'

The stranger made an odd, vaguely affirmative expression, one eyebrow half-raised. 'Once, not so long ago. Decided to head out on my own. Not much point having a career structure in this day and age.' He took a long draught of his bitter and smacked his lips.

'What are you doing here?' Church wondered if it had anything to do with the encounter with the police in Callander; he was ready to leave immediately if the situation called for it, and he tried to convey this surreptitiously to the others, but all their attention was on the spy.

'Why, to see all of you, dear boy.' He chuckled at their uncomfortable expressions. 'That would be a little bit of a lie, actually. Stumbled across you by accident in town earlier. Thought I'd drop in on you . . . see how you're getting on.' The chuckles subsided into a smile that made them even more uneasy.

Shavi leaned across the table curiously. 'And the security services know who we are?'

'Well, of course. They know everything that's worth knowing. That's their job, isn't it?' He looked around at their faces, still smiling in a manner that might have seemed jovial until it was examined closely; it was a social pretence. 'You really don't know what's happening, do you?'

'We have a good idea,' Church replied.

'No, you don't. You just think you do.' He took another sip of beer, playing with them. His eyes narrowed thoughtfully. 'Let me cast my mind back, remember all those reports and discussions. So much said and written, it's hard to believe it's only been going on for three months, give or take. Right, I have it. The M4, back in March. Terrible pile-up, cars and lorries and buses all mangled. A conflagration that blocked the entire motorway, caused traffic chaos for days. You remember it, don't you?'

Church gave nothing away.

'And what caused all that carnage?'

Church's eyes flickered towards the others; no one spoke.

The spy chuckled again. 'I understand your reticence. Really. It's not the kind of thing one talks about, is it? Well, let me answer the question for you. You believe the disaster was caused by some kind of flying creature out of a fairy book, blasting gouts of flame from its mouth.'

'And you're saying it wasn't?' Church made an attempt to pierce that jovial mask, but all he could see beneath it was more lies and deceit.

'Perception is such a funny thing,' the spy mused. Their uneasiness had started to turn to irritation at his undisguised patronising manner. 'We have all these faculties which paint a picture of the world for our mind.' He made a fey, airy gesture. 'Something we can make sense of. But can any of them really be trusted, that's the question? If there is one fact known by all security agencies around the globe, it is that there are no absolutes. Sight, sound, smell, touch, taste, all can be manipulated to present a view of the world as real as the *real* one.'

'What are you saying?' Church bristled. 'That we didn't see what we thought we saw?'

'Come on, old chap! It was a creature from a fairy book!' The spy aped disbelief. 'It all depends how you see things. Fire streamed down from the sky and blew up a chunk of motorway and some poor commuters. Well, of course, it *could* be some kind of mythical beastie. But, really, come on now, we are all intelligent people here, are we not? What would you say is the most rational explanation? The flames of a dragon's breath? Or a missile fired from a plane or a helicopter?'

His words struck them all sharply, prising open the doubt and dislocation they had felt in the early days. 'We saw—'

The spy silenced Church with a furious shake of his head. 'No, no, no, that's not good enough. Can't be trusted. After you witnessed the murder under Albert Bridge, you and the young lady went to see a therapist, did you not? And he attempted to recover the hidden memory of the incident—'

'How do you know about that?' Church's angry indignation masked a growing concern; how long had he been spied upon?

'He told you about screen memories,' the spy continued. 'False memories created by the mind to hide a truth which is unbearable. Or false memories created by an outside source to hide a truth which they do not want to come out.'

'You make it sound as simple as flicking a light switch,' Laura said.

'It is. Drugs, mind-control techniques, subliminal programming, targeted microwave radiation, post-hypnotic signals. The mind is a very susceptible organ.'

Veitch snorted derisively. 'Bollocks. That's what it is, mate, whoever the fuck you are. You're saying we can't trust anything we see or hear. Or think—'

'Exactly.' The spy settled back in his chair and smiled triumphantly.

'You speak as if you are saying something new.' Tom surveyed the spy with a face as cold and hard as marble; the spy looked away. 'But that is exactly how it has always been in life. You simply have more ways of manipulation now.'

Church shook his head. 'Everything we've experienced – everything supernatural – is just a big lie created by a lot of jumped-up public schoolboys with too much free time? I don't believe you.'

'That's your prerogative. But you know the old adage about big lies working the best. And it's not just a few jumped-up public schoolboys. It's . . .' The words dried up, and he waved his hand dismissively. 'Occam's Razor. The most likely explanation is the correct explanation. Dragons or attack helicopters? Shape-shifting demons or special forces assassins? Wizards juggling occult forces or very clever scientists? Demon torturers in underground dens or a few rough lads who've lost their natural calling in Ulster, making the most of the peace and quiet in high-security converted mines? Listen to me again: drugs, post-hypnotic programming, screen memories. Lies heaped on lies.'

'And this is the biggest one of all.' Church went for his drink to give him a moment to think. Wasn't this the kind of thing he first feared in the aftermath of that night beneath Albert Bridge? Suddenly he wanted to smash the glass and turn the table over. All that suffering, and they still couldn't trust what was happening.

'Tell me,' the spy continued, 'when you look at one of these shape-shifting demons, do you feel queasy? Does your mind protest that it's not seeing the right thing? When you look at one of those glorious god-like beings, do you occasionally think you see the truth behind it? The bottom line is: do you want to carry on living a lie because it's easy and comforting to believe? Lots of lovely magic and heroic derring-do, just the kind of way you dreamed the world really was when you were children. Or do you want to face up to the harsh facts about how life *really* is? No magic at all. Just lots of cynical, powerful people manipulating you on a daily basis for their own ends?'

'That's a difficult choice,' Laura said acidly. 'And not in the way you think.'

'There have been too many facts which uphold—'

'Don't argue with him, Shavi,' Church snapped. 'He's enjoying screwing with your mind.'

'I admit it is a very carefully constructed scenario,' the spy mused. 'In fact, it would even fool someone who knew how these things were done.'

Shavi, however, seemed to be enjoying the intellectual game. 'If what you are saying is true, then why is so much effort being expended?'

'Power. Control.' The spy smiled. 'You should never raise to high office, either democratically or through promotion, people who *want* high office. That desire is a signifier of some very unpleasant character traits.' He paused while he finished his beer. 'We have martial law now. The democratic process has been suspended. For how long? Until the crisis is over. Oh dear. Let me posit a scenario: there has been a coup. Those sick old aristocrats couldn't take losing their seats in the Lords . . . Friends in the military, the security services, the judiciary, all those Chief Constables . . . Late-night chats in the Lodge—'

Church shook his head vehemently; he realised vaguely that he looked like a sullen schoolboy.

'Think about it for a minute. Doesn't it make a certain kind of sense? Can anything that you've experienced be perceived in another way? Think *deeply* about every incident you've experienced. Could it have happened in a different way, from another perspective?' He raised his hands, prompting their introspection.

'Interesting,' Shavi said with what the others thought was undue excitement. 'But that would imply that we five have been specifically targeted for mind control. That begs the question, why us? We are nobody special.'

'Perhaps the powers behind the curtain believe you *are* somebody special. But no, more people than you five have been influenced. Just to keep the grand illusion growing. A big lie is the best lie, and this is the best lie of all.'

Church could see from the faces of the others that the spy's words were disturbing them, destabilising a world view which had already been fragile in its unreality; he had to admit, he felt the world was moving under his own feet. Only Tom seemed unaffected.

'Give me one reason why we should believe you,' he said.

'Oh, God, you shouldn't. That's the subtext of what I'm saying, isn't it? Don't believe anyone, don't believe anything. Not even yourselves. This is my reality. We all make our own. Perhaps it's yours, perhaps not.'

'You're a victim of your own disinformation,' Church said harshly. 'There's no point us questioning you at all. You're either lying to us or lying to yourself.'

The spy rattled his empty glass on the table, as if he were expecting one of them to buy him another. 'Do you know people can die of sadness? We find them all over the place, just sitting, slumped, a blank expression, no evident sign of death. They stopped believing in their reality. Switched themselves off—'

Veitch's growing confusion triggered the anger that was always just beneath the surface. When he leaned across the table there was such repressed violence in his movement that the spy was taken aback. 'This is just bollocks. You're screwing with our heads just to knock us off course. You're working for the Bastards, aren't you?'

'Believe what you want—'

'Shut up.' Veitch jabbed a finger in the spy's face. 'Get out of here before I break something.'

The spy shrugged, rose, still smiling, but there was now an obvious wariness behind his patina of chumminess; he glanced once more at Veitch, almost relieved to be moving away. 'Think about what I said—'

'Get out,' Veitch said coldly.

The spy made a gesture of reluctance and moved off, but when he was far enough beyond their arc to feel safe once more, he turned back and flashed the same arrogant smile. 'Be seeing you.' And then he was swallowed up by a crowd of drinkers heading towards the bar.

They played with their drinks in silence for a moment and then Shavi said, 'What do you think?'

'You know what I think,' Veitch replied. 'He's a liar. How can you believe any of that bollocks?'

'You know how it is with these gods and mystical items and all that stuff that's supposedly crossed over. We all see them in different ways.' Laura gently rubbed the scar tissue on her face, a mannerism she had developed whenever she was feeling particularly uncomfortable. She rapped her head. 'All this stupid grey matter up here can't begin to grasp what they really are.'

Tom adjusted his spectacles thoughtfully. 'I've had more occasions of altered perception than most people so I have little fondness for some over-arching view of reality. He was right – everyone has their own reality, none more valid than any other. Personally, I find it hard to believe that all my memories have been implanted, but it's certainly possible. I could be a carpenter from Wigan or a used-car salesman from Weymouth who only *believes* he's the mythical Thomas the Rhymer. Who's to say? But I do believe this – you can chase your tail round in circles for the rest of your life trying to find out what the *truth* really is, or you can just deal with it the way you think it is. Paralysis or action. And does it really matter what the higher power truly is – some incomprehensible power seen as dark gods by ancient man or corrupt humans? Surely the aim is to defeat it, whatever it is.'

'It matters to me,' Laura said. 'If I can't put a head in the target sights, I can't pull the trigger.'

The confusion had brought an air of despondency to the table. Church knew he had to take some action to prevent the paralysis Tom had mentioned. 'Tom's right. There's no point sitting here like a bunch of pathetic losers. We've operated in a state of permanent confusion for the last few months, so this isn't going to make any difference.' He turned to Laura, although his words were meant for all of them. 'Okay, if you want to believe somebody who turns up out of the blue and frankly admits his life is based on telling lies, then that's your prerogative. But at least keep it at the back of your mind until you find some evidence to back it up. I don't believe we should mention it again. What do you say?'

Laura shrugged. 'You're the boss, boss.' A ripple of agreement ran through the others.

As the clock neared midnight, the bar began to thin out. Church watched the drinkers hovering near the door as if they were reluctant to venture out into the night, making jokes about watching out for the 'bogles' waiting to chase them home.

'It's as if they all secretly know there's something frightening out there, but won't admit it to themselves or anyone else,' he mused aloud.

90

'Normal human nature,' Shavi said. 'Who would *want* to believe the world is how it is?'

Laura finished her drink and slammed the glass down theatrically. 'So are you really trying to fool yourself this was anything other than a night's serious drinking?'

'We have actually learned a great deal with this reconnaissance,' Tom said indignantly. 'Would you rather rush into danger blindly? We know that in the New Town Edinburgh seems untouched by what is happening. Yet the Old Town is transformed, corrupted. That tells me the Fomorii are here as we suspected, and here in this particular quarter of the city.'

'You better not be saying we need to get out on the streets at this time of night.' Although Laura was as combative as normal, Church could hear the uneasiness in her voice.

'I don't think it would be wise after midnight,' Church said.

'So far the Fomorii have confined themselves to the out-of-the-way places, the lonely places,' Shavi began. 'Why do you think they are here, at this time?'

'Because,' Tom replied, 'the Well of Fire makes this one of the most significant places in the land. In times past the Fomorii would not have been able to come within miles of this site, but now the Earth-blood is dormant. So, I presume, there is a certain frisson in colonising a place that was so important to everything they despise.'

'The dark overcoming the light,' Shavi noted.

They finished their drinks and left, their heads swimming with too much alcohol and all the doubts implanted by the spy. Outside, the unseasonal chill had grown even colder. Laura shivered. 'Jesus, it's like winter.'

The Royal Mile was deserted. Church had visited the city with Marianne for the Festival and he knew it was never so dead. An eerie stillness lay oppressively over everything; no lights burned in any windows, the late-night coffee shop was closed, even the street lights seemed dim.

They didn't need any prompting to move hastily back to the hotel. But as they made their way up Lawnmarket towards the spotlit bulk of the castle, the night dropped several more degrees and their breath bloomed all around them. A dim blue light seeped out of Ramsay Lane, although they couldn't tell if it was some optical illusion caused by the stark illumination of the castle. As they drew closer, however, there was no doubt. The sapphire glow emanated from somewhere along the road they had travelled earlier that evening, casting long shadows across their path; the shadows moved slightly, as if the light was not fixed.

'Police?' Shavi suggested.

Tom was unusually reticent. 'I don't think so.'

A deep hoar frost sparkled on the road and gleamed on the windows near where Ramsay Lane turned sharply. They marvelled at the display of cold in the first thrust of summer, but then a dark shape suddenly lurched into view and they all jumped back a step. Veitch quickly moved in front of them, lowering his centre of gravity ready to fight. The shape moved slowly, awkwardly, in a stiff-limbed manner; they saw it was a man with long black hair and a bushy beard they had seen drinking in the pub – except now his hair and beard was white with frost and his skin had a faint blue sheen that shimmered in the street light. He slumped against a wall, saw Church and the others and reached out a pleading hand. A faint strangled sound escaped his throat which they presumed was a cry for help.

As they ran forward, he crumpled to the pavement, still.

Laura went to turn him over, then snatched back her hand. 'Ow! Too cold to touch.'

Shavi blew on his hands, then quickly pressed two fingers against the man's neck. 'No pulse.'

'What do you think, Tom?' Church said.

It was only when the Rhymer didn't answer that they realised he wasn't with them. They looked up to see him standing at the top of Ramsay Lane, staring towards the source of the blue light. His expression had grown even more troubled.

As the others ran back to his side they were shocked to see the whole of Ramsay Lane was covered in ice, as if it had been transported to the middle of the Antarctic. At the bottom of the winding street the blue light glowed brightly. It was bobbing gently in their direction and at the heart of it they thought they could make out a dark figure. As it moved, the ice on the surrounding buildings grew noticeably thicker.

'What is it?' Church asked in hushed amazement.

Tom's voice was choked so low Church could barely hear the reply. 'The Cailleach Bheur.'

'In English,' Laura snapped.

He looked at her with eyes shocked and wide. 'The Blue Hag, spirit of winter. Quickly, now!' He roughly pushed them until they were moving hurriedly back down the Royal Mile, the way they had come. Tom kept them to the middle of the road and only calmed once they had turned off the High Street on to the broad thoroughfare of the North Bridge. Once they were firmly over Waverley Station he slumped against a wall, one hand on his face.

'What was that?' Church asked forcefully.

It was a moment or two before Tom answered, 'One of the most primal forces of this land.'

Church couldn't help glancing over his shoulder towards the shadow-shrouded Old Town. 'Fomorii?'

'No, nor of the Tuatha Dé Danann. Like the Fabulous Beasts, the Blue Hag and her sisters are a higher power, almost impossible to control. Yet the Fomorii have somehow bent her to their will, like they did with the first Fabulous Beast you encountered. They have her patrolling the Old Town like some guard dog, leaving them free to carry on their business.'

'She's some kind of evil witch?' Veitch said hesitantly.

Tom turned a cold gaze on him. 'If the deepest, coldest, darkest, harshest winter is evil. The Cailleach Bheur is a force of nature. Nothing can survive her touch.'

'You know, *hag* doesn't sound too frightening when you think about it. It makes you think of bath chairs and whist drives that never end—'

Tom's glare stopped Laura in her tracks. 'The Cailleach Bheur controls the fimbulwinter. If she unleashes it the entire planet will freeze and all life will be destroyed.'

'That sounds like a tremendous power for the Fomorii to influence,' Church said.

'It's a mark of their confidence. Or their arrogance.' Tom put his head back and took a deep breath. Some of the strength returned to his face. 'It will have taken a tremendous ritual, an appalling sacrifice, for them to control her, and even then it will undoubtedly be for only a short while. They really are playing with fire this time.'

'Bad joke, old man.' Laura rattled a stone across the road with her boot. 'And this thing has sisters?'

'Black Annis, the devourer of children, who makes her home in the Dane Hills of Leicestershire. And Gentle Annie, who controls the storms.'

'I think I prefer that last one,' she said.

'The name is ironic,' Tom said, 'and designed to placate her. You wouldn't want to be caught in one of her storms.'

Church recalled Black Annis from his university studies. 'But the scholars believe the myth of Black Annis grew out of the Celtic worship of Danu or Anu, the Mother of the Danann.'

'The same provenance,' Tom snapped, 'but very different.'

The night in the New Town was summery and relaxing, but a blast of wind filled with icy fingers rushed down from the hill, as if to remind them what lay only a short distance away.

'Then to get to the Fomorii, wherever they might be, we have to go past the Blue Hag,' Church said.

Tom nodded. 'And in the minds of the old people, the Cailleach Bheur was another name for Death.'

His voice drifted out on the chill wind that spread out across the city.

chapter four

the perilous bridge

In daylight the Old Town seemed less oppressive, but there was still an uneasy undercurrent which made them keen to move through it quickly. Veitch wondered if the authorities had any idea what was happening among the jumbled clutter of ancient buildings; although it hadn't been sealed off, the tourist office was closed and the crowds that moved in the historic sector were even thinner than on the previous day. The body of the frozen man had been removed.

From the Royal Mile they stopped to survey their destination. The extinct volcano of Arthur's Seat presented them with the curve of Salisbury Crags, dark and formidable.

'At least 350 million years since it last erupted,' Laura said, consulting the tourist guide she had shoplifted earlier; Church had been forced to return to the bookshop to pay for it. 'But with our luck . . .'

'This is an ancient landscape,' Tom mused. 'There were people hunting here nine thousand years ago.'

'Wow, that's even older than you,' Laura jibed.

He harrumphed under his breath. The others couldn't understand how he always fell for Laura's jibes. 'You know, the Celts recognised the importance of this place,' he continued with his back to Laura. 'The Castle Rock was a stronghold for the Gododdin tribe, who named it *Dunedin*, the hill fort. But they weren't here because the high ground was easily defendable. It was that.' He pointed to the soaring heights of Arthur's Seat. 'The sacred place of power.'

With the help of Laura's guide book, they ignored the steepest paths to the top. Hiring a car for quick passage along the winding route of Queen's Drive, they drove up through the increasingly rough countryside towards the 823-foot summit. At the start of their journey they passed an odd grille set into a wall before being drawn by the placid waters of St Margaret's Loch, overseen by the grim ruins of St Anthony's Chapel. Not long after they arrived at Dunsapie Loch, where they found a path with a gentle gradient. The summit presented them with an astonishing view across the city and beyond, to the Borders and Fife. When he saw it, Tom grew still as he quietly studied the homeland he had left so many hundreds of years before, and after a moment or two he wandered off to be alone with his thoughts. Veitch and Shavi set off in a different direction to explore the surroundings.

'This is amazing.' Church was surprised to hear wonder had driven the cynicism out of Laura's voice. 'We're right in the middle of the city!'

'I didn't expect you to be bowled over by lyrical views,' Church said.

She glanced at him from behind her sunglasses. 'Shows how much you know. Nature is the only thing worth believing in in this shitty life.'

She slumped down on a rock in her usual couldn't-care-less manner, but Church knew she wanted him to join her. He sat close, feeling her body slowly come to rest against him. 'Nature girl, eh?' He mentioned the unusual desktop wallpaper of interlinking trees he had seen on her portable computer not long after they met. 'You nearly took my head off when I asked you about that before, but it was an environmental thing, wasn't it?'

'Oh, you're so sharp. It's an Earth First design.'

'What's that?'

'A radical environmental group. I'm a member. We believe in taking action where it's called for, like when some developer is ripping up ancient woodland or some farmer's trying to make a fast buck growing GM foods.'

This surprised him. 'You're good at keeping secrets, aren't you? I didn't think you believed in anything.'

'Everybody has to have something to believe in. And that's mine.' She adjusted her sunglasses slightly, then let her fingers stray to her scar tissue. 'So do you still think I have something to do with Little Miss . . .' She caught herself. '. . . with Ruth disappearing?'

'I never said I thought that.'

'No. You never say much of anything that's important.' There was a sharp edge of bitterness in her voice.

'It was just seeing you with all that blood. I knew you weren't getting on—'

'So naturally I'd go and slit her throat and hide the body. That makes a lot of sense. For the leader of this sorry little clan, you really are a moron.' She

96

sighed. 'I just want a little trust, you know. Is that too much to ask? I know I've not gone out of my way to endear myself like some perky, eager-to-please tele-sales girl, but that's my way. You should be able to see through that.'

'I'm sorry. I—'

'Everybody else can act like a moron, but I have high expectations for you.'

Her words contained a weight of emotion that was in conflict with the blandness of the surface meaning; so much, it was almost too charged for him to deal with. He felt attracted to her, cared for her, certainly, but beyond that he had no idea what she meant to him. The pressure of events made his own deep feelings seem like a foreign language to him.

He searched deep in himself for some kind of comfort to give her, but all he could do was put his arm around her shoulders and pull her closer. That simple act appeared enough to satisfy her, and that made him feel even more guilty.

'So what do you reckon our chances are?' Veitch clambered on to an outcropping of rock, his muscular body compensating for the buffeting of the wind; he was fearless despite the precariousness of his position. 'You know, of finding her alive?'

'I can tell you care for her a great deal.' Shavi smiled mischievously; he knew his words would plunge Veitch into a clumsy attempt to talk about his emotions.

'She's a good kid.' Veitch kept his gaze fixed on the landscape spread out before them.

'And you feel that way even though she treated you so harshly for killing her uncle?'

'I deserved it. I did kill him. Are you going to answer the bleedin' question or not?'

Shavi squatted down on his haunches and absently began to trace the cracks in the rock. 'I have hope.'

'You know, I'm going to kill the bastard who did that to her.'

'Revenge never does much good, Ryan.'

'It makes me feel good. Do you reckon Blondie had anything to do with it?' He glanced over to where Church and Laura were sitting.

'I do not know. My instinct says probably not.'

'I just want to be doing something. All this sitting around is driving me crazy.' He found a pebble and hurled it with venom far out across the landscape. After he had watched the descent of its arc, he said, 'After we find her . . . if we find her . . . do you think, you know, me and her could ever get together? I know we're chalk and cheese and all that, but you never know, do you?'

'No, you never know.' Shavi watched Veitch fondly; for all his rage and barely repressed violence, at times he seemed like a child; inside him Shavi could sense a good heart beating, filled with values that were almost old-fashioned.

Veitch laughed. 'I don't know why I'm talking about stuff like this to a queen.'

For the first time Shavi sensed there was no edge to the slur; in fact, it was almost good-natured. 'I don't—'

'Yeah, yeah, I know what you're going to say. Men, women, they're all the same to you.'

'And emotions are all the same as well, whoever you care for.'

Veitch eyed him thoughtfully for a second, said nothing.

Shavi came over and sat next to him on the rock. 'There is a belief in many cultures that we create who we are through will alone.'

'What do you mean?'

'That we are not a product of breeding or environment. That if we wish ourselves to be a hero or a great lover, and wish hard enough, than we will transform ourselves into our heart's desire.'

Veitch thought about this for a second. 'And if we mope around thinking we're a nothing, loser, stupid, small-time crook, then that's what we end up as well.'

'Exactly.'

'So why are you telling me this?'

Shavi shrugged. 'I just want to help.'

Veitch looked at him curiously, but before he could speak, Tom wandered up to them along a muddy path worn into the scrub. Shavi and Veitch made no attempt to read his mood; at times his thought processes were as alien as those of the Tuatha Dé Danann or the Fomorii.

''s up?' Veitch asked.

'I can't find any sign of the gate to the Well.' Tom stood next to them, as detached as ever.

'You didn't have any problem down in Cornwall,' Veitch noted.

'The power here has been dormant for a long time. There are no structures or standing stones to keep it focused. It may even be extinct.'

'So, what? We're wasting our time? Those haunts wouldn't have bothered mentioning the place if that was the case.'

'The Aborigines have a similar view of an earth energy. In fact, it is an extremely widespread cultural belief around the world.' Shavi brushed his wind-whipped hair from his eyes. 'The Aborigines call it *djang*, the creative energy from which the world was formed. In their stories of the Dreamtime, *djang* spirit beings transformed into things in the landscape – rocks and trees, bushes and pools. That residue was always there so the people could tap into their spiritual well at any moment. And like the ley lines we have discussed before, there were *dreaming tracks* and *song lines* linking sacred sites. But the *djang* could also be conjured up with correct, traditional dances and rituals.'

Tom's eyes narrowed thoughtfully. 'Your shamanic abilities are very potent. Do you think you could find the *dreaming tracks* that would lead us to the source?'

'If I have that ability I do not know how to access it. Yet.'

Veitch noticed Shavi's faint smile and tapped him firmly on the chestbone. 'But you could learn!'

'Possibly. Given time—'

Tom shook his head. 'We have little time for you to fritter away meditating. You'll need to do what shamans have done throughout history when they were searching for information or guidance.'

Shavi looked at him, puzzled.

'Ask the spirits of the dead.'

They made their way down from Arthur's Seat in the early afternoon. The day had grown cloudy and thunderheads backing up in the east suggested a storm was approaching. Just off the comforting modernity of Princes Street they located a small café where they discussed Tom's suggestion.

'Why are you asking Shavi to do it?' Church asked Tom between sips of a steaming espresso. 'You seemed to have a good-enough handle on it when you called up the spirits at Gairloch.'

'To continually contact the dead allows them to learn to notice you. And then they will never leave you alone.' Tom's tone suggested this was not a good thing.

'So it's all right for the Shav-ster to set himself up for a lifetime's haunting, but you have to protect yourself,' Laura said sharply. 'You sound like one of those First World War generals sending the boys off to die.'

'I may be remarkably talented,' Tom replied acidly, 'but Shavi is the one with true shamanistic abilities. He is more able to cope with the repercussions.'

Laura began to protest, but Shavi held up his hand to silence her. 'Tom is correct. I fully understand my responsibilities. It is the role of the best able to do all they can for the collective, whatever the outcome.'

'You sure you're all right with this?' Veitch said with a note of concern. 'Nobody ought to be bleedin' bullied into doing something they don't want.'

'I will not deny that the prospect is unnerving, but then everything about life at the moment is very frightening. There are no longer any certainties.' Shavi smiled to himself. 'Perhaps there never were. I have had difficulty adjusting to my new-found abilities.' His face darkened. 'On the way to Skye, when I gained control of the sea serpent, I felt like my mind had been spiked. That sense of losing control, of finding yourself in something so alien, it was like waking entombed beneath the earth, of giving up your body and never knowing if you could ever get back . . .' His voice drifted away, but after a moment his smile returned. 'It was a little like dying. But now I am resurrected.'

Laura snorted derisively. 'You're saying something like that isn't going to screw you up for ever? Yeah, right.'

'Only if I let it. The shadow is still there, the fears. But not to do something because of fear is even worse.'

Laura's expression suggested she didn't understand a word he was saying. She focused on her cappuccino.

'Okay, it's agreed,' Church said. 'But where's all this going to take place?'

'Somewhere suitable,' Tom replied. 'Somewhere regularly frequented by the dead.'

Laura threw the guide book across the table. 'It's all in there,' she said with an odd note to her voice. 'God help you, you poor bastard.'

Early evening sunlight streamed into the hotel bedroom, catching dust motes in languid flight. Through the open window came the gritty sounds of the city, rumbling and honking with optimism and stability; the normality was powerfully soothing. Church and Laura lounged in the tangled sheets, listening to their subsiding heartbeats, daydreaming of the way the world used to be. The sweat dried slowly on their skin as they held each other silently. For a long while nothing moved.

Even then Church couldn't find complete peace. The thoughts that had been creeping up on him since that evening on the quayside at Kyleakin had gathered pace; of Niamh and the kiss that had filled his entire being, almost forgotten in the upheaval of Ruth's disappearance; of Laura and her slowly revealing deep affection for him; of his own strained ambivalence. For too long it had seemed like events were uncontrollable and now he was beginning to feel his personal life was going the same way. After so many months trapped in the sphere of his grief and guilt over Marianne's death, his emotional landscape was an uncharted territory. He knew he felt an attraction to Niamh, but whether it was physical or emotional, or even pure curiosity, he wasn't entirely sure. And the same with Laura – why couldn't he read what he felt about her? The only time he was truly in tune with her was during that moment in sex when his conscious mind switched off and the shadow person at the heart of him took over.

'What are you thinking about?'

He glanced down to see her eyes ranging over his face. 'Life, death, and all things in between.'

She nodded thoughtfully.

He slid down and threw one arm across his eyes; the darkness was comforting. 'What did you think I was thinking about?'

'It would have been nice if you'd said, me.'

'Sorry.' There was a stress-induced unnecessary sharpness in his voice which he instantly regretted.

He felt Laura's muscles tense next to him and a second later she had levered herself up on her elbow to fix an incisive eye on him. 'What's on your mind?'

'What isn't? The weight of the responsibility on our shoulders. All that bullshit the spy told us last night – I can't get it out of my head, even though I know I should. The fact that I'm eaten up with vengeance for whoever it was killed Marianne and your mum.' He caught himself. 'You've never told me how you feel about that.'

'I don't feel anything. I'm not even numb. Don't get me wrong, I'm glad it wasn't me who did it to the old bitch – at least I can still look at myself in the mirror – but it's not as if I'm tearing myself apart that she's dead. After all she did.' She shifted selfconsciously to hide the original set of scars on her back.

The tone of her words made him feel uncomfortable. 'That sounds a little—'

'What? Cold? Psychotic? Don't criticise me. You don't know anything about my life.'

'I'm trying—'

'Not hard enough.'

He suddenly felt angry that he constantly had to pussyfoot around her; it was more strain that he didn't need. He knew she had her own problems – the rumbling trauma from the scars Callow had inflicted on her face, the doubts over why Cernunnos had marked her – but all of them had problems and no one else acted like a spoiled brat.

They sat in silence for five minutes watching the dust motes dance in a sunbeam, and when she spoke again she sounded calmer. 'Anything else on your mind?'

He paused for a long time, then admitted it aloud, to himself as much as to her. 'That I should be sending us all to look for Ruth instead of—'

'What? Trying to save the world and everyone in it? That makes sense.' Another whiplash in her voice; he felt the irritation rise again.

'I'm on your side. Why do you always give me such a bad time?'

'I'm having a bad life.'

'It's not all about you, you know,' he snapped. 'I sit here with my thoughts and I can't even tell who I am any more. Thanks to that stuff I drank from the Danann cauldron, sometimes I think I can hear alien voices chattering at the back of my head, saying things I can't understand but I know they're terrible. Then everything flips on its head and I feel the rumblings of whatever the Fomorii did to me with the *Roisin Dubh*, deep in the same place—'

'Well, boo-hoo for you.'

Unable to contain the building rage any longer, he hammered his fist into the mattress. 'Shit, why am I here?'

'Yes, why are you here?' She gave him a harsh shove to the other side of the bed. By the time he'd turned back, angrily, she was out and starting to get dressed. He wanted to shout at her, that *she* was the one destroying the relationship, but then her mask of cold aloofness dropped slightly and he saw the hurt burning away underneath. He had never seen such emotion in her face before.

The shock of it calmed him instantly. 'Look, I'm sorry. We're all under a tremendous strain.'

She muttered something under her breath as she marched to the door, then turned and said, 'Go fuck yourself,' before slamming it behind her.

Laura hated the way she had to blink away tears of anger and hurt as she marched out of the hotel. For years she'd been good at battening down any emotion so that even those closest to her had no idea what she was thinking. But now it seemed as if the stopper had come out of the bottle and wouldn't go back in again. And Church seemed to have a particular talent for painfully extracting feelings, even when he wasn't trying; and somehow that made the process hurt even more.

However much she tried to pretend to herself she didn't like him, she realised she felt something closer to a childish ideal of love than anything else she had experienced in her life. At first she had hoped it was purely sexual, like so many of her previous relationships. Then she wished it was born of circumstances; of fear; of desperation. But it wasn't. Emotionally she'd suffered enough at the hands of her parents. And now everything was happening just as she'd feared.

She headed directly towards Princes Street, hoping to lose herself in some of the trendy bars which were still doing a roaring trade. Shavi and Tom, who had been in search of psychoactive substances for their respective rituals, hailed her as they returned to the hotel. She pretended she hadn't seen them.

She opted for the noisiest, most crowded bar and forced her way to the front to buy a Red Stripe. Although her attitude never wavered, it wasn't long before the locals were trying to pick her up. She fended a few off with acid comments, but as the drink took hold a little company that was interested in her seemed increasingly attractive.

For the next two hours she found herself at the centre of a group of young men and women whose only concern in life appeared to be having a good time. The conversation was sharp and witty, the jokes raucous, the flirtation charged. There was no talk of darkness or death. Laura found herself gravitating increasingly towards two of the most powerful characters in the group: Will had short brown hair and blue eyes that were gently mocking, a supremely confident demeanour and a certain sexual charisma; Andy was more openly loud and humorous, taller and bigger-boned, with corkscrew hair and a wispy goatee.

After a long, sparring conversation, Will grinned at Andy knowingly before turning to Laura. 'So, you up for going on somewhere else?'

'Subtle. Wouldn't happen to be your sweaty, beery bedroom, would it?' Laura sipped on her beer, enjoying the game.

'You've got me all wrong.' Will's grin suggested she hadn't got him as wrong as he'd like her to think. 'We're going on to a club. Great fucking place. Different venue every week. Cool fucking crowd. Good beats. You'll like it.'

'Ah, I don't know . . . I'm getting a bit old for clubs. I'm usually tucked up long before now with something hot and comforting.'

'You can't pull out on us now. Or we'll have to call you a big, blonde, soft, southern saddo.' Andy pushed his face into hers in a mock challenge.

'There might be another way we can convince you,' Will interjected. 'Come to the toilet with us.'

'Like I haven't heard that one before.'

He took her by the hand and led her through the crowded bar to the toilets at the back. Laura whistled at the men at the urinals before they herded her into a cubicle. Once the door was locked Will surreptitiously pulled out a small plastic bag from his Levi's pocket. Inside were five or six yellow capsules.

'Es?' Laura said.

'Like none you've ever tasted before. The best MDMA cut with a little something extra. Same loved-up strength with a little more trips. Straight off the boat from the States.' Will waved the bag in front of her face. 'Our gift to you, just to show you how much we want you along.'

The sight of the Ecstasy made her suddenly uneasy. Too many unpleasant memories surfaced of the months she'd spent in Salisbury and Bristol blasted out of her head, driving herself to the brink with a wilful disregard for her own health, both mental and physical, before she'd finally cleaned herself up. Drugs weren't good for her; or rather, she wasn't good for drugs; and she didn't want to go down that road again. But she'd had enough of all the repression and fear of the last few months. She wanted to celebrate life with abandon, forget Church and the stupid mission that was ruining her life, forget who she really was. She just wanted to have fun.

She dipped her hand in the bag and then, fighting back the nagging doubts, she popped one of the capsules on to her tongue. 'Let the good times roll,' she said with a grin.

The grim shadows that gripped the Old Town by day had merged seamlessly into the oppressive darkness of night as Shavi made his way cautiously along the Royal Mile. He had attempted to put on a brave face for the sake of the others, but he felt a nugget of dread heavy within him. Each new experience since he had discovered his aptitude for the mystical and the spiritual seemed to have taken him another step away from the light of humanity into a tenebrous zone from where he feared he would never be able to return. All he had to see him through was an outsider resilience honed through the disenfranchised days of his youth. He hoped it was enough.

He started as the slam of a door echoed along the length of the near-deserted street. Someone emerged from one of the pubs further down the way, glanced around uneasily at the gloom, as if surprised by the lateness of the hour, then broke into a jog towards the bright lights of North Bridge.

Shavi sucked in a deep breath to calm himself. He had read and reread the guide book entry for his destination, but its terrible story had done little to ease his anxieties. The handful of mushrooms taken to enhance the shamanic experience hadn't helped either. At the cobblestoned Heart of Midlothian at Parliament Square he paused briefly and spat, as custom dictated, to ward off the spirits of those executed at the old Tolbooth Prison. It might have been ineffective – the customs of the Unseen World were unknowable – but he thought it wise to proceed with caution; he had no desire to be confronted by the spectral severed heads of those dispatched and later exhibited in the area.

Across the road loomed the Georgian façade of the City Chambers. It spoke of elegance and cultured discourse, the best humanity had to offer; like all of the modern world it hid a multitude of sins. Beneath the chambers was what remained of an entire city street, Mary King's Close, locked away in darkness. The guide book described it as the most haunted place in all Scotland, which was hardly surprising. The City Chambers had been built there to seal off for ever a part of Edinburgh history the people hoped to forget, couldn't bring themselves to face, with all its shame, guilt and suffering. But like all bad memories it refused to stay buried.

In 1645, when Edinburgh was in the grip of the Black Death, the filthy, overflowing tenements of the Old Town were filled with the diseased and the dying, and Mary King's Close was worse than most. *A sickening plague pit*, the city fathers had said. The rich, cultured, upstanding Great Men of the City had a view of the poverty-stricken that was less than human, and in an act of brutality that reverberated down the years they ordered the entire close blocked up. They called it quarantine. The truth was not so clean: every resident was left to die without food or water in the hope that the disease could be contained. And if that was not enough of a monstrosity, when the moans of the inhabitants had finally drifted away, two butchers were sent in to dismember the corpses.

Shavi shivered at the extent of the cold-hearted cruelty. No wonder the spirits of those who had suffered couldn't depart the prison of their misery. For hundreds of years, visitors to the hidden street had reported the most awful, shrieking spectres, accusing revenants, a little girl, her china doll face filled with such overwhelming sadness it caused physical pain in those who saw it, watchers from the shadows whispering threats and prophecies of suffering and pain; an oppressive atmosphere of despair hung over all, and even the sceptical left the place changed on some fundamental level.

Shavi surveyed the City Chambers carefully, then let his gaze slowly drop to ground level. If even normal, rational people experienced such dread, what would he find, with his super-charged perceptions? With apprehension tightening a band around his chest, he set off across the street.

The entrance to the buried close was a nondescript, rickety wooden door off Cockburn Street. He flicked on his torch the moment it opened, listening to the echoes disappear into the depths. Spraying the light around inside, he was confronted by a path that rose steeply to another entrance. To his left, about halfway up, was an ancient front door almost lost in the gloom. Dust was everywhere, in thick layers on the floor and hanging in choking clouds in the air, so that he continually had to stifle coughs; the resultant noise, twisted by the echoes, was like the bark of a beast prowling nearby.

Slowly he moved through a maze of bare rooms, claustrophobic in the dark, where an oppressive atmosphere gathered among the creaking timbers that propped up the ceilings. He tried to shake off the knowledge that he was alone there, far beneath the road where no one would ever hear him if he yelled, but the thought kept creeping back.

The mushrooms turned the echoes of his footsteps into percussive bursts rattling off the confining walls in a syncopated rhythm that rose and fell, grew and receded; there was something about the quality of the reverberations that didn't seem quite right and in the brief snatches of silence that lay inbetween them he was sure he could hear other disturbing, muffled sounds. He didn't pause to listen too closely. The air grew dank as he moved deeper into the heart of the Close's system of ancient bedrooms, living rooms and kitchens, where families of ten or more were forced to live together in abject poverty.

After a while he stopped to try to get his bearings; the last thing he wanted to do was get lost down there. In the darkness that lay beyond the beam of his torch he thought he could see sparks of light swirling like fireflies; he dismissed it as a trick of his eyes, although it continued to nag at him. The atmosphere was even worse than he had anticipated, alive with dismal emotion and sour memory, brooding for centuries, ready to lash out with bitterness.

Shavi attempted to maintain his equilibrium. His gradual understanding of the Invisible World told him that whatever power lurked there away from the light would see anything less as a sign of weakness; and that could, very possibly, be a fatal mistake.

He sprayed the beam around. He was in a small room next to an old fireplace. The plaster on the walls was cracked and flaking. There was nothing out of the ordinary until something caught his eye in a flash of the torch beam: one corner was filled with an incongruous collection of dolls, teddy bears, photos, dollar bills, Tamagotchis: a pile of offerings left by those who had been there before him. It was just rubbish, but there was a strange, eerie atmosphere that surrounded it.

The place was starting to affect him; his breathing had grown shallow. A compulsive desire to flee came in waves, forcing him to grip the torch tightly as he fought it back. Briefly he stared at the torch, trying to clear his mind; despite years of meditation, in that spot, it was almost impossible. His heart was pounding so wildly, the throb of his blood made his head ache. But somewhere he managed to find the reserves of strength for which he was searching. He switched off the torch.

The darkness was all-encompassing.

His breathing stopped suddenly, until his head spun and he thought his lungs would burst. And when the ragged inhalation did come, it sounded so loud he wanted to tear the air from his throat for fear it would mark him out. Cautiously, he lowered himself to the ground and sat cross-legged, and through an effort of pure will he managed to calm himself a little; at least enough to remain in that awful place.

The dark gave him the destabilising sensation that he was floating in space. There was no up or down, no here or there, just a sea of nothing, with him at the centre of it. Gradually his other senses became more charged to make up for his lack of sight: distant, barely perceptible echoes bounced off the walls which seemed, unnervingly, to have no particular point of origin, but which he attributed to changes in the temperature of the building fabric; the floor was dusty and icily cold beneath his fingertips; his nostrils pierced the cloying mist of damp to pick up subtler smells which intrigued him – tobacco smoke, perfume, leather – which he confidently told himself were the fading memories of visiting tourists.

But he knew what he was really sensing: the smells and sounds and textures of the resting body of that place, which was, in a very real sense, alive, more than an amalgamation of bricks and mortar, a creature bound together with the bones of pain and the blood of suffering, guts of despair and the seething, sentient mind of hatred. He knew. And he knew he was there at its mercy.

For nearly half an hour, he sat in the deep dark, listening to the sound of his own breathing. He had just started to wonder if the place would keep him there in torment without presenting itself to him when his nerves began to tingle; his heightened senses had picked up a subtle change in the atmosphere. The temperature had dropped by a degree or two and a strange taste like milky coffee had materialised beneath his tongue.

There was no sound or movement, but he suddenly felt an overwhelming presence looming behind him. His mind demanded that he turn round, defend himself; somehow he managed to hold still. He could feel it, he was sure; it wasn't his imagination. Whatever was there seemed to rise up over him, poised to strike, still silent but radiating a terrible force. It hung there, his hair prickling at faint movements in the air currents. The effort to turn round almost drove him insane, but he continued to resist. And in that instant he knew, although he didn't know how, that if he had turned, he would have been struck dead immediately.

Although it was dark, he closed his eyes and concentrated. He could feel it above him, frozen, waiting for him to make any move that would allow it to attack. Shavi sensed oppressive, primal emotions, but not what it truly was.

And then, when he thought he could bear it no longer, it receded like a shadow melting in the dawn sun, slipping back and back until Shavi felt alone once more. He released a tight breath of relief, although he knew it was not the end.

He didn't have long to wait. At first he couldn't tell if the odd movement his eyes registered were the purple flashes of random nerves sparking on his retina or if it was some external phenomenon. White dots sparkled in one spot, like dust motes in a sunbeam, but moving with a life of their own, coming together almost imperceptibly, coalescing into a shape. His heart began to beat faster.

The shape glowed with an inner light, took on a pale substance, until he realised he was looking at the form of a small girl. Her blonde hair was fastened in pigtails, her face as big and white as the moon, from which stared the darkest, most limpid eyes he had ever seen. She wore a plain shift dress and had her hands clasped behind her back. More than her presence, it was what she brought with her that truly disturbed Shavi: an atmosphere of suffocating despair. It didn't simply make him sad; he felt as if it was being curled into a fist and used to assail him.

'Hello,' he said in as calm a voice as he could muster.

Her eyes didn't blink. The more he looked into them, the more he felt they were not human at all: alien, demonic, too dark and deep by far.

'I hope you will help me,' he continued.

'Ye shouldnae have come here.' It was not friendly advice.

Knowing what was at stake, Shavi arranged his thoughts carefully. 'I understand your pain. I recognise the wrong that has been done to you. But I come to you with open arms, seeking aid. Would you turn your back on another who walks the long, hard road?'

Shavi's heart seemed to hang steady in the long, ringing silence that followed. He couldn't tell if the girl was ignoring him or if her dark, luminous eyes were coldly weighing his presence.

Eventually the glass sliver of her voice echoed once again. 'You're a wee hank of gristle and bone. There's no a handful of meat on ye.'

There was something about her words that made him shiver.

The little girl looked away from him into the sucking dark. 'I can hear Mama calling. Always the same. "Will ye no come here? Marie. Marie!"' Her voice rose to a sharp scream that almost made Shavi's heart stop. 'But I've no had any food for days and my poor belly hurts! And then the night closes in and still Mama calls!' Her face filled with a terrifying fury. 'And now the men with the choppers are coming, with the sound of squealing pigs in their ears and dirty old rags tied across their faces!' She turned the full force of her regard on him and his head snapped back involuntarily. 'Are ye sure ye wish tae lay your heart afore us?'

Her question was weighted with some kind of meaning he couldn't discern, but he felt he had no choice. 'I am.'

There was another unnerving period of silence and then she suddenly cocked her head on one side, as if she had heard something. A few seconds later Shavi heard it too: a sound like chains rattling. It was accompanied by the overpowering, sickly-sweet stink of animal blood.

The little girl looked back at him. 'They're coming. Ye better run now. Ye better run.'

And then she took a slow step back and the darkness folded around her until she was gone.

The appalling claustrophobic atmosphere of pain and threat grew even more intense. Shavi realised he was holding his breath, every muscle in his body rigid. Then, in the blink of an eye, he was abruptly aware he was no longer alone. He couldn't see who was out there in the dark, but he felt that if he did perceive their forms, he would go instantly insane. He swallowed, unable to ignore the feeling that his life hung by a thread.

'Welcome,' he began.

'Ye come with death at your heels and darkness like a cloak.' The hollow voice cut Shavi off sharply; there wasn't a hint of warmth or humanity in the sepulchral tones.

'We hate all life.' Another voice, even colder. 'Here, in the deep dark, we are imprisoned. Abandoned tae shadows, forgotten by almost all. We have nothing tae believe in but revenge. So we wait. And we remember. And we seethe.'

Shavi steeled himself. 'I know your story. You were the innocent victims of abject cruelty.' Somewhere distant came the dim sound of chopping, growing louder, becoming distorted before disappearing; bitter memories, trapped but continuously recurring. 'There is nothing I can say to assuage your suffering, but my heart goes out to you.'

'And ye think that is enough?'

Shavi swallowed again; his throat was too dry. 'It is all that I can do, apart from offer my prayers that you will soon be freed from this Purgatory to find the rest you deserve.'

A heartrending shrieking erupted all around. Shavi's heart leapt and he wanted to clutch at his ears to shut out that terrible sound. After a few seconds it died away and then there was just the tinkling of nonexistent chains and faint movement in the dark. He hoped what he had said was enough.

Then: 'Ye have fair eyes and ears tae sense us. Most only feel us like a shiver on the skin.'

'What d'ye want?' Another voice, gruffer, more uneducated; a hint of threat.

'Knowledge,' Shavi replied. 'I can see some, but not all. From your dark place, you can see everything. You have great power. I bow to you and ask for your aid.' Shavi smelled woodsmoke and that disturbing stink of animal blood once more.

'Speak.'

'The world is plunging into darkness—'

'Why should we care?'

'Not everyone is like your persecutors. Somewhere, descendants of your friends and family still live. Do not forget the good—'

'Dinnae preach tae us!' The voice cracked like a gunshot.

The atmosphere of menace grew stronger; Shavi knew he was losing control. 'Then I will not argue my case at all. I will simply say, we need you. And the world needs you.' In the absence of a reply, he continued talking, hoping that at least the sound of his voice would keep them at bay. 'The old gods have returned and they are already wreaking havoc across the land. But now some of them are attempting to bring back the embodiment of all evil. Balor.' The dark susurrated with their whispers. 'You must have sensed all this?'

'Aye.'

'And if *he* returns, it will truly mean the end of everything. He will draw the darkness of the abyss across all existence. Somehow we have to stop the Fomorii. Whatever they are planning is beginning here, in this city. But where? And how *can* we stop them? They are so powerful, we are so weak. But there must be a way. We will never give up while we breathe.' Shavi tried to order his thoughts. There were so many questions he wanted to ask, but he had to be selective; the dead would have only limited patience, if they told him anything at all. Yet there was only one other question that truly mattered. 'And I would beseech you to answer one more thing. One of our number is missing, presumed dead. Ruth Gallagher, a good, decent woman. We hope in our hearts she is still alive. Perhaps you could guide me towards the truth.'

As his words drifted out into the dark, he was sure that whatever was out there had drawn closer while he spoke. Every sense told him if he reached out a hand he would touch . . . what? He shook the thought from his head.

'There is a price tae pay for anything gleaned from the other side.'

'I will pay it.'

'Do ye not want tae know what it will be?' The words were laced with stifled triumph and sharp contempt, which unnerved him greatly, but it was too late to back out.

'It does not matter. I have my responsibilities. This information has to be uncovered. I will have to bear the burden of whatever you demand, however great.'

'So be it.'

Shavi felt a wash of cold. He couldn't shake the feeling he had agreed to something he would come to regret, but what he had said was correct: he had no choice. Whatever the price, he would have to find the strength to pay it.

'The woman lives, but only just. And her future looks very dark. Hold out little hope.' Shavi had not heard the voice before. It was clearer, younger and had an intelligence that wasn't present in the others.

Shavi didn't know whether to feel joyous or disheartened by the answer. 'If there is anything we can do to save her we will do it,' he said. Odd, muffled noises which sounded like mocking laughter echoed away in the gloom.

'Seek out the stones from the place that gave succour tae the plague victims if ye wish to find the path beneath the seat.' A woman's voice this time. The words were cryptic, but Shavi had expected no less; the dead were helping and hoping to torment at the same time.

'But the Well of Fire will not be enough tae help ye. The worms have burrowed deep in their nest and the Cailleach Bheur is tae powerful for even the blue flames.'

'Then, what?' Shavi asked.

More mocking whispers rustled around the edge of his perception. When the woman spoke again, her voice was tinged with a dark glee. 'Why, call for the Guid Son, Long Jack. Only he can help ye now.'

Shavi hoped Tom could make some sense of their cryptic words. 'I thank you for all the aid you have given me. But one thing still puzzles me—'

'The where,' the educated voice interrupted. 'Know this: the girl and the worms keep their counsel together, deep beneath Castle Rock.'

Shavi felt the tension ease slightly; he had all he came for. But his muscles still knotted at the prospect that the dead had merely been toying with him and, having given up their secrets, would not let him leave alive. Tentatively, he said, 'You have been most gracious in your aid.' He took a deep breath and steeled himself. 'I am ready to pay the price you requested.'

'That has already been put intae effect. Your time here is done. Get thee gone before we rip the life from ye.'

Shavi bowed slightly, then made his way in the direction of the exit as hastily as he could muster without breaking into a run. The hatred of the jealous spirits was heavy at his back and for a few steps it felt like they were surging in pursuit of him, unable to contain themselves any longer. Anxiously he flicked on the torch, which appeared to make them hold back beyond the boundary of the light. But he didn't breathe easily until he was up in the empty street, sucking in the soothing night air, his body slick with cold sweat. The intensity of the experience had left him shaken, even after everything else he had been through over the past few months; he had never believed he could suffer such mortal dread.

But he had come through it and that alone gave him strength. Knowing it wasn't wise to tarry in the Old Town any longer than necessary, he hurried back towards the hotel, desperate to tell the others everything he had learned; but most of all that Ruth was still alive.

As he marched back towards the lights of the New Town, he didn't notice a dark shape separate from the shadows clustering the entrance of an alley. It began to follow him, shimmering in the light, insubstantial, as it dogged his every step. If he had thought to glance behind him, curious at what price the spirits had asked of him, he would have recognised it instantly: his friend and lover, murdered in a South London street two years before.

There were no longer songs, just drum and bass suffusing her brain and body, mixing with the drug, driving reality away on waves of sound. Laura couldn't even recollect a conscious thought for the past hour; she had given herself up to the trip of flashing lights she could hear and noise she could see, dancing, sweating, not even an individual, just a cell in the body of the crowd-beast.

Will and Andy had led her to an old building on the eastern edge of the Old Town. From the outside it didn't appear to have been used for years, but inside it had been transformed by vast batteries of lights, stacks of speakers fifteen feet tall and machines pumping out clouds of dry ice and occasional frothing spurts of bubbles. The place was big enough to cram in several hundred people, yet managed to avoid feeling impersonal. By the time they arrived, the trip had already started and the two young Scots were growing animated.

Will leaned forward to whisper in her ear, 'This drug always makes me feel horny. Come on, let's away to the toilet for a bit of slap and tickle.'

He was right; her pleasure centres were already being caressed by the warm waves that washed through her and she felt herself grow wet at the thought of him between her legs. It wasn't as if she hadn't had numerous other episodes of seedy, horny, loveless sex while off her face in some club or other. She wasn't a prude; it was fun, like taking the drug in the first place; nothing more. At least that's what she had always told herself, but although it would have been the easiest thing in the world to give in to, she suddenly realised she felt strangely reluctant. Part of her was telling her to do it to punish Church, but even then, she couldn't bring herself. It didn't make sense to her at all, and the more she thought about what it meant, the more uneasy she felt.

In the end she grabbed hold of his right hand and raised it in front of his face. 'This is more your scene.'

She flashed a fake smile and left hurriedly to get a drink of water.

On her way back she got drawn into the heart of the dance floor where she lost herself in the music. It was the relief of nothingness, but as the trip reached one of its plateaus, she was irritated to discover occasional thoughts leaking through to her foremind. Most of them concerned Church, but she didn't want anything to bring her down. Angrily, she looked for something to distract her, losing the rhythm of the music in the process. Stomping off the dance floor she leaned against a pillar with her arms folded, where she waited for the trip to pick up again. A goodlooking young man with an annoyingly untroubled face came up to talk to her, but she couldn't hear a word he was saying over the unceasing thunder of the music. She waved him away furiously.

After a few moments, she was relieved to feel the drug begin to take her to the next level and her mood calmed. A smile sprang to her face; she was surprised at how good it felt. The closeness of all the other clubbers cheered her, made her feel part of something. She surveyed the moving crowd warmly, then found her gaze drawn to the flashing lights which a moment ago had seemed dissonant, but now, with the music, made perfect sense: red, green, blue, purple. A white flash. Red again. A strobe. The meaning of life. Slowly she raised her eyes heavenwards, revelling in the growing sense of bliss. And there, as if in answer to her feelings, was an astonishing sight. The entire ceiling was sparkling like a vast canopy of stars in a night sky. She caught her breath as a revolving light splashed upwards, adding to the coruscation. 'That's amazing,' she whispered in wonder.

In the throes of the trip she suddenly became obsessed with sharing her breathtaking vision with Will and Andy. The crowd was so densely packed she felt a moment of panic that she wouldn't be able to find them, but after pushing her way back and forth through the dancers for a few minutes, she spied Andy sitting at a table near the door with a glass of water before him and a cigarette smouldering between his fingers.

'You've got to see this!' she called out. He didn't respond, even glance her way. She guessed her voice had been dragged away by the rumble of the music. She waved excitedly to catch his eye. Still nothing.

The trip started to roll with force and she was almost distracted by the music and the lights, but one thing stuck in her mind and wouldn't shake itself free: the sparkling that had glimmered across the ceiling had now transferred itself to Andy. His corkscrew hair glistened in the occasional beam of light, stars gleamed in his goatee.

'Amazing,' she whispered once more.

But the thing was still niggling at the back of her head, like fingernails scratching on a window pane. It was something more than the spangly effect; something discordant. *What was it?* she mused. She tried to take a step back through the effects of the drug. His skin, too, had that faint twinkling quality. It wasn't that he had been dusted with the gold make-up some of the women dancers used, nor was it the drug. She *was* seeing it. Wasn't she? Her inability to distinguish reality from mild hallucination began to irritate her, throwing the drug off-kilter.

Be careful, she warned herself. *You don't want this trip to go bad.*

She concentrated, focused. The effort twisted the trip a little more.

And there it was. The water before him had risen a full half-inch above the level of the glass. And there it hung, suspended in time.

First the scratching at the back of her head turned to an insistent hammering. Then the trip turned, sucking up the anxiety from the pit of her stomach. She knew. If only she hadn't been drugged she would have seen it long before. She wouldn't have gone there at all. She would have known better.

The water hung, suspended. *Frozen.*

She took a step back, desperately trying to stop herself falling into full-scale panic. Her heart was thundering like it was going to burst out of her chest. She was finding it difficult to breathe.

Andy's stare was locked on the dancefloor. It didn't waver, he didn't blink. There was no movement in him at all.

Frozen, she thought.

Behind him, the walls, too, glistened. It was spreading out gradually from the doorway like an invisible field, creeping across surfaces, leaving its tell-tale sign.

Poor Andy, she thought obliquely. Then, a drug-induced twist: *My God! He's dead!*

And now that she knew, she could feel the bloom of it on her skin; the temperature had dropped several degrees and was still falling fast.

She's coming. The notion drove her into action. She ran for the door, but as she neared it the cold was almost unbearable; her skin appeared to sear from its presence. It was more than winter, more than Arctic; it seemed to Laura to represent the depths of space. She took another few paces and then gave up as the hoar frost thickened on the door. She began to shake as cracks developed in the wood. She was already backing away rapidly when it was torn apart by the freezing moisture and burst inwards with a resounding crack.

The Cailleach Bheur was framed in the doorway, painted red, then blue, then green, then purple by the club's lights, like some hideous MTV video effect. Laura's breath caught in her throat. At first she couldn't quite make out the creature's appearance as the shape shimmered and danced, becoming briefly this and then that. But then her mind settled on a form which it found acceptable and Laura saw an old crone hunched over, dressed in tattered, shapeless rags, her face a mass of wrinkles, her hair as wild as the wind across the tundra. She supported herself on a gnarled wooden staff that was bigger than she. And all around her the air appeared to shift with gusts from unknown origin, suffused with an icy blue illumination that seemed immune to the club's lights; in the glow were flurries of snowflakes that came and went eerily without leaving any trace on the floor behind her.

She moved forward spectrally, almost as if her feet weren't touching the ground. And then she slowly turned her terrible gaze on everyone in the room. In the depths of those swirling eyes, Laura saw nothing remotely human; they contained the desolation of the ice-fields, of the depths of frozen seas. And the sight triggered the trip to bring up a fear so powerful and primal it wiped out all conscious thought. Laura turned and drove herself wildly through the crowd, knocking people over, punching and gouging to get away, oblivious to the angry shouts directed at her.

She was on the other side of the club, huddled behind a table on the beer-puddled floor, when some semblance of sense returned to her, and even then the panic was coming and going in waves. She cursed the drug, but knew she had no option but to ride it out; and that could last for several more hours.

The lights were still flashing, the music still pounding, but through it she became aware of sudden frenzied activity. The dancers had recognised the threat of the Cailleach Bheur. They were surging around crazily, searching for an exit, trampling anyone who fell before them in their panic. Raw screams were punching through the beats like some hellish mix. Laura tipped over the table in front of her to offer her some kind of protection and then desperately tried to order her thoughts enough to get out of there. An emergency exit. Surely there must be one somewhere. But it wasn't a regular club, probably wasn't even legal. What if there was only one way out?

That brought another wave of panic which almost sent her fleeing into the tumult, but she'd used enough drugs in her shady past to know how to calm herself a little. She focused on one of the flashing lights and did deep breathing to clear her mind. When the wave had passed, she peeked above the lip of the table to get her bearings.

What she saw filled her with dread. The walls, floor and ceiling shimmered with ice, reflecting the flashing lights in a breathtaking manner that was amplified by the drugs coursing through her system: it was the ultimate light show. But the wonder was corrupted by the grisly piles of frozen bodies heaped across the floor, faces locked in final expressions of terror, hands clawed, legs bent ready to thrust forward, taken by the cold in seconds. Laura instantly flashed back to sickening images of World War I battlefields she had seen in a history lesson.

And moving through the scene slowly was the Cailleach Bheur, her face as dark as nature. The cold came off her in waves, metamorphosing at the tips into snaky tendrils which reached out to anything not yet touched by the icy blast of eternal winter. The speakers fizzed and sparks flew off the decks. A second later the ear-splitting music ended in a shriek of feedback. That only revealed the awful screams of the surviving clubbers huddled in one corner of the room. Laura covered her ears, but couldn't drive out the sound. She couldn't even tear her eyes away as one of the tendrils wound its way along the floor like autumn mist before wrapping itself around the ankle of a young man who was futilely trying to kick it away. It was followed instantly by an odd effect which, in her state, she found both fascinating and horrible: ice crystals danced in the air before forming around his leg, moving rapidly up to his waist. Yelling, he tore at it, but it simply transferred to his hands where he touched the crystals, turning the skin blue, then forming a film of ice over it. A second later he fell to the floor with the same rictus, catching the light like a gruesome ice sculpture.

Laura was convinced she was going insane from the magnified panic and terror. Irrationally, and with desperation, she threw herself over the table and ran to the men's toilets. The door slammed behind her just as a rapidly pursuing wave of cold crashed against it. She heard the familiar cracking sound as the wood froze, but when it didn't burst in she guessed the Cailleach Bheur had turned her attention back to the remaining clubbers.

Frantically she tore around the small room and was overjoyed when she discovered a tiny window over one of the cubicles. She wrenched it open gleefully, oblivious to the breaking of a fingernail and the spurt of blood as it ripped into her skin. When she saw the solid bars that lay on the other side she burst into a bout of uncontrollable sobs.

'I can't think straight!' she yelled at herself between the tears. 'Why was I so stupid? I'm a loser! A fucking loser!'

The screams echoing dimly through the walls were bad enough, but when they finally faded away, the silence that followed was infinitely worse. Laura collapsed into a corner of the cubicle and hugged her knees, realising how pathetic her whimpers sounded, unable to do anything about it.

The silence didn't last long. The telltale sounds of forming ice and cracking wood gradually made their way towards the toilet door. Laura pressed her back hard into the wall as if, just by wishing, it would open up and swallow her. Her cheeks stung from the tears which had soaked her top. She was already making desperate deals with God: no more drugs, no more stupidity, if He whisked her out of there to safety, turned the Hag away from the door, did anything, anything – when she suddenly noticed a curious sight which broke through the panic. The blood which dripped from her cut finger was green. It wasn't a trick of the light or a vague visual hallucination; an emerald stain had formed on her top. Cautiously she touched the tip of her tongue to it; it didn't even taste like blood. It reminded her, oddly, of lettuce.

'Jesus Christ, what's going on?' It seemed like the final straw of madness. And an instant later she heard the toilet door begin to break open. Her breath clouded around her; the temperature was plummeting.

Clarity crept back into her mind as the drug entered one of its cyclical recessions, and with it came a decision not to die screwed up on the floor of a toilet like some pathetic junkie. She jumped up on to the toilet seat and began to wrench at the bars on the window in the hope that they were looser than they appeared.

By now she was shivering uncontrollably. The door groaned and began to give way.

'Come on,' she pleaded, but the bars held fast. Then another strange thing happened. Where her blood splashed on to the bars it appeared to move with a life of its own, spreading over the metal, changing into something which, in the gloom, she couldn't quite make out; all she could see through the shadows was movement and growth. Instantly the bars began to protest and a few seconds later they burst out of the brick.

The sound of the toilet door bursting inwards and the wave of intense cold that followed drove all questions from her mind. She pulled herself through the opening and fell awkwardly into a dark, litter-strewn alley that smelled of urine. Pain drove through her shoulder where she hit the ground.

Ignoring it, she forced herself to her feet and hurried away just as a white bizzard erupted out of the window above her.

The relief that hit her was so overwhelming she burst into tears again, but by the time she stumbled out on to a main road her head was spinning; there was no point trying to make sense of what had happened until the trip was over. Yet she couldn't resist one last look at the green smears across her hands. An involuntary shudder ran through her that did not come from the cold.

chapter five

storm warning

There was neverending darkness, and pain, more than she thought she could bear. How long had it gone on for now? Months? Ruth's head swam, every fibre of her body infused with agony. At least the sharp lances that had been stabbing through her hand where her finger had been severed had subsided, a little. She didn't dare think how the wound had healed in the dirty confines of her tiny cell.

Since she had been snatched from the hotel in Callander she had cried so many tears of pain and anger and frustration she didn't feel she had any more left in her. Through all the hours of meaningless torture, it was the hope that kept her going: that she would find a way out, however futile that seemed; that the others would rescue her. But it had been so long— She drove the thought from her mind. *Stay strong*, she told herself. *Be resilient.*

It would have helped if all the suffering had been for a reason, something she could have drawn strength from by resisting, but the Fomorii holding her captive seemed merely to want to impose hurt on her in their grimly equipped torture chambers. They had held back from inflicting serious damage – they always stopped when Ruth blacked out – but she felt it was only a matter of time before they lost interest in their sport.

Feeling like an old woman, she shuffled into a sitting position. Her straw bedding dug into the bare flesh of her legs. She'd mapped the cell out in her mind long ago: a bare cube carved out of the bedrock, not big enough to allow her to lie fully out, smelling of damp, scattered with dirty straw, a roughly made wooden door that had resisted all attempts to kick it open.

There's still hope. It was her mantra now, repeated every time the despair threatened to close in.

She couldn't remember anything about her capture, who did it, how it happened, where she had been brought. Her recent memory began with the shock and dismay when she discovered her missing finger and she wondered if it was the upheaval of that discovery which had driven out all the other thoughts.

Somewhere distant the deep, funereal tolling of a bell began. Soon they would come for her again. Tears sprang to her eyes unbidden and she hastily wiped them away with the back of her hand. She wasn't weak, she would survive.

There's still hope.

Afterwards, with the pain still fresh in her mind and her limbs, she enjoyed the cool, anonymous embrace of the darkness, where thoughts were all; this was the place she could live the life she wanted to live. But, as had happened so many times, the balm was soon disrupted by the familiar voice which made her think of the serrated teeth of a saw being drawn across a window pane.

'Does the light still burn?'

'It burns,' she replied. 'Not brightly, but it's there. You're a good teacher.' She caught herself. 'Teacher. I still haven't worked out what our relationship is. Are you a teacher, aide, confidant—?' She wanted to add *master*, but a frightened part of her made her hold back.

'All of those, and more. I have been entrusted with your well-being.' The sound of his words made her think he was smiling darkly, wherever it was in the gloom he existed. Though he had been helpful and supportive, she had an abiding sense that buried within him was a contempt for her powerlessness.

'What are you?' she asked, as she always did in their conversations.

And he replied as he always did: 'I am who you want me to be.' It had almost become their little joke.

But she didn't know, and that unnerved her. She remembered all she had read throughout her life about *familiars* being demons or sprites doing the Devil's bidding, and however much she had grown to realise that was propaganda put out by the early Church, she still couldn't shake the irrational fears it had set in her. Whatever, she knew she would have to stay measured and protective in her dealings with him.

'I think I prefer you as an owl,' she noted. When the Goddess had gifted her the familiar in the dark countryside outside Bristol, she hadn't realised what she was taking on; certainly with regard to what the Goddess had planned for her, but she had grown into it, reluctantly. And after her meeting with the woman who practised the Craft in the Lake District, she had seen its benefits. But still, she was scared. There was so much she didn't know, so many repercussions she couldn't begin to grasp. And she was afraid that when they did happen they would be terrible; and it would be too late to go back. 'So what's the lesson for today?' she continued hesitantly.

The voice began, telling her dark, troubling secrets: about the way the world worked, about nature, some things she didn't feel comfortable hearing at all, for they hinted at greater, darker mysteries which under-pinned every aspect of existence. But her body of knowledge about the Craft was growing. There in the dark she had learned how to use thorn apples and white waterlilies to make flying ointments, how Christmas roses could convey invisibility, how periwinkles could spark passion in the right potion and how henbane could be used to conjure spirits and intensify clairvoyance. She had discovered which plants could be used for healing and which for protection. And she knew the release of sexual energy was the core of all magick, linked directly to the blue fire that bound together the spirit of the world. Amazingly, she seemed to understand it all on first hearing and forgot none of it.

Time passed. There was a brief discussion about the raising of storms and communication with animals, enough to pique her interest and to make her realise how much there still was to learn.

'And all of this works as you say?' she asked.

'All works if applied in the correct manner by the right strength of will.'

'If I don't get out of here all this information is going to be a complete waste, isn't it?'

He ignored her question. 'This secret knowledge exists to be put into practice and it will be meaningless to you until you do so. Do you understand the message that underpins this gift I give you?'

She thought for a moment. 'No, I don't. I don't understand anything.'

'Listen, well. There is no reality. There is no shape to anything, except the shape you give it. In these matters, your will is all-powerful. If you learn to apply it—'

'I can do anything.' She weighed his words carefully. 'If you're to be believed . . .' Her voice faded. Then: 'There's always hope. That's what it means. It's down to me.'

In the dark, he concurred. 'There is always hope.'

Church paced around the hotel room before coming to rest at the window, as he had done repeatedly over the last three hours. The sun was just beginning to tint the sky pink and pale purple away to the east.

'You are worried about her,' Shavi stated.

'She can look after herself.' The words sounded hollow the moment he uttered them. He knew Laura was resilient enough to cope in almost any situation, but the danger she always carried with her was the dark, self-destructive demon buried in her heart. And after their argument he feared she had been prepared to give full vent to that side of her nature, to punish both herself and him.

He turned back to Shavi, whose face was still bloodless an hour after he had returned to the hotel. Church knew that there was much more to his experiences in St Mary's Close than the bare bones of information he had told them. But Shavi was defined by his decency and he wouldn't tell them anything that might burden them; his suffering was his own. Church couldn't resist clapping a supportive hand on his shoulder as he passed. When everything else seemed to be falling apart, he was glad for the people he had around him. It was more than he could have hoped for; he was surprised by the warmth of the feeling.

'Look, forget all the bollocks the spooks spouted,' Veitch said with a grin. 'Ruth's alive and kicking. That's the good thing, right? That's the important thing.' He grew irritated when he looked around the room to see only gloomy expressions. 'What's wrong with the lot of you?'

'The spirits implied her situation was dire,' Shavi began. 'We should not get our hopes—'

'Why should we believe them? All they do is talk in bleedin' riddles anyway—'

'She's with the Fomorii, Ryan,' Church cautioned. 'We've both been there.'

Veitch fell silent.

Shavi ran his fingers through his long hair. 'What could they possibly want with her? I was under the impression we were beneath their notice since we failed to win over the Tuatha Dé Danann.'

Tom waved a hand dismissively. 'Her situation is not paramount—'

Church stepped in before Veitch could jump to his feet angrily. The South Londoner's eyes were blazing with the barely controllable rage he always carried close to the surface. 'What's wrong with you? She's a friend, you bastard.'

'This is about more than any of us. We're all dispensable.' The coldness in Tom's eyes made Church shiver; the emotional detachment was so great he wondered how apart from them Tom really was.

'I thought you were supposed to be the big mythic hero,' Veitch sneered. 'Turning your back on a girl in trouble isn't very heroic, is it? You weasel.'

Tom turned to Church. 'Tell him. You understand.'

Of course he understood, but he could barely put it into words because it was the antithesis of everything he felt: they *were* all disposable, their petty little human concerns, hopes and fears meaningless against the end of everything. He felt like he was trading off his humanity little by little. If they succeeded, would it be worth it if there was nothing of him left to appreciate it?

Before Church could open his mouth, Veitch saw in his face what he was about to say. With a contemptuous shake of his head, Veitch stalked over to the other side of the room where he stood with his back to them.

Tom pushed his glasses back up the bridge of his nose. 'Now that's out of the way—'

'Have a little heart, for God's sake,' Church snapped. 'Just because you're right doesn't mean you have to stamp all over people's feelings.'

Tom eyed him coolly. 'Keep a level head,' he cautioned.

'Let us examine the evidence,' Shavi said diplomatically; his smile was calm and assured. 'Do we have enough to move forward?'

Church sighed wearily. 'Every time we try to get some information from anything supernatural it always ends up as mysteries wrapped in smoke and mirrors, so vague you can never be sure you've deciphered it correctly.'

'They do it on purpose,' Tom said. 'They want to see us misinterpret their words and fail or suffer. It's a power thing. Good sport. But they have given us enough.' He nodded to Shavi. 'You did well.' Coming from Tom, it was like a cheer.

Shavi looked down shyly. ' "Seek out the stone from the place that gave succour to the plague victims." Do you have any idea what that means?'

'Something particularly relevant to the residents of St Mary's Close. A little research should turn it up.'

'Then that will lead us to the Well of Fire,' Church said. 'And if we can find some way to bring that back to life, then we stand a chance of disrupting the Fomorii stronghold which we now know is somewhere beneath the castle.'

'Destroy that,' Tom said, 'and we will prevent Balor returning. They would not have guarded the place with something as terrifying as the Cailleach Bheur if this was not the location for the ritual of rebirth.'

Since they had been in Edinburgh they had all felt a darkness pressing heavily at their backs. It was something more than a premonition, almost as if the threat of Balor were reaching out from whatever terrible place his essence inhabited; as if he were aware of them. It left them desperate to win the struggle ahead, and dreading what would happen if they failed.

'And then we get Ruth,' Veitch chipped in pointedly without turning from his investigation of the mini-bar. He pulled out a bottle of lager.

'But the spirits said the blue fire was not enough,' Shavi noted. He stretched out his legs and rested his head on the back of the chair. 'They said we should call for the Good Son, whatever that means.'

Out of the corner of his eye Church saw a flicker cross Tom's face; it was like a cloud obscuring the sun. 'What is it?' he said to Tom.

'Nothing.' Tom looked at his feet. 'A story I heard once long ago.'

'Oi. Spit it out then. You were the one who said all those old tales were important,' Veitch said irritatedly.

Tom walked over to the window where he seemed to be eyeing the rising sun suspiciously. 'The Good Son was the name given by the ancient worshippers to one of the most important of the Tuatha Dé Danann. The Celts knew him as Maponus or Mabon – which simply means *Son* – or Oenghus. He was, in their stories, the son of Dagda, the Allfather, and the Great Mother. The Son of Light. When the Romans came into the Celtic lands he became associated with Apollo. When the Christians came, he was the Christ. He was linked to the sun, the giver of life. More double meanings, you see. The Good Sun.'

'What, you're saying Jesus didn't exist?' Church asked.

'Of course not,' Tom snapped. 'I'm simply saying Maponus was an archetype. An original imprint that other cultures drew on for their own myths.'

'Well, I'm glad you answered that one, then,' Veitch said sarcastically.

'He was widely worshipped throughout the world,' Tom continued. 'The Divine Youth who would lead the world back into the light; he was a great musician, *the player of the lyre*, a great lover, a patron of the arts, worshipped at the sacred springs and seen as a direct line to the powers of creation. Beautiful, witty and charming. But there was another side to him.' He paused. 'The Irish used to call him the Lord of Love and Death.'

The sun broke through the window, casting his distorted shadow across the wall; Church had a sudden vision of something monstrous moving across the room. 'What happened?' he asked quietly.

'I have no idea. After the great sundering, when all the old gods and creatures of myth left here for Otherworld, some of them, the ones with the greatest bond to our world, returned. Maponus was one of those. His links were possibly the strongest of all. There was a reason he, of all the Tuatha Dé Danann, was seen as a saviour by mortals. And then, suddenly, he disappeared.'

The others waited for him to continue. 'What happened?' Church prompted.

'The Tuatha Dé Danann would never speak of it,' he said hesitantly. 'In all my time in Otherworld it was the one question I dared not ask.' A shadow crossed his face. 'That's wrong. I did ask it once. But never again.' Church caught a glimpse of the same terrible expression Tom had worn when he had first told them about the suffering he underwent during the gods' *games*.

124

'The Tuatha Dé Danann indulged me. I was an amusement, a curiosity, but certainly not an equal. They considered me so far beneath them they would never discuss something they considered important. And this, whatever it was, was obviously of vital importance.'

'If he disappeared, how the hell are we supposed to find him?' Veitch asked.

'When I returned to this world and was inducted into the secret knowledge of the land by the Culture . . .' He looked at them sharply as if he had given something away. '. . . the people of the Bone Inspector, I learned another strange story which perhaps shed a little light on it. One of the great old gods had been bound by the Culture in a place just south of Edinburgh, sealed in the earth for all time.'

'I don't fucking understand.' Veitch's irritation was growing. 'If this geezer was so loved, why was he banged up?' He glared at Tom as if the hippie was personally setting out to confuse him.

'I never learned why. That information was kept by the highest adepts within the Culture. I never stayed with them long enough to rise that high.'

'The Culture . . . the people of the Bone Inspector . . . they seemed to have a lot of influence. Power,' Church noted.

Tom nodded. 'Supposedly eradicated by the Roman forces, they simply went underground, for centuries. But in the time when they bound the old god, they were at their strongest, worshipping in their groves, tending to the people, turning to face the sun at the solstice, standing proud, no longer stooped in hiding.'

Veitch drained his lager and tossed the bottle into the waste bin with a crash. 'I don't get it. I've seen these things in action. You can't just stand up and wave a sword at them.'

'At that time, the keepers of the knowledge had unprecedented control of the lifeblood of the Earth. They used the blue fire to shackle a god.'

'Then he is imprisoned still,' Shavi noted, 'waiting to be released?'

Tom merely looked out of the window towards the sun, closing his eyes when the light caught his face.

'Sounds a bit dodgy to me,' Veitch said suspiciously. 'He's not exactly going to be of a mind to help us after being underground all that time.'

'I thought you were the one prepared to risk anything for your lady-love?' Tom said curtly.

'*Can* we control him?' Church asked. 'How do we know the dead weren't lying to us, playing another of their games so we'd actually get into an even bigger mess? Like having an angry god giving us a good kicking for his unjust treatment.'

'We don't know.' Tom sighed. 'But it makes a queer kind of sense. If the Fomorii are preparing for the rebirth of Balor in their fortress beneath the castle, it will have been deemed impregnable. They will not risk losing their sole reason for existing. The Cailleach Bheur . . .' He swallowed hard; his mouth had grown unfeasibly dry. 'She is a power of nature, greater even than many of the powers you have already witnessed. Of all the gods, Maponus is possibly the only one who could hold her at bay, contain her so she didn't unleash the fimbulwinter. And if, at the same time, we could awaken the Well of Fire then the shadows might finally be turned back.'

'Alternatively, everything could go to hell in a handcart,' Church said acidly.

Tom shrugged. 'Did you expect easy choices?'

'No, but I don't expect you to be glib, either,' Church replied. He knew the decision would ultimately rest with him and he didn't feel up to making it. So much seemed to lie on every choice. He wished he could just return to the pathetic little life he had before.

'Do you know where Maponus is imprisoned?' Shavi asked.

'Not exactly. Not to the foot. But I know the place.' He took off his glasses and rubbed a hand over his tired eyes. 'A place called Rosslyn Chapel.'

'I have heard of it,' Shavi mused. 'A place of many mysteries. But it was founded many years after the time of which you speak.'

'And the Good Son was there long before the first stone of Rosslyn Chapel was laid. The building was devised as a resting place.'

'I remember now.' Shavi took the bottled water Veitch handed him from the mini-bar. 'The chapel is famous for its blend of Celtic, Christian and Masonic iconography in its structure. For a supposedly Christian place of worship there are pagan symbols everywhere, more representations of the Green Man than anywhere else in the land.'

'And The Green Man,' Church said, 'is another way of saying Cernunnos—'

'Cernunnos was an important element in the ritual of binding. He is, to be glib—' he glanced at Church '—the flip side of Maponus. The thick, dark forests to the sunlit plains. Winter to summer. Night to day.'

'His brother,' Church ventured.

'As if that term means anything to them.'

'I am impressed that the memory of Maponus survived the centuries strong enough to prompt the erection of such a magnificent, codified building,' Shavi said.

Tom nodded thoughtfully. 'A good point. Of those few who held the knowledge, a separate group was established in perpetuity. The members were called, in our parlance, Watchmen. Their aim was not only to keep the knowledge of the old god's imprisonment, but that a line of civil defence would be established to prepare for any further incursions from Otherworld. They were of their own creed to begin with, but as the role was essentially spiritual, when Christianity began to become established, representatives were chosen from the new Church. And from all the other faiths that eventually set up roots in this land. Over time, each faith's Watchmen became almost separate entities, unaware of those groups formed by their rivals. But they all kept the same knowledge and the same mission.'

'It was one of the Watchmen who pointed us in the right direction at Glastonbury.' Shavi moistened his throat with the water. Some of the blood seemed to have returned to his features, much to Church's relief. 'And it was another group which built Rosslyn Chapel?'

Tom nodded. 'Under the direction of Sir William St Clair, a prince of Orkney. In the increasingly Godless twentieth century most of the groups have withered. I have no idea if one still exists at Rosslyn—'

The faint knock at the door made him tense, as if he had heard a gun being cocked. Before anyone could speak, Veitch was already moving on perfectly balanced limbs until he was poised at the door jamb, ready to act. He looked to Church for guidance.

Church waited a moment then called out, 'Who's there?'

'Laura.' Her voice sounded like paper in the wind.

Veitch wrenched open the door and she almost collapsed in. Church moved forward quickly to catch her.

She looked into his face before her eyelids flickered and a faint smile spread across her lips. 'You know, I always saw it like this.'

It was midmorning before she had recovered. Faintly contrite but determined not to show it, Laura sat in a sunbeam on the bed, wrapped in a blanket, her skin like snow, her pupils still dilated so much her eyes seemed black. She had attempted to tell them the full horror of what had happened at the club, but so much had been tied into her trip she couldn't separate reality from hallucination herself. 'Maybe that spy was right,' she said. 'Maybe it is all how we see it in our heads. Who knows what's really happening?'

'Exactly!' Shavi began excitedly. 'Liquid nitrogen would cause—'

Veitch pushed forward, barely able to contain his irritation. 'What's wrong with you? Look at the state of you – off your face, talking bollocks. This isn't a holiday. You can't just carry on having a good time—'

Church clapped a hand on his shoulder. 'Not now, Ryan.'

Veitch glared. 'Jumping to her protection just because you're shagging her, even though you know I'm right?'

'It's not like that. We all know she could have made some better choices, but this isn't the time.'

Veitch shook his head angrily. 'This is war. We've got to have some strict rules. Because if one person fucks up, it could drag the rest of us down.'

'He's right,' Tom said. 'We have to have discipline—'

'And that's one thing I haven't got, right?' Laura said sharply. 'You lot are such *blokes*.'

She desperately wanted to talk about her fears, about what was happening to her body, but everyone seemed more ready to criticise than to listen. She didn't feel any different, but the shock of seeing what happened to her blood lay heavy on her. Part of her wondered if she had contracted some hideous new virus which had crossed over from Otherworld; there were so many new rules, so many things still hidden, it was impossible to put any event into any kind of context. Perhaps it had lain in her, dormant, but was now beginning to ravage her body. But with all their talk of discipline and missions and responsibility to the cause, how could she even bring it up? It was something she had to deal with herself.

Veitch leaned against one of the lobby's marble columns, adopting a look of cool detachment while secretly believing the attendants were all sneering at him, whispering behind their hands that he shouldn't be there, that someone ought to throw him out. It made him feel angry and hunted and at any other time he wouldn't have subjected himself to it, but those feelings paled in comparison to the betrayal he felt at Church's dismissal of Ruth's plight. He understood in an oblique way what Church said about obligation and responsibility, but loyalty to friends overrode it all; and love was even more important than that.

He was suddenly aware of an old man moving across the lobby towards him. His gait was lazily elegant, although he looked in his seventies. The sharp cut of his expensive suit, the delicate way he held his silver-topped cane, the perfect grooming of his swept-back white hair and old-style handlebar moustache, all suggested a man of breeding.

Here we go, Veitch thought. *Somebody who wants the riff-raff thrown out.*

But as the elderly gentleman neared, Veitch saw he was smiling warmly. 'I am an excellent judge of a man's face,' he said in the well-formed vowels of a privileged Edinburgh brogue, 'and I can see we've both been touched by magic.' His eyes twinkled as he took Veitch's left hand in both of his; Veitch was so shocked he didn't snatch it back as he normally would have. 'I can see troubles too,' the gentleman continued. 'And if it is any comfort, hear the words of someone who has grown wise in his long life: never give up believing.' He tapped Veitch once on his forearm and then, with a polite nod, turned and moved gracefully back across the lobby.

'What was that all about?' Church had come up on Veitch while he curiously surveyed the gentleman's retreat.

'Dunno. Some old duffer who's had too much sun.'

As they wandered in the morning sunlight towards the sandwich shop to pick up lunch, Veitch put on the cheap sunglasses he had picked up at one of the department stores on Princes Street. He couldn't contain himself any longer. 'I don't know how you can dump her, mate.'

Church nodded, relieved it was finally out. 'I know how you feel, Ryan. More than you might think. But after how I almost screwed things up before Beltane because I was so wrapped up in my own problems, I've got to keep my eye on the big picture. I learned the hard way that we all come second.'

Veitch shook his head; the sunglasses masked his emotions from Church. 'I hear what you're saying, but it's not right.' His feelings were heavy in his voice, but he was managing to control himself. 'She's one of us. We should look after our own.'

'And maybe we can. There might be a way we can do what we have to do and save Ruth at the same time. I just haven't thought of it.'

'Well, you better get thinking. It's your job.'

'Why *is* it my job?' Church bristled. 'Did I miss the election? How come I ended up leading this pathetic bunch?'

Veitch looked surprised, as if Church had asked the most stupid question in the world. 'Course it had to be you. Who else could do it?'

'Shavi.'

'He's got his own responsibilites. Listen, you know your strengths. Thinking, planning. Seeing the *big picture.*'

Church grunted, looked away. 'Well, I don't like it.'

'You're good at it. Accept it.'

'Okay,' Church said. 'Well, you accept this. The Pendragon Spirit, or whatever it is, is pushing all our strengths out into the open and yours are obvious too. You're not just the fighter, the warrior, you're the strategist. I've seen it in you – you're a natural at choosing the right path whenever we're in a tight spot. So here's your job: sort out how we can save Ruth *and* do everything else we need to do.'

Veitch looked even more surprised at this, but after a moment's thought he said seriously, 'All right, I'll take you up on that. But if I do it, you've got to give me a good hearing.'

'Deal.'

The relief on Veitch's face was palpable. As they crossed Princes Street, he said, out of the blue, 'So what's happening with you and the big-mouthed blonde?'

Church shrugged. 'We get on well. We've got a lot in common.'

'I don't trust her.'

'I know you don't. But I do. Is that what you want to hear?'

'Yes.' He paused outside the sandwich shop and turned to Church. 'She's got it bad for you, you know.'

'So you're an expert on affairs of the heart now, are you?'

'I know what I see. Do you feel the same about her?'

Church shifted uncomfortably, then made to go into the shop, but Veitch stood his ground. 'Everything is a mess these days,' Church said irritably. 'All I can do is get through each day acting and reacting, not thinking at all.' He missed Ruth much more than he might have shown, but he kept quiet because he didn't want to give Veitch any more fuel for his argument; but Ruth was the only one to whom he could truly talk. Her listening and gentle guidance had helped him unburden numerous problems. 'Is that the end of the inquisition?' he asked sharply.

'One more thing. Something that's been on my mind. That dead girlfriend of yours. How you coping with that?'

Church winced at Veitch's bluntness. 'You have got this strategy thing, haven't you? Checking up I'm not a liability?'

'No—'

'Yes, you are. You just don't realise it. Marianne's death doesn't haunt me any more. Neither does she, if that's what you mean. Since the Fomorii stopped bothering with us they've not sent her spirit out to make me suffer. But that doesn't mean I've forgotten they've still got her.' He tapped his chest and then his head. 'It's in here and it's in here. And one day soon I'm going to set her free *and* get my own back.'

This seemed to satisfy him. 'I just wanted to be sure.'

Church watched him disappear into the shop with an increasing sense of regard. His skills as a warrior were growing stronger with each passing day, as if ancient history were shouting through his genes. The Pendragon Spirit had chosen well, each of them maturing into a different role, the resources most needed for the task at hand. Perhaps there was a chance after all.

As they made their way back to the hotel they noticed signs of activity on The Mound just beyond the National Gallery. Two police cars were parked across the road, lights flashing, and armed soldiers had been discreetly positioned near walls and in shadows in the vicinity. A crowd had gathered near the cars with a mood that seemed at once irritated and dumbfounded.

'Looks like trouble,' Veitch said. 'We should stay away.'

'I want to find out what's happening.'

He grabbed the arm of a man at the back of the crowd to ask for information. 'They're closing off the Old Town,' he replied, obviously troubled by an event which seemed to shake the natural order. 'Public safety, they say. If the Old Town isn't safe, what about the rest of us?'

'I hear there was some kind of Government laboratory up there doing top secret experiments and they had an accident,' a middle-aged woman whispered conspiratorially.

'Now why would they do experiments where people live and all the tourists go?' another woman said with a dismissive snort.

A young man with a shaved head and a pierced nose butted in. 'No, it's a serial killer. A pal o' mine went to a club up there last night and he dinnae return home. The word is a whole load of people were murdered.'

Church listened to the theories bouncing back and forth until he was dragged away by Veitch tugging insistently on his arm. 'One of the cops spotted us and went for his radio,' he said. 'Looks like we're still on the Most Wanted list.'

Church was back soon after, this time with Laura. After discussion, they had decided that, despite the risks, they had to get to the Central Library in the heart of the Old Town to search for the information they needed. At least in the daylight the supernatural threat was minimised, but it increased the danger of them getting picked up by the police.

'Why couldn't they have closed the place off tomorrow?' Church grumbled as they surveyed one of the road blocks.

Laura fixed a relentless, icy glare on a woman who had been staring at her scars; the woman withered and hurried away.

'Don't pick on the locals. They don't have your power,' Church said drily.

'I always use my powers wisely.' Laura looked around surreptitiously, then fixed her sunglasses. The blockade at the foot of Cockburn Street was manned by one young policeman who kept glancing uneasily up the steeply inclining road behind him.

'God knows why I chose you. That blonde hair stands out like a beacon. It's not the best thing for subterfuge.'

'Actually, I chose you, dickhead. And it's my beauty that attracts all the looks, not my hair.' She scanned the street briefly before picking up an abandoned beer bottle at the foot of a wall. 'What we need is a diversion.'

Before Church had time to protest she hurled the bottle in an arc high over the policeman's head while he was glancing round. It exploded against the plate-glass window of a record shop, which shattered in turn. The policeman started as if he had been shot. Once the shock had eased, a couple of seconds later, he ran to investigate the shop, still obviously disorientated.

'There we go.' Laura ran for the shadows of Advocate's Close, which disappeared up among the buildings.

'You like taking risks, don't you?' Church said breathlessly when he finally caught up with her at the top of the steep flight of stairs.

'Life would be boring without them.' They both came up short against the eerie stillness which hung over the normally tourist-thronged Royal Mile. 'Spooky,' she added.

'The Fomorii are getting stronger. They're slowly spreading their influence out from the castle to secure their boundaries. That's what you saw last night at the club.' Church suddenly glanced back into the shadows clustered at the foot of the steps.

'What is it?'

'I don't know . . . thought I saw something. I'm just jumpy.'

'If the copper was after us we'd know by now.' She strode out across the street. 'So you've forgiven me, then?'

'There's nothing to forgive.'

'What, apart from my stupidity?' She didn't meet his eye.

'Come on, anybody could have done what you did. It's hard to adjust to all the new dangers that are out there.'

'Veitch doesn't think so. The Cockney bastard wants me dead.'

'You're overreacting. He's our tactician and warrior. It's his job to be cautious.'

'*Tactician and warrior?*' she sneered. 'That's a strange euphemism for wanker.'

As they made their way up to George IV Bridge Church couldn't help looking behind him again. The apprehension he felt from the moment they entered the Old Town was increasing rapidly.

'Stop being so jumpy,' Laura cautioned sharply. 'No one's behind us.'

Church found himself involuntarily grasping for the locket the young Marianne had given him before she died; it felt uncommonly hot in his hand, as if it, too, was responding to something that couldn't be defined by the five senses. Despite its cheapness, with its crudely snipped photo of Princess Diana, it gave him some comfort. Infused with the power of faith, it represented to him the tremendous power of good that had come from the terrible changes in the world, a counterbalance to everything else they experienced. Instinctively he felt it had even stronger powers than the inspirational ones he attributed to it.

They walked quickly to the Central Library. The evacuation had obviously taken place hurriedly that morning after the discovery of the carnage at the club, for the swing doors at the front were unlocked. They slipped in and ducked beneath the electronic barriers to reach the stacks in the sunlit room at the back. It didn't take them long to find the section dedicated to Edinburgh history.

'It's like technology never happened,' Laura said with distaste as she glanced at the rows of books.

Church ignored her; she was only trying to get a reaction, as usual. He pulled out a pile of general history books and heaved them over to one of the reading tables. They spent the next hour wading through the tales of murder, intrigue and suffering which seemed to characterise Edinburgh, reading beyond just the plague years in case the spirits had been less than direct in their guidance.

While Church quietly immersed himself, Laura attempted new levels of irritation by announcing every time she came across something of interest. 'Listen to this,' she said, ignoring his muttered curse. 'This used to be the most crowded city in Europe. There're six thousand living in the Old Town now. Back then there were nearly *sixty* thousand. That's like Bombay or something. No wonder the plague went through here like wildfire. They were all crammed inside the city walls so instead of spreading out, they just built the houses up and up. Eight, nine, ten storeys. Sometimes just shacks of wood on top. They were collapsing all the time or catching fire, killing—'

'Fascinating.'

'Hey, there's another great fact here.'

'Really.'

'Yes. It says all people with the surname Churchill are pompous windbags.'

It took a second or two to register and before he could say anything she'd grabbed him and pulled him halfway across the table to plant a kiss on his lips. 'Get the poker out of your arse, dull-boy. Just because it's the end of the world doesn't mean we can't have fun.' There was almost a desperation in her comment. She glanced around, then leered at him. 'A good place for sex. How many people can say they've done it on a reading table at the public library?'

'You're only saying that to get out of doing boring work.'

'You reckon.'

He gave her a long kiss, but as he pulled away his gaze fell on a passage in an open book next to them. 'There it is!'

'That's it. Change the subject—'

'No, listen.' He levered her to one side so he could read: 'Down where Princes Street Gardens are now there used to be a lake, the Nor' Loch, which was the main source of drinking water for the city. It was also where all Edinburgh's sewage used to flow—'

'Very tasty.'

'—so everyone's immune system was low, particularly those who were close to the Nor' Loch, like the residents of Mary King's Close – which is why they suffered particularly badly when the plague came.' Church traced his finger along the tiny print of the book. 'There was a nearby village called Restalrig, which has been swallowed up by the city now. Next to Restalrig's church was a natural spring which was a major source of clean water during the plague years.'

'So that's *the place that gave succour to the plague victims.*'

'Sounds like it.'

'Now there was a stone surround to the spring and when they decided to build a railway depot on the site in 1860 they moved it to another natural spring. At the foot of Arthur's Seat.'

'We saw it!' Laura exclaimed. 'When we drove past on our way to the top. There was a grille and a big pile of stone shit set in the hillside—'

Church grinned triumphantly. 'That's the way in. A natural spring which was always seen as somewhere sacred, probably because it was a potent source of the earth energy—' They were distracted by a faint sound.

Laura looked round anxiously. 'What was that?'

Church silenced her. Nothing moved in his field of vision across the library. No sound came through the windows from the normally bustling Old Town. Cautiously he moved forward, motioning to Laura to investigate one side of the library while he looked down the other.

He soon lost sight of Laura among the stacks. Although he could *feel* on some instinctive level they were not alone, there was no sign of anyone else in the building with them.

He'd got to the edge of the stack dedicated to religion when he heard Laura cry out. He sprinted across the library to find her slumped against the wall in a daze, her eyes flickering with fear as they focused on some inner landscape.

'The black wolf,' she said, as if she were drugged. 'He looked at me. And his eyes were yellow.'

Once Church was sure she was physically unharmed he quickly turned his attention back to the room. It was still empty, but there was an increasing air of tension; someone was definitely nearby.

'Don't worry,' he whispered distractedly, 'it'll be okay.'

'No,' Laura said forcefully. 'It's the Black Wolf.' The fear surged up in her; she covered her face with her hands.

Church moved on. The stacks rose on all sides; the interloper could be round any corner. His attention was drawn to a door away to his right which seemed to be moving gently; it might have been simply the result of an air current. Holding his breath almost involuntarily, he approached. The movement of the door stilled. Apprehensively, he reached out for the handle.

The door crashed against him, forcing a yell of surprise. Before he could recover, boney fingers were clamped around his wrist, wrenching him towards the gap. Through the shock Church registered the bizarre sight of what appeared to be tracings of black veins against parchment-white skin. By the time he reacted, his hand was already through the gap and the door had been yanked back sharply against his forearm. He cursed loudly and struggled to drag his hand back, but it was held tight.

'One for the unified force of my anger. And one for revenge.' Church's blood ran cold. The voice was barely human; it was like hot tar bubbling in a pit. 'And five is the number of my despair. Each digit a catechism in the ritual of salvation. A symbolic death to be followed by a real one.'

A new pain, harsh and focused, erupted in Church's hand. With horror, he felt the skin of his middle finger break open, the blood start to trickle down into his palm.

He's trying to cut it off! The terrible thought burst in his mind, and with it came the certain knowledge that this was the one who had mutilated and abducted Ruth.

He wrenched at his hand with increasing desperation, but it was pinned with an inhuman strength. And the blade bit deeper. Red hot needles danced across his skin. His forehead felt like it was on fire, his vision fracturing around the edges as he started to black out.

No, he pleaded with himself.

It felt like the blade was down to the bone now. His head started to spin, his knees grew weak.

Somehow he found an extra reserve of strength to give one last pull, but it was not enough. Just as he started to lose consciousness, arms folded around him, adding to his strength. Laura set her heels and heaved and somehow he found the will to join in. His wrist felt like it was going to snap, his arm like it was popping from its socket.

But then something gave and he found himself flying backwards. He landed on the floor several feet back, with Laura pinned beneath him.

'You big bastard,' she gasped.

Desperately he rolled off her and pulled out his handkerchief to stem the flow of blood. The cloth was soaked crimson within seconds, but the blood slowed enough for him to tie it tight.

Laura was anxiously watching the door which had swung shut. 'I think they've gone,' she ventured. Then: 'What *was* that?'

'I don't know.' Church still felt nauseous at the memory of the voice. It had sounded like something from *The Exorcist*. Fighting off the rolling waves of pain that were rising up his arm, he moved forward cautiously and pulled open the door. There was no one on the other side. Splatters of his own blood, that had run off his attacker, marked a trail out of the building.

'Whatever it was, it's not going to be satisfied until it's had us all,' he said.

'I need my fingers. They're a lonely girl's best friend.' Although she was trying to make light, there was no humour in her words. 'Come on, we've got to get some stitches in that.'

In spite of having found their next step forward, their confidence had ebbed as they made their way up the street from the library. Apprehension almost prevented them crossing the Royal Mile, with its clear vista from the imposing bulk of the castle at the top, but they pulled themselves together enough to continue towards the worrying darkness of Advocate's Close.

Halfway across the road Laura caught at Church's sleeve and whispered, 'Look at that.'

Above the castle, grey clouds were roiling unnaturally, unfolding from the very stone of the place, rolling out across the Old Town. Within seconds the hot summer sun was obscured. The temperature dropped rapidly and Church felt the sting of snow in the cold wind.

They raised their faces up to stare at the dark skies, suddenly shivering in the heart of winter.

only sleeping

Dawn came up over Calton Hill like gold and brass. Summer heat quickly dispelled the cool of the night, and the air was soon filled with the chorus of waking songbirds and the aroma of wild flowers. Amongst the treetops that clustered to the south-west side of the hill, tiny figures danced and swooped on the warm currents, their gossamer wings sparkling in the sun's first rays.

For Veitch, it was a transcendent moment that pointed up the hollowness of the world before the change. His hard face softened as he followed the winged creatures' magical trail; the tension eased from his muscles. His smile transformed him into the kind of man he might have been if he hadn't grown up at a certain time in a certain place, trapped by destiny, punished by reality for no crime apart from existing.

And Shavi watched Veitch, and he too smiled. And the others looked to Shavi and felt the genuine warmth and hope he exuded, even in the darkest moments. It was he who had suggested the ritual to greet the sun as a way of marking the next phase of their life, and as a memory of something good to carry with them into dark places. Tom had helped out with the details of the ancient rite which had been carried out at the stone circles in the long-forgotten days, and they had chosen Calton Hill, where every year Edinburgh residents gathered for a pagan rite of seasonal renewal on Beltane. It was the place, it was the time.

And there, in the aftermath, they all felt stronger and they could turn their eyes away from the still-sleeping, geometrical streets of the New Town to the clouded, chaotic and thunderous bulk of the Old. Above it, the winter clouds still churned.

'We will always remember this moment.' Shavi's voice was a whisper but it carried through the still air with a strength and clarity that sent a shiver down their spines. 'This is not just an age of darkness and anarchy. It is a time of wonder and miracles too. Never forget. Light in dark—'

'The best of times, the worst of times.' Church smiled.

'Sweet and sour,' Laura chipped in. 'Cabbage and chocolate—'

'All right!' Shavi laughed. 'You have no sense of occasion!'

'And you'd get on a pretentious spiral up your own arse if we'd let you.' Laura rolled on to her back, chuckling playfully.

For that brief time, Church forgot his brooding nature and turned to look through the twelve Doric columns of the National Monument towards the sun, pretending it was Athens, dreaming of Marianne – but no longer in a bad way.

Tom, stoned and grinning, looked more like a Woodstock refugee than he had done in weeks. When he smiled, the lines of suffering and despair turned to crinkles of good humour and his piercing eyes sparkled with a blissed-out hippie's playfulness. 'Shavi's right.' His voice, too, became less sombre, and more of its original Scottish brogue was evident. 'Make the most of it.'

'Okay,' Church said. 'Pop quiz. Favourite golden oldie. I'll start: *Fly*—'

'—*Me to the Moon*, you predictable Sinatra dickhead,' Laura chided. 'You hadn't mentioned the *great man* for a while. I thought you'd grown out of that.'

'We haven't had much time to kick back and listen to music.'

'*Scooby Snacks*.' Veitch's voice surprised them all, floating out dreamily and distracted while he watched the sprites in the trees. 'Fun Lovin' Criminals.'

'*Strange Brew* by Cream,' Tom grinned.

Laura stared at him as if he was insane. 'No, wasn't that Beethoven?' she said sarcastically.

'Stop criticising and chip in so we can criticise your musical taste,' Church said.

She wrinkled her nose. 'Oh God, I don't know. *Hey Boy Hey Girl* by the Chemical Brothers. Or maybe something by Celine Dion,' she added with a sneer. 'What's yours then, Shav-ster?' Laura raised her sunglasses slightly to get a clearer view of his expression. 'Some Andean pan pipe music? Kashmiri drum and bass? Tibetan chants? Aboriginal didgeridoo solos?'

'*Move On Up* by Curtis Mayfield, if you must know,' he said with mock playfulness. 'The ultimate positivity in music.'

'Oh God, can't you just say you like the beat?' She pulled off her boot and threw it at him. He ducked with a laugh and crawled behind Tom, who suddenly looked very perturbed.

Church didn't want to break the mood, but it had to happen sooner or later. 'We need to talk about divvying up,' he began. Nobody looked at him as if he had only thought the words, but he sensed a change in the atmosphere, as if everything was suddenly hanging in stasis.

'I think it's up to me to go into Arthur's Seat—'

'And you said that with a completely straight face, Church-dude.' Laura's voice was suddenly weary. 'I always said you had no comic timing.'

'—and I think Tom should go to Rosslyn Chapel—'

'No,' Tom said firmly.

'But you know the history of what happened there. You've been taught some of the knowledge of the people who did the binding. It's obviously yours,' Church protested.

'No,' Tom said again.

Laura scanned his face for a moment. 'He's scared.'

Tom glared at her. 'Yes, I am, and I don't mind admitting it, as any wise man would do. But that's not the reason. We've all got a part to play here and mine is as teacher, as guide to the ways of the land, the earth energy. I need to go with Jack to show him, tell him, teach him. I may not be the embodiment of the Pendragon Spirit like you, but I am bound to it for all time. It lights my way. And I, in turn, help it in any way I can.'

'So it's not about you being scared at all, then,' Laura said, with a false smile. Tom looked away.

'Veitch, Laura and I can go to Rosslyn Chapel,' Shavi began, but this time it was Veitch's turn to refuse.

'I'm staying here.' He turned towards them, his face set.

'Why?' The fresh stitches in Church's finger began to ache.

'Someone has to get Ruth out.'

'On your own!' Church exclaimed. 'I know I asked you for a plan, but I expected it to be one you'd thought about for more than five minutes.'

'I know what I'm doing—'

'Right. So you're going to waltz into a stronghold filled with Fomorii out to tear you limb from limb, go directly to Ruth and carry her out like at the end of *An Officer and a Gentleman*.'

'Something like that.'

'And, of course, it'll be no problem that when the Well of Fire is ignited or redirected or whatever I'm doing, you'll be right at ground zero.'

Veitch shrugged. He obviously wasn't going to be deterred.

'Muscle boy's in love,' Laura mocked in a singsong voice. Veitch flashed her a cold, hateful stare, but said nothing.

'Ryan—' Church began.

'I'm going to find a way in to that place and I'm going to do my best to get her out. Because it's the right thing. Just like you're trying to do the right thing for everybody else. If I can get in just before the shit hits the fan, there's a chance—'

'How will you know the right time?'

'I'll know. I feel things. You know, the right way to act. The right thing to do at the right time. I don't know where it's coming from, but it's getting stronger. You said it yourself.' He stared into the middle distance, faintly uncomprehending. 'I'm different now. Better. I'm not going to let it go to waste.'

Church searched his face for a moment, then nodded. 'It's decided, then. I go to the Well with Tom. Laura and Shavi head south to Rosslyn Chapel. And Veitch—'

'Attempts *Mission: Impossible*. I don't fancy your chances, even for a big, tough, street boy.' Church heard a surprising note of concern in Laura's voice. 'A nest of Fomorii. Their biggest stronghold, protecting the thing most valuable to them. And you.' She paused. 'Shall I order the pine box?'

'I'll take my chances. Let's face it, I'm the only bastard who actually has a chance among you bleedin' lot. If I kick the bucket, well, you know, it was for the right reason. That's what this is all about, right?' He turned to Church. 'That's what you keep saying, innit? Do it for the right reason. This is *my* right reason.' He seemed surprised to see admiration in their stares and grew uncomfortable.

Laura attempted to break the mood with some glib, mocking comment, but for once the words escaped her. Church watched her face sag as she bit her lip; he wondered what lay behind her sunglasses.

'Where are we gonna meet up afterwards?' Veitch asked optimistically.

'Greyfriars Churchyard.' Church had spent most of the previous afternoon planning, armed with a map of the city and the guidebook, while fighting back nausea from the pain in his finger.

'Why there?'

'Because I always wanted to see that statue of the little dog that sat by his master's grave. Greyfriars Bobby – what a great tourist attraction that is.' He tried to make light of the conversation, but he couldn't shake the feeling that Veitch wouldn't be meeting them. 'I think we can pick a quick route out of town from there. And it's an easy place to find if the shit really is hitting the fan.'

They all thought about this for a moment.

Nobody wanted to be the first to go, but eventually Shavi shouldered the responsibility. He knelt beside Veitch and gave his shoulder a brief squeeze before setting off down the hill. Tom followed, resting one hand on Veitch's head in passing, a restrained show of respect that was surprisingly voluble in a man normally so emotionally detached. Laura paused, but couldn't bridge the gap and hurried uncomfortably after the others.

It was only then Church realised how truly strong were forged the bonds that joined them. Their communication was silent, but deeply expressed; powerful emotions united them, of respect and trust, friendship and faith, even love. It was even harder to believe the Celtic spirits' accusation that one of them was a traitor.

'Are you going to be okay here on your own?' he said.

Veitch grinned with fake confidence. 'No, but fuck it.' He stripped off his shirt to feel the sun on his skin, his tattoos gleaming across his torso. 'See this?' He pointed to a pentacle picked out in an intertwining Celtic design. 'I always wondered what that was. But it's us, innit? See, five points, all separate, but all joined together, and stronger for it.'

Church gave him a friendly clap on the shoulder. 'You're a smart bloke, Ryan. You shouldn't hide it so much.'

'Yeah, smart like shit.' He fumbled for Church's hand and shook it awkwardly. 'You know, I never thought I'd ever be a part of something like this . . . fuck it!' He shook his head, embarrassed. 'You better get going. It's time to go to work.'

Church set off down the hill. Halfway down, where the trees began to close in around the path, he glanced back to see a figure silhouetted against the dawn sky, framed by the soaring Athenian columns. It was such a sad, lonely sight he quickly turned and hurried after the others.

It was already early afternoon as Shavi and Laura made their way south. The sun had started to give way to the sea mist the locals called the haar. It swept in from the north-east, obscuring Arthur's Seat and the castle, rolling out across the rooftops and clinging hard to the streets. They had considered hiring a car, but Church had cautioned them about keeping a low profile, so Shavi had convinced Laura to walk the six and a half miles towards the misty, purple bulk of the Pentland Hills. She refused, however, to carry any of the camping gear which was mounted on a framed rucksack on his back. As they set out through Tollcross the Old Town seemed uncomfortably close; Laura was convinced she could feel a wintry chill radiating out from the streets that emptied on to Lothian Road. They kept to the other side, near to the comforting modernity of the new financial district, until the blackened, ancient buildings of the Old Town were far behind.

Although it was not raining, the haar infused the air with so much moisture their clothes soon became damp and Laura's spikey hair sagged on to her forehead.

'You can probably remove your sunglasses now,' Shavi said wryly.

'When you get the pomposity out of your arse.' She looked around. 'Not much traffic for a capital city.'

'People are only making journeys when they feel it is absolutely important. They subconsciously sense the danger that is all around.'

'And it hasn't got so bad yet.'

The street rode the rolling hills, past rows of smart shops where a few people seemed at ease enough to hover outside the windows, up towards the ring road. Laura leaned over the barrier, still curious to see such little transport.

'Well, the airport is shut now all the flights have been grounded,' Shavi pointed out. 'And with the Old Town closed off I suppose they have lost the parliament, the newspaper offices, many businesses—'

'Don't they realise they can't carry on with their lives?'

'I think they probably do. But it is human nature to carry on with routines in an attempt to maintain normalcy, often in the face of all reason.'

A little further on Laura began to complain of aching feet, and from then on, as they left the city behind and wound out into the countryside, they had to take numerous long breaks while she nursed her burgeoning blisters.

'I've never walked this far in my life,' she moaned.

'I once walked the entire length of Kashmir—'

'Oh, shut up.' She was limping away before she had to listen to any more of his tale. 'It hurts enough already,' she muttered.

It was late afternoon before they reached the Rosslyn Chapel sign which pointed down a lane off the main road. Between wet fields and under a slate-grey sky, it took them in to the village of Roslin.

'Did you know,' Shavi began, 'that the Roslin Institute is nearby, where they cloned Dolly the sheep. A place of mysteries both old and new.'

'Whoop de doo.'

They were barely in the village when another tiny lane led them off to the right. A little way down it they reached the chapel car park; they could tell they were nearing their destination from the stark change in atmosphere: it grew oppressive and brooding, as if the mystery that lurked there was potent enough to affect the air itself. The chapel was completely obscured by trees, a visitor centre and high fences which made it difficult for anyone to get inside. The custodians had already locked up for the day.

Shavi checked the sky and rubbed his chin thoughtfully, but before he could speak, Laura said, 'Pull yourself together. We're not going in there today. I'm not going to be caught anywhere near the place after night has fallen.'

Shavi smiled. 'Then we make camp.'

They needed to find somewhere where they wouldn't be stumbled across or reported to the authorities. Picking their way down a steep path, they came to the graveyard, with its neatly tended plots, ancient and new stones mingling together. Another footpath led off to one side where the trees grew thickest. The whole area was still. No traffic rumbled, no birds sang.

'Maybe it's just the weather, but I can feel something like . . . despair.' Laura glanced into the thick vegetation beneath the tree cover where the water dripped from the leaves in a steady rhythm.

Shavi nodded, said nothing.

The path wound around until the graveyard was lost behind them and the branches closed over their heads, sealing them in a gloomy, verdant world. A rabbit started at their approach and dived into the undergrowth. Eventually they could hear the splashing water of a stream or falls, and then they were out of the trees again, suddenly confronted by the breathtaking view of a tree-clustered glen far beneath them. The haar drifted eerily in white tendrils among the treetops. Everywhere was still, waiting.

'It's beautiful,' Laura said. 'But there's something not natural about the place. Which is a pretty stupid thing to say about the countryside.'

The path wound round until it crossed a tiny stone bridge which soared high above the glen. On the other side, hanging over the steep sides of the valley like some fairy-tale fortress, were the majestic stone ruins of Rosslyn Castle. Just beyond the broken turrets and fallen walls they could see lights; part of the building was still in use. They picked up a rough track just before the bridge which led them scrambling down into the glen and then the trees were closing over them again. Oak, ash and elm mingled all around, hinting at the great age of the woodland, and this was reflected in the diversity of the undergrowth that prospered beneath the tree cover: wood sorrel, ransoms, golden saxifrage, dog's mercury and wood-rush.

The place was so lonely Laura couldn't help but feel unnerved and when she glanced at Shavi she could see it reflected on his normally stolid face too; it was in the air, in every tree and rock. They trekked along the floor of the glen by the banks of the white-foamed North Esk until they found an isolated clearing where the smoke from any fire would not be seen from the castle.

'Are you sure we shouldn't go back and find a B&B?' Laura ventured. She was even more disturbed when she saw Shavi almost considered it.

They pitched the tent with its rear end in an impenetrable cluster of undergrowth to prevent anyone approaching them from behind. To Laura's growing anxiety, the flora all around was so dense, the noise from the swishing leaves and the thundering river so great, it would have been impossible to discern strangers until they were almost upon them.

'If this was a movie,' Laura began, 'I'd say, "I can't shake the feeling there's somebody watching us."' Shavi nodded. 'You're supposed to say, "Don't be so stupid, it's just the trees,"' she added irritably.

'I think we should take a chance and light the fire now.' He looked up at the streaks of drifting white in the gloomy treetops. 'It will get dark here much quicker than if we were out in the open.'

'You can build a beacon they could see in Holland for me.'

Shavi spent the next half hour collecting enough wood to last them all night while Laura sat morosely in the mouth of the tent. Her anxiety eased a little when he finally had a small fire glowing in the clearing a few feet away from them. They boiled up a little rice while Shavi roasted kebabs of peppers, onions and tomatoes, which they ate while listening to the crack, drip and shiver of the living wood around them.

Shavi was correct about the dark, which swept in unnervingly quickly until it was sitting just beyond the glimmer of the campfire, breathing in and out oppressively.

After a while Laura found herself leaning against Shavi; she had shuffled up to him almost unconsciously, for comfort. He slipped an arm around her shoulders, out of friendship; there wasn't a hint of any of the passion they had shared in Glastonbury. And she leaned her head gently against his shoulder, glad he was there, for so many reasons she could barely count them.

'You seem unhappy,' he ventured.

'And you look like a dickhead, but do I take it out on you?'

He smiled and waited for a few moments while the rushing of the river took over. 'Romance is by necessity difficult.'

'Everything is difficult.' Then: 'Why "by necessity"?'

'The value of anything is defined by the effort it takes us to get it. And romance is the most valuable thing of all.'

'That's one opinion. Me, I'd go for an iced bottle of Stolichnaya, an ounce of Red Leb and some peace and quiet.'

'Jack is going through a difficult time. He has suffered an extreme emotional blow—'

'We've all got our problems.'

'—and a great deal is expected of him, more than he thinks he can possibly give. He is torn between the things he wants to do, the things his heart is telling him, and what he feels is the right thing to do.'

'He's too wrapped up in this whole "heroes have to sacrifice" thing.'

'Yes, he is.' Shavi gave her a faint, comforting squeeze. 'But he is a good, decent man. The best of all of us.'

'I know that.'

'Everyone knows it. Except Jack.'

'And you're about to say I should cut him some slack.'

'No. I am just saying this by way of explanation.'

'You think I've done the wrong thing by getting in with him, don't you?' She looked round at him, but his gaze was fixed firmly away in the trees.

'I think your romance would have a better chance at a different time. There are so many obstacles being placed before it by external events.'

She looked away so he couldn't see her face.

'But you know your heart better than I.' He turned and stared at the back of her head, hoping she would look at him, but she kept the barriers up. 'And if there is any lesson from all this hardship we are experiencing, it is that things are worth fighting for and fighting to the last, and tremendous things *do* happen.'

'Who do you think he should be with?'

'I—' He struggled to find words that would not hurt her. 'My opinion does not matter.'

'It matters to me.' When he didn't answer, she said in a barely audible voice, 'He's my last chance.'

'What do you mean?' he asked curiously.

'Nothing.'

Shavi thought about what she said for a moment. 'You are a good person,' he stated firmly.

'No, I'm not. I'm a bad girl. And I've got coming to me what all bad girls get.'

'No—'

Her face flared with long-repressed emotion. 'Don't give me all that redemption shit! Don't even begin to tell me everything will turn out bright and sunny. That's not how it works!'

'It does in my world.'

That brought her up sharp. She eyed him askance, then looked away, her expression so desolate with the flood of uncontrollable feelings and ideas that Shavi wanted to pull her tightly to him to comfort her.

But before he could act he caught a movement away in the trees. It was barely anything, a shift of a shadow among shadows in the gloom, and it could easily have been some small animal investigating the fire, but his instincts told him otherwise.

Laura felt his body stiffen. 'What is it?' she asked, sensing his urgency.

'I do not know.' He rose and advanced to the fire.

'Didn't you ever see *Halloween*?' she cautioned. 'Don't go any further, dickhead.'

'I am simply trying to see—' The words strangled in his throat in such an awful manner Laura didn't have to see his face to know he had glimpsed something terrible.

'What is it, for God's sake?' she hissed.

The fear surged into a hard lump in her chest, but it melted into burning ice when she saw him moving quickly away from the firelight into the dark.

'Don't go!' Her yell trailed away in dismay and disbelief. How could he be so stupid?

And then she was alone in that dismal place with the dark pressing tight around her, feeling small and weak in the face of all the awful things loose in the world. She couldn't bring herself to move even a finger. Instead, she strained to hear the sound of his returning footsteps, any sound from him that proved he was still alive. But there was nothing. Just the constant rustle of the leaves, the creak of branches under the wings of the wind, the rumble of the river; the lyrical sounds oppressed her. It was too noisy, too alive with nothing.

'Shavi,' she whispered, more to comfort herself with the sound of a voice than in the hope he might hear. *Don't do this to me*, she wanted to say. *I'm not strong enough to deal with this on my own.*

She sat there for an age while she grew old and wizened. Her rigid muscles ached, her stomach was clenched so tightly she thought she was going to vomit or pass out. And still there was no sign of him. He could have been swallowed up, torn apart; there could be things feeding silently on his remains right then, waiting to finish their meal before moving on to her.

And then he suddenly lurched into the circle of light and all of it erupted out of her in a piercing scream.

'Don't worry,' he croaked.

'You stupid bastard!' she shouted in a mixture of embarrassment and angry relief.

But then, as he clambered down next to her, she saw his normally dark, handsome features were grey and there was a strained expression which made him look fifteen years older. 'What was out there?' she said, suddenly afraid once more.

He couldn't seem to find any words. Then: 'Nothing.'

It was such a pathetically inadequate response she hit him hard on the arm. 'Don't treat me like an idiot. Don't try to protect me like some stupid little girlie. That's the worst thing you can do to me.' She swallowed, glanced fearfully beyond the firelight.

'It is nothing. Nothing for you to worry about.'

'Then, what?' She searched his face and saw things in his eyes which unnerved her on some deep plane. With his philosophical outlook, Shavi had always seemed immune to the terrors that plagued the rest of them; he was an anchor for her, a sign that it was possible to cope better. And suddenly all that fell away. 'What is it, Shavi?' She reached tentative fingers to his cheek. 'What did you see out there?'

'What did I see?' His voice sounded hollow. 'I saw Lee. My boyfriend. Two years dead now, two years dead. His head smashed out in the street. And he spoke to me. The things he said . . .' His voice was dragged away by the wind.

Laura recalled how Shavi had told them of the murder arranged by the Tuatha Dé Danann, one of the deaths that had prepared them all for their destiny. 'He was really there?' Her concern for Shavi was suddenly overtaken by the sudden fear that if Lee was there, her dead mother could be too. And that really would be more than she could bear.

Shavi seemed to sense what she was thinking, for his face softened a little. 'It is my burden. The price I had to pay for getting the information from the spirits in Mary King's Close.'

'But that's terrible! That's not a price, it's a sentence! It's not fair!'

'It is my burden. I will cope with it.' It was obvious he couldn't bring himself to speak any more, and however much she wanted to ask him what the spectre had said, she knew it was something he would never tell. But she could see from the expression on his face that it must have been something awful indeed. How much longer would he have to put up with it, she thought? The rest of his life? The thought filled her with such pity that all she could do was hug him tightly and bury his face in her shoulder.

When she awoke in the dead of the night, she was surprised she had actually managed to fall asleep. Shavi's haunted face had hung in her mind, feeding every deep, mortal fear she had about death and what lay beyond it. She remembered stroking his head as it lay on her breast, desperately trying to comfort him, although he gave no voice to his fears; but then she looked in his eyes and she knew there was nothing she could do that would ever make him feel better.

The thoughts faded with the realisation she was awake, and the knowledge that she had woken for a reason. At first, in her sleep-befuddled state, she had no idea why. Shavi slept soundly beside her. Outside the tent the wind moaned gently among the trees and the leaves and branches sighed, but no more nor less than at any other time during the night.

As she went to lower her head back to the pile of clothes she was using as a pillow she realised . . . it was there on the edge of her senses, barely audible, almost a hallucination. Her fingers felt the gentle yet insistent throb of it from deep within the ground. When she lowered her ear towards the groundsheet, she could hear it. *Lub-dub, lub-dub.* So distant, which made her realise how powerful it must be; never ceasing. She tried to tell herself she was mis-sensing it on the edge of a dream, that it was a water pump, that it was the reverberation of the river through the soil and the rock.

Lub-dub, lub-dub

It seemed to be calling out to her and issuing a warning at the same time. And then she knew what it really sounded like. The beating of a heart that would never know death, buried far beneath the ancient landscape. The image spawned a wave of terror. Laura screwed up her eyes and covered her ears, but it was there inside her head and there was nothing she could do to get it out, and she knew she would not sleep again that night. *Lub-dub, lub-dub.* The relentless rhythm of death and madness.

While Laura and Shavi were just winding their way out of the city centre, Church and Tom skirted the edge of the Old Town before cutting across its easternmost edge to break into the green expanse of Holyrood Park. The sedate mass of the Royal household loomed up silently through the haar which obscured all of Arthur's Seat apart from the lowest twenty feet. The area, normally a haven for joggers and dog-walkers, was deserted. In its desolation it seemed unbearably lonely and ancient.

No words passed between them until they were standing before the well-head, feeling unseasonably cold.

'Here we are then,' Church said banally.

Now they were there, they could see how out of place the well-head looked, surrounded by the wild grass and bare rock of the wilderness that soared up above the city: a defiant statement that man would not be bowed by nature. Iron bars ran on both sides of the forecourt before the well and up the hillside over the top of it. The well-head itself was dark stone stained with the residue of years; the water trickled out into a small pool just out of reach beyond more vandal-proof bars. It smelled of cold iron and dark tombs. Above it was a plaque which said:

St Margaret's Well
This unique Well House dates from the late 15th century. It
originally stood at Restalrig, close to the church, and its design is a
miniature of St Triduana's Aisle there. In 1860 it was removed from
its first site, which was then encroached upon by a railway depot, and
was reconstructed in its present position near a natural spring.

Church read it carefully then said, 'When they moved it, did whoever was in charge know this was the entrance to the path beneath Arthur's Seat? Or was it coincidence?'

'There is no coincidence.' Tom surveyed the well-head carefully, as if he were looking for a lock.

'So someone did know?'

'Perhaps. A great deal of secret knowledge has been maintained down the years. There are numerous societies which keep their version of the truth close to them, many secret believers passing words down from mother to daughter, father to son. Or perhaps the people who moved the well-head were simply guided by an unseen hand.'

A few weeks earlier Church would have met such a comment with derision, but now he was more than aware of what lay behind the visible. 'So how do we get in? Can you see the switch like you did at Tintagel?'

'I can, but I'd be remiss in my job if I didn't start teaching you.'

'I can't see anything!'

'That's because you are not looking correctly,' Tom replied with exasperation.

Church squinted in the feeble hope it would reveal some hitherto obscured detail, but it only brought an irritated snort from Tom. 'Haven't you learned anything yet?'

'I've learned you're an annoying bastard,' Church snapped.

'The mistake you people constantly make is that you see the five senses as separate, and as the only tools at your disposal. Haven't I told you to trust your intuition? Sense where the switch is. Feel the power of the earth energy in this spot, its arteries and veins, where it pulses the strongest. Then let it inform each sense in turn, until they are all working together. Smell the switch, taste it in the air. Hear it calling to you.'

Church attempted to do what Tom said. After a few seconds he said, 'It's not working.'

Tom cuffed his shoulder so that Church spun round in irritation. 'You're not trying hard enough. Concentrate. Open your mind and your heart to it. If you don't *believe*, you won't do it.'

'Why should I be able to do it?'

'Why? Because you're special, though God knows why. You are a manifestation of the Pendragon Spirit. Its force moves through you. You're closer to the land and the energy than I am. In an ideal world, you should be teaching me!'

Church sighed and turned back to the well-head. 'It's not easy to believe in something like that.'

'Stop whining. Get on with it.'

Church concentrated. After a while he gave up trying to look at the detail in the stone and closed his eyes; that seemed to help. In the dark behind his eyelids he imagined he could see blue tracings like the trails left by firework sparklers. But then he realised it wasn't his imagination, and if he concentrated, he could make the paths stronger, see the faint web they made. A little more concentration and he could hear them fizzing, as if he were standing near a high-tension power line; they smelled and tasted like burnt iron.

And then he opened his eyes and he could still see the blue trails glowing beneath the surface of the stone and the surrounding grass. 'It's there.' His awed voice was hushed. He let his gaze slip slightly to the side and he could see the blue arteries continuing out and up into Arthur's Seat, across the ground behind him towards the city. 'It's in everything. Everywhere.'

He noticed that some of the arteries and veins glowed with a paler blue and others appeared oddly truncated, as if they had withered and died. With this realisation and the conscious stream of thoughts it generated, he began to lose control of the vision. It flickered as his senses fragmented, became individual units again. Desperately he launched himself forward and hammered the palm of his hand on to the point on the well-head where the blue fire had appeared to converge. There was a surge of needle-pain in his fingertips and blue sparks flew. With a deep rumble, the well-head split open, flooding water out, but giving access to a dark tunnel which lay beyond the spout of the spring.

Tom grabbed his elbow and propelled him in. The moment they set foot in the tunnel the well-head ground shut behind them. Church had expected stifling darkness, but there was a faint phosphorescent glow to the slick rock walls which gave the passage the gloomy appearance of the last minutes of twilight. But it was enough to see by, and Tom was already marching ahead.

Church caught up with him with a double-step, breathing in the dank air and shivering slightly. His footsteps echoed off the walls. 'That was amazing.' Although there was no reason for it, he spoke in a whisper. 'Is that how you see things?'

'Sometimes. When I allow myself.'

'It's—' He searched for the right word, but couldn't find one to match the immensity of what he felt. He settled for, 'Tremendous. I can understand how people could get all religious about that. It showed the interconnectedness of everything. That blue, spiritual fire, in the land, in the rocks.' He gazed at the back of his hand. 'In us.'

'It's the neolithic mindset. Once everybody could see things that way.'

'Then what happened? Why did we lose it?'

Tom shrugged. 'The more we developed the rational side of the brain, the more we lost touch with the intuitive. We simply forgot the skill to combine the senses, to be holistic in feeling. It's one of the great arrogances of man that we consider we are constantly evolving, that to dwell wholly on reason and science and logic is somehow *better*. But what would you think of a man who chopped off his left arm to make his right arm stronger? That ability to combine the senses, to *feel*, that was the most amazing skill of all. Man hasn't been whole for a long time, yet everyone in this century thinks they're some kind of superman, the pinnacle of existence. If it wasn't so bitter, the irony would make me laugh.'

Church thought about this. The passage began to slope down, but just as he thought they were going to head into the bowels of the earth it rose up sharply, then descended again. Soon he'd lost all sense of direction.

'I've got a question,' he said eventually.

'Go ahead.'

'In all the stories there's a myth that the fairies are scared of iron. The Fomorii and Tuatha Dé Danann don't seem to have any problem with it.'

'Correct.'

'But I noticed the earth energy seems to smell and taste of iron—' Tom's sudden grin brought him up sharp.

'Very perceptive! You've found the source of the myth! It's the blue fire and everything it represents that fills them with fear. That's what can bind them. And in its most potent form, that's what can destroy them.'

Church surprised himself with the awe he felt. 'I didn't realise the power of it. Then if we can control it—'

'The Brothers and Sisters of Dragons truly can be the defenders of the land.'

'We have to awaken it,' Church said firmly, almost to himself.

'That's your destiny,' Tom added.

Ahead of them the tunnel dipped down into the darkness again. Church found himself subconsciously going for the locket given him by the young Marianne; it filled him with strength in a way he still couldn't quite understand.

'What lies ahead, then?' he said uneasily.

Tom shrugged. 'It won't be an easy journey. This close to such a powerful source of the earth energy, time and space will warp. It will be disorientating. We will have to keep our wits about us.'

'And when we get to where we're going, how are we supposed to get the blue fire moving again?'

'Do I look like the fount of all knowledge?' Tom said irritably. 'We'll find out when we get there. Hopefully.'

And with that he set off into the darkness.

The hotel seemed empty without the others around. Veitch ate dinner early, steak and potatoes with a good red wine, but the high life he could never have afforded before did little to raise his spirits. With everything in such a state of flux, so many pressures and so much at risk, there was too much even to think about. And it wasn't just that the world was changing, it was the deep things shifting within him. Here, finally, was a chance to change; he could leave behind the Ryan Veitch he had despised all his life and become the person he always dreamed he would be: good, decent, unselfish, caring. Until chaos had descended on the world, he had dismissed the idea with the certain knowledge that he was who he was – he would never change. But now he had a chance, he was determined not to let it slip through his fingers.

When the sun started to go down he took his brooding with him to the bar. The room was near-deserted. It would have been wiser to stick with wine, but he couldn't resist ordering a pint of lager, which he took to a table where he could see the door; an old habit.

He'd got halfway down his drink when he noticed the elderly gentleman who'd come up to him in the lobby the previous day. He was smiling at Veitch from a nearby table, as elegant as ever with his smart suit and his swept-back white hair. He sat with his hands crossed on top of his cane.

'You know, this old place used to be thronging at this time of year,' the man said. Veitch smiled politely, but he had never been one for small talk, particularly with a higher class. Toffs always made him feel insignificant, stupid and uncultured, whatever his better judgement. But this man seemed pleasant enough; his smile was warm and open, and there didn't seem any judgment in the way he looked at Veitch. 'Do you mind if I join you?' He smiled at Veitch's reticence. 'Oh, don't worry. I'm not some predatory shirtlifter. I merely wish to share your company and, well, and perhaps my thoughts.' His smile changed key, but Veitch couldn't read what it signified.

'Okay,' Veitch said, recognising his own loneliness. 'I'll have a drink with you.' He took his lager over to the man's table and sat opposite him. Up close, he could see the man's eyes sparkled with a youthfulness that belied his age. He smelled of expensive aftershave and pipe tobacco.

'Gordon Reynolds,' the old man said holding out a well-tended hand. Veitch shook it and introduced himself.

For the next hour they exchanged small talk: about how Veitch was finding Edinburgh, about the weather, the best tourist sites, the malts that really ought to be sampled and a host of other minor issues. Reynolds broke off to sip at his whisky and when he replaced his glass there was a gleam in his eye. 'You look like a bright young man,' he said. 'You are aware, of course, that something very strange is going on in the world.'

'I've seen some funny things.' Veitch sipped at his lager.

'They closed off the Old Town today.'

Veitch nodded.

'You're very reticent.' Reynolds smiled. 'I suspect you know much more than you're saying.'

'I know a bit. Don't like to talk about it.'

'It's bad, then. No, don't bother telling me otherwise. I've some friends in Wick who used to keep in touch before the telephones went down. They were keen hill-walkers, used to go off into the wilderness. Well, rather them than me. Give me a warm fire and an old malt by it any day. But one day, not so long ago, they went off into the wilds and saw some . . . quite terrible things. Quite terrible. Now they never leave the town. No one does. The wilderness is off-limits.' He scanned Veitch with a dissecting gaze, taking in every minute movement of the Londoner's face. 'But you know all this, I can see. Then you know it's not just happening up in Wick. There's word coming from all over. Here in Auld Reekie, with our sophisticated ways, we could laugh at the superstitions of our country cousins. And now they've closed off the Old Town.'

'It's going to get worse before it gets better.'

'I'm sure it is, I'm sure it is. And there's the Government with the hints and whispers and "it's a crisis, we can't give you too much information", trying to make us think it's the Russkies or the Iraqis or God knows who while they desperately flounder around for an answer that will constantly evade them. Never trust the Establishment, my boy. They're in-bred with arrogance. They think we're too stupid to be told anything as radical as the truth.'

'I'll drink to that.' Veitch drained his pint and glanced towards the bar, hoping for a lull in the conversation so he could get a refill.

'The ironic thing is that most of the people are starting to know better than they. The Establishment is too inflexible and this new age needs people who are prepared to take great leaps forward. They'll be left behind. Only the fleet of mind will survive. What do you think of that?'

'I think—' Veitch raised his glass '—I need another lager.'

Reynolds looked up and motioned to the barman. A minute later another round of drinks arrived at their table.

'How did you manage that?' Veitch asked. 'They don't do table service.'

'Oh, I've been a resident here for many years, my boy. They grant me my little indulgences out of respect for my great age and my deep wallet.'

Veitch laughed. 'You're all right, Gordon.'

'That's very decent of you to say, my boy. But tell me, you're troubled, aren't you? I could see it written all over your face whenever I saw you around the hotel. Share your burden. I may, *may*, I stress, be able to help.'

Veitch sighed, looked away. 'No, best not.' But when he caught Reynolds' eye, the elderly man seemed so supportive he said, 'Oh, bollocks, what's the harm.'

He wasn't sure it was completely wise of him, but over the next hour he proceeded to tell Reynolds everything that had happened since he had encountered Church in the old mine beneath Dartmoor. He was sure some of it made no sense – he could barely grasp the intricacies himself – but Reynolds kept smiling and nodding.

'So that's the way it is, Gordon,' he said after he had related the latest impending crisis. 'Sometimes I wonder, what's the fucking point.' He caught himself and smiled sheepishly. 'Sorry. Bad habit.'

Reynolds dismissed his apology with a flourish of his hand. 'So, you feel it's hopeless. Hopeless in that you feel there's only five, or six, or whatever, ineffectual people facing down the hordes of hell. And hopeless because the girl you love is locked away in some dismal place with no chance of a rescue.'

'I never said I loved her!' Veitch said indignantly.

Reynolds waved him away again. 'Of course you do! It's obvious!'

Veitch coloured and shook his head. 'And I'm not saying it's hopeless. I mean, I'm going in there to get her, you know. I'm giving it my best bleedin' shot.'

'But you don't hold out much hope of getting out again.'

'Ah, who knows?'

Reynolds sat back in his chair and thought for a moment, sipped at his whisky, then thought again. Veitch watched him with growing impatience. Eventually, tweaking his moustache, Reynolds said, 'Are you in the mood for a story, my boy?'

'A story?'

'Yes. A true-life story. Like they have in the women's magazines. It's about a young man of style and elegance, dashing and debonair, not really one for books, but a whizz with the girls—' He laughed richly. 'Now I can't fool you, can I? Yes, it's my story. Still interested?'

Veitch nodded. He had warmed to Reynolds; his old prejudices had been forgotten for the moment.

'Let me tell you then. I was twenty-four, from a very good family with a little money in my pocket and a lot of confidence. A dangerous combination. My mother and father had always considered me for a career in the law. Edinburgh is the lawyers' city, after all. But, you know, that thing with the books . . .' He shook his head. 'No, not for me. I wanted something a little more colourful. Why should I consign myself to a prison of dusty old books when I could run off to sea or enlist in some war in an exotic clime? And that's just what I did. I set off on foot for Leith with a head full of Robert Louis Stevenson and dreams of hiring aboard some tramp steamer to the Orient.'

'Nothing wrong with that,' Veitch mused. 'Better than getting stuck in a rut at home.'

'Exactly! But then the strangest thing happened to me. As I walked towards Leith with the sun climbing in the sky, I came across a vision of such beauty it made me stop in my tracks. Now this wasn't film star beauty, do you understand? But she was beautiful to me.' Veitch nodded. 'Even to this day I don't know why I did it. Perhaps it was because I was filled with the kind of joy you can only experience when you embark on something new, or perhaps it was the quality of light, or the fresh tang on the wind, or all those things aligned in an unrepeatable harmonious conjunction. But that moment was so special it felt like my skin was singing.'

He caressed the ornately styled head of his cane for a long moment, so deep in thought he appeared oblivious to the people around him. But when he spoke again, his voice was so infused with happiness Veitch felt warmed simply to hear it. 'Her name was Maureen. She had red hair that fell in gorgeous ringlets and skin so pale it made her eyes seem uncommonly dark. She was walking into town on the other side of the street. What did I do? Why, I threw all my plans in the air and ran across the road to talk to her.'

'You're an old romantic, Gordon.'

'Oh, indeed,' he chuckled. 'I thought perhaps I'd pick up my plans later in the day, or the next day, or the next week. But as we walked and talked, and as she laughed, and as we recognised, in our looks and our gentle touches, that we were carved from the same clay, I realised I would never set sail from Leith. It takes someone very, very special for you to give up all your dreams in a single moment. But it was there, love at first sight, like all the poets say. Do you believe in that?'

Veitch sat back in his chair and looked up into the dark sky through the window. 'I'm not sure, Gordon. I think I'd like to, but it's not the kind of thing you get to think about too much in Greenwich, know what I mean?'

'I think you're not being very honest with yourself,' Reynolds said with a knowing smile. 'Maureen and I quickly became inseparable. On the surface we had very little in common. She came from a good, upstanding family, but they had little money, little of any material possessions. She had been forced to leave school at thirteen to help earn the family's keep. But those things don't matter, do they?'

'S'pose not.'

He pressed his fist against his heart. 'These are where the real bonds are made.' Then he touched his temple. 'Not here. But there was one difference even we could not overcome.' He paused; the muscles around his mouth grew taut with an old anger. 'I was a Protestant and Maureen was a Catholic, you see. That means nothing to you, I can see, and that's good. You're a modern man – you're not burdened with centuries of stupidity. Everybody thinks of that kind of prejudice as the Irish problem, but it's always been here in Scotland, even to this day. You told me you'd heard the stories in the city about Mary King's Close, the street boarded up to let the Black Death sufferers die.'

Veitch flinched at the coincidence. He nodded.

'The people of Mary King's Close were Catholics. Demonised, made less than human. Mothers of the time would frighten their children by saying the terrible people of Mary King's Close would get them if they weren't good. Would the horrors inflicted on them have happened if they were Protestants in this most Protestant of cities? I think not.'

'But Protestants might have got it in a Catholic city.'

'Of course, and I've damned them both to hell many times.'

Veitch tried to read his face. There was a seam of ancient emotion fossilised just beneath the surface. But he kept smiling, his eyes kept sparkling. 'What happened to her?' Veitch asked.

'Ah, you see which way the story is going. We kept our romance a secret from my family and friends for as long as we could, but in a city as watchful and atrociously gossipy as Edinburgh it was bound to come out sooner or later. To say it was a scandal would be to overstate the case. In the wider sense, no one cared about a thing like that, and that is to the general population's merit. The people of Edinburgh *are* good people. But in my own particular circle . . .' He sighed.

'You got a hard time from the folks,' Veitch said with understanding.

'My father was apoplectic. My mother took to her bed for days. The rest of my family treated me as if I'd developed some severe, debilitating mental illness. My close friends, who came from the same social circle, were acidic in their comments, but they directed most of their vitriol towards Maureen, who must, quite obviously, have led me astray.'

'And there was trouble.' Veitch took a long swig of his lager, trying to delay what he knew was coming.

Reynolds's face crumpled, but only for an instant before he brought the smile back; in that tiny window Veitch saw something that made him flinch. 'There was blood. They found her with her head stoved in on the edge of Holyrood Park. She'd been raped, several times, they said, not just murdered, but humiliated. Taught a lesson, in the good old-fashioned way.' His words were bitter, but his tone was as gentle and measured as ever.

'God Almighty!' Veitch went to take another drink, then had to put his glass down. He was overwhelmed by a terrible sense of injustice against a man he was sure, in the short time he had known him, was better than most. He felt a surge of anger, a desire to rush out and gain retribution in the most violent way possible, forgetting the crime had happened decades earlier. 'Who did it? Who fucking did it?'

'Oh, no one was caught. Understandably. The rich and well-to-do are always protected by the law. There was an outcry in the city, but it blew over when the next scandal came along, as these things do. Who did it?' He raised his eyebrows thoughtfully. 'One of my friends, several of my friends, all of them, my family. I would suppose they are the prime suspects. They were all guilty, whatever the detail.'

'Didn't you try to find out who it was? Didn't you try to get them?' Veitch felt the heat rising up his neck to his face.

Reynolds shook his head dismissively. 'No, of course not. It didn't matter, you see. Nothing mattered. Maureen was gone. My life was over.'

The baldness of the statement made Veitch bring himself up sharp.

'I loved her, you see. I loved her in all the clichéd ways – more than life itself, more than myself. We'd devoted ourselves to each other in a way that, I think, people find hard to understand these days. The night before her death we'd spent six hours talking about our life, about what we meant to each other, about the here and now and the sweet hereafter. In all the world she was the only person that mattered. And a few hours later I was more alone than anyone could be.'

There was a long silence which Veitch couldn't bear to fill. After a while the emotions between them became unbearable too, so he said in a quiet voice, 'How did you carry on, mate? I don't know what I'd have done . . . Blimey . . .' His words failed him.

'Why, I carried on. As Maureen would have wanted me to do. But I carried on a different person, as you would have expected. I went into the law, which made my family very happy. And I never married, which was better than they feared, but not what they hoped. I never kissed another woman. I never smelled another woman's perfumed hair. I never touched a woman's skin.'

Veitch felt a lump rise in his throat. He thought he might have to go to the toilet before he made a fool of himself.

But then Reynolds said, 'Come up to my room for one last drink. I have a bottle of malt that is quite heavenly. I retire early these days. It gets lonely when the night falls.'

They moved slowly through the quiet, deserted hotel, their thoughts heavy around them. 'You're a better man than me,' Veitch said as they reached the lifts.

'No,' Reynolds said assuredly. 'I lived a life without hope and thus wasted it. In what you told me I can tell you have hope, or at least the potential for hope. And perhaps I can help you.' They entered the lift and he punched the floor number. 'I lived a life with nothing to believe in,' he continued. 'How could I believe in anything? Family? Friends? Religion? What kind of God would let a thing like that happen? What kind of God was worshipped by the people closest to me?'

The thick carpet muffled their footsteps. It was comfortingly bright in the corridor.

'There is a gun in the drawer of my bedside table.' It seemed like a non sequitur, but Veitch was suddenly alert, Reynolds was going somewhere. 'An old service revolver. A family heirloom.' He laughed. 'Fitting, really.'

Veitch looked at him, but he kept his pleasant gaze fixed firmly ahead. 'I'd made my plans, composed my mind and a few nights ago I was ready to kill myself.' His smile made it sound as if he was discussing attending a picnic. 'I'd had enough of the drudgery of days. The emptiness of thoughts. The coldness of life. It seemed time for a Full Stop. Wrap things up neatly. The end of my story.'

'So why didn't you do it?'

Reynolds looked at him in surprise. 'My, you are a blunt man. I like that. You wouldn't get that in my family. They'd just pass the brandy and someone would see fit to mention it a few days down the line. Why didn't I kill myself? Why *didn't* I?' he mused, as if he had no idea himself. 'Because of my very last conversation with Maureen, that's why.'

Reynolds unlocked the door and they stepped into his suite. It was spacious and well turned-out, but still a hotel room; there were no personal touches to show it had been his home for so long. It spoke of an empty life lived for the sake of it.

'Nice place,' Veitch said uncomfortably.

Reynolds poured two large glasses of twenty-year-old malt and handed one to Veitch. 'It's a place to rest my head.'

Veitch perched on the edge of a desk. 'So, are you going to tell me, or punish me for a bit longer?'

Reynolds laughed heartily. 'I wanted you to hear my story before I got to the crux of the matter. Stories are important. They provide a framework so we can't easily dismiss the vital messages buried at the heart of them.' He pulled open a bedside drawer and took out the service revolver, which he tossed to Veitch so he could examine the archaic weapon.

'Blimey, that's a museum piece. You're just as likely to have blown your bleedin' hand off as your head.'

Reynolds gave a gentle laugh. 'The last conversation with Maureen has never left me.' He lowered himself into a chair on the other side of the desk, put his head back and closed his eyes. 'All those years and I can still smell her hair, feel exactly how her hand used to lie in mine. And I can remember every word we said. Most of it, I'm sure, would seem nauseatingly cloying out of the context of our lives, but it held meaning for us. But there was one point . . .' He drifted for a moment, so that Veitch thought he had fallen asleep, but then his voice came back with renewed force. 'The only thing left to discuss was what would happen should one of us die. We knew our situation, that anything could happen. And we made a pact that whoever went first would send a sign back to the other that love survived, that there was hope beyond hope, a chance, at the end of the long haul, of being reunited. Love crosses boundaries, that's what we felt. Our feelings were so strong, you see. So strong. How stupid you must think we were.'

'No—' Veitch began to protest, but Reynolds held up a silencing hand.

'After her death I waited every day for that sign. Weeks passed, months. Of course, there was no sign. Two people in love create a fantasy world where anything can happen, one that has no connection with reality. In reality there is no hope. Love does not cross boundaries.'

Veitch stared into the golden depths of his drink, his mood dipping rapidly. Gradually he became aware that Reynolds was staring at him and when he looked up he saw the elderly man was beaming.

'And then the other afternoon, when I woke from my nap, I found this on my pillow in a slight indentation.' He dipped in his pocket and held up something almost invisible in the light.

'What is it?' Veitch said squinting.

Reynolds summoned him closer. Between the elderly man's fingers was a long, curly red hair. Reynolds brought it gently to his nose, closed his eyes, inhaled. 'And here I am, all those years ago.' When he opened his eyes they were rimmed with tears. 'Her scent was on the pillow, and again this morning.'

'You're sure—?' Veitch began, but he saw the answer in Reynolds's face.

Reynolds traced away one of the tears with a fingertip. 'I wasted my life believing in nothing when there was everything to believe in. I wasted my life by not holding hope close to my heart. Don't make the same mistake, my boy. Don't wait until you're too old and wrinkled to appreciate what life has to offer, and don't wait until you're nearly on your deathbed before you gain some kind of salvation. There really is a bigger picture. We might have no idea what it is. It might not fit any of our past preconceptions. But knowing it's there changes the way we look at the world, the way we deal with each other, the way we face up to hardship. It changes everything.' He smiled as another tear trickled gently down his cheek.

Veitch took a hasty swig of his whisky as another lump rose in his throat.

'In the last few weeks nothing has changed, really, truly, apart from a way of seeing the world. An old way, made new again. We forgot it for so long, settled for a new reality that seemed better, but was much, much worse,' Reynolds said quietly. 'There may be a lot of trouble that has been introduced into the world in recent times. But everything is defined by its opposite, and with the fear and terror have come hope and wonder. These times are not all bad, my boy. There are a lot of wonderful things out there. And perhaps, for all the suffering, this new world is better than what existed before: all its machines that made our lives so easy, yet no wonder, no magic. This is what we need as humans, my boy. Hope, faith, mystery, a sense of something greater. *This* is what we need. Not DNA analysis, faster cars, quicker computers, more consumer disposables, more scientific reductionism. *This* is what we need.'

'I've been thinking,' Veitch began; he struggled to find the right words. 'Maybe it's not all as bad as people have been making out. You know, for me, personally, I think it might be better.'

'Then go into your big quest with a strong heart,' Reynolds said, 'but don't try to make things back the way they were, for all our sakes.'

Veitch drained his malt slowly, thinking about Ruth, about the terrors they were facing. 'Something to believe in,' he said quietly, almost to himself. 'That's all we need.'

chapter seven

good son

In her deepest, darkest, most testing time, Ruth plumbed the depths of her character for reserves she never knew existed. Every hour seemed torturous, trapped in a minute world that encompassed only the claustrophobic confines of her cell, the ever-present darkness, the chill that left her bones aching to the marrow, the foul odours that occasionally drifted through from beyond the door. Part of her resilience, she knew, came from her ability to view her crucible of pain as a chrysalis. She would store up as much learning from her invisible companion as she could and when she emerged she would be wiser, more confident, stronger; no longer the weak-willed Ruth Gallagher who was living her life for the sake of other people. When she emerged.

She had grown numb to the regular periods of suffering inflicted on her by the Fomorii. Her body bore numerous wounds which would scar over into a mural of pain that would never leave her. The stump of her missing finger ached constantly and sometimes she almost imagined it was still there. But in a way the routine was almost comforting: the dull sounds of bodies moving towards her door, the insane shrieks and grunts growing louder, the feeling of nausea as the door was thrown open to reveal the almost unbearable visage of a Fomor. And then the long drag to the chamber where the instruments were kept, where the furnace burned in one corner, the atmosphere sticky and foul.

This time it was different. When the door burst open, the first face she saw was the corrupt beauty of the hybrid Fomorii priest Calatin, his expression contemptuous and cruel. He wore a filthy white shift top and leather breeches; his long hair was greasy and infested, a parody of a sophisticated aristocrat.

'*Serith Urkolim*,' he said in his guttural dialect as he nodded to Ruth. 'I thought I had seen the last of you. You proved a minor irritation until your grand failure exposed how truly pathetic you were. An insult to the very essence of the Pendragon Spirit. Oh, how your world must have mourned and wailed and cursed your name into the cold void. In that most important hour, you proved yourself as insignificant as the rest of your kind – we needed waste no more time on you.

'But then there you were, delivered to our door, at a turning point in our plans.' He chewed on a fingernail and giggled. 'And a notion came to me of great irony. Oh, to strike a blow against the feeble order of nature! To throw up an abomination! To show our contempt for all existence!'

'Just get it over with,' Ruth spat.

This time they dragged her to a different room. No furnace, no torture instruments; it was almost stately by Fomorii standards. Rough wood and stone, a tapestry hanging on the wall depicting scenes Ruth couldn't bring herself to examine, and, in the centre, a strange curved bench which appeared to be made of polished obsidian. Flickering torches cast a sickly, ruddy glare over the room.

Ruth was so weak she could barely stand. The Fomorii strapped her to the bench with harsh leather straps that bit into her flesh. Her head was spinning so much from her fragility she couldn't begin to understand what was happening. Instead she focused on the small joy that came from the knowledge there would be no torture that day.

Through watery eyes she watched Calatin pacing the room, suddenly intense and serious. He examined the bench, the straps, and then gently stroked a long, thin finger down her cheek and smiled cruelly. 'You have proved you are ready.'

He stepped to one side and motioned to the rear of the chamber. Two Fomorii emerged from the gloom carrying an ornate wooden chest which they placed somewhere below her feet. Through the thick stone walls Ruth heard a deep, slow rhythm, as if an enormous ceremonial drum was being hit. Every few beats it was followed by the grim tolling of the distant bell she had heard before; there was something about the relentless sound that made her very frightened.

'What are you going to do?' she croaked.

Calatin merely smiled. He motioned to the other Fomorii, who bent down to open the chest. A second later they rose with a purple velvet cushion on which lay an enormous black pearl, the size of a child's bowling ball. When Ruth saw it, she was overcome by an irrational wave of terror. Unable to control her feelings, she tried to drive herself backwards and off the bench, but the straps held fast.

Two more Fomorii moved in on either side of her and held her head fast. 'No,' she gasped.

One of the Fomorii forced some kind of metal implement between her lips and then ground it between her teeth. With a snap he forced her mouth open so sharply pain stabbed through the tendons at the back of her jaw.

Almost tenderly, one of the other Fomorii lifted the pearl and brought it towards her.

Ruth had a sudden flash of what Calatin intended. Her eyes widened as panic flooded through her system, but she couldn't move, couldn't even scream; the only sound that emerged from her throat was a desperate, keening whine.

'If it will not go in, break her jaw,' Calatin said curtly.

Ruth watched in terror as the pearl came towards her. It was so big it would choke her instantly. She thrashed from side to side, but the Fomorii held her fast.

And then the pearl was so close it was all she could see; the darkness engulfed her every sense. Her lips touched it and it felt as cold as ice, but it tasted of nothing. It pressed hard into her mouth, grinding against her teeth. Her muffled gasps grew more laboured. Her panic obscured all rational thought. There was simply the constantly increasing pressure, the pain as they forced her mouth wider and wider still, the thought that it would never fit, the horror if it did.

And then somehow her mouth was around it and just as she waited for them to retreat, they increased the pressure and began to ram it further, trying to force it down her throat.

She choked, felt her lungs protest at the lack of oxygen. And still they pressed and rammed and forced.

And then a strange thing happened. Through her overwhelming anxiety, she felt an odd sensation deep in her throat; it seemed like cotton wool at first, and then as if her throat was coming apart in gossamer strands.

And then the black pearl began to go down.

The last thing Ruth felt was an enormous pressure and a terrible coldness filling her neck. And the last thing she saw was Calatin's face swamping her vision, grinning triumphantly.

Shavi and Laura woke at first light, entwined together as if they were desperate lovers afraid to face the world. No words were exchanged as they crawled out into a land of drifting white mists and thick greenery. The morning was chill, despite the season, and an eerie stillness hung over all, punctuated only by the occasional mournful cry of a bird and the regular drip of moisture from the leaves. The nagging atmosphere of lament and loneliness had not dissipated in the slightest.

They ate a breakfast of beans and bread in silence against the dull rumble of the river which was so unceasing they no longer heard it. Laura kept a surreptitious eye on Shavi, who still appeared pale and drawn, but whenever he saw her looking he flashed his open, honest smile; even so, she could tell the weight of the night and what was to follow lay heavy on him.

After breakfast they washed the pots in the river and packed up the tent with a meticulousness that suggested they were both playing for time. Eventually they had no choice but to pick their trail back along the glen until they reached the steep path up to the bridge.

Ten minutes later they stood outside the chapel compound trying to get a glimpse of the building, but it was obscured by trees and high walls as the current custodians intended. The mist collected even more tightly around them, so it was impossible to see beyond the perimeter of the small, stoney car park outside the visitors' centre. It had the odd effect of distorting sounds so that at times they felt someone was approaching, only for the noise – whatever it was – to materialise yards away. They waited and listened, but after a while they had to accept there was no one else in the vicinity.

'I guess we climb over the wall,' Laura said tentatively.

Shavi nodded, rubbing his chin introspectively.

'But what then? Where do we even begin to start looking for . . .' She glanced over her shoulder uncomfortably, as if she had sensed someone standing there '. . . that thing we're looking for?'

'The chapel is consistently described as an arcanum, a book in stone. The carvings that cover the building are a code designed to be pondered upon. They may offer religious guidance, or fables—'

'Or they may tell us where the prison cell is.' Laura hugged her arms around her. 'Okay. Now don't get me wrong – you're a mustard-sharp guy, Shav-ster. But if people have been trying to decipher this place for centuries, what makes you think you can waltz in and do it in a few minutes?'

Shavi wagged a finger at her, smiling. 'I never said I could decipher it in minutes. But we have two things denied the searchers who came before us.'

'Yeah? And what's that?'

'Firstly, we know what we are looking for.' He took the wagging finger and tapped the side of his nose. 'And secondly, intuition.'

'A shaman's intuition, you mean. You going to be doing some more of your funny stuff?'

His smile grew enigmatic as he looked towards where the chapel was hidden. 'I intend to allow the building to speak to me.'

'Well, give it my regards.' She turned and walked towards the compound wall. Shavi heard her mutter, but obviously loud enough for his benefit, 'You nutter.'

She gave him a leg up on to the wall and he pulled her up behind him. A second later they had dropped into the chapel grounds. The building lay just a few feet away across the wet grass, a grim, Gothic pile that looked like it had been designed for some thirties Expressionist movie; it was breathtaking, despite the ugly, silver scaffolding that clung to it. An oppressive, brooding aura rolled off the building, dampening their spirits, almost physically forcing them to bow their heads. It was both threatening and frightening, Laura decided.

'You know that supercharged feeling we got at all the other sacred sites, whatever the religion? I don't get it here.' She could see Shavi felt the same.

Slowly they advanced on the chapel, as if it were sleeping, as if it could turn on them and bite. Despite his growing anxiety, Shavi marvelled at its intricate design. Rows of spired columns ranged around three sides like sentinels, or missiles waiting to be launched: the last defence against an uncaring higher power? Towards the west end, a towering wall separated the baptistry from the rest of the chapel. It seemed oddly out of place, like a shield to repel invaders from the west; Shavi could tell from its design that from above, each end of the wall was shaped like a cross.

'A bit over the top, isn't it?' Laura ventured. 'I know these old piles were thrown up to show the glory of God and all that bollocks, but this is even more ornate than York Minister. And it's just a tiny chapel in the middle of nowhere.'

'It is special,' Shavi replied distractedly. 'But the architecture itself is a message, or many different messages. Everything has been included for a reason, every stone, every tiny carving.'

'Well? Is it talking to you yet? Because I'd really like to get out of here as soon as possible.'

'What are you doing?' The stern voice made them both start. They whirled to see a man standing near the door into the visitors' centre. He was in his sixties with a pale, wrinkled face and thinning silver hair, and he was wearing a dog collar beneath an unsightly purple anorak.

'Shit. Rumbled.' Laura hissed to Shavi, 'You better do the talking. He'll probably think I'm Satan incarnate.'

Shavi walked forward, smiling, proffering an open hand. The cleric eyed it suspiciously. 'We apologise for the illicit entrance, but time is of the essence,' Shavi said.

'The chapel doesn't open until ten a.m.,' the cleric said in his mild Borders accent. 'I'll have to ask you to leave until then. And to be honest, you're lucky I don't summon the police.'

'We are not tourists,' Shavi continued. 'We are on a mission of vital importance—'

'We get a lot of strange types round here,' the cleric interrupted, 'and they all say they're on some kind of mission or other. The legends that surround the place seem to attract all sorts of unsavoury types and, frankly, many of them are distinctly unbalanced.' Despite his words he seemed to be eyeing Shavi a little more thoughtfully; he made no further attempt to move them on, as if he was waiting to hear what Shavi had to say.

'We would like to meet with a Watchman.' Laura could tell Shavi was shooting in the dark, but his words seemed to have an effect.

'What do you know of the Watchmen?'

'I know they are the secret guardians of places like this. We met one of their number in Glastonbury. He helped us in our mission.' Shavi paused. 'Are you a Watchman?'

'I may be. What would you be wanting?'

'You know of the change that has come over the world?' The cleric nodded. 'Your traditions talk of five people who will fight to save mankind. At least that is what the Watchman in Glastonbury told us. We are two of the five.'

The cleric's gaze flickered briefly towards Laura. 'You don't look like much.'

Shavi held up his hand to silence Laura before she let forth a stream of bile. 'Nevertheless, we are a Brother and Sister of Dragons, and we are here at a time of great peril.'

'A Brother and Sister of Dragons, eh?' The cleric smiled disbelievingly, although they could see the name resonated deeply with him. Shavi spent a further ten minutes convincing him of their credentials until they saw his expression become confused, then troubled. 'Perhaps you are who you say. Then what has brought you here to Rosslyn?'

'You know why this place is?' Shavi turned to face the building. 'You know what it hides?'

'I know some of it. Stories, traditions. It is hard to pick truth from myth sometimes. And every tale has a different meaning, depending which mouth tells it.' The cleric walked over and peered deeply into Shavi's eyes. 'You know,' he began with a new seriousness, 'I believe you actually might be who you say you are.' He suddenly appeared flustered. 'Then this is an important time. I've been remiss. To be honest, I never really expected this to happen in my lifetime.' He caught Shavi watching him intently. 'I never expected it to happen at all,' he backtracked. 'When you get as old as I am and you don't see any sign of all the things you've been taught, you start to lose your . . .' He made a gesture with his hand to fill in the missing word. 'But how would you know the traditions of the Watchmen, if there was no substance to all I've been taught?'

He was obviously finding the psychological and philosophical repercussions of the sudden revelation troubling. Shavi recognised his growing anxiety and held out his hand once more to deflect the cleric's thoughts. 'My name is Shavi. This is my companion Laura. We would appreciate any help you can give us.'

This time the cleric took the hand. 'Seaton Marshall. Of course I will give you any help I can. But what can Rosslyn offer you?'

'There is trouble in Edinburgh. We are doing what we can, but we are not strong enough. We were told there was power here that could help us, if only we could locate it.'

'Power?' Marshall looked puzzled. 'Really? Well, I always wondered . . . You know, I've been coming here on my rounds at this time every day since I took on the responsibility of the Watchman thirty years ago, and never once have I encountered a soul. It was such a surprise to see you, such a surprise.' He was clearly overjoyed at this exciting break in routine. 'Then the stories *are* true? That's amazing, that truly is. Come.' He took Shavi's arm and led him towards the North Door. 'Let me show you one of the most puzzling and marvellous buildings on God's earth.'

The interior of the chapel was illuminated only by subdued lighting which had obviously been installed for the benefit of the tourists; it smelled of damp, stone and candles. It was also small, which added to the sense of claustrophobia; gloom collected in the roof and corners like bats. It took a second or two for Shavi's and Laura's eyes to adjust to the shadows, but then they were instantly hit by the true wonder of the place. Everywhere they looked there were intricate carvings in the stone: grinning devils, beatific angels, Green Men peering from the foliage, daisies, lilies, roses and stars, too much to take in. As Shavi slowly surveyed the amazing detail, though, he began to get a sense of the allegories and messages coded in the stone. Books get lost, parchments turn yellow and crumble, but here was something that would carry its meaning for centuries; and how important was that meaning if such a place had to be constructed at such great cost and effort to preserve it?

He felt a *frisson* that could have been excitement or unease when he realised how many of the carvings translated to their own experience: the Green Men that were everywhere, peering down with the terrifying beneficence of Cernunnos, the angels and devils that bore a disturbing resemblance to the Tuatha Dé Danann and the Fomorii. He stopped and caught his breath. There, at the foot of a pillar, was the image with the greatest resonance: a dragon, so out of place in any church, yet at the foundation of the great edifice, as the blue fire and the dragons that represented it were at the root of everything. 'Amazing,' he whispered. It was all there. Stories and legends, teaching and warnings. It was nominally a Christian place, but here it was speaking of things that were potent long before Christ walked the earth. What did it mean; for them; for all the great religions that sprang from that time?

'Ask me any question you want,' Marshall said. 'I know the history of this place back to front. I've mulled over every carving until my head hurt, trying to understand what Sir William St Clair meant when he had the place built. Sometimes I think I've got it. I see God in the great scheme of it all, but—'

'But the Devil is in the detail,' Laura said coldly. Shavi was surprised; she was normally at best silent and at worst openly virulent in the face of religious authority.

Marshall coughed uncomfortably. 'Not quite what I meant to say, but, yes, I do get a sense of great unpleasantness in certain areas.'

'And that's not what I meant,' Laura replied, but her attention had already been drawn by the disturbing iconography.

'Why did Sir William decide to build it?' Shavi asked. 'There must be some records.'

'Many of them went missing in 1700 after a cleric drew on them to write a history of the St Clair family,' Marshall said. 'Just one of the mysteries that surround the place.'

'Perhaps he uncovered something that others wanted to remain hidden.'

'Perhaps. But it may have been that the St Clairs remained Roman Catholics instead of giving in to the Reformation. The religious divide has always remained strong in Scotland and many Catholics have suffered persecution down the centuries. The desire to remain secure in such a volatile atmosphere has led both the truth and the history to be obscured.' His eyes were bright and intelligent; he seemed to have been transformed by boyish enthusiasm at the hope that some of the mysteries might finally be unveiled. 'But the St Clairs also had very strong links to the Freemasons, who guard their secrets jealously. And, some say, to the Knights Templar. And the Rosicrucians. It has been said that the true history of the world is the history of secret societies and if that is true, then all history converges here at Rosslyn.'

'Are you going to keep me in the loop or carry on speaking in this foreign language?' Laura asked tartly. 'In which case I'm going off to find an icon to kick.'

'In the Middle Ages there were many stories about the existence of *Enlightened Ones*,' Shavi explained patiently, 'the Rosicrucians, an intensely secret society whose leaders were only known to an innermost circle of adepts and the great and good leaders of society who protected them. They were supposedly highly advanced alchemists who were former members of the Knights Templar.' Laura gave a weary sigh and made a hand motion for him to continue.

But it was Marshall who carried on: 'The Knights Templar were the warrior priests of Christianity, established to protect pilgrims travelling to the Holy Land. Experts at fighting, but also intellectually superior. As well as armourers and knights, their number contained cartographers, navigators, doctors and learned clerics. But the Church became jealous of their growing power and turned on them in 1307. They were accused of taking part in blasphemous rituals—'

'That sounds interesting.' Laura's smile was a challenge Marshall chose to ignore.

'The penalty for helping them was excommunication. That is an example of how seriously the Church attempted to eradicate them. It is rumoured that an entire fleet of Templars fled to Scotland, where they went into hiding. There is a village near here called Temple which owes its name to their presence.'

'There was much more to it than that, though, was there not?' Shavi said.

Marshall nodded. 'It was rumoured the Templars had learned great secret knowledge in the Holy Land which terrified the Church, which threatened belief in the entire religion. And they were supposed to have brought that knowledge back here to Rosslyn and secreted it somewhere within the chapel.' He paused. 'And some even say what they brought back was the preserved head of Jesus Christ himself.'

'Oh, gross!' Laura made a face.

'And the Templars were linked to the Rosicrucians *and* the Masons. And the St Clair family had close links with the Masons,' Shavi noted.

'This is all rumour and hearsay,' Marshall stressed. 'Writers have built an edifice of *proof* by linking disparate and fragmentary evidence.'

'We have learned there is truth in all legends, and the constant truth here is that the chapel hides something of great importance. I feel we have come to the right place,' Shavi said.

'Is there any way I can help?' Marshall asked excitedly.

'Yeah, a coffee would be nice.' Laura nodded towards the door.

Marshall's brow furrowed for a moment, but if he felt her antagonism, he suppressed it. He nodded and slipped out.

'You should not treat people so harshly,' Shavi cautioned. 'There is no malice in him.'

'The way I see it, anybody who stands up for the Church is some kind of hypocritical bastard, so that makes them fair game.'

She wandered away from him, not wishing to discuss it further. When he caught up with her she was staring at the stained-glass windows above the altar which depicted the Resurrection. The one on the left showed three women arriving at the sepulchre; in the right window two angels sat, one holding a scroll which read: 'He is not here but is risen.' She shivered.

'It's true what he said about secret societies,' she noted thoughtfully. 'Not just the ones that you said, but the Watchmen, that freakish geek the Bone Inspector's people, all this shit going on behind the scenes. You can't get anything straight any more. They teach you one history at school like that's all there is and then you find out there's a whole 'nother load of crap going on.' She shook her head, the thoughts suddenly coming fast and furious. 'You know, you can't even trust your eyes any more. Everybody sees the so-called gods differently, all those magical items we found – it's like nothing is real. So what can you believe in?' She turned to him. 'How can you go on when you can't trust anything at face value? When you don't have any idea what's real or not? What's important or not?'

He shrugged. 'Faith.'

'In what?'

'That is the question, is it not?' He slipped an arm around her shoulders and she rested against him briefly before pulling away.

Marshall walked in with two steaming cups of coffee. 'There's a little café section in the visitors' centre,' he said. 'But there's no fresh milk at the moment, unfortunately.'

Laura thanked him, a little curtly, but with no real sharpness.

'Can you show us some of the things of interest?' Shavi asked the cleric.

'Certainly.' He took them over to the south door and pointed to the top of a pillar. 'See there. A lion and what appears to be a unicorn. The lion's often linked to the Resurrection. The unicorn is symbolic of Christ. Yet the two are fighting. What do you think that means?'

'I do not know,' Shavi replied thoughtfully.

'It seems like a warning,' Laura noted. 'Fighting, you know. Not a good thing. Christ fighting against the Resurrection.'

'That doesn't make any sense,' Marshall said.

He led them around to the north aisle and pointed out the burial stone of William St Clair, which contained both a Templar insignia and the carved outline of the Grail; Laura glanced at Shavi, but he gave no sign that it was important. Two more dragons; an angel with a scroll. 'There are carved images of open books everywhere,' Marshall explained. 'One line of thought is this is supposed to refer to the Book of Revelation and the Day of Judgment. *I could see the dead, great and small, standing before the throne: and books were opened.*'

'So, you have an ambiguous reference to the Resurrection and constant reference to the Apocalypse.'

'Christians of that time were obsessed with these issues,' Marshall said.

Laura snorted. 'They still are.'

'Up here.' Shavi pointed to a carving of angels rolling away the stone from Christ's tomb. And on the pillar to the right, three figures, one without a head, observing the crucifixion scene.

'No one knows who the three figures are,' Marshall said. 'Here's one I've always admired.' He indicated sixteen figures dancing up and down a ribbed arch; next to each one was a skeleton. 'It's the danse macabre, the dance of death, showing death's supremacy over mankind.'

'Hey, Happy Jack.' Laura wandered away, wishing she was with Church, the two of them on some beach miles away from everyone else. Suddenly she felt a cold flood wash over her, pinpricks dancing up and down her spine. It was as if her subconscious had seen something she wasn't aware of, something exciting, stimulating or important. She looked around, saw nothing. Then, slowly she raised her head and there it was; but there was no way she could even have glimpsed it.

Looking down at her was the biggest, finest example of the Green Man she had yet seen in the chapel. Branches protruded from his mouth like tusks, curling back in an abundance of leaves across his head. The face was darkly grinning, the eyes black slits beneath plunging eyebrows. She couldn't tell if it was supposed to be evil, mischievous or threatening.

Something about the eyes, she thought. Almost as if it were looking directly at her, communicating with her.

'Y'know, maybe this isn't such a good idea,' she called out. But Shavi and Marshall were immersed in examining two unusual pillars. The doubts suddenly began ringing through her. The carvings all seemed to suggest something bad, some warning not to disturb what had been sealed there. To release it could bring about the Apocalypse, that was the message, wasn't it? she thought. Why couldn't Shavi and Marshall see it? It seemed so obvious to her. But maybe she was just being stupid. They were both smarter than her, more perceptive. She glanced back up at the face of the Green Man and shivered once more.

'Explain to me about the two pillars,' Shavi was saying as she approached. The one on the left stood tall and straight, with intricate carvings rising in tiers from the base. But the one on the right was even more elaborate and sophisticated in its design. Instead of rising in straight lines, the detailed carvings twisted around the column in what must have been a display of the prowess of a master mason.

Yet Marshall indicated differently. 'The one on the left is called the Mason's Pillar, the one on the right the Apprentice Pillar. There's a story that goes along with them: in the absence of the Master Mason, his apprentice set about working on the pillar, creating this perfect marvel of workmanship. On the Master Mason's return, instead of being delighted at the success of his pupil, he was so overcome with envy he flew into a rage and killed the apprentice with one blow of his mallet. And of course he paid the penalty for his actions.'

'The sacrifice of something good. An act of betrayal sealed in blood,' Shavi said. He ran his fingers through his long hair as he tried to read more meaning in the story.

But Laura's attention was drawn by the dragons and vines wrapped around the base of the Apprentice Pillar, binding it with the symbols of the Green and the Earth Spirit. Now her doubts were starting to make her feel queasy.

'This is where we need to look.' Shavi indicated the Apprentice Pillar.

'Are you sure?' Marshall said. 'People have pondered over the meaning of this place for centuries. You've drawn your conclusions rather quickly, if you don't mind my saying.'

'Perhaps. I am simply making an intuitive leap. But here is my reasoning: this pillar cries out that it is unique in its very design – twisted, while all the other pillars remain straight and true. It even has its own legend, which sets it apart as something formed under special circumstances. And myths and legends, as a friend of mine repeats incessantly, are the secret history of the land.'

'Then what do you suggest? Digging beneath it?' Marshall looked uneasy at this act both of sacrilege and the destruction of an ancient monument.

Shavi nodded. Laura and Marshall both winced for different reasons.

'This floor is stone. The pillar . . . Lord! You might bring the whole roof down! As if we haven't had enough structural problems with this place over the last few years.'

'Nevertheless. Our need is great. We must find a way.'

'And I have no power here,' Marshall continued. 'I am, I suppose, at best tolerated. Someone will try to stop you. The police will be here in minutes.'

Laura glanced at her watch. 'The place doesn't open till ten. We've got hours yet.'

Shavi looked beyond the Apprentice Pillar to a flight of stairs leading down into the gloom. 'Where does that lead?'

'The sacristy. It's believed to be even older than the chapel,' Marshall said.

'So the chapel was built around it,' Shavi mused.

'It's not so important. I mean, it's completely bare of ornament, unlike this place. It's just a rough rectangle of stone some thirty-six feet long. Records say there are three Princes of Orkney and nine Barons of Rosslyn buried down there.'

Shavi went to the top of the stairs and peered down. 'Buried where, exactly?'

'Why, no one knows exactly.' Marshall gestured as if it was such an unimportant fact it was barely worth discussing.

Shavi rested his cheek against the cold stone of the door frame and weighed the place and dimensions of the room below before glancing back at the Apprentice Pillar. 'So,' he began with a faint smile, 'the burial chamber could be a walled-off extension from the back of the sacristy.'

'Possibly.'

'Which would put it somewhere beneath the Apprentice Pillar.'

Marshall thought about this for a moment, then nodded fulsomely. 'You could be right. And of course that would make it a little more accessible from the sacristy.'

'Well, I wish we could hang around to hear you explain the big pile of rubble and the hole in the wall,' Laura said snidely.

'There are tools available. Near the graveyard there's a store for those who've been working on the repair of the building,' Marshall said. He slipped out and returned soon after with two pick-axes and a shovel.

Cautiously Marshall led the way down the treacherously worn steps into the dank, bare sacristy. Shavi followed while Laura took up the rear with a feeling of growing apprehension. 'Are you sure about this?' she hissed to Shavi once Marshall was far enough ahead to be out of earshot.

'I am not sure about anything. All I know is we have no alternative. We do not have the power to oppose the Fomorii directly, certainly none that could deflect the Blue Hag.'

'Yeah. You're right, I suppose. I just have a feeling this is going to be a frying pan/fire scenario.'

Shavi searched her face. She was surprised to see he was taking her views seriously. 'Would you like to turn back?' he asked genuinely.

That surprised her even more. 'Let's see how we go. We can always pull out if things get too hairy.'

They identified the spot on the sacristy wall that corresponded with where Shavi guessed the burial chamber lay. The wall was old stone, sturdy enough, but the cement between the blocks was ancient and would crumble easily. They stood in silence for a long moment, attempting to come to terms with what they were about to do. Then Shavi raised the pick-axe above his head and swung it at the wall.

The moment it struck an echo ran through the building that sounded like an unearthly moan filled with anguish. It was surely a bizarre effect of the chapel's acoustics, they told themselves, but it had sounded so vocal it made them all grow cold. Shavi and Marshall glanced at each other, saying nothing. Laura backed a few paces away, wrapping her arms around her.

Shavi swung the pick again. This time the moan seemed to be outside, all around the chapel, caught in the wind. It grew palpably darker in the already gloomy sacristy.

'There's a storm coming,' Marshall noted, but it didn't ease them. Almost at his words, the wind picked up and began to buffet the outside of the building.

The stone wasn't as resilient as it had first appeared. Large chunks had fallen to the ground and the cement had all crumbled away; they would soon be able to remove an entire block and from then on the job would be relatively easy.

Shavi raised the pick for the third time.

A tremendous boom resounded through the main body of the chapel above them. They realised at the same time it was the sound of the chapel door being thrown open. Shavi threw down the pick and hurried up the steps with the others close behind.

Framed in the doorway was a man of indeterminate age, although Shavi guessed he must have been in his sixties. His greasy, grey-black hair was long and hung in an unkempt mess around his shoulders, framing a skull-like face that was sun-browned and weatherbeaten from an outdoor life. He was thin but wiry and exuded a deep strength that belied his age. Shavi would not have liked to have been on the receiving end of a blow from the six-foot, gnarled staff that the man clutched menacingly. At first sight Shavi guessed he was some kind of itinerant; his well-worn baggy trousers had long lost their original colour to become a dirty brown; he wore tired sandals and a dingy cheesecloth shirt open to the waist. But then Shavi noticed the warning issued by his dark, piercing eyes; the power within showed he was a man with a mission.

'I've come to stop you two doing something you probably won't live to regret,' he said with a rural accent Shavi couldn't place.

Laura tugged at Shavi's arm. 'Here's a word of advice: stay out of the way of that staff.'

'You know him?'

'We met in Avebury before you came on board,' she said.

And then Shavi recognised him. 'The Bone Inspector.' He smiled and held out his hand in greeting.

The Bone Inspector didn't take his eyes off Shavi's face.

'Who is he?' Marshall asked.

'The custodian of the land's old places, the stone circles, the longbarrows and burial mounds. The last in a long line of wise men who kept the knowledge of nature's ways.' Shavi tried to read him, sensed a threat, though he didn't know why.

'Do you know what you're doing here?' the Bone Inspector asked.

'Trying to save the world,' Laura said from the back. 'You should try it some time.'

'I couldn't believe it.' His voice was low, trembling with repressed emotion. 'When I felt it in the land, like a shiver running through the soil, I came as quick as I could to stop you, you damn fools. I'll ask you again: do you know what you're doing?'

'We have been guided here to free the hidden power—'

The Bone Inspector snorted derisively. 'Hidden power! Then you don't have any idea what's beneath your feet. Or why this place was built to keep it there.'

'Then tell us,' Shavi said firmly.

The Bone Inspector laughed contemptuously. 'It's beyond you, boy. It's bigger and darker and more dangerous than you could ever imagine, and if you had any idea what it was, you wouldn't even be within ten miles of this place. All of you, you're like mice, getting into things you shouldn't, causing trouble. I knew you weren't up to the job.'

'We're up to it,' Laura said adamantly, 'so you can take your staff and shove it—'

Shavi silenced her with a cut of his hand. 'I mean to find what is here and take it with me. Everything turns on this. If we return without it, all is lost.'

The Bone Inspector's face grew harder. 'And I mean to stop you. I could sit quietly and explain why what you're doing is a mistake of nightmarish proportions, or I could beat the shit out of you. Either way you'll get the message – and I know which one will be more effective. So let's see who's up to the job, eh? Boy.' There was arrogance in his voice; he was not used to being opposed. He raised his staff aggressively and in a liquid movement rolled on to the balls of his feet, primed and ready to attack. Shavi could see he knew how to use the staff; there was something in the way he held his body which suggested the rigid discipline of the martial arts, although Shavi guessed the fighting style was uniquely British, and very ancient. 'How do you plan to fight, then, boy?' the Bone Inspector asked.

Shavi stood calmly with his arms by his side. He registered no fear, no sense of urgency at all. He knew he would be no match physically for the Bone Inspector. Instead of tensing, he let his muscles relax, pushed his head back slightly and closed his eyes.

'You do that,' the Bone Inspector said. 'Pretend I'm not here.'

Shavi had never tried it before, but the fact that his abilities were improving each day was unmistakable. It was difficult to attempt something untried in the crucible of conflict, but he was growing increasingly confident. He knew in his heart what he *should* be able to do. It was only a matter of seeing if he could.

At first nothing seemed to be happening. Then, gradually, the Bone Inspector's sneering voice seemed to fade until it sounded as if it were coming from the depths of a long tunnel. At the same time Shavi's vision skewed like it was being twisted through a kaleidoscope. Dimensions stretched like toffee, turned on an angle. Once the distortion took over, different, deeper senses took over. Time appeared to be running slowly. He could hear sounds, whispers, that had not been there before, although he had no idea who was talking; and he suddenly seemed to be able to see *through* the dense stone of the wall and out across the land for what appeared to be miles. In that dream-like state he was beyond himself, beyond the chapel; although he had touched on it with his experiments he had never achieved such clarity before. And then he was ready: he put out the call with a voice that was not a voice.

'Shavi! This is no time to zone out on me!' Laura shook his arm but he didn't even seem to feel it.

'What's going on?' Marshall said. Then, to the Bone Inspector, 'Why are you threatening these people?'

The Bone Inspector grinned, his staff still levelled at Shavi's throat. 'Hold your voice, church-man. Your kind act like you know everything about everything when you know nothing about nothing. Don't go sticking your nose in where it doesn't belong.'

'This is sanctified ground!' Marshall said irately. 'I will not have fighting here!'

'No, but you'll let these two take a pick-axe and shovel to the place. Hypocrites, your kind, always have been.'

Laura was distracted from the confrontation by a movement outside the door: a shadow flitting against the background of clipped grass and mist. Another one, too quick to pin down the shape. There was something outside, several things, and they were drawing closer.

'Shavi?' she muttered.

'Playing dead won't help, lad,' the Bone Inspector mocked. 'You'll have to learn your lesson soon enough.'

'What lesson's that?' Laura's eyes darted back to the door. *Closer.* 'That sooner or later everyone turns into a bitter old git?'

The Bone Inspector's grin soured. He opened his mouth to speak. And in that instant something flashed through the door and hit him, and then he was howling in pain. Everything moved so fast it took a few seconds for Laura to register what was happening. A large russet fox was scrabbling wildly at the Bone Inspector's torso, its teeth sunk deeply into his forearm. Blood trickled down his brown skin. He flailed around with the staff, trying to thrash it off, but it was holding on too tight and the pain was throwing him off-balance. Before he could toss away the staff and grapple it with his free hand, a large mongrel and a Great Dane still trailing its owner's lead burst through the door and set about him with snapping jaws. Laura could tell they were not really trying to hurt him, but they kept him reeling and gave him enough nips to make his skin slick with blood and saliva. More shapes were moving towards the chapel; she glimpsed another fox, a badger, bizarrely, several rabbits, all heading towards the Bone Inspector. In the whirlwind of fur and fang, snapping and snarling, he was driven backwards by sheer weight of numbers until he was on the threshold. Laura picked up his stick and ran forward to jab him with it so he went spinning out on to the grass.

'Quick!' Shavi gasped. 'The doors!' He pitched forward, spraying spittle, his eyes rolling, and grabbed the back of a pew for support.

Laura and Marshall ran together and slammed the doors shut, then helped each other to drag pews in front of them. When they had finished it would have taken a bulldozer to plough the doors open.

And then, eerily, the crescendo of awful animal noises ended suddenly, to be replaced by the dim sound of paws padding quickly away. There was a choking moan, quickly stifled, as the Bone Inspector started to feel the full pain of his wounds.

Laura whirled. Shavi still clung to the pew, pale and weak. 'You did that!' she said incredulously.

He nodded, tried to force a smile. 'I never realised I had it in me.'

'Good Lord!' Marshall muttered. He slumped down on to a pew blankly.

Laura and Shavi hurried round and piled pews against the west and south doors too. 'He's going to find a way to get in as soon as he recovers,' she said.

Shavi nodded. 'Then we better get moving.'

Back in the sacristy, Laura felt cold, queasy, barely able to continue. Shavi, though, seemed oblivious to the growing anxiety which hung over the chapel like a suffocating fog. He swung the pick-axe at the wall with force; the reverberations exploded to the very foundations. Up in the choir Marshall still sat in a daze, staring at the floor, his arms hugged tightly round him. And at the door the Bone Inspector hammered and hollered, his voice growing increasingly fractured. It was a terrible sound, filled with a growing sense of fear. Laura covered her ears, but even that couldn't block it out.

'What's in there, Shavi?' she asked, but he didn't seem to hear. His face was fixed, almost transcendent.

And the pick-axe rose and fell, rose and fell. Shards of stone flew off like bomb fragments and clouds of dust filled the air. He coughed and choked and smeared his forehead with sweaty dirt. 'Nearly there,' he hacked.

Laura wanted to say *Don't go any further*, but with that thought there was a sudden crash and several stones collapsed into a dark void beyond. Laura jumped back in shock, not quite knowing what to expect. Shavi paused in mid-swing. Slowly the dust settled.

As their eyes adjusted to the gloom beyond, Laura saw Shavi had been correct in his assumptions. He had uncovered a large tomb filled with dusty stone sarcophagi; on several were carved the sign of the sword which Marshall had attributed to the Knights Templar. The atmosphere that swept out was so unpleasantly stale it forced Laura to clutch her hand to her mouth. But it was more than just the odour that choked her; there was a wave of oppression and threat which came on its heels. She couldn't bear to stay any longer. She hurried back up the steps; Shavi didn't even notice. His gaze was fixed on an intricately carved column of death's heads, Green Men and dragons which he guessed from its siting was a continuation of the Apprentice's Pillar above. Halfway up the column was an area where nothing was carved at all. Gently he touched it. It appeared to vibrate coldly beneath his fingertips.

'Here we are, then,' he whispered.

★

Marshall still sat with his head in his hands, didn't even look up when Laura walked by. She wanted to be out in the open air, where she could breathe, but the Bone Inspector didn't show any sign of giving up. If anything, his hammering against the wooden door had grown even more frenzied, his yells hoarse and broken.

'Give it a rest,' she said angrily. 'This is supposed to be a place of peace and serenity. We can't hear ourselves think in here.'

At her voice he subsided. It was so sudden Laura felt a brief moment of panic that he had something planned, but then he spoke in a voice that was full of such desperation she was shocked. 'You musn't go through with this. You have to stop now. I'm begging you.'

'If you hadn't acted so up your own arse and told us exactly what was wrong we might have listened.' She chewed on her lip. 'So what's the big deal?'

'Listen, then.' His voice echoed tremulously through the wood. 'It is not *what* lies here, but *who*: The Good Son.' He laughed bitterly. 'A name of respect given to placate, to keep something terrible at bay.'

'He was supposed to be a good guy,' Laura noted.

'You should know by now,' the Bone Inspector said with thin contempt, 'that when it comes to the old gods there is no *good* or *evil*. They are beyond that.'

'You know what I mean,' Laura replied sourly.

'If you could trust any of the Tuatha Dé Danann, then he was the one,' he conceded. 'He *was* loved. As I said, it would be wrong to attribute human emotions to these gods. They're alien in the true sense of the word, unknowable—'

'But you're going to,' Laura noted slyly.

'The Fomorii loathed Maponus—'

'Jealous of his good looks and way with women, I'd guess,' she said humourlessly.

'In their bitterness at their overwhelming defeat at the second battle of Magh Tuireadh, the Fomorii were determined to launch one last desperate strike at the Tuatha Dé Danann,' the Bone Inspector continued. 'And Maponus as the favourite son of the Tuatha Dé Danann was the perfect target. They attacked as he attempted to cross over from Otherworld to visit his worshippers here.'

'Attacked how?'

'All that's known is that Maponus was struck down as he crossed the void between there and here—'

'If he was killed—' Laura interrupted.

179

'Not killed. These gods never truly die anyway. What the Fomorii planned was much worse. Whatever they did to him in the void, when he arrived here, he had been driven completely, utterly insane. That's the ultimate punishment: eternal imprisonment in a state of suffering. The world never knew what had hit it. The first sign of what had happened was a small village in the Borders. Every inhabitant was slaughtered, torn apart in so vile a manner it was impossible to identify the dead, even to estimate how many had died. In his dementia Maponus roamed the wild places and in the long nights people spoke of hearing his anguished howls echoing among the hills. Every attribute he had was inverted. He was not the giver of light and life, but the bringer of darkness and death. No love, only mad animal frenzy, no culture, only slaughter. It is impossible to guess how many died during his reign of terror. Tales passed down through the generations told how the fields ran red with blood. And the Good Son, once a name to be revered, became a source of fear.'

'What happened to him?' Laura's voice sounded oddly hollow, as if the room had mysteriously developed other dimensions which allowed it to echo.

'He couldn't be allowed to continue in this way,' the Bone Inspector replied darkly. 'He may have been seen as saviour once, but now he was cast in the role of destroyer, and if humankind wanted to survive, it had to destroy him. Or the next best thing.'

'We're a fickle bunch, aren't we?' Marshall was suddenly next to her, his voice painfully sour. 'If salvation doesn't arrive just how we expect, we bite that outstretched hand.'

'My people gathered in their college, first at Anglesey, then at Glastonbury,' the Bone Inspector continued. 'It was their time, you see. After so long in the dark, the Sundering had allowed them to grow in strength and hope. Their sun-powered cosmology, their worship of that bright side of Maponus, allowed them to turn their backs on the night and the moon and hope for a greater role for mankind in the mysteries of existence. They weren't going to see all that swept away, especially by a god whose time had passed, even one so close to their hearts.

'In a ritual which took seven nights to prepare, they eventually drew up enough power to bind Maponus in one spot. Even so, it cost the lives of two hundred good men, so the legends tell, reduced in Maponus's frenzy to a shower of blood, bone and gristle. But the others held fast, and Maponus was caught.'

Laura glanced over her shoulder towards the steps to the Sacristy. The flinty clink of pick-axe on stone echoed up. 'Jesus.' Her voice sounded pathetically small.

'You have to stop him!' Marshall hissed. 'For the love of God! Before it's too late!'

'But we don't have a choice.' Laura repeated the mantra, her head spinning. 'If we don't do this here, everything goes fucking pear-shaped.' And then she was running towards the steps, yelling, 'Shavi!'

Shavi couldn't hear anything, not even the sound of his own frenzied attack on the pillar. His concentration was drawn into the stone and nothing beyond existed. He coughed through the clouds of dust he was raising, scrubbed at the sweat that was dripping from his brow, and swung, and swung. And then finally, with a crack that seemed to tear through the very foundations of the chapel, a sound almost like a human roar, the pillar burst apart. Shavi staggered backwards and fell. And as the dust gradually cleared he saw what lay inside.

'They cut off his head!' the Bone Inspector was bellowing. 'They cut it off while he was still alive and sealed it in a pillar. And it was still alive even then! Still screaming! And they buried his body nearby—'

Laura reached the top of the steps, still shouting Shavi's name, just as the first tremor rattled through the building. A shower of dust fell from the roof as a large crack opened up in the stone floor, pitching her to one side. She hit the flags hard, knocking the wind out of her.

Marshall was already moving past her, his arthritic joints cracking under the strain. Laura caught a glimpse of wild emotions in his face as he headed down the stairs. Another tremor hit and he fell from halfway down, banging his head against the stone. Blood spattered from a deep gash as he slammed into the sacristy floor.

The tremors came faster, building in intensity. As she hauled herself to her feet, Laura had a sudden image of the chapel crashing down on top of her, crushing every bone beneath the enormous weight of stone.

Shavi's head was spinning and for a brief moment it felt like he was surfacing from a dream until reality suddenly jolted him alert. The clouds of dust that swept through the chamber were almost choking, and the intense vibrations running up through the floor made him nauseous. But it was the sound that disturbed him the most; it moved effortlessly from a barely audible bass rumble to a high-pitched keening. There was something in the quality that filled him with an overwhelming despair, while making his gorge rise; he could hardly bear it.

And then the dust cleared and he saw the origin of that awful noise.

Where he had smashed away the stone of the pillar lay a dusty space, and within it was a severed head. It took him a second or two to make any sense of the features, but gradually they fell into relief: full lips, perfect cheekbones, large eyes, a straight nose. There was something about the face that was incredibly beautiful, yet at the same time sickeningly corrupt. The skin seemed to glow with an inner golden light, but near the jagged skin of the severed neck the hue was queasily green. And the eyes, though dark and attractive, moved from an angry red to purple. The rear and sides of the head were still trapped in the stone, so only the face peered out, as if the owner was comically peering through some curtains. Long hair turned white and matted with stone dust poked out on either side.

Shavi could barely tear his eyes away from those full lips, which moved sensually to make that foul sound. He could feel it rumbling in his stomach cavity, vibrating through his teeth, deep into his skull. He pressed his hands against his ears, but it made no difference.

Although the spectacle was hideously mesmerising, Shavi realised instinctively he ought to get out of there. Before he could move, the largest tremor of all opened a massive fissure in the floor. Chunks of stone dropped from the ceiling and Shavi threw up his arms to protect himself. When he next dared look, he realised a golden light was rising up slowly out of the fissure. The apprehension held him fast; he *had* to see what was coming.

Within seconds a hand protruded from the dark, and then slowly Maponus's headless body hauled itself out of the hole. For a brief moment it staggered around as if it were learning to walk and then it moved to clamp its hands on the pillar. The remaining stone that held the head crumbled away. Its eyes ranged wildly; there seemed to be no intelligence there at all.

The thin, delicate fingers clutched until they caught on to the head. A second later it was placed firmly on the shoulders, the eyes still rolling. A sickly light eked out from between the head and the body as the two knitted together. And then Maponus stood erect and whole for the first time in centuries, slim and beautiful and golden and filled with all the terror of the void.

Shavi thought his eyes were about to be burned from his head at the wonder of what he saw. 'Please,' he whispered. 'Hear me.'

Maponus fixed his monstrous gaze upon Shavi. The eyes flickered coldly; Shavi saw nothing human in them at all. Slowly the god began to advance.

'In Edinburgh, the Fomorii await,' Shavi continued. His voice sounded like sandpaper. 'We call on you to help us defeat the Cailleach Bheur. Defeat the Fomorii.'

Maponus listened, and then he smiled darkly.

Shavi sighed, relieved his message had been understood. But when he raised his eyes back to the glowing figure he saw Maponus was still advancing, his features frozen and murderous. The god stretched out his arms and golden sparks spattered between his hands. Shavi could taste the ozone on the back of his throat. One more step and he began to feel the temperature rise, the pressure build in his head. Deep inside, a part of him was trying to drive him out of there, but he was held in the stress of that dazzling regard. The hairs in his nostrils began to sizzle.

'No! If you have to take anyone, take me!' Somehow Marshall was there, trying to interpose himself between Shavi and the god. His face was scarlet with the blood from his wound, and with his staring, terrified eyes, in other circumstances, he would have cut a comical pantomime figure. But there, in the light coming off the creature, he looked like some tormented soul from a painting by Bosch. Despite his fear, he managed to raise his frail, trembling body until he could look Maponus in the eye. 'Take me.' His voice was quiet, gentle. He stretched out his arms in a posture of sacrifice, not supplication.

Maponus clamped his hands on either side of Marshall's head. In an instant Shavi could smell the sickening odour of cooking flesh. Marshall howled as the blood began to boil in his veins. Those sparks danced and sparkled all over the cleric's twitching body, raising plumes of grey smoke.

The horrific sight broke the spell. Shavi rolled over and scrambled out of the chamber, throwing himself up the steps from the sacristy two at a time. Laura was waiting for him at the top, her face streaked with tears.

'That smell,' she choked.

He grabbed her and drove her towards the door. As they madly threw the pews away from the exit, the chapel began to shake wildly. Enormous chunks of masonry fell from somewhere above, and rifts opened in the walls and floor.

Laura glanced over her shoulder just once at the light gradually rising from the sacristy. 'He's coming!' she moaned.

The last pew was thrown aside just in time and then they were hurtling out into the chill, misty morning air. The Bone Inspector was waiting for them, his face showing all the horror that they felt in their hearts. With a deafening rumble, the chapel fell in on itself, shaking the ground like an earthquake.

The three of them were already at the perimeter wall, pulling themselves over to safety. Shavi paused on the summit to look back at the devastation, hoping against hope that the monstrous thing they had unleashed would be trapped under the rubble.

He was overcome by an awful sickness when all he saw was a golden light fading into the mist, moving out across the countryside.

chapter eight

the deep shadows

The first sign that all was not as it should be hit Church twenty minutes after they had entered through the well-head. No longer stale, the air in the tunnel smelled of cinnamon and mint. And it almost seemed to be singing, harmonious melodies bouncing back and forth off the walls. 'Is this the start of it?' he asked.

' "This is the best part of the trip".' Tom's voice echoed curiously behind him.

'What?'

'Nothing. Just remembering the sixties.'

'This is no time to be getting nostalgic.' Church was tense with apprehension.

'If you'd enjoyed the sixties to the full you'd be a little mellower in dealing with everything life has to throw at you now.'

'Sorry. I was born too late for the summer of love.' There was a *shush-boom* effect deep in the stone walls, like a giant heart beating.

'You missed a great time. That smell, it reminds me of Californian nights, hanging out at Kesey's parties when he and the Merry Pranksters set up shop after they did the Magic Bus ride. Jerry Garcia doing the music. Two kinds of punch – normal and *electric*. That was before the Hell's Angels moved in and ruined it.'

'What are you talking about?' Church said distractedly. 'You *have* done too many drugs, haven't you.' He reached out to touch the tunnel wall; strange vibrations rippled up his fingers.

'You know, Kesey, Leary, all those psychonauts, they set things in motion that could have changed the world before the Establishment stamped it down. They believed the psychedelics could help them see God, did you know that? And by doing that they were just like all those people who threw up the great monolithic structures around the world where the earth energy is at its strongest. Before our feeble *modern* culture, psychedelics fired civilisation.'

'Are you saying all those hippies were right?' Church said distractedly.

'We all need to be neo-hippies if we're going to cope with this new world that's being presented to us, Jack.'

The note of tenderness in Tom's voice surprised Church so much he looked around and was instantly disoriented. He appeared to be viewing Tom through a wall of oily water, the image stretched, skewed, distorted.

'Tom?' He reached out a hand, but his friend seemed to recede with the action until he appeared to be floating backwards along a dark corridor, growing smaller yet glowing brighter.

'It will be all right, Jack.' Tom's voice grew hollow, deep and loud, then faint, as if it were cycling between two speakers. Church blinked and Tom was gone.

Unable to understand what was happening, he was overcome by a sudden wave of panic. They had been walking along quite normally, and now he was alone; it made no sense.

Desperately, he clamped his eyes shut, focusing on Tom's advice to be *mellow*, and then he remembered how Tom had warned him that space and time could warp that close to such a potent source of the earth energy. He composed himself with a deep breath, accepted that he was on his own, and forged on down the tunnel.

After following its undulating path for about fifteen minutes, lulled by the background harmonics of the air, he suddenly rounded a corner into a large cavern. He could tell it was enormous from the change in the quality of the sound of his breathing and footsteps, although the roof disappeared into the deep shadows above him. The danger of getting lost in such a place was a distinct possibility. He could follow the walls with their faint phosphorescent glow around the perimeter, but he instinctively felt the correct path was directly across the floor of the cavern, through the darkness that could hide treacherous fissures, sinkholes and pits. His fears were confirmed when he glanced down and noticed a carved rock set in the floor by his feet. It was well-made, polished and indented. It showed a dragon, its tail curling to form an arrowhead which pointed the way into the centre of the cavern. He hesitated for just a moment, then strode off into the shadows.

It seemed like he had been walking for hours, although he guessed it was only about fifteen minutes. In the enveloping dark the going was laboriously slow, feeling with each foot before taking another step. At times the visual deprivation was so hallucinatory he felt his head spinning and he had to fight to stop himself from pitching to the ground; in that warped atmosphere he was having trouble discerning what was happening in his head and what was external.

Without eyes, sound took on added meaning and he was alert to any aural change in his surroundings. When he first heard the distant, reverberating *ching-ching-ching* of metal on metal he froze instantly.

Listening intently, he held his breath as the noise grew louder until it was accompanied by the trudge of heavy footsteps. A faint light began to draw closer, which he at first thought was just his eyes playing tricks on him. Gradually, though, an enormous figure presented itself to him, but it seemed unreal, like an obvious movie effect, with the light buried deep within it and seeping out through its surface. As it came into focus he felt a sudden pang of fear. From the sickening waves that rolled off it, it was undoubtedly a Fomor, but it was encased in black, shiny armour; the chainmail that glinted darkly beneath the plates was making the metallic sound that had alerted him to its presence. The oddly shaped armour with its gnarls and ridges was like a carapace, making the figure resemble a giant insect; on the head was a helmet which concealed most of the hideous face, two curved horns reaching out from the temple with a row of six smaller ones beneath. It was gripping in both hands an unusual but cruel weapon with on one side a nicked and sickly smeared axe-head and on the other a line of sharp tines of irregular length. Church heard its breath rumbling like a traction engine, the vibrations churning in the pit of his stomach.

The figure was terrifying to see. Church had the sense it was more powerful than any of the Fomorii he had encountered before. And as it advanced, the threat around it grew until he felt queasy from the potency of the danger.

His shock at what he was witnessing finally broke and he took a couple of staggering backwards steps before turning and running. He hadn't gone far when he stumbled over an outcropping rock and crashed down, winding himself. But as he glanced back to see how close the Fomor warrior was behind him, he saw the figure begin to break up into tiny particles, as if it were made out of flies. There was no sound, and a second later it had completely disappeared.

Church rolled on to his back, breathing heavily, trying to make sense of what had happened. He had felt the Fomor was definitely there, yet it didn't seem to have been aware of him. Was it simply a hallucination or a by-product of the strange atmosphere that existed in that place?

As he climbed to his feet a more important concern pushed all those questions from his mind. In his attempt to get away he had done just as he had feared – lost his sense of direction. It was impossible to tell where he had been going. There was nothing for it. Despondently, he selected a path at random and set off.

The mesmerising darkness became claustrophobic. He was flying, he was falling. He was hearing voices singing from the void, fading, rising again in anger or despair. There was Marianne, his Marianne, saying, 'So the real Dale is still in the Black Lodge?' He scrubbed at his ears and it went away.

To his right he saw a dim golden glow pulsating with the beat of the blood in his brain. As he drew near, figures separated from the light, all shining, all beautiful. He recognised faces he had seen when the Tuatha Dé Danann had swept to his rescue at the Fairy Bridge on Skye. Lugh stood, tall and proud, reunited with his spear, which he held at his side. And behind him was the Dagda, a starburst from which features coalesced, alternately ferocious and paternal, always different; his own father appeared there briefly. And there were others who seemed both benign and cruel at the same time; some were so alien to his vision it made his stomach churn. They were talking, but their communication was so high-pitched and incomprehensible it might as well have been the language of angels.

He almost stumbled among them, but they were oblivious to his presence. He had the sudden urge to lash out, a childish desire born of his own powerlessness, but he knew it would be futile, and so restrained himself; if he admitted it to himself, there was some fear there too.

But were they hallucinations? Or was the potent energy drawing him towards real moments plucked from the flow of time? As if to answer his unspoken question, Lugh pointed to an image which coalesced among them. It was Veitch, obvious despite the mask that covered his face, clutching a shotgun, his nervousness masked by anger. Church knew instantly what he was seeing: the moment when his friend had his life torn from him. Veitch waved the gun back and forth. In the background the building society was still, tense.

One of the Tuatha Dé Danann Church didn't recognise leaned forward and said something in the angel-tongue. On cue, Veitch whirled and fired the gun. An elderly man was thrown back as if he'd been hit by a car, trailing droplets of blood through the air.

Ruth's uncle, Church thought. *The act that brought on her father's heart attack.* Two lives ruined by the arrogance of power.

He watched the faces of the Tuatha Dé Danann expecting, hoping almost, to see cruel glee or contempt there, but there was nothing. It was an act inflicted on beings so far beneath them that there was no call for any response; it was nothing more than a brushing away of a dust mote.

Sickened, he turned and hurried away.

He hadn't gone far when an idea struck him. If what he was viewing was random, such a turning point in all their lives would have been too much of a coincidence. In some way the events were arriving before him like lightning leaping to the rod on a church steeple, summoned by his subconscious, or some other vital part of his being.

Maybe we're operating on the quantum level, he thought, *where everything is linked.* But if that was true, what did the first terrifying image mean? *Maybe I can make this work for me.*

He concentrated until he dredged up images from his subconscious, some so painful they brought tears to his eyes. He remembered how Tom had used the blue fire to warp space before, drawing them along lines of power from the stormy sea off Tintagel to the top of Glastonbury Tor in the wink of an eye.

Do it for me now, he wished, feeling like a boy, not caring.

For long moments nothing happened. And then, suddenly, he was falling. When the descent stopped he was standing in his old flat. But it didn't have the familiar look of bachelorhood, the secret layers of dust, the scatter of magazines, piles of videos and CDs, and odours that wouldn't shift. It was before. When Marianne lived there.

His heart leapt, but that was just the start of a complex flood of emotions that overwhelmed him. He breathed in deeply. He could smell her! That brought a fugitive tear, which he hastily rubbed away.

Stay focused. This is where you find the truth, he thought. *If you can bear it. If you can feel your heart ripped out, see things that will scar your mind for the rest of your life.*

He wished he could let it go, move on, but Marianne's death had destroyed him and not even a saint could turn the other cheek to that. Here was something he *could* believe in: revenge. Cold and hard.

The flat appeared empty. One of her acid jazz CDs played innocuously in the background. And then he could hear her moving around, humming to the music, at peace with herself and the life they had.

Don't cry, he told himself futilely.

He remembered where he had been at that moment: in the pub two streets away, drunk on booze, drunk on life, singing old Pogues songs with Dale and thinking what it would be like to be married.

Don't cry, he told himself futilely.

He wiped his face, forced himself to stay calm in the centre of a room a lifetime away, when he had been whole; listened intently. Soon. Soon.

Marianne singing now, in perfect harmony with the track. Leaving the kitchen where she had been washing up. Crossing to the bathroom. He

189

strained to see, then averted his eyes at the last moment. Then regretted it a second later.

The bathroom cabinet opening. She was taking out something. Bath oil? No taps yet. There had been no water in the bath.

There it was: the bare, brief click of the door. Nausea clutched his stomach.

'Church? Is that you?' Her voice; he couldn't bear it.

Take me away. His eyes were flooded, blurring everything.

He took a step forward. A dark shape flitted across the hall towards the bathroom. The damp ebb of his emotion was replaced by a cold hatred that surprised him; but it was better, definitely. It allowed him to act.

He moved quickly. He was going to find out who the bastard was who had destroyed everything. It didn't matter that he was a puppet. He was a killer of dreams and he was going to pay the price.

Don't scream, he prayed.

Marianne screamed. And then he was running, and running, but the bathroom was a million miles away, and he knew if he reached it, what he wanted most in the world would destroy him. Every sight, every experience stays with you forever; that one would ruin him for all time.

I have to see, I have to see, he pleaded with himself. And still he ran, but he knew he couldn't bring himself to do it. And then the bathroom, the flat, everything that had ever mattered to him was receding, and he was falling, upwards this time, yelling and crying, like some drunken fool, brutalised by the pain of his emotions.

And then he was back in the dark once again.

He wandered for what seemed like hours. If that were the case, the cavern would have been enormous, but he had the unnerving feeling he was no longer walking through that place; his meanderings had taken him much, much further afield. He didn't dare think too hard about that; the chance that he might be lost and walking for all time hovered constantly at the back of his head.

Sometimes he thought he was about to break through into another solid place; shadowy figures moved in the distance, lighter than the surrounding dark, but he never seemed to draw near enough to reach them. Sounds continued to burst through the void, fading, then growing louder, as if they were being controlled by a mixing desk: psychedelic aural hallucinations. Briefly, he heard Ruth calling for his help, but it was lost the moment he thought he recognised her voice.

And still he walked, until he heard something enormous moving away in the dark, circling him. A chill insinuated itself into his veins. There was a sound like the rough breathing of a wild animal and when he turned suddenly, he glimpsed a giant wolf. He knew instinctively this was the thing that had taken Ruth and attacked him in the library. But he also knew, although he did not know how, that it was not really a wolf, nor any kind of supernatural creature; it was mortal, and more, it was someone he knew.

For the briefest instant a yellow eye glinted in the dark and he was filled with an immeasurable dread. He turned and ran in the opposite direction until he was sure he had left it far behind him.

'Jack!'

The voice came as a shock because he had seen no sign of any other figure after fleeing the wolf that was not a wolf. It was crystal clear, unlike the other hallucinations, and when he spun round there was Niamh, arms outstretched towards him, her normally placid face filled with concern; it made him fearful to see it.

'It is a maze,' she was saying. 'If you do not pick your way through, you will be lost.'

Unlike the other visions of the Tuatha Dé Danann, she was able to see him. In fact, he felt she had come looking for him, to lead him out of there, back to safety.

'Your own thoughts are trapping you,' she continued.

'How do I get out of here?' he called.

But before she could answer, her face grew scared and she was pulled apart, as if she were nothing more than smoke caught in the wind. Even she did not have power over that place.

After a long while he came to the conclusion that he was not making his way through a maze. It was a whirlpool. The blocked earth energy was causing eddies in the very fabric of reality, sucking him back and forth. How *was* he ever going to get out of it?

He finally realised the futility of walking and getting nowhere, so he simply sat on the cold, stone floor and tried to think his way out. No further scenarios presented themselves to him, nor did doors open, but during a meditation on the nature of the blue fire, a possible solution presented itself.

Gently he closed his eyes, which seemed a bit unecessary in the uncompromising dark, but it was the only way he could do it. Then, with as much willpower as he could muster, he tried to focus on the earth energy as he had done at the well-head. It was a long shot, but Tom had told him the energy was in everything. Perhaps there was some kind of pattern he could see that would show him the way out.

He thought it would be hard, but it took much longer in coming than it had before; the anxiety gnawing away at him seemed to be a barrier. Eventually he saw the first familiar blue streaks, just flashes against the blackness, like tracer bullets in a night-time air-raid. Slowly, though, his perception came into focus and he recognised that the earth energy was as prevalent there as it had been out on the land.

It seemed that his analogy of a whirlpool had been correct. The tracks of light were sucked into different eddies that formed complex patterns, reminding him of Mandelbrot set illustrations he had seen: chaos every-where, yet, paradoxically, an overriding pattern to it; a blueprint for existence. The marvel of it was mesmerising; he could certainly see how the ancients had been in awe of its power and majesty. The lifeblood of everything.

Even so, in places the traces of light fragmented or seemed to dry up completely. There was none of the pulsating vitality he had seen when Tom had first introduced him to the blue fire at Stonehenge. Was this what had been happening all over the land, all over the globe: the gradual break-down of the fundamental essence of the world, driven to extinction by people with an increasing morbidity of spirit?

His dreamy musings came to an abrupt end. There was one area where the light was brighter and more forceful; it seemed to be driving in to the confluence of tiny whirlpools that made up the bigger maelstrom. He hurried towards it and was pleased to see that beyond that area there was a definite flow, although it was more of a trickle than a torrent.

He moved as quickly as he could, not knowing how long he could maintain his altered perception. Occasionally it flickered and threatened to fade and he had to fight to bring it back, but he was buoyed by his progress.

The visual and aural hallucinations appeared to have been left behind in the whirlpool area, so he was surprised when an insistent voice came echoing through the darkness to him. Its familiarity was more of a shock: it was his own. As he turned suddenly, the view of the earth energy fizzed out. And there he was, coming towards himself through the void. His ghost-image was subtly changed: longer hair, a goatee, the drawn, pale face of a man who had seen too many terrible things; it was the same Church he had seen watching a burning city in his vision in the Watchtower.

'Is this it? Is this the right time?' his future-self was saying to him passionately; Church couldn't decide if it was fear or anger or a mixture of both he was hearing in the voice. 'You have to listen to me! This is a warning!' He looked around, confused, as if trying to work out where he was. '*Is* this the right place? Am I too late?'

His words fell into relief and Church said quickly, 'Tell me what you have to say.'

The future-Church shook himself, regained his focus. 'When you're in Otherworld and they call, heed it right away! They're going to bring him back! They're—'

'Calm down! You're babbling!' Church yelled. '*Who* is going to bring *who* back?'

The other Church suddenly looked terrified, glanced over his shoulder. 'Too late!' he yelled.

And then he was gone.

The encounter disturbed Church immensely. The message was garbled, disorienting, but he felt he had missed a vital opportunity to discover something important, perhaps something that would be a life-or-death matter. He vowed to keep the message in his head so that if any fitting situation arose, he would be able to act instantly.

When they call, heed it right away.

At least he had managed to maintain his sense of direction. He continued walking along the path he had been following and soon he saw the gently glowing cavern walls approaching from either side. They met at a rough opening where the tunnel continued. And on a boulder near the entrance sat Tom, quietly sucking on a joint.

'How the hell did you get here?' Church asked in disbelief.

'I walked.'

'You know what I mean!'

Tom shrugged, giving nothing away. Then he couldn't seem to resist, and said with a faint smile, 'You were the one who had to go through it. It was a test.'

'It was a natural obstacle caused by the backed-up earth energy. Wasn't it?'

'It was. But you were drawn into it for a reason. I told you, it was a test.'

'Why was I being tested?'

'You know,' Tom snapped.

Church tried to make sense of it. 'The things I saw out there! It was—'

'I know. I've experienced that kind of thing before. We can carry on now. We've been allowed access.'

'You're talking like the blue fire's got some kind of intelligence,' Church laughed mockingly.

'It has. Of a kind. Everything thinks, everything feels, everything hurts.'

'More hippie bullshit!' Church snorted with derision, but the concept stayed with him. They set off along the new tunnel and after a moment or two, he said, 'So tell me, is it God?'

'Call it that if you want,' Tom said dismissively. 'If you want to reduce something so enormous and complex to such pathetically, childishly simplistic terms.'

Church chopped the air with his hand and cursed under his breath, picking up his step so he didn't have to walk in irritation at the older man's side.

And then, suddenly, they were at a blockage in the tunnel. Boulders of varying size were piled up to the tunnel roof.

'Is this what we have to clear to get things flowing again?' Church said.

'Don't be an idiot,' Tom replied. 'Did you think it would be that easy?'

Through the rock, Church perceived a sound like an engine running. In a moment of *frisson* he realised it was the sound of breathing.

'Change is the important thing,' Tom continued. 'You have to bring things out into the open, for good or bad.'

Church tried to read his face, but he knew how futile an exercise that was. 'I don't like the way you said that,' he noted.

The walk back from the strange, ritualistic room had been a blur to Ruth. The pain and shock of her experience had, for a brief while, almost wiped her mind clear. Only one thing had struck her through the haze: a sound from behind a heavily padlocked door, like a flock of birds crazily flying around the confined space.

She barely noticed they had taken her to a new cell, as depressing as her old one, but almost palatial in size; although it was pitch dark she could tell how large it was from the bouncing echoes of her footsteps. After the cramped confines of her last prison, it should have been cause enough for joy, but her every thought was taken up with the struggle to accept she was still alive. When the black pearl was being forced into her mouth, she had so convinced herself she was going to die her survival had left her disoriented, shocked and, in an odd way, depressed.

She could still feel the awful weight of the pearl deep in her stomach; it was radiating cold into every fibre of her being. She turned to one side and vomited on the flags, sickened by the pressure and the changes taking place in her body. The nausea never left her. What did it all mean? They'd be coming for her again soon and she really didn't know how much more she could bear.

She crawled away to the other side of the cell, trying to avoid the smell of vomit, but the stench was too strong. She retched again. Shaking, she lowered her head on to the cold floor and hoped sleep would come soon to save her from the nightmare.

Veitch's instincts had been sending sharp prompts throughout the morning, and by late afternoon he had already made up his mind to move by sundown. Scarcely had he accepted the decision than he heard a tumult echoing across the city from the Old Town. From his window he could see nothing but scattered groups of people looking up to the old, grey buildings that crested the great ridge which ran down from the castle, so he quickly made his way outside.

Dark storm clouds hung oddly over the Old Town, while the rest of the city was bathed in the reddish light of the setting sun. Further down the Royal Mile towards Holyrood those clouds seemed to be churning and there were flashes of light that were not lightning erupting among them; each flash was accompanied by a rumble like distant gunfire.

The crowds were uneasy and apprehensive. It was a manifestation of all their deepest fears that had grown since the Old Town had been so mysteriously sealed off. 'What's going on up there?' one man asked darkly, of no one in particular. Those nearest looked at him fearfully, looked back at the disturbance, said nothing.

Veitch watched it for a moment or two longer, until he decided it might well be the diversion for which he had been waiting. He didn't know if it was the doing of Shavi and Laura or Church and Tom, but he should move fast to seize the moment. He broke away from the crowd and hurried in the direction of the Old Town.

He realised how much had changed the moment he began to climb the steep steps of Advocate's Close. Within the space of a few feet the temperature had changed from summer balm to deepest winter; his breath clouded and the steps shimmered with hoar frost. When he reached the summit he was startled to see thick, fresh snow drifting across the Royal Mile, unspoilt by footprints or tyre tracks. The mist had quickly descended, casting a spectral pall over the entire area.

Shivering, he zipped his leather jacket to the neck and waded out into the street. The covering of snow was crisp; it was several degrees below zero.

Another flash and rumble startled him. The battle, or whatever it was, was still raging at the foot of the Royal Mile, obscured by the haar. His first instinct was to head straight to the castle, but he knew he had to be sure the Cailleach Bheur was being distracted. He made his way out into the middle of the road where the snow wasn't so deep and set off towards the disruption.

About halfway down the Royal Mile the mist had thinned out enough for him to see what was happening. The Cailleach Bheur stood with her back to him, both hands grasping her gnarled staff, which was planted firmly in front of her. Bubbles of blue energy were forming around her, increasing in size rapidly, then rushing out in waves. Whenever they burst, the deep rumble rolled out, making Veitch's ears hurt. That close to her, it was almost unbearably cold; Veitch convulsed with shivers.

The object of her attack was a gloriously beautiful young man floating several feet above the road, his long hair whipped by the force of the energy. He seemed to glow with an inner golden light, but there was some unpleasant quality in his face which disturbed Veitch immensely. The flashes of light appeared to be generated somewhere within him; they were diffuse, like a heat haze on a summer day. Veitch occasionally felt their warmth breaking through the cold. He guessed this was the power Shavi and Laura had been despatched to find and was pleased by their speedy success. The first strike went to the underdogs, he thought; perhaps things weren't so bad after all.

Although the two forces were obviously in battle, Veitch saw no anger, no emotion of any kind that he recognised. But he was relieved to see the new arrival was more than a match for the wintry ferocity of the Cailleach Bheur. With renewed vigour, he left them to their fight and hurried back up the steep road.

Edinburgh Castle stood at the very summit of the Royal Mile on a mound of volcanic rock created three hundred and forty million years before. The Fomorii had chosen their location well. Surrounded on three sides by sheer cliffs, its position was impregnable. And if the Fomorii had somehow burrowed into the very rock beneath the castle, Veitch knew they would be almost untouchable. His comfort came from the knowledge that he didn't have to defeat them – that would be up to the others – he must merely get Ruth out.

To that end he had spent his time well since the departure of the others, reading up on the fortress's history and studying its layout in intricate detail until he had his strategy well mapped out in his mind. Subterfuge was the only way forward. In the times when the garrison had fallen into English hands, the Scots had only been able to retake it through stealth, once by scaling the cliffs and taking the defending troops by surprise, once by disguising themselves as merchants and using their supplies to block open the castle gates so a larger force could sweep in. Deception went against his nature – a direct assault always made him feel much better – but he was learning rapidly.

The approach to the castle was across the wide-open forecourt where the Tattoo was held every year. In normal weather Veitch would not have been able to cross it unseen, but the drifting thick mist provided reasonable cover. He sneaked into an entryway near the Camera Obscura for a few minutes while the sun set completely. Then, with the night providing added protection, he crept around the perimeter wall.

It was an eerie scene. The castle was ablaze with light reflecting off the thick snow, a Christmas confection designed to lure tourists from across the city, but there wasn't a sound in the vicinity. The drifting mist that resembled smoke on a battlefield muffled any sound from the New Town and obscured any view of the modern city. Veitch felt like he had been transported back in time.

The castle gates were open – the Fomorii obviously feared no direct assault. Veitch ducked below the level of the low stone wall and crept beneath the dark arch of the gatehouse. Adrenalin was coursing around his body; he felt revitalised, ready for anything. In the Lower Ward he paused and glanced through a window back into the gatehouse. A guard in military uniform stared blankly across a bare table. Veitch couldn't reconcile the army presence with the Fomorii until he recognised the waxy sheen to the guard's face; on close inspection, it resembled a mask: it was a shape-shifted Fomor. This was obviously how the Fomorii had managed to take the castle in the first place, quietly, unnoticed, while the Old Town bustled around them. Somewhere, he guessed, there lay a charnel house filled with the bodies of all the soldiers who had been replaced.

He kept to the shadows as he climbed the stairs towards the Middle Ward, trying to muffle his footsteps as much as he could. If he allowed himself to recognise it, he would have had to admit he was terrified, but every sense was fixed on the here and now, smelling the wind for the familiar reek of the Fomorii, listening for even the slightest sound, constantly scanning for any movement in the shadows. He had no idea if the Fomorii had established any kind of secret defence which would alert them to his presence, but he put his faith in moving fast, so he didn't stay in one place too long.

As he rounded the corner into the Middle Ward he was brought up sharp by a patrol moving in step across the windswept expanse. Quickly, he pulled himself back against the wall, praying he had not been seen. With foreknowledge, it was obvious the patrol did not consist of human soldiers; there was a brooding presence to it which set his nerves on edge.

He held his breath, let the darkness settle on him; the cold bit sharply and he could no longer feel his feet where they were covered by the blanket of snow. As he scanned the battlements, towers and building, it was clear the Fomorii were everywhere. It would take all his skill and a large dose of luck to slip by them unseen; if he were spotted at this early stage he wouldn't stand a chance.

His task was to find where the Fomorii had established their entrance to whatever lay beneath the castle; his only chance of discovery was to follow some of the Bastards to the location. He guessed, though, that entrance could lie in the Castle Vaults, which were on the closest level to the base rock. But his progress wasn't going to be easy – the Fomorii patrol was marching back and forth across the Middle Ward, barring his advance. At least his detailed preparation had left him with a fairly comprehensive knowledge of the castle's labyrinthine byways. Slowly, he edged backwards through the shadows until he found the Lang Stairs, seventy mediaeval steps that led up into the mist. Cautiously he advanced up them; if a Fomor was coming in the opposite direction, the haar would prevent him knowing until they were on top of each other.

By the time he reached the top he was covered in a cold sweat. Somewhere ahead he could hear the crunch of footsteps in the snow. Quickly he dashed past the rows of cannon lining the battlements until he found another hiding place. At that point he was off the beaten track and the chance of another Fomorii patrol passing by was slim. He squatted down and caught his breath, wondering what Church would have done in the same situation. The tension was so high it would have been easy to turn back, but his evening of conversation with Reynolds had filled him with an uncommon, fiery hope; he really believed he could reach Ruth, get her out, even. And then, perhaps, she would recognise him for who he truly was.

It was too cold to remain in one spot for long. Crown Square, with its clustering, towering buildings, was his best chance for cover as he made his way towards the Castle Vaults. At the square's east entrance he paused to survey the scene. It was quiet and deserted, the snow deep and unbroken across the broad expanse. The mist drifted hazily along the rooftops. To his right, the Scottish National War Memorial loomed up, dark and foreboding; there would be no one in there at least, among the silent monuments to those who had died in defence of the realm. The other buildings around the square could well be occupied, but they were all dark too.

Warily, he stepped out; the snow crunched unnervingly loudly under his feet. The exit to the vaults was directly opposite him, just a stone's throw across the way. He had made it halfway across when he came up sharp. The lights from the Upper Ward that filtered into the square were suddenly throwing a large, distorted shadow on to one of the walls ahead of him. Veitch had only an instant to think before launching himself to his left and his only possible hiding place: the Great Halls, where the door hung open.

The shadow was across almost the entire square as he threw himself through the opening. He prayed he had been quick enough, but as he scurried into the gloom his foot clipped the door and it swung shut. It must have been seen by whoever was approaching, for it was followed by the insistent, nauseating barks and shrieks of the Fomorii dialect. Veitch propelled himself into the main hall and searched for a hiding place. If he could lie low, the Fomorii guard might simply think the door had been blown shut by the wind.

The darkness in the hall was magnified by the oppressive wooden panelling beneath the deep red walls and heavy beams which supported the vaulted roof. Stained-glass windows along one wall allowed dull beams of light to filter through. The hall was a museum to armoury: swords, pikes, spears, shields, breastplates and helmets were everywhere. Two heavy wooden chairs stood in front of an enormous stone fireplace at one end. Veitch dived behind them into the shadowy hearth and waited there.

A second after he'd settled, footsteps echoed across the room. He peered under the chairs to see a Fomor disguised as a Royal Scots Dragoon march into the centre of the hall and slowly survey it. Veitch held his breath, every muscle of his body tense. The moment was suspended for what felt like hours until the creature turned and began to walk back towards the door. Just as Veitch was about to breathe again, the guard stopped, threw one more glance around, then began to fumble for a radio at its belt. Veitch knew instantly from the body language what was intended: a warning of a potential intruder, or just a call to be more vigilant; either way, it was bad news.

The thought had barely registered when he was stealthily slipping out from behind the chairs. As the guard brought the radio up, Veitch pulled a stout short sword silently from a baize-covered display table and began to creep across the floor. He could catch it unawares, drive the sword into the base of its skull before it had a chance to raise the alarm. He'd seen how powerful the things were; he didn't want to risk a face-to-face confrontation.

He slid quickly across the room, raising the sword as he moved. He was almost ready to put his shoulder behind the plunge when the radio suddenly let out an ear-piercing shriek. In a split second it had changed form, like mercury being dropped on to the floor. A silver sheen flooded over it as it sprouted legs like a spider before scurrying up the guard's arm, where it proceeded to shriek.

Veitch only had the barest instant to realise the thing was a Caraprix – one of the symbiotic shape-shifting creatures which both the Tuatha Dé Danann and Fomorii carried with them – before the guard was whirling. In the same fluid motion his human face began to melt away like candle-wax, rolling, pluming, becoming something so hideous it made Veitch's gorge rise. He tried not to look as he continued with his sword stroke, driving it towards the creature's head. But the Fomor had shifted enough for the blade to glance off its shoulderbone or whatever the unpleasant ridge was that was materialising under the guard's shirt, splitting it open.

The creature swung something that had been an arm but now resembled a scorpion's tail, still changing, catching him hard on the side of the head. He flew sideways, hitting the floor hard as purple stars burst in his brain.

He rolled on to his back as the Fomor advanced like a reptile, indistinct and dark and sickening, smelling of raw meat. Veitch gave himself wholly over to instinct, that strange fighting prowess that had gradually emerged from deep within him. He propelled himself forward, tangling himself in the creature's legs. Its momentum carried it forward and over him. As it fell, he held up the sword, then rolled out of the way at the last moment. The Fomor's own weight drove the sword through its neck and into its skull. It lay on the floor twitching and shrieking, leaking a substance that smelled so bad Veitch had to fight back the nausea.

The Caraprix, too, was wailing. It leapt from the fallen guard and scuttled across the floor. Veitch reacted instantly. He jumped forward and stamped down hard with one heavy boot, splattering it in a burst of grey ichor; its wail of alarm was cut off mid-note.

Veitch allowed himself one moment of relief, scarcely able to believe he had killed one of the creatures, though he still didn't fancy his chances in a direct fight. Then he hurried over to the wall display, selected another short sword and a dagger which he tucked into his jacket, then a crossbow and some bolts, which he hung on a strap over his shoulder. And then he headed hastily to the door to see if anything had responded to the creature's dying cries.

The square was as quiet and deserted as when he had first seen it. The only tracks were the guard's and his own. Quickly he ran to the west exit from the square. He could hear the patrol still moving around the Middle Ward, but there was nothing between him and the Castle Vaults.

He kept close to the walls until he reached the entrance, still amazed he had made it so far. The vaults were dark and dank and smelled of wet stone and earth. The first section consisted of a long arched corridor; there were two rooms leading off it. After the wide open spaces, the place felt claustrophobic. Water was dripping from the ceiling in a constant rhythm and echoes bounced wildly off the stone.

His teeth went on edge when he heard the Fomorii dialect reverberating from the furthest room. Guardedly, he crept to the corner and peered round. Two more Royal Scots Dragoon guards stood talking next to an enormous cannon, which he knew from his reading was the mediaeval siege gun, Mons Meg. Beyond it was a ragged hole in the stone floor from which cold air currents drifted. He had been right. Here was the entrance to the Fomorii's subterranean lair. But how was he going to get past the guards?

He noticed the room had a door near the far wall, which he guessed connected with the other chamber that led off the corridor. He returned to the first room, where there was a tourist display detailing the vault's history as a prison, a bakehouse and barracks. Steeling himself, he used the haft of the sword to smash the glass, then hurried back to his original position outside the second room. As he had guessed, the guards took the back route to investigate the disturbance, allowing him a free run to the hole in the floor. Rough steps led down into the dark.

There was no time to deliberate. It had been a gamble to do anything which might alert the Fomorii to his presence, but it had been the only option; he would deal with the consequences later. Fighting back his anxiety, he put his foot on the top step.

Seconds later he was in dark, freezing tunnels only occasionally lit by a barely flickering torch. Branches broke off on either side from which drifted foul smells like the cooking of rotted meat; from the distance he could hear odd sounds of indiscernible origin which made him strangely fearful. It was a maze. The chances of finding Ruth were slim, of returning alive even slimmer.

chapter nine

the well

Night had fallen by the time Shavi and Laura made it back to Edinburgh on the back of a lorry delivering builders' supplies to Leith. The Bone Inspector had long since abandoned them, loping across the fields in the direction of the city, one backward glance of contempt and horror showing them what he felt of their actions.

From more than five miles from the city centre it was obvious something terrible was happening in the Old Town. The sky was filled with flashes and rumbles and as they drew closer they could see the wintry clouds that obscured the area were churning as if violent winds were gusting in that one spot.

'What do you reckon?' Laura said as they stood on the pavement where the driver had dropped them off.

Shavi could tell from her voice she feared the worst. 'We will see when we get closer.'

'We're going in there, then?' She didn't wait for an answer. 'Do you think the others will be all right?'

'I do not know.'

'That's him, isn't it? That freak?'

Shavi said nothing. He felt complicit in the awful things that were happening, were bound to happen. If he had listened to Laura's doubts, if he had not been so driven in his desire to accomplish their mission, the mad god might not now be loose. Perhaps Maponus had been subtly influencing him, drawing him in until his free will was compromised, but that was not enough of an excuse. His mind was strong; he could have resisted.

'Come on.' He walked away from Lothian Road into Bread Street. Shivering in their light summer clothes, they hadn't gone far through the shadowed, twisty-turny streets before they noticed a building which had crumbled into a pile of rubble, as if it had been hit by a bomb.

Shavi ran forward to inspect the wreckage, then noticed a curious sight. It took a second or two before it dawned on him what he was seeing. 'Look here,' he said as Laura joined him.

She followed his pointing finger over the debris and saw another crumpled building beyond it, and more beyond that. A swathe had been cut through the city to the outskirts. She turned a hundred and eighty degrees and realised the path continued in the opposite direction to the heart of the Old Town. They looked at each other, but couldn't think of any way to express the thoughts that were colliding in their heads. After a moment of silent contemplation they scrambled across the bricks, stone and tiles towards the Royal Mile.

In the next street they found the body of an old man who had obviously refused to abandon his home during the great evacuation. It wasn't simply crushed by the housefall; it had been lovingly rendered into its component parts. The head was missing, but there was a fine red dew across an arc of virginal snow. Shavi and Laura both blanched.

'We're going to burn for this,' she said.

They could see the battle raging through the gap in the buildings long before they clambered up on to the Royal Mile. It was furious in its intensity: a clattering of light and dark, summer and winter, two different aspects of hell; Shavi and Laura could barely look at it. Maponus' beautiful face was contorted by an expression of such overwhelming hatred it made their blood run cold. His eyes were ranging wild, his fingers flexing, unflexing, as the energy or whatever it was rolled off him. Sometimes his attention wavered and he would let off a venomous blast at one of the abandoned buildings nearby, as if his pent-up hatred was for everything in existence. But then the Cailleach Bheur would strike again in her coldly emotionless way and his skittering attention would return to her.

At that moment the crone seemed less human than ever; her features had dissolved into the sucking darkness of the void, her limbs were black and angular like the branches of a wind-blasted tree on a wintry heath. Her power was awesome to experience; even at a distance they could feel the cold like knives in their skin. The way the blue illumination shimmered drove Laura's mind back to the club, as the flashing lights had been refracted then obscured by the hag's relentless ice. For the first time she truly realised how close to death she had come. Before the power of these old gods, they were nothing. She wiped a stray tear away hurriedly before Shavi had a chance to see it.

They scurried for cover behind a tumbled-down wall, their breath clouding in the cold air. 'What's going to happen if he gets by her?' she asked.

'At the moment they seem fairly well matched—'

'But sooner or later—'

'We put our faith in the others. In Church and the blue fire.' It was the first time she had heard an edge to his voice.

'What about Veitch?' They both looked into the depths of the thick mist that shrouded the castle.

'We should head to the rendezvous point. Just in case.'

Laura snorted derisively. 'Is it me, or is this a head in the sand situation? You know, I hope one of us bastards has a Plan B. Otherwise I'd say, in our fine tradition, we've made things even worse.' Shavi was already departing. 'Don't walk away, you bastard! If that thing we set free gets away from here, we're going to be knee-deep in killing fields.'

He turned slowly; his eyes were brimming. 'I know,' he said quietly. And then he was moving away into the night once more and she had no option but to follow him.

Veitch could barely control his shivering as he progressed along the freezing, gloomy tunnels. The torches on the walls were too far apart to give him any comfort, but at least he didn't encounter any Fomorii guards. That unnerved him even more, because he knew it was only a matter of time – he would have expected the place to be swarming with them. Were they all hiding to lure him in there so they could sweep down to tear him apart? He drove that thought out quickly.

The entire place was a maze. All the tunnels looked the same, all were filled with the foul stench of spoiled meat cooking. Roughly constructed wooden doors were occasionally spaced on both sides. He had tried some of them tentatively, but they had all been locked. In the end he had been forced to hiss Ruth's name, expecting to be answered by a Fomorii roar, but there had been no response from any.

In a way he almost wished he *would* be confronted by something; that would be better than the unbearable tension of expecting an encounter around every corner, of constantly straining to hear footsteps approaching from behind.

When the side tunnel loomed out of the dark it came as a shock. Its surround was ornately carved with writhing things and disturbing twisted shapes; over the top there was a stone face so unbearably hideous Veitch had to look away. The cold air currents which swept from its depths suggested it opened on to a large space. As he took a few steps in, trailing one hand along the wall for support, he picked up a strange, deep bass rumble like heavy trucks rolling; it made his stomach curdle. A few paces later and he recognised voices, scores, perhaps hundreds of Fomorii, but instead of the chaotic jumble of their usual dialect, it was controlled, two conflicted notes repeated over and over again. They were singing.

In a strange way, that was worse than anything he could have anticipated. There was something about that sound that made him want to flee back to the lights of the New Town, but he forced himself to press on. By the time he emerged from the tunnel, he was shaking uncontrollably, his body once again covered in sweat. He was at the top of a flight of rudely carved stairs leading down into a large chamber. And the room was filled with Fomorii. He had been right: hundreds of them. The sum of their presence was so terrible the bile surged into his mouth and he had to shuffle back to retch where he would not be seen. When he looked down into the chamber again, his vision became liquid; he couldn't fix on their forms and for an instant he was convinced there was just one beast down there, enormous and black and filthy with all the evil of existence.

He averted his gaze as his eyes swam, then they fell on what appeared to be a raised dais at the far end, flanked by two flaming braziers. On the centre was Calatin; the corrupt half-breed had his arms raised in some act of worship. When he dropped them, the intolerable singing stopped on one drawn-out note which slowly faded into the dark. Then he began to speak animatedly in the barks and shrieks of the Fomorii dialect. Veitch couldn't bear any more, but just as he began to retreat he glimpsed something in the shadows beyond Calatin: an enormous Fomorii dressed in black battle armour and resembling some giant insect.

Back in the main tunnel, he fought to control his nausea and spinning head. He couldn't work out what he had witnessed – a rallying of the troops? A prayer session? – but it had left him thoroughly disquieted. There was no point wasting time considering it. He returned to his mission with a renewed vigour born of dread.

Lost in his thoughts, he almost walked straight into a Fomorii guard as he rounded a corner. At the last minute he threw himself back, praying he hadn't been seen. The guard had been at the end of a tunnel which was reached down a short flight of steps. Veitch had only glimpsed him, but he had been alerted by a buzzing in his head and the now-familiar sickening in his stomach; it could have been instinct, but it was more as if the Fomorii existed on some level beyond the corporeal, as if they were a foul gas he could smell or a discordant sound constantly reverberating. But it was more than both those things; the creatures offended some fundamental, instinctive part of him.

Peeking round the corner as much as he could dare, he watched the dense area of blackness and the suggestion of a shape at the heart of it. The creature was so big and threatening, its position in the tunnel was almost impregnable; a full-frontal attack would undoubtedly be suicide. He could sneak by, continue exploring the tunnels, but a guard suggested the first site of importance he had come across. He gnawed on a fingernail, desperately urging himself to make the right decision, at the same time aware that he had never made the right decision in his life.

Church and Tom scrabbled away at the rocks that blocked the tunnel until their fingers and knuckles bled, but eventually they had cleared a large enough path to crawl through. It was warmer on the other side and the air smelled of lemon and iron. The breathing sound that had first alerted Church was now so loud it made their ears ring.

Tentatively, he advanced down the tunnel. More rubble crunched underfoot and the walls were cracked and broken open; there were holes so big he could put his hand through them.

'We must be right in the heart of Arthur's Seat now,' he said, suddenly claustrophobic at the weight of rock lying above his head.

'You would think,' Tom replied.

'You have a remarkable knack of sounding superficially like you agree with me while at the same time suggesting I'm completely wrong and an idiot into the bargain.'

'It's a skill. I've had centuries to perfect it.'

Church suddenly noticed an unusual texture on the rock that lay at the end of one of the fissures in the wall. Squinting, he could just make out a strange diamond pattern. 'That's odd.' Cautiously he reached in and ran his fingers over the surface; it was rough and cool to the touch, but the pattern was certainly regular.

'Jesus!' he exclaimed, snatching his hand back.

Tom was instantly at his side. 'What is it?'

'It moved! No, the rock didn't move, but something just beneath the surface of it did. It was like . . . It was like . . .' He blanched.

'What?' Tom stressed.

Church leaned forward and peered into the fissure, shaking his head.

'Like what?' Tom repeated. There was an irritated edge to his voice.

'Like . . . Like muscles moving beneath skin.' He swallowed, moved to another fissure further along the wall. Bending down, he peered into it, then hesitantly held his hand over the opening, wondering if he dared. Slowly he reached in, all the time watching where his fingers were going.

'Oh my God!' This time he threw himself back, shaking his hand in the air in disgust. The movement had been greater, something seemed to roll up. In the dark of the fissure he could see something red glinting. He crept forward. 'Oh my God' – a whisper this time. The red glowed brighter, shifted slightly.

'What is it?' Tom hissed.

'An eye.' Church swallowed, repulsed. 'I touched an eye and it opened.'

Suddenly there was a tremendous rumbling deep in the rock and the tremors rippled out so powerfully it threw them off their feet. Showers of dust fell from the ceiling, choking them, blinding them, as the wall cracked and finally crumbled.

'Get down!' Church threw himself over Tom to protect him. But the ceiling held steady and only a few tiny rocks from the wall bounced across his back. When he eventually felt safe enough to look up, coughing and spluttering, he instantly realised what the unnerving sound had been.

On the other side of where the wall had been lay a long, sinuous figure, its muscles and tendons shifting under the scaled skin that reflected the faint light in bronze and verdigris with a touch of gold. The Fabulous Beast breathed in and out, regularly, peacefully, moving gently in its deep sleep, but its bulk was so big even the slightest tremble of its lithe body sent tremors through the rock. Church couldn't even get a sense of its true size, for much of it was hidden under the fallen rock; even that had not disturbed it.

He took a step forward, overcome by the sudden wonder of what he was seeing.

'You feel it?' Tom was watching him curiously.

'What?'

'An affinity. You may not be of the same blood, but you are of the same spirit.'

And he did feel it, tingling in his fingers, up his spine, singing in the chambers of his head; he felt like a tuning fork ringing in harmony with the sleeping beast. 'A Brother of Dragons,' he muttered.

'Your heritage.' Tom moved in next to him, clapped a grounding hand on his shoulder. 'You are learning, growing. It's been a slow process, but you're getting there.'

'Why hasn't it woken?'

'It hasn't woken for a long, long time. It is kin to the old one that lies beneath Avebury, younger, but only just. This place was once almost as potent a source of the blue fire as Avebury, but for some reason the energy dried up quicker here once the people turned away from the spirit.'

'And the Fabulous Beast went into hibernation?'

'Hibernation? I suppose that's one way of looking at it. It is detached from the world and everything in it.'

Church dropped to his haunches to examine the creature's flank. 'It's magnificent . . . beautiful—'

'And dangerous. Make no mistake, the Fabulous Beasts are not pets. They are wild and untamed, a force of nature.'

Church stood up, sighing. 'Where did they come from? They don't fit in with how we thought the world operated.'

'They fit in with the way the world should be, and once was.'

'What are we supposed to do now?' Church asked, looking down the steep slope of tunnel where it disappeared into the gloom. 'I don't know how the hell I'm supposed to get the earth energy moving again. And to be honest, even if we could find a way, I still don't see how it's supposed to help us.'

Tom set off walking, his voice floating back ethereally. 'Perhaps it won't help us. But healing the wounded land, perhaps, is a mission that exceeds opposition to the Fomorii. Your prime mission.'

'If Balor returns, there won't be a land left to heal,' Church said sourly, trying to keep up.

The tunnel pitched downwards steeply until there were points when Church had to grab hold of the walls to stop himself slipping out of control. The air grew colder and dustier and at times he felt the blast of strong air currents, although he couldn't begin to guess where they were coming from. As they descended they seemed to move into an oppressive doom-filled atmosphere; their sporadic conversation dried up accordingly, so the only sound was the soft tramp of their feet.

The air currents grew worryingly stronger until gusts surged up the tunnel, knocking them against the walls. It was almost as if they were coming to the edge of a cliff. Church had a sudden vision of the vast underground sea in *Journey to the Centre of the Earth*. And then the tunnel ended abruptly and the the source of the wind became clear.

They were standing on a small ledge which ran around a yawning hole so big they couldn't see the other side. It plunged away from their feet in a dizzying drop into darkness, but the rush of air and odd, disturbing echoes suggested it was very deep indeed. It may well have gone down for ever. Church closed his eyes and threw himself backwards into the tunnel mouth as a rush of vertigo made his head spin.

'Here we are,' Tom said. 'The well of fire.'

Church eventually found the strength to creep forward on his hands and knees to peer over the edge into the abyss. The wind rushed up, buffeting his face, tugging at his hair. His head reeled as he fought the sensation that he was being sucked over the lip.

'There are spirit wells like this all over the country, all across the world.' Tom's voice floated distantly behind him; Church felt like the darkness was swallowing him whole. 'Few as mighty as this, however,' Tom continued. 'And fewer still that are actually alight.'

Church sat back, pressing himself firmly against the rock wall. 'What am I doing here? It's a dirty, big hole in the ground. This is hopeless.'

'Hopeless?' Tom said. 'Haven't you learned anything yet?'

'You're great at tossing out cryptic advice. Why don't you say something useful for a change – tell me what I'm supposed to do.'

'Sort it out yourself,' Tom snapped. 'You're the one who's supposed to be learning.'

Church cursed under his breath and returned his attention to the abyss. He peered into it for inspiration, but nothing came. Slowly his mood dipped. Was he going to fail again? Then thoughts surfaced like bubbles on that black, oily pool. This was a source of the blue fire. It wasn't truly a hole in the earth; they weren't really under Arthur's Seat. It was a place between worlds, beyond reality, like Otherworld. Perhaps it was Otherworld, but somehow he doubted it; it was more likely the well was a channel through to wherever the blue fire originated. He looked up at Tom who was standing with his hands behind his back, as if on a stroll through the park. 'Where does that go?' he said, pointing into the well.

Tom smiled like a teacher whose favoured pupil had just made a great leap of logic. 'Where do you think it goes?'

Church cursed again and waved him away; answering questions with questions was Tom's favourite type of conversation and over the months it had not diminished in irritation factor.

Church pondered some more; gradually his thoughts seemed to come together. What was the nature of the blue fire? That was obvious, if everything Tom had said was true: it was the essence of the spirit. And the blue fire had dried up here and stagnated across the land, once the people had turned away from believing.

'Can we ignite it again . . . can we draw back the blue fire . . . by doing . . .' The words failed him and he held up his hands in irritation. Then: 'An act that touches the spirit, that resonates in that plane.'

Tom nodded thoughtfully. 'Perhaps. In this new world a leap of faith can have as far-reaching an effect as a leap of logic. Will it work? Perhaps, if you want it enough.'

The strain of the responsibility began to seep into Church's shoulders. He wanted out of it, back to the life he once knew, but there was no hope of that, ever again. He closed his eyes, feeling his emotions and thoughts wash over him, then he dipped into his pocket and pulled out the locket given to him by the young Marianne.

'This saved my life.' He held it up so it spun gently. 'A cheap piece of jewellery with a cut-out magazine photo of Princess Diana stuffed inside. Meaningless, really. And then suddenly infused with meaning and power. Why? Because a little girl put her heart and soul and dreams into it? It's like some stupid fairy story.'

'We now live in a time of myth,' Tom began quietly, 'where archetypes live and speak with a power that can bend reality, where thoughts take shape. If something is wished to have meaning, then it will have power. Things were like that before the change, but the power was muted. Myth has always shaped us, you know that. You can see it in Diana's life – the years of suffering, the sacrificial death, the mourning that became almost worship. The resonances and coincidences shout out loudly, so much so that you would not believe them. Diana, the name of the moon goddess, the goddess of hunting and woodlands and fertility, worshipped by women. Which Diana are we talking about?' He shrugged. 'There have always been powers moving behind the scenes, ordering our lives. We call them by different names, trying to make sense of them, but we never will. The only way to proceed with any equanimity is to accept that we exist at the heart of magic and mystery and nothing will be revealed, certainly not before death, and perhaps not even after. Enjoy the moment, go with the flow—'

'And all the other hippie values.' Church shook his head. 'I should make this locket my offering in the hope that somehow its power, its spirit, can set things in motion. But that girl, she changed my life in just one meeting. She was a kid, but she was everything I wasn't. Brave in the face of death, positive, filled with some kind of faith. It was magical to see.'

'And the name connection reminds you of your girlfriend,' Tom said pointedly.

Church nodded slowly. 'Yes, they're both tied up in my mind. I can't see where one ends and the other begins. With Marianne's spirit still trapped, I don't know if I can give this up. It feels like my only connection with her. Maybe I'm supposed to have it to free her.'

He looked at Tom for some kind of support and guidance, but the face he saw was impassive and unreadable.

'I know what you're thinking,' Church continued. 'That I screwed everything up before Beltane because I was so wrapped up in my own problems and Marianne. I promised myself I'd shake all that, but some things run too deep.' He looked back at the locket, spinning gently, catching the light like a tiny star. 'I wish I was better at this.'

A noise echoed along the tunnel behind them, just a tiny sound, but in the acoustics of the well chamber it sounded like thunder; they both snapped alert immediately. Breath held tightly, eyes staring unblinkingly up the tunnel, they waited. For a moment there was nothing. And then another sound, a crunch of a foot on the grimy tunnel floor, but so faint it suggested whoever was there was walking cautiously, so as not to be discovered. That alone sent uneasy signals running through them.

'Someone's coming,' Church whispered redundantly. 'Who else could be in here?'

'No one,' Tom replied. 'Unless we were followed.'

Church looked around hastily; the tunnel was the only way out. 'This isn't the best place to get caught. I wish Veitch was here.'

Tom surveyed the thin ledge. 'We could edge around to the shadows on the other side.' His voice was barely audible.

Church glanced into the deep dark of the well and felt his head spin again. 'Or we could greet them here with open arms. It might be nothing . . . it might be somebody . . .' His voice faded; he was being stupid. The chances were, in that place, at that time, whatever was coming was a threat. He looked at the ledge and winced. 'I don't know if I can do it.'

'And the alternative is?' Tom said, irritatedly. He grabbed Church's arm to try to drag him, but Church shook him off so violently they both almost fell into the well.

'Jesus!' Church hissed. 'Leave me alone! You're going to kill us both!'

'*You* are if you make us stay here.' Tom forced himself to stay calm. 'Face the wall. Feel with your feet and don't look down.'

'That's easy for you to say!' But Tom was already inching his way along the ledge. Church froze. The path seemed unbearably thin; the tip of Tom's heels hung over the drop. Sweat grew chill down his back and on his forehead.

Then he glanced up the tunnel and saw something which cut through his fear with a greater terror. A glint of yellow, gone, then yellow again, something small and insignificant, but he knew instinctively what it was. The thing he had glimpsed earlier in the cavern that had the shape of a great wolf, but was not a wolf; the terrible cutter of fingers that had taken Ruth. He had thought it another hallucination, or a glimpse across time and space caused by the bizarre rules of the whirlpool cavern, but it had really been there. And now it was coming for them.

And still he hesitated. The magnetic pull of the well's vertiginous depths was almost unbearable. The more visceral danger of what was approaching down the tunnel stabbed him with sharp knives. But if he could find his rational mind somewhere among his primal fears, he knew what the only route could be.

Feeling he was saying goodbye to his life, he put his first foot on the ledge.

Slowly he edged round the lip of the immense hole, feeling his heart beat so loudly in his ears he thought he was going to go deaf. His view alternated between the backs of his eyelids and the cold, dark rock of the cavern wall which repeatedly brushed the tip of his nose. Every sensation was heightened, almost too painful to bear. He felt sick. Every few seconds his mind told him he was going to die; he couldn't shake the feeling he was going to flip over backwards.

More than anything he wanted to glance back to the tunnel mouth; he could hear the rough breathing of the thing approaching, the scraping of its feet on the rock; it was making no attempt to hide itself now. But he couldn't bring himself to look, so all he was left with was the approaching noise and the feeling that he wasn't moving fast enough, that it would follow him on to the ledge, and then he truly would be trapped.

Suddenly his left shoulder hit a body. It was Tom, who had stopped, but the shock of it when he was lost in his thoughts broke his concentration and he made a startled sound. And then he was moving slowly away from the rock wall, and although he held his muscles rigid, it was not enough to drive him back. He strained to grip the wall, but it was moving away. He was going over.

Tom's arm came from nowhere and slammed between his shoulder blades, propelling him back upright. The strangled gasp that rushed from his throat was a mixture of relief and terror.

'Hush.' Tom's voice was so low it was almost a faint exhalation, which Church had to strain to hear.

'Why did you stop?' he responded in kind.

'If you could tear your eyes away from the rock you'd realise we can't see the tunnel any more. Which means it can't see us. Did you see what it was?'

Church swallowed, composed himself, repeated the mantra in his head: *Don't look down!* But there they were, hanging over an abyss, trying to have a normal conversation; it was madness. 'I got a glimpse . . . the eyes . . .' His mouth was too dry; he swallowed again. 'It's whatever took Ruth, what Laura thought was a giant wolf. And I saw it that way too, in the big cavern. But it's not. I know . . . somehow, I know . . . that it's human.'

'Sometimes, when the old gods have *tampered* with someone, it's hard to get a handle on them,' Tom mused. 'It screws up the mind's perceptions. It's like they've changed in some fundamental way and the mind is struggling to make sense of all the confusing signals so it imposes an image on it. The closest one that seems to fit. But it's a lie, a desperate lie, to preserve sanity.'

'Then what does it really look like?' Tom's use of the word *tampered* made Church shiver. He remembered the age-old man's account of his suffering at the hands of the Tuatha Dé Danann Queen, when he had been taken apart and put back together again, for little more than sport. *Frail Beings*, the Danann called them. Frail. Easily broken. Never put back quite right again.

The conversation died in the face of the threat. And so they listened to sounds that really did seem to issue from an animal, but then, eerily, intermingled with a guttural, warped human voice. It was muttering to itself. For a second they thought it might retreat up the tunnel, but after a moment's lull the breathing began to draw closer and they heard the scrape of a foot on the ledge, the click of nails on the cavern wall.

And then Church did tear his eyes away from the wall to stare wide-eyed into Tom's face. Tom moved off with the fast, supple movements of a man who had already experienced things worse than death. Church tried to keep up, but every muscle ached from forcing to keep himself close to the wall, and with movement his head had started spinning again. His throat seemed pencil-thin; he couldn't suck in enough air. And behind them the pursuer was drawing closer. He wondered if they could travel all around the well and head back up the tunnel to lose their pursuer in the cavern.

His foot slipped off the ledge and he had to grip on to the wall so tightly he was sure the delicate skin under the tips of his nails was bleeding. He was moving too fast, making stupid mistakes. But whatever was behind was relentless. He moved on.

And the well sucked at him again, sucked and inhaled and wished him off the ledge. And only a gossamer-thin wish was holding him on.

How much further? he wondered. It was impossible to tell how far around the arc they had travelled.

And then he heard the sound behind him, just a heavy breath, but in it a dark, malevolent triumph. He glanced to his right and saw, suspended in the black, the cold, yellow eyes, staring at him.

Their awful pull was destabilising. He tried to move away faster, but his foot slipped again and this time he went down on one knee. Off-balance, he was scrambling at the wall, shifting his weight wildly, trying to throw himself forward, shifting to the side, having to overcompensate, and then his knee was slipping off the ledge too, and the weight of the well was dragging him down.

For an instant time seemed to hang, pictures dropped from a hand, caught in midair. He looked up, saw Tom's face ahead of him frozen in horror. Realised some noise was coming from his mouth that made no sense. Felt his weight go completely over the edge. Looked down, saw nothing but dark, dark, dark, pulling him in. Falling.

At the last moment he reached out and slammed both hands on the ledge; his body swung hard against the wall, winding him. Tendons strained. His shoulders felt like they were going to explode. His fingers blazed with fire, seemed to be snapping. And his heels kicked wildly over nothing at all.

'Tom,' he croaked.

Tom looked at him, then slowly up at their pursuer. The ragged breath was so close now, Church swore it was almost above him.

'Tom,' he said again. Then: 'Go on. You can't help me.'

There was a look in Tom's eye as if all the repressed emotion in his body had come rushing to the surface, of more than tears, more than despair. But he remained, caught.

Church closed his eyes, knew he didn't have long. If the drop didn't get him, the Big Bad Wolf would. This was it. The end. He thought of Marianne and Marianne and Laura and Ruth and Niamh and all his new friends and his old ones and his family, and then he removed one hand from the ledge and somehow, through force of will, managed to keep hanging. *For just an instant longer*, his mind sparked.

The free hand swept into his pocket and pulled out the locket.

'I wish, I wish . . .' he whispered, but there were too many tears in his eyes.

And then he let it go, and it went spiralling down, the last star disappearing into the inky void.

A second later he joined it. His stomach shot up to his neck, his brain felt like it was twisting in his skull, and the air was rushing around him and somewhere Tom was yelling and . . .

Ruth had tried not to weep throughout all her ordeal and she had survived until that moment when she remembered the meal she had had with Church at Wodka in London before the whole mess had truly started. For some reason that triggered the tears and she hadn't been able to stop for a good quarter of an hour.

At least she had been provided with a rough bed of sacking and straw. Things seemed to be moving within it, but after the cold floor it seemed like paradise. That small piece of special treatment from creatures without even the slightest shred of humanity disturbed her more than anything; it was as if they were giving her a brief respite to build up her strength before something even more terrible. That brought another flood of tears. The black pearl had almost destroyed her. What could be worse than that? How much more could she take? Sometimes, although she dreaded to consider it, suicide almost seemed an option.

As if in answer to her thoughts, she heard a noise beyond the distant cell door, lost in the overpowering gloom. It was a Fomorii voice, insane and bestial. There were notes in it she had never heard before, so terrifying she clutched at her ears to drive it out, but the tumult continued until it ended in sudden silence. They were coming for her again.

'No more,' she pleaded in a broken voice. 'There's nothing left in me. I can't take anything else.'

She blinked away the tears, felt her head spin with the nauseating noises, waited, waited. There was a sound of metal on stone, some terrible torture instrument being dragged in. Blades, growing slicker, cogs turning, sparking pain that would consume her. The sounds grew closer, right outside the door now.

'Please,' she whimpered.

The lock turning. Click; a note of finality. Then slowly, slowly, swinging open. The light flooding in from outside, burning her eyes. And then the unbearable wait. She battened down her emotions, tried to think and feel nothing.

A figure was silhouetted in the flickering torchlight at the top of the flight of stone steps that led from her cell. It didn't make sense. Her head spun, her heart leapt with the rush of a hope she hardly dared accept.

The figure shifted, the torchlight sweeping over its torso, illuminating its face; a disbelieving grin of triumph. Words coming to her across the void between them.

'And the crowd went wild.'

Tears, no longer despairing, burned her cheeks. It was Veitch.

'Jesus Christ!' The jubilation on Veitch's face turned to horror when his eyes finally adjusted to the gloom enough to see Ruth huddled on the other side of the cell. It took a second for him to take in her filthy, matted hair, the dirt smeared across her skin, the unclean rag tied around her hand across the stump of her finger, but it was her face that affected him the most; it carried the weight of punishment and suffering to a degree that was painful to see. Yet despite that, at its core there was the defiance and strength he had recognised the first time he met her; diminished certainly, restrained, but still there. She had not been broken.

'Thank you.' Her voice sounded delirious.

Veitch threw himself down the stairs and sprinted across the cell, scrubbing at the spots of foul black ichor on his bare skin that burned like nettle sting.

'What's that?' Ruth said weakly, watching his actions; she seemed so detached she was barely conscious.

'Shit that came out of one of the Bastards. Blood, I suppose. Burns like fuck.' He knelt down and gripped her shoulders. 'Look, I know it's been a nightmare for you, but you've got to pull yourself together till we get out of here. I got in, but I don't know if I can get out again, and we're going to have every Bastard in here on our heels soon.'

'You came for me?' She couldn't seem to make sense of what he was saying.

'Couldn't leave you down here, could we?' The way she held her face up to him, slightly puzzled, slightly relieved, filled him with emotions he had never experienced in such an acute form before; there was a sharpness to them that almost made him wince, but a warmth too, and he knew at that moment that this was what he had been searching for all his life. He couldn't bear it if those feelings slipped away from him. 'Come on, girl,' he said softly. 'You and me against the world.'

At first he was afraid she wouldn't be able to walk and he'd have to carry her, but after he helped her to her feet she quickly grew steadier and soon she was moving across the cell without any aid. Outside the door she wrinkled her nose at the gruesome mess that smeared the corridor. Black and green slime was everywhere, along with chunks of matter and what looked like the horned, twisted remains of a Fomor; it appeared to have been hacked to pieces. Three crossbow bolts protruded from one part of it she couldn't recognise. Veitch retrieved them quickly and held them in the flame of one of the wall torches to burn the ichor off them.

'You did that?' she said.

Veitch couldn't tell if it was astonishment or horror he heard in her voice. 'You can't go in halfhearted. They'll tear you apart.' He paused, then added almost apologetically, 'I had to disable it with the bolts before I could move in. Probably wouldn't have stood a chance otherwise. You know, wouldn't fancy one of them in a fair fight . . .' He realised he was starting to ramble and caught himself. 'Come on.'

He attempted to lead them back the way he had come, but the tunnel system was a maze and every turn looked alike. He had the horrible feeling they were going deeper into the heart of the complex. 'There was some big hall where they were all praying or something. If I could find that I'd know we were on the right track.'

'So we're lost?'

'Blimey, it's not Oxford Street down here!'

'It's okay. I wasn't criticising.' Her voice sounded weary; a wave of pain crossed her face.

He instantly felt guilty at bristling. 'I just need to get my bearings.'

They headed down the tunnel a little further and stopped outside a heavily sealed door. From behind it, they heard the unmistakable sound of birds; it was as if a whole flock had been imprisoned within.

'I've heard that before,' Ruth said.

'Want to check it out?'

'Best not.'

They both felt oddly uneasy in proximity to the door, even more than the heightened sense of tension they had experienced in their journey from the cell. But before they could decipher the clues presented to them, the very walls of the tunnel reverberated with the crazed sound of a tolling bell. It wasn't how Ruth had heard it before; it was relentless, jarring, and she wanted to clutch at her ears to drive the sound out.

'Shit, we've been rumbled.' Veitch recalled the first time he had heard the noise in the abandoned mines under Dartmoor, just before the Fomorii swarmed in pursuit. 'Come on!' he said insistently, grabbing her wrist. 'We haven't got any time now!'

They hurried onwards, Ruth desperately attempting to keep up, but they hadn't gone far when they heard a rising tide of Fomorii grunts and shrieks approaching them. Veitch cursed under his breath and pivoted, heading back the way they had come. He took the first side tunnel he came to, sighing with relief when the faint slope appeared to go upwards. Yet as they rounded a bend to the right they came up against a stream of fast-approaching Fomorii at the end of a long stretch of tunnel. The sudden roar that erupted from the mass as it surged like oil along the corridor was terrifying.

Veitch spun round again, putting his arm across Ruth's shoulders to propel her forward. 'It's like a fucking ant hill.' He took another branching tunnel and tried to batten down the cold weight of fear rising in his chest so Ruth wouldn't see it, but he knew they were rapidly running out of options.

This tunnel was sloping up too, but the clamour behind them was increasing in intensity, drawing closer. Even if they made it out of the tunnel, they had to get through the castle before they were safe.

Suddenly Ruth grabbed his arm and hauled him to a halt. 'We can't stop!' he snapped.

She was pointing to a trapdoor in the wall they had just passed. It was about four feet off the floor, the size of a domestic oven. Seemingly oblivious to the approaching noise, she pulled herself away from him and wrenched the door open. A cold blast of air surged out of a dark tunnel. 'We could hide in there,' she said exhaustedly. 'We're not getting anywhere running around.'

He could tell from her face she was aware of all the thoughts he had been trying to hide from her, but she seemed more determined than scared. He nodded. 'Let me go first, though. Just in case . . .'

He boosted himself in and Ruth followed immediately behind his boot heels. She pulled the trapdoor shut behind them, plunging them into an all-encompassing darkness. It was freezing cold in the tunnel, and intensely claustrophobic. Veitch had to wriggle to get his shoulders forward; he was uncomfortably aware of the weight of rock pressing down upon his back.

Shivering, they lay as still as they could, until they heard the awful sound of the pursuing Fomorii rushing up the tunnel. Their blood ran cold; it was like the screech of demons surging out of hell, hungry for souls. As the creatures approached the trapdoor, Veitch screwed his eyes tight, listening to the noise, wishing he couldn't hear it, waiting for the flood of light as the trapdoor was pulled open. And then they would be torn from their hiding place, ripped apart in a blood-frenzy of tearing claws and rending jaws. Any second now. He winced, waited.

But the sound carried on, up to the door, past it, and along the tunnel until it dwindled into the distance. 'They'll realise they missed us in a minute or two and they'll be back. We have to get out of here,' he hissed.

'We can't go out there.' Ruth's disembodied voice floated on the air. 'They'll be looking everywhere. We don't stand a chance. You'll have to crawl on to see where this tunnel goes.'

Veitch's heart suddenly went up into his mouth. He inched forward slightly as a test and his shoulders rubbed painfully on the walls. 'We'll get stuck,' he protested.

'The alternative's going out there and getting eaten alive.'

'I prefer that to getting trapped in here and dying slowly.' He had a sudden vision of how it would feel, the rock pressing in at him from every side, unable to move backwards or forwards, the rising panic, the sudden clutching insanity at the certain knowledge of one of the worst deaths imaginable. 'Anyway,' he choked, 'it's so small it won't go anywhere.'

'Of course it goes somewhere.' Ruth's voice had a school teacher snap. 'There's a trapdoor on it, for God's sake! They wouldn't put a door on a tunnel that went nowhere.'

He couldn't argue with her logic, however much he wanted to, and it was a certainty that there was no refuge for them back in the tunnels. 'You better be bleedin' right,' he said.

'Just get on with it and stop whingeing.'

'Oi, can't you control that tongue even at death's door?'

'Shut up.' She gave his calf a gentle punch; despite her words there was something reassuring and supportive in her manner. Veitch recognised a growing bond, or thought he did, and that was enough to drive him on.

With an effort, he dragged himself forward, shifting the muscles in his back and shoulders until they ached. There wasn't even the faintest glow of ambient light ahead of them, which made him wonder how far the tunnel actually went. And the more they progressed, the more he became aware of the tiny space embedded in the rock, the size of a coffin, barely enough air to breathe. His chest began to burn; he was working himself up to a panic attack.

'How ya doin'?' he called out to deflect his mind. But all that came back was a gasp of assent that suggested Ruth was having as hard a time as he was.

Don't panic, he told himself. *There's no way you can back out of this place in a hurry. You'll go fucking mad if you lose it.*

And just when he thought he couldn't bear it any more, it got worse. It was the width of the tunnel that had been causing him the most problems, but at least he had been able to crawl on his hands and knees. Now the ceiling was getting lower. He tried to tell himself it was just a by-product of the panic he was holding in stasis, but soon it was impossible to crawl, and it seemed to be getting tighter and tighter.

He sucked in a deep breath, then another, then another, trying to calm himself enough to speak; he couldn't let Ruth see how weak he was. 'Bit of a problem here.'

'What?' The word was barely a gasp.

'The roof's coming down. I think it just comes together, a dead end. We're going to have to back up.'

'That doesn't make any sense!'

He heard tears in her voice; she was running on empty and a failure at this point would destroy her. He couldn't bear to hear that sound again. 'Look, I'll give it a bit longer, right? It's not closed up all together.' The words felt like pebbles in his throat.

Slowly, on shaking arms, he lowered himself down until he was slithering like a snake. There was a brief moment of relief at the few spare inches above his head, until the ceiling came down so sharply there was only a gap of about seven inches. If he turned his head on its side he could just about keep going. His panic was on the verge of raging out of control; a band of steel was crushing his chest so tightly he was sure he was having a heart attack. He knew if he allowed himself to speak it would turn into a scream, and then he would be scrabbling at the rock until his fingers bled, and kicking and yelling, and then the last bit of thin air that seemed to be in the tunnel would finally go and he would be left choking and dying.

He felt Ruth's hand on the back of his leg, so supportive he almost cried. 'You can do it.' It was as if she could read his thoughts. There was such belief in her words it snapped him out of the panic. Focusing his mind, he pressed his cheek firmly against the floor and pushed with his toes. He moved forward an inch or two. He tried again, but this time the going was more painful. And then, suddenly, he was wedged. He tried to wrench his head back, but the rough rock of the ceiling only dug into his flesh like the barbs of a harpoon. He couldn't go back.

In the flash of terror he was immobilised.

'Stay calm,' Ruth whispered behind him. 'You can do it.'

Couldn't she see? He started to writhe as he fought for some way to free himself, but any movement backwards only made the situation worse. There was no air at all; however much he sucked in, it felt like only a thin rasp reached his lungs. The rock pressed down on him, crushing harder and harder. Sparks of light started to flash in front of his eyes. He was blacking out; dying.

He didn't know if it was a spasm or some last rational thought crashing through the chaos, but suddenly he gave one final push forward with his toes. It drove him an inch or so. Through the haze he discovered he could move his head a little. He pushed again, and after a tough moment when he thought his shoulders were going to jam, he slipped forward even further. He could barely believe it; the ceiling had started to rise again.

'It's all right!' he yelled with barely concealed relief. 'It's getting higher again!'

Scrambling forward, he was soon back on his hands and knees, and although he couldn't turn to help Ruth through, he gave her enough verbal encouragement to bring her past the scariest part.

The blast of cold air was stronger there, and a faint light glowed. 'Why's it so cold?' Ruth asked.

'Trust me on this – it's winter up top, summer everywhere else. The whole world's gone crazy. Situation normal.'

Veitch moved forward as fast as he could until the tunnel came to a sudden end. He smelled the clear, cold night air, heard distant sounds. 'We're through,' he said.

'Where are we?' Ruth whispered.

Cautiously, he leaned out of the tunnel. It opened into some tubular, stone structure. There was a drop beneath them into what appeared to be water; he could see the black surface reflecting light from above. Twisting, he looked up into a circle that framed the drifting, white haar, lit by the castle's lights.

'It's a well,' he said, retreating back into the tunnel. 'Least, I think it is.

Right, there are two wells at the castle. One's too small, more like a cistern really. So this must be the other.' After the strain of the tunnel crawl, it took a second or two for the details to surface. 'The Fore Well. The main water supply a few hundred years ago, but it's out of use now so there shouldn't be too much water in the bottom. Just in case we slip, like. Now if only we can climb out of the bastard—'

'How do you know all this?'

'Did my research, didn't I? I wasn't going to come waltzing into this place without knowing what I'm doing.'

'I'm impressed.'

He shrugged, but inside he was enjoying her praise. 'It opens out on the Upper Ward. When I was up there a while back there weren't any guards in that area, so we could be on to a winner. If we can get past the cover.'

'Cover?'

'There's a grille fastened on top to stop all the tourists falling in—'

'Oh, shit,' she said, dismal again.

'Hang on, don't start getting negative already. We've come this bleedin' far. Just give me a chance, all right?'

Without waiting for an answer, he dropped in to the water. The icy shock almost made him call out. He was saved only by the fact that he had misjudged the depth. He plunged down beneath the surface and had to kick back up, spluttering and shaking from the cold.

'Are you okay?' Ruth asked worriedly. Her pale face was framed in the dark of the tunnel opening.

'Yeah, but it's like fucking ice.' He blew the water out of his nose, treading hard to prevent the weight of the sword and the crossbow pulling him down.

'You need to get out quick before you get hypothermia.'

'Thanks for the advice.' He dug his numb fingers into the grooves between the stones, braced his back against one side of the well and set his feet against the other. Then, with a tremendous effort, he began to edge himself up. Twice he fell back into the freezing water with a loud splash and a foul curse, but no one came to investigate. The newly discovered steel inside him pulled him through and finally he had made his way to the top. Gripping the grille with his left hand to give him some support, he slid the sword under the area next to the fastening and heaved. It was hard to get leverage from his precarious position and he was afraid that either the sword would snap or the lock would hold fast, but after a moment or two he heard the sound of protesting metal. A second later he was heaving the grille off the well-head and climbing out into the freezing night.

He didn't bother to rest from his exertions. Checking there were no guards in the vicinity, he rushed over to the Great Hall where he remembered seeing some netting in the armoury display. The corpse of the Fomor guard had still not been discovered.

Back at the Fore Well, he lowered the netting so Ruth could tie it round her. Then, bracing himself, he hauled her to the surface. Weakly, she rested against the battlements, looking round anxiously.

'Are you sure it's safe?'

'Not for long.'

She brushed a frail hand across her eyes. Veitch winced when he saw the space where her finger should be. 'Thank God,' she said. 'I thought I was going to die in there. I thought I was going mad. How I didn't panic, I don't know.' She gulped in a mouthful of air. 'I'm babbling now.'

He slipped an arm round her shoulder; she didn't flinch. 'It's okay,' he said.

Her eyes sparkled when she looked up at him; was that a connection he saw? He felt warmth rise up into his cheeks. 'You were great,' she said. 'You were like a rock. I wouldn't have got through it without you.'

The irony made him wince, but he couldn't break the illusion. For the first time she thought he was somebody who was worth something, who was capable, decent. But the conflict made him feel like a cheat. Even when he was getting what he wanted, his guilt and self-loathing got in the way. 'We've still got a way to go yet. That was the easy bit,' he said flippantly.

Before she could answer, her attention was distracted by something in the sky towards the bottom of the Royal Mile. The haar had started to drift away from that area and the black, star-sprinkled sky was clear.

'What is it?' Veitch asked.

'I don't know. I thought I saw something.' She scanned the sky uneasily. 'There it is again!' she said, pointing. The heavens were fleetingly lit by a strange, blue glow. In it, dark shapes seemed to be moving. 'What do you think?'

'I don't know.' Veitch had a sudden *frisson* which he couldn't explain. 'But I reckon we need to get to the rendezvous site pronto.'

The air was rushing so fast it ripped the breath from Church's mouth; his stomach flipped and twisted. The initial shock and terror was wiped away in a second by the helter-skelter sensations and the adrenalin that surged through him; the whole world seemed to be moving so fast he didn't have a chance to think. Beneath him, above him, all around him was darkness so intense he could have been plunging through space. Some hidden, rational part of him was scanning the shadows for any sign that could prepare him for the terrible moment of impact and it was that which caught the faint glimmer of blue light far, far away in the acheronian tunnel. It resembled a slight rip in black silk and it was growing wider, as if the fabric were rending.

The sight mesmerised him, driving out all other sensations, and his mind suddenly began to churn out notions to fill the vaccuum. *It's the blue fire,* he thought. *Is that the bottom?*

But it didn't look like the bottom; the well appeared to carry on past the growing speck of light. It grew wider still, the rate of tear increasing rapidly. *The locket did it!* he realised.

And at that moment the blue fire suddenly burst through. It was like a geyser rushing up towards him. He had only a split second to marvel at the wonder of it and then he was hit full-force by the eruption of splendour. It knocked all sense from him for a while, and when he finally came round he was hurtling back up the well even faster than he had dropped down; the velocity tore at the muscles of his face, pulled his lips back from his teeth, stole even more of his breath until he thought he was going to black out again. The coruscating energy licked all around him, yet astonishingly it hadn't burned him as he had feared in the instant before it had hit him. Instead he experienced an almost transcendental sense of wellbeing; it felt cool and like honey at the same time.

He couldn't tell if he was hallucinating from the wild sensations, but there seemed to be things moving in the fire all around him, large, dark shapes that twisted and turned sinuously. He almost felt he could hear their alien thoughts whispering in his head, accompanied by an overwhelming sense of freedom and jubilation.

He caught the briefest glimpse of Tom's dazzled face as the energy exploded out of the well and then it rocketed up and curled around the roof, the waves protecting him. He tried to suck in some air, but all he could get were a few gasps. And then he was hurtling along the tunnel, through the cavern, which seemed smaller when lit with the burning blue light, up to where the Fabulous Beast was sleeping. Only it wasn't asleep any longer. Fleetingly he saw its blazing eyes, its mouth roaring, spitting fire, in a tremendous display of exultation, and then it unfolded its wings just as it was caught in the flood.

And then he did black out. When he came to he had the briefest sensation of flying through cold night air and landing in a bone-jarring impact on the mist-damp grass, the wind smashed from his lungs. Finally he sucked in a lungful of air, his head swimming as he stared up at the vast, sparkling arc of the sky, waiting for his thoughts to catch up with the rush of sensation.

When he could, he rolled over and jumped to his feet. Tom was lying in a tangled heap nearby. Church ran over, worried, but the old man stirred and shook himself, muttering some curse under his breath. Smoke was rising from their skin, as if they had been singed by the fire, but they felt no pain. The disorientation was still swamping Church's head as he looked around and recognised they were once more at the foot of Arthur's Seat near the spring.

Tom pulled himself to his feet and instantly grew still. 'Look,' he said in a voice filled with awe.

Church followed his glance. At first he didn't see it, but when the peculiar perception came on him it was unmissable. Streams of blue fire were running from Arthur's Seat into the Old Town, where they were growing stronger, until they became a burning river heading towards the castle. And all along, tributaries were breaking off, flowing into Edinburgh, out across the country into the dark distance: a magnificent tapestry of blue fire. The land was coming alive.

And overhead, swooping and diving in the currents that followed the energy lines, was the Fabulous Beast. It let forth an enormous blast of fire which showered down among the buildings and in the red glare Church saw it was not alone. Three other, smaller beasts twisted and turned in complex but unmistakably jubilant patterns. And they were all heading towards the castle.

the substance of things hoped for

The night was filled with awe and fire. The Fabulous Beasts rose up from Arthur's Seat like a bell tolling the passing of an age now out of time, subsumed with righteous wrath and primal fury. And all across the city people threw open their windows or pulled over their cars to watch the end of it all.

The first column of fire came from the oldest of the creatures, sizzling through the air like a missile strike. It hit the centre of the Palace of Holyroodhouse, which ended its long life in an explosion that was heard twenty miles away, ballooning debris as far away as the New Town; it spiralled down in flaming arcs like celebratory fireworks, crashing into the streets, demolishing cars and roofs. The fire itself was almost liquid as it cascaded through the ruins, swamping those who tried to flee.

And high overhead the beasts swooped and soared in a display of freedom, occasionally pausing to roar another blast at the corrupted zone beneath. Their intricate flight patterns almost looked like a form of communication as they slowly worked their way up the Royal Mile. Tron Church became a needle of flame. The City Chambers, which buried the spirits of Mary King's Close, rose up in a bonfire of past hatred. St Giles's Cathedral exploded in a shower of rock and slate and superheated stained-glass. And among them the smart shops and houses of the regal street dissolved in fire. The remnants of the haar burned off, to be replaced by a thick, black pall of smoke which glowed red and gold on the underside.

A few very privileged souls were astonished to see what appeared to be a river of blue fire surging up the Royal Mile to the castle, as if it were seeking out its destination with sentience; and where it passed, the shadows that had clung to the Old Town in recent times seemed to leap back in horror from the burning light.

All of it was converging on the castle with a rapidity that left onlookers breathless and disoriented.

At the foot of Arthur's Seat, Church and Tom watched the growing conflagration with an odd mixture of dismay and relief.

'It all depends on the others doing their job now,' Church said, coughing as the wind gusted charred, sooty air into his face. 'I hope Veitch got out.'

'If he did, he had God on his side. If he didn't, there's nothing we can do for him now. Nor for the girl.'

Church bit his lip, said nothing. Then he covered his mouth with his handkerchief and set off in the direction of the rendezvous point, praying silently that someone would be there to meet them.

Shavi and Laura were sitting morosely on South Bridge when the attack began, still trying to make head or tail of what had happened at Rosslyn. Laura was concerned at how badly Shavi had been affected by the experience, which lay heavily on the already deep scars of his encounter with his dead friend. Neither thing would go away easily; during their short walk she had seen him continually glance into empty doorways or down shadowed alleys, as if someone were standing there. But the moment Holyroodhouse exploded, all that was forgotten. They ran back through the deserted, snowy streets to see what was happening, only to be knocked flat on their backs by a blast of heated air as another house went up in flames.

'This is too dangerous,' Shavi said. 'We need to be away from here.'

'He did it!' Laura could barely hide the jubilation in her voice. 'I knew the old bastard would pull through!' She watched the Fabulous Beasts for a moment, tracing their flight path back to Arthur's Seat. 'Church-dude – a hero, not a zero.' She brushed hair away from her eyes, grinning broadly. 'At least one of us isn't a fuck-up.'

Her pleasure was sharply interrupted by a terrible sound of pain and anguish that left them both clutching their ears. 'What the fuck was that?' she said when it had died away. But Shavi was already slipping and sliding through the snow closer to the Royal Mile.

Laura caught up with him at the vantage point they had occupied before. The source of the sound was two Fabulous Beasts, circling, blasting the spot where Maponus and the Cailleach Bheur had been involved in their titanic struggle. At ground zero was an enormous smoking crater, so hot at the core the stone was turning to molten lava. To one side lay what Laura guessed was the Blue Hag, but her shape seemed to be shifting constantly, desperately trying to hold on to the appearance Laura knew. A blizzard whirled frantically around the tight core of her being where a blue light glowed brightly; the awful sound came off her intermittently, like an alarm threatening imminent meltdown.

Of Maponus she could see nothing at first. But then the smoke cleared to reveal a terrible sight: the beautiful god was also in semi-fluid form, but whether it was because of his own madness or the ferocious heat of the blasts, he had been transformed into a twisted, grotesque shape from which three faces and several limbs protruded obscenely. His mouths opened and closed noiselessly, the silent screaming even more disturbing than the Blue Hag's shriek. Laura wondered why his writhing was so constrained until she saw he was half-fused into the wall of a house.

'He has fallen!' Shavi said triumphantly.

But the words had barely left his lips when a smell like frying onions filled the air and the dim golden light that always suffused Maponus' skin began to grow slowly more intense. The god's skin began to melt from his bones, then the bones themselves, and the odd things that vaguely resembled organs, all of them dissolving into one pure white light. The shapeless radiance pulled itself into a tight orb as it released itself from the wall and then began to move away across the debris.

Another blast from one of the Fabulous Beasts blinded them with a shower of dust and choking smoke for a moment, and when it had cleared they saw the Bone Inspector loping more like a beast than a man across the rubble in pursuit of the diminishing white light.

'Do you realise what this means?' Shavi said, aghast. 'He cannot be destroyed. None of them can.' His face was drained of all blood.

Laura grabbed his arm and began to pull him away; the heat was so intense she could smell her hair singeing. 'There's nothing we can do now.' She had to shake him hard to stop his protests. 'Mister Freak is on his tail. He can carry the can for a while.'

'We have a responsibility—'

'That's all we do have! Later, before I hit you with a rock. You've gone all *Apocalypse Now* combat crazy, and if you start mumbling like Marlon I really will be forced to cause pain.'

Shavi fell silent, but his eyes remained troubled.

'This isn't over,' she continued. 'Think of it as a brief retreat, right?'

'It is not over,' he agreed firmly.

Veitch and Ruth had barely moved several yards along the ramparts before they had once again become transfixed by the Fabulous Beasts.

'Shit, they're blowing the whole place up!' Veitch wrapped his arms around himself to stop shivering; the water from the well freezing on his clothes and hair made him resemble a walking snowman.

Ruth watched carefully for a moment, then said, 'They're coming this way.'

Veitch grabbed her arm and dragged her to the Lang Stairs, and although they were lethal with ice and snow, he took them three at a time. At the bottom he paused briefly to scan the Middle Ward. The Fomorii patrol were rooted near the Cartshed, their waxy human faces turned to the approaching threat. Their statue-like appearance was emphasised by their lack of emotion, but in one second they began to change, the flesh and clothes falling away as horns and carapaces and bones began to emerge amidst a sudden cacophony of monkey-shrieks. Mid-transformation, they scattered like a disturbed ants' nest.

Their stomachs were turning, but Ruth and Veitch were already moving down to the Lower Ward before the change was complete.

'I'll never get used to that,' Ruth said queasily.

Veitch paused near the Gatehouse and Old Guardhouse. 'Maybe we can sneak—'

The words caught in his throat as the Fomor guard emerged from the doorway and barked, 'Arith Urkolim!' the moment he caught sight of Veitch. The Londoner tensed, torn between going for the crossbow or the sword, knowing either would be useless as the Fomor advanced relentlessly.

But before he could move, the glaring, reflected light from the snow suddenly darkened and a deep shadow fell over them. It was accompanied by what sounded like giant sails unfurling in a heavy gale.

Ruth dragged him back just as the oldest of the Fabulous Beasts swooped down in a blaze of glittering bronze and green scales. The Fomor and the Gatehouse were caught up in a furious firestorm that left Veitch and Ruth huddled in the snow, choking for breath as liquid fire and rubble rained down all around them. The crashing of mighty wings grew even more intense above them. Ruth rolled on to her back and peered through the billowing smoke. Four Fabulous Beasts were circling the castle.

'Let's move,' she choked.

They clambered to their feet, shielding their faces from the blazing ruins of the Gatehouse. 'We'll just have to put our heads down and run,' Veitch gasped.

The flames closed around them for a second, the heat searing their lungs, but then they were out in the bleak, snow-swept Esplanade, slipping and sliding down the slope towards Lawnmarket.

Behind them they heard the terrible sound of the Fomorii raising the

alarm. Ruth glanced back briefly and saw Calatin standing on the battlements of the Upper Ward, shrieking at the darkness that surged around
him, pointing in fury at the circling Beasts.

'I hope those monsters don't hurt the Beasts,' Ruth said.

Her fears were unfounded. A second later the purifying fire rained down
from the heavens. The entire castle was engulfed in an inferno of living
flame. Stone which had stood firm for centuries flowed like water or
exploded in the instant heat. The lights popped out and windows crashed
in.

Ruth and Veitch scrambled down the Royal Mile, trying to put distance
between them and what they knew was to come. Ruth guessed the Scots
Guards must have had an ammunition store in the castle, for a moment later
there was an explosion that felt like the city was being levelled. They were
knocked flat on their faces by the pressure wave, which also drove them
momentarily deaf. In a world of eerie silence, Ruth rolled over to see a
column of fire reaching up to the heavens where the castle had once stood. It
shimmered red and gold as the Fabulous Beasts did soundless rolls and
turns around it.

At the base there was an odd sight. The flames there were blue and they
reached deep into the core of the rock on which the castle had stood.

'It's over.' The tears of relief came with the words. She scrubbed them
away with the back of her hand, then turned to Veitch, smiling and crying at
the same time. 'It's over,' she repeated, even though she knew he couldn't
hear her.

The temperature rose dramatically within minutes as the summer rushed
back in to replace the fleeing winter. The near-instantaneous thaw sent
water gushing into the drains and pouring in torrents from the rooftops. As
their hearing returned, Veitch and Ruth were enveloped in the thunderous
sound of the castle and the Royal Mile burning, filling the air with choking
particles, obscuring the stars with thick, oily smoke.

They hurried down George IV Bridge as fast as they could, but in the
aftermath of their victory the adrenalin retreated rapidly and Ruth, in
particular, was overcome with a powerful exhaustion. Eventually she was
clinging on to Veitch as he almost carried her the last few yards into
Greyfriars Kirkyard.

The graveyard sprawled away from the overpowering presence of the
kirk, surrounded by high stone houses that made it a peaceful backwater
untouched by the city. Ancient trees clustered all around, their thick cover
blocking out the glare from the inferno. The choking fumes hadn't reached
it either. There was only the sweet scent of the rose garden that lay before

the main jumble of stones, mausoleums, obelisks and boxes that glowed eerily white, like bones, in the gloom.

None of the others had arrived, so Veitch and Ruth collapsed on to a stone box; he slid his arm around her and she rested her head on his shoulder.

After a second or two, he said, 'I know what you went through. Back at Dartmoor, when those bastards were dragging me through their torture mill . . .' He exhaled loudly. 'You did fine.'

'It doesn't feel fine. It was like, hanging on, you know?'

'You'll put it behind you soon.'

'Is that right?'

A pause. 'No.'

She retched and dipped her head between her knees.

'Are you okay?'

'No, I feel terrible.'

He laid her down on the box and put his jacket over her. Her skin was so pale it was almost the colour of the stone her cheek was touching. She huddled up into a foetal position and a second later she was asleep.

Veitch kept watch over her, his eyes flickering from the gentle rise and fall of her chest to the dark shadows that clustered all around. He wished the others would hurry up. Despite the destruction of the castle, he couldn't believe that was the end of it. With Ruth asleep, the kirkyard seemed too quiet and exposed; an attack could come from any direction. The rustling of the leaves and the shifting of the branches in the faint breeze made him think there was something moving around in the gloom. And the more he sat in silence, the more he thought he could hear faint noises on the other side of the kirkyard.

Another sound nearby warned him that it wasn't all in his mind. It could have been a squirrel or a cat, but over the last few weeks he had learned to expect the worse.

At first there was nothing. Then he glimpsed movement around the kirkyard, shapes flitting among the trees, appearing and disappearing behind the grave markers. He started to count, then gave up, although there was nothing to suggest they were Fomorii. But whatever was out there seemed to be moving closer. His grip grew tighter on his sword.

'Unclean.'

The word was just a rustle caught on the wind. He looked around suddenly in the direction it had come from, but the area was deserted.

'Who's there?' he called firmly.

No answer. The nerves along his spine were tingling; he had the uneasy sensation that he was being watched. More movement. He couldn't put it down to imagination; there was definitely someone out there.

'You better come out,' he said forcefully.

'What's going on?'

Veitch started at the voice. Church had just marched through the kirkyard gates, beaming broadly, Laura hanging on his arm, looking honestly happy for once. Behind them was Tom, as impossible to read as ever, and then Shavi, who seemed uncommonly downcast. 'Did you see it? Did you see what we did?' Church continued. 'All those screw-ups and bad luck and this time we got it right!'

Church suddenly noticed Ruth asleep under Veitch's coat and threw off Laura's arm to run to her side. Laura's expression changed to one of irritation before she managed to mask it.

'Is she okay?' Church gently touched her wrist where it poked out from beneath the coat.

'She's had a bad time.' Veitch kept one eye on the kirkyard; all the movement had ceased. 'The bastards really put her through it, but she's tough. She'll be okay.'

Church grinned. 'Then we're celebrating! Everything worked out fine. I don't believe it!'

'Unclean.'

This time the voice was clear and unmistakable. Church looked round, puzzled. 'What was that?'

'There's somebody out there.' Veitch pulled out the sword where it could be seen. 'I don't think it's the Bastards, but I don't have a good feeling about it.'

The others gathered around. 'I sense something—' Shavi began.

'Can't you see them?' Tom snapped. 'Amongst the trees?'

And then they could all see them: grey figures moving slowly, some of them raising their arms to the heavens as if they were in some kind of distress. They moved forward, silently at first, but as they drew closer faint whispers sprang up like echoes in their wake, growing louder until their voices were clear. They were protesting about something, frightened, outraged.

'What are they?' Church asked.

'The dead,' Tom said. 'The spirits of the kirkyard.'

'Eighty thousand of us.' The voice came from behind a mausoleum. Gradually a figure emerged, hollow-cheeked and staring, with eyes that made their blood run cold. He was as grey as the stone, wearing clothes which dated his time to the turn of the century. 'That's how many of us are buried here. Eighty thousand.'

The spirit of a woman rushed up to them, wailing so loudly they all flinched, but at the last minute she turned away and fled among the stones.

'What's wrong with them?' Laura's voice was hushed, frightened.

The spirits were in a semi-circle before them now, tearing at their ghostly hair, beating their breasts; their anguish was palpable.

'Leave now.' The man near the mausoleum was pointing at them accusingly. 'You are damned!'

'They are coming for you! They are not departed!' a woman shrieked, her hair as wild as snakes. 'They will not let you go!'

'Coming into this place, so unclean!' the man continued. 'Foul! Besmirched! And the Night Walkers will follow in your wake, hunting you. You will bring them here!'

'What's wrong?' Veitch yelled at them. 'We've actually done some bleedin' good for a change—'

He was cut off by more shrieking.

'Come on,' Church said, 'let's go.' He shook Ruth, who struggled to stand, barely able to keep her eyes open.

The spirits followed closely as the six of them started to back away to the kirkyard gates; the voices became more shrill and intense, wailing like sirens, enough to set teeth on edge.

'Unclean!' the man yelled so loudly Laura jumped back a step. 'You corrupt this sacred ground! Your black trail scars our home!'

The dead crowded in suddenly, and although they appeared insubstantial, their clawed fingers caught at the group's clothes, tore at their hair. Church and the others broke into a run, pursued by the shrieking spirits, which were dipping and rising across the kirkyard like reflected light on mist. It was as if the spirits were being tortured by unimaginable pain.

Only when the group was resting against the foot of the bridge outside the kirkyard gates did the sound subside; and even then the spirits could be glimpsed flitting around the kirk in a state of distress.

'That freaked me out,' Laura said. A flicker crossed her face and she glanced to Church, hoping perhaps that he would deny her thoughts. 'They were saying the Fomorii were going to hunt us down.'

But he seemed more concerned by something else. 'What made them act like that?' He looked to Tom for an answer.

'It doesn't matter about any of that,' Veitch said animatedly. 'We did it.'

They all turned to him.

'There was some ritual going on under the castle—'

'Ritual?' Church's eyes gleamed.

232

Veitch nodded, smiling tightly. 'Something big. I reckon it was *the* big one. And we stopped the Bastards doing it.'

A ripple of relief ran through the group; they could hardly believe it. Church turned to Tom, questioning silently.

'You saw the place.' He was almost smiling. 'All that's there now is a big crater.'

'We stopped them,' Church said quietly, as if the words would break the spell. After all the weeks of failure, disbelief hung at the back of his voice. But it was true. 'We burned out the nest. They won't be able to bring Balor back.' He dropped to his haunches, one hand over his face while he assimilated the words. The moment hung in the air, and then Laura draped a tentative hand on to his shoulder. It was as if that was the signal; suddenly they were hugging each other, slapping backs, laughing and gabbling inanely as the tension rushed out of them. Veitch let out an ear-piercing yell of triumph that bounced among the buildings.

'But those spooks—' Church hugged Laura off her feet and crushed the rest of the sentence inside her. She tried to look aloof, but she couldn't keep the smile in.

'The Fomorii are still here,' he explained. 'You saw the nest in the Lake District – they're all over the damn place. We've just stopped them getting the upper hand, that's all. That's all!' He let out a whoop. 'We've kicked them so hard it's going to take them a while to get back on their feet! Now *we*'ve got the upper hand! All we've got to do now is find a way to get the Tuatha Dé Danann on our side and kick the Bastards out for good.'

'Oh well, it's almost over then,' Laura said with a smile that dripped irony.

'Ah, shaddup, you miserable git.' He kissed her and that surprised both of them.

'We owe ourselves a bleedin' big piss-up,' Veitch said, his arm tight around Ruth's shoulders. She was smiling wanly, still scarcely able to believe what she was hearing.

But they all agreed Veitch was right. Swept up in their jubilation and relief, they turned towards the south and began to move out of the city.

They had travelled barely a quarter of a mile when it became apparent they wouldn't get far on foot. Church and Veitch had been supporting Ruth, but with each step they were doing more dragging than carrying.

They eventually halted on a corner while Veitch and Laura disappeared down a side street. Forty-five minutes later they pulled up in a pristine Transit.

'Who'd you kill for that?' Ruth croaked.

'God, even half-dead she's Mother Superior.' Laura raised her eyes in an exaggerated response.

They loaded Ruth in the back and made her as comfortable as possible, then Church joined Laura and Veitch in the front. 'Just like old times,' she said, without a hint of sarcasm.

Beyond the reach of the Old Town, the streets gave way to well-heeled neighbourhoods where the houses were rambling and set well back from the road, and beyond that were the plain, structured streets of suburbia. By two-fifteen a.m., they were crossing the ring road, enjoying the balminess of a warm summer night after the chill environment of the Cailleach Bheur.

Unlike most English cities, the built-up area ended abruptly and they were plunged immediately into rolling green fields punctuated by peaceful woods. The tyres sang on dry roads through tiny villages. Away to the east, the remnants of the haar still clouded the horizon, but overhead the skies were clear and iced with stars.

At the sign for Roslin Village, Laura glanced over her shoulder to see Shavi's chin droop on to his chest. He was normally so bright and optimistic, it pained her to see the dismay etched into his features. More than anything, she wanted to clamber over the seat and give him a hug, but there was no way she could in front of the others.

After a long journey through thick woods, they entered a desolate valley plain where sheep wandered morosely over the clipped, yellow grass. In the distance the hills rose up steeply while, nearer to hand, train lines cut a swathe through the heart of the valley. At 4 a.m. they broke off to make camp for the night. Veitch and Church had been determined to keep going until dawn, but the decision was made for them by another technology failure which left the van drifting aimlessly on to the verge. They pushed it for a little way until they found a lane which led behind a small copse of trees where they could hide; even after their success, paranoia still hissed in the background. They'd abandoned all their clothes, camping equipment and provisions at the hotel, so they made themselves as comfortable as they could in the confines of the van. Tom was particularly concerned about Ruth, but she appeared to be sleeping easily enough. After their exertions, they drifted off within an instant of resting.

By the time they rose the sun was high in a clear blue sky and the interior of the van was beginning to bake. Although still weak and exhausted, Ruth was much brighter. They helped her outside where she propped herself up against a wheel and before too long she was exchanging banter with Shavi and Church and baiting Laura and Veitch. On the surface it was like old times, but something had changed; where there had been malice, now there was affection, however well-hidden.

They were eager to exchange details of their experiences. Veitch was reticent in his description of his assault on the castle, and when Ruth emphasised the extent of his bravery his ears turned red. They all did their best to boost Shavi, but his account of Maponus and the thought that he was still at large cast a chill over them all.

Tom listened carefully, then said, 'He is beyond our remit now. If anyone can find a way to restrain him, then it would be the Bone Inspector. He has knowledge denied to you and I, and it was his people who imprisoned Maponus initially.' He paused. 'But he is just one man.'

'But Maponus cannot be killed – we saw,' Shavi stressed. 'None of the gods can.'

'No,' Tom agreed, 'not in the way you mean. Although the lowest of the Fomorii, the troops, if you will, *can* be eradicated, as Ryan found out at the castle.'

'How can we be guerrillas if we can't hurt the ones that really matter?' Laura protested. 'We're just an irritation—'

'Situation normal for you, then,' Veitch muttered.

'We've done what we can,' Laura continued, 'done a good job. Can't we leave it up to somebody else, now? We've earned a rest, haven't we?'

Nobody seemed comfortable debating this line and the conversation drifted on to Church and Tom's encounter beneath Arthur's Seat.

'It was the weirdest experience,' Church said. 'The way reality, time, space, everything, seemed to be fluid in proximity to such a powerful source of the blue fire.'

'Maybe that's how reality really is,' Ruth mused. 'God knows, we've had enough proof we can't trust our senses to perceive anything correctly. When you think about it, it's scary. We're prisoners in our heads, completely at the mercy of our brain functions, and beyond that little bit of bone, the universe might be completely different to how we imagine it.'

'There is a line of scientific thought, currently growing in popularity,' Shavi mused, 'that suggests time does not exist. We perceive it as flowing constantly because that is the way our brains have been structured to understand it. But we are really living in all times at once. That would explain precognition—'

'But how does it work?' Ruth said.

'I wish you lot would shut up – you're making my head hurt,' Veitch said irritably. 'Talk, talk, talk, like a bunch of bleedin' students. Things are how they are, that's all. We've got more important things to think about.'

A hawk hunted for prey over an area of scrubby undergrowth in the middle distance. The image triggered a succession of disturbing thoughts in Church.

'Tom and I weren't alone beneath the Seat,' he said.

'Yeah, the old git took along the chip on his shoulder,' Laura said tartly.

'The one who took Ruth was there.' Church flashed a glance at Ruth, not quite knowing how she was going to react.

Veitch bristled. 'What did he look like?'

Church exhaled through the gap in his teeth. 'You know what he looked like. A bloody big wolf, just like Laura said. With yellow eyes and everything.'

'You should never have left the path, little girl,' Laura said to Ruth with a faint smile. From the corner of his eye, Church caught Veitch watching the two of them intently, coldly.

Church nodded to Tom. 'You tell them what you told me.'

Tom took off his spectacles and cleaned them on his shirt. Without the glasses he looked less like the sixties burn-out case and more like the erudite, thoughtful aristocrat he was. 'When the old gods have . . .' There was a long, jarring pause while he searched for the right word. '. . . *adjusted* someone, it is often difficult for the mind to fully fix their shape. It's as if something fundamental has been altered on a molecular level, something so in opposition to nature it seems to set up interference patterns for the senses. The first few times you see something like this, unless you're prepared, it's like a punch in the stomach. To make sense of it, the mind gives it a shape which is closest to the essence of its being—'

'So it's a wolf at heart?' Ruth asked. There seemed to be a stone pressing at the back of her throat.

'Is this the origin of werewolves?' Shavi interjected.

Tom shook his head. 'The *Lupinari* are different. This creature was mortal once. And the ones who have been altered sometimes seem so enamoured of this inner self, they grow into it. Physically.'

'I've met a few guys like that,' Laura said. 'They don't need a full moon. Just seven pints.'

'You don't remember anything?' Church asked Ruth.

She shook her head. 'Just Laura—'

'Laura?' Veitch's voice was a whipcrack.

'Laura was around somewhere. That's all I remember.'

They sat in silence for a few moments, weighing the evidence. And then, once they had exhausted all possibilities, they were forced to turn to Ruth again, although none of them wanted to hear what she had to say.

'How was it in there?' Church asked tenderly.

She smiled weakly. 'Oh, you know . . . You can guess.'

He nodded. 'Do you want to talk about it?'

She shook her head. 'I just want to get back on my feet.'

'I might be able to help there.' Tom gave her a faint smile, but it was warm and honest, a rare sight. He headed off into the countryside. They watched him for a while, dipping down occasionally to pluck something from the ground.

'Hmmm, grass and weeds. You're in for a treat,' Laura said. 'What is it with the old git? He knows all about these herbs and shit like he's some old witch.' Ruth flinched, but no one noticed.

'He's had a long time to learn.' Church continued to watch Tom. Their relationship had always been abrasive, but he had respect for the Rhymer's wisdom.

'He learned it from the Culture, the people of the Bone Inspector,' Shavi said. 'It is age-old knowledge, from the time when people were close to the land.'

'We need to sort out the way forward.' Veitch cut through the small-talk sharply.

'What's to sort out? I'm so hungry I could eat you.' Laura let the double-entendre hang in the air teasingly, her sunglasses obscuring her true meaning. 'Calm down, big boy. That wasn't meant in a nice way.'

'Laura is right,' Shavi said. 'Hot food first, then provisions, camping equipment, clothes. We need to replace everything we left at the hotel.'

'Yeah, because that city is not going to look very pretty after the air-raid,' Veitch said sharply. 'We need to find a place to lie low while we work out what we're going to do. Somewhere the Bastards can't find us.'

Church nodded in agreement. 'We should head south.'

'Yeah, I'm sick of heather and tartan,' Veitch said. 'And all the bleedin' Jocks hate us anyway.'

Tom returned half an hour later with two handfuls of vegetation while Ruth was vainly searching the sky for her owl. He used the wheel brace in the van to pound them into two piles of pulp. One he applied as a poultice to Ruth's finger, the other he made her eat, despite her protests.

'Stop whining,' Laura said. 'As soon as you get past the gag reflex it'll be fine.'

Eventually she ate it, and she did retch noisily for a while, but nothing came back up. They helped her back into the van and she fell asleep as soon as they set off.

The journey was not easy going. They stopped at a roadside café for a large meal that doubled as breakfast and lunch, before they were hit by two technology failures, lasting two hours and forty-five minutes respectively. In Peebles they used their credit cards to stock up on everything they needed, but the shop assistants were wary of taking the plastic; with the failure of the phone system it was impossible to check their validity, and everyone seemed to suspect the whole system was collapsing anyway. To recognise that fact was a blow too far so the cards were swiped in the old-fashioned way, with an unspoken prayer that everything would sort itself out soon. But it was obvious to Church and the others that the balloon was on the point of going up.

As they passed through Melrose, Tom waxed lyrical about his home area until Laura yawned so loudly and repeatedly it brought him to cursing. Jedburgh passed in a blur and they crossed the border in late afternoon.

There was a heated debate about which route to pursue after that, but everyone bowed to Veitch's strategic decison to head into the wide open spaces of high hills and bleak moorland that comprised the Northumberland National Park. They swept from the rolling fields of the Scottish Lowlands into a majestic landscape of purples, browns and greens, brooding beneath a perfect blue sky. It was a place of rock and scrub, wind-torn trees standing lonely on the horizon, and a howling gale that rushed from the high places as if it had a life of its own.

The hardiness gave way to the pleasant shade of the Border Forest Park, where the play of light and dark through the leaf cover on to the windscreen made them all feel less hunted. There was a deep peace among the thick woods that was a pleasure after the omnipresent threat of Edinburgh.

While Shavi drove, Veitch took charge of the map book. He made them follow a circuitous route through the quiet villages that must have added fifty miles to their journey, but he insisted if there was any pursuit it would make their destination less apparent. Laura noted tartly that he'd already baffled the rest of them about where they were going.

They eventually came to a halt at an abandoned railway station at High Staward, eight miles south-west of Hexham. They loaded all their possessions into four rucksacks which Church, Veitch, Tom and Shavi shouldered with much protesting. Laura taunted their lack of manliness, and even Ruth tossed out a few quips, and eventually they were marching along a footpath northwards through the deserted countryside.

Veitch had selected the location after careful study of the maps, and they all had to agree it was so off the beaten track it was as good a hiding place as any. They plunged down into thick woodland where the dark lay heavy and cool and the only sound was the eerie soughing of the wind, like distant voices urging them to stray from the path. A mile later they emerged to a breathtaking sight: the Allen Gorge. Four miles long, its precipitously steep sides soared up two hundred and fifty feet, covered with so many trees it looked like an Alpine landscape. Secluded pathways wound along the riverside and away into the trees.

'We could hide here for weeks if we wanted.' Veitch's voice held a note of pride that the reality matched up to his expectations.

They followed a path into the area with the thickest tree cover and then ploughed off into the wild. They finally halted when they couldn't see the path clearly any longer. The tents went up quickly in a circle, and at the heart of it Veitch dug a pit for a fire.

In the early evening sun, Church and Shavi went exploring. They found an outcropping rock in a clearing on the side of the gorge where they had majestic views over the entire area. They were both instantly struck by the immaculate beauty of the place.

'You know, if we lose all the technology, maybe it won't be so bad,' Church mused. 'We'll still have all this.'

Before Shavi could reply, the tranquillity was shattered by the roar of two jets burning through the sky in the direction of Newcastle. 'I bet they're not test flights,' Church said. 'Looks like trouble.'

Fifteen minutes later another one followed, but before it had crossed the arc of the sky, the technology chose that moment to fail once more. They saw the jet plummet from the sky like a boulder, hitting the ground with an explosion that made their ears ring despite their distance from ground zero. They stood in silence for a long time, watching the black pall of smoke merge with the clouds. Wrapped up in that incident was the failure of everything they knew; Church found himself questioning his earlier statement. They couldn't put it into any kind of perspective, and in the end, they didn't even try. They wandered back to the camp, thinking about the poor pilot, wondering what was happening in Newcastle, glad they were hidden in their perfect isolation.

Dinner was beans and bread, and sausages for all except Laura and Shavi. They ate around the campfire in the balmy summer evening atmosphere, enjoying the fading light as it filtered down through the canopy. The crack and pop of the fire was relaxing as the night drew in. It was the first time in weeks they had been able to eat peacefully without a very real fear of pursuit or some other pervasive threat hanging over their heads; they found it hard to adjust.

After the meal, they sat drinking coffee for a while, listening to the sounds of the owls coming alive in the trees and then they broke up for some time to be alone with their thoughts. They agreed to meet up later in the evening to celebrate with the good supply of beer and whisky they'd brought with them.

Church was the first back to the camp after a quiet stroll among the trees, where he had forced himself not to think about anything too troubling. Ruth was still resting where they had left her, staring into the flames. She looked up and smiled when he approached.

'How are you feeling?' he asked.

'Much better. My stump's stopped aching and I feel quite rested – my energy's coming back. Whatever Tom puts in those foul concoctions he makes up, he should sell it in bulk to the NHS.' She paused thoughtfully. 'If there still is an NHS. Apart from that I've just got a queasy feeling in the pit of my stomach, like I've eaten sour apples. That's the least I expected, to be honest. I could be up and about like normal in a couple of days.'

He dropped down next to her and slipped an arm around her shoulders. They had grown easy in their friendship since the night they had met under Albert Bridge, drawing comfort from the many similarities between them, enjoying the differences. They both felt that when the situation was at its worst, they could always turn to each other for support.

'I'm glad you're back,' Church said matter-of-factly.

Ruth dropped her head on to his shoulder, remembering a similar scenario on Skye, not so long ago, but a world away in experience. 'There was a time I thought I wasn't going to make it back. I thought they were going to torture me and torture me until I died just because I couldn't take it any more.'

'Ryan's right, Ruth. You came through it. You've shown what huge reserves you've got inside you. It may seem like a nightmare now, but in the long term, that's a good thing.'

One thing still troubled her, but she didn't see any point in telling Church; it seemed so minor after everything else. Since she had left her cell there had been no sign of her owl, or whatever creature it was that took that form. She was surprised at how distressed that made her feel. It wasn't just that it hadn't found her yet; she felt instinctively that some deep bond had been broken.

What could have happened to cause that? The education she had been receiving in her cell still sang in her mind, so powerfully had it been learned. She had been rapidly growing closer to the way the familiar had wanted her to be.

One thought did worry her: that there had been no familiar; it was all a hallucination caused by her suffering, and the owl that had followed her for the last few weeks was simply a bird and nothing more.

Church lounged back on his elbows. 'It feels good to know we've done something right for a change.' He glanced down at her hand and winced. 'Even though we paid a big price for it.'

'What are we going to do now? We can't call ourselves losers any more.' Ruth butted him gently with her head; their easy familiarity soothed her almost as much as Tom's herbal remedies. 'Don't tell me you've finally shaken that miserabilist streak.'

'What, and change the habits of a lifetime? It's just taking a few days off.' He laughed quietly. 'And I'm certainly not going to let anything ruin the celebration tonight. After all the shit we've waded through over the last few weeks, this is going to be the party to end all parties.'

Laura had found a boulder near to the river where she could sit and think. The sound of rushing water always calmed her. As a girl she'd dreamed of living near the coast and taken every opportunity to let her parents know how she felt. Her father had even agreed once, and they'd sat together looking at his *AA Book of the Road*, searching for the perfect home. If she remembered rightly, they'd decided on somewhere in South Devon. But that was before her mother had truly let God move her in mysterious ways – all the way from sanity to the other end of the scale. The failure to uproot, despite her father's promises, was just the first and most minor of a lifetime of disappointments. Since then there had been so many she'd become inured to them; any happiness was an aberration to be questioned.

She'd never really thought her cynical outlook actually brought about her disappointments, but if it was the case, it was too late to change. After she'd met Church, it had seemed her life's route had taken a sudden detour to the sunny side of the street and things really could work out as she hoped. But perhaps that had just been the desperation influencing her. She'd long ago learned wishing and hoping didn't make things real, and now it all seemed to be slipping back to the old ways. Church didn't love her, not the way she loved him. The others, she was sure, secretly hated her; she certainly hadn't done anything to make them think otherwise, however much she secretly admired them. She was always screwing up, dragging them into bad situations.

And now there was the thing with her blood. What was happening to her? It terrified her to the core of her being and she desperately wished there was someone she could talk to about it. But there wasn't, not even Church. Her thoughts and emotions had to stay locked up, same as they always had; it was the only true way to protect herself.

She would have expected a degree of bitterness, but now that she examined her state of mind she realised there was only a damp, grey acceptance. And wasn't that the most pathetic thing?

A vague movement among the trees caused her to turn suddenly. It was only Veitch, his face a curious mask that hinted at emotions but gave nothing away.

'I thought you were supposed to be the big warrior-strategist-whatever,' she sneered. 'You couldn't creep up on a deaf, blind person.'

'I wasn't creeping.'

Now she thought she did see emotions: anger, suspicion, hatred, although that was perhaps too strong. Suddenly, inexplicably, she felt frightened. 'Yeah, well, don't try coming a-wooing. I've already told you where I stand on that front.'

'I wouldn't dirty myself.'

'Ooh, bitchy. Well, you're not exactly the catch of the century, believe me.'

He grabbed her arm so roughly she let out a sharp squeal.

'What the fuck do you think you're doing?' She shook him off angrily.

His eyes blazed coldly and suddenly she was aware of the hardness of his body, the tendons like steel wire. She jumped off the rock and began to march back in the direction of the camp. He made another lunge at her, but she anticipated it and dodged beyond his fingers.

'Don't fucking walk away from me.'

'What's the matter? Can't get laid the normal way so you have to take it like some Neanderthal?' She fought to keep the tremor from her voice.

Her words, though, seemed to shock him. A puzzled expression crossed his features, as if he was struggling to understand her meaning. Then the anger returned harder than ever. 'I'd never do anything like that!' The words hissed between his teeth like steam from a fractured pipe. 'Is that what you think of me?'

'You're not exactly acting like Prince Charming.' She couldn't resist turning to face him, knowing she had a clear path to the camp if she needed to make a run for it.

'You've got a smart mouth.' He took a step forward, but he restrained himself from making another lunge for her.

'Come on then!' Suddenly it was impossible to control herself and all the pent-up rage, all the self-loathing and despair erupted. 'Give it to me! What's rubbing you up the wrong way?'

'You!' He jabbed a finger at her face. 'You wander around throwing out smart comments, acting so cool and aloof like you're better than everybody! But I've got you sussed! I know you had something to do with what happened to Ruth—'

She threw up her arms in amazement. 'You are so off the fucking mark you're on another planet!' She turned and set off through the trees, her head spinning from the rush of emotion.

The roar of breath expelled from Veitch's mouth was animalistic, the sound of someone who couldn't cope. And then she heard the crash of his feet on the ground as he set off after her. She didn't wait any longer. She put her head down and ran, glad she was wearing boots and jeans, weaving through the trees as fast as she could go. But it was too dark. She slammed against a tree, winded herself, smashed a shin against an outcropping rock. Behind she could hear the grunts and yells of Veitch's angry pursuit; he was moving swiftly, avoiding all obstacles like some night-hunting panther. He'd be on her in a minute.

The fear sluiced all the hot emotions from her in a cold wash. And what would he do when he caught her? Her heart hammered as she leapt a fallen tree, ducked beneath a low branch.

'Bitch!' The word was low and hard.

In her rising panic, her thoughts flatlined. She made a move to jump a hollow, twisted her ankle, and then she was falling off-balance. She hit the ground hard, saw stars, slid through the undergrowth that tore at her face and hair, and came to a halt against a pile of rocks. Pain flared through her side and involuntary tears sprang to her eyes.

Veitch was over her a second later, rising up dark and empowered like some monstrous creature from a forties horror movie. His fists were bunched, raised to hit her. 'I know you did Ruth somehow! Did it yourself, or fucking sold her down the river! You're the traitor they told us about! But I'm fucking on to you!'

Something seemed to explode in his face and then the fist was swinging. Laura cried out, closed her eyes, threw her head to one side.

When the blow didn't come, the chaotic jumble of her thoughts fell quickly into place and she looked up. Veitch was sitting down, his head in his hands and when he looked up a few seconds later, his eyes shone with tears. 'Fucking bitch! You've brought me to this!' His voice was a croak of repressed emotion. 'I'd never hurt a woman. Never!'

'You have a good way of showing—' For the first time she managed to bite off her comment. 'I didn't have anything to do with what happened to Ruth. And I'm not a traitor.' She tried to keep her voice measured.

'I don't believe you.' By the time he'd stood up and walked a few paces through the trees he'd composed himself. 'I don't believe you,' he repeated; the threat in his voice made her blood run cold. 'I've been watching you. I'll keep watching you. I'm not going to let the others get hurt. I'm going to make sure someone pays for Ruth. One sign, that's all I need. One sign. And you're dead.'

He disappeared into the gloom among the trees, silently, dangerously.

243

Once he was out of sight, Laura crumpled and all the tears she had held in for a lifetime came flooding out.

After she had managed to collect herself, the golden glow of the fire drew her back to the camp. But as the trees thinned towards the clearing her heart caught in her throat. There was Church, his arm around Ruth, her head on his shoulder. It wasn't jealousy she felt; she could see there was nothing furtive about their body language. Instead she was hit by the aching revelation that she could never attain the depth of Church and Ruth's relationship: the easy familiarity, the emotional honesty, the warmth were all apparent, even at a casual glance. And she could see there was love there, a kind she would have given anything to experience, so subtle Church and Ruth seemed oblivious to it themselves.

She couldn't blame Church. The fault was within herself. Something had been broken during those lean years of childhood and early teens; however much she tried, she couldn't give up her emotions honestly, and so she had consigned herself to a life of being shut in the prison of her body, feeling something keenly, hearing a corrupted version emerge from her lips; an emotional synaesthesia.

As she watched them, she hurt so profoundly she felt there was a physical pain deep inside; the hopelessness for herself was even more overwhelming than when she had realised she could never attain the loving family life of her school friends, so deep there was no point fighting it; acceptance was the only option.

She rubbed her face muscles, as if that would break up the desperate expression, fixed an ironic smile and stepped out from the shadows.

'Well, Siamese twins,' she said sharply. 'You should get on the waiting list for the operation.'

Within the hour they were all sitting around the heartily blazing campfire. The night was balmy, dreamlike, alive with the crackle of the burning wood, the calls of hunting owls, the flitter of moths and crane-flies. It felt like a time of peace, a time when anything could happen.

Church lounged on his side and threw twigs into the flames. Next to him was Ruth, who seemed to be getting brighter with each passing moment, except for the occasional queasy expression. Laura and Veitch sat on opposite sides of the fire, never making eye contact, yet acutely aware of an atmosphere of suspicion and threat hanging over them like a poisonous cloud. They both knew, whatever happened, they would never overcome it.

Tom sat cross-legged, rolling a joint, alone with his thoughts. Shavi was beside him, handing out the cans of beer when needed, ensuring the bottle of whisky never stayed in one place too long. When he had first returned to the camp, his face was grey and haggard, as if he was suffering from some debilitating illness, but Laura recognised the truth instantly. She knew in the dark woods he had encountered the thing that would never leave him alone, and she knew how deeply it had affected him, yet he never complained to any of the others about his private burden. She wished she had some of the inner strength that saw him through it. When the others weren't looking she gave his hand a secret squeeze; his smile made her night.

The drink flowed freely, the conversation ranged across a variety of subjects: archaeology, drugs, music, films, sex, football, but nothing dark or threatening; it was a celebration of all the things that made their lives worth living.

Shavi became animated when the talk drifted on to some of the places they had seen in their travels: the wonders of Stonehenge and Avebury, infused with history, meaning and mystery, the rugged beauty of Cornwall, the joys of little seaside towns, the majesty of the Lake District and the Scottish Highlands.

'There is nowhere in the world that is richer in natural beauty than Britain,' he said. 'Stories of the people live on in the shape of the hedgerows, in the cut of fields, in the landscape itself. The place is a living mythology, constantly changing with the weather. The fens in a storm, Oxfordshire in winter, London on a summer night. Mountains and marches, beaches and flood plains, rivers and gorges and chalk downs. Where else can you find all those in a short drive of each other?' He sighed, tracing his fingers along the soil. 'There is magic infused in the very fabric of the place.'

'The history adds to it for me,' Church noted. 'It's not just about the beauty of the landscape. It's the places where humanity and nature have interacted.'

'Exactly,' Shavi said passionately. 'Which is why an industrial landscape can be as exciting as a natural one. It all comes down to single images, frozen in time. Step back, look at them, and you can see the magic instantly. Power stations gushing white clouds at sunset. Wildfowl skimming the glassy surface of the Norfolk Broads. People trooping home from the tube after work on a cold winter night, smelling cooking food, hearing music and TV noise coming from a hundred windows. Tractors rolling down a snow-covered lane.' They drifted with his lyrical words, conjuring up the pictures he described. 'And that,' he said firmly, 'is what the blue fire represents.'

The conversation came to an abrupt halt when Veitch saw the light. It floated among the trees like a golden globe, slowly and silently, almost hypnotic in their drunkeness. But they had seen too much to accept any phenomenon at face value; threats lurked in even the most mundane sight. Veitch leapt to his feet instantly, his sword gripped firmly. Church and Shavi joined him a second later.

'What is it?' Ruth whispered, but Veitch waved her silent.

The globe bobbed and weaved directly towards them, and as it drew closer they realised it wasn't alone. They could hear a faint, melodious singing, and although they couldn't understand the words, the music made them feel like they were filled with honey. The sword gradually fell to Veitch's side. Only Tom remained alert.

A second later they spied the outline of two figures approaching through the shadows. The globe was a lantern one of them was holding to light the way. The singing grew louder as they neared, and it seemed like it was a song of joy with the world, of great experiences savoured, of drinking in all life had to offer.

Veitch's languor disappeared the moment the two arrivals stepped into the light from the campfire. They were both of the Tuatha Dé Danann, their skin faintly golden, their features breathtakingly beautiful. They were obviously of the caste closest to humans, for none of them felt the squirming alien thoughts in their heads or experienced the warping perception caused by the more powerful of the gods.

One of the visitors had long, flowing fair hair and a face which seemed to permanently beam. The other looked more sensitive and thoughtful; his hair was tied in a ponytail. They both wore loose-fitting blousons open to the waist, tight breeches and boots like movie buccaneers.

'What have we here? Fragile Creatures? Alone in the woods at night?' The smiling one turned his open face from one to the other and they all found themselves smiling in return. 'Do you not realise the seasons have changed? The dark is no longer a time for Fragile Creatures to walk abroad.'

'We are not as fragile as you think.' Tom stepped from behind Shavi to present himself to the visitors.

'True Thomas!' His smile grew broader, if that were possible. 'We have missed your rhymes in the Far Country. How have you fared, good Thomas?'

'As well as could be expected, Cormorel, under the circumstances.' Tom gestured to the others. 'You have heard of the Brothers and Sisters of Dragons?'

Cormorel looked surprised for an instant, but then the smile returned and he bowed his head, politely and formally. 'It is indeed a great honour to meet the blood-champions of the Fixed Lands. The fame of the Pendragon Spirit's vessels has extended even unto our home. Hail, Quincunx. The faithi have spoke proudly of the five who are one hero.'

Veitch surveyed the two new arrivals suspiciously, poised to move at the slightest sign of danger. Church was afraid Veitch's barely contained rage would force an unnecessary confrontation, until he realised his friend was surreptitiously watching Tom for his lead.

'This is my good friend and fellow traveller, Baccharus,' Cormorel continued. The other golden one's bow was more clipped than that of his colleague.

Church and the others introduced themselves hesitantly. Tom motioned to the campfire. 'Will you join us?'

'Gladly, True Thomas. It has been too long since we enjoyed the company of *people*.' Cormorel pronounced the last word as if it were alien to him.

Cormorel and Baccharus sat together next to the fire, seemingly revelling in the event. Church took a position next to them with Tom on the other side, while the others gathered around the rest of the fire with varying degrees of discomfort; only Shavi seemed truly at ease.

Church picked up his beer to take a sip, then noticed Cormorel's eyes following his hand. 'Would you like a drink?' Church said. 'Can you drink?'

'We can eat, drink, make merry in many ways.' Cormorel eyed Ruth and Laura slyly. 'Of course, we may not appreciate the sensations in quite the same way as you Fragile Creatures. But it is the experience we seek, the keys to existence.' Church opened two cans for him and Baccharus, which they took gratefully. They sniffed the drink, sipped at it cautiously, then nodded to each other. 'When we were last here there was something made of honey,' Cormorel noted thoughtfully. 'This is more to my palate.'

'What brings you here, Cormorel?' Tom asked.

'We are reacquainting ourselves with the Fixed Lands, True Thomas. It always held a special place in our hearts. We have been denied its pleasures for too long.'

Baccharus leaned forward and said quietly, 'Here, with your truncated existence, lives burn brightly. Experience is savoured. There is a potency which we find invigorating.'

'And you are all so much fun!' Cormorel added with a flourish.

'Glad we entertain you,' Veitch muttered coldly. If Cormorel and Baccharus noticed the offence in his voice, they didn't show it.

'We are revisiting the places we knew before the Sundering,' Baccharus said, 'but so much has changed. The air is filled with unpleasant particles. The water in the rivers is sour. Even the trees are in pain. I can hear the dryads whispering their distress as I pass. You have not fared well without us.'

'Things haven't gone well on a lot of fronts,' Church agreed. Baccharus' words touched a nerve with him that made him uncomfortable. Was humanity really better off when the gods ruled over them?

Cormorel suddenly noticed Ruth staring at him curiously. 'What is it?' he asked.

'We don't know anything about you,' she replied. 'The only ones of your kind we've met before weren't exactly easy to talk to.'

'And as you can see,' Cormorel said, raising his hands, 'we are not all cut from the same cloth.'

'Tell us about you, then. About your people. Where you come from, what excites you.' Church recognised the incisive gleam in her eye; she was using her lawyerly skills to extract information which might be of use to them later.

'You are trying to define us in your terms and we cannot be defined. We simply *are*. A part of the universe and outside the universe, outside of time and all reality. We move among the stars, slipping between moments. As great as the fabric of existence, as fluid as thought.' He winked at Tom. 'It is hard to know us, eh, True Thomas? However long you spend at our side.'

'But you seem comfortable with the way we perceive reality,' Ruth continued, undeterred. 'Try to express it in terms which make sense to us.'

Cormorel nodded thoughtfully. 'Then I will try to tell you of the glory and the wonder and the anguish and the pain. Of a race cut adrift from its home, condemned to wander existence for all time.' His voice took on a mournful quality which made their hearts ache; there was something in the way the Tuatha Dé Danann manipulated sound which had a dramatic effect on human emotions; Church wondered if this explained his confused feelings for Niamh. 'We have always been, the Golden Ones. There when the universe winked into life. And we will be there when it finally whispers out. Our storytellers spin vast accounts of our days when all was well with Creation and we resided in four cities of wonder. It is the arch-memory, the homeland, to which we all dream of returning. We have never found it in our wanderings.' His voice grew sadder still. 'And I for one would say we probably never will. But the Far Lands, with their ebb and flow, and, strangely, the Fixed Lands too, are the closest in our hearts. And so we move between one and the other, and we stay and go, and we yearn. And though we remember our home and see the connections, we are always an echo away. That is our curse. Never to be at peace. We exist in the great turn of the universe. Our lives are lived at the heart of everything. And so our joys are great, and our sorrows too.' He fixed a sad eye on Ruth. 'Can you understand what it is never to have the only thing that makes you whole? Without our home, we cannot understand our place in the scheme of things. We are bereft. That is our character.'

'That is everybody's character,' Shavi said.

Baccharus began to sing in their lyrical, alien tongue; there was so much sadness in every syllable they felt as if their chests were being crushed by despair. Their heads bowed as one, and in that song they finally felt the true pain of the Tuatha Dé Danann.

When the last note of Baccharus' magical singing finally faded away, there was a brief moment of ringing silence, and then Cormorel brightened instantly. 'Come. We have driven the sadness from our being for a time and now we are free to drink deep!' He raised his beer and emptied the can, letting forth an enormous belch. Church handed him another one, which he glugged eagerly.

'Now let me tell you of joy and wonder!' he continued. 'Would you like to hear how our greatest warriors crushed the Night Walkers beneath their heel at the second battle of Magh Tuireadh? Or perhaps a personal tale of my great wassailing? Or perhaps something of the Fragile Creatures who preceded you?' He gave a strange, weighted smile that none of them could quite understand. 'Not so fragile, some of them. For your breed at least. They did not accept us with kindness in the early days.'

'I heard they resisted you quite forcefully,' Tom noted.

Cormorel mused on this for a moment. 'They were slow to appreciate the true order of things. They were, I think, quite brutal in spirit. There was something of the Night Walkers about them.'

'A matter of perception, I would say,' Tom persisted.

Cormorel didn't seem offended by his tone. 'We crushed them in the end, you know.'

Tom nodded. 'Yet they still exert an influence. Knowledge encoded in the landscape for future generations to decipher. Information to be used to resist you.' Church and the others all looked at Tom, but he wouldn't meet their eyes. 'Their bravery is beyond question, but perhaps you have underestimated their intelligence. They were playing a very long game.' Tom let the words hang, but it was obvious he was not going to elucidate.

Cormorel maintained a curious expression for a moment, then shrugged as if it were nothing, but Church could tell Tom's comments were still playing in his mind.

'Tell me why some of you are almost like us and some are just . . . unknowable,' Ruth said.

Cormorel smiled condescendingly. 'None of us are truly like you.'

Baccharus held up his hand to silence his partner. 'No, that is a good question. Some of us are very like the Fragile Creatures, if only in our joys and sorrows. How many of our brethren would take pleasure in this, here, tonight, around this fire? Yet to me this is a moment of great pleasure, to be savoured and discussed at length once we are back in the Far Lands.' He smiled sweetly. 'We love our stories. They are the glue that holds the universe together.'

Tom bent forward to intrude in the conversation once again. 'There is a hierarchy among the Tuatha Dé Danann. They have a very complex society which is layered depending upon the power they wield. At the top is the First Family. At the bottom . . .' He motioned towards Cormorel and Baccharus.

Church flinched; it sounded distinctly like an insult. Cormorel seemed to feel the same way, for he eyed Tom askance as he sipped his beer.

'Do you hold no grudges, True Thomas, for the time you spent with us?' he asked pointedly.

'I have learned to be at peace with my situation.'

Cormorel nodded. 'That is not quite an answer to my question, but I will accept it nonetheless.' His smile grew tight. 'Did you know, True Thomas, your Queen has returned to her court under Tom-na-hurich, the Hill of Yews? Your white charger still resides there, as vital as the last day you saw him.' His eyes never left Tom's face.

Tom's face remained as emotionless as ever, but Church recognised a faint hardening. 'The point I was making,' he continued, turning to the others, 'is that power seems to come with the extent of time they have existed, and some of the Tuatha Dé Danann are much more powerful and alien than us. Although they say they have all existed since the dawn of time, it would appear that some are much older than the others. Dagda, the Allfather, was there at the beginning, and he has no connection to us at all. These two, I believe, came later.'

'Then perhaps there is an evolution, even among the gods,' Shavi mused.

Church was struck with a moment of clarity. 'And perhaps one day we will evolve to be like the Danann.'

Cormorel laughed faintly, patronisingly. 'And perhaps the arc of sky will rain diamonds.'

'It is unwise to be so arrogant, Cormorel,' Baccharus said. 'Though it is easy to accept our place in the universe, we of all races should know there is a cycle to everything. Powers rise and fall, influences ebb and flow. And the Fragile Creatures have shown their resilience in the face of the uncaring hand of existence. You see these here, you know the power they represent.'

Cormorel shrugged dismissively. 'You are a dreamer, Baccharus.'

In the brief lull that followed, Church saw his opportunity. 'How are you dealing with the Fomorii?'

Cormorel took the whisky and sipped it, smacking his lips. 'They leave us alone. We do not bother them,' he said as he passed the bottle on.

'They won't leave you alone for long. They were trying to bring Balor back. Now we've stopped them they'll just turn to something else. And you could be the target next time.'

'Oh, most certainly. And when they dare raise their hands against us, we shall strike them down.'

Church couldn't believe Cormorel's arrogance. 'Surely it would be better to attack first, before they can—'

'There are too many things to do, too many places to visit here in this world that has been denied us. We need to be making merry, drinking this fine . . .' He held up the can, then shook his head when he couldn't summon a word to describe it.

'They beat you once before. When they first emerged into this world.'

Cormorel's gaze lay on Church coldly. 'We did not fully realise the extent of their treachery. Now we are prepared.' He sighed, his annoyance dissipating quickly. 'However much I meet *people*, I find it hard to understand your inner workings. You have so little time and indulge in so little enjoyment. But you are entertaining, for all your foibles. We will continue to try to understand you.'

'Have you heard what the Fomorii are doing now?' Shavi asked.

Cormorel smiled and shook his head. 'They may burrow into the deep, dark earth and wrap themselves in shadows until the stars fall, for all I am concerned. The Night Walkers are a poisonous brood, given to plotting and hating, but they are wise and would not seek to challenge us unnecessarily. We can afford to leave them alone.' He peered at Church, his brow furrowed. 'Strangely, I see you have the taint of the Fomorii about you.'

Church explained how the Fomorii had infected him with the Kiss of Frost and how, although the *Roisin Dubh* had been destroyed, some of its dark power still lay within him.

Cormorel shook his head sadly. 'Very unwise, Brother of Dragons. You will not find any of the Golden Ones aiding you until you have expunged that taint.' He wrinkled his nose as if there were a bad smell.

'And how do I do that?' Church asked.

Cormorel shrugged. 'Perhaps if you travelled to the Western Isles, immersed yourself in the Pool of Wishes . . .' His voice trailed off; the question was obviously of no interest to him. 'Now,' he said animatedly, 'have we more drink? This is a celebration, not a conference!'

They drank deep into the night, with Cormorel and Baccharus taking it in turns to entertain with wild songs and great stories which carried with them the vast movement of the depths of the ocean or the shifting of tectonic plates. Church and the others were entranced with stories of the four lost cities of wonders, of the many, deep, mysterious mythologies which the Tuatha Dé Danann kept close to their heart, of puzzles and tricks, great battles and terrible failures, of passion and love, cruelty and hatred. The Tuatha Dé Danann, for all their alienness, were a race of powerful emotions and Church and the others could not help but be awed by the things they heard. Even Veitch gave in to a broad grin during one song, while Laura had to hide the tears that came to her eyes during another particularly sad lay. Only Tom remained impassive throughout.

And when the birdsong rose in earnest and the shadows receded at the first lick of dawn, Cormorel and Baccharus stood up and bowed, thanking the others profusely and politely for their hospitality.

'The next time you are in the Far Lands we will return the favour,' Cormorel said.

'I fear not,' Tom interjected.

Cormorel eyed him cunningly and nodded, but said nothing. And then the two of them turned and set off through the woods, their melodious singing eventually fading into the sounds of nature awakening.

'They were very charming,' Ruth said. 'The stories they told were wonderful. You could yearn for everything they've experienced, the sights they've seen. Otherworld could be such a magical place to live.'

Tom turned his back on them and headed towards the tents. 'Yes, and that is the greatest danger of all.'

chapter eleven

along darker roads

Their dreams were filled with spires of silver and gold, of giants who cupped spinning suns in their palms, of wonders so bright and startling they could not bring them back to the world of waking. When they did finally emerge from their tents, dry-mouthed and thick-headed, the day seemed more vital than even the blazing sun and clear blue sky promised. They bathed in the cool, rushing river, ate a lazy lunch of beans on toast and drank tea while gently reminding each other of the stories they had been told, like old friends remembering favoured times.

By one p.m., Veitch was starting to get anxious. He scanned the trees continuously, and while the others laughingly told him to unwind, he refused to rest. 'We've been here too long,' he said, packing his bag. Using belts and rope and a few other items they'd picked up in town the previous day, he made a makeshift harness to hold his sword and crossbow. His jacket hung over it awkwardly – he looked like a hunchback, Laura gibed from afar – but he could reach the weapons easily.

Eventually he'd dampened the mood enough that everyone reluctantly packed up and returned to the van. 'I *liked* it here,' Ruth said with irritation. 'There was some peace and quiet for a change. And lots of nature.'

'There'll be other places.' Veitch spoke without looking at her directly, but he'd been watching her all day, surreptitiously. Her health seemed to have improved immeasurably, thanks to Tom's potions. She'd still vomited among the trees on emerging from the tent, but she was sure that was the alcohol she'd downed. He felt good to see her so well, especially knowing he'd contributed to it. He still wished she'd look at him sometimes, talk to him in the close, confiding way she'd done when they first emerged from the castle. But there was time. And he actually felt like there was hope.

They picked up the A68 heading south. Traffic normally streamed along the route, but vehicles were sparse; fewer and fewer people seemed to be travelling any great distance from their homes. The landscape was green and rolling, with a fresh breeze blowing in from the coast. Yet despite the wind, Tyneside was obscured by unnaturally dark clouds which looked suspiciously like smoke.

Veitch had studied the maps intently before they set off, weighing strategies, discarding options. He eventually decided they should head to the Peak District, where they could find enough of a wilderness to lose themselves but would be close enough to several major conurbations if they needed the security of people.

With Shavi driving they sped past Consett, which was still reeling from the terrible deprivations of the eighties, and through the open countryside west of Durham. As they passed the branch road to Bishop Auckland the traffic began to back up.

'Probably an accident,' Church mumbled, leaning forward in his seat so he could peer over the roofs of the cars ahead. A few hundred yards away a blue light flashed relentlessly. The van crept forward a few feet. Shavi wound down the window; exhaust fumes and the stink of petrol wafted in. Above the sound of idling engines, voices carried. 'Is it an accident?' Church asked.

Shavi strained to hear, then shook his head. 'I cannot make out what they are saying.'

The van moved forward again, jerked to a halt as Shavi pulled on the handbrake. Church could see blue uniforms moving around; a few standing in a huddle. There didn't seem any sense of urgency.

'No ambulances. No fire engine.' He wound down his window and hung right out for a moment. 'Can't see any wreckage,' he called back.

Eventually the van had crept forward enough for him to get a clear view. He slammed into his seat, his face concerned. 'It's a police roadblock.'

'They're not going to be doing a traffic census with the country falling apart around them.' Ruth leaned over from the back to see. They were only a few cars away from the checkpoint now.

'I've got a bad feeling about this.' Church glanced in the side mirror. There was a solid queue of cars behind them.

'Why should it be anything to do with us?' Laura said. 'No one even knows we're coming this way.'

'For all we know, there could be blocks on every road south.' Church turned to Shavi. 'When they wave the next car through, don't pull up any further. We'll play it by ear.'

Everyone's attention was focused on two policemen with clipboards who were peering into the cars to check the passengers. Church watched them for a moment; a skittering at the back of his head told him his subconscious had glimpsed something else more important. Slowly he surveyed the scene. At first he saw nothing, but a second sweep picked out a subtle detail that sent ice water running down his spine.

Three policemen stood in a tight group away from the others, watching the proceedings carefully. There seemed nothing untoward about them at first glance until one became aware of the odd way the bright sunlight was striking their skin. It created an odd sheen on the flesh that made it appear like a wax mask.

'Fomorii!' Church hissed. Without drawing attention to himself he carefully indicated the bogus police. 'They've arranged this for us, like the trap they set at Heston services. They're using the report from the Callander cop as a pretence to pull us over.'

One of the policemen with the clipboards was marching towards them, irritated that they hadn't pulled the van forward. He started to gesticulate angrily, then paused as his gaze flickered across the faces framed in the windscreen. He glanced down briefly at his clipboard, then spoke hurriedly in the radio pinned to his breast pocket.

'Shit,' Church muttered.

Shavi didn't wait for instructions. He pounded his foot on the accelerator and thrust the van into gear. There was a screech of tyres and the stink of burning rubber as he threw the wheel to one side. The van squealed out of its starting position and hurtled forward. Church braced himself on the dashboard, but everyone in the back was thrown across the floor amidst yells and curses.

Bollards went flying in all directions as the van rattled from side to side. Church had a glimpse of the fake policemen's curiously dispassionate faces as the van whirled by. Voices rose up above the whine of the engine.

'Don't hang about, Shav. Put your foot down,' Laura called out sourly from a heap somewhere in the back.

They sped down the road at ninety, but the sirens which had risen up in the background were growing louder.

'We're not going to outrun them,' Veitch said, glancing over his shoulder.

'I know.' Shavi took one look in his side mirror, then threw the van across the opposite lane in the path of a lorry. Its horn blared. Church and Veitch both swore as they instinctively threw their heads down.

The van missed the lorry by a few inches, bounced over a kerb and careened down a B road leading into the heart of the fells. Shavi gunned the engine along the deserted road and didn't let up until they had put a few miles between them and the main road. A village called Eggleston flashed by and the road branched in several directions. Shavi chose the southern route; the police would have to be lucky to follow them immediately. By then the others had just about recovered from the chase.

'You mad fucking bastard!' Veitch looked angry, but there was a note of respect in his voice.

The others in the back were fine, if bruised, but they were all aware their predicament had taken a turn for the worst.

'We're going to have to abandon the van,' Veitch said. 'After that stunt they're going to be looking out for it on every road.'

Laura peered through the rear windows at the landscape, a windswept smudge of greens and browns, patches of firs, areas of dark scrub beyond the fields that lined the road, leading up to the high country in the north. 'Great. We're back in *Deliverance* country. Where are we going to find another van round here?'

'We aren't.' Veitch motioned for Shavi to pull up a rough side lane which led behind a thick copse. 'We're going to keep well off the roads. All roads.' Aghast, Laura dreaded what was coming. 'We've got plenty of supplies, tents, we can live rough. If we lose ourselves out there, with all the shit that's going down they're not going to have the time or equipment to find us.'

Church nodded thoughtfully. 'It's a good plan.'

'It's *a* plan,' Laura said in disgust. 'So's lying in the middle of the road until something runs us over! Listen, I'm not a camping kind of girl. What we've done so far, fine. At least there was, you know, civilisation nearby.' She looked back out the windows. 'All I can see are blisters, no bathrooms, cold wind and rain.'

'You'll live,' Veitch said dismissively. He grabbed the books of maps. 'We'll have to use this to navigate. The way I see it, we can pick a good route south from here to the Pennines. They'd have to really want us to come after us.'

'They really want us,' Church said.

They removed all their rucksacks, tents and provisions, shared them out, then drove the van as deep into the copse as it would go. The leaf cover was thick enough to ensure it would take a while for it to be discovered. Sirens wailed across the open landscape as they moved hurriedly south away from the road. They crested a ridge where the wind gusted mercilessly, and then they were in open countryside.

The going was slow. Although Ruth was much recovered, she flagged easily and had to take many long rests, even over the first five miles. The A66, the main east-west route across the north country, appeared in the late afternoon. They waited in the thick vegetation by the roadside for nearly ten minutes until they were sure there was no traffic nearby, and then scurried across, ploughing straight into the fields beyond.

According to the map there were only four villages between them and the next main road ten miles away. The rest of the area was eerily deserted: just fields and trees and the occasional scattered farm. Although they needed to be away from the main thoroughfares, the isolation unnerved them. They knew the old gods were not the only things that had returned with the change that had come over the world; other things best consigned to the realms of myth were loose on the land; some of them frightening, if harmless, others sharp of tooth and claw, with a wild alien intelligence. None of them relished a night in the open countryside. That thought stayed with them as they marched in silence, trying to enjoy the pleasant birdsong that rang out from the hedgerows and the aroma of wild flowers gently swaying in the field boundaries.

As twilight began to fall they neared the first of the villages marked on the map. Ruth suggested they pitch camp somewhere within the village boundaries, for safety. If they were going to risk a night in the wild, there were plenty of opportunities ahead. She looked ghostly white in the fading light and she had twice headed over to the hedgerow to be sick; the whole journey was taking its toll.

Her voice sounded so exhausted they all agreed instantly, whatever their private doubts.

Darkness had fallen completely by the time they reached the village and the golden lights were gleaming welcomingly across the night-sea of the fields. They hurried down from the high ground with an exuberance born of the potent desolation that emanated from the deep gloom shrouding the rest of the landscape; sounds which they could not explain by bird or foraging mammal pressed heavy against their backs; movements of shadows against the deeper shadow seemed to be tracking them in adjoining fields.

Laura cried out at one point when a figure loomed out of the night. It was only a scarecrow; even so, there was something about it that was profoundly unnerving. The clothes seemed too new, the shape of the limbs beneath oddly realistic; as she passed she had the strangest sensation it was turning to watch her. She could sense its disturbing presence behind her as she continued down the field and suddenly she was thinking of the man on the train turned into a figure of straw. When she felt a safe distance from the scarecrow she glanced behind her, and instantly wished she hadn't. Although it could have been her troubled imagination, she was sure there were two red pinpricks staring out of the shadows beneath the pulled-down hat. Watching her.

The village was an odd mix of country money and rural decline: a handful of run-down sixties council houses cheek-by-jowl with sprawling ancient dwellings, overlooked by an Elizabethan manor house. There was only one main street, not blessed by street lights, and a couple of brief offshoots. Somehow a small pub and a tiny shop had survived the decline that had afflicted many similarly sized villages. There warm night air was thick with the aroma of clematis and roses which festooned the houses on both sides of the road. Everywhere was still and silent; although lights shone from the occasional undrawn curtains or crept out from slivers between drapes, there was no movement anywhere.

'We ought to ask if it would be all right for us to pitch our tents within the village boundaries,' Shavi said with his usual thoughtfulness. He selected a house at random and wandered up the front path among the lupins and sunflowers. His rap on the door was shocking in the stillness. A second later the curtains at the nearest window were snatched back with what seemed undue ferocity to reveal the face of a middle-aged woman. She bore an expression not of surprise or irritation at being disturbed, but of unadulterated fright. When her searching gaze fell on Shavi she waved him away furiously and drew the curtains with a similar, and very final, force. He returned to the others, looking puzzled.

'I told you,' Laura said, '*Deliverance* country. Don't bend over to tie your shoe laces. You'll be squealing like a little piggy.'

'There's always one miserable battleaxe in every village,' Ruth said. 'Knock somebody else up.'

'You don't have a trace of innuendo in your body, do you?' Laura noted.

Shavi tried the next house, then one a few doors up the street and one across the road; the response was the same in all of those that deigned to peek through the curtains: fear.

'Look, this is bleedin' crazy,' Veitch said with irritation. 'Let's try the boozer. I could do with a pint. At least they won't turn us away.'

As they moved down the main street towards the creaking sign and bright lights of the pub, Church slipped in next to Tom. 'Looks like they've been having some trouble here.'

'Hardly surprising, an isolated place like this. They should count themselves lucky they're still hanging on. Remember Builth Wells?'

Church recalled the deserted town, the preying things lurking in the shadows waiting for new blood. 'From their reactions I don't think it's the kind of place we should be out sleeping under canvas.'

'I think you're right. Let's hope the inn has some rooms.'

★

The pub was The Green Man, echoing the name of the tavern on Dartmoor devastated by the Wild Hunt; another strange, disturbing connection in a world now filled with them.

Church led the way in to the smoky bar; flagged floor, stone fireplace with cold ashes in the grate, dark wood tables, chairs and bar, an old drinking den, a hint of establishment. Small wall lamps provided focused pools of light which threw the rest of the place into comforting shadow.

Drinkers, mainly men, were scattered at tables and along the bar, a surprising number for a small village pub at that time of night. They heard the hubbub of hushed voice as they swung the door open, but the moment they were all inside every conversation stopped and the drinkers, as one, turned and stared, their expression shifting through the same emotions: fear, relief, suspicion, surprise.

'*Deliverance*,' Laura repeated in a singsong voice as she marched over to the bar.

Veitch leaned over to whisper to Church. 'Nah, it's like that other film. *American Werewolf.* The Slaughtered Lamb. Rik Mayall. And that bloke who did the tea adverts.'

'Brian Glover.'

'Yeah, him.'

Church glanced round, not sure whether to smile at the ludicrousness of the response or feel disturbed at whatever lay behind it.

'You know,' Ruth broke into the conversation, 'sooner or later someone's going to say *Folk don't come round here much* in a hick accent.'

Laura fixed a cold stare on the barman, who appeared to have frozen midway through pouring a pint of bitter. 'You see these scars?' she said pointing to her face. 'The last landlord who didn't get me a drink quick came off much worse.'

'Sorry.' The barman was a side of beef in his fifties with curly ginger hair and rock 'n' roll sideburns. 'We don't get many new faces in here these days.'

Ruth exchanged a secret smile with Church.

The barman checked his watch. 'Just stopping off for a quick one on your way to . . . ?' He waited for her to finish off his enquiry.

She ignored him, glanced along the optics. 'Better get me a big vodka. Ice, no mixer. Make it a treble. I've had a day of hard labour and I'm a wilting flower who's not used to that kind of treatment. Oh, and whatever this lot want.'

The barman didn't make any other attempt at conversation; he seemed thrown by Laura's demeanour, as if she were speaking to him in a foreign language. They took their drinks to a gloomy corner and the only two free tables, which they pulled together.

'It certainly has character,' Shavi noted as he scanned the room while sipping on his mineral water.

'If you like wall-to-wall crazy and forties horror movie cliché.' Laura swigged her drink gloomily. 'I don't know why we couldn't have stayed in the city.'

'What do you think's going on?' Church asked.

Tom wiped the cider from his drooping, grey moustache. 'Just a local problem. Otherworld was filled with the detritus of a million nightmares, little ones and big ones, and I presume most of them have found their way back here.'

There was something comforting about the age-old atmosphere of the pub after the fearful atmosphere out in the night. They settled back in their chairs to enjoy their drinks, appreciating the half-light which gave them a measure of cover from the suspicious glances. While Laura amused herself by staring out the few locals who dared to look their way, the others discussed their apparent success in evading the Fomorii. 'They're obviously determined to catch us,' Church noted. 'But it was interesting they used subterfuge. We must have set them back so much in Edinburgh they're afraid of taking an over-the-top approach.'

'When have you known them not to be over-the-top?' Veitch noted.

'He's right,' Ruth said. 'There was something about this that reeked of desperation, not revenge. You'd think they'd have gone for the nuclear option.'

Tom pressed his glasses back against the bridge of his nose. 'I think their true motivations will become apparent very quickly.'

'So in the meantime let's make the most of this lull and enjoy ourselves,' Laura said sharply. 'You lot, you're like, *Let's look for some big, heavy stuff to depress us.* You know, fun is an option.'

Church smiled, gave her leg a squeeze under the table. He was surprised to see the palpable relief on her face.

Before they could say any more a man sauntered over, holding a half-drunk pint. He was in his late twenties, with a soft, rounded face and a conventional, side-parted haircut. Unlike many of the others in the bar, he seemed relaxed and easy-going. 'Hello,' he said, 'I'm the official welcome wagon. Max Michaels. My parents had a thing about alliteration,' he added half-apologetically. 'You probably think it's all a bit strange in here. Which it is, make no mistake. Mind if I sit down?' Once they'd agreed he pulled up a chair; there was an old-fashioned politeness about him.

'Look, can I be blunt?' he said. 'You all look like intelligent people. You obviously know there are some very strange things going on all over.' He warmed when he saw the recognition in their faces, then asked them further questions until he was sure they understood the change that had come over the world. 'That's a relief. There's nothing worse than having to tell some unbelieving idiot the world has become a fairybook. So I can talk plainly, that's good. Now I haven't quite figured out what's happening, but the way I see it, for some reason reality has skewed away from science to the supernatural. The way appliances, cars, everything, fails suddenly for no apparent reason. The sudden rise in coincidences, premonitions, prophetic dreams. Do you get where I'm coming from?'

Church nodded. 'We've experienced all that. And more.'

'Good, good. If that was the end of it, it would have been bearable.' A shadow crossed Max's face. 'A few weeks ago a local farmer came in here raving about this strange sighting he'd had in one of his fields. It was a great laugh for everybody. We all thought he'd been inhaling too many organophosphates. Then some of the other farmers claimed they'd seen something. So then we decided we'd got our very own Beast of Bodmin. You know, some escaped panther living in the wild. Only it didn't really fit with the descriptions . . .' He chewed on a knuckle briefly, his thoughts wandering. 'And then things just went crazy. People went crazy. You can't just adapt overnight to having the whole world turned upside down. There were . . . a lot of casualties. Psychologically speaking. Depression, wouldn't leave their houses—'

'We saw that on our way here,' Veitch said.

'No, that's because it's dark. You don't move round much after dark, not if you can help it. A few of us meet up here mob-handed, to plan. I suppose, really, just to keep some kind of normality ticking over. We see each other home.' He took a deep draught of his beer, then grew animated. 'The problem's been the isolation. When all the phone systems went off-line and the postal system was suspended, and all the media, we were just left to stew in our own juices. It would have helped if we could have found out if other people were suffering too. Misery isn't so bad if you know it's been spread around.' He laughed humourlessly.

'Believe me, it's been spread around,' Ruth said. There was something about Max that she was warming to; a geniality, perhaps, or a lack of cynicism.

'Yeah, so I gather. I'm a reporter by trade, a stringer for the nationals. 'Course, when the phone lines went down, that put paid to that career. Thank God for the food-sharing system we've got going. Anyway, journalism, you know, it's in your blood. I *wanted* to know what was happening, and I wanted to let everybody else know. So we set up a jungle drums news service, passing information to the next village along, and they would pass it along to the next, and so on.' He shrugged in embarrassment. 'It was the best we could do. We *had* to know.'

'I admire your ingenuity,' Ruth said. 'Getting it set up so quickly. Most people wouldn't have bothered.'

'Information is power. I've had that drummed into me ever since I started on a local rag.' He seemed warmed by the praise. 'We've managed to stretch from Appleby to Durham so far. And you wouldn't believe how much trouble we had setting that up. Some bloody civil servant or council twat stumbled across it at some point and tried to stop it. Can you believe it? He was ranting on about D Notices and not causing a panic. Then he set out to the next village in his car at twilight and we never heard from him again.' There was a long pause while he sipped his beer. 'You've got to adapt, haven't you? Nothing makes sense, but if you don't get your head round it you're just . . .' He searched for the right words. 'Driving in a car to the next village, thinking it's a normal trip.'

'You've done a good job here,' Ruth said. He seemed to need the comfort; when he relaxed the strain was evident on his face.

'So tell me what you know,' he said, suddenly excited. 'Anything will help. Any little thing.'

'Any little thing,' Church repeated with an amused expression.

They didn't see anything wrong with filling Max in on many of the things they'd experienced since they'd got together. A hour and a half had passed before they'd finished and Max looked shellshocked. 'That's amazing. Stupendous.' He eyed them suspiciously for a moment, but it was obvious from their expressions that they weren't spinning him a yarn. 'So you're some kind of heroes. Basic, day-to-day people standing up against unimaginable odds. This is just what people have been waiting to hear!'

'You've got it all wrong,' Church said with a dismissive laugh. 'From our perspective it looks very different.'

'You're right there,' Laura added grumpily.

'No, don't you see! This is something I can do! Tell the world about what you're doing – or at least the world as far as I can reach. Give people hope. You know, war reporting. Because that's what it is.'

Veitch shook his head with irritation. 'We don't need that. A bloody spotlight shining on us all the time! No way. Anyway, we wouldn't even recognise ourselves once you've finished. I know what bleedin' reporters are like.'

'You owe this to the people. It's part of your job—'

'We don't owe anybody anything.' There was an unpleasant harshness to Veitch's voice.

'We were thinking about camping in the village somewhere,' Ruth said to change the subject.

'You can't do that.'

'No, you're probably right there. How about getting some rooms here?'

Max glanced over at the barman. 'I'll have to ask Geordie. I don't know . . . In the current climate I'm not sure how keen he'll be to have strangers in the place.' He sighed. 'But we can't send you out into the night either, so he'll have to.'

Tom leaned across the table to catch his attention. 'You haven't told us what's going on here.'

'Yes, of course.' He scrubbed the hair at the nape of his neck, suddenly uneasy. 'Well, it's not like we *really* know. We've all glimpsed things out there in the fields, but what they truly are—'

'What do they look like?' Ruth asked.

'We've only seen flashes, but we pieced things together from different accounts. When they move they're like sheets blowing in the wind. They seem to change and twist all the time, so they look, you know, not really solid, like they're not quite there. But they are.' He took another swig of beer to moisten his drying mouth. 'They've got teeth. One of the farmers saw them go through a sheep like it was a threshing machine. Turned the poor beast into chunks. That was the start of it.'

'But not the end,' Church said.

Max shook his head. 'While they were out in the fields they were terrifying, but we could deal with it. They weren't *here*, you know? We were safe in our castles.'

'But once they'd found their footing they began to come into the village.' Tom nodded at the familiar pattern. 'More prey, and easier to catch.'

'They came into town one night like a storm blowing in, sweeping up the High Street, swirling around all the houses. Everyone knew what was out there in the fields, so they didn't really venture out that much at night. Anyway, they found their victim. Mrs Ransom. She lived on her own in the big house at the top of the High Street. Quite well-to-do, but everyone got on with her, I suppose. There was a lot of blood, and . . .' His words dried up. As he stared blankly into the dregs of his pint, the awful strain was apparent on his face. 'After that the place just shut down. It was hard to go anywhere during the day. A farm hand, Eric Rogers, went missing in the fields. They found him. Part of him. Some people thought they'd try to drive away to the city . . . some did, but most were afraid even to go anywhere in their cars. We were virtually prisoners in our houses. Every night we barricaded ourselves in, and every morning we'd run out to meet here.'

'It's a wonder you managed to carry on living your lives,' Veitch said.

'We didn't, at first. But we began to get an idea of their patterns. They'd be in the village every night after dark, but we didn't actually see them in the environs during the day. Just on the outskirts, in the fields and the roads. Then we realised something. After Mrs Ransom, they hadn't taken anybody else from their house, even though a lot of the barricades were pretty flimsy things. But one night Jimmy Oldfield, who was this old lush from Recton Close, he got a bit funny in the head from all the pressure. He'd been in here drinking all day, telling everybody he'd had enough, that he was going to make a stand. Everybody thought it was just the booze talking.' A guilty expression crossed his face.

'Anyway, that night they seemed to know Jimmy had the least defences because they hovered all around his door for ages, but they couldn't get in, didn't even try, really. That's what the people holed up across the road said. But Jimmy . . .' Max shook his head slowly. 'I reckon he'd pickled his brain with all the whisky he'd drunk. He came to the door with his shotgun. All those awful things were gathered on his front garden, poised, like. Ready to attack. Jimmy opened the door just a crack to shove the shotgun out and that was it. They were in. There wasn't anything left of him the next day.' He sighed, finished his beer. 'So the upshot is, they only come into the village at night, and however dangerous they are, they can't get into your place if the door's shut tight.'

Veitch shrugged. 'It's a bit of a bastard not to be able to go out at night, but it shouldn't be too much trouble to keep everyone safe.'

'You'd think, wouldn't you?' Max waved his glass for the barman to pour him another pint. 'Anyway, after somebody got killed they never bothered us for a while so we could pretty much go about our lives as normal. We used the time to tell everybody in the village what we knew and to make sure all the old folk had good defences. They all got the rule: nobody opens their door after sunset.'

They could all see what was coming. 'But somebody else died,' Church said.

'Not just one, three people. It doesn't make any sense! The things can't get inside if the house is shut up. And everybody knows they have to keep their doors locked at all times. So tell me how people are dying?' He took his drink from the barman and drained half of it too quickly.

'People do silly, dangerous things even when they know they shouldn't,' Ruth suggested.

Max shook his head. 'One of them, Dave Garson, I was only speaking to him the afternoon he died. He was terrified. There was no way he was going to open his door. But he was gone the next day. His wife and kids were

264

hysterical. They said the things came bursting in after they'd gone to bed and Dave was finishing off his beer in the kitchen—'

'Maybe you're wrong about them getting into locked houses,' Church began.

Max shook his head furiously. 'That's not it. We're as sure as sure about that. We've been watching them. They can't get in.' He turned around to call over an aristocratic-looking man who was drinking a short at the bar. He was tall and thin, probably in his late sixties, with white hair and a handlebar moustache. He reminded Church of an ex-army type.

'This is Sir Richard,' Max said as he made the introductions. 'He lives in the Manor House on the green. We decided to form an action group to gather information on these things.'

'Surveillance is one thing I am *very* good at,' Sir Richard stressed. 'We set up a good team around the village, keeping watch all night long. We tracked the movements of these things. Took a few pot-shots at them to see if we could do them any damage. No luck, unfortunately. Like shooting fog.'

'And they definitely can't get into shut-up houses, right, Sir Richard?' Max said.

'Absolutely. They'll gather at the door, but never go inside. The most damnable thing. We honestly have no idea what to do next.'

Having made his point, he retreated to the bar. Max leaned forward and whispered, 'Ex-Tory MP for his sins, but he's a pillar of the community, great at organising things and getting people involved. In fact, I'm surprised how much this nightmare has brought everyone together. I used to think this was a right stuffy place, but since all this started I've seen a different side of all sorts of people. It seems to have brought out the best in everyone. Ironic, isn't it?'

For the rest of the evening they mulled over this point. They had all seen the good that had come out of hardship and suffering, but however much they argued, they couldn't agree if what they had lost was a fair price for what they had gained.

Geordie the barman had some spare rooms he used to let out to foreign tourists touring the area, but he agreed to give them up reluctantly. He was a little warmer when they promised to pay handsomely if he could arrange some food. He disappeared into the kitchen and forty-five minutes later came back with some cold ham, mashed potatoes and peas. Laura moaned about the meat 'infecting' her vegetables, but after their hard day's walking the others polished off their dinner and washed it down with more beer.

Max left them alone while they ate, returning to the other drinkers to pass on what he had learned. Church watched their expressions move through disbelief to a dumbfounded acceptance and then something approaching awe. It made him feel uncomfortable.

At eleven p.m., all the drinkers gathered together at the door. Church could see the apprehension jumping from one to the other like electric sparks, lighting their faces for just a fleeting moment. Max maintained his cheeriness somehow and threw a bright wave before wrenching open the door and peering out into the oppressive darkness of the street. They all hovered for a moment, and then some kind of circuit was thrown in their minds and they surged out. Church could almost hear the unified exhalation of fear. Then, with a rustle and a bang, they were gone and the door was shut.

'Will they be all right?' Ruth asked.

Geordie leaned his heavy frame across the bar. 'With a prayer. They've done it enough times, got it down to a fine art. They don't take any risks.'

'It would be easier to stay at home.' Church was surprised how concerned Ruth appeared.

'That'd be a bit like giving up, now wouldn't it?'

'I suppose so.'

After he'd finished wiping up, Geordie led them through the back and up a twisting staircase to a roomy first floor. Several bedrooms lay off a dog-leg corridor. They were all Spartan – a double bed, chair, dresser, wash basin – but they were clean and the beds were all made up with crisp linen.

'What time's breakfast?' Veitch asked.

'You're paying, you decide,' Geordie said grumpily. 'Gi' me a knock when you're ready.'

Church and Laura took the first room. Veitch angled to share with Ruth, but she opted for Shavi.

'Looks like it's you and me, son,' Tom said wryly.

'Whoop de doo.' Veitch kicked the door shut. 'He's definitely a queen, right?'

Laura made love to Church voraciously, pinning him to the mattress and riding him so roughly the clatter of the bedframe against the wall left no one in the building in any doubt what was happening. After ten minutes, Veitch hammered on the wall and shouted something indecipherable but obviously angry and obscene.

'Just 'cause you aren't getting any!' Laura yelled back. 'One-hand boy!'

Her passion brought Church to an early climax, but she didn't seem to want anything in return. She collapsed next to him, flushed and laughing at her exertion. 'Just call me Rodeo Girl.'

Their breathing subsided slowly as they stared at the ceiling until all they could hear were the creaks of the old house settling in the night. During the sex, Church's doubts had drifted to the back of his head, but there in the silence they returned in force. More than anything he didn't want to hurt Laura. He knew her better than all the others, her well of insecurity, her secret fears and lack of confidence, the kind of things she would be horrified if he said he recognised in her. Yet he seemed incapable of getting any handle on his emotions as far as she was concerned.

She seemed to sense what he was thinking, for she smiled and put a hand firmly across his mouth. 'Less is more. Don't ruin things with intellect.'

He took her hand away gently. 'I just want to be honest with you. You know . . . no false pretences. I—'

She clamped the hand down even more firmly. 'Churchill, this is me you're talking to. Do you think I'm going to be led up the garden path like some dreamy-eyed girlie? I'm a mature adult. Without wishing to define mature. I'm able to make choices. I know what I'm getting into. I know the inside of your head looks like something out of *Saving Private Ryan*. Back in Edinburgh I let the pathetic . . . yes, even desperate . . . side get out of control. But if it happens again, I'm going to put my own eyes out.'

She took her hand away. He went to speak and she clamped it down again, laughing in enjoyment at the small power.

'So the bottom line is, don't worry. No strings. If things work out, that's fine. If not, well, at least we tried. So let's just enjoy the moment.'

He wriggled free and buried his face half in the pillow so she couldn't get at him again. Laughing, he said, 'You're sure.'

'Sure as shit, big boy.'

They play-fought briefly, unable to represent their feelings any other way, before falling back side by side, giggling. Once they'd quietened again, Laura said thoughtfully, 'You know what, I don't take anything for granted any more.'

'What do you mean?'

'I used to drift through life accepting everything that came my way. Didn't get too excited because that was the way it was. It was just . . . nice. You know that tingly feeling you get in the pit of the stomach? I get that all the time these days. Sometimes just looking at shit, like the way the sun hits the fields. Like the smell of really good food. Or woodsmoke? Have you noticed how good that smells? I get excited when we all have a good conversation, you know how it is when the ideas are bouncing around and I'm bitching like hell and people are batting it back at me. The world's falling apart and people are dying out there, and I'm sitting thinking these are the best days of my life. What does that say about me?'

'It's not just you.'

'What?'

267

'I feel it too. I think we all do. What does it say? Something about the way life should be lived, I guess.'

'Urrp. Heaviness alarm. Why can't you just say it means I'm fucked in the head and leave it at that?'

'Because you're not.' He felt a sudden wave of affection for her. 'You don't do yourself any favours, you know. Why do you keep acting out this, shall we say, *difficult* persona?'

'It's a natural selection process. I know anybody who fights their way through that crap has got to be all right. Anybody who gets turned away by it isn't worth the time or effort.'

'There are easier ways—'

'No, there aren't. You can't trust anybody at face value. They might be smiling and pleasant and say nice things, but what's going on inside? It's a life lesson, idiot-brain. I'd have thought you would have learned that by now. This is the only way I can work out who's all right.'

The thought stayed with him as he floated in the warm peace of the room. The complexities of her character intrigued him, but there was something deep in her words that kept nagging at him, hinting at something important. He wrestled with it for a while, but it was stubbornly resistant and before he knew it he was drifting off into sleep.

Veitch relaxed once the sound of Church and Laura's love-making faded, but it had obviously left him with a surfeit of irritation. He prowled the room like an animal, stripped to the waist, the brilliant colours of his tattoos rippling with the movement of his muscles.

'Will you sit down! You're making me feel uncomfortable,' Tom snapped.

Veitch glared at him, said nothing at first. He slumped in the chair and removed the crossbow from the harness hanging on the end of the bed. From a little leather bag he took an oily rag and proceeded to carry out his nightly ritual of cleaning the weapon and ensuring it was in full working order. The routine seemed to give him some comfort.

'Your skills as a fighter seem to be coming on apace,' Tom noted. 'Do you think you're up to it?'

Veitch grunted, but didn't rise to the obvious bait. 'You're supposed to be the hero of a country – or so the stories say. Why don't you do something fucking heroic?'

Now it was Tom's turn to grow cold. 'You don't believe stories. They're there to *make* heroes so weak people have something to look up to. Try the real world some time. You'll see people making difficult choices, compromises, trying to do the best they can, despite everything.'

'So you're not a hero? You've got a rep based on a pack of lies.'

'Don't stick your ignorance on a flag. You'll regret it. Believe me.'

'You're dead weight, if you ask me.'

Tom took out the tin in which he kept his drugs and began to roll himself a joint. 'You have too much anger.'

'Life makes me angry.'

'You make yourself angry.'

Veitch focused on the crossbow.

'You wish you were something else,' Tom continued. 'You're angry with yourself that you're not.'

'You sound like a fucking social worker.'

Tom lit the joint and inhaled. 'You know that old story about the scorpion being given a ride across a rushing river by some other animal . . . I can't remember which one now.'

'Yeah, I know it. The scorpion promises not to sting, but halfway across he does because he can't help himself so they both die.'

'People always reel out these trite little stories as if they're supposed to be some great, unshakeable wisdom. There is no great, unshakeable wisdom, not that anyone on this planet can see, anyway. Everything is open to debate. That story was supposed to show people are prisoners of their nature. It's a sad story really. It says there is no hope for redemption. You will keep repeating your mistakes until you die. Don't you think that's sad?'

Veitch said nothing.

'I happen to believe people can change. That they can grow wise with the years, slough off the skin they were presented with as children. If they really want to.'

Veitch continued working on the crossbow as if he hadn't heard Tom at all. The room slowly filled with the fragrant hash smoke. When he did finally speak, Veitch's voice was miraculously drained of all the rage that had fractured it before. 'I think that Laura tart is the one who's trying to sell us down the river.'

'Why do you say that?'

'It's obvious, innit?' A pause. 'Don't you reckon?'

'I don't know. I think it might be you.'

Veitch looked up in shock. 'What are you talking about?'

Tom shrugged. 'Just an instinct.'

Veitch searched his face for a moment to see if it was another wind-up, but as usual couldn't tell a thing from Tom's impassive features. 'Listen, I'm doing the right thing here.' His voice trembled again from the repressed emotion. 'I know everybody thinks it must be me because I never played it straight before. These people mean more to me than anything. What we're doing . . . for the country, you know . . . for everybody . . . I'd give up my life for that.' His stare challenged Tom to argue.

'I stand corrected,' Tom replied in such a way that Veitch couldn't tell whether he meant it or not. 'But it's not wise to go pointing the finger without evidence.'

'Aren't you worried about the fact that one of us might be fucking everybody up?'

'I'm aware of it, certainly. But you can't take everything the dead say at face value. You've seen evidence of that. Be patient. As long as we remain on our guard then we will be better placed to protect ourselves. But a constant and high level of suspicion for those we are relying on is not helpful.'

'Is this some kind of pep talk?'

'See it how you want.'

Veitch finished the crossbow and returned it to the harness. 'I'll take your advice. Fair enough?'

Pain, terrible pain. Torture instruments that flared in the dark with the glow of heat. The animal stink, and those voices that were not voices, like the jungle at twilight. And Ruth thinking, *I can't take any more hurt. It would be easier to be dead.*

But they wouldn't relent. Another cruel blade, another corkscrew attachment, and hammers. Tears burning her eyes, throat constricting so tightly there was no air for her lungs. And then the scream, raw and bloody.

The scream.

'It is okay. You are having a bad dream.'

Thrashing wildly, still screaming, still torn between the hell of the torture chamber and the darkness of the room. And then, gradually, reality intruding, Shavi's face forming out of the pale shape that appeared before her eyes.

'It is okay,' he repeated. Gently, he pulled her towards him. Her tense muscles slowly relented and she laid her head against his chest, her mind spinning, her heart thundering, the tears still rolling down her cheek.

'I'll never forget,' she whispered. 'Never.'

It might have been Ruth's scream that woke them all, but within minutes in their separate rooms they all became aware of something going on in the street beneath their windows. At first it was hard to see anything in the deep dark, but they could pick out movement swirling up and down the street in shallow gusts. It took a second or two to realise what they were seeing until Max's description came back to them: *like sheets blowing in the wind.*

The motion itself was eerie in its unworldliness, but occasionally they picked out tiny sparks of red light they all knew must be eyes. Laura felt the *frisson* most acutely when she remembered the scarecrow they had passed on the way in.

Whatever the creatures were, they were like a force of nature in the way they howled along the streets, sending gates crashing open and shut. But Sir Richard had been right: they did not enter any houses.

That was almost enough to calm the group's jangling nerves, until ten minutes later they all heard an unmistakable sound, high pitched and insistent like the wind in the trees, yet somehow strangely unnatural; it made them all feel queasy. A second later the creatures began to sweep back towards the fields. But as they passed the pub, another noise rose up, briefly, along with a flash of something pale caught among the flurry of movement. It sounded very much like a child crying.

chapter twelve

a heap of broken images

Despite the danger, Veitch and Church were out of the pub and racing up the High Street within seconds, but there was no sign of where the creatures could have gone. The night was too dark, the countryside too empty. It didn't take them long to locate the victim's home; the shrieks could be heard across the village.

A woman in her late twenties clutched at the door jamb of one of the council houses, her face ruptured by grief. She was trying to propel herself out into the street while a man and another woman fought to restrain her, their expressions of deep dread revealing their motivation. Her dyed black hair flailed all around as she howled like an animal: sometimes Veitch and Church picked out the name Ellie among the incomprehensible wailings of a ruined life.

Lights were coming on all around and soon other neighbours were at the scene. One of them forced some tablets into her mouth and shortly after they managed to calm her enough to get her inside. Veitch and Church waited patiently until the man who had been holding the mother back ventured out, hollow eyes staring out of a chalk face. He was barefoot, still wearing grey pyjama bottoms and a Metallica T-shirt.

'What happened?' Church asked quietly.

It took a second or two for him to register their presence and even then he seemed unable to focus on them. Tears leaked out of the corner of his eyes. He furiously scrubbed them away, saying, 'Sorry, mate, sorry. Fuck.' He leaned on the gatepost, shaking. 'She said it was locked! Fuck.' He turned round to look at the open front door. It had once been painted white, but now it was a dirty cream, scuffed with old bootprints near the bottom, some of them very small. Inside the hall the light was stark and unpleasant. The man turned back, stared at them for a long moment as if he were about to say something and then he staggered towards the house next door.

Once he was inside, Veitch slipped down the path to examine the door. 'Look at this,' he said pointing to the jamb. The wood was splintered. 'They forced it open. That Max was wrong.'

Church ran his fingertip over the damaged jamb. 'Maybe those things are learning new tricks.'

The smell of frying bacon, eggs and sausages filled the pub. As the group sat around the tables in the bar, they felt convinced that even aromas were more vibrant in the new world. But even that simple joy couldn't dispel the dismal air that had grown after the night's events. Talk turned quickly to whether the village should be evacuated en masse if the safety of the occupants could no longer be guaranteed.

'That's up to the villagers,' Tom pointed out, 'but I would say they would be loath to leave their homes, even in the face of such a trial. In this time of crisis, stability is vitally important.'

'That poor woman. Her only child.' Ruth's face still looked a little grey; since her ordeal she rarely gained her colour until after breakfast. 'We have to do something to help.'

'As if we haven't got enough on our hands,' Laura said sourly.

'No, I agree with Ruth,' Church said, to Laura's obvious annoyance. 'We can't leave these people high and dry if there's anything at all we can do.'

'Max said the creatures leave the village alone for a while after they have secured a victim,' Shavi reiterated. 'That gives us a little time.'

'Then we should start straight away.' Church broke open his egg with his fork. 'Talk to everyone we can. There must be something we can use, some kind of defence that will keep these things out—'

'I don't believe you lot,' Laura snapped. 'One minute you're talking about this big mission to save the world, the next you're taking time out to save the waifs and strays. Anything could happen here. You saw what was going on last night. There's no guarantee one of us won't get hurt or worse, and then we won't be able to do what's expected of us. I say we save ourselves.'

Veitch eyed her coldly. 'It's all about doing the right thing too.'

'What must it be like to be you?' Laura sneered. 'All those echoes from that one thought rolling around your head—'

'Least it's a good thought.'

'Okay, okay!' Church held up his hands to calm the bickering. 'Let's see what we can do.'

★

273

As they filed out into the sunlit street, Shavi hung back until he caught Church's eye. They stood behind in the pub doorway while the others went off to explore the village. The air was already hot and filled with clouds of butterflies drawn by the heavy perfume of the roses. Bees buzzed lazily from bloom to bloom.

Church could see from Shavi's expression it wasn't going to be good news. 'What's wrong?' he asked.

'I find this very hard to say,' Shavi began hesitantly, 'but as soon as we have finished our duties here I am afraid I will have to leave.'

Church's heart sank. 'You can't leave, Shavi! For God's sake . . .' He floundered around for the correct words. 'We're relying on you. You're the backbone of the whole team. The only stable one among us!'

'I fear you are not doing yourself or any of the others justice. Please do not make this difficult for me. I understand my responsibilities to you and all, and to the mission destiny has delivered to us. It is just—'

'What?' There was an unnecessary hardness to Church's voice.

'It was I who freed Maponus. And every life that is cut down by his hand is on my conscience.'

'Look, we asked you to seek him out and free him. You couldn't have—'

Shavi held up a hand to silence his friend. 'Whether I knew what I was unleashing or not is immaterial. I certainly exhibited arrogance in my approach which allowed me to be manipulated. Even without apportioning blame, any deaths are my deaths. I have to do something to make amends—'

'Like what?'

'Help to imprison him again.'

'Shavi, with all due respect, what can you do? It took a collection of the most powerful people in the land to bind him originally. And not all of them survived.'

'I do not know what I can do. But if there is a chance that I can do anything I have to seize it. I will seek out the Bone Inspector and offer my help. Perhaps the two of us can find some way—'

'Shavi, I'm not having any of this.'

Shavi smiled. 'This goes far beyond our friendship and your leadership, Jack. I am burdened by this responsibility.'

Church tried to dredge up some relevant argument. He felt massive failure for all of them staring him in the face. 'The Pendragon Spirit called us together to complement each other with our abilities. Losing you would be like losing an arm – there's no way we'd be able to carry on.'

'I am not leaving for ever, Jack. Just until I have found a solution. Then I will return to help in—'

'Okay, stay a little longer. Take some time to weigh things up—'

'I have—'

'No, listen. The woman in the Watchtower who set us on this path originally. Her name's Niamh. There's some kind of bond between us. Before you make any move, let me contact her. She might have a solution. For God's sake, Maponus is one of their own. They have to help!'

Shavi looked unsure.

'I'm not asking you to change your mind. Just defer it until I've tried this path.'

Shavi nodded politely. 'All right. I will do that.'

As Church watched Shavi wander down the summery street towards the others, he couldn't escape the feeling that the burdens which had been placed on him as leader were growing with each day. Sooner or later he knew he would be found lacking.

'We should question all the information we've been given. Go back to first principles.' Ruth checked the list of victims Max had given her. She was enjoying the opportunity to use her naturally incisive abilities on a problem rather than dwelling on the queasiness and weakness that afflicted her too often now.

Tom sighed in a manner which suggested he could barely find the energy for the task at hand.

Ruth knew him too well to rise to the bait. 'I think I've found out your special ability, Tom,' she said without raising her eyes from the list.

'Oh?'

'Directional irritation. You turn it on, pick out a target, boom.' He snorted in such a comically affronted way Ruth couldn't help a smile. 'Look,' she continued, 'we know nothing about these things. If the information is flawed, any response we decide on could be flawed too. And that might be the *fatal* flaw.'

He shrugged dismissively. 'There are more important things—'

'Don't start that again. We've made the decision. Let's stick to it.'

He snatched the list from her and compared the addresses to the village around him. 'At least the last three are in the same area. We can turn this around quickly.'

With Laura and Veitch talking to some of the villagers who had seen the creatures and Shavi already at the house of the first victim, Mrs Ransom, they headed off to the cluster of other victims. The addresses were all in the vicinity of Recton Close, where the drunk Jimmy Oldfield had lived and died. His council house stood empty, the garden gate wide open, one window shattered from what was probably a randomly thrown stone; one of the local kids, Ruth guessed.

Not too far away they could see the house of the previous night's victim.

The curtains were tightly drawn. They thought it best not to trouble the recently bereaved mother and instead concentrated on the neigbours of Oldfield and the other two people who had died.

There was little to distinguish those who had been taken. Oldfield might have been an alcoholic, but he was fondly regarded by those who lived in the small pocket of sixties housing. Of the other two, a young milkman who had been laid off by the local dairy just before the troubles and a middle-aged cleaning woman who worked at some of the more well-to-do houses, there was little to suggest they would have been foolish enough to allow access to their houses after dark.

Ruth and Tom pored over the information they had gathered on a bench overlooking the village green. 'It's too much of a coincidence to think all these people could have mistakenly let those things in,' Ruth said. 'And that poor woman last night . . . She'd seen at first hand what could happen with her neighbours—'

'Unless the child opened the door,' Tom ventured.

'Maybe these things are some sort of sirens,' Ruth mused. 'Something about them hypnotises people into letting them in.'

'Possibly. But Ryan said the door he inspected last night had been broken open.'

Ruth chewed on her knuckle, watching the ducks waddle down to the pond in the centre of the green. It was quiet and lazy in the late-morning sun and there was no sign anywhere across the picture-postcard village of any of the suffering that descended on it with nightfall. 'Then everyone *must* be mistaken,' she said. 'These creatures have to be able to get in when they want.' Even as she said it something didn't seem quite right, but whatever it was stayed hidden in her subconscious.

'No, I cannot stress strongly enough that these creatures cannot get into any property that is shut off. Even a closed but not locked door seems to deter them.' Sir Richard stood erect and still, as if he were on parade outside the sprawling, detached house of Mrs Ransom at the far end of the High Street. The residence was cool beneath the shade of several mature trees around the low-walled front garden, while the building itself was covered in a sweet-smelling mass of clematis.

Shavi nodded politely. 'I hope you do not mind me going over this again—'

'No, no, old chap, not at all.' Sir Richard adjusted the Panama hat that shaded his eyes. 'I know you're only trying to help. But, really, we have got a very efficient defence force here. We've done everything in our power to protect the village. As to those creatures, well, I've watched them with my own eyes, and I am a very well-trained observer. I am in no doubt of their limitations.'

'Then how can—'

'No idea at all. People make mistakes, leave a door ajar at twilight. It's easily done.' There was a note of sadness in his voice.

Shavi looked up at the dark face of the large, old house. 'A lovely property.'

'It certainly is. Been in the Ransom family for generations. Sadly Alma was the last of the line. I come down here every now and again to keep an eye on the old place, make sure the local yobs don't start tearing it apart. It's a very, very sad situation.'

'She was the first?'

He nodded. 'An awful wake-up call to all of us.' He motioned to the rambling, well-heeled properties that lay all around. 'You think you're impregnable here, in this beautiful countryside, and this historic village. It was such a safe haven away from the rigours of modern society. I retired here after I lost my seat at the last election. Somewhere to tend the roses, enjoy a relaxing life for a change. And now . . .' His words dried up.

'Everyone has suffered,' Shavi agreed, 'all across the country, but people are finding ways to survive.'

'True. Very true. It has been an extraordinarily testing time, but I cannot stress enough how much my faith in human nature has been restored. The way everyone in the village pulled together once we understood the nature of the threat facing us. It's been the Blitz spirit all over again.' His eyes grew moist as he looked around the quiet street. 'I fear for the future, though. If things carry on as they are, all of this could be swept away. It's not fair at all, is it? What's to become of us?'

After the surprising kiss in Callander, Church had been wary of having any further contact with Niamh, but he couldn't see any alternative. Shavi was the backbone of the team: resilient, dependable in every circumstance, fully aware of all his obligations; they couldn't afford to lose him. The real problem was how he should contact her. He had no idea how the system of transfer worked between Otherworld and what he laughingly called the *real* world, nor what the abilities of the Tuatha Dé Danann were in hearing communication between the two places. Were they as omnipotent as some of them sometimes appeared? Would it be enough just to call her name? She had, after all, stressed the bond between them; perhaps that was enough.

In the end he decided at least to make things a little easier. He asked around the village for any site that carried folk tales of fairies or supernatural activity. An old woman directed him to a small, overgrown mound on the outskirts where she had seen 'the wee folk' playing one night when she was a girl.

He sat on the summit and closed his eyes, feeling the sun hot on the back of his neck. His instinct told him he needed to be in tune with the spiritual power of the blue fire, although he was unsure of attempting it without Tom around to guide him. But after a few minutes trying to clear his mind, he found it surprisingly easy. Perhaps it was a skill that grew commonplace with repetition, or perhaps it was simply that the blue fire was stronger in the land since his success at Edinburgh, but as soon as he could concentrate he was aware of the tracings of power shimmering across the countryside, casting a sapphire tinge across the golden corn, adding new depth to the rich, green grass. When he finally felt he had tapped into it, he whispered her name. At first there was nothing; and not for the first twenty minutes. But just when he was about to give up, a strange vibration hummed in the air, like the sound around an electricity sub-station. An instant later she was standing before him, her smile as mysterious and deep as the ocean.

'You called, Jack. I came.'

Before her, he was suddenly aware he felt awkward and faintly embarrassed, his emotions and thoughts stumbling over each other like a schoolboy before his secret sweetheart. 'I need help.'

She nodded, her eyes heavy-lidded. She took his hand and led him down to the warm grass. As he sat, she leaned near to him, not quite touching, but close enough so that he was constantly aware of her presence; close enough for him easily to breathe in that pleasing aroma of lime and mint. 'Why are you interested in me?' He hadn't meant to ask the question, but it had appeared on his lips almost magically.

She gave a soothing, melodious laugh, as if it were the most ridiculous question in the world. He enjoyed the way her eyes crinkled, her face innocently lit up. In that moment it was hard to see her as one of a race so alien they treated people with oblique contempt. 'I have seen you grow, Jack. I was there, in the half-light, the moment you were born. I saw your potential take shape, your good heart grow stronger. I stood a whisper away the first time you cried from hurt emotion. I saw you develop decency and honesty and love for your fellow man. I saw you suffer broken hearts, and persevere even at that terrible point when you felt your world was coming to an end. And you came through, Jack. You became the best you could be. So few Fragile Creatures can say that. And I was there in every moment, so much a part of your life in the highs and the lows that I knew every secret thought, every half-wish and barely remembered dream. I was a part of you, Jack. No one knows you better. No one.' There was almost a pleading quality to her voice.

'But I don't know *you*.'

'No. No, you do not.' And now sadness, so fragilely potent he almost felt it. She looked away briefly, too much going on behind her eyes for him to see.

'What is it you are saying, Niamh?'

'There is nothing I can say. I merely reveal to you the slightest fragment of the minutest strand of my feelings. Our races are as far apart as Otherworld and here. And as close. No good has ever come of any bond forged between the two. One passes so quickly, the other goes on for ever, both are bound in tears.'

Her voice filled him with a deep melancholy. For the first time, in her eyes, in her body language, the way she held her mouth, he could see how deeply she felt for him and it was monumentally shocking. To be loved so much and not know it was astounding, and truly moving, to such a degree he felt he should seek deep within him to see if there was any way he could repay such a profound investment. But all he found inside was confusion. He thought of Laura and the desperate scramble of emotions he felt around her. And, oddly, Ruth, whom he thought he considered a friend, but when he attempted to examine his emotional response he found it was too complex and deep-seated. And now this woman, who was so open and honest, she was like a cool desert oasis he wanted to dive into and slough off all the corruption that had mired him over the weeks and years.

'I don't know how I feel,' he said honestly.

'You are fortunate.' More sadness. 'To know and not to have is the hardest thing.'

He tried to find something comforting to say, but nothing came.

She looked around, at the rolling summer fields, and some of the sadness eked away. 'This world is changing. Soon it will be a land of myth once more, where magic lives in every turn.' She turned back to him, her smile sweet once again. 'A land where anything can happen.'

He nodded thoughtfully. 'When you put it like that, it doesn't seem such a bad thing.'

'How can I help you, Jack?'

He felt almost guilty asking for something when she had bared her soul to him. But once he had told her about Maponus, and seen her face register surprise, then darken, all other thoughts were wiped away.

'The search for the Good Son has never ended,' she explained. 'The Golden Ones were riven by despair when he was lost, the brightest of all our bright stars, our very hope for the future. There was no knowledge of his disappearance – he was simply there, then not. Of course we must bring him back to us. There will be much rejoicing, scenes of wonder not witnessed since the victory celebrations after the second battle of Magh Tuireadh.' The notion excited her greatly, but gradually her face darkened as the implications of Church's information wormed their way through. 'If he has been so severely damaged by the Night Walkers, there may be little even the Golden Ones can do to restore the Good Son to his former glory. The Night Walkers' revenge is swift, cruel and usually irreversible.'

'But you will attempt to get him back to Otherworld?'

'Of course. He is the jewel of the Golden Ones.' She was positive, yet Church could see she was troubled. 'Yet he is so powerful.' Her voice faded into the wind.

'You're saying even your people might not be able to restrain him?'

'He could cause great destruction to this world. Your people will fall before him like—' she looked around '—like the ripe corn.' She turned to Church with fleeting panic in her eyes. 'You must not go anywhere near the Good Son. Do you understand?'

'At the moment I'm going where I'm called. We have an obligation—'

'You have an obligation to defend this world. You cannot do that if you are no more.'

'I'm asking you for help.' He looked her directly in the eye; her irises seemed to swirl with golden fire.

'Then I will help. But I ask something of you in return.'

'All right.'

'A chance to show you my heart, to prove that universes can be crossed. To show that the love of a Golden One and a Frail Creature can surmount all obstacles.'

Church searched her face; suddenly events seemed to be running away from him.

'I know you have a dalliance with another Frail Creature. You must end it. You must give your love solely to me for a period. A chance, that is all I ask. And if our romance does not rise up to the heavens, then we will go our separate ways.'

Dismally, Church thought of Laura, how much it would hurt her. Could he do that when there was still a chance they were right for each other? Could he hurt her, knowing how much she would suffer? And once more he thought of Ruth, and wondered what she would think of him. Niamh was watching the play of his thoughts with innocent, sensitive eyes.

He wondered why he was even bothering to deliberate; there was no real choice. He couldn't afford to let Shavi leave. And if he could do anything to stop Maponus's rampage, he had to try. He had learned through bitter experience over the last three months that he couldn't put his own feelings

280

first; that was the burden of his leadership. Sacrifices had to be made. Always. 'Okay,' he said. 'I'll do what you say.'

The sudden swell of emotion in her face surprised him, and in that instant he wondered if he really could feel something for her. She took his hand, an act that to her was obviously filled with meaning; it was as if she was some Victorian heroine whose every gesture was infused with import to make up for her stifled emotion. 'Much deliberation will need to take place if we are to bring Maponus back with us,' she said. 'I will need to devote myself to the planning and to attending my brethren in this. You will not see me for a while. But then . . .' Her cool fingers grew tighter around his hand and her smile deepened. She nodded politely, stood up and walked slowly away. Briefly she turned and flashed him a smile weighted with emotion, and then she was gone in the blink of an eye, as if the sky had folded around her.

Laura and Veitch didn't quite know how they ended up interviewing villagers together, but they managed to do it with as little communication between the two of them as they could manage. If anything, Veitch seemed to Laura a little contrite in his body language and whatever gruff comments he made, but after his rage in the gorge, she wasn't taking any chances. She was thankful for her sunglasses which hid the fear she knew was flickering in her eyes.

Eventually, though, they found themselves walking alone down the sun-drenched High Street and there was nothing for it but to make conversation. 'Nothing new there, then.' Laura broke the silence, stating the obvious because she couldn't think of anything else to say that wasn't heavy with all sorts of difficulties. 'Another morning of my life wasted.'

Veitch grunted. His own cheap sunglasses gave nothing away.

Laura was suddenly struck by the absurdity of the image. 'Look at us. It's like Tarantino meets *Emmerdale*.' That brought a smile to him. It was only a chink, but she felt she had to give it a shot. 'About the other day—'

'I'm sorry, all right.' It was as if someone had pulled the blinds down on his face. 'I've got a bleedin' awful temper and half the time I can't control it. I don't know where it came from. I never used to have it.'

'Stress, probably. But that wasn't what I wanted to say. You're right for worrying about one of us selling the others down the river. Nobody else seems to worry about it too much, but it's there – can't ignore it. But it's not me, all right? That's what I wanted to say. It's not me. I don't care if you believe me or not, but I've got to say it out loud. I'm a big fuck-up – and I'll deny I said that if you ever bring it up – but I wouldn't screw over any of us in this group.'

Her normal reticence made the honesty in her words palpable. Veitch was

281

taken aback for a moment, but he didn't show it. 'Who do you think it is, then?'

She paused, unsure whether to continue, but it wasn't worth turning back at that point. 'Are you going to bite my head off?'

'No.'

'Okay. I know you've got the hots for Ruth, I know she's been through the worst fucking shit imaginable, but I think it's her.'

'Bollocks.'

'Thank you for that measured response.' She bit her tongue; she could feel the power in his hard body at her side. 'I'm not just being a jealous bitch, which I am, but not right now. Here's what I think. She's been waking up with nightmares about what those bastards did to her—'

'Wouldn't you?' He was already starting to bristle. She had to get to the point.

'I think those nightmares are caused by something real. You remember what the Bastards did to Tom under Dartmoor? They stuck one of those creepy little bugs in his head so he'd do everything they wanted.'

Veitch's head snapped round. For a second Laura's blood ran cold until she saw the troubled expression on his face. 'You think they did that to her?'

'Makes sense.'

He considered it for a moment, then shook his head vehemently. 'Bollocks.'

'Just think about it, that's all. It could've happened. Someone needs to keep an eye on her, and seeing as you've appointed yourself official judge, jury and executioner—' She caught herself. She'd done enough. She could tell from Veitch's expression that the notion was already burrowing its way into his head.

'Come on, I need you.' Ruth caught Veitch's arm when they all met up outside the pub. She pulled him over to one side where the others couldn't hear them, oblivious to the odd way he was looking at her.

'What's wrong?'

'I want us to have sex.'

Veitch's expression was so comical she had to stifle a giggle and that wouldn't have helped at all; he was sensitive enough as it was. His mouth moved, no words came out; his whole, stumbling thought process was played out fleetingly on his face. 'You're taking the piss now.'

That was the first response she expected. 'No, I'm not. I'm deadly serious.'

Veitch shook his head. There was a pink flush to his cheeks. He was eyeing her askance, still trying to read her motives.

'When we started out on this whole nightmare I was just a normal girl, but I've changed, like we've all changed. I've learned some things. Powerful things. How to change the world around us, things . . . things I don't want to talk about because I can hardly believe it myself. You know the owl that followed me around?'

His eyes ranged across her face; he seemed to be trying to peer into her head. He nodded.

'That wasn't just an owl. It was . . . Well, I don't really know what it was. I'm not making much sense, am I? I wish I could understand it all better myself.' She became lost in her own confusion of thoughts briefly. 'Look, the owl's some kind of familiar. You know what that is? A demon . . . I don't know . . . Some kind of supernatural creature, anyway. That took the form of an owl to be with me. But when the Fomorii had me under the castle I found out what it was really like. Not what it looked like. I mean, I couldn't see it. But . . . it taught me things—'

'What kind of things?'

Her mind sparked and fizzed with wild current when she considered the answer to the question; it was suddenly as if she could look into the infinite. 'Things that could help us. Only the trouble is, now the familiar has gone away and I don't know why, but there are still so many things I need to know.'

'Well this is all very fucking nice, but what's it got to do with us shagging?'

She sighed. 'I'm sorry, Ryan. I really am making a mess of this, aren't I? Let me try again. Sex is at the heart of all magic. Throughout history it's been used in all sorts of rituals. The earth energy, the blue fire in the land is the same energy we have inside us. In our spirits, our souls. It runs in grids over our bodies the same way it does in the land. Like the stone circles are areas where it's at its most powerful, there are places on our bodies where the power is strong. In eastern religion they're called chakras—' She watched him start to glaze over and quickly picked up the pace of the conversation. 'Normal sex fills us with this energy which we can use. But a particular kind of sex – it's called tantric sex – supercharges these chakras and—'

'And you know how to do this?'

'The familiar told me. I mean, I've never tried it, but—'

'There has to be a first time.'

'Right. Look, I don't want to take advantage of you. This isn't an emotional thing. But you get a good screw out of it and all the experiences you could want. And I get—'

'What?' His brow furrowed. 'If you don't want it to be anything serious, what do you get out of it? You're not some slapper—'

'You're so sweet,' she said with a mock-smile. 'I get knowledge, hopefully. Power I can bend to my will.'

The incomprehension was chiselled into his face. He felt uncomfortable. It wasn't what he wanted, in the slightest, but it seemed important to Ruth.

'Look, don't waste time thinking about it now. If you're up for it, I'll fill you in as we go along. Are you?' He nodded, unsurely. 'Right. Then let's do it.'

Back in the pub bedroom she drew the curtains and locked the door. None of the others would even think of disturbing them at that time of day. They were downstairs in the bar, picking over the remainder of their lunch, having a quiet drink, chewing over the village's problem. Her breath was ragged from apprehension and, if she admitted it to herself, a sexual charge.

'You're sure about this?' She could hear faint nervousness in Veitch's voice. She sensed that if she called it off he would be more than happy.

'I am. Are you?'

'Yes.'

Not exactly a ringing endorsement, but what did she expect. 'I know this isn't how you expected, Ryan. It's not exactly every maiden's dream either. Not that I'm a maiden.' She blushed, looked away. 'But it's the only way I can think of—'

'It's okay. You don't have to explain any more.' She smiled; underneath it all he was quite sweet. 'So how do we start?' he continued.

'Take our clothes off first, I suppose.'

It felt unduly uncomfortable, so artificial in the way it was drained of all passion, but she knew she couldn't afford to be selfconscious, for Veitch's sake. If he saw her being embarrassed, the atmosphere would completely fall apart and he probably wouldn't be able to perform. She set her mind and tried to act as brazen as possible. She pulled her T-shirt over her head and threw it on the bed, then unhooked her bra. Her nipples were already hard; her breasts almost ached. She tried to fool herself that her instant and powerful arousal was because it had been so long, but she knew in her heart she was physically attracted to Veitch. As he pulled his own T-shirt off she let her gaze run over his lean, muscled torso, watching the flex and ripple of the tattoos, like cartoons in animation. There was a hardness to his body she hadn't experienced in any of her previous lovers; it wasn't even the kind of hardness that came from working out in a gym. It was the kind of compacted yet supple muscle that came only from a life lived at street level, in onerous situations that tested the body on a daily basis in a way the fitness trainers couldn't even imagine. His own nipples were hard; that excited her even more. Briefly, his clear, powerful eyes caught hers and there was no embarrassment there at all. Energy crackled between them. She saw his own passion laid bare as his gaze dropped to her breasts.

She undid her loose belt, unpopped the buttons and dropped her jeans to her ankles. In the same motion she slipped down her briefs and stepped out of them. She felt the chill of the wetness between her legs send a tingling fire into her belly.

Veitch removed his trousers and his shorts. He was very hard, aching for her. A shiver ran through her. He seemed filled with vitality, as if the blue fire burned in every cell, nuclear fission raging out of control, ready to consume her.

She took his hand and pressed him towards the floor. When he was sitting with his legs out in front of him and his hands behind, she climbed astride him and gently lowered herself on her taut leg muscles, gripping his erection in her fist and feeding it into her. His hardness was shocking; it seemed to go in so deep she felt it was almost in her chest. She wrapped her legs around him and supported herself on her hands behind her. Her heart was thundering, the passion crackling through every fibre of her.

'Don't move,' she said. 'This is the hard part. The aim is to achieve orgasm without moving, through meditation, directing the energy. I've had some guidance how to do it. Normally it takes a long period of training and discipline. Do you think you can do it?'

'I can try.' He closed his eyes, his body rigid, still.

Ruth took the opportunity to scan his features; in relaxed mode there was a surprising tenderness to his expression, almost an innocence. In that moment she could imagine how he would have turned out if not for the privations of his early life. And then she lowered her gaze to the startling colours of his torso: the Watchtower was there, swimming in a sea of stars, some kind of sword, a bulky creature in an insectile armour that made her feel so uncomfortable she moved on quickly, a strange ship skimming blue waves, a burning city and, most disturbingly, a single, staring eye which she knew represented Balor.

She put all thoughts out of her mind, leaned forward and kissed his clavicle. A slight shiver ran through him. She moved up, kissed the curve of his throat. Then up further to gently brush his lips. She felt his erection throb inside her.

Leaning back, closing her own eyes, she focused her sharp mind in the way the familiar had told her, the way she had practised during those long, terrible hours of imprisonment. It came to her with surprising ease. She felt the world moving beneath her, the shifting of subtle energies deep in the rock and soil. Whatever Church had done in Edinburgh had worked. The Fiery Network was slowly coming to life, breaking through the dormant areas, joining up the centres that had remained powerful, like blood filling a vascular system. She saw in the darkness in her head the flicker and surge of the blue fire as it ran in the earth, came up through the ground, through the walls of the building, along the floor, burst in coruscating sapphire into the base of her spine. And gradually it started its serpentine coiling up towards her skull.

Time was suspended; they had no idea how long they were there. Their very existence was infused with the dark, shifting landscapes in their heads, the feeling of the engorged blood vessels in their groins. Veitch fought the urge to thrust, although every fibre of his being was telling him to drive hard into her. Her vaginal muscles seemed so tight around him, massaging him gently. Even with his eyes closed he was aware of her body as if he was staring at it: the flatness of her belly, the heaviness of her breasts, the hardness of her nipples, electric sexual signals driving into the depths of his mind.

And then everything came in a rush, the blue fire suddenly crackling up the final inches of their spines, erupting in their heads like the birth of stars; every nerve bursting with fire, rushing back down to their joined groins. Veitch ejaculated in such a fierce manner he felt as if his life was being sucked out of him. The sudden crackling current inside Ruth's vagina danced jaggedly to the tips of her fingers and then to the front of her brain. Their orgasm brought a fleeting moment of blackness that felt like the end of everything.

And in the following instant, Ruth was consumed with a power she had never experienced before. It felt like she was flying high above the earth, deep into the depths of space. And there she saw the thing that had the face of a man and the face of an owl simultaneously, and it was frantically tracing a strange sigil in the air with its hands, desperate to keep her at bay.

'I cannot come near you,' it said in its half-shrieking voice. 'You are tainted. Seek help now. Seek help or die.'

She fell into Veitch's arms and he held her tightly while their thundering hearts subsided. But Ruth couldn't enjoy the warm honey glow that infused them both in the aftermath of their passionate experience. She pulled herself back and looked Veitch deep in the eye; he was horrified to see the fear shining brightly within her.

'Something's gone badly wrong,' she said in a fractured voice. 'What the Fomorii did to me under the castle . . . it isn't over. It's still going on inside me.'

★

They dressed hurriedly and found the others sunning themselves on the steps in front of the pub while Tom finished his cider.

'Where did you two scuttle off to?' Laura asked suspiciously.

Ruth turned straight to Tom and Church and began to explain her fears, and for the first time told them about the black pearl. Her heart sank as she saw Tom's face at first darken and then blanch.

'Why didn't you tell us this before?' Tom hissed.

'It was too traumatic!' she protested. 'I could barely get my head round it myself!' She tried to look him in the eye. 'What's going on?'

'I don't know. But it was a ritual the Fomorii carried out. They wouldn't have done it without a reason.'

'You have your suspicions,' Ruth pressed.

'I have ideas, but it's best not to say them right now. Not until I'm sure.'

Tears stung Ruth's eyes. 'It's going to get worse, isn't it? I thought the sickness was just a natural result of all that trauma. I thought it'd pass.'

Church stepped in and put a comforting arm round her shoulder. Both Laura and Veitch flinched. 'What are we going to do?' he said to Tom.

Tom took off his glasses and cleaned them while he thought. 'She needs to be examined by one of the Tuatha Dé Danann. They are the only ones who might reasonably be able to tell us what the Fomorii have done.'

'And they might be able to help,' Ruth said hopefully, 'like Ogma helped you when you had the Caraprix in your head.' Veitch's gaze grew sharp.

'Will they help us?' There was an edge to Church's voice.

'They might.' Tom rubbed his chin, his gaze fixed firmly on the ground. 'If I asked them.'

'But what if they don't help?' Church continued. 'What's Plan B?'

Tom said nothing. After a long moment he wandered off down the road to weigh his thoughts.

The shadows were growing longer when he eventually returned to them. Ruth had been away to throw up twice in the meantime; Church guessed the stress was already contributing to what was wrong with her. The others waited anxiously around the pub table.

Tom looked around their concerned faces, then said, 'One of the Prime Courts of the Tuatha Dé Danann can be reached through a door not far from here. The Court of the Final Word is the closest translation of its name. Unlike the usual Tuatha Dé Danann courts, it is a place of quiet reflection, of study. If there is anyone who can provide an insight into Ruth's condition we will find them there.'

'Where is it?' The concern in Veitch's voice was palpable.

'Beneath Richmond Castle.' Tom glanced at the clock over the bar. 'If we move quickly we can be there before nightfall.'

'Is it that serious?' Church asked.

Tom's silence was the only answer he needed.

chapter thirteen

where the devil is

'I'd been keeping the full tank of petrol for emergencies,' Max said ruefully. 'The way things are going, I think it's going to become a priceless commodity.' He cast a worried glance at Ruth's drawn face. 'But if this isn't an emergency, what is?' He smiled, trying to bolster the atmosphere.

The car was a red Fiesta, peppered with rust on the wings and sills. The inside was a mess. He opened the doors with some embarrassment, then swept the crumpled maps and fast food wrappers out on to the pavement. 'Sorry. You can always tell a hack's car.'

Tom climbed into the passenger seat while Church took the back seat with Ruth. He slipped an arm across the top of the seat; her head fell naturally on to his shoulder. The others stood on the pavement; Veitch and Shavi were grim-faced, but Laura was impossible to read.

They eventually picked up the B6270 through the ragged, romantic countryside of Swaledale, heading south-east. During the journey Church and Tom tried to explain to Max about Tir n'a n'Og, the Otherworld, and the alien ways of the Tuatha Dé Danann to prepare him for what lay ahead. In other circumstances his dumbfounded expression would have been comical, but it soon fell away as he assimilated every detail with a speed that surprised them both. It wasn't long before he was babbling excitedly about a new way of seeing the world.

The scenery flashed by in a blur of rolling fields and green hedges; seeming normality. While Max and Tom passed the time in sporadic conversation, enthusiastic on Max's part, barely tolerable on Tom's, Church and Ruth slid down in the back seat and spoke in hushed voices.

'I can't believe this is happening,' she said, staring out of the window at the blue sky.

'You're right. You've suffered enough,' Church said.

'No, the people out there have suffered enough. I've had a little pain, but at least I know what's happening in the world. What's a few aches and pains compared to having your life turned on its head? I mean, I want to get back to doing something that matters and there's all this—' she gestured irritatedly '—holding me back.'

The weariness was evident on her face. Slowly she lowered her head back on to his shoulder, but Church continued to watch her while she rested, feeling a sense of deep respect that almost overwhelmed him.

They'd just moved on to the A6108 when Tom exclaimed loudly.

'What's wrong?' Church threw himself forward between the seats. He quickly saw it wasn't the right thing to do. Tom was already sliding down as low as he could go. On the side of the road, three policemen stood stiffly around a patrol car. They were gone so quickly Church had no way of telling if they were Fomorii, nor if they had seen him. He ducked down, turned and crawled up the seat just enough to peer out of the back window. The police all appeared to have got into the car, but it wasn't in pursuit. He held his breath and watched until it was out of sight.

'Close shave,' he said, still not wholly sure.

Shavi had spent an hour doing his best to boost Veitch's spirits, but the Londoner still wore the broken expression of someone who had seen ultimate victory snatched from his fingertips. 'We have to believe Ruth will be all right.' Shavi's voice rolled out softly across the quiet bar. His arm rested comfortingly around Veitch's shoulders, and Veitch made no attempt to shake it off. Laura watched them both carefully from behind her sunglasses, but added nothing to the conversation.

'You saw the old man's face. He looked like it was already over.' Veitch gently massaged his temples. There was an intensity about him that made the atmosphere uneasy.

'We have to have hope, Ryan. That is the message of this whole era.'

Veitch looked up suddenly and curiously into Shavi's face. He seemed surprised at what he saw there. After a moment's contemplation, he said, 'Okay, you're right. Course you are.' In the centre of the table where they had been abandoned earlier, he noticed the sheaf of notes Ruth had prepared. 'We've got to sort this out. Help these poor bastards.'

Shavi could see it was merely a displacement activity for the futility Veitch was feeling at his inability to do anything to help Ruth, but if it kept his mind focused on something positive, it was worthwhile. Veitch examined the notes with gusto, making observations as he read before handing each paper he finished to Shavi or Laura. No obvious conclusion presented itself to them, but they continued to turn it over while they ate the dinner Geordie had prepared for them.

'There's nothing new here,' Laura protested. 'Unless you're thinking of tracking them out to their lair, and then we wouldn't know how to kill them.'

'We don't even know where the *lair* is,' Veitch said. He shovelled a forkful of mashed potato into his mouth.

'It must be somewhere in the vicinity of the route we came in.' Laura told them about the scarecrow and the glowing red eyes.

'That's something,' Veitch said, 'but you're right, we don't know how to wipe them out yet. No point looking for them until we get a handle on that. It didn't look like we'd get much of a result with the sword or the crossbow.'

Laura re-examined one of the pages of notes. 'At least we know where the feeding ground is.'

Veitch perked up at this. 'What do you mean?'

Laura pointed out the rough sketch of the village lay-out with the victims' houses highlighted.

'That's a bit of a coincidence, isn't it?' he said.

'I don't know what you're talking about.'

'All those poor bastards in one place.'

'The old biddy wasn't anywhere near them. It's probably just that they've settled on this area because it's near to where they come in to the village. Or something.' She stared at the map intently, turning it this way and that.

Veitch chewed on a jagged nail thoughtfully. 'I'm getting a very fucking unpleasant idea,' he said.

The evening was warm and still as they moved through the village. The chorus of birdsong filled the air, but there was no sound of cars or human voices. Even though it was still light, everyone had retreated to their homes.

Veitch first took them to the large, detached house of Mrs Ransom, quiet beneath its canopy of old trees. They slipped through the creaking iron gate and up the brick path to the front door. Instead of knocking, Veitch simply inspected the door jamb before growing suddenly excited. He ran back down the path and vaulted the low brick wall on to the pavement. Shavi and Laura hurried to keep up with him as he ran the two streets to the collection of council houses which had provided all the other victims.

Oldfield's house was the first to be inspected. Veitch ran from there to the other two. He didn't bother checking the door of the young mother who had lost her child. Finally he rested breathlessly against the wall of one of the houses. He'd obviously figured something out that everyone had missed, but there was no jubilation in his face; instead, he seemed intensely troubled, and when he looked up Laura saw the familiar glint of cold, hard anger in his eyes.

'Fucking hell,' he said.

Max gunned the Fiesta into Richmond just as dusk was falling. The town was dominated by the ruins of the Norman castle which overlooked the River Swale, the keep towers soaring up a hundred feet into the darkening sky. Beneath it, the cobbled market was filled with people enjoying the warm summer evening as they made their way to the pubs.

Max scrutinised the scene. 'People carry on trying to be normal even when they realise something is badly wrong,' he mused.

'Nothing there to write about,' Tom muttered.

A tight, knowing grin crept across Max's face. 'That's where you're wrong. That is something to write about. That's something that speaks loudly.'

'Yes. And it says "Sheep to the slaughter",' Tom noted sourly.

Max laughed easily in disagreement. 'And that's just what I'm going to do. Write about it. About all this. This is something I can do, let the people know the truth. It's a kind of—'

'Calling?' Church knew just how he felt. Max nodded, still smiling.

They left the car in the centre and headed towards the castle on foot, Ruth trailing apprehensively between Church and Tom. Church surveyed the broken stone silhouetted against the blackening sky.

Tom followed his gaze. 'Do you feel it?'

Church nodded. 'The blue fire.'

'All the clues are there in the legends. The secret history. The story goes that a potter by the name of Thompson found a secret tunnel under the castle. He followed it and found a large cavern where King Arthur and his knights lay asleep. Sound familiar?'

'What are you talking about?' Max asked.

'All the legends have truths stitched up inside them. Important information, vital lessons.' Church could see the reporter was soaking up all the information. 'The King Arthur legend is a metaphor for the power in the land, what we call the blue fire. The legends surround all the places where this earth energy is most potent, many of them with links direct to Otherworld.'

'Like here,' Tom said.

'So when the legends say the king needs to be woken to save the country in the bleakest of times, they're really talking about waking the power in the land?' Max looked up at the castle in a new light.

'Thompson found a horn and a sword near to the sleeping knights,' Tom continued, obviously irritated that his story had been interrupted. 'When he picked up the horn, the knights began to wake. Naturally, he was scared to death. He dropped the horn and ran back down the tunnel, and as he did so a voice came after him. It said, "Potter Thompson, Potter Thompson, If thou hadst drawn the sword or blown the horn, Thou hadst been the luckiest man e'er born".'

'Good story,' Max said warmly.

They wound their way up for a while until they looked back and saw the lights of the town coming on before them. They all found it uncannily comforting; Richmond looked bright and at peace in an inky sea.

Tom followed the lines of blue fire as Church had done at Arthur's Seat until he located their confluence on an open spot on the hillside. The sparks flew like molten metal as he pressed his hand down hard. Within seconds, to Max's obvious amazement, the grass, soil and rock tore apart with a groan, revealing a dark path deep into the hillside.

Max peered in nervously. 'Are you sure it's okay?'

'No,' Tom said, and gave Max a shove between the shoulder blades that propelled him into the shadows.

Otherworld was bathed in the crisp, creamy light of an autumnal morning just after sunrise. Swathes of mist rolled across the wet grass at calf-height. The air was rich with the perfume of turning leaves, fallen apples and overripe blackberries. Melodic birdsong floated out from a nearby copse that was painted gold, red and brown in the dawn light.

Max looked around, disoriented. 'I don't get it.'

'Time moves differently here.' Church strode out towards gleaming white Doric columns he could just make out through another thick copse. 'Sometimes faster, sometimes slower. It's not fixed.'

Max's face showed his difficulty in grasping the concept of this new reality.

'Here are the rules,' Tom said curtly. 'Eat and drink nothing. If you are offered anything, politely refuse. Treat everyone you meet with respect. Never, ever raise your voice in anger. It would be best if you said nothing at all. Try to stay in the background.'

'I'm getting a little nervous now,' Max admitted.

'Just pretend you're in a different country with a culture you don't know,' Church said. 'You have to be cautious until you know the rules of the society, right?'

They moved quickly through the trees, the curling leaves crunching underfoot. Beyond, they had to shield their eyes from the glare of the sun reflecting off the polished white stone of their destination which rested in majesterial splendour among intricately laid-out gardens. The Doric columns supported a portico carved with an astonishingly detailed tableau showing aspects of the history of the Tuatha Dé Danann. Behind it, the Court of the Final Word spread out as far as the eye could see, like some Greek temple reflected in infinite mirrors.

'It's enormous.' Max's voice was laden with awe.

'It would seem.' The door was made of polished stone. Tom was there first and hammered on it. His fist barely seemed to make a sound, but they could hear the echoes rumbling through the structure into the distance.

When dim footsteps approached Church and Ruth both caught their breath. Despite all they had seen, they were not inured to the wonders and terrors of Otherworld. The life forms were myriad and astonishing in their complexity; even with the Tuatha Dé Danann, one could never quite be sure what would present itself.

The door swung open silently, as if it weighed no more than a feather. It framed two figures standing in a cool, enormous hall dominated by a large, tinkling fountain and tall trees which oddly seemed to be part of the structure. The young man and woman looked barely in their twenties and were dressed in what appeared to be gleaming white togas, edged with gold braid. Church and the others' eyes had no trouble accustomising to their appearance, which meant the Golden Ones were of low level and low power.

'Frail Creatures?' the young man said curiously, his beautiful face like marble, his heavy-lidded eyes moving slowly, like a lizard in the sun.

'I am True Thomas,' Tom began. 'You may have heard of me. I have been granted the freedom of your realm.'

The woman bowed courteously but a little stiffly, her long, black hair shimmering as she moved. 'Greetings, True Thomas. We are aware of your prestigious position.'

Tom winced at this, although there was no irony in the woman's words. 'My companions and I seek the aid of the Council of the Final Word. Are any of them present this day?'

'All the council members are concerned with the business of study, True Thomas,' the man said. 'A great deal was lost in the storm that followed the Wish-Hex and now so much has been opened up to them once more. The Fixed Lands for one. I am sure you understand.'

Tom nodded slowly; Church was puzzled to see a grey cast fall across his face. 'They are not involved in any dissections?' The young man said nothing. Tom composed himself and continued, 'With the freedom granted to me, I would wish to wait.'

'It may be some time. In your perception.'

'If you would inform the council of my attendance I am sure one of the Venerated Ones would eventually find a way to greet me.'

The man nodded and stepped aside so they could enter. They were led to a room off a long, lofty atrium. It was filled with marble benches and sumptuous cushions piled alongside rushing crystal streams cut into the gleaming stone floor.

'I wish I'd brought Laura's sunglasses,' Ruth said feebly.

'How are you feeling?' Church gave her a hug.

'Still sick.'

They arranged some of the cushions in a circle and lounged. 'They're like the worst kind of arrogant aristocrats,' Max whispered. Tom made a silencing move with his hand. Max nodded and continued, 'How long are they going to keep us waiting?'

'Hours. Perhaps days. Maybe even weeks.'

'Weeks!' Ruth said dismally.

Yet it was only twenty minutes before they heard movement in the corridor without. 'Looks like you've still got some clout,' Church whispered.

A deep, unfocused light glimmered across the white walls, as if whoever was approaching held a lantern, but when the figure emerged he carried nothing. And this time Church did experience the unnerving shift of perception; faces seemed to float across the figure's head, some of them sickeningly alien and incomprehensible, others cultured and sophisticated. Eventually he settled on a set of educated, aristocratic features that centred on a Roman nose and a high forehead with piercing grey eyes and full lips; his hair was long and grey and tied at the back in a ponytail. There was a sense of tremendous authority about him that made Church almost want to bow, although he was loath to debase himself before any of the invaders.

Tom, however, was already down on one knee. 'You honour me, master.'

'True Thomas. It pleases me to see you so hale and hearty after everything.' His smile was broad and warm; Church felt instantly at ease. 'And these companions, are they as resilient as you, True Thomas?'

'Oh, more so by far.' Tom stood up and gestured to Church and Ruth. 'A Brother of Dragons, a Sister of Dragons.' Tom introduced them by name, studiously avoiding bringing any attention to Max. Then he motioned to the gentle, kindly figure while keeping one eye on Ruth. 'You are honoured. This is Dian Cecht, High Lord of the Court of the Final Word, seeker of mystery, master healer, supreme smith, builder of the silver hand of Nuada—'

Dian Cecht waved him silent with a pleasant laugh. 'There is no need to trumpet my successes unless you also tell of my many failures, True Thomas, and those I would rather leave to the shadows. I would thank you, Brother and Sister of Dragons, for the part you played in freeing us from the privations of the Wish-Hex.' Church winced at the memory of how the Tuatha Dé Danann had manipulated them, made them suffer in the extreme, just for such an occasion. Dian Cecht gestured magniloquently. 'Now, tell me your request.'

Tom laid a hand on Ruth's shoulder and pressed her forward. 'The Night Walkers have inflicted their corruption on this Sister of Dragons, Good Lord. We ask your favour in helping to remove it.'

Dian Cecht nodded thoughtfully. 'I sensed the whiff of the Night Walkers' presence. Their vile trail is too distinctive to hide. I would not have thought a Sister of Dragons would have allowed herself to be so tainted.'

Ruth felt as if she had failed in his eyes.

'There is nothing ignoble in this suffering,' Tom said in her defence. 'This Sister of Dragons has proved the most hardy of her companions. She succumbed only in the face of overwhelming force.' He paused, then added, 'Much in the way the Tuatha Dé Danann succumbed to the first onslaught of the Fomorii.'

There was a flicker of coldness in Dian Cecht's eye as he cast it suddenly in Tom's direction. 'Ah, True Thomas, one would have thought you would have learned diplomacy during your time among us. Still, I am sure there was no offence intended, and I understand your point.' He turned back to Ruth, now smiling warmly. 'The Filid I am sure will sing loudly of your courageous struggle. I will do for you what I can.'

As he turned to go, he spied Max hovering behind the others. 'I see you have left this Fragile Creature out of your accounts, True Thomas.'

Tom had the expression of a schoolboy who had been caught out. 'He is here to keep a record of these great things transpiring in this world of ours.'

'Ah,' Dian Cecht nodded thoughtfully. 'Then you maintain the traditions of the Filid. Good, good. Wisdom and knowledge needs to be recorded and disseminated.'

Once he had glided out of the room to make his preparations, Ruth turned to Tom. 'Who is he? Can he do the job?'

'I was speaking correctly when I said you were honoured. Dian Cecht is one of the greatest of the Tuatha Dé Danann.' Tom flopped down on to a cushion as if his conversation with the god had wearied him.

'He seemed . . . wise,' Max ventured.

'Wisdom is the essence of him. He has a vista into the very workings of existence. He sees the building blocks that make up everything, the spirit that runs through them. That is why he is the greatest of physicians, the deepest of thinkers, the best maker of all things.' Although his words seemed on the surface to be filled with awe, there was a sour note buried somewhere among them.

'All of the Tuatha Dé Danann seem very different from each other,' Church noted.

Tom nodded. 'While obviously a race, they are all set apart as individuals—'

'So he's a top doctor?' Ruth interjected.

Tom sighed at her phraseology. 'He is the god of healing in the Tuatha Dé Danann pantheon. He was renowned for guarding the sacred spring of health, along with his daughter, Airmid. It is believed it has its source here, within this temple complex, though no one knows for sure. Its miraculous waters can cure the sick and bring the dead back to life.' Church stirred at this, but he didn't dwell on the thoughts that surfaced. 'It can, so they say, even restore the gods.'

Ruth could barely contain her relief. 'So he shouldn't have any problem with whatever those dirty bastards did to me.'

'Then he's one of the good guys,' Max said.

'You could say that,' Tom replied contemptuously. 'The truth is buried in the old stories. When Nuada lost his hand in the first battle of Magh Tuireadh, Dian Cecht made him a new one out of silver. The Tuatha Dé Danann were impressed by his handiwork, but it was not enough. Because he was not truly whole, Nuada was no longer allowed to lead them into battle. He coped as best he could with the shame, but eventually he turned to Dian Cecht's son, Miach, who was believed to be an even greater physician. And it was true. Miach knew the workings of existence even better than Dian Cecht. He grew Nuada a new hand, a real one, and fixed it on to him. A remarkable feat, even for the Tuatha Dé Danann. Nuada was whole again and once more took up the leadership of the race. A time of celebration, you would think? Instead, Dian Cecht promptly murdered Miach for upstaging him. So, yes, a good guy. That's a fair description, isn't it?'

They all fell silent while they considered this information. Then Church said, 'If he's such a big shot, why did he come so quickly when you called instead of sending out some menial?'

'Perhaps,' Tom replied, 'he was stricken with guilt.' But he would not elaborate on his comment any further.

The young man and woman who had greeted them at the door were sent to fetch them an hour later. With Church supporting Ruth, who had been overcome by another bout of nausea, they were led into a massive precinct with a ceiling so lofty they could barely see it through the glare that streamed in through massive glass skylights. Vines crawled around the columns which supported the roof, while some seemed to have trees growing through them as if the stone had formed around the wood.

Dian Cecht stood in a shaft of sunlight in the centre of the room, next to a spring which bubbled up out of the ground. The water was crystal clear and caught the light in a continually changing manner. Although it had no odour, the air near it seemed more fragrant, clearer. They found their gaze was continuously drawn to its sparkle and shimmer, as if it were calling them on some level they didn't understand.

Dian Cecht was wearing robes of the deepest scarlet, which made Ruth instinctively uneasy; he was like a pool of blood in the whiteness of the room. A scarf of red was tied around his head, hiding his hair. He motioned to Ruth to come forward. She glanced briefly at Church for support, then moved in front of the tall, thin god. His eyes were piercing as he silently surveyed her face; she felt he was looking deep into the heart of her, and that made it even more worrying when a troubled expression crossed his face.

'What is it?' she asked.

He shook his head, said nothing. Beside him, a strange object lay on a brass plate that rested atop a short marble column. Ruth tried to see what it was, but her eyes strangely blurred every time she came close to focusing.

He bent over the object and muttered something that sounded like the keening of the wind across a bleak moor. It seemed to respond to the sound, changing, twisting, folding inside out, until it settled on the shape of a bright, white egg with waving tendrils. Ruth instantly recalled the creature she had seen in Ogma's library immediately after the operation to remove the Fomorii equivalent from Tom's brain. 'A Caraprix,' she said.

Dian Cecht smiled when he looked on it. 'My own faithful companion.' He said something else in that strange keening voice and the creature glowed even brighter.

'What are you going to do with it?' Ruth asked, suddenly wary.

'Do not worry. You will not be harmed.' He took her hand to comfort her, but the moment they touched a shudder ran through him. 'The Fomorii have weaved the darkness tightly inside you. I cannot see through it.' He retracted his hand a little too quickly. 'But my friend here should be able to penetrate to the periphery of the shadows and return with the information we need.'

Church's heart leapt when he saw the pang of fear in Ruth's face. 'What is inside me? What have they done?' Her voice sounded as if it was about to shatter.

Dian Cecht smiled a little sadly, then gentle brushed her forehead with his fingertips; she went out in an instant, as she had when Tom had utilised the same technique at Stonehenge. Church started forward, but Dian Cecht caught her easily in his deceptively strong arms and carried her to a pristine marble bench nearby. Church was shocked to see her skin was almost the same colour as the stone on which she lay.

The atmosphere grew more tense and Church had the uncomfortable feeling that a cloud had passed across the sun, although the light in the room remained as bright as ever. Dian Cecht knelt down beside Ruth's head and held the gently throbbing Caraprix in his palm. Church glanced to Tom for support, but the Rhymer would not meet his eyes; Max's face was still with queasy concentration.

The Caraprix was brought slowly towards Ruth's right ear. When it was almost touching, the creature burst into life, snapping like elastic in a wild blur before becoming something like a tapeworm that darted into the waiting orifice. Even unconscious, a spasm crossed Ruth's face.

Dian Cecht stood up and took a step back, fingering his chin as he watched Ruth with resolute thoughtfulness. Church fought to contain his digust. He imagined the Caraprix wriggling through the byways of Ruth's body, probing into the nooks and crannies as it sought out the Fomorii corruption. But he guessed it wasn't like that at all. Instinctively he knew that if a surgeon cut Ruth open he would find no sign of anything unusual in her body at all; the shadow Dian Cecht sensed was lodged in the invisible shell of her spirit.

The moments went by agonisingly slowly. Neither Dian Cecht nor Tom moved, which made Church realise how very alike they were, although he would never have told Tom that. Max, it was obvious, was forcing himself to watch the proceedings: a trained observer, lodging every incident for posterity.

The tableau seemed frozen in time and space; and then everything happened at once. There was a sound like a meteorite shrieking through the atmosphere to the ground. Ruth's face flickered, then grimaced; finally she convulsed, jackknifing her knees up as if she had been punched in the belly. There was a blur in the air erupting from Ruth's ear and then a *shush-boom* as the shrieking sound crashed into the room with them; Church clutched at his aching ears.

The Caraprix, once more in its egg shape, lay on the floor, surrounded by a pool of gelatinous liquid, throbbing in a manner that Church could only describe as distress. Dian Cecht's face contorted, ran like oil on water until Church found it unrecognisable; it settled only when he was on his knees beside the Caraprix, scooping it up into his hands like a broken-winged sparrow, and then he was hurrying out of the room, the air filled with the terrible keening of the wind.

Ruth came round soon after with the sluggish awareness of someone waking from a deep anaesthetic. She made no sense at first, talking about a ship skimming across the sea, and then her wide eyes focused and locked on Church. He held her hand tightly, brushed a strand of hair from her forehead. Beads of sweat dappled the pale skin.

'What did he find?' Her voice was a croak. Church maintained his demeanour; she looked past him, at Tom, and then Max, and a single tear crept on to her cheek.

They wondered if Dian Cecht was ever going to return. He kept them waiting for more than two hours in the cathedral silence of the precinct. When he did finally arrive, he was not alone. On either side were the young man and woman who were obviously his attendants, and behind them at least twenty others, some with the stern, shifting faces that signified high power. A grim atmosphere wrapped tightly around them.

Dian Cecht spoke in moderate tones; the others remained silent, but it felt as if they were on the verge of screaming. 'We cannot help you or your companions, True Thomas.'

Tom stepped forward and bowed slightly. 'Thank you for the assistance you have given, High Lord of the Court of the Final Word.'

Church couldn't believe what he was hearing. 'Hang on a minute,' he said incredulously, 'you can't just brush us off like that!'

Dian Cecht surveyed him with aristocratic coldness, his warm nature suddenly departed. 'It would do well to maintain respect—'

'No,' Church said firmly. 'You respect me. I represent this world, these people. I'm a Brother of Dragons.'

Tom stepped in quickly. 'He has not learned the ways of—'

Dian Cecht silenced him with an upraised hand. 'For all your power, Brother of Dragons, you are powerless. You are a Frail Creature. Your voice may crow louder than your stature prevails, but in essence that is what you are and that is what you will always be. And even by your own meagre horizons you have failed so dramatically that you are not worthy of whatever position to which you so feebly aspire.' His freezing gaze washed over Church's face. 'You have no notion what has happened?'

'What did you find?' Church tried to maintain equilibrium in his voice.

300

His contempt for the Tuatha Dé Danann was growing; he wanted to drive them all from the land at that moment, Niamh included.

Ruth's hand closed tightly on his forearm. 'Church. Don't.' He ignored her.

'The Sister of Dragons has been corrupted beyond all meaning of the word.' Dian Cecht's stare fell on Ruth, but he seemed unable to keep it there. 'She is the medium for the return of the Heart of Shadows.'

His words fell like stones in the tense atmosphere. There was a sharp intake of breath which Church guessed came from Tom. Church watched the Rhymer's hand go involuntarily to his mouth, but slowly, as if it were only confirmation of an idea he had not dared consider.

'What do you mean?' Church didn't want to hear an answer.

'The black pearl—' Ruth began.

'Was the essence of Balor, the one-eyed god of death, Lord of Evil, Heart of Shadows.' Dian Cecht's face filled with thunder.

Church's head was spinning; he looked from Dian Cecht to Ruth to Tom, who seemed to have tears in his eyes, then back to Ruth.

'The black pearl, the Gravidura, was distilled over time by the Night Walkers to maintain the consistency of whatever essence remained from the Heart of Shadows,' Dian Cecht continued. Church recalled the drums of the foul black concoction they had come across in Salisbury and under Dartmoor. 'It is the seed. He will be reborn into the world at the next festival of the cycles.'

Ruth turned to him, her face filled with a terrible dawning realisation. Tears of shock rimmed her eyes. 'What are you saying? That I'm pregnant?' Her hands went to her belly; she watched them as if they belonged to someone else, with a look of growing horror. 'Inside me?' She started to scratch at her stomach, gently at first, but with growing manic force until Church caught her wrists and held them tight. The look in her eyes was almost unbearable to see. 'What will happen?' she asked dismally.

'When the time comes, the Heart of Shadows will burst from your belly fully formed.' Church wanted to run over and hit Dian Cecht until he removed the coldness from his voice. 'No Fragile Creature could survive that abomination.'

Ruth looked dazed, like she was going to faint. Church slipped an arm around her shoulder for support. 'Why are you treating her this way? She's a victim, not a—'

'She allowed it to happen.'

'Don't be ridiculous—!' Church caught himself, tried a different tack. 'Look, you've got him here, your arch-enemy. If you can get the essence . . . the seed . . . out of her—'

'We will have nothing to do with the corruption. Even to be in the same presence fills us with . . .' He made a gesture as if there was a foul smell under his nose.

'But it makes no sense! If Balor is reborn he's not going to leave the Tuatha Dé Danann alone for long. He'll wipe you out like he's going to wipe out everything—'

The words dried in Church's throat when he saw Dian Cecht's face flare with rage, become insubstantial, shift through a range of alien visages. He suddenly acted as if Church were no longer in the room. 'We will deal with the Heart of Shadows and the Night Walkers if they become a problem, True Thomas—'

'If!' Church raged.

Tom moved quickly to push him and Ruth towards the door. 'Quiet, you idiot!' he hissed. 'You're close to having your blood boiled in your veins!'

'Leave now, True Thomas, and do not bring this foul thing to this place again.' Dian Cecht turned sharply and led the others from the precinct.

The silence that lay in their wake was all-encompassing. Ruth dropped her head heavily on to Church's shoulder. 'God . . .'

'Are you going to tell us your blinding revelation or what?' Laura tried to keep apace with Veitch as he marched back towards The Green Man. His face was flushed with anger and there was determination in every fibre of his being.

'I'll do more than tell you.'

Laura glanced back at Shavi, who shook his head dumbfoundedly.

Veitch burst into the pub like he was looking for a fight. Most of the action group had already gathered there, hunkering in serious conversation at the bar. They looked up in shock as Veitch marched up. He muttered something to one of the group which Laura and Shavi couldn't hear and then he spun round and was heading out of the door again. Laura thought about catching his arm to slow him until she glimpsed his expression. She dropped back several feet and let Shavi move ahead to keep up with the Londoner.

Night had almost fallen by the time they had reached the area of large, old houses at the top of the High Street. Only a thin band of pale blue and gold lay on the horizon and that was disappearing fast. Veitch ranged back and forth along one of the streets, his fists bunching then opening, his breathing ragged. Eventually he found the house he was looking for. One boot burst the wooden gate from its hinges and then he was racing up the path.

302

The door was locked. He hammered on it so loudly the glass in the front windows rattled. 'Open up!'

A hollow voice echoed somewhere inside.

'I said open up or I'll kick the fucking thing down and then you'll have nothing to protect you!' he raged.

Footsteps approached quickly and they heard the sounds of bolts being drawn. The door had opened only a crack when Veitch kicked it sharply, smashing it into the face of whoever was behind it. There was a groan as someone crashed back against the wall of the hall. Veitch pushed his way in with Laura and Shavi close behind. They didn't recognise the man who was desperately trying to staunch the blood pumping from his nose; it had streamed down over his mouth so that he resembled a vampire from some cheap horror movie. He was in his fifties, balding and overweight, with large, unsightly jowls.

But instead of berating him, Veitch marched past, glancing into the first room he came to before moving on to the next. He stopped at a large drawing room at the rear of the house. French windows looked out over a garden so big they couldn't see the bottom in the dark. The room was decorated with an abundance of antiques on a deep carpet; large, gilt-framed paintings hung on the walls and a log fire crackled in the grate, despite the warmth of the day. A piano stood in one corner.

Several people were gathered in the room, their apprehensive, pale faces turned towards Veitch, Shavi and Laura. There were four women, one in her forties with blonde hair so lacquered it resembled a helmet, the others in their sixties or older, but still well turned-out. The rest were men of different ages and shapes, but they had one thing in common which only Veitch could see: the vague air that the world belonged to them.

'I say, what do you think you're doing?' Sir Richard stepped forward from the back of the group, a glass of brandy nestled in his palm. His cheeks were slightly flushed; Laura couldn't tell if it was from the fire, the brandy or the interruption.

Veitch stepped forward and smashed the glass from his grip with the back of his hand. It shattered on the floor.

'Good Lord, are you mad?'

'I fucking hate toffs and rich bastards,' Veitch spat. There was a note in his voice which made Laura's blood run cold.

Shavi stepped forward. 'Ryan, are you sure—'

He whirled. 'Yes, I am fucking sure! You two wouldn't even have thought of this because you've got a good outlook on life. You were brought up right in a modern world where everybody treats each other at face value, and that's how it should be. But there are still people out there, even in this fucking day and age, who think they're better than others, because they were born that way or because they earned a bundle of fucking cash.' He turned back to Sir Richard. 'Am I right?'

Sir Richard flustered indignantly. 'If you're implying that I—'

'Shut the fuck up.'

Laura watched the scene with a terrible fascination. The sense of irrational, uncontrollable threat that Veitch was radiating scared even her, so God knows how frightened the great and good of the village felt. She looked round and saw the dismay and worry marked in their faces; they looked as if Veitch was about to shoot them, then rob them; and with her hand on her heart, Laura couldn't say that he wouldn't.

Veitch turned to Shavi, but he was obviously talking to the whole room. 'Let me tell you what happened. When the rich old lady was the first to catch it, this lot were horrified. They thought they were fucking untouchable here in their little sanctuary. But that was a big alarm: anybody could get it now the whole world had been turned on its head, and they had no special fucking privileges to protect them. And then when the drunk got it the little lightbulbs started popping over their heads. He was a fucking undesirable, a piss-head and a burden on fucking society. Maybe it wasn't even so *bad* that he got it. The village would look a lot prettier without his piles of puke in the gutter. And then they thought, it didn't *have* to be them who ended up as dead meat. There were a few more that the village could do without. Lazy layabouts without a job for a start.' He put on a mock high-class voice, but it was still laced with venom. 'Wasn't there a little pocket of them down in that part of the village we never went to, where those cheap, dirty little houses were?'

'Now hang on a minute! Those were our neighbours!' a tall, thin man in a dark suit said sharply. 'We always got on well with them.'

'You tolerated them because you were on top,' Veitch snapped. 'But when your backs were against the wall, you didn't have far to look for sacrifices. You knew those fucking creatures left you alone for a bit after they'd eaten. But you knew they couldn't get into a house without the door open. So what did you do? One or two of you fucking cowards went down after dark and jimmied a door open.'

Laura suddenly realised why Veitch had been examining the door frames; he'd been looking for splinters where the locks had been forced. And she guessed from his past experience he had a perfectly good idea what a jimmied door looked like.

'So you consigned those poor bastards to be meat for another scavenging class we've all had dumped on us.'

Shavi was looking from Veitch to the faces of the assembled group and then back; the truth of Veitch's account was in the guilt that was heavy in every feature. But Shavi was still puzzled. 'I do not understand. If all the doors were locked, the creatures would not have been able to get to anyone—'

Veitch shook his head. 'You're too much of a good bloke, Shav. You've got to think like these bastards. They like cash. They'll do anything for cash. It's their fucking god. They hated being prisoners in their own homes. Couldn't make any lucre. But if those creatures laid low for a few days they had a chance to see if they could get their businesses going. Working their fucking big farms or trying to keep their fucking wine-importing business going or whatever the fuck it was.' He turned slowly around to them. 'That was it, wasn't it?'

Sir Richard began to protest. Veitch stepped forward and hit him sharply in the mouth; his lip burst open and blood splattered on his clean, white shirt. A gasp rippled round the room, and Laura realised she had joined in, so shocking was the image.

One of the old women started to cry. 'I'm sorry—'

'Bit fucking late for that. Thought you'd get rid of a single mum last time, didn't you? Instead you got a poor kid.'

'We didn't mean—'

'Shut up. Whose idea was it?'

There was a long silence while everyone in the room tried to read what his next actions would be. Finally Sir Richard stopped dabbing at his lip. 'It was all of us. We discussed it together.' There was an unpleasant defiance in his face that gave the truth to everything Veitch had said.

'Yeah? Fair enough.' Veitch nodded reasonably. Then he slowly drew the crossbow out of the harness, loaded it and pointed it at the thin man in the dark suit; his face turned instantly grey. 'We'll start here then.'

'No, Ryan,' Shavi cautioned. Veitch ignored him. He slowly tightened his finger on the trigger.

'No!' The thin man pointed a shaking finger at Sir Richard. 'It was his idea! Yes, we all went along with it! But it was his idea!'

'You know what? I fucking thought as much. I'm a good judge of character like that. I know scum when I see it. And I knew you slimy fuckers would all be jumping to save your own skin when the shit hit the fan.' He motioned to Sir Richard with the crossbow. 'You're coming with me, matey.'

'I certainly am not!' Sir Richard's eyes darted round like a hunted animal. Before he could move Veitch had loosed the bolt into the floor and had clubbed him on the side of the head with the crossbow. Sir Richard slumped to the floor unconscious.

Veitch coolly reclaimed the bolt and slipped it back into the harness with the crossbow. Then he bent down and effortlessly slung Sir Richard over his shoulder. He turned to Shavi and Laura as he marched towards the door. 'I'll see you at the pub later.'

'Where are you going, Ryan?' Shavi asked darkly.

'I said, I'll see you later.' He tried to mask what was in his face with a tight smile, but Laura and Shavi both saw, and wished they hadn't.

The journey through the temple, across the autumnal fields, and out into the wide world, resembled a funeral procession. Ruth's face was like jagged shards of glass, her eyes constantly fixed on an inner landscape. She leaned on Church, for emotional rather than physical support, but his tread was heavy. Tom followed behind, unusually disoriented, with Max looking poleaxed at the rear.

In Richmond it was midmorning, the air heavy with an unpleasant heat. Insects buzzed in from the surrounding dales, and traffic fumes choked the market place. They had no idea if it was the next day or several weeks hence; although it remained unspoken, they all knew the date was now mightily significant.

In the back seat of the car, Ruth could no longer contain herself. She undid her jeans and pulled them down over her belly; there was an unmistakable swelling there.

'It doesn't make any sense!' Church protested to Tom. 'There's nothing actually, physically inside her! Is there?'

Tom looked away, shaking his head; it could have meant anything. Ruth broke down in sobs of shock.

After they had subsided, she slumped on the back seat in desperate silence. Tom caught Church's eye and the two of them slipped out, leaving Max to keep an eye on her.

'There must be something we can do,' Church said when they were far enough away from the car not to be overheard.

'Perhaps. But there is a more immediate problem. The Fomorii will never leave us alone until they have Balor back. Inside her is their entire reason for existence, the Heart of Shadows. They *must* have regrouped after the devastation in Edinburgh. Once they locate us their pursuit will be relentless.' He paused. 'They can't take the risk that you'll kill her to prevent Balor being born.'

'Kill her?' The thought hadn't even entered Church's head.

Tom nodded gravely. 'At the moment it's the only option.'

Church cursed Tom furiously for his cold-heartedness, but his reaction was so extreme because he knew, if he could bear to examine his thoughts rationally, that the Rhymer was right. The rebirth of Balor meant the End of Everything. To prevent that, Ruth's life was a small price to pay. Rationally, objectively, from a distance. But from his close perspective she was so dear to him her life was more important than everything. How could he kill her? And he knew, with a terrible, hollow ache, that ultimately the decision would come down to him; one of the burdens of leadership. And whatever his choice, he also knew it would destroy him for ever.

The atmosphere on the way back was thick with unspoken thoughts. Church could see Max was seething with questions, but he didn't feel like answering anything; it was too big to consider even in the privacy of his head. Ruth had dried her eyes and was coping with the shock remarkably well; somehow, that made Church feel even worse.

'That's why my familiar has disappeared,' she muttered, almost to herself. 'It won't come anywhere near me while that thing's inside me.'

They drove with all the windows down, but even that couldn't disperse the oppressive heat in the car. They were sleeked in sweat, sticking uncomfortably to the seats, flushed and irritable. There wasn't even a breath of wind across the lush landscape; the trees remained upright, the crops and hedgerow flowers unmoving.

Max drove speedily along the empty roads, leaning forward to peer through the windscreen that was streaked yellow and orange with the remains of a hundred bugs. But as he rounded a corner, he cursed loudly and slammed on the brakes, the Fiesta fishtailing to a sudden halt. A stream of cars filtered past the turning they needed for the route home: ahead were the unmissable signs of another police roadblock.

'They did see us on the way here.' Church grabbed Max's shoulder. 'You need to back up and get out of here. Find a different route.'

The words were barely out of his mouth when a spurt of blue activity broke out at the road junction; someone had already spotted them. Officers wearing body armour and helmets were tumbling out of the back of a van parked on the edge of the road; Church thought he glimpsed guns.

Max slammed the car into reverse and stepped on the accelerator. With a screech of tyres, they shot backwards, but they'd only travelled a few yards when he hit the brakes. Church and Ruth crashed into the seats in front. Roaring out of a field behind them where it had been hidden was another police van, lights flashing.

'What now?' Max shouted. Before Church could answer he engaged gears, threw the car to the right and shot through an open gate into another field. The going was easy on the sun-baked ground, but they were still thrown about wildly as the car propelled itself over ridges and furrows.

Church gripped on to the ridge of the back seat so he could watch through the back window. The police were drawing closer. 'I hope you watched *The Cannonball Run*,' Church said.

Max grunted something unintelligible. All four wheels left the ground as the car crested a rise. They came down with a bone-jarring crunch and careered sideways on the dusty soil for a short way. 'It always looked easier in the movies,' Max said.

The police were only yards away when Max swore fitfully and suddenly drove directly at the barbed wire fence ahead. They ploughed through it with a rending and scratching and slid down a steep bank, bouncing over a small ditch on to the road with a shower of sparks.

The police vehicle followed suit, but when it hit the ditch its higher centre of gravity flipped it over. It smashed upside down and slid along the tarmac. Max gave a brief cheer as he watched the scene in the rearview mirror.

'Don't celebrate too soon,' Tom said gruffly. They followed his gaze to the bottleneck of traffic at the police checkpoint.

A shadow had risen up ten feet off the ground beyond the vehicles. Its outline shifted ominously in a manner Church had seen too many times before. Max started to retch loudly.

'Don't look at it!' Church snapped. 'Whatever you do. Keep your eyes on the road. Drive!'

Max couldn't resist one last look and vomited on to the floor between his feet. It deflected his attention from driving. The engine idled while he wiped his mouth, shook his dazed head.

The shadow moved, began to take on a sharper form. It was enormous, powerful, dense, seeming to suck in all light from the vicinity. It accelerated towards them, oblivious to the vehicles lined up in its path. A Renault flipped up end over end with a sound like a bomb going off, then a Peugeot and a Mondeo. A Jag folded up like paper in an explosion of glass and a rending of metal.

Church was transfixed; it was like a shark ploughing through water, leaving carnage in its wake. Cars flew like sea spray as it surged onwards. 'Drive, Max.' Church's voice was almost lost beneath the orchestral crashing of metal on tarmac.

It was relentless; as it built up speed it began to change, parts of the dense shadow detaching themselves and folding out, unfurling then reclamping themselves around the figure. It was like the horny carapace of an insect slowly building before their eyes, impenetrable plates, then something that looked like a helmet, but with horns or claws, and all of it in shimmering black. And still it moved.

Finally Church recognised his vision of the monstrous Fomorii warrior in the distorting cavern beneath Arthur's Seat; the same creature Veitch had seen at the ritual under the castle.

A People Carrier went over as if it weighed no more than paper. *How powerful is it?* Church thought. 'Come on, Max!' he yelled again.

The urgency in his voice finally shocked Max into activity. The car shot forward, throwing them all around once more.

'Don't look in the mirror,' Church cautioned; he knew Max, who was not inured to the terrible sight of the Fomorii, would black out instantly. 'Give it all you've got.'

The car began to race just as the Fomorii smashed through the last of the cars and started on the open road between them. Church could feel the thunderous vibrations from its pounding feet through the frame of the car.

'Is it gaining?' Ruth asked. She was clinging on to a corner of the seat to stop herself being thrown around.

'It's making the car jump around!' Max shouted over the racing engine. 'I'm having trouble controlling it!'

Agonisingly slowly, the car began to move faster. It didn't appear to be fast enough, but Max kept his foot to the floor, bouncing up and down in his seat as if trying to add to the momentum. And then, although they hardly dared believe it, the bone-jarring vibrations began to subside a little. Church glanced back once more at the nightmarish image of the beast and saw it had started to fall back; but it was still driving on, and he knew that even if they escaped this time, it would always be somewhere at their backs until it had completed its frightful mission.

'We're doing it,' he said. 'Just pray we don't have another technology failure. And be thankful we've got an open road ahead of us.'

Eventually the twists and turns of the road took them out of sight of the pursuing creature, although they could still hear it for several minutes after. Gradually, Church's heart stopped racing and he rested his face on the back of the seat.

'That's it,' he said. 'That's what they've sent after us.'

'One of the things,' Tom corrected. 'Every resource will be marshalled—'

'Oh, God!' There was a note of hysteria in Ruth's voice.

Church took her hand gently. 'Once we get back to the village we need to get moving again,' he said. 'We can't stay in one place too long.'

'Why? We've only got to kill time until Lughnasadh. Then it will all be over,' Ruth replied bitterly.

He didn't know how to answer that.

'We thought you lot were never coming back,' Veitch said when the car pulled up in the dusty High Street. He tried to hide his concern behind an irritated façade.

'How long have we been gone?' Church helped Ruth out, wondering how he was going to break the news to the others, in particular to Veitch.

'Three days.' Veitch couldn't contain himself any longer. He stepped up so he could look Ruth in the eye and said tenderly, 'How are you?'

She forced a smile. 'Pregnant.' Veitch looked shocked, then worried, and that made her laugh. They retired to The Green Man where Church, Tom and Max had a steadying drink and Ruth attempted to put a brave face on the end of her life.

Veitch's face never flickered when they told him what they had learned, but Church knew he would never forget the look buried deep in the Londoner's eyes; it was the mark of someone who had discovered there wasn't a God. Veitch took a drink, put his arm round Ruth, cracked a joke and said they'd find a solution – they always did; all the right noises. But that deep look never went away. Church wondered how Veitch would cope the closer it got to Lughnasadh; and what his response would be if that terrible decision had to be taken.

The mood remained sombre while they caught up over drinks. Shavi's account of what had taken place in the village left the returnees horrified. Max looked dazed, then queasy. 'I've known Sir Richard since I've been here. All those others too. I can't say I ever really got on with them, but I thought we were all coming from the same place. And I'm supposed to be a trained observer and a good judge of character.' Despite the shock, his spirits soon raised as they always seemed to, and it wasn't long before he was feverishly scribbling everything down in his notebook.

Their attention turned to Veitch's success in uncovering the deception. His ears coloured when Church congratulated him effusively; he looked genuinely touched by the praise.

'And I always thought he'd been clouted with the stupid stick,' Laura said. 'Looks like I'll have to find some other insults. Good job there's a long list.' She was getting braver once more; and Veitch, for his part, seemed to take her words in good humour.

'But you haven't told us what happened to Sir Richard,' Church said. 'You couldn't really take him to the cops, could you?'

Shavi and Laura watched Veitch intently. 'I convinced the bastard to leave town,' Veitch replied coldly.

Finally it was time to go. Max offered them his car, an act of generosity that brought a warm hug from Ruth and a back-slap from Veitch, but Church knew the police would be watching for it. After a heated discussion they decided to make their way on foot across the deserted countryside far away from the roads, cities and towns, despite the dangers that might lie away from the centres of population; it would give them a better chance of evading the Fomorii while they decided what to do next.

It was midafternoon and still unbearably hot when they left the cool confines of the pub. There was still plenty of the day left to put them deep into the heart of the wild upland country. They shook Max's hand, waved to Geordie, who grunted gruffly, and then they wound their way wearily towards the horizon.

Max stood with Geordie in the middle of the street until they had disappeared from view. 'Bloody rum bunch,' Geordie muttered.

'No, mate, heroes,' Max said. 'They might not know it, but they are. They just need writing up. Some of the rough edges taken off them so people can see the wood for the trees.'

Geordie grunted dismissively. 'Not my kind of heroes.'

'You're not seeing it right, Geordie. We're at war now. Under siege. In times like this the people need someone to look up to, someone who'll give them courage to keep fighting.' He smiled tightly. 'I reckon that lot fit the bill – if their story is told in the right way. And I'm just the man to tell it.'

As they passed the outskirts of the village, Laura glanced up at the scarecrow which had unnerved her so much on her way in. She was surprised to see it looked different, although she at first wondered if it was a trick of the glaring sun. Squinting, she tried to pick out what had changed; gradually details emerged. It was no longer just a scarecrow. Something had been tied to it. She squinted again. Another scarecrow appeared to be hanging at the front of the original in the same crucified position, only the bottom two thirds of it was missing. And the head of the second one didn't look very good either.

But something was still jarring. Curious, she took a few steps forward so the sun was away from it. And then, in a moment of pure horror, she realised what it was. It wore a white shirt splattered with something dark near the collar. Instead of straw, something gleamed in the sun; bone that had been picked clean by the creatures in the fields.

Unable to mask her queasy thoughts, she snapped round at Veitch, suddenly aware of the dark, hidden depths of his character. She knew from his body language he realised she was watching him, but he never turned to meet her gaze. His eyes were fixed on the horizon, his expression cold and aloof.

chapter fourteen

wretched times

The clear blue sky was so near they felt like they were in heaven, the air so clean and fresh it burned their throats, which were more used to the particles and fumes of city living. There, high up on the dinosaur-backed ridge of the Pennines, they felt like they had been sucked into the thunderous heart of nature, or into the past where no chimney belched, no meaningless machine disturbed the stillness. Amidst outcropping rock turned bronze by the unflinching sun they picked their way through swaying seas of fern, down sheep-clipped grassy slopes, across bleak upland moors where the wind cut like talons.

Tom navigated by the sun and the stars, leading them on into the remotest parts of the land where the sodium glare had never touched. At night the vast spray of stars looked like a milky river leading them back to the source. They made their camps in hidden corners, dips below the eyeline, behind boulders and in low-hanging caves; all except Ruth took turns keeping watch over the dying campfires.

At times they saw things moving away in the dark or heard sounds that had little to do with any animals they knew; one night Shavi had a conversation with someone unseen whose voice switched between the mewling tones of an infant and the phlegmy crackle of an old man. When the sun began to rise, Shavi heard the mysterious stranger scurry away on many legs, an insectile chittering bouncing among the rocks.

Their decision to steer clear of any centre of population meant finding food was a constant problem, though they were thankful that Tom had an encyclopaedic knowledge of the roots, plants and herbs which grew in secret places where no one would have thought to look. He taught Veitch his many skills at catching rabbits and the occasional game bird, and how to snatch fish from the sparkling streams and rivers they crossed. When cooked on the campfire, the fare was mouth-watering; even so, they soon yearned for a richer and more varied diet.

'This feels like *Lord of the Flies*,' Shavi remarked one calm morning as he watched Veitch carve a spear with his knife; he refused to use his crossbow for hunting.

'Let's hope it doesn't end the same way,' Church replied; he attempted to take the edge off his words with a smile.

'Say, why don't you focus on the black side?' Ruth chipped in with cheerful sarcasm. After the initial shock she had put them all to shame with her bright mood, refusing to be bowed by what had been inflicted on her. Church kept waiting for her to crack as the black despair he was sure lurked within came rushing to the surface, but it never did, and as time passed he came to think it wasn't there at all.

'Look around,' she continued. 'This is the best there is in life. Stars you can see, food and water you can taste, air you can breathe. I've never felt as much at peace. You know, despite everything. Back in London, with work and all that, life had a constant background buzz, like some irritating noise that you force yourself to get used to because it's always around. Now . . .' She held out her arms. 'Nothing. It's not there.'

'It always takes a disaster to show you what you're missing in life.' Laura's voice dripped with irony, but they all knew she was speaking the truth.

Ruth's health continued to be up and down: morning sickness as if she had a normal pregnancy, which always made her laugh darkly, aches and pains in a belly that continued to grow by the day, then times when she felt as robust as she usually did.

Despite the urgency they all felt with Lughnasadh approaching rapidly, they hadn't been able to reach any decision on what to do next. It was almost as if they were paralysed by the enormity of the task before them, and the certain knowledge that the repercussions of one wrong step would be more than any of them could bear. Instead, most of the days and nights passed in the denial of reality that was small-talk, as if they were on a pleasant summer hike. If they could have brought themselves to examine what was in their hearts they would all know they felt there was only going to be one awful, unbearable option.

It was always Tom who was expected to find a solution; he was, after all, the one with the most knowledge of the new rules that underpinned reality. After five days of brooding and weighing of options, of trying to read the stars and muttering away in the thick groves, he thought he had a plan, but the others could tell from his face that he didn't give it much weight. He refused to discuss it there in the open, dangerous high country.

'Talk of such dark matters needs somewhere secure and comforting, where energies can be recharged and preparations made for what lies ahead,' he said. Any questions were simply met with a finger pointing towards the horizon.

That night they made their camp in a sheltered spot on the southern slopes of Pen-y-Ghent not far down from the summit. It was a clear evening and after they had eaten they sat looking at the brilliant lights of the West Yorkshire conurbation spread out to the south-east.

After a long period of thought, Ruth said, 'It's too big, isn't it?'

'What are you on about?' Veitch put the finishing touches to another spear; he was becoming expert in the construction of weapons.

'Look at it.' She outlined the extremes of the lights with a finger. 'They used to be just a few settlements. Then they became villages, then towns and cities, and now they're all merging into one. They're driving nature out completely. There's no human scale at all. People need to feel close to nature to be healthy, psychologically and physically.'

'I thought you were a city girl,' Veitch said.

'I was.' Ruth closed her eyes for a moment. 'I've changed.'

'Perhaps this whole disaster happened for a reason,' Shavi mused.

Ruth eyed him, her eyes bright, waiting for him to say what she was beginning to think herself.

'We have had Government after Government concreting over huge swathes of the countryside,' he continued. 'How many acres have been lost since the Second World War? How much of the ancient woodlands have been cut down? How many hedgerows torn up by greedy farmers? How much moorland destroyed by Army firing ranges? How many rivers polluted, chalklands debased, coastal floodplains disrupted? There was a relentless advance of urbanisation, of what was laughingly called *progress*—'

'And now it's stopped,' Church said thoughtfully.

'Perhaps something drastic had to happen to redress the balance. To save the land.' Shavi lay back with his hands behind his head to stare at the stars.

'What are you saying?' Veitch looked confused and a little irritated. 'That the Bastards invaded us and slaughtered all those people just to save a few bunny rabbits?'

'Oh, *they* do not know about it,' Shavi mused. 'Perhaps they are just part of the plan.'

'Plan?' Veitch looked to Ruth for guidance.

'The great scheme of things,' she said.

Laura slapped her forehead theatrically. 'Tell me you're not going to start talking about God!'

'*There is always something higher,*' Ruth mused. 'That's what Ogma said in Otherworld.'

Shavi leaned up on his elbows to laugh gently at Veitch's expression. 'We are only throwing ideas around, Ryan. Do not let it trouble you.'

'Well, it does,' Veitch said moodily. 'I get worried when people start talking about God. There's enough to worry about down here.'

'Exactly!' Shavi said. 'We are all crabs living in an enclosed rock pool. Occasionally water rushes in, changes things around, adds something new. We do not know it is the sea. Because the rock pool is all we see, we think it is all there is. We are puzzled by the mystery, but comforted by the regularity of our existence. We could never see that an infinite variety of wonder lies just feet away, that intelligent beings roam that place doing miraculous things. We are stuck in the rock pool and we can never see the big picture. So why try to make sense of something we cannot grasp? Why not just enjoy the wonders the next tide brings in?'

There was a long pause and then Laura said, 'You're getting up your own arse again, Shav-ster.'

'What I don't get,' Veitch said, 'is how any of this magic shit really works. I mean, somebody does something, then miles away something else happens with no connection between the two. What's that all about?'

'Look at it this way.' Shavi was growing excited that the conversation was moving away from mundane matters. 'You play computer games, no? The same as Laura. You both know about cheat codes. You type the code in and it cuts through the reality of the game. You can do anything you want – walk through walls, get all the weapons or secrets. Be a god in that fantasy world. There is a writer by the name of Warren Ellis who described magic as the cheat code for reality, which, I think, is a perfect analogy.'

Realisation dawned on Veitch's face. 'I get it! Blimey, why didn't you put it like that before?'

Even Laura seemed intrigued by this line. 'Now those are the kind of cheat codes I could do with.'

'This whole world now, it's all about mystery and discovery. It's like being a kid all over again,' Church said. He thought for a moment, then added, 'When I fell into the pit under Arthur's Seat, feeling like my life was going to be over in an instant, I saw the blue fire come out of thin air. Not thin air, that's wrong. From somewhere else, like Otherworld, but not there.' He looked from Ruth to Tom to Shavi. 'Where do you think that was?'

'The source of it all?' Tom shrugged, the ashes of his dwindling joint glowing red in the dark. 'Is it really worth asking that question? Do you think we'll find out the truth? Not in this life.'

'It *is* worth asking,' Church insisted, 'even if we can't find the answer. The asking is important. It—'

'Look at that.' They followed Ruth's pointing finger into the sky. A serpentine silhouette curled among the stars, riding the night currents on leathery wings. Although they could pick out no detail of the jewelled scales, the Fabulous Beast still filled them with an inspiring sense of wonder; it was a sign of a connection with the infinite that always surrounded them. 'You look at that,' she continued dreamily, 'and then all those city lights destroying the night . . . there's no comparison, is there.'

Instantly the entire landscape was plunged into darkness; it was just another technology failure, but they all audibly caught their breath, the coincidence with Ruth's words seeming unnervingly meaningful.

'Spooky,' Laura said. 'Now make them come on again.'

The brief tension punctured, they all burst out laughing, then lay back to watch the Fabulous Beast gently tracking across the arc of the sky.

Exhausted by their daytime exertions, Ruth, Tom, Veitch and Shavi drifted off to the tents long before midnight. Once they were alone, Laura slumped next to Church, her head resting on his thigh. She had trouble making any first move which might lead to affection, so her actions always followed the same pattern of casual contact. Church tried not to flinch or give any sign things had changed, but he felt guilty he hadn't yet brought the relationship to a close as he had promised Niamh. It was odd; once Niamh had left his side he felt less of an attraction, more inclined to stay with Laura. He was sure Niamh hadn't been consciously manipulating his feelings; it had simply happened, in the same way they had all been subtly influenced by the musical tones of Cormorel and Baccharus. Perhaps there was something in the nature of the Tuatha Dé Danann that made humans fall under their spell. The old fairy stories that had been based on the ancient memories of the Tuatha Dé Danann often told how hapless night-time wanderers were bewitched by the soft voices of the Fair Folk. Even so, he had given Niamh his word. Could he break it? Did he want to risk offending someone so powerful?

'You're starting to become a cliché, Churchill. Sitting there brooding while you've got the world's most glamorous woman lying next to you.' He realised she had been staring up at him while he had been lost in his thoughts.

'Sorry. You know . . . so much to think about . . .' It sounded feeble, almost insulting. She laughed, but he suddenly realised he could see something squirming deep in her eyes. 'What's wrong?'

'We never really talk, do we?'

'You don't like talking.'

'No.' That look again, even though she was trying to hide it.

'Tell me what's wrong.'

Her eyes flickered away from him; she pretended she was watching the dying embers of the campfire away near the tents. Then: 'I'm scared.' A pause. 'And that was about as easy to say as swallowing nails.'

'We're all scared.'

'Do you think you can be any more glib?'

He sighed. 'Don't try to pick another fight. There are easier kinds of sport.'

'I'm not. You are being glib.' Her voice sounded hurt, the first time he had heard that tone. 'I'm scared something's happening to me. Inside.'

'What, you're ill?'

'I guess.' She flinched, looked unsure. 'When that winter witch came after me in the club in Edinburgh something happened that I didn't tell anybody about—'

'Why not?'

'Because I was scared, you dickhead. Are you going to hear me out or talk bollocks for the rest of the night? I was trying to get out, thinking I was dead, regretting being a stupid bitch like usual, and I cut myself. Nothing much.' She held up her finger and drew a faint line on her skin where the scratch had been. 'Only the blood wasn't red, it was green.'

'Some kind of poisoning?'

She shook her head forcefully. 'When it splashed, it seemed to have a life of its own. It moved all over some bars on a window, broke them open.' She stared at her hand as if it belonged to somebody else. In a quiet voice, she added, 'I think I'm jinxed for life.'

Church took her hand and examined it closely. Slowly, he turned it over; there was the tattoo of interlocking leaves that had been burned into her flesh on the island in Loch Maree, the mark of Cernunnos.

Gradually realisation crossed her face. 'The bastard did something to me! I was so worried I didn't even think of that.'

'Maybe. Seems like too much of a coincidence.'

'And there are no coincidences,' she added bitterly. 'So what's happened to me? God . . .' She slammed her fist against the ground angrily.

'I don't know, but I'm betting we'll find out sooner or later. The way Cernunnos acted, he must have something in mind for you.' He felt a surge of anger at how the gods continued to manipulate them all. 'Look, you're obviously still healthy, still walking about, try not to worry about it—'

'That's easy for you to say! How would you feel if you'd suddenly got anti-freeze for blood?' She brushed at her eye before he saw the stray tear, the only honest admission of all the churning emotions in her.

Suddenly he was aware of how fragile she felt, alone and worrying, trying to do her best for everyone else while keeping her personal fears deep inside. She was more of a mess than all of them and that was saying something: filled with self-loathing, unable to see even the slightest good in her character. Yet still trying to do her best. He brushed the hair from her forehead; she wouldn't look at him. He had responsibilities here too; no one else was looking out for her and she wasn't up to doing it herself. Once again he was trapped by doing what was right and damning the consequences. He couldn't abandon her; that would be inhuman. So what if Niamh found out? He could explain the situation. How bad could it be? Certainly not as bad as leaving Laura to fend for herself when she was at her lowest ebb.

'Come on,' he whispered. 'Let's go to bed.'

Morning came bright and hard. Tom was up before everyone else, lighting the fire and boiling up the remnants of the rabbit stew they'd eaten the night before; it met with uniform disapproval, but there was no alternative so they forced it down despite their protesting stomachs.

By seven a.m. they were on their way. Using Veitch's book of maps in conjunction with the sun, Tom strode out confidently. He still refused to give them even a hint as to their destination.

'I don't get it,' Laura said. 'Yesterday my feet were two big, fat blisters. Today they're fine.'

Tom snorted derisively from the front of the column. 'Don't you *ever* pay attention? Why do you think your esteemed leader healed so quickly after the Fomorii masters of torture were loose on him under Dartmoor? Do you think they simply didn't do a proper job? Why do you think Ruth has regained her—'

'What's your point, you old git?'

'It's the Pendragon Spirit,' Church said. 'It helps us heal.'

'Pity Tom Bombadil up front hasn't got it, then. He could grow himself a new head when I rip this one off.'

Tom replied, but it was deliberately muffled so Laura couldn't hear.

'Keep walking, old man,' she shouted. 'And watch out for those sudden crevices.'

Not long after, Veitch and Shavi broke off from the others to see if they could catch something for lunch. They were wary of getting lost, so they arranged a meeting place they could easily pick out on the landscape. After an hour of futile tracking for rabbit pellets and scanning the landscape for any sign of game birds, they gave up and rested against a young tree which had been so battered by the wind it resembled a hunched old man.

Veitch cracked his knuckles, then progressed through a series of movements to drive the kinks from his muscles. Shavi watched him languidly.

'Do you want to talk about what has happened to Ruth?' he asked eventually.

'No.'

'You should. It is better to get these things out in the open.'

'You sound like the counsellor my mum and dad dragged me to when I was a kid.'

Shavi laughed gently. 'I am talking as a friend.'

This seemed to bring Veitch up sharp for a second, but then he carried on as before. 'I never thought I'd have a queen for a friend.'

'These times have changed us all.'

Veitch sighed. 'You better not say any of this to the others, all right?'

'Of course not.'

' 'cause you're the only one I could talk to about it. Yeah, it's doing my head in, course it is. I thought after going through hell to get her back from the Bastards that would be the end of it. And now this. It cuts me up thinking what she's going through. She doesn't deserve that. She deserves . . .'

He seemed to have trouble saying what he was thinking so Shavi gently prompted him: 'What?'

'The best. Whatever makes her happy.'

'Even if that is not you?'

Veitch looked away. 'Yeah. I just want her to be happy.' He was lost in thought for a moment, but then his brow furrowed. 'What do you think's going to happen to her?'

'I do not know. I do know we will do our best.'

'I know it looks black, but I just can't believe she's going to die. Everyone thought she was a goner when the Bastards had her. They didn't say it, but I know they did. But I never doubted we'd get her out for a minute. And I reckon we'll do it this time.'

Shavi smiled; there was something heartwarmingly childlike about Veitch beneath his steely exterior. 'You believe in happy endings.'

'Never used to. I do now, yeah.'

A sound like the roar of some unidentified animal thundered across the landscape. They both started, the hairs standing on the back of their necks. Something in the noise made them instantly terrified, as if some buried race memory had been triggered.

'What the fuck was that?' Veitch dropped low to peer all around.

They could see nothing in the immediate vicinity, so they crawled to the top of a slight rise for a broader vista. At first that area too seemed empty, but as their eyes became used to the patterns of light and shade on the landscape they simultaneously picked out a black shape moving slowly several miles away. The jarring sensation in their heads the moment their eyes locked on it told them instantly what it was.

They squinted, trying to pick out details from the shadow, but all they got were brief glimpses of something that seemed occasionally insectile, occasionally like a man. Yet there was no mistaking the dangerous power washing off it.

Veitch, who had seen it more clearly before, realised what it was. 'It's that big Bastard, the warrior, that almost got the others on their way back from Richmond.'

'It is hunting,' Shavi said instinctively.

'Do you think it knows we're here?'

Shavi chewed his lip as he weighed up the evidence. 'It seems to have an idea in which direction we are going, but it does not seem to be able to pinpoint us exactly.'

'They've sent it after Ruth, the biggest and baddest they've got to offer. What the fuck are we going to do now?' He answered his own question a moment later. 'Keep moving. We can't hang around.'

They retreated down the rise, then hurried back to tell the others.

There was no further sighting of whatever was hunting them, its path had appeared to be taking it away to the west while they were moving south-east. Even so, they were now even more on their guard.

As the day drew on, dark clouds swept in from the west and by midafternoon the landscape had taken on a silver sheen beneath the lowering sky. There, on the high ground, the wind had the bite of winter despite the time of year; they all wished they had some warmer clothes, but they had only brought a few changes of underwear and T-shirts.

Dusk came early with the clouds blackening and they knew it was better to find shelter and make camp rather than risk a lightning strike in the open ground. The rain fell in sheets, rippling back and forth across the grass and rocks; the clouds came down even lower and soon visibility was down to a few yards.

Not even Tom's outdoor skills could find any wood dry enough to make a fire. They sat shivering in their tents, observing the storm through the open flaps. Eventually the rain died off and the clouds lifted, the storm drifting away to the east. They watched its progress, the lightning sparking out in jagged explosions of passion, the world thrown into negative, the martial drumroll.

Laura's voice drifted out across the camp site. 'We need a band. You can't beat a light show like that with any technology.' The wonder in her words raised all their spirits.

It took two more days to reach their destination. The first was dismal with occasional downpours. The going was hard in the face of the gale and the landscape was treacherous in the intermittent mists. They made camp early and slept long.

The second day was much brighter from the onset and by midmorning even the smallest cloud had blown away. Veitch, Shavi and Church stripped to the waist in the growing heat, prompting them to tease the women to follow suit. A mouthful of abuse from Laura brought their jeering to a quick end.

For the first time in days they had to cross major roads and avoid centres of population. They wound their way by Shipton and Ilkley, and whenever the moorland gave way to lanes they ducked behind stone walls every time they heard the sound of a car. After their enforced isolation they felt oddly unnerved when they realised the most populous areas of Yorkshire were close. Tom even claimed to smell Bradford and Leeds on the wind.

Ilkley Moor was almost mystical in the way it responded to the weather conditions and the shifting of light and shade across its robust skin. The green fields on the edge gave way to romantic bleakness the higher they rose, where gorse and scrubland looked copper in the midafternoon sun. There, in the midst of it, the sense of isolation returned, potent yet oddly comforting.

They knew the spot the moment it came into view. The standing stones glowed brightly, their shadows like pointing fingers. But it wasn't the sight of them; after only a few days away from the trappings of the modern age their senses were attuned to changes in the world around them, the crackling energy in the atmosphere that instantly seemed to recharge their flagging vitality, the feel of a powerful force throbbing in the ground as if mighty machines turned just beneath their feet; a sudden overwhelming sense of wellbeing.

Church closed his eyes and had an instant vision of the blue fire flowing powerfully in mighty arteries away from the circle. 'There's nothing dormant about this spot.'

Although he tried to hide his emotions as usual, Tom seemed pleased by Church's sensitivity. 'This has always been a vital spot. Welcome to the Twelve Apostles of Ilkley Moor.'

★

The twelve standing stones which Tom called the Apostles were roughly four feet high and hacked from the local millstone grit. 'There were originally twenty,' Tom said. 'In the nineteenth century they thought it was a calendar and christened it the Druidical Dial.'

Amongst the stones they felt instantly secure and relaxed, as if they instinctively knew nothing could harm them there.

'It feels like Stonehenge on a smaller scale.' Ruth felt comforted and hugged her arms around herself.

'All the sacred sites used to be like this,' Tom said. 'Places of sanctuary. Linked to the Fiery Network. So many have been torn down now.'

Shavi stood in the centre of the circle, closed his eyes and raised his arms. 'The magic is vibrant.'

'It's one of the places that remained potent, even during the Age of Reason,' Tom continued. 'In 1976 three of the Royal Observer Corps were up here. They saw a white globe of light hovering above the stones. Throughout the eighties there were many other accounts of strange, flashing lights and balls of light descending. That helped the circle regain some of its standing in the local community and every summer solstice there used to be a fine collection of people up here for celebration.'

Church drifted away from the others to press his hand on one of the stones; he could feel the power humming within as if there were electronic circuitry just beneath the surface. It seemed so long since Tom had introduced him to the blue fire at Stonehenge, although it was only a matter of weeks, yet now it felt such a part of his life he couldn't imagine living without it. The image of Tom manipulating the blue flames that first night had haunted him and he had begun to realise it was something he desperately wanted to be able to do himself. Cautiously he removed his hand an inch from the stone and concentrated in an effort to produce that leaping blue spark.

Nothing came. Yet he felt no disappointment. He was sure it was only a matter of time.

They set up camp within the tight confines of the circle. In no time at all the earth energy had infused them, recharging them, healing their aches and pains, and Ruth felt better than she had done since Callander; the nausea had almost completely gone. Yet the moor stretched out so bleakly all around and the camp was so exposed they couldn't shake their sense of unease and the feeling they were constantly being watched.

For long periods, Veitch sat half-perched on one of the stones scanning

323

the landscape. 'See anything?' Church asked him while the others were preparing dinner.

He shook his head without taking his eyes off the scenery. 'Look at it out there. There could be somebody ten feet away lying in the scrub and we'd have trouble seeing them.'

'At least if that big Fomor comes up we won't miss seeing him.'

'Yeah,' Veitch said darkly, 'but then where do we run, eh?'

When darkness fell, the sense of isolation became even more disturbing. There was no light, no sign at all of human habitation; they might as well have been Neolithic tribesmen praying to their gods for the coming of the dawn.

Their small-talk was more mundane than ever, with none of the usual gibes or abrasiveness, as they all mentally prepared themselves for the discussion to come. Eventually Tom took out his hash tin and rolled himself a joint, which they all recognised as the signal that they were about to begin. Ruth suddenly looked like she was about to be sick.

'Over the last few days we have all done a remarkable job in avoiding the severity of the problem that faces us,' Tom began. 'That's understandable. It's almost too monumental to consider. But let's speak plainly now so we know exactly where we stand. Here in this circle we have the chance for ultimate victory in the enormous conflict that has enveloped us. And we face a personal, shattering defeat that will devastate us.' Church was surprised to hear the raw emotion in Tom's words; the Rhymer had always pretended he cared little about any of them.

'What you're saying,' Ruth said, her face pale but strong, 'is that if I die, Balor dies, the Fomorii lose, we . . . humanity . . . wins. But if you're overcome by sentimentalism and you can't bring yourself to kill me, Balor will be reborn and everybody loses. And I get to die anyway, in the birth. That last point pretty much makes any debate unnecessary. Either way I die. So . . . we should get on with it as soon as possible.'

'Hang on a minute—' Veitch protested.

'Yes,' Church said. 'I know you'd just love to be a martyr, but maybe we should see if there are any other options before we rush to slit your throat and bury you out on the moors.'

'I'm just letting you know I'm prepared,' Ruth said.

Shavi leaned forward. 'The Tuatha Dé Danann, certainly at their highest level, seem almost omnipotent. Can we ask them to help us?'

'You didn't see Dian Cecht.' The contempt in Church's voice was clear. 'The Fomorii are corrupting in their eyes, and Balor is the ultimate corruption. They're not prepared to get their pristine hands dirty, even if they *could* do something.'

'They're like a bunch of toffs telling the labourers what to do,' Veitch said venomously.

Laura had been watching Tom closely while the others spoke. He had been drawing on his joint, inspecting the hot ashes at the end, as if he wasn't really listening. 'You've got something in mind, haven't you?'

Tom seemed not to hear her, either, but the others all turned to him. 'The Tuatha Dé Danann will not be able to destroy Balor's essence in its current form unless the medium for the rebirth is destroyed,' he began. 'But, as Shavi said, their abilities are wide-ranging. It is possible they may be able to do something to help. I've seen some of the wonders they can perform . . .' His voice faded; he bit his bottom lip.

'How are we going to get them to help us?' Church said. 'They don't want anything to do with anyone who's been touched by the Fomorii.'

'I may be able to help.' Tom drew on the joint insistently; it was obviously no longer about enjoying the effect or using it for some kind of consciousness-raising – he was trying to anaesthetise himself. 'You recall around the campfire in the Allen Gorge, Cormorel told me my *Queen* had returned to her court?'

'She was the one who first took you into Otherworld,' Church said. Whose immense power had taken Tom's body and consciousness apart and reassembled it, who had treated Tom like a toy in the hands of a spoilt but curious brat, his torment so great his mind had almost shattered. And the woman he had grown to love in his captivity and suffering. Church shivered.

'The Faerie Queen, humans called her. She was also known as the Great Goddess by the older races, and a legion of other names.'

'So, she's, like, a bigshot?' Veitch said. 'The Queen.'

'There are many queens among the Tuatha Dé Danann, all with their own courts, although that term is about as relevant as any other when discussing them. But, yes, she is higher than most.'

'And you think she will help?' Church asked, watching Tom carefully for the truth behind his words.

The Rhymer smiled tightly. 'How could she not when her pet returns, rolls over and asks so nicely?'

The bitterness in his voice stung them all. Church knew what a sacrifice Tom would be making; after both the agonies and the crushing blow to his ego, to put himself at risk of facing it all again was more than anyone should be expected to do.

Ruth recognised it too, for there were tears rimming her eyes. She wiped them away, stared at the ground desolately.

'There is no guarantee that she can help, though?' Shavi asked.

Tom raised his hands. 'There are never any guarantees.'

'Then we should have an alternative plan.' Shavi rested a comforting hand on Ruth's back; she shivered, seemed to draw strength from it. 'We already have patrons among the Tuatha Dé Danann. Niamh—'

'I don't think I can ask her for any more help. She's trying to sort out Maponus,' Church said; but he had a pang of guilt knowing that he was afraid to approach her after failing to end his relationship with Laura.

'More importantly,' Shavi continued unfazed, 'there is Cernunnos. Ruth saved him from the control of the Fomorii. Now she is in difficulty, perhaps he will return the favour.'

'Yes.' Ruth's eyes grew wide. 'He said *the Green* was inside me.' She struggled to remember his exact words. 'He said *in the harshest times, you may call for my aid. Seek me out in my Green Home.*'

'That's it, then!' Veitch said excitedly. 'Plan A and Plan B. One of 'em's got to work!'

'We have to be wary not to get too in debt to any of the Tuatha Dé Danann.' The weight in Tom's words gave them all pause.

'This is a desperate situation,' Church said. 'We have to take risks.'

'I know,' Tom said. 'But you have to be aware there is always a price to pay, and that price may be very high indeed. Do not go into this blindly.'

'Then what's the plan? How do we get to these freaks?' Veitch had latched on to the suggestions with the simple hope of a child; the brightness of relief lit his face.

Tom cursed under his breath. 'I think a good starting point would be for you to learn how to treat them with respect. If you open your mouth like that you won't have a second chance to speak.'

'Right.' Veitch looked suitably chastened.

'The Queen's court is accessed under Tom-na-hurich, the Hill of Yews, in Inverness,' Tom said. 'It will be a long, difficult journey, so I propose to set off at sunrise—'

'You're not going alone.' Church didn't leave any room for debate in his tone, but he was still surprised when Tom didn't argue. Church quickly looked round the others, then stopped at Veitch. 'Ryan, you had better go with him. We can't risk the Queen hanging on to him. There needs to be someone to bring back the goods in an emergency.' He hated speaking so baldly, but he could see Tom knew exactly what the potential risks were.

'Not back up to Scotland,' Veitch moaned. 'We've only just scarpered from there.'

'What about Cernunnos?' Ruth asked. 'Where's this Green Home?'

'Cernunnos has been most closely linked with the site of the Great Oak in Windsor Park,' Tom said. 'The oak is no longer there, but the god is rumoured to appear at the spot which was the prime centre of his worship in antiquity. They say,' Tom added, 'he appears there most at times of national crisis.'

'I remember,' Church mused, 'another legend linked to that site. About Herne the Hunter.'

Ruth nodded. 'Cernunnos said that was one of the names by which he was known.'

'The legends say Herne was a Royal huntsman who saved a king's life by throwing himself in front of a wounded stag that was threatening to kill his master,' Tom said. 'As Herne lay dying, a magician appeared who told the king the only way he could save his huntsman's life was to cut off the stag's antlers and tie them to Herne's head. He recovered and became the best huntsman in the land. But he was so favoured by the king, the other huntsmen, overcome by jealousy, eventually persuaded the king to dismiss him. Herne was so broken by this he went out and hanged himself. And the king never had the same kind of success in his Royal hunts.'

Shavi mused over this story for a moment, then said, 'I feel that legend is more metaphor than fact.'

Tom agreed. 'There is secret information in all these stories that has the power to survive down the years. That one tells of how the people turned their back on the resurrective and empowering force of nature, how they suffered for it, and how nature suffered too. It was a warning, albeit a gentle one, compared with some of the legends.

'You see,' he continued, as if the information buried under centuries of experience in his mind was starting to come out in a rush, 'Cernunnos and his bright, other half are, if you will, the bridge between the Tuatha Dé Danann and the natural power of this world. In many ways, they are closer to us than they are to their own. It was a joining that happened in the earliest times, when the two gods pledged themselves to this world and, in doing so, the best interests of the people.'

'You'd be good for this one, Shavi,' Church said. 'You're the shaman. You've developed all those links to nature. You should be able to communicate with Cernunnos.'

Church felt Laura shift next to him and he knew exactly what she was thinking: Cernunnos had put his mark on her too; Ruth obviously wasn't in any condition to undertake the journey, but as a favoured of Cernunnos, Laura would have been a natural choice. Church hadn't chosen her because he felt she wasn't up to the task, couldn't be trusted with something so important; and she knew exactly what his reasons were. He felt a pang of guilt at hurting her, but he had to focus on the best interests of the group.

'When I get to the park, how do I contact Cernunnos?' Shavi asked.

'There is a story I recall from my long walk around the world in the sixties,' Tom replied. 'In 1962 a group of teenagers found a hunting horn in the forest on the edge of a clearing. They blew it and were instantly answered by another horn and the baying of hounds. It was Cernunnos and the Wild Hunt, with the wish-hounds. The boys fled in fear.'

'And the Hunt, I presume, did not depart until they claimed a life,' Shavi noted darkly. 'A price to pay indeed.'

'Perhaps he won't appear in that form,' Ruth suggested hopefully.

Shavi shrugged. 'Then I seek out the horn.'

Laura avoided Church's gaze when he looked from her to Ruth. 'That leaves just the three of us,' he said.

'You're sure we're up to protecting the Queen Bee,' Laura said acidly.

'We'll do our best, as always.' It wasn't a question he really wanted to consider too deeply.

Thunder rolled across the moor; a flash of lightning lit up the northern sky. 'Looks like we're in for a storm.' Veitch seemed happier now he felt he was doing something positive.

They watched the sky for a while, but the bad weather was skirting the edge of the moor, moving eastwards. Another flash of lightning threw the landscape into stark relief.

'What's that?' Ruth said suddenly. But the night had already swallowed up whatever she had seen.

'What did it look like?' Church asked.

'I don't know.' Her voice sounded like she had an idea. She moved to the edge of the circle to get a better look.

'Don't go beyond the stones!' Tom said sharply. 'The earth energy gives a modicum of invisibility here if there's anything supernatural in the vicinity. They'd have to stumble right across us to see us.'

'I don't know . . .' Ruth peered into the dark, but it was too deep.

Another flash of lightning, moving away now, so the illumination was not so stark. Even so, Ruth caught her breath; this time it was unmistakable. A large black shape like a sucking void was moving rapidly across the bleak moorland.

'It's here.' Her voice barely more than a whisper. She turned, eyes wide; the others could read all they needed in her face.

Tom rushed over and kicked out the campfire. 'Stay down, stay quiet! It may pass us by.'

At that moment twin beams of light cut through the night, rising high up into the sky like searchlights. A second later they lowered sharply as a car came over a rise and started to head towards them. The headlights briefly

328

washed over the stones as the car came on to the road that ran within sight of the circle.

'Shit,' Veitch said under his breath.

Across the quiet landscape music rolled from the car's open windows. Church unconsciously noted it was New Radicals singing *You Get What You Give*, but that thought was just a buzz beneath a wash of rising panic. The car's engine droned. Young voices sang along loudly, male and female, four, maybe five of them.

'Shut up,' Laura hissed to herself.

'Turn off the headlights,' Veitch said.

As if anything will do any good, Church thought.

The car continued its progress, a firefly in the night.

Veitch spun round, his face contorted with anxiety. 'We've got to get out there and do something! The Bastard will be on them in a minute and those poor fuckers won't stand a chance!'

Church hesitated; he was right, they ought to try.

Tom seemed to read his mind. 'No! No one leaves the circle! If you go out there you will surely die. Even here, your chances are slim—'

'Fuck! We have to do something!' Veitch protested. Church thought he was going to cry.

'You go out there and die in vain, everybody else dies with you!' Tom's voice was a snarl that would brook no dissent. 'You're too important now! You have to think of the big picture!'

Veitch was starting to move. Tom gripped his shoulder and Veitch tried to shake it off furiously, but Tom held on so effortlessly it seemed incongruous. Veitch half-turned, eyes blazing, but he didn't move any further.

Another diminishing flash, an instant's tableau: the dark hulk of the Fomorii warrior had risen up, started to change as its insectile armour clanked and slid into place, preparing to attack. The car trundled along, the occupants oblivious.

Ruth's eyes were tear-stained. She stared at Church, aghast. He winced, looked away.

'Maybe we could . . .' Laura stopped, shook her head, walked away until she was out of the others' line of sight.

Shavi was like an iron staff, his face locked, his eyes fixed on the feeble beams of light.

Suddenly there was a sound like aluminium sheeting being torn in two. Several stars were blotted out. And then the ground trembled. There was an instant when they all had their eyes shut, praying. But they had to see, so they would never forget. The darkness swept down like a pouncing lion. There was a crunching of metal. The headlight beams shot up in the sky. Singing voices suddenly became screams that must have torn throats. New Radicals were still singing, just for an instant longer, then snapped off at the same time as the screams. A second later the lights blinked out. More crunching. Silence. And then an explosion which rocketed flames and shards of metal high into the sky as the petrol tank went up.

Everyone in the circle was holding their breath. The universal exhalation came slowly, filled with despair.

'Get down!' Tom hissed.

They dropped flat so they could feel the vibrations in the ground, fast, growing slower. They didn't stir until they had died away completely. When they eventually sat up, everyone looked shell-shocked; faces pale, eyes downcast.

'We did that,' Veitch said bluntly. He walked over and leaned on one of the stones, staring out across the moor. The crackling fire cast a hellish glare across the scrub, the smoke rising to obscure the stars.

Ruth leaned in to Shavi who put his arms around her. Church looked over to Laura, but she had her back to him, wrapped in her own isolation.

'You were right,' Church said to Tom, 'but I don't know how you can be so cold.'

All Tom would say as he slumped down at the foot of a stone was, 'Life's much more simple when you're young.'

It was over an hour before they felt able to talk some more. Veitch still looked broken, the others merely serious.

It was Ruth who voiced the thought that was upmost in all their minds. 'If that thing is hunting us, what chance do Church, Laura and I stand? Do you think we can possibly keep ahead of it until one or the other of you gets back?'

'No,' Tom said baldly. 'But I have a plan—'

'Well, yippee,' Laura said flatly.

'There is a place not too far away that has the potency of this circle. Another blindspot. It is big, very big, and if you choose your hiding place carefully you should be able to avoid detection for . . .' He chewed on a knuckle for a second or two. '. . . Quite a while.'

'That's not the wholehearted answer I was hoping for,' Ruth said irritatedly.

'Where is it?' Church asked.

'In the High Peaks. It's a magical hill, more a mountain really, called Mam Tor, the *Heights of the Mother*, rising up 1,700 feet. The most sacred prehistoric spot in the entire area.'

'A mountain to hide in!' Veitch said in astonishment.

'Great. We can play at being the Waltons,' Laura said.

'The ancients recognised it as a powerful spot. Nearby there is a hill dedicated to Lugh, now known as Lose Hill. All around there are standing stones and other ceremonial sites, all looking up to the hill of the Mother Goddess. At the foot is the Blue John Cavern, where the semi-precious stone originates. A landscape filled with magic and mystery. The perfect hiding place.'

'Great,' Church said. 'Now all we have to do is get there.'

Church woke in the middle of the night with a familiar, uneasy feeling, but one he hadn't felt for a few weeks. He crawled out of the tent, feeling his stomach churn. Laura was on watch, but she was dozing near the dying embers of the fire; he would have to have a word with her in the morning.

Slowly he looked around the darkness that pressed in tightly against the stones. Nothing. The wind blew eerily across the moor, making an odd sighing noise in the scrub. He prayed he was wrong, but in his heart he knew.

'Where are you?' he said softly.

A second later a figure separated from the dark: indistinct, almost blurred, as if he were looking at it through a curling sheet of smoke. He thought after all his brooding, all the weighing of emotions, the logical acceptance, he would feel nothing, but the pang in his heart was as sharp as ever.

'How are you, Marianne?' He held the tears back successfully.

The smoke appeared to clear and there she was, as beautiful as when they had shared a home; when she was alive. She didn't speak, she never did, but he felt he could almost read her thoughts. Her face was so pale, by turns frightening and filled with despair.

'I should have known when they'd failed to find anyone with the big beast, they'd send you to hunt me out,' he said softly. 'Do they have a message for me, Marianne? Anything? Or have they just sent you here to break my spirit?'

A sighing. Was it still the wind, or was it her?

He smiled sadly, wishing he could leave the circle to try to touch her hand one final time, although he knew that was impossible; he had learned his lesson. He wouldn't break the protection of the stones and put himself under the malign Fomorii influence that inevitably surrounded her. 'Did they think I'd fall for it all again?' His voice was low and calm; he didn't even know if she could hear it, anyway. 'Tell them it won't work any more – I'm not as weak as I was. If anything, seeing you here, knowing what they've done to you, gives me more strength to carry on. I'm going to set you free, Marianne. And then I'm going to make them pay. If you can take anything back to them, tell them that.'

He couldn't be sure, but he hoped, and he hoped: her face seemed to register the faintest smile.

And then she was gone.

chapter fifteen

the RAVENING

Beneath the soaring vault of a gold-and-blue dawn sky they said their goodbyes. Less than a month remained until Lughnasadh. Conflicting emotions darted among them like electricity between conducting rods, but although the currents ran far beneath the surface, they all recognised the secret signs. Few words were said, but hands were shaken and backs slapped forcefully.

Church surprised himself by the depth of his affection for Shavi, Veitch and even Tom; there was the mutual respect of the survivors of desperate times, certainly, but also a recognition of qualities of decency and bravery which often lay hidden in modern life. It was uplifting to realise even damaged goods carried with them the blueprints for rectitude. He feared for their safety, but he had no doubt that if anyone could overcome such adversity, it was them.

Ruth hugged them all, although Tom looked uncomfortable at the contact; he walked away a few paces so the unpleasant experience would not be repeated. Laura too tried to appear aloof, but her repressed nods to each of them shouted as loudly as if she had thrown her arms round their necks. Then Shavi turned to Veitch with a broad grin.

Veitch brandished his hunting knife threateningly. 'If you try to hug me I'm going to kill you. I'm not joking.'

Shavi laughed as he pushed the knife to one side. He put his arms around Veitch and pulled him tight. Veitch was like a rod for a second, then relaxed and hugged Shavi just as warmly. It was an act of deep friendship, yet no one was surprised; they had all watched each boundary fall over the weeks until only Veitch had been left to recognise it.

'Fuckin' queen,' he muttered as they broke off.

'Thug,' Shavi responded.

333

Despite the gravity of the situation, there was more hope around than they truly deserved to feel.

When they finally felt ready, Veitch and Tom turned to the north and set off across the uneven terrain, carefully avoiding the blackened, still-smouldering wreckage of the car. Shavi, who was to accompany the others to Mam Tor before continuing to Windsor, led the way south.

Away across the moor a lone figure watched the two parties, as they had been watched for so long. The choice was difficult, but eventually the selection was made. As the figure set off across the scrub anyone could have been forgiven for thinking they were seeing an unfeasibly large wolf loping after its prey.

Mam Tor rose up majestically from the stone-walled, patchwork green of the surrounding countryside, a slab of imposing rock, brown and grey against the brilliant blue sky. None of them could believe how tall it was, how sheer were the cliff faces. Far beneath its imposing summit the two valleys of the Hope and Edale rivers stretched out, cool and verdant in the heat of the day.

'I can see what the old git meant.' Laura's sunglasses protected her eyes as she peered upwards. 'Nobody's going to scramble up there on a whim.'

'Bronze Age people forged a settlement there because it was impregnable as long as food supplies lasted,' Church said, harking back to his archaeological studies. 'An excavation up there in the sixties found a stone ceremonial axe and other bronze axes. It was a ritual place for the Great Mother that protected them all.'

'Let's hope it protects us as well,' Ruth said.

Their journey to Mam Tor had been without incident, but they all felt exhausted from helping Ruth along the rugged route which wound like a clear, rushing river between the overpopulated, overbuilt sprawl of Greater Manchester and the industrial zone of West Yorkshire. As the days passed, her stomach had started to swell rapidly, straining at her clothes. With it had come a sapping of energy, as if her very life force were being leached from her; but somehow she still managed to keep going. Her nausea, particularly in the morning, had become debilitating, and they had to find regular supplies of clean water to keep her from dehydrating. By night she shook as if she had an ague, her face ghostly white, her skin almost too hot to touch, sweat soaking through even her jeans.

There, looking up at Mam Tor, she had somehow found the strength to stand unaided. It seemed right, important. The place was sacred to her ancestors. And the Mother Goddess, or one of them at least, was her patron now. She prayed this was the place she was supposed to be to survive her ordeal.

'Are you going to be all right from here?' Shavi brushed his long hair from his face where the wind whipped it continuously. He looked remarkably fit despite the exertions of the journey, standing straight and tall, his body lithe, his limbs loose. The others felt calm just being near him.

Church nodded. 'We'll be fine.'

'Speak for yourself.' Laura surveyed the steep, precarious path that rose up to the summit.

'Watch how you go,' Church said. 'I'm sorry you've got to go on your own.'

Shavi smiled. 'I am comfortable with my own company. And I can travel faster alone.' He hugged Church tightly before giving both the women a warm kiss. Then he turned and continued his journey south.

The wind became more merciless the higher up Mam Tor they ascended. 'Well, it's going to be a lot of fun living up here,' Laura said sourly. 'There's nothing like the harsh elements to give a complexion that wonderful ruddy bloom.'

'Just be thankful it's not winter,' Church said as he strode off ahead. The truth was, he didn't know how well they would do. None of them had the trapping skills of Tom or Veitch and the environment was truly bleak and exposed. His only plan was to find a sheltered spot to pitch the tent, one which couldn't be seen from any great distance. Beyond that, it would be a matter of taking things a day at a time, which didn't seem the best strategy in the world when so much was at stake.

With Church and Laura virtually having to drag Ruth with each step, it took them nearly two hours to get a significant way up the tor, and by that time the sun had started to set. They turned and looked back over the breathtaking vista as the huge sweep of the country slowly turned golden in the fading light. It was an instant so beautiful they felt a brief *frisson* of transcendence that pushed their troubles to one side.

But then the high peak called again and they continued on their way. 'We need to find a good site by dark.' Church scanned the rugged, unforgiving slopes.

'Why don't you just go ahead and state the obvious?' Laura muttered.

'And why don't you just keep on sniping until I get *really* irritable?' Church snapped. 'What's wrong with you?'

'Please don't argue,' Ruth said weakly. 'Let's just try to get somewhere quickly.'

They bit their tongues for her sake, although the tension between them had not been given vent since Church had selected Shavi for the mission to Cernunnos. Church knew Laura had been hurt by the decision, but he couldn't understand why she didn't see it as a tactical choice instead of the personal blow she obviously considered it.

The night seemed to come in uncannily quickly, pooling like an inky sea across the countryside, rising rapidly up the tor. They were all too exhausted to look around much more and their calves felt like they were being burnt by hot pokers after the steepness of the climb.

Church was just about to select a campsite at random when he spotted a series of regular dark shapes among the gloom, hidden in a fold in the mountainside. They were too stark to be natural. He led them over to the place amidst Laura's protestations and was surprised to see an abandoned house hidden in the shadows. It looked like an old hill farmer's home, just three stark rooms on a single level. It had obviously been empty for some time; the door sagged on its hinges, the windows had been put out and the inside was strewn with the detritus of the years: a few slates from the roof, Coke cans, plastic bags, old newspapers, a couple of shrivelled condoms.

'Home, sweet home,' Church said, slapping his hand cheerily on the door jamb. 'Hey, I *can* believe in serendipity.'

'I don't like it.' Ruth stood a few feet back from the shadow the house threw, her arms wrapped around her. She looked it over like it was going to jump out and bite her. 'It's spooky.'

Laura marched past them both. 'Well, I'm sick of tents and if it'll keep the rain and wind off, it's good enough for me.'

'It's a good hiding place.' Church could see he wasn't going to convince Ruth easily. 'Nobody will be able to see us unless they're right on top of us.'

'Look at this.' Laura's voice floated out from the dim interior.

Ruth followed Church in with some trepidation, unsure if it was worse to be outside in the open night. Laura was pointing to a wall lit by the last meagre rays of the sun. It was covered in a mass of writing, some in huge letters, but vast swathes in an almost microscopic scrawl; most of it seemed unintelligible.

'Kids,' Church said.

Laura leaned forward to try to read the tiny print. 'They really don't have much to do round here, do they?'

Ruth stood in the corner, her arms still wrapped around her. From the corner of his eye, Church could see her gaze jumping back and forth, as if she was expecting something to come out of the corners of the room. 'I feel like something bad has happened here,' she said.

And at that moment the sun set and darkness claimed the land.

The rain started as Tom and Veitch reached the lowland slopes with twilight drawing in. By the time they had arrived at a main road, their clothes were soaked through and their hair was plastered to their heads; it was a hard, unforgiving downpour, uncommonly chill for that time of year. The cars hissed by, steaming in the spray, their headlights blazing paths through the night. Most of them were driving too fast for the conditions, desperate to get to the safety of their destinations before the deep night encroached.

After long deliberation during their walk, Tom and Veitch had decided to eschew the established policy of tramping through the wilderness. With only two of them, they felt they could move quicker and with a greater chance of being unseen by picking up a vehicle and following the main roads north, at least up to the Scottish Highlands.

But after forty-five minutes standing on the roadside in the splash zone they began to question their choice. No one was prepared to stop to pick up a hard-faced, muscular young man and his older companion who looked like he'd done too many drugs.

'We're going to be here all bleedin' night.' Veitch's voice was thin with repressed anger as a Volvo hurtled by in a white glare and a backwash that showered him from the waist down. 'This was a stupid idea.'

Tom removed his glasses to wipe the droplets off them for the third time in as many minutes. He kept his attention fixed on the stream of traffic.

'It's hardly bleedin' surprising, though, is it? We could be anything here. Everyone must know by now you can't trust stuff at face value. Once we were in the car we could tear their faces off.' He took a perfectly timed step back to avoid the splash from a Golf. 'I haven't seen this much traffic for ages. Probably 'cause it's a main route. Safety in numbers and all that. I bet the back roads are deserted—'

'You're talking too much.'

'Nerves, all right? I'm worried about Ruth.'

Tom stuck out his thumb once more with undiminished optimism.

'We don't stand much chance of winning now, do we?' Veitch continued. 'I mean, I'm still staying hopeful we can help Ruth, but what's inside her . . .' He looked into the middle distance. 'If it finds its way back, what's it going to be like?'

Tom didn't seem to hear him at first. Then he said, 'When Balor led the Fomorii across the land in the first times, it was said daylight was driven from the land. In the eternal night there was only the stink of burning flesh

337

and the rivers ran red with blood. Humanity was driven to the fringes of existence.' His pause was filled with the rushing of the wind and the rain. 'If he returns once more, there is no hope for anything.'

Veitch chewed this over while the cars sped past, and when he spoke again it was as if it hadn't even been mentioned. 'How long are you planning on sticking it out here before you realise nobody's going to help us? Come on. We better find some shelter.'

'People haven't changed. There are still some who'll help out a fellow in need.'

'Yeah—' Veitch began cynically, just as a 2CV indicated and pulled over sharply.

The passenger door opened on to a man in his early thirties, his face surprisingly open and smiling. His cheeks were a little chubby, his eyes heavy-lidded beneath badly cut jet-black hair which made him look more like a boy.

'Where are you going?' he said loudly over the white noise and rumble of the road sounds.

Tom leaned in. 'As far north as you can take us.'

'Okay. Hop in.'

Veitch clambered into the back, scrubbing the excess moisture out of his hair, while Tom took the front. It was only when they were both settled that they saw their driver was wearing a dog collar.

'You must be mad hitching at this time, in this weather,' the driver said as he pulled away.

'Needs must.' Tom glanced at him askance. 'We were counting on a Good Samaritan,' he added wryly.

'There're still a few of us around.' The driver laughed. 'Actually, I had selfish motivations too. I wanted some company.' He stuck a hand out sideways. 'I'm Will.'

Tom and Veitch introduced themselves, then fell silent, but Will was keen to talk. 'I've been down to London. Came down yesterday and stayed overnight. I've got a parish in Newcastle. Rough area, good people though. I'd be the first to admit it's been a struggle. Still, the last few months have been a struggle for all of us, haven't they?'

'There's been some trouble up there, hasn't there?'

A rawness sprang to Will's face and he shifted uncomfortably; he didn't appear to want to talk about that. 'They've closed off part of the city. Terrible business. Terrible. But that's nothing new today, is it? Have you heard any news about what's happening?'

'Only what we've seen with our own eyes.' Tom was enjoying the warmth of the heater on his feet.

338

'They say the Government is on the verge of giving up the ghost. Apparently they've set up a coalition, a Government of National Purpose. As if that will do any good. They're all politicians, aren't they?'

'Anybody who seeks out power should never be allowed to have it,' Tom agreed.

'I don't think they've any idea what's going on at all.'

'Does anybody? Do you?' Tom watched him curiously. He seemed a little naïve and idealistic, like many younger clerics.

'Nobody knows the details, but we have all seen what we've seen. We know science is on the back foot. What should we call it – the supernatural, the strange, the wondrous? Those who believed in that kind of thing always struggled to identify it on the periphery of life. Now it's right there at the heart.'

'I would suppose,' Tom noted, 'that you were one of those believers. Being a clergyman and all.'

Will grew quiet, his face lost in the shadows between street lights. After a moment's contemplation he said, 'Actually, that's not true. I considered myself one of the new breed. You know, trendy, the papers called us, because we had raves, flashing lights and dry ice instead of hymns. No time for the miracles and magic of the Bible. There was no truth in it, just a true way of living, little stories to teach decency.'

In the back, Veitch began to doze. After the exertion of the last few weeks, the warmth, the rhythm of the wipers and the hiss of the wheels created a soothing atmosphere that made his limbs leaden. Will's voice was calming too; he began to drift in and out of the conversation.

'And now you think differently?'

'You're damned right.' He paused. 'Must watch my cursing these days. My basic belief before was: God is a supernatural entity. If there's no evidence of the supernatural – and I've never seen any – how could there be a God, a virgin birth, even an Ascension? But I carried on because the Church still did good, important work. And then the miracles happened. All over the country – lame people walking, blind people seeing, the dead reviving. All the clichéd stuff. But this time there was evidence.' He hammered the steering wheel passionately to emphasise his words. 'There was a meeting in London. The General Synod was discussing all the monumental events that have been happening all over. I was still quite cynical until I heard all the personal testimonies, from every single part of the country.'

'And you think these are some signs from your God?' Tom did little to hide the faint contempt in his voice.

'I honestly don't know. I'd like to think that. Some of my colleagues think

339

the opposite. They say everything they've seen in the world proves there *can't* be a God – not our God, anyway. How can miracles be special . . . be miracles . . . if they're happening randomly every day? It's magic, they say, not God's work. And the reports presented at the meeting of—' he eyed Tom unsurely '—powerful beings—'

'Not God's creatures,' Tom said.

'So *they* say.'

'And you think differently?'

'Until I've seen them with my own eyes . . . If you believe God created the universe and everything in it, then he could have created the most bizarre, alien beings. Who are we to begin to wonder at His reason for putting them here? The scheme is too big, our perspective too small.' He glanced at Tom. 'I take it from your words you don't believe in God.'

Tom grunted. 'I believe in a higher power. Call it God if you will. The common belief is that people who have seen great suffering cannot believe in God, for how could God allow such things to exist? That is shallow and misguided. Only people who *have* seen great suffering can know without a doubt that God truly exists.'

The vicar's brow furrowed. 'How can you say that?'

'Work it out for yourself. That's the only way true wisdom comes.' Tom watched the dark hedges and closed-off villages flash by.

Will didn't seem offended by Tom's brusque manner. 'All I can tell you is what this means for me. Two days ago science told me there was no place for miracles. Now we live in this world where wonders are commonplace. And they may not be caused by *my* God, as you put it, but the fact that they are happening means that for me miracles are now truly possible. Anything is possible. And once I realised that, I just had to rush back to my church to tell everyone about it.'

'Well, isn't that a conversion on the Road to Damascus,' Tom said drily.

'I can understand your cynicism, I really can,' Will stressed. 'But despite all the misery that's been caused – and I accept there's been a lot – on a spiritual level, there's also so much more hope. All the things the Bible teaches aren't abstract concepts any more. Life has just become so much more, I don't know, vital. How can you worry about making more money or seeking out power when all this is happening? It focuses the mind on the truly important things.'

They continued northwards, the rain finally drifting away to leave a cloudy, warm night. The conversation was punctuated by long periods of silence when they each wrestled with their own thoughts, but that was often too uncomfortable and they would be forced to return to discussing the state of the country and how much life had changed. Veitch was oblivious to it all as he slept soundly, stretched out across the back seat.

As the midnight hour passed and Newcastle drew nearer, the air being sucked in by the heater gained an unpleasant tang of chemicals and burning, Tom glanced over at Will; the vicar's face, oddly, seemed to have lost some of its youthfulness and his expression had grown darker.

'How bad is it back at home?' Tom asked.

A pause. 'Very bad.'

'You're aiming to pass on some of that hope you feel.'

He nodded. 'Something magical. The Church lost touch with that, with the reason why people needed it. There's been too much looking inward, too much rationalising and reasoning and not enough heart. Not enough magic.'

The sky overhead was briefly lit up, as if it were daylight.

'Good Lord.' Will leaned over the wheel to peer up into the sky. 'Was that a flare?'

They travelled on for another five minutes without any further disturbance, but then something else caught Will's eye and he slowed the car down. 'Look at that.' There was awe in his hushed voice.

Lights were moving in complex patterns across the sky. Some were balls, glowing red or white, others cylinders that seemed to have all the colours of the rainbow on them as they rotated slowly.

'UFOs,' Will noted.

'That's what they used to call them. Keep going, they won't disturb you.'

Will glanced sharply at Tom. 'You're saying they're alive? They're just lights.'

'Just lights? There is no *just* anything in this world.'

'Then what?' He looked back up to the heavens, slowing the car even further.

'Spirit forms, I suppose you would call them. Sentient beings that reflect what is taking place in our heads.'

'How do you know this?'

'I've seen them before.'

'They look like cherubs. Or angels.' Will chewed on a knuckle excitedly. 'Perhaps that's what they are. If they were seen in ancient times . . .' He paused, holding his head to one side. 'I can feel something. Can you feel something?' Will didn't seem to notice Tom's lack of a reply. 'It fills me with a sense of wellbeing. Almost of transcendence.'

'That's part of their nature too.'

A tear trickled from the corner of Will's eye. 'You say they're, what, spirit forms? But if I say they're angels, who's to say which of us is right?'

Tom shrugged disinterestedly.

'It's all a matter of perspective.' He pulled the car over to the side of the road, transfixed. The lights continued to bob and weave across the sky, their flares lighting the clouds like fireworks. Then, as Will watched intently, their movement ground to a halt. There was a brief period when they hung suspended in the heavens, and then gradually they shifted in unison towards some kind of alignment. A few seconds later they formed a blazing cross of many colours, hanging in the eastern sky.

Will caught a sob in his throat, but the tears streamed down his cheeks. 'I've been so wrong.'

The lights stayed that way for a long moment, and then the cross slowly broke up and they drifted away to lose themselves among the billowing clouds. Will chewed on the back of his hand; he appeared to be shaking all over.

Tom winced, then sighed, unsure quite how to say what he felt. 'It might—'

'I know what you're going to say. It might not be what I think. I might be putting my own interpretation on it. But can't you see – that doesn't matter! It's a sign of something bigger. That's all we really need.'

He sat for a while with his head resting on the steering wheel. When he did finally look up, he was transformed, beaming and optimistic. Seeing him, Tom couldn't help but think that perhaps he was right.

Will left them on the outskirts of Newcastle, where Tom caught up on his sleep in a back garden shed. The next morning they picked up a succession of lifts that took them north. They crossed Hadrian's Wall without incident and made better going across the Scottish Lowlands, with several other lifts taking them north of Stirling. They were dogged by repeated technology failures on the outskirts of Perth and, in frustration, decided to proceed on foot. Although it was rough going as they moved into the foothills of the Cairngorms, they knew it was also the best option for safety. With only the A9 as the main route northwards, their chance of discovery would increase tenfold in a vehicle.

The pines in the Forest of Atholl were cool and fragrant and filled with game birds. Veitch even brought down a deer with his crossbow and that night they enjoyed a royal feast, with enough meat left over to last them days. Beyond the trees they headed across the deserted countryside towards Ben Macdui, which dominated the skyline, rugged and brown against the blue sky. Crystal-clear springs plummeting down from the peaks provided them with a plentiful supply of refreshing water and away from the pollution the clear air was invigorating; they both felt much better for it.

Their relationship passed through raucous humour, anger and mild bickering, often in the course of a single hour. Veitch couldn't work Tom out at all; he got lost in the hidden depths of his companion, found himself unable to navigate the subtleties of his intellect and moods. But he couldn't shake the feeling that the stone-faced, grey-haired man was a fraud, trading on his reputation as some hero of myth. Tom seemed to have a great deal of knowledge about every subject, but he rarely volunteered it when it was needed, which was anathema to Veitch, who believed at all times in acting quickly and decisively.

With only twelve days remaining, they had been through a period of uncomfortable silence brought on by an argument over which was the quickest route to take across the hills. The uneasy atmosphere dissipated sharply when Veitch caught sight of a swathe of constant motion, passing across the lower reaches of the mountain range far below them. At first glance it appeared as if the land itself were fluid, rippling and changing in a dark green wave moving slowly across the landscape.

'What is that?' He tried to pick out detail from the glorious sweep of the countryside.

'Look.' Tom pointed to what appeared to be a tiny figure moving ahead of the wave.

Veitch continued to stare until he realised what was happening: the wave was actually vegetation; trees were sprouting from the ground and shooting up to full maturity in a matter of minutes, and the uncanny effect seemed to be following the tiny figure.

'The Welsh knew her as Ceridwen,' Tom said.

Veitch glanced at him disbelievingly. 'How can you tell that from here?'

'My vision is better than yours.' Tom made no effort to convince Veitch. 'Better than any human's.'

'Okay, what's she doing then?'

'She's one of the Golden Ones – she comes from the family of Cernunnos. What is she doing? It looks to me like she's returning the primaeval forest to the Highlands, the way it used to be before all the trees were cleared for agriculture and industry.'

'What for?'

'To her branch of the Golden Ones, nature is very special, and the trees and their living spirits are the best representation of that. She's bringing magic back to the land in a way that people will truly be able to appreciate. For wherever trees grow, magic thrives.'

Veitch dropped to his haunches, balancing himself with the tips of his fingers. He caught a glimpse of black hair, flowing like oil, and what appeared to be a cape swirling behind Ceridwen, sometimes the colour of sapphires, then emeralds. 'I don't get it. If they're supposed to be the enemy, how come they're looking after the land? I thought that was our job.'

Tom shrugged. 'On most levels they're higher beings. They understand the things we take for granted.'

The Rhymer wandered off, but Veitch stayed watching the verdant band spread back and forth across the desolate landscape. It filled him with a tremendous sense of wellbeing that he couldn't quite explain, and when he took his leave five minutes later, he did so reluctantly.

They spent half an hour looking for a place sheltered enough to make camp in the bleak uplands and by that time twilight had turned to near dark. Despite the season, the wind had turned bitter again and there was a hint of icy rain in the air.

'I don't like this,' Veitch said as he tramped breathlessly up an incline.

Tom grunted; he was in one of his moods where conversation was a burden.

'The dark, out here in the country.' Veitch knew he was talking as much for himself, but it made him feel a little more easy. 'I'm a city boy. It never gets dark in the city, even when it's night. You've got other things to worry about there, but at least they're always easy to see.' He looked up. 'The moon's full. It'd give us more light if not for the bleedin' clouds.'

'You're not afraid of a few shadows, are you?' Tom snapped. His brogue had grown a little thicker now he was back in his homeland again.

'Ah, fuck off.'

'City boys. You think you're so hard,' Tom taunted.

Veitch's anger flared white and hot for an instant; sometimes he was afraid of it and the way it seemed to take him over completely. He wondered, when he was in its grip, what he was really capable of. Before he could respond with a comment that would bring about another raging argument, he glimpsed a light high and away to his right that was quickly lost behind an outcropping. He pulled back until he saw it again.

'There's a place up there.' The light seemed more than welcoming in the sea of darkness. 'Maybe they'll let us bunk down for the night.'

Tom wavered for a moment, but the prospect of a night with a roof over his head seemed too attractive. He pushed past Veitch and marched briskly towards the white glow.

It was a crofter's cottage, built out of stone, but still looking as if it had been hammered by the elements almost to the point of submission. Smoke curled out of the chimney to hang briefly and fragrantly in the air; it smelled of peat or some wood they couldn't quite identify. The ghostly outlines of prone

344

sheep glowed faintly on the hillside all around. They both watched the place for a few moments while they weighed up any potential dangers, then, finding none apparent, Tom strode up to knock on the door.

There was a brief period of quiet during which they guessed the occupant was shocked that someone had come calling to such an out-of-the-way place. Then heavy footsteps approached. 'Who is it?' a deep voice said in a hesitant Highlands accent.

'We were out walking. There looks to be a storm blowing up,' Tom said politely. 'Do you think you could give us shelter for the night? We—'

'No. Be off with you.' There was a sharp snap in the voice that could have been anger or fear.

'Miserable bastard,' Veitch muttered. 'Come on, I thought I saw somewhere to make camp just over there. He's probably in-bred anyway.'

Before they could move away another, unidentifiable, voice rose up from somewhere at the back of the house. They heard the man move a few steps away from the door and a brief, barely audible argument ensued. A few seconds later the door was jerked open so sharply they both started.

A man in his late forties with dark, unwelcoming eyes barked, 'Get in. Quickly now!'

They jumped at his order and he slammed the door behind them, throwing a couple of bolts as if to emphasise his order. He was wearing a faded *Miami* T-shirt with old blue braces over the top holding up a pair of dirty grey, pin-striped suit trousers. His hair was curly black and grey, but his three-day stubble made him appear harsher than he might otherwise have been. He sized them up suspiciously, then beckoned them over to the fireside with a seemingly approving grunt. 'Better get y'sen warmed up. It gets cold up here at night, even in summer.'

He disappeared into another room and came back with a woman in her early twenties who had obviously been the source of the argument. Her face was bright and confident, as welcoming as the man was suspicious. Her hair was long and shiny-black, her eyes dark, and she was slim, in a clean white T-shirt and faded Levi's. There was something about her that reminded Veitch of Ruth, although her features had more of country stock in them.

'You'll have to forgive my dad. He doesn't know the meaning of hospitality.' The father began to speak, but she silenced him with a flashing glare; a fiery temper clearly lay just beneath the surface. 'I'm Anna. Dad here, he's James. Jim.'

'Mr McKendrick,' the father mumbled in the background.

Tom and Veitch introduced themselves. 'You've been having some trouble,' Tom noted, slipping off his rucksack.

'Something's been worrying the sheep.' Looking uncomfortable,

345

McKendrick wiped his mouth with the back of his hand. 'Worrying? Savaging more like. Six dead in the last two nights. Eight gone last month.'

'A wild dog,' Tom suggested, not believing it for a minute.

'Sat up with my gun last night. Never saw a damn thing. Found what was left of the carcasses at first light.'

Tom nodded. 'I can see that would be a problem. And you thought the culprit had come knocking at the door?'

McKendrick ignored him. Anna stepped in. 'Have you eaten? I could do you some bacon sandwiches?'

They both agreed this would be a good idea. While McKendrick pulled back the curtains to peer outside, Tom disappeared to use the toilet. Once Veitch heard the spattle of hot oil and smelled the first singe of the bacon he followed Anna into the small kitchen, which was barely big enough for the two of them.

She smiled when he entered and asked him to slice the bread. 'You'll have to excuse Dad. He's been under a lot of pressure. You don't make any money with a croft at the best of times, and the last few years certainly haven't been the best of times. He cannae afford to lose sheep at this rate.'

'You help him out here?'

'Don't look so surprised!' She slapped him playfully on the shoulder. 'My mum died earlier this year. It was a shock to us all, but Dad took it really hard. Went to pieces, really. I was living down in Glasgow, having the time of my life, but I jacked it all in to come back here and get him back on his feet.'

Veitch took the spatula from her hand and turned the bacon, but he couldn't take his eyes from her face. Her own eyes matched his, move for move. 'That was good of you.'

'Don't make me out to be a saint. Anybody would have done it for family. But no good deed goes unpunished, right? Now he doesn't want me stuck in a miserable life like crofting miles away from anything anybody could call society, and he doesn't want to lose me and be on his own either. So we sit here every night stewing in our juices.'

'Must be pretty hard.'

She shrugged. 'So what about you? You don't look the kind to be hill-walking in these times.' She looked him in the eye. 'Nobody would be up here alone at night in the Troubles. Unless they had a very good reason.'

'I have a very good reason.'

'Tell me about it, then.'

'I'm a big bleedin' hero trying to save the world from disaster.'

Her eyes ranged over his deadpan face as she tried to pick the truth from his comment. Eventually she held his gaze, while a smile crept across her lips, and then she turned back to the cooker. But she never told him what she thought.

They ate the sandwiches in front of the fire. McKendrick thawed a little and even offered around a shot of malt which looked, from its unlabelled bottle, as if it had been distilled locally. Veitch still couldn't take his eyes off Anna. He didn't know if it was because she reminded him of Ruth or because of some other attraction, and that thought filled him with guilt about how fickle he really was. For her part, Anna seemed truly taken by him. While Tom and her father talked in quiet, serious tones by the fire, the two of them sat in creaking, threadbare armchairs in one corner, their lighthearted conversation punctuated with humour.

But at one point Veitch looked up and found McKendrick watching him with a cold annoyance bordering on anger. Veitch knew why, didn't care; life was too short.

They were disturbed shortly after midnight by a wild commotion outside: the undeniable sound of sheep in torment, deep rumbling from some unrecognisable animal throat that turned into a guttural roar. Veitch was the first to the window, but the light inside made it impossible to see more than a few feet. McKendrick had his gun and hovered hesitantly at the door, but Veitch was by his side before he had his fingers on the handle.

'Let me go first, all right?' The crossbow was in his hand as he slipped out into the chill night. He regretted it instantly. Even outside it was impossible to see much beyond the small circle of illumination from the croft's windows; he could almost feel the darkness pressing hard against him. He had advanced to the edge of the light before McKendrick came out with a powerful torch. He had never heard the noise the sheep were making before; it was frenzied and high-pitched and at times almost sounded like the shriek of a woman.

'Quick! Over there!' He pointed redundantly in the direction of the noise.

The determination in McKendrick's face didn't quite mask the underlying fear as he swung the torch round wildly. It flashed over undulating grass, the ghostly grey shapes of fleeing sheep, past something that was just a glimmer, but a splash of colour and a jarring shape that shouldn't be caught Veitch's eye. 'Back! Back!' he yelled.

McKendrick retraced the arc. They caught a glimpse of a low shadow that moved away like lightning. Left behind was the carcass of a sheep, gleaming slickly, the white bones protruding like enormous teeth. It had been so torn to pieces they had trouble recognising which part was which.

'Holy Mary, Mother of God!' McKendrick hissed. 'It *is* a dog!' He nestled the barrel of his gun over his forearm while still trying to manipulate the torch.

'Careful,' Veitch said. 'It might be rabid.'

The white light washed over more grass, its movement jerky with McKendrick's anxiety, so at times it looked like they were glimpsing images illuminated by a strobe: a rock that made them all start; a sheep running in their direction. The carcass again. The wind had whipped up and was moaning across the high land, scudding the clouds across the moon and stars so it became darker than ever. And against it all was the sound of the sheep's hooves constantly driving across the grass, disorienting them so it was impossible to tell where the dog was.

McKendrick gritted his teeth in frustration. 'Stay behind me. If I see it I'm just going to let rip with both barrels. Might scare it—'

They had heard tell of animal sounds that could chill the blood; McKendrick had thought it poetic license, but when the howling rose up, at first low and mournful but then higher and more intense, they felt ice-water wash through them. The primal sound triggered some long-dormant race warning that was so overpowering that their instinct rose to the fore and instantly drove them towards the house.

Just as their backs were at the door, McKendrick's final sweep with the torch locked on to a prowling shape, so fleeting they caught only a glimpse of golden eyes glowing spectrally in the light. McKendrick fired instantly, but they didn't wait to see the result. They slipped through the door and locked it firmly behind them.

'I think I got it,' McKendrick said breathlessly with his back pressed hard against the door. 'Winged it, at least.'

Veitch wasn't so sure. Anna and Tom waited anxiously in the centre of the room; it was apparent from their faces they had been as disturbed by the howling. McKendrick and Veitch looked at each other, but it was the older man who finally gave voice to what they were both thinking.

'It was a wolf, I'm sure of it.'

Anna shook her head furiously. 'You're joking! There haven't been wolves here for centuries.'

'But this was once their homeland,' Tom mused. 'Perhaps they've returned.'

'With the forests,' Veitch added.

'How?' Anna asked. 'That's crazy!'

McKendrick went to the window and peered out cautiously. 'Crazy things are happening all the time these days,' he mumbled.

'Are you sure it was a wolf?' Tom said pointedly. 'Not a man?'

Veitch knew what he was implying. 'Bit bigger than normal, but nothing out of the ordinary.'

Anna looked at them both curiously, but said nothing.

'If you did hit it, we might be able to track it at first light. Follow the blood,' Veitch said confidently. 'It would be easier if we could see the bleedin' thing. We don't stand a chance out there in the dark.'

This seemed like the most sensible course of action, so while Anna retired to the kitchen to make a pot of tea, the men sat by the fire, slowly feeling their heartbeats return to normal.

McKendrick retired an hour later, and while Tom dozed fitfully in a chair in front of the fire, Veitch attempted to make up a bed on the floor in one corner. Anna helped him, talking animatedly in a hushed voice.

'Sorry if I'm rattling on,' she said with a giggle. 'It seems like ages since I've had a body to talk to. Apart from my da', that is.'

Veitch lay back on the collection of cushions with his arms behind his head. 'He seems like he's got it pretty much together now. He's a tough bloke. Bit of a no-nonsense life he's got going up here. Maybe it's time to get back to your life.'

She looked wistful. 'I don't know. I can't be selfish—'

'You've got to be, sometimes. Otherwise you can just give up your life to all these responsibilities everyone throws at you. They'll never stop.'

She stifled a yawn, then lay down next to him, staring up at the ceiling. 'That sounds like a lot of sense. Right now. But then I'll catch him looking at Mum's photo and crying when he doesn't think I'm around—'

'Don't you get lonely?'

She turned to look at him with her deep, dark eyes. 'Sometimes.'

He rolled on to his side and propped his head with his arm. 'You look like you like big fun. You're gonna go stir crazy in this place after a while.'

'Sometimes I think I already have.' She shrugged. 'You know how everybody needs something in their lives they believe in? Well, this croft is Dad's thing. For all the blood and sweat that goes into it and the poverty that comes out, he loves it. He'd die if he moved away. It looks boring, bleak, hard. But then you get up on an autumn morning to see the dawn slowly moving across the mountains in orange and brown. And you hear the wind across the hillsides on a winter's night, almost like it's a real person.'

'So what do you believe in?'

'Right now, looking after a man who raised a bairn while managing to keep body and soul together in a place like this. He's sacrificed for me. It's the least I can do in return. The very least.'

Veitch rolled back, his expression faintly puzzled, vaguely troubled.

'And what do you believe in?'

That question troubled him even more. 'Still looking for it, I reckon.'

She leaned over and gently touched the tattoo on his forearm; her fingers were cool, the contact hot. 'Tell me about these.' She smiled with mock lasciviousness. 'Do they go all the way down?'

Before he could reply, the door to the bedroom swung open and McKendrick glared out. 'Anna! To bed. Now,' he hissed.

She smiled at Veitch a little sadly, but there was nothing else to say.

The gale picked up during the night, whistling in the chimney and clattering around the eaves. Veitch woke repeatedly, reminded of Anna's description of the wind as a real person; at times he was convinced he could hear an insistent voice, warning or challenging. Over near the dying embers of the fire, Tom grumbled and twitched in his sleep. Veitch checked his watch: three a.m. Shouldn't be too long until dawn.

A rattling ran along the length of the roof. He sat bolt upright in shock an instant before he realised it was still the wind. He wouldn't be surprised if half the tiles were off come morning. He lay back down, but the rattling sound came back in the opposite direction.

His instincts jangled. Slowly he raised himself on his elbows and listened. It didn't sound like the wind at all. It sounded like there was someone on the roof.

A shower of soot fell down the chimney and the fire flared. His attention snapped to it, but his mind was already racing ahead. The resounding crash against the front door had him to his feet in an instant; it was so hard he thought it was going to burst the door from its hinges.

Tom staggered to his feet, still half asleep. 'What . . . what in heaven's name . . . ?'

Veitch ran to the window and peeked out. A large grey wolf which looked, in his state of heightened tension, as big as a Shetland pony, was hurling itself at the door. With each impact, the hinges strained a little more. Veitch struggled briefly to make sense of the wolf's unnatural actions before jumping back and yelling, 'McKendrick! Bring your gun!'

But the crofter was already half out of the bedroom with his shotgun, looking dazed. 'You better see this,' he said.

Veitch ran into the bedroom. Anna was sitting up in a Z-bed, trying to make sense of what was happening. The curtains had been dragged back and outside Veitch could see several sleek wolves circling, all as big as the one battering the front door. The rattling on the roof echoed again; at least one of them was up there too.

'There must be eight or nine of them!' McKendrick said in disbelief.

'Have you got another gun?' Veitch snapped. The crofter shook his head.

Cursing, Veitch ran back to the living room and scrambled for his crossbow, suddenly aware of how feeble it really was. He barely had time to load a bolt when the door burst open and the wind howled in; the curtains flew wildly. The wolf struck him full in the chest with the force of a sledgehammer. He went down, winded, and then it was on top of him, jaws snapping barely an inch from his face. Its meaty breath blasted into his nostrils, its saliva dripped hot on his chin. He could barely breathe from the weight of it.

He forced his face to one side in desperate, futile evasion, anticipating the enormous power of the jaws stripping the meat from his skull. And then the strangest thing happened: deep in his head he felt an uncomfortable tickling sensation, like a dim radio signal on the end of a band. Slowly he found his face drawn back round until he was looking deep into the wolf's eyes, golden with the cold circle of black floating at the centre; they drew him in until he was lost in a gleaming intelligent soup, at once alien, yet a part of him.

The terrible spell was broken with the sound of smashing glass. Another wolf burst through the window and sprawled in the centre of the floor before righting itself. And then the rest of the pack was inside, circling low and fast. Tom tried to fend one off with a wooden chair. The wolf played the game for a second, then suddenly unleashed its jaws in a frenzied snapping that turned the chair to splinters in an instant.

From the corner of his eye Veitch could see his crossbow where it had fallen. Slowly he crept his hand spider-like along the floor towards it; it was already loaded, so he could put a bolt through the wolf's head with just one hand.

He was halfway to it when the wolf noticed what he was doing. A low, bass rumble started somewhere deep in its throat then rolled upwards into a bloodchilling snarl. Its movement was so swift Veitch barely saw it. Those golden eyes were shining before him, and then suddenly he was encompassed in darkness and the foul stink of the beast's breath. He felt its fangs sink into the flesh at the top of either cheekbone; fiery pain ran deep into his temple. It had his entire head in its mouth; it had to exert only slightly more pressure and his skull would shatter.

It held him like that for a few seconds while every desperate thought he had ever had rattled through his mind, and then, mysteriously, it released its grip. Before he could begin to fathom what was happening, it had released the crushing pressure on his chest and was padding away and out of the door.

All the other wolves had gone too, but the room looked as if it had been torn apart by a tornado. Shattered furniture lay all around, covered with shards of glass and torn material. Tom was slumped in a daze in one corner, but as he struggled to sit up it became apparent he wasn't badly hurt.

McKendrick, however, lay on his back half in, half out of the bedroom. His face was covered in blood and his gun was nowhere to be seen. Veitch scrambled over to him and raised his head so he could dab at the wounds with a remnant of curtain. After the shock of his appearance, the cuts seemed mainly superficial and it wasn't long before his eyes flickered open. Veitch began to speak, but the panic that flared in McKendrick's face silenced him instantly.

'They've taken Anna,' he croaked.

The winds had moved off across the mountains with the first light of dawn as they picked their way across the chill, dew-laden hillsides in search of Anna. Veitch took pole position with Tom at the rear; between them was McKendrick, who looked like a spectre, his skin grey, his eyes filled with a painful desolation; it was the face of a man who had seen his entire world destroyed in an instant.

They hadn't been able to bring themselves to discuss Anna or what was likely to have happened to her after the wolves took her. Instead they had attempted to understand why the pack had acted so unnaturally, and there were no easy answers there either. And so, silently and unanimously, they had agreed to pursue the creatures to bring back Anna, or what was left of her.

Veitch felt numb. His emotions about Anna and Ruth had been so confused, although even his usually superficial self-analysis admitted that Anna's minor problems were a psychological substitute for Ruth's more intractable ones; solving the former had been his unrecognised key to achieving his heart's desire. And he had been thwarted again.

The track was easy to pick up, even for the untrained eye: flattened grass and too many splatters of blood, which they tried to convince themselves belonged to the wolf McKendrick had wounded. They made quick progress downhill, but there was no sign of the wolves ahead of them. The pack had moved away from the croft with alarming speed.

They soon found themselves on the perimeter of the new-grown forest, which already seemed to have attained its own ecosystem: thick forest floor vegetation, woodland flowers and a wide array of birds. Mist had settled in the depths of the valley and among the trees like candyfloss. The more they penetrated the shade beneath the verdant canopy, the thicker it became, blanketing all sound, obscuring what lay on every side.

After they had moved through it a little way, Tom pulled Veitch on one side. 'This is insanity. If the pack attacks here we don't stand a chance. They could be circling five feet away from us now and we wouldn't know.'

Veitch agreed, but he couldn't turn back. 'If we retreat now we'll lose the trail.'

'You can't help saving damsels in distress, can you?' Tom said sourly. 'It's a pathological obsession.'

'I might listen to what you're saying if you weren't so fucked up yourself.' Veitch marched back into the lead with an irritation that came from knowing Tom was right. He had to save Anna because that was what heroes did. And if he couldn't be a hero, he had to be the person he always had been, and who could live with that?

They'd progressed about half a mile into the thickest part of the forest when they first heard movement, all around. McKendrick's finger jumped to the trigger and Veitch had to rest his hand on the barrel to calm the crofter; he looked like he was about to have a breakdown.

'Take it easy, mate,' he whispered in a strong, calm voice. 'You'll end up blowing one of us away.'

McKendrick's bottom lip was trembling. He plunged his teeth into it and a trickle of blood ran down on to his chin.

The mist continued to distort the forest sounds; the birdsong seemed to come and go, and when they heard the vegetation crushed beneath loping paws it was impossible to pinpoint the location. But the pack was undoubtedly nearby, possibly surrounding them, as Tom had feared. Twigs cracked from somewhere behind them, grass or a bush swished just ahead. Yet despite the muffled nature of the sounds, something about them didn't sound right to Veitch's heightened awareness; the weight burden was wrong, the movements not as sleekly lupine as he would have expected.

'They're moving closer,' he hissed.

'How can you tell?' McKendrick's gun was wavering so much Veitch thought there was more danger there.

'I can hear things clearly.' *These days*, he mentally added. He truly did feel a different person to the woolly-minded, sluggish old Ryan Veitch. The Pendragon Spirit had given him the chance to rise above himself.

Tom moved in close so only Veitch could hear him. 'So what's the big strategy now, warrior-boy?'

A large figure shimmered in and out of the tendrils. 'There!' McKendrick cried and raised his gun.

Another shape erupted out of the mist and knocked McKendrick flying; the gun disappeared into the undergrowth. Veitch lashed out instinctively

353

and caught the attacker a glancing blow. It howled sharply before it was gone.

He dropped low, whirling around. 'That wasn't a wolf!'

As if in response to his words, another figure dropped out of the air in front of him, obviously from a tree branch above. It was a man, but oddly different to any man Veitch had seen before. His long, matted hair was a deep black and his skin swarthy, with an excess of body hair. His bone structure was clearly defined above his sharp jaw, forming handsome features which suggested both pride and an incisive intelligence. He was naked, his body lithely muscled, filled with power. But it was his hands and feet that caught Veitch's attention; they were over-sized, the fingers long and gnarled, with sharp, jagged nails that more resembled talons. He was sweating profusely from his exertions and there was a sheen of forest dirt across his skin. Gradually Veitch's attention was drawn to his thick, dark eyebrows which menacingly overhung glowing golden eyes; Veitch knew instantly he had seen those eyes before.

Veitch went to lift his crossbow in warning, but the man raised his arm quickly with a strange hand gesture that had the little finger and index finger extended while the others were folded back; oddly, it was filled with a threat Veitch didn't feel comfortable opposing, and he let the crossbow drop.

'Who is this?' McKendrick said in a broken, uncomprehending voice. Tom helped him to his feet.

'The *Lupinari* have returned to the deep forests,' the man said in a deep, almost growling voice which rang with an unplaceable accent.

Recognition suddenly dawned on Tom's face and he took a step towards the strange, beast-like man to communicate, but he was halted in his tracks by the same threatening hand gesture.

Tom held his open hands up, palms outwards; a primal gesture. 'I never encountered your people in the Far Lands.'

The man eyed him coldly. 'Then you never ventured into the forests of the night.'

'No, I never did.'

The man let his hand drop slightly and used it to gesture around. 'The Far Lands, for all their twilight appeal, were uncommon grounds to us. These are our homelands. This is our world, where we have hunted since time began.'

Other figures began to appear out of the mists, both men and women, all naked, dark-haired and swarthy-skinned; they moved low and sinuously, like animals; occasionally their eyes gleamed like cats'.

'In the days of our ancestors, we lived side-by-side with humankind. The wild men of the woods, you called us, and in the dark wintertime you even came to look upon us fondly, as you yet feared us. For sometimes we would bring gifts to your door, and keep away the privations of the long, dark nights. For it is in our nature to help fellow creatures of intellect.' There was a hint of anger in this last sentence. 'Your people knew us, and our powers, and never hunted us, for they knew we never ate human flesh. For if we did, the taste of it would consume us and we would desire it ever more and there would be nothing but war between our races.'

The other members of the pack circled round, filtering in and out of the mists. Veitch kept a wary eye on them; the mention of human flesh had unnerved him.

'And if one of our people turned rogue, and ate mortal meat, we would hunt him down and destroy him ourselves,' the leader continued. There was a long pause while he looked into each of their faces, and then he said, 'But this night gone you did attack us.'

Veitch suddenly noticed the splatter of dried blood across his left ribcage. 'You attacked his sheep.'

The leader fixed his cold eyes on Veitch. 'But we never ate human flesh.'

Tom took a cautious step forward to attract the leader's attention away from Veitch's lack of diplomacy. 'We had no idea the *Lupinari* had returned to these lands,' he said in as conciliatory a tone as he could muster. 'We would never wish to offend you. We would hope to live in peace, as we always did in times past.'

Golden eyes blinked slowly, implacably. 'Nevertheless, a blow has been struck. There must be some retribution before we agree a pact.' His face contained no emotions they could understand, and they all feared the worst.

McKendrick had seemed in a daze to this point, but in that moment he appeared to grasp what was happening. 'Not Anna,' he whimpered.

'His sheep, given freely,' Tom suggested hastily.

The leader shook his head slowly. 'We had no knowledge they were his beasts or we would not have taken them. We can easily find other prey. For that is what we do.'

'Not Anna,' McKendrick said again.

'You better not have killed her,' Veitch snapped.

The leader's eyes flashed towards him, filled with such bestial rage Veitch instinctively went to protect his throat. 'I held your head in my jaws,' the leader growled. 'You are nothing to me.'

'You don't eat human flesh,' Tom noted. 'You said.'

As if on cue, another figure advanced from the mists; it was Anna. At first she moved with the sluggish pace of someone who had been hypnotised, but when she neared them, recognition dawned in her eyes and she ran to her father. They held each other, crying silently.

355

'What do you require?' Tom asked quietly.

The leader fixed his unflinching stare on the Rhymer. 'For one night, every year, she will leave her father to be with us.'

McKendrick's eyes grew wider. 'What will happen to her?'

'She will learn to hunt with the *Lupinari*.'

'To hunt?' McKendrick brought the back of his hand to his mouth. 'My wee girl?'

Veitch saw something else. 'She isn't going to stay around here for ever.'

The leader's eyes narrowed. 'If the pact is broken the *Lupinari* will seek retribution through the hunt.'

'It is agreed,' Tom said.

'No!' McKendrick was blazing with righteous anger now. 'I won't leave my daughter with these things!'

Tom placed a firm hand on his shoulder. 'There isn't another way. If you want to save her life, and yours, then you'll do this.' He turned back to the leader and repeated, 'It is agreed.'

The leader nodded slowly. 'Then perhaps in times to come our peoples can live closely and wisely once more.'

There was a note of conciliation in his voice. Veitch herded McKendrick away before he could put up any opposition, relieved that it hadn't come down to a fight, knowing they wouldn't have stood a chance if it had.

After a few paces he glanced back, just to be sure they were not being followed. But all he saw were vague impressions as the *Lupinari* melted back into the mist, and not a single footfall was heard to mark their passing.

Back at the croft McKendrick was in a state of shock, but Anna seemed to have accepted her tribulation with equanimity. When she saw Veitch watching her intently, she left her father sitting on the floor next to the hearth and pulled him to one side.

'No grim faces now,' she cautioned with a gentle finger on his cheek. 'It's not the end of the world.'

'You don't know what they'll be expecting of you on your nights with them.'

'I'll deal with it when it happens.'

'And it's going to be hard for you ever to get away from here now.'

'What's to stop me coming back just for the night?' But they both knew it wasn't going to happen. 'I just wanted to say, thanks for helping us.' She seemed to read every troubled thought passing through his head. Then she took his face in her hands, stood on tiptoes and gave him a long, deep kiss. Afterwards she said, 'It's a shame you have to go—'

'I have to.'

'I know. But it's a shame.' And then she smiled once and turned to her father. Veitch watched her for a while, kneeling next to McKendrick, one hand round his shoulder, whispering comforting words that only the two of them could hear. But then Tom caught his eye and nodded towards the door.

They made their goodbyes as best they could, and then when they were out walking over the sun-drenched hillsides, Veitch asked, 'Is this always how it is?'

'What do you mean?'

'When you're trying to do the right thing in the world. When you've got all these responsibilities. Like a big fucking rock on your shoulder.'

Oddly, Tom appeared pleasantly surprised by the comment. He clapped Veitch warmly on the shoulder. 'That's how it is. You get your reward later.'

'How much later?'

Tom's tight smile seemed filled with meaning, but Veitch couldn't understand it at all. 'Much, much later,' the Rhymer said before turning his attention to the path ahead.

They walked nonstop for the next day across the exhausting mountainous landscape and made camp in a gorge as night fell. They hadn't seen or heard anyone since they had left the croft; in the desolation, humanity could have been stripped from the face of the planet and they would never have known.

Since he had left Anna, Veitch hadn't been able to settle. He had found his thoughts turning to the others he had spent so long with over the past months. Why did they act the way they did? Why did they say one thing while believing another? His own thoughts had always moved swiftly and directly into words, and in the past he had judged others by the same standard, although he had known subconsciously that was rarely the case. And finally his attention had turned to Tom; he had spent the day secretly watching the way he moved, the subtleties of his facial expressions, his strange choice of words, and by the evening he knew that he didn't know the man at all.

As they sat around the fire finishing up the last of the provisions McKendrick had given them, the questions were plaguing Veitch so much he couldn't keep them in any longer. 'You said yesterday your eyes were better than mine.' Tom nodded. 'How much else has changed?'

The Rhymer prodded the fire, sending the sparks soaring. 'A great deal.'

'Like what?'

'I can hear better. Smell things more acutely. Can't really taste very much any more, though.'

Veitch gnawed on a crust while he thought. 'If a doc cut you open,' he began, 'what would he find inside?'

Tom stared into the fire, said nothing.

'If you don't want to talk about it—'

'I don't think I'm quite human any more.'

'Don't think?' Veitch watched Tom's face in the firelight, wondering why it was always so hard to tell what he was thinking or feeling.

'I don't know. I don't know if I should be here with people, or back in Otherworld with the rest of the strange things. I don't know if I can trust my feelings, if I really have any feelings, or if I just pretend to myself I have feelings. I don't know if I cut myself open if I'll find straw inside, or diamonds, or fishes, or if all the component parts are there, just in the wrong order.' He continued to watch the flames.

Veitch had a sudden, sweeping awareness of Tom's tragedy. He had lost everything; not just his family and friends, who were separated from him by centuries, but his kinship with humanity, his sense of who or what he was. He was more alone than anyone ever could be. Yet he still wished and hoped and felt and yearned; and he still tried to do his best for everyone, despite his own suffering.

'I think you're just a bloke, like me and the others,' Veitch said.

Tom looked at him curiously.

'And I think you'll find what you're looking for.'

Tom returned his attention to the fire. 'Thank you for that.'

'It must be hard to go back to that bitch who wrecked your life.'

Tom remained silent, but Veitch noticed the faint tremor of a nerve near his mouth.

'You know when I said I couldn't understand why everybody thought you were a hero. I'm sorry about that.'

Tom threw some more wood on the fire and it crackled like gunfire. 'We need to get some sleep.'

'Okay, I'll take first watch.' He stood up and stretched, breathing deeply of the night air. 'What are we going to find when we get where we're going?'

'Everything we ever dreamed of.' Tom wandered towards the tent. 'And everything we ever feared.'

Tom had been in the tent barely five minutes when an awful sound echoed between the steep walls of the gorge. All the hairs on the back of Veitch's neck stood erect instantly and a queasy sensation burrowed deep in the pit of his stomach. Veitch hoped it was just an unusual effect of the wind rushing down from the mountains, but then Tom came scrambling out of the tent, his face unnaturally pale, and Veitch knew his first instincts were correct: it was the crying of a woman burdened by an unbearable grief.

At first he wondered if it was Anna, who had followed them, but Tom caught at his sleeve as he made to investigate. 'Don't. You won't find anyone.'

'What do you mean?' Veitch felt strangely cold; his left hand was trembling.

'You can always hear the Caoineag's lament, but you will never see her.'

Veitch peered into the dark. The wailing set his teeth on edge, dragged out a wave of despair from deep within him. He wanted to crawl into the tent and never come out again. 'What is it?'

'She is one of the sisters of the Washer at the Ford.' Tom's voice was so low Veitch could barely hear it. 'A grim spirit.'

'Is this her place, up here in the mountains?'

Tom shook his head. 'She is here for us.'

'For us?' Veitch dreaded what Tom was to say next.

'Those who hear the sound of the Caoineag's mourning are doomed to face death or great sorrow.' And with that he turned and dismally retreated to the tent.

chapter sixteen

on the night road

The light from the fire glowed through the trees like a beacon in the darkness of the night. Another technology failure had left Shavi breathless as the sea of illumination that spread out across the Midlands winked out in an instant; even after all this time it still chilled him deeply to see it.

He had just been coming down the final, gentle slopes of the Pennines after Ashbourne when it happened. He never travelled at night, particularly in the wild country, but he wanted to complete the last leg of that difficult part of the journey before he reached the more comforting built-up areas that lay towards the south. Now he wondered if he had made the wrong decision.

More than anything, he was aware of time running away from him; Lughnasadh was only eleven days away, little enough time to put everything right. He still found it hard to believe their great victory in Edinburgh had turned to such a potentially huge failure. His mind kept flashing back to Ruth and the suffering she must be feeling. But more, he was aware of the looming presence of Balor, in the shadows beneath the trees, or the chill in the wind, or the deep dark of a cloudy night. There had been no sign of the Fomorii, but he knew they were out there, searching for him. He could palpably sense the god of death and evil close to their reality. He felt it like a queasiness in the pit of his stomach and in the many dreams that had increasingly afflicted his sleep. An overpowering atmosphere of dread was beginning to fall over everything he saw and heard.

Although the night was warm and there were plenty of stars, a smattering of clouds kept obscuring the moon. That made the darkness almost impenetrable and he was sure he could hear something moving nearby. On several occasions he had been convinced someone was following; not too close, but tracking him from afar, sometimes off to one side, sometimes the other, always out of sight. He tried to pretend it was paranoia, but he had learned to trust his sharpened senses.

His main comfort was that if it were some kind of stalking beast, it had had plenty of opportunity to attack him while he slept. Yet it kept its distance, almost as if it were sizing him up. A twig snapped, too loud in the still of the night. He looked round briefly, then hurried towards the fire.

Almost forty people were seated around a blazing campfire next to a copse on the edge of a field. In the gloom beyond were parked a motley collection of vehicles: a black, single-decker bus of fifties vintage, a beat-up Luton van spray-painted in Day-Glo colours, other coaches, obsolete and heavily modified, minibuses stocked high with effects. The gathered crowd were obviously travellers, camouflaged by old army fatigues, leather and denim, hair long, spikey or shorn, piercings glinting everywhere, tattoos glowing darkly in the flickering light. They were all ages: children playing on the edge of the firelight, a few babes in arms, several pensioners, and a good selection of those in their twenties, thirties, forties and fifties. The hubbub of conversation that drowned out the cracking, spitting wood dried up the moment Shavi stepped into the circle of light.

Shavi scanned their faces, expecting the suspicion and anger that came when a tight-knit group was disrupted, but there was nothing. He looked for anyone who might be a leader or spokesman.

A thickset man with long black hair and a bushy beard waved Shavi over with a lazy motion of an arm as thick as Shavi's thigh. He wore a cut-off denim jacket over a bare chest and had a gold band straining around his tattooed bicep; a matching gold gypsy earring shone amidst the black curls. He was grinning broadly; one of his front teeth was chipped.

'The last brave man of England!' His voice had the rich, deep resonance of a drum. 'Come over here and tell us what it takes to walk alone in the countryside at night!'

Shavi squatted down next to him, perfectly balanced with the tips of his fingers on the ground. 'I did not intend to be out so late—'

The man's bellowed laugh cut Shavi short. 'Now how many times have we heard that before?'

The others laughed in response, but it wasn't directed at Shavi. 'Come on, pull up a pew.' The man slapped the dry ground next to him. 'You don't want to be going back out there in a hurry, do you?'

Shavi accepted his hospitality with a smile. The easy conversation resumed immediately, as if he were an old friend who had just returned to the fold. A second later a cup of warm cider was pressed into his hands. He could smell hash on the wind and soon someone switched on an eighties beat-box. It pumped out music which seemed to switch without rhyme or reason from upbeat to ambient, jungle to folk. There was a strange, relaxed mood that was oddly timeless. He felt quite at home.

Shavi's host introduced himself as Breaker Gibson. He'd been with the convoy for six years. As a group, the travellers had followed the road for most of the nineties, their number ebbing and flowing as people tagged along at different sites or drifted away without explanation; an extended family that owed as much to a gaggle of mediaeval itinerants as it did to any concept of modern grouping. Their neverending journey was seasonal, taking in most of the festivals: Glastonbury and Reading, some of the counter-culture get-togethers in Cornwall and Somerset, the summer solstice at Stonehenge, Beltane in Scotland. They had their own code of conduct, their own stories and traditions that were related and embellished around the campfire most nights, their own myths and belief systems: a society within a society.

Breaker didn't want to talk about his life before he joined the collective; Shavi got the sense it was an unhappy time that he was trying to leave far behind, and the constant motion of his new existence appeared to be working. But of his time with the group he was robustly happy to discuss, and had a plethora of stories to tell, most of which he wildly exaggerated like a storyteller of old, all of which seemed to involve some kind of run-in with the law. After an hour Shavi liked him immensely.

For his part, Shavi was completely open about what had happened to him over the long weeks since he had hooked up with Church and the others, but he said nothing about the reasons for his mission south, nor his destination; it was too important to trust to someone he had only just met.

Breaker peered into the night beyond the light of the campfire. 'Aye, we've seen some rum things over the last few weeks. We stopped to pick up a guy hitch-hiking near Bromsgrove. Dressed all in green, he was. But each to his own – I'm not a fashion cop.' He chuckled throatily. 'We got to the point where we'd promised to drop him off. Looked around – he wasn't anywhere on the bus! And we hadn't stopped anywhere he could have jumped off. Next thing, someone discovered all the pound coins had turned to chocolate! The kids had a feast that night, I tell you!' His chuckle turned to a deep laugh. 'Could have been worse, I suppose.' A shadow suddenly crossed his face. ''Course, we've seen some rotten things at night.' Now a tight smile; Shavi knew what he meant.

'Still,' he said, raising his mug of cider, 'it's wonderful to be alive.'

As they drank and chatted, two women came over. One was in her late twenties, with a pleasant, open manner and sharp, intelligent eyes. She had a short sandy bob and wore a thick, hand-knitted cardigan over a long hippie skirt. Her name was Meg. With her was a Gothy woman about ten years older with a hardened face and distinctly predatory eyes, but a smile that was welcoming enough. She said her name was Carolina. They both seemed eager to talk to Breaker, who obviously had some standing within their community.

'Mikey doesn't want to do the late watch,' Meg said, drawing out a list of names and quickly running her eyes down it.

'The little git says we keep picking on him to do it,' Carolina interjected sharply.

'But I've checked the rota and it's been divided up fairly,' Meg added.

Breaker sipped on his cider, suddenly serious. 'I'll have a quiet word with him. We can't afford to have too much dissent in the ranks.' He turned to Shavi. 'We had to instigate the watches a few weeks back after some bad shit happened.'

Shavi could feel the eyes of the women sizing him up. 'What was it?' he asked.

'Woke up one morning, hell of a commotion. Penny over there—' he motioned to a thin, pale woman whose eyes bulged as if she had a thyroid problem '—she was in a right state, understandably. Her baby, Jack, he'd gone missing. Taken in the night. And in the cot where he'd been lying was a little figure made out of twigs tied up with strands of corn.' Breaker's cheerful face sagged for a second. 'Naturally we told the cops, went through all their rigmarole, getting the usual treatment that it was partly our fault for the way we lived. It was just going through the motions. Everyone knew what had really happened. Since then we've had the watches going through the night. No more trouble, so I suppose you can say it's worked. But some of our . . . less-committed . . . friends don't like having their sleep disturbed.' This was obviously a source of great irritation for him, but he maintained his composure.

'So what's your deal?' Carolina said to Shavi bluntly. 'Why are you walking the land?'

'A friend of mine is very ill. I need to find some way of helping her.'

'Medicine?' Meg asked.

'Something like that.'

'So where are you going? Maybe we could give you a lift.' Carolina glanced at Breaker, who nodded in agreement.

Shavi weighed up whether to tell them. 'South,' he said. 'To Windsor.'

Breaker tugged at his beard thoughtfully. 'We could do south.'

'Yeah, haven't been that way for a while.' Carolina winked at Shavi. 'We tend to steer clear of some of the posher areas. The residents used to run us out with pitchforks in case we robbed them blind.'

The two women were called over by a teenager who looked as if he hadn't bathed for days; thick mud coated his face and arms like some Pictish warrior. Once they were out of earshot, Breaker said, 'They just about run this place, those two. We couldn't do without them, though I wouldn't say it to their faces. Give 'em bigger heads than they've got.' He looked Shavi in the eye. 'So, are you with us?'

'I would be honoured.'

'Good. One more for the watch rota!'

The camp was already alive when Shavi awoke from the best night's sleep he'd had in days. In the light it was easier to get a better handle on the people roaming around, and to see the vehicles, which looked like they would have trouble travelling a mile, let alone thousands. He ate a breakfast of poached eggs on toast with Meg, who had an insatiable desire for information about what was happening in the country; she was bright and sparky and he warmed to her. Afterwards he had his first mug of tea since The Green Man; it made his morning complete.

Once everyone had started preparing for departure, Breaker hailed him to invite him to sit up front in his sixties vintage bus, which had been painted white and vermilion like an ice cream van. The back was jammed with an enormous sound system and what appeared to be the cooking and camping equipment for the entire community.

'Hell-bent or heaven-sent,' Breaker said with a grin as he clicked the ignition. He pulled in behind the black fifties bus and the convoy set out across the country.

The open road rolled out clearly ahead of them, with no traffic to spoil the view of overhanging trees and overgrown hedges.

'You have experienced the technology failures,' Shavi said with a teasing smile, his gaze fixed ahead.

Breaker eyed him askance, then laughed at the game that was being played. 'Oh yes, we've had our fair share of problems with that.' He winked. 'Some of us were even kinda happy to see it. Bunch of Luddites, I ask you! Travelling around on the Devil's Machines!'

'And what happens if the technology fails completely?'

'Well, that's why God invented horses, matey! If it's good enough for the old ancestors, it's good enough for me and mine. I can see it now: a big, old, yellow caravan . . .' He burst out laughing. 'Bloody hell! Mr Toad! Poot, poot!' He was laughing so much tears streamed down his cheeks and he rested his head on the steering wheel to calm himself. Shavi had a sudden pang of anxiety and considered grabbing the wheel, but Breaker pulled his head up a second later and righted the bus as it drifted towards the hedge.

Shavi noticed an ornate Celtic cross hanging from the rearview mirror. 'For safety on the road?'

Breaker nodded. 'Though not in the way you think. That symbol was around long before the Christians got hold of it.' He muttered something under his breath. 'Bloody Christians stamping all over any other religion. Some of 'em are the worst advert there is for Christianity. On paper it's not a bad religion. Love thy neighbour, and all that. But once they start mangling the words, anything can happen. Having said that, we've got a few Christians here, but they're not the kind where you can see the whites of their eyes, if you know what I mean. The rest of us are a mixed bag of Pagans and Wiccans, an Odinist, a few Buddhists, some I don't even bloody well know what they're called, and I don't reckon they know themselves either!'

'In these times faith has come into its own. It really can move mountains.'

'What do you believe in, then?'

Shavi rubbed his chin thoughtfully. 'Everything.'

Breaker guffawed. 'Good answer! I tell you, the people you have to watch are those bastards who don't believe in anything. You can see them all around. Scientists who reckon they know how the universe works 'cause they know how one molecule bumps into another. Bloody businessmen who think they can screw anyone over in this life to get what they want because there's no afterlife so no comeuppance. Property developers flattening the land . . .' He chewed on his lip. 'Making a fast buck, that's too many people's faith.' He raised a hopeful eyebrow in Shavi's direction. 'Looks like they could have a few problems in this new world.'

'Oh, let us hope.'

They laughed together.

The convoy avoided the motorways and kept to the quiet backroads. It was a slow route that involved much doubling back, but Breaker explained it meant they could more easily avoid undue police attention. As they cruised down the A444 towards Nuneaton they passed another convoy coming in the opposite direction, but these were the army. Grim-faced soldiers peered out from behind dusty windscreens; they looked exhausted and threatened.

'We live in a time of constant danger,' Shavi said.

'Something big's been happening, but we never get to hear about it. They go bringing in martial law, then they haven't got the resources to police it because everybody's off fighting somewhere. At least that's what the rumours say.' He glanced at Shavi. 'You hear anything?'

'I have seen signs . . . a little, here and there. The authorities have no idea what they are doing. They are trying to fight with old thinking.'

'They don't stand a chance, do they?' He mused for a second. 'We always wanted the Establishment to leave us alone. I wonder what the world's gonna be like without them?'

As they rounded a corner they were hit by a moment of pure irony: a police roadblock barred their way.

They were held there for half an hour. Everyone was forced out of their vehicles on to the side of the road while they and all their possessions were searched. Nothing untoward was found; those who did carry drugs had found much better hiding places, after years of bitter experience. Even so, the indignities were ladled on: verbal abuse, women pushed around, homes turned upside down and left in chaos. All the travellers remained calm. They had obviously learned any opposition would result in a rapid escalation into a confrontation they could never win.

Shavi expected the police to pounce on him in a second, but they seemed to have no idea who he was. Eventually, once the police had had their sport, the convoy was turned around for no good reason that anyone could see; other cars and lorries were waved right through.

Breaker's face was stony as he headed back north and looked for a side road. 'Just like the bleeding miners' strike. And they call this a free country.'

They eventually made their way around the blocked area and pitched camp for the night in the deserted countryside to the east of Stratford-on-Avon. The area was thickly wooded enough for their vehicles not to be seen from any of the roads in the area.

'One of the good things about all this – we never get hassled at night any more,' Breaker said. 'Everybody's too afraid to leave their homes once the sun goes down.'

Once they were all parked up, they assembled for the tasks to be handed out. Three went off to dig the latrines while others scouted the area for wood for the fire; no one was allowed to touch any living tree. The cooking range was erected from Breaker's bus and several volunteers set about preparing a vat of vegetarian chilli. The mouth-watering aromas drifted over the campsite.

After everyone had eaten their fill, Shavi sat with Breaker, Meg and

Carolina next to the fire, watching the gloom gather. He had spent the day mulling over the story Breaker had told him about the abducted child and he had grown increasingly disturbed that so little had been done.

'What could be done?' Carolina said dismally.

Meg agreed. 'We've seen the things away in the field. Enough of us have come across all the strange, freaky shit that hovers around the camp at night. We're not stupid.'

'I am not suggesting you are,' Shavi said. 'But if you believe in the reality of the things you talk about, then you should not be surprised when I tell you I have certain abilities which may be of use to you.' He explained the gradual development of his shamanic skills over the weeks since the world had changed. It was a difficult task – he knew most people were still mired in the old way of thinking – but after all he had seen of the travellers' nonconformist lifestyle, he guessed they would not be so blinkered.

'So what do you suggest?' Carolina suggested. 'A shamanic ritual?'

'That might be effective. It is a matter of trying to peel back the layers to achieve contact with the invisible world, where all knowledge lies.'

'And you think you've got what it takes?' Carolina gave a wry smile.

'Bloody hell, Carolina! Give the bloke a chance!' Breaker berated loudly. 'He's right – we've done bugger-all so far. It wouldn't hurt to take a shot at this.'

Meg nodded. 'I'm in agreement. We can do it tonight, if you like. What do you need?'

'A quiet place among the trees, a handful of us to provide the focus of energies, some mushrooms or hash preferably, natural highs to alter consciousness. If not, we will have to make do with alcohol.'

The others looked from one to the other and laughed. 'Yeah, I think that's doable,' Carolina said with a smirk.

Penny broke down in a sobbing fit once Meg told her what was planned. She pushed her way past the others to clutch at Shavi's clothes, her tearful face contorted by all the emotions she had not been able to vent. 'Please God, help me find Jack!' she wailed.

Meg led her away to calm her down with a cup of tea while Breaker rounded up a few people to help with the ritual. By the end there were eight of them: Shavi, Breaker, Meg and Carolina, a woman in her sixties with long white hair tied in a ponytail, the mud-covered eighteen-year-old, who was known as Spink, a ratty-faced man with curly ginger hair and his partner, a heavyset woman who smiled a lot.

They found a clearing in the woods where they couldn't see the camp or hear any voices. Breaker had been wary of straying so far from the safety of the fire, but Shavi had convinced him the ritual would protect them as much as any physical defence.

The evening was warm. They sat in a circle, breathing in the woody, verdant aroma of the trees, listening to the soothing rustle of the leaves in the cooling breeze. It wasn't as dark as they had feared under the trees. The night was clear and the near-full moon provided beams of silver luminescence that broke through spaces in the canopy like spotlights picking out circles on the wood floor. The patterns of light and shade it created provided an attractive, stimulating backdrop to what they were about to do.

Breaker had rustled up a plastic bag of dried mushrooms and a block of hash, which they shared out equally. They didn't have to wait long for it to take effect. Shavi had primed them to begin a regular, low chant. He knew, instinctively, that the insistent vibrations coupled with the psychoactive drugs stimulated the particular region of his brain he needed to achieve the higher level. He didn't know how he knew that, but it was there in the same way that he knew it was the technique employed by their ancestors in the stone circles and chambered tombs millennia ago.

The chant moved among the trees until it became a solid, living thing, circling back and forth, then inserting probing fingers deep into his mind. He closed his eyes and raised his face so the breeze caressed his skin. The blood was singing in his veins as a tremendous sense of wellbeing consumed him; he felt roots going down from his body into the soil, moving underground until they joined with the trees and the shrubs. He felt a part of it all.

The next step was the hardest. There was a deep anxiety locked inside him from the time his mind had been almost lost to the sea serpent just off Skye, and he had to fight to ensure the drugs didn't amplify it to the point where it overwhelmed him. He regulated his breathing and focused, riding the waves with mastery. And then it was just a matter of falling back into his head, and back and back, as if he were plummeting into a deep well. Paradoxically, that journey deep within saw him suddenly out of his body. He was in the air over the clearing, looking down at himself and the others, still chanting. The view was strange, fractured; colours seemed oddly out of sorts and the dark was almost a living, breathing thing. He had only the warped perspective for an instant before his mind was jumping like lightning through the woods. There was a sensation like pinpricks all over his body, and then he was blinking, seeing the world at ground level; a wrinkle of his nose and a bound; he was a rabbit investigating the strange scene. Another lightning leap and suddenly he was up in the treetops, seeing with astonishing precision. There was the rabbit, white cotton-tail twitching. He was consumed by raptor-lust; his big owl eyes blinked twice and then he was on the wing. The lightning leap plucked him away again, to a badger snuffling in the undergrowth further afield, to a fox probing the outer reaches of the campsite for any food to steal, to a moth battering against the windscreen of a bus, trying to reach the light inside.

And then, suddenly, he was jolted back into his own body, only this time he was seeing with different eyes, feeling and hearing and smelling with completely new senses. The invisible world was opening to him.

'Come to us,' he said loudly. There was a ripple in the chanting, but he felt Breaker glance round the others to maintain the rhythm.

Above him, in the centre of the clearing, the air seemed to be folding back on itself. What looked like liquid metal bubbled out and lapped around the edges of the disturbance. There was an odour like burned iron. Shavi could feel the nascent fear of those sitting near him, but to their credit they all held firm in their trust in him. A hand thrust out of the seething rift with the white colour and texture of blind fish that spent their lives in lightless caverns. Then another hand, followed by arms, elbows wedged, heaving itself out into the night. A head and shoulders protruded between them, featureless, apart from slight indentations where the eyes, nose and mouth should have been. Shavi knew from experience it was one of the human-form constructs shaped out of the aether that the residents of the Invisible World often used to communicate.

'Who calls?' It was suspended half out of the rift, as if it were hanging from a window.

'I call.' Shavi knew better than to give his true name. 'I seek knowledge. The whereabouts of a mortal child.'

The white head moved from side to side in a strange pastiche of thinking. 'Know you there is a price to pay for information.'

Shavi held up his hand and slit the fleshy pad of his thumb with a hunting knife he had brought from the camp. Several droplets of blood splashed on to the ground.

'Good,' the construct said. 'A tasty morsel of soul. How is Lee?'

Shavi winced at the mention of his dead boyfriend's name. 'No games. Now, information. The mortal child was stolen from this group several weeks ago. A twig doll was left in its place.'

'The child is in the Far Lands.'

'Alive and well?'

'As well as can be expected.'

'Who took him?'

'The Golden Ones enjoy the company of mortals.' There was a faint hint of irony in its voice. 'They pretend they like to play with their pets, which they do, but that is not the true reason.'

This sounded like it could be dissembling, but he pressed on anyhow. 'What is the true reason?'

'That answer is too large and important for one such as I to give.' This gave Shavi pause; he made a mental note to consider it at a later date. 'Rather you should ask me if there is hope the child will be returned,' the construct continued.

'Is there?'

'No hope.'

'None?'

'Unless the Golden Ones can be made to bow to your will. Or you can provide them with something they need in exchange.' There was none of the mockery Shavi had expected in these comments. What was the construct really saying?

'Where is the child?'

'In the Court of the Final Word.'

Where Church and Tom had encountered Dian Cecht. Where the Tuatha Dé Danann carried out their hideous experiments on humans.

'I thank you for your aid. I wish you well on your return to the Invisible World.'

'One more thing.' There was a note of caution in the construct's voice. 'Turn quickly when the howling begins or the world will fall beneath your feet.'

Before Shavi could ask about this unsolicited, oblique advice, the construct had wriggled back into the rift and it had folded around him. The warning, if that was what it was, turned slowly in his mind, but he didn't have a second to consider it. Carolina yelled sharply; Shavi followed her wide-eyed, frightened stare.

He was shocked to see Meg, who had been sitting cross-legged at the foot of a mighty oak, was now being swallowed up by the tree. The wood appeared to be fluid and was sucking her into it like quicksand. Her eyes were wide with horror, but she couldn't scream for what looked to be a hand made out of the wood of the trunk had folded across her mouth. It dragged her further in; soon she would be lost completely.

Breaker leapt to his feet and grabbed her right arm, but to no avail. Then all the others joined in, but however much they tugged, they couldn't halt Meg's inexorable progress.

'Wait!' Shavi yelled. He pushed past them and placed his hand on the rough bark. It slid like oil beneath his fingers, attempting to pull him in too. The others fell back, waiting to see what he would do. 'Be at peace, Man of

Oak. We summoned the Invisible World for information. There is no harm intended to you.'

For a moment the repellent sucking at Shavi's hand continued, but then gradually it subsided. The trunk appeared to ripple and an unmistakable face grew out of the ridged bark, overhanging brow shadowing deepset eyes, a protruding nose and a gash for a mouth.

'We know of you, Brother of Dragons.' The voice sounded like wood splintering.

There was a gasp of surprise from the others. 'I know of your kith and kin too, Man of Oak, though I have never spoken with any of you before,' Shavi said.

'We remain silent when mortals walk beneath our leaves. They have never treated the Wood-born with respect.' A sound like the sighing of wind in branches escaped the mouth. 'But we know you are a friend of the Green and the people of the trees and the people of the lakes, Brother of Dragons. Do you vouch for these others?'

'I do.'

There was a moment's pause, and then Meg was slowly ejected from the tree trunk. She fell gasping on to the ground, where Breaker and Carolina ran to help her to her feet. She looked unhurt, but Shavi asked gently, 'Are you all right?' She nodded, bewildered; her eyes were still rimmed with tears. Shavi felt a wave of relief that she was safe. He'd read of the dryads and naiads, the tree and water spirits, and he had sensed them at times during his previous explorations of his abilities, but it was the first time they had manifested. This time he had responded instinctively and it seemed to have worked.

'Those who move within the Invisible World are dangerous to call, Brother of Dragons,' the tree-spirit said.

'I proceed with caution, as always, Man of Oak. How do your people fare?'

'In our groves, our woods and deep forests we are as strong as we ever were in our prime. Strong enough to repel any who try to fell us. Already blood has been spilled in the north country and in the west, and after nightfall the people have learned to avoid the coppices where our fallen bodies lie.'

The grim note in the creaking voice was so powerful the others blanched and took a step away. But Shavi sensed an opportunity and persevered. 'Our stories say there was not always such enmity between man and tree.'

'In the days before your people turned away from the wisdom of the land we were treated with respect and we, in turn, respected the men who moved among us.'

'It could be that way again.'

'It may still be too early, Brother of Dragons. The new season has not been long in the—'

'No.' Meg stepped up to Shavi's side. The tree creaked in protest at being interrupted. 'I'm sorry for speaking out of turn,' Meg continued hurriedly, 'but not all people are the same. We've always respected trees, nature. It's part of our belief. We never cut green wood. We don't pollute the land.' Shavi saw the wild intelligence bright in her eyes; she knew, as he did, that the Oak Men would be strong allies.

A whispering like the crackling of dry leaves seemed to run through the ground to nearby trees, then out through the wood. 'They're talking,' Carolina said, a little too loudly.

Soon after lights appeared in the deep dark, far among the trees, flickering will-o'-the-wisps that, oddly, put them all at ease. 'Spirit lights,' Shavi said in awe. 'The spirits of the trees moving out from the wood.'

'It has not been seen by mortals for many lives, even by how the Wood-born measure time,' the oak said. 'We accept your words. We call you to come to us as friends. Embrace the wood. Move through our home, listen to the whisper of our hearts. Show respect for us, men and women of flesh and bone, and we in turn shall forever grant you the good fortune that comes from our protection. Let this be the first act of a new age.'

'I thank you, Men of Oak, for your good grace in forgiving the sins of the past.' Shavi rested his hand on the bark once more; it was warm and comforting to the touch.

'Seasons come and go. A fresh start will be to the benefit of both our people.'

Shavi turned to face the others. They were watching the lights floating gently among the trees, their faces almost beatific. Race memories, long buried echoes of wonder and awe had been released in them. In one moment they had become their ancestors.

Gradually, one by one, they drifted off lazily among the trees. Shavi watched their transcendental expressions as they reached out to the lights, touched the wood, caressed the leaves, lost to the mystery. The Oak Man had been right: this was a moment of vital importance for the new age, the reforming of a bond that had been so powerful in times long gone.

Shavi followed a little way behind, observing the change that had come over the travellers as they wandered in and out of the circles of moonlight; they were more at peace than he would have believed. Deep in the woods some of them came across a glassy, moonlit pool where water trickled melodically over mildewed rocks from a tiny spring, a green and silver world that smelled as clear and fresh as a wilderness mountaintop.

Carolina sat on a rock at the edge and trailed her hand dreamily in the water. She retracted it suddenly when she saw a face floating just beneath the surface, big eyes blinking curiously. The figure was not solid; in fact it seemed to be continuously flowing and reforming. But no sense of threat came off it. Cautiously, Carolina reached out her hand and paused a few inches above the surface. The water rose up in a gentle crystal spiral to touch her fingertips briefly before rushing away. There was a sound like gently bubbling laughter. Carolina looked up and smiled, her face as innocent as the moon.

Hours later, back at the camp site, the eight of them tried to express to the others what had happened. Amidst the gushing enthusiasm it wasn't hard to communicate the overwhelming sense of wonder that possessed them, and by the time midnight turned they all felt they had been part of an epochal shift.

Penny was overjoyed that her son was still alive, but the thought that he wasn't even in the world left her dismal. 'You've got to help me,' she said to Shavi, clutching at his sleeve like he was the Saviour; her face was pitiful, broken.

'I will do what I can,' he replied, and it wasn't quite a lie. He didn't tell her what was likely to be her son's fate in the Court of the Final Word, that even if he could find some way to bring the boy back, his mother might not recognise him.

Still, his brief words seemed to cheer her. She left the fireside hurriedly to wander among the trees in the hope that the Wood-born's promise of good fortune would find its way to her.

Shavi retired to his tent early, exhausted by his experience. As the firelight began to die he had also seen a grey shape flickering like reflected light among the vehicles, and he did not feel strong enough to deal with Lee that night. His guilt at his boyfriend's death had not been assuaged by the knowledge that it had been part of some overarching scheme by the Tuatha Dé Danann; he still could have done something to save Lee, he was sure of it, but fear for his own safety had paralysed him. If being taunted and berated by his dead lover on a nightly basis was the price he had to pay to purge the emotions that were eating away at him, then that was how it would have to be; even if the words he heard were driving him insane.

There was a faint scratching on the canvas. A silhouette he would never forget. He buried his face in his bag and tried to sleep.

And then the whispering began.

At some point he must finally have dozed off for he woke with a start to a
rustling at the entrance to the tent. His first befuddled thought was that it
was Lee until Carolina pushed her way in past the flaps. Behind her was
Spink, now miraculously cleaned of the mud that had grimed him from
head to toe. He was handsome, dark-eyed and black-haired beneath his
disguise. Shavi switched on his torch and positioned it so it illuminated the
tent.

'Do you mind if we come in?' Carolina said when she was already inside.

Shavi gestured magnanimously; if truth be told, he was keen for
company. 'How can I help you?'

Spink seemed awestruck in his presence, so it was Carolina who did all
the talking. 'The people out there are talking about you like you're some
kind of Messiah.' Her eyes sparkled in the torchlight.

'I am no Messiah.'

'They saw what you did in the wood. You've got powers of some kind.
You do things that no ordinary person can do.'

Shavi nodded. 'But inside I am just a man. Flawed, frightened, unable to
know what is the right decision.'

She shook her head; her black hair shifted languorously. 'You're not
convincing me. You told us yourself, you're a man with a mission. You're
here to deliver us all from evil.'

'Not like that.'

'Not a Messiah, then. But a mystic, a wise man. Shaman. You used the
word yourself.' This he had to concede. 'Then you could teach us all
things—'

'I am not a teacher.'

'Look at us all here!' she protested. 'Why do you think we've opted for
this kind of life when we could be living in warm homes where there's
always plenty of food on the table, where there's always some nice loving
husband or boyfriend there to make sure everything's all right?' There was a
sliver of bitterness in her voice; she swallowed it with difficulty and
continued. 'We're all searching for something, something better. It was a
spiritual choice. You must understand that?' He nodded. 'We've been failed
by society, failed by the Church, all the religions. But there's a deep hole
inside us that we want filled.' She hit her chest hard. 'You can help fill that.'

Shavi was humbled by her passion and eloquence. 'So you are saying that
you want to be my disciples?'

She glanced at Spink, whose eyes brightened. 'That's exactly what we're
saying.'

'Let me tell you something,' he began slowly. 'I grew up in West London

374

in a family of brothers and sisters and aunts and uncles and nieces and nephews and . . . too many even to count. As a child, it was quite idyllic. I never wanted for love. I studied hard at school to make my father proud of me, and he *was* proud, and I was happier than any boy had any right to be. My father . . . The thing I remember about him sometimes when I am drifting off to sleep is the way his eyes would light up when I would bring him my school books to show him my work. They would crinkle round the edge, and then he would smile and pull me over to him. There was such integrity and honesty in his face, all I wanted was to be like him.'

He closed his eyes, the memories flashed across his mind almost too painful to bear. 'My family was very strictly Muslim. It was the glue that held everything together. The mosque was as much a part of our life as the kitchen. And for my father and mother, for all my relatives, it was the thing that gave them strength to face all the privations the world brought to their door. But it was not right for me. I tried. I tried so hard I could not sleep, I could not eat, because I knew it would make my mother and father proud. But it did not speak to me, here . . .' he touched his chest, then his forehead '. . . and here. It did not feel right, or comforting, or secure, or even begin to explain the way the world works. For me. For I still believe, of all the religions, it is one of the strongest. But it did not speak *to me*. And so, in all good faith, I could not continue with it.'

Carolina and Spink watched every flicker of his face, his deathly seriousness reflected in their own.

'I told my father. The shock I saw in his features destroyed me. It was as if, for one brief instant, I was a stranger who had washed into his room. And I never saw his eyes light up again. At first he tried to force me to be a good Muslim. And then, when that did not work, at sixteen he drove me out of the house for good. I stood crying on the doorstep, the same good son who had pleased him all his life. And he would not look me in the face. And he would not speak a word. And when the door closed it was plain it would be for ever.'

'What a bastard,' Carolina said.

'No. I could never blame my father. He was who he was and always had been. And there is not a night goes by that I do not think of him warmly.'

'Why are you telling us this?'

'Because I have spent all my life since then searching for something which would give me the same feeling of warmth and security I felt as a child, and which would fill that void inside.'

'But you've found—'

'No. I have not. Once you set off along that path to enlightenment it is a very dark road indeed, and I have not seen even the slightest glimmer of light at the end. It is a journey we must all make, alone. What worked for my father did not work for me. What will be right for me, will not be so for you. Do not seek out masters. Look into yourself.'

There was a long pause. Then she said, 'Can't you see? That's just the kind of guidance I was looking for—'

He sighed.

'Okay, okay, I hear what you're saying. But I tell you now, we are going to be your disciples. We'll just do it from a distance.' Her smile was facetious, teasing; he smiled in response.

He could see in her face there was something else. 'What do you want?'

'We want to be with you.'

It took him a second or two to realise what she was truly saying. 'That may not be a good idea.'

'Why? Because you think we're being manipulated somehow? We know what we're doing. This isn't an emotional thing, it's a . . . it's a . . .' She searched for the right words.

'A ritual thing,' Spink said suddenly.

Shavi nodded. He understood the transfer of power through the sexual act and he certainly understood the power of directed hedonism. But he was uncomfortable with how they were elevating him to the position of some potent seer and hoping that some of whatever he had would rub off on them during intimacy.

Before he had a chance to order his thoughts, Carolina had stripped off her T-shirt. Her breasts were small and pale in the torchlight. Spink followed suit; his chest was hard and bony, the ribs casting strips of shadow across his skin.

'Spink's bi,' Carolina said. 'Or maybe gay, I don't think he's decided yet.'

She leaned forward and kissed Shavi, her mouth open and wet. Spink moved in and began to nuzzle at Shavi's neck. There was too much sensory stimulation for Shavi to keep his thoughts ordered and eventually he gave in to the pleasures of the moment.

The torch was switched off. His fingers slid over warm flesh. Hands caressed his body, stripping him naked. Their bodies moved over his, both of them hard, at times impossible to tell who was whom. The atmosphere became heightened with energy and for that brief moment he felt renewed.

The scream cut through the early morning stillness, snapping Shavi out of a deep sleep. He untangled himself from draping limbs, only just stirring, before pulling on his clothes and scrambling out on to the dewy ground. The air was chill; it couldn't have been long after dawn.

The first thing he saw brought that cold deep into his veins. There, in the tufted grass by the tent opening, was a slim, pale, severed finger.

All over the campsite people were falling out of camper vans, buses and cars, staggering bleary-eyed into the light. Shavi lurched past the finger, barely able to take his eyes off it, then tried to estimate the direction from which the scream had come. He didn't have to look far. In the no-man's land between the vehicles and the wood, a woman silently dipped down, then rose up, dipped down, rose up, a surreal image until Shavi saw her face was contorted with such grief she couldn't give voice to it. A shapeless mass lay at her feet.

Shavi ran as fast as he could, but several people reached the site before him. He pushed through them a little too roughly. Lying at the centre of the shocked circle of travellers was Penny, the ground stained in a wide arc around where her finger should have been. She was white with death.

Shavi felt his stomach knot, his mind fizz and spark with the awful realisation that he had brought this horror to the gentle, peaceful travellers. The ground seemed to shift beneath his feet and he had to stagger away where he could no longer see the body.

chapter seventeen

δust of cReeδs outwoRn

What do you mean, it's all your fault?' Breaker's face was shattered, his cheeks still stinging red from tears. Carolina stood beside him like a ghost while Meg squatted nearby, her hands pressed against her eyes, as if she were trying to stop the image from entering her brain.

Shavi explained everything, from when it had all begun on the banks of Loch Maree. The others listened intently, their faces impassive; Shavi couldn't tell if they were judging him. Afterwards Carolina asked in a breaking voice, 'So why is it hunting you?'

'I have no idea.' He swallowed, composed himself. 'I thought we had seen the last of it in Edinburgh. I had no idea it was following me or I would not have brought it to your door. You must believe me—'

'We do.' Meg came forward and hugged him tightly. 'We can all see you're all right. You wouldn't have put us at risk if you'd known.' She glanced over to where the body lay covered by a sheet. 'Poor Penny. Just after she'd found out what'd happened to Jack.'

'That is why it happened,' Shavi said morosely.

'What do you mean?' Breaker asked.

'The attack was meant to show there is no hope. Penny was snuffed out just as she achieved it.' Shavi chewed his lip until he tasted blood. 'It was a message for me. The finger was left outside the tent, a sign that the killer could have come for me while I slept.'

'But why?' Carolina looked like she was about to vomit.

'To make me suffer, I would think. To make me frightened, always looking over my shoulder, so never knowing when the attack will come.'

'What's the obsession with fingers?' Breaker asked.

'I have no idea. Are you going to report this to the police?'

Breaker toyed with his beard, but it was Meg who gave voice to the thoughts in all their minds. 'There's no point. With all the shit going down, the cops haven't got time to look into this. They'll probably just use it as another excuse to harass us.'

'Then I would suggest we bury her among the trees. The Wood-born will watch over her,' Shavi suggested.

The grave party ensured the hole was six feet deep, carefully avoiding all the roots that criss-crossed the area. There were enough of them to ensure the work was done quickly, then everyone in the camp gathered for the ceremony; their faces were disbelieving, angry, distraught. Their lives had been disrupted so suddenly and completely no one had quite been able to assimilate what had happened. Breaker and Meg said a few words in a ritual which echoed the cycles of the seasons and spoke to the overwhelming force of nature.

Once the grave was filled, everyone was surprised to see a spontaneous shower of leaves from all the surrounding trees, until the overturned soil was covered by a crisp blanket of green; it was an act of such respect several people wept at the sight. Shavi felt, in a grimly ironic way, that the bond between the two groups had been strengthened further.

They decided to postpone any wake until everyone had had time to come to terms with what had happened. Instead, Breaker, Carolina, Meg and Shavi gathered around a makeshift table in the back of Breaker's bus.

'Of course, I will be leaving shortly,' Shavi announced once they were seated.

'Why?' Meg's eyes blazed.

'This sickening thing is pursuing me. When I leave he will follow me and you will be left to return to your lives.'

'No,' Meg said forcefully.

'I agree,' Carolina added. 'You're one of us now. We're not going to desert you.'

'They're right,' Breaker said. 'They're always right about everything, that's why we love them.' His words seemed honest rather than patronising. 'There's safety in numbers, Shavi. You go off on your own across that deserted countryside, well, that bastard could pick you off at any time. We're organised here. We can do more, better, watches. We'll get you where you need to go.'

'But—'

'Don't fucking argue,' Carolina said wearily. She wiped her eyes with the back of her hand. 'Think of your friend. Think of the big picture, all you're trying to do. Here's where we do our bit too.'

Shavi sagged back against the window and slowly rubbed a hand across his eyes. 'Thank you. You are true friends.'

'Just do one thing for us,' Breaker said.

'What is that?'

'If you get a chance, any time, ever, bring Jack back. For Penny.'

Shavi put one hand on his heart and held the other up, palm out. 'For Penny.'

Church perched on a rocky outcropping over a precipitous drop, contemplating how quickly the remaining nine days would pass. Before him the Derbyshire countryside rolled out in the hazy, late morning sunshine, a patchwork of green fields, shimmering water, ribbon roads and small, peaceful villages. But it wasn't the great beauty of the scene that caught his attention.

Nearby, houses were burning. The tangled wreckage of vehicles glinted in the sunlight. Things he couldn't quite comprehend moved along the hedgerows or kept to the dark at the edge of copses. Occasionally one would be forced to cross a field, like a cloud-shadow moving across the land. It always made him shiver to see it.

The Fomorii appeared to be growing in force, more daring in their desperation as Lughnasadh neared. They sensed Ruth and what she contained were somewhere in the area, but the magic Tom had identified at Mam Tor was, so far, enough to blind them to the exact location. But if he allowed himself to admit it, he knew it was only a question of time. For once, he could do nothing; it was a matter of placing his faith in Shavi, Veitch and Tom.

Sometimes he saw the Fomorii hunter-warrior circling the area, more intense and threatening than the other shifting shapes, like a localised storm filled with lightning fury. It left him feeling fearful and nauseous. And something more than that: he was starting to feel the bitter taint of hopelessness. Only days to go. What could they do? They were going to fail again, and it would be the end of everything.

Cautiously he crept back from the edge. What would he do when the black tide did begin to surge up the mountain? Fight them off with sticks and stones like schoolboy war games? Or sit back and pray there really, truly was a God in His heaven?

Ruth lay in her sleeping bag on a bed made of flattened fern in a corner of the room. Her skin was ashen, her hair matted from the bouts of sweating and delirium that were coming with increasing regularity. Her eyes flickered, her features trembled; terrible thoughts that did not seem to come from her own mind stumbled through her head.

They had cleaned up the place as best they could. Church and Laura had spent a morning sweeping out the rubbish and depositing it in the shadows at the back of the house. Church had patched up the roof with dead wood and vegetation, but the wind still whipped through the broken windows and sometimes it was uncommonly cold for that time of year; perhaps it was the altitude. Food was a problem. There was little to trap on the mountain and none of them were any good at it anyway. Church had made several forays into a nearby village and had stocked up the larder as best he could. The increasing Fomorii activity in the area made it too risky to go foraging any more. They all prayed the provisions would hold out.

Laura squatted in the corner, occasionally casting a subdued glance to Ruth's restlessly sleeping form. The sunglasses rarely came off these days, even at night. Her brooding consumed her. She hated the way Church cared for Ruth; there was real tenderness in his touch, an honesty in his words that made her yearn; the feeling between the two ran so deep it was as if it had formed when the earth was just cooling. She knew it was jealousy, pure and simple; it was the kind of relationship she had always dreamed about, had expected once she had hooked up with Church, yet even though all the facets seemed in place, it had never materialised, and that was the bitterest blow of all. If she couldn't find it with Church, who could she plumb those depths with?

And she could see Ruth was dying; they all knew it, though no one spoke it aloud. Yet there she was, being petty and jealous and bitter. That filled her with guilt and self-loathing, which once more fed all those negative emotions; a terrible, dark spiral that had no end.

'What are you thinking?'

Laura started; she hadn't realised Ruth was awake. 'I'm thinking, "Boy, I hope she doesn't start whining any time soon".'

Ruth managed a weak laugh; her voice sounded like autumn leaves. 'You'll never change, will you?'

'Count on it.'

Ruth tried to lever herself into a sitting position. Her arms were feeble and her belly was enormous; she seemed to have gone almost full-term of a natural pregnancy in a matter of days. Eventually she gave up and settled for half-sitting, half-lying. She snorted with laughter at her own pathetic attempt.

'How do you keep so up? You've had the bum deal to end all bum deals. Some psycho slicing off your finger. Getting tortured by the Bastards. Now this—'

'Now I'm pregnant with the one-eyed God of Death and he's going to burst out of my stomach in a few days and tear me apart. Well, when you put it like that . . .' She laughed again, before breaking into a coughing fit.

'What is it with you? When I first met you, you were such a poker-up-the-arse kind of girl. Some spoilt little middle-class moron. I thought you'd fall apart at the first sign of trouble.'

'What's the matter? Jealous?'

Her words were lighthearted but they stung Laura as if she'd been slapped. 'You have a real sense of the absurd, don't you?'

'I'm dying. You're supposed to be nice to me.'

Laura watched her impassively.

'That was the point where you were supposed to say, "Course you're not dying. Everything will work out in the end".' Ruth threw an arm across her eyes. Laura couldn't tell if she was trying to hide her emotions, but she felt bad anyway.

But not bad enough she could bring herself to be nice. Nice was for losers. 'What do you expect me to say?'

'I don't know. Nothing to say, is there? I'm dying. I know I'm dying. And any chance I have is the longest of long shots.' She removed her arm and Laura was surprised to see a remarkable peace in her face.

That twisted the knife in her gut even more and suddenly she felt like crying; the words just bubbled out. 'What is it? Church, you can see he's a hero. It's stitched right into the heart of him, always beating himself up about responsibilities and obligations and doing the right thing. Shavi's just Mister Decency. You know he'd give up his life if the cause was right. Even Veitch, the Testosterone Kid, a fucking murderer by his own admission! Even he's fighting against type to be good, to be a hero. And despite all his very obvious limitations, you know he's going to come through, when the chips are down and all those other clichés. And then there's you, kicked around and tortured from pillar to post, taking all this shit that *nobody* should have to take. And dying with dignity. I don't fit in here. You give me a choice between saving my own skin and doing the right thing and you watch my dust!' The self-pity was sickening, but she seemed unable to control herself.

'You're not being fair on yourself—'

'Don't start analysing me. I don't need it. And for God's sake, don't start being *nice* to me.'

'I won't—'

'Just don't.'

'Look, can't we just be friends? Even now?' Ruth's eyes filled with tears; despite her calm, her emotions were on a knife-edge.

Laura remained silent, staring at the wall. The mass of scrawled writing disturbed her immensely and in all their time there none of them had felt up to making any effort to decipher it. It was just part of the oppressive mood that lurked in the corners of the house. She was sure Ruth sensed things there that she wasn't talking about, and there were times when she felt it acutely herself, and she was less sensitive than anyone she knew. *Something bad had happened,* Ruth had said, and something bad was *going* to happen. Perhaps that was it: not an echo of the past, but a premonition. She felt it so strongly she could almost touch it.

'You've always hidden yourself away from all of us.' Ruth's voice was hazy and Laura could tell she was on the verge of drifting into one of her intermittent periods of delirium. 'Hiding behind your sunglasses, trying to be smart and glib all the time so no one knew what you were really thinking. Even that name – Laura DuSantiago. That's got to be an alias, a new persona to hide in.' She swallowed; her mouth sounded sticky with mucus. 'Tell you what,' she continued weakly. 'You tell me your real name now. I won't tell a soul. A dying woman's last wish.' She laughed hollowly.

Laura sat quietly for a moment, then moved to the bedside and knelt so her mouth was close to Ruth's ear. Ruth strained to hear.

'Go fuck yourself,' Laura said softly.

Then she rose and calmly walked out of the room in search of Church.

Breaker cursed under his breath as the lead bus began another difficult three-point turn in the middle of the road. About half a mile ahead they could see the tailback leading up to the police checkpoint. It looked like the police were barring every road they tried; Shavi had lost count of the times they had turned around and sought an alternative route. But that wasn't what was troubling him. It was the things he increasingly caught glimpses of from the corner of his eye, moving as fast as foxes, or slipping back into shadows when he half-turned his head. He hadn't mentioned them to Breaker or the others, but he knew what they were: the Fomorii were abroad.

He took some relief from the fact that they were still wary enough to stay out of plain sight; just. They must be terrified about having let the essence of their god slip through their fingers, if it were possible for such creatures to feel fear. But he was concerned about how widespread they were and how their number appeared to be increasing. If they were this close to the surface now, what would happen when desperation set in as Lughnasadh neared?

He knew they were searching for any sign of Balor, but was it possible they could *sniff out* the Pendragon Spirit too?

'You look worried.' Breaker cast a sideways glance as he pulled up behind the bumper of the bus in front.

'I was merely trying to second-guess the obstacles which might lie between us and my destination.'

'You reckon the Finger Hunter is somewhere nearby? I don't see how he could be keeping up with us unless he's smelling us on the wind.'

Shavi thought that was a distinct possibility, but said nothing.

'The biggest problem is the cops. We need to stay out of their way. I don't know what's happened to them. They were always bugging us, but now they seem to be hassling *everyone*. All these checkpoints. What the hell do they think they're trying to do?'

Some of the police at every checkpoint had waxy faces, Shavi had noticed; it was obvious to him what they were trying to do. And it appeared that there was some link between what Breaker called the Finger Hunter and the Fomorii too. Shavi had an overpowering image of a net closing around him. Perhaps he would never reach Windsor at all.

After leaving the camp where Penny had been buried, they had taken a couple of days to pick a relatively short route past Banbury before cutting through the lanes between Oxford and Bicester to reach their current position just north of the M40. On the map Windsor looked to be only forty minutes' drive away. Two rapidly successive technology failures slowed them down even more, but every attempt to cross the motorway failed and they were continually pushed east towards London. With only a week remaining before Lughnasadh Shavi could ill afford any more delays.

'We can't get too close to the Smoke,' Breaker said, concerned. 'A convoy this size'll draw too much attention. We'll get snarled up and they'll have us off the road in a minute. Plus, some of our valued members get very uneasy whenever they're near any built-up area. All that pollution.'

Shavi barely spoke any more; his attention was directed at the apparently empty countryside. Thoughts were piling up inside his head, forcing him down a very worrying path. The one who killed Penny was obviously not Fomorii, but possibly had some kind of link with the Night Walkers. The killer knew who Shavi was travelling with, probably knew exactly where he was. What if the killer decided to point the Fomorii in his direction? Shavi scanned the fields cautiously. He had not seen any sign of the Fomorii for some time. Perhaps they too were wary of getting too close to the Capital. Still, he would be on his guard.

They paused in a lay-by on the A40 east of Postcombe to weigh up their options. Most people stayed in their vehicles, taking the opportunity to have a quick snack or a drink, but the ones who had naturally gravitated towards the leading group gathered on the roadside for a conference. There were Breaker, Meg, Carolina, and four others whom Shavi didn't know by name. While they spoke heatedly, Shavi circled the group, focusing his attention on the fields that swept out to the north and east.

It was late afternoon and the sweltering temperature of the day had been made worse by thick cloud-cover rolling in to trap the heat. They would have to consider making camp soon, and that was a prospect Shavi did not relish.

Exhausted by the day's driving, still shattered by what had happened to Penny, the travellers' nerves were fraying, their voices growing harsh. Shavi tried to ignore them to concentrate on the darkening landscape, but their debate grew louder and more hectoring until he turned and snapped, 'Quiet!'

They all looked at him. A car roared by and then the road grew still. 'What is it?' Carolina said. 'There's nothing—'

He waved her quiet with a chopping motion of his hand. Something was jarring on his nerves, but he couldn't quite put his finger on what it was. There was the wind in the trees. Distant traffic noise from the motorway. Nothing, nothing . . . And then he had it. The field birds were cawing harshly; on the surface it was not unusual, but instinctively he seemed to know what they were saying. He could hear the tonal differences, the faint nuances, almost as if it was speech. They were frightened.

He spun round to the others. 'Back to the vehicles. Quickly. It is not safe here.'

The words had barely left his mouth when there was movement along all the hedgerows of the fields: darkness separating from the shadows near the hedge bottoms, rising out of ditches; the Fomorii were moving.

Most of the travellers obeyed him instantly and ran towards their vehicles. One of the men whom Shavi didn't know turned to look at the fields curiously; his eyes started to roll and nausea passed across his face. Shavi gave him a violent shove in the direction of his camper van before he could see any more.

'Do not look at the fields!' Shavi yelled. 'Get on the road and keep driving! Follow Breaker's lead!'

He threw himself in beside Breaker and the bus lurched out on to the road. A horn blared furiously as a Porsche overtook at high speed. 'What's going on?' Breaker asked.

'The Fomorii are attacking,' Shavi said darkly, one eye fixed on the wing mirror. 'They want me. And they will destroy you all to get at me.'

The vehicles surged on to the road in a wave of creaking, protesting metal. But age lay heavy on some of them and their response was poor. Shavi held himself tense as he watched the trail pull out of the lay-by as the fields turned black with movement; it was as if a termites' nest had suddenly been vacated.

'Are they all with us?' Breaker asked anxiously.

Shavi counted the vehicles out. 'Nearly there.' A bus. Another. A mini-van. 'One more.' The straggler was the camper van belonging to the traveller Shavi had forced into action. It was slow, weaving unnecessarily, and Shavi knew the driver was trying to see what was in the fields through his mirror. 'Do not look,' he prayed under his breath.

The camper van slewed suddenly to one side and came to a halt. Shavi pictured the driver vomiting, then passing out. He slammed a hand against the side window as if it would jolt the driver awake.

In the mirror Shavi watched the darkness sweep over the hedgerow into the lay-by. He had an impression of teeth and body armour, wings and too many legs, all shimmering sable, and although he had grown almost immune to the appearance of the Night Walkers, he still felt his stomach churn.

The Fomorii hit the camper van like a tidal wave. It crumpled as if it were made of paper, then shredded into a million pieces. Shavi looked away quickly.

Breaker glanced at him, but didn't have to ask. After a long silence, the traveller said, 'Do you think they'll follow us into London?'

'They will not be able to keep up with the vehicles if you travel at speed. But now they know I am with you they will continue to hunt you down. If we go into London there is a danger we will be obstructed, slowed down.'

'Then what?' Breaker's thumb was banging on the wheel in an anxious rhythm.

Shavi thought for a moment. 'We must speed up, but not go completely out of sight. They must see you drop me off—'

'We can't abandon you to them!' Breaker flashed him a dismayed glance.

'I will have a better chance of hiding from them alone. There must be somewhere near here where I can attempt to lose them.' He snatched up Breaker's dog-eared book of maps and hastily riffled through the pages. When he found the page they were on, he pored over it for a minute, then stabbed his finger down. 'Here.'

When Breaker was convinced the convoy was going to go straight into the centre of High Wycombe, Shavi indicated a turning. They came to a stop at West Wycombe and waited anxiously, with constant reference to the

386

mirror. Meg and Carolina could contain themselves no longer, and ran from their respective vehicles to see what was planned. They pleaded with him not to go, but he would not be deterred; his leaving was the only chance they had.

When he spied movement in the countryside on either side, he kissed them both, shook Breaker's hand forcefully, then sent them on their way. His last view of the travellers was a series of pale, frightened faces trying to comprehend what was happening in their lives.

He waited alone in the road for as long as he could. It quickly became obvious the dark stream of Fomorii had realised he had left the convoy, for they hurtled towards him relentlessly, without heeding the disappearing vehicles.

Once he was sure of that, he dashed through a gate and ran as fast as his legs would carry him.

The lowering clouds made the late afternoon into twilight. The very air around him seemed to have a gun-metal sheen and he could taste iron on the back of his tongue; a storm was brewing, which he hoped would be to his advantage, although he had the unnerving feeling the Fomorii could see in the gloomiest weather conditions.

But at least he was sure he could make the location work for him. Once he saw the name on the map, the information about myths, legends and history that he had amassed over a lifetime instantly came into play.

He was sprinting through the classically designed grounds of West Wycombe Park in full view of the gleaming Palladian mansion where the Dashwood family had made their home for hundreds of years. It was one of their ancestors who had earned the place such notoriety. In the mid-eighteenth century Sir Francis Dashwood founded a private brotherhood of the upper crust, which he ironically named the Knights of St Francis. There was little of the chivalrous about a secret society dedicated to orgies and blasphemous religious ceremonies, acts which earned it the nickname the Hellfire Club and a motto *Do what thou wilt*. The truth had turned into legend, which had haunted the family and the area ever since, but somewhere in the grounds was another part of Sir Francis' grim legacy which Shavi thought might save his life; if only he could find it.

He headed for the unmistakable landmark of St Lawrence's Church, built by Dashwood, with a meeting place for ten of his Hellfire Knights in a gleaming, golden ball on the top of the tower. Shavi had half-expected to be met by security guards or someone trying to make him buy a ticket, but things were falling apart quickly all over; what was the point of maintaining tourist locations when everyone was trying to live on a day-to-day basis in a climate of increasing fear?

At the church he stopped and glanced back. The shadowy shapes were closer now, massing as they flowed down the sweeping green slopes of the garden. Quickly he scanned the area.

Eventually he found what he was looking for: an entrance cut into the hillside overlooking the park. Within lay a network of artificial caves going deep underground where the Hellfire Club had held its magic rituals and orgies. It was tucked away at just such an angle that the approaching Fomorii would not see him take the detour and would presume he had continued on through the grounds; and it was discreet enough that unless they knew it was there, they would not see it. He hoped.

He skidded inside, his chest aching from his ragged breathing; even fit as he now was, he hadn't moved at such a clip for a long time. The catacombs were filled with an inky darkness. Lights had been installed for the tourists, but he didn't dare attempt to put them on, even if he could have located the light switch. He moved as swiftly as he could while feeling his way along the chill, dank walls. When he rounded a corner and the ambient light was extinguished, the gloom was complete. He had a sudden flashback to the grim ruins of Mary King's Close and felt his heart begin to pound. He had attempted to bend the supernatural to his will, but the more he had learned about the Invisible World, the more he realised how much there was that terrified him. He wondered if any remnant of the monstrous rituals carried out by the Hellfire Club had been imprinted in the rock walls; if Sir Francis Dashwood's spirit still walked the place, trying to expunge his lifetime's sins; if there were other, worse, things there that had been called up by the Club's desire to be an affront to natural law.

But more than the otherworldly threat was the certain knowledge that if the Fomorii did enter the catacombs he would not be aware of them until they were upon him.

When he felt he had progressed deep enough into the heart of the tunnels, he slumped down against the foot of the wall and took a deep breath. His whole body was shaking from the strain and the fear, his blood pumping so loudly he didn't think he would hear if a column of hobnailed soldiers were marching towards him; he forced himself to do a series of breathing exercises to calm himself. Once he had relaxed as much as he could he tried to concentrate all his energies on his hearing. In his mind's eye he pictured the scene above ground: the oppressive force of Fomorii smashing down small trees, tearing through shrubs and flowers, sweeping up and around the church. By now they should have reached the entrance to the catacombs.

He listened intently. Nothing.

Perhaps they had already passed, thundering through the rest of the grounds, not stopping for miles, like robot drones pointed in one direction and turned on. Of the Fomorii he had encountered, there appeared little of independent thought and cunning; that rested in large quantities with their leader Calatin, and Mollecht, the Fomor who appeared as a swirling mass of crows, whom Shavi had not seen since that night in the Lake District when they thought they had snatched victory.

Time passed in deep silence. How long should he wait there, he wondered? In the dark he found he was losing track of the hours. If the Fomorii had not already found him, it would be logical, he supposed, to wait until morning before attempting to leave. They would be scouring the countryside for him and the night was not the best time to be trying to evade them. But even if he did make it through the night undiscovered, what chance would he have of reaching Windsor Park? It was not far on the map, but if there were an army of Fomorii between him and his destination, it might as well have been a million miles away.

At some point he fell asleep, and he must have been out for a while, for on awakening suddenly his mouth and throat were uncommonly dry and every muscle ached. When he opened his eyes he was completely disorientated by the dark and had to struggle to recall where he was. But as soon as his memory clicked into action he became alert; he knew something had woken him.

His first thought was that the Fomorii had finally tracked him down, but the dark caves around him seemed as empty as they ever had been. His next thought was of some supernatural presence; his instincts were as attuned to the Invisible as the visible world. But he didn't have that queasy sensation which always materialised in the pit of his stomach whenever something uncanny was nearby.

He held his breath and listened. At first, nothing; then a sound, just the slightest scuffle of dust from a footstep that many would have missed, but his own hearing had grown hyper-sensitive in the dark. There was someone else in the caves, and they were creeping, so as not to be discovered.

The construction of the caves meant all sound was distorted, so it was impossible to tell from which direction the footfall had come. In the all-consuming darkness Shavi was loath to move one way or the other in case he bumped into the intruder. But then neither could he sit there and wait to be discovered.

Weighing the odds, he decided to attempt to make his way back to the door; at least then he would have the option of fleeing if necessary. He stood up and rested his left hand on the wall before moving forward a few paces. He paused and listened. Another few paces and he stopped again.

The unmistakable scrape of a foot on the gritty floor. A tingle ran down his spine. It seemed to come from somewhere over to his right. Cautiously he continued ahead, placing each foot down slowly and carefully, so as not to make even the slightest noise.

His breath was held tightly in his chest. He half-expected to come face to face with something terrible; the dark was so deep he wouldn't have known if there were someone standing motionless even six inches in front of him. With an effort he drove those thoughts from his head; it would do him no good; he had to stay calm.

Another noise, this time in front of him. The echoes were mesmerising. He couldn't tell if the intruder was circling or if he was misreading the direction of the sounds. He moved back a few paces and waited again.

In the claustrophobic space of the caves, Shavi knew it was only a matter of time before his pursuer caught him. Yet there was a slim chance to weight the odds a little more in his favour. He closed his eyes and took a deep, calming breath, focusing far within himself. He still couldn't turn his nascent shamanistic abilities on and off like a light switch, but with concentration there were little tricks he had practised. He felt the force rising within him like a billowing sheet, filling him, moving out through his mouth, to wrap itself around him. The first time he had attempted this he had been standing within a few feet of Veitch, yet the Londoner had not even noticed him, at least for a moment or two. He didn't know *how* it worked, but he perceived it as a cloak which made him merge in with the surroundings. It was a subtle trick and easily punctured, yet in the gloom of the cavern it might have more force. He hoped it would be enough.

His throat had grown painfully dry. After several minutes without a sound, he moved off again. This time he progressed a long way through the caves, but somewhere in the dark he must have taken a wrong turning, for he knew he should have come across the door by then. There was no point retracing his steps – he wouldn't have any idea when he arrived back at where he had slept anyway. His only option was to keep going left, in the hope that it would lead him to an outside wall which would eventually take him around the perimeter of the catacombs to the exit.

As he moved he listened as intently as he could, but there was no sign of anyone; at the same time he had an overwhelming and unpleasant sense of *presence*. And then he froze as every nerve seemed to fire at once. Was someone standing right behind him? His mind screamed at him to run, but somehow he held his ground. In that heightened moment his senses started playing tricks on him. Was that the bloom of a breath on his neck? An involuntary spasm ran through him; he didn't even dare swallow. The most natural thing in the world would have been to run away, but he was as sure as anything in his life that that would be the end of him.

And so he waited, and after several minutes the feeling slowly ebbed away. He didn't know if the intruder had been there, just inches away, listening, unable to see him, or if it was all in his mind. But the nausea he felt at the strain was certainly real.

He began moving again, hugging the wall, straining not to be heard.

His journey seemed to take hours, punctuated by long pauses brought on by dim echoes, the faintest footfalls, that might very well have been all in his mind.

And then, just as he was about to dismiss the entire experience as a flight of fancy, he happened to glance behind him, though his eyes were useless. The intensity of the darkness was almost hallucinatory and for a while his mind had been conjuring up flashes of colours, streaks of light, that were just brief electrical bursts on his retina. He could have dismissed it as another mind-flash, but what he saw made him stop and stare. No flash, no streak. Two tiny points of yellow away in the dark.

But then they disappeared and reappeared and he knew what they were: eyes, glinting with an awful inner light.

In his shock, he turned back and there was a thin grey band of dim light. It was seeping through the entrance. He moved towards it as quickly but as quietly as he could.

Steeling himself, his hand hovered over the handle. Then he wrenched it open and hurled himself out into a world just coming to life. On the threshold, he couldn't resist making the most of that pre-dawn light and threw one glance over his shoulder before sprinting across the park as fast as he could go.

And then he ran and he ran, that briefest glimpse staying with him as he put as much distance between him and his pursuer as he could. What he half-saw in the gloom was a shape that looked like a giant wolf, its eyes growing with a malignant fire. But an instant later his mind had started to rearrange it into something else: a human figure. The killer was still close behind him, as relentless in its pursuit as the wolf his mind presumed it to be.

But what troubled him more than the knowledge that he had escaped death only by a hair's breadth was that in that instant when the shape had started to change he was almost convinced he knew the person it was becoming. In the gloom and the fear, he hadn't been able to harden up the vision, and the connection remained disturbingly elusive.

To his infinite relief, there was no pursuit; nor were there any Fomorii in the immediate vicinity. But what he had half-seen continued to haunt him long after the sun had driven the greyness out of the landscape.

chapter eighteen

the court of the queen of elfland

Inverness appeared out of the dark Highlands landscape like a small island of light in a vast sea of shadows. Veitch and Tom walked down from the hills with leaden legs, burdened with the crushing weight of exhaustion. They had spent the last few days endlessly dodging the Fomorii, who were swarming across the purple moorland in increasing numbers. Tom had utilised some of his tricks – a ritual, some foul-tasting brew made from herbs and roots – which made the two of them oblivious to the Night Walkers unless they were in direct line of sight. But that still entailed endless hours of creeping along rocky gullies, taking the hard route over peaks or skulking in woods until the danger had passed.

It was a far cry from the first leg of their Scottish journey, when they had dined out on wholesome provisions from the villages they dropped in on. Now Veitch was heartily sick of wild game, roots and herbs, however well Tom cooked it. He had an almost unbearable craving for pizza or a curry, washed down with a beer.

'You reckon we'll get time to stop off for a ruby?' he said wearily as they trudged into the outskirts of town.

Tom looked at him blankly.

'Ruby Murray. Curry. It rhymes.'

Tom shook his head contemptuously. 'Eight days left. Why don't we go on a pub crawl while we're at it? We could have a few drinks for Ruth. That should make her well.'

'All right. No need to act so bleedin' crabby.' He took a few steps, then muttered, 'Twat,' under his breath. That made him feel better.

The truth was, their nerves were growing frayed. Time was running away from them. Lughnasadh was close, and the presence of Balor was almost tangible. They had both dreamed of a single eye watching them malignantly from the dark, and had woken sweaty and sick, with the feeling that the monstrous god of the Fomorii was *aware* of them. Even when they walked, they could feel his attention sweeping over them, the air thick with dread; with it came an overpowering sense of black despair that conjured thoughts of suicide, which they had to fight constantly to repel.

The weariness shucked off their shoulders the more they progressed into town. It felt good to see sodium lights after the oppression of a country night, to smell motor oil and the aroma of home cooking. But the closer they got into the centre, the more they began to realise something was wrong. No cars had passed them at all. Nobody walked the streets, even though it was only just past ten. The pubs were all locked, the curtains drawn, although Veitch could hear people drinking within; when he hammered on the doors a deep silence fell, but no one ever came to answer.

Eventually an old man swung open an upstairs window and hung out, his face filled with such fear Veitch gaped for a second.

'For God's sake, man, get yourself to your hearth!' The old man glanced up and down the street; he hadn't noticed Veitch wasn't alone. 'Can you not see it's after dark!' He slammed the window shut and drew the curtains before Veitch could question him; Veitch shouted to him several times, but there was no further response.

'What's up?' Veitch asked Tom with disquiet.

Tom continued to walk briskly, seemingly oblivious to the sense of threat. '*What's up?* Old friends have come to visit Inverness and they won't leave until they've expressed their infinite kindness.' Sarcasm dripped from his words.

'You're talking about the ones we're going to see?'

'The Queen of Elfland—'

A curiously amused expression jumped on Veitch's face. 'You're kidding me.'

'The Queen of Elfland. That's what they used to call her in the old stories. As if to pretend she was some kind of nice, acceptable *fairy*—' the word was filled with bitterness '—would somehow deflect her attentions.'

'So what would you call her?'

'Nothing she could hear.' He looked away so Veitch could not see his face. 'The moment we cross over, we must be on our guard.'

'You make her sound like some witch ready to tear our bleedin' heads off.'

'She will be filled with charisma, magnetic and alluring. That is her danger.'

'Okay. No problem.'

'No, you do not understand. The slightest wrong move could be the end of you. Every court of the Tuatha Dé Danann is different. The Court of the Yearning Heart embraces chaos and madness, which is why it is given over to pleasure. It is very easy to be seduced by it.' The deep tone of personal experience was unmissable. 'Listen carefully. You know the rules of Otherworld, and they go doubly here. You must accept no food nor drink from anyone or you will instantly fall under the power of the Queen. And she will find it greatly entertaining to trick you into doing so. You have to be sharp, Ryan. You have to be sharp.'

Veitch was shocked by the familiarity of Tom's use of his Christian name. For the first time, he felt the Rhymer was truly concerned about his safety. 'What'll happen, you know, if I do—?'

'Don't.'

'But if I do?'

Tom sighed. 'You will not be allowed to leave the Court of the Yearning Heart, at least not until the Queen has taken you apart down to your very molecules and has rebuilt you in whatever way her whims take her at the time. Until you have suffered every pain and pleasure imaginable, until it has become such a way of life that you *want* such suffering. And when she has finished, you will no longer be the man you are. You will no longer be a man.'

If Tom had tried to scare him, he'd succeeded.

'There isn't a man alive who couldn't love her,' Tom continued. 'But she dishes out joy and cruelty in equal measure; sometimes she isn't even aware that's what she's doing. The gates at Tom-na-hurich remained intermittently open long after the Sundering. There is a story of two itinerant fiddlers who crossed over. The Queen paid them to entertain the Court and allowed them to eat one of the sumptuous meals that are always laid out there. The fiddlers played their hearts out for the rest of the night. But when they were taken back to the Hill of Yews come the morning, they crumbled into dust. Two hundred years had passed without them knowing, and the Queen had taken great pleasure in hiding this from them.'

Veitch was silent for a moment. 'So how come you didn't turn to dust?'

Tom laughed hollowly. 'Why, only humans suffer such fates! The Queen has seen that I can never fit that bill.' He stopped in the middle of the road and looked out across the city to beyond the River Ness; Veitch guessed their destination lay in that direction. 'The legends say I lie under

Tom-na-hurich with my men and white horse, ready to save Scotland in her hour of need.'

'Well, that's what you're doing, ain't it?'

Tom snorted. 'Heroes only exist in stories. There's no nobility in what people do. We're all driven by a complex stew of emotions and it's down to fate whether people see us as good or bad.'

'You're a cynical git,' Veitch said dismissively. 'And you're wrong.'

They continued in silence for the next fifteen minutes until Veitch noticed a golden glow washing over the shops of the High Street. It was moving gradually towards them, casting strange shadows up the grim brick walls of Eastgate Centre. 'What's that?' His hand went to his sword under his coat.

'The welcoming committee.'

As the glow drew nearer, Veitch saw it was coming off a small group of people wandering along the road, although there was no sign of any light source. The moment he looked at the figures he experienced the now-familiar disorientating effect.

Tom drew himself up; the faintest tremor ran through his body, but his face was a mask of calmness. Veitch moved in next to him, tight with apprehension.

Five figures were approaching, all of them wearing outlandish clothes which mixed golden armour and red silk, topped by unusual helmets like enormous sea shells.

'The Queen's guard,' Tom noted. 'Out hunting for entertainment.'

Veitch took his lead from Tom, although his instinct was to hide. He watched as the guard progressed down the street, glancing into alleyways and side streets, shining their terrible regard into windows.

When they first clapped eyes on Tom and Veitch, sly smiles spread across their faces and they picked up their step as if they expected their quarry to flee for their lives. As they neared, their expressions became even more triumphal with recognition.

'True Thomas!' the leader of the guard exclaimed; there was a dark glee in his words, a contemptuous sneer shaping his mouth.

'Melliflor,' Tom said in greeting, giving nothing away.

'Why, we thought you had gone from our doors for all time, True Thomas!' Melliflor smiled with barely disguised mockery. 'The many wonders of the Court of the Yearning Heart are hard to resist, are they not? It calls to you always, even when you do not want to hear. Or,' he mused, 'is it your mistress who has brought you back? Our Lady of Light would be overjoyed to see you, True Thomas.'

Two of the guards had moved behind Veitch and Tom, to prevent any retreat. Veitch watched them suspiciously from the corner of his eye.

'Then take me to her, Melliflor,' Tom said. 'It will be good to see my Queen again after so long.'

Melliflor made an exaggerated sweeping gesture with his right hand to allow Tom to lead the way. After a few steps he arrived by Tom's side; Veitch might as well not have been there.

'May I enquire why you have returned to our doorstep?' Melliflor asked artfully.

'To renew acquaintances, Melliflor.'

'I hear you played a significant part in our return to the solid lands. I am sure our Queen will wish to offer her gratitude in her usual way.'

'Lead on, Melliflor. I have come far these last few days and I am too weary for conversation.'

Melliflor's sneering smile suggested he knew the meaning behind Tom's words; Veitch could quite easily have loosed the crossbow at him there and then.

They moved silently at a fast pace through the deserted streets, crossing Ness Bridge with the water rolling silently beneath, then along Glenurquhart Road, past suburban houses all deserted; some were merely burnt-out shells. Tomnahurich Cemetery loomed up suddenly, the white ghosts of stones gleaming. Melliflor led them past the neatly tended plots to a road running up a hill which looked strangely unnatural on the flat valley bottom. It soared steeply, cloaked in a thick swathe of trees: yews, oaks, holly, pine, sycamore, all interspersed with thick clumps of spiny gorse; the air was heady with the summery aromas of the wood. Hundreds of graves were hidden among the trees right up the hillside, as if they too had grown there. The road curved in a spiral dance around the hill to the summit, modern in construction but hinting at an ancient processional route. 'Welcome to the Hill of Yews,' Melliflor said respectfully, 'known by the local people as Tom-na-hurich.'

They followed the road round until they were swallowed by the trees and the lights of Inverness were lost. It was a strange, mysterious place, eerily still, yet their footfalls echoed in an unusual and unnerving manner; no one felt like talking until they had reached the summit. Here a large area had been cleared at the centre and filled with the jarringly regimented rows of a Victorian cemetery. The fringes were thickly treed with the oldest yews and oaks. At the highest point a cross had been raised to mark Remembrance Day.

They stopped at a nondescript spot among the crumbling, brown gravestones. Melliflor took a step forward and bowed his head before muttering something under his breath. A second later the ground vibrated with a deep bass rumble, as if enormous machinery had come to life, then the grass and soil prised itself apart. From within the long, dark tunnel which had materialised Veitch could hear faint music that immediately made him want to dance; the tang of rich spices wafted out into the balmy night and he was suddenly ravenously hungry. But then he glanced up at Tom and all his desires were wiped clean; the Rhymer's face was as white as a sheet and taut with the effort of keeping in his fear; a faint tick was pulsing near his mouth which, in the emotionless dish of his face, made him look like he was screaming.

At the other end of the tunnel were a pair of long, scarlet curtains. Melliflor held them aside for Veitch and Tom to pass into a great hall which appeared to be the venue for a riotous party. The music was almost deafening; Veitch heard fiddles, drums, a flute, other instruments he couldn't quite place, although he could see no sign of a band. A roaring fire in one corner made the air very warm, but not as uncomfortable as he would have expected at the height of summer. It was filled with an amazing range of scents, with each fresh waft bringing a new one: lime, pepper, roast beef, strawberries, cardamom, hops – so many it made his head spin.

So much was happening in the hall, he couldn't concentrate on one sense for too long. Long tables ranged around the outside of the room on which were heaped every food imaginable, though many he couldn't recognise and some made him turn away, although he couldn't explain why. In the centre of the room the Tuatha Dé Danann were dancing. Scores of them whirled round and round with wild abandon to the odd music, which occasionally flew off the register of Veitch's hearing. It was like a turbulent sea of gold waves crashing against the tables and the walls; it made him queasy to watch.

The assault on Veitch's senses was so great he felt his knees go weak and for a moment he was afraid he was going to faint. But then the rush hit him powerfully and he was swept up in it all. His body was reacting as if he had taken a cocktail of drugs, some mild hallucinogen and an amphetamine; he wanted to fling himself into the seething mass.

He was vaguely aware of someone on his right proffering a goblet of deep, red wine. Unconsciously he reached out to take it, his gaze still fixed on the dance floor.

He was jolted alert by the weight of Tom's hand on his forearm. The Rhymer was already thanking the young girl who had offered the wine with the studied politeness which seemed necessary to prevent any retribution. The girl looked disappointed and her face darkened as she turned away.

Veitch bowed his head sheepishly as Tom glared at him; he couldn't believe how quickly he had almost gone against all of Tom's deeply stressed cautions. He would not forget again.

His attention was drawn back to the dancing, and beyond it to the shadows that clustered along the edges. There he could just spy writhing bodies; the gods looked to be in coitus. He could just make out bobbing heads, violent thrusting, sensuous movements, and occasionally the sounds of passion broke through the music; but there was something about it which did not seem quite right, as if the bodies were not penetrating and enveloping, but flowing in and out of each other like mercury; merging. He looked away.

Melliflor was at Tom's side, hands cupped, falsely oleaginous. 'The Queen was overjoyed to know you had returned, True Thomas. She will see you shortly. In the meantime, you and your companion be accepted as our guests. There is food and wine aplenty, the finest music in all of the Far Lands. Make merry, True Thomas, and be a perfect son of the Court of the Yearning Heart.'

'And is it all given freely and without obligation?' Tom asked dispassionately.

'Ah, True Thomas,' Melliflor said cunningly, 'you know we can make no promises here.'

Veitch and Tom found a pile of luxurious cushions in one corner from where they could watch the dancing. Veitch felt so comfortable after the exhaustions of the previous weeks he could have fallen asleep in an instant, but he was sure that was not wise. He was afraid to do anything in case he committed himself to something unpleasant and he wished he had listened more carefully to Tom's instructions during the long walk to Inverness.

Several times revellers walked up to offer jugs of wine or plates lavishly filled with juicy fruit or spiced meat, but always Tom politely refused. It was like a game the Tuatha Dé Danann were playing to see if they could catch their guests out; Veitch could see them talking excitedly and pointing at him before an even more tasty offering was brought up. By the end Veitch's mouth was watering and his stomach rumbling, and all he could do was think how long ago his last meal had been.

Eventually Melliflor glided up. He bowed deeply. 'The Queen will see you and your companion now, True Thomas.'

The two of them were led out of the great hall along stone corridors hung with intricately embroidered tapestries and rich brocaded cloth. Braziers burned with scented wood so the atmosphere was constantly heady. They passed many closed doors and from behind them came strange, unnerving sounds; some sounded like yelps of pain, others like moans of pleasure; some it was impossible to distinguish.

They were eventually presented to a chamber draped throughout its length and breadth with gossamer ivory silk which filtered the flickering light of the torches on the walls so that the room was infused with a dreamy white glow. The material was almost transparent, but hung in so many places it was impossible to see what lay at the centre. Melliflor bowed and retreated, silently urging them to continue. They pushed their way through the gently swaying silk, which felt like the wings of butterflies when it brushed their skin. As each layer was passed they could see shapes more clearly. Veitch's heart began to beat hard in anticipation.

Finally they were through to the middle of the room. The Queen lay on a bed made of luxuriant cushions, so deep they looked as if they would swallow her. Her face was more beautiful than anything Veitch had seen in his life; there was a cruelty there which counterpointed the beauty in such a way it made her even more desirable. Her black hair was long and lustrous, her lips full and red; her eyes sparkled with an inner green light. And she was naked, her golden skin shimmering in the filtered light. Her breasts were large, her nipples tautly erect, her waist slim, her hips shapely, her belly flat; the epitome of what many would consider a male fantasy, truly the Queen of Desire. Veitch wondered if that was how she really looked, or if it was a form she thought could manipulate him; he tried to tell himself that with the Tuatha Dé Danann nothing could be trusted.

But then his eyes were drawn to her sleek, black pubic hair. She lay with her legs curled round so he could see her vagina. She made no attempt to hide herself; indeed, she seemed to be presenting herself to them. Veitch could see how Tom had been so entranced by her.

'It is wonderful to see you again, True Thomas.' Her voice was lazy and filled with strange, enticing notes.

'My Queen.' Tom bowed.

'Come.' She waved them nearer. 'Who is your companion, True Thomas?'

They stood so close Veitch could smell the warm perfume of her skin. She looked at his face intently, her eyes dark beneath half-lids; Veitch felt sucked in by them.

'This is Ryan Veitch, my Queen. He is a Brother of Dragons.'

'Ah, one of the champions of the solid lands.' There was none of the mockery or contempt in her voice that Veitch had heard in so many of the other Tuatha Dé Danann. She sounded honestly interested, even impressed. He attempted an awkward bow, which seemed to please her. 'You did us a great service by freeing us from the Night Walkers' place of exile,' she said directly to Veitch. 'You are in our gratitude. If there is anything you require here in my court, you only have to ask.'

'Thank you.' Veitch was embarrassed his voice sounded so strained.

The Queen suddenly noticed the colourful tattoos only half-covered by the sleeve of his jacket. Her brow furrowed in curiosity. 'What have we here? Is that the Staff of Heart's Desire?' She looked up brightly into Veitch's face. 'Please. Remove your shirt. I must see.'

Veitch glanced at Tom who nodded curtly. Selfconsciously he slipped off his jacket and shirt; on his naked skin, the tattoos gleamed vibrantly. The Queen leaned forward until her face was close to his hard stomach muscles; Veitch could feel her breath. 'The Watchtower,' she mused. 'And here, the sword, Caledfwlch. Amazing. You are a walking picture book.'

She smiled seductively. Then, while her eyes were fixed firmly on his, she reached out gently until her fingers touched his skin just above his belt. A deep, uncontrollable shiver ran through him. Within an instant he had an erection so hard it was painful. The Queen kept her fingertips there a moment longer, then withdrew them just before he came. Veitch took an involuntary step back and sucked in a juddering breath.

Her little game won, the Queen turned from Veitch as though he were no longer there and spoke directly to Tom. 'You were always my favourite, True Thomas.'

He bowed. 'You are gracious, my Queen.'

'Why have you returned to me? I thought it likely I would never see you again. I presume you are not here to seek my affection?'

'We request your aid in a matter of great importance, my Queen.'

'*We*, True Thomas?' Her gaze was incisive.

'*I* request your aid, my Queen. And I will be forever in your debt if you will help *me*.'

'That is indeed a gift worth having, True Thomas.'

Veitch had the impression of an owner curbing her dog. Suddenly he could see the huge edifice of power and malice that lay behind her eyes, but that did not stop him desiring her.

'One of the Sisters of Dragons has been infected with the taint of the Night Walkers,' Tom began. He paused while he formed his argument, knowing that everything depended on it. 'That understates the situation. It is not a taint, it is the ultimate corruption. The essence of the Heart of Shadows grows within her. The Night Walkers seek to bring back the End of Everything.'

'That is indeed a serious development.' Her gaze never wavered from Tom's face; she didn't seem even slightly troubled by the news. She shifted her position, raising her behind slightly so Veitch once again had a perfect view of her sex. 'What is your primary wish?'

Tom collected himself before he said, 'To destroy the End of Everything.'

Veitch started. 'To save Ruth's life,' he corrected sharply.

The Queen's smile grew as she looked from one to the other. 'A disagreement?'

'No disagreement.' Tom fixed a cold eye on Veitch.

'There is no need to argue.' Her voice was like honey. 'There is a possibility I may be able to help you achieve both your aims.'

Tom bowed again. 'Anything you can do to help us would be gratefully received, my Queen.' She glanced at Veitch and he realised he was supposed to prostrate himself too. He bowed awkwardly once more and muttered something that approximated Tom's statement.

It appeared to please her; she nodded and smiled. 'There are many secrets here in the Court of the Yearning Heart, some which are hidden even from my brethren; even from the Court of the Final Word. Here, all things are given up eventually.' She sucked on her index finger as she thought deeply for a moment. 'The Eddy-Ball,' she said with a certain nod. 'A gift of great value to me.' A smile; the game had begun. 'The orb opens out into the void between worlds. It has the ability to suck the essence from the solid.'

'And this could be done without harming the Sister of Dragons?'

'Of course. And the Heart of Shadows will find itself in a place where no shadows are cast.' This amused her.

Veitch could barely contain his relief. Although Tom maintained his plain expression, Veitch could see the signs in the Rhymer's face too.

'Thank you, my Queen,' Tom said.

'And you will do something for me. True Thomas?'

His face grew taut. 'Of course, my Queen.' Tom waited for her to demand he stay behind.

She pretended to think, toying with him. 'No, True Thomas, not you. This Brother of Dragons.' She glanced seductively at Veitch. 'I will give the Eddy-Ball to him and him alone, and in return he will carry out a simple request for me.'

'Anything,' Veitch replied before Tom could stop him.

There was a triumphant note in her smile that made Veitch uneasy. 'The Questing Beast has again escaped from the pits beneath us. It is loose in the solid world. It is my heart's desire that this Brother of Dragons seek it out and destroy it, or at least lead it back here to the Court of the Yearning Heart.'

Veitch could hear her words, but all he could see was Tom's face, which had grown eerily bloodless. 'The Questing Beast—' he began.

The Queen silenced him with an upraised hand, her eyes watching Veitch's face intently. 'Will you do this for me?'

Whatever doubts Tom felt, Veitch knew he didn't have an option. 'All right.'

'Then I will make the arrangements. Go with Melliflor and he will provide you with all you require.'

They moved slowly away until the gently stirring sheets of silk had swallowed up the Queen once more. As they walked, Veitch brushed against Tom and felt the trembling that was running through the Rhymer's body.

They were provided with two connecting chambers far from the noise of the Great Hall where they could rest and prepare themselves. They were both ravenously hungry, made worse by the plates of food left for them on tables in the corners of the room. Tom plucked from his ever-present haversack two bags of roasted peanuts he had been saving as a last resort, and they munched on them hungrily.

Veitch was filled with questions, but at first Tom wouldn't speak to him; it was almost as if he couldn't bring himself to do it. He retreated to his chamber for an hour where he smoked a joint quietly on the deep, comforting bed.

Veitch couldn't begin to rest. His mind turned over all that he had experienced, but kept returning to the image of the naked Queen; it was beginning to torment him. And when he forced himself not to think about her, his eyes drifted to the food.

When Tom finally walked in, he sat bolt upright with relief and said, 'Come on. Spill the fucking beans. What am I up against?'

Tom pulled up a chair and sat on it backwards, folding his arms on top of the backrest. 'You and your big mouth, agreeing to anything she said.'

'We didn't have any choice.'

'Of course we had a choice. They play games, barter, throw things back and forth. You don't take the first thing offered. You were too hypnotised by the sight of her cunt.'

'And you weren't? You were almost down on your knees with your tongue hanging out!'

Tom cursed under his breath and put a hand on his eyes. 'There's no point arguing about it. It's done. We have to find a way to make sure you survive.'

Veitch kicked the other chair so hard it flew across the room. 'Come on, then. Talk. What's this thing I've got to hunt?'

'The Questing Beast. It's a living nightmare, something that even the Tuatha Dé Danann are wary of facing head-on. Their own legends say it was there in Otherworld long before they arrived, one of the first creatures to exist after the universe was formed. They call it a Rough Creature. A prototype for what was to come, if you will. Not fully formed.'

Veitch sat carefully on the edge of the bed. 'If it's in *their* legends—'

'Exactly.'

'So they're sending me out there because they don't want to have a go themselves. That's par for the course, isn't it? Those Bastards don't like getting their hands dirty. So if they're so wary of it, what was it doing here? And how the fuck am I going to kill it?'

'The Queen keeps many dangerous things here at the Court. It's a mark of prestige. How are you going to kill it?' He shrugged wearily. 'I don't know enough about it. Neither do the Tuatha Dé Danann. But their distaste for it isn't because of its power, it's because of its imperfect form, which they find abhorrent in the same way they react to the Fomorii. Us, they can just about tolerate. Anything less is to be despised.'

'So how dangerous is it?'

'Very. Make no mistake about that. It escaped into our world several centuries ago, before my time, and many people died before it was driven back to Otherworld. The general belief of the time was that a mortal girl gave birth to it after having sex with the Devil. The legends that grew up around it described it as having the head of a snake, the body of a big cat and the hindquarters of a lion, which is just another way of saying the people of the time couldn't describe it. It was said to give off a sound like forty hounds baying, or questing, in its stomach, and that's how it got its name.'

'So we don't know what it looks like, just that it's very fucking bad.' Veitch jumped to his feet and started pacing round the room; his eyes repeatedly strayed to the appetising food. 'Well, it was driven off, so it can be done. It sounds like a big deal, but I'll be hunting it, not the other way round. Anyway, it's got to be, for Ruth, for Church and everything. Can't fuck up now.'

Tom realised he was talking to himself, planning, bolstering; it was like the ritual of a boxer preparing for a fight.

After another moment's pacing, he turned to Tom and said, 'Okay, I've got my head round it. I'm going to get some Zs in now. We'll do it when I wake.'

As he left the room, Tom hid the fact that he was secretly impressed; once a conflict situation had been established Veitch's developing abilities made him like a machine. Fear or overconfidence didn't burden him; he simply weighed up all the available evidence and decided what needed to be done. Tom hoped that would be enough.

In the court it was impossible to know if it was night or day. But when Veitch woke his body told him he had had a good rest; the exhaustion had seeped from his muscles and he felt ready for anything. He was still hungry, but he knew he could find something to eat back in the real world.

Tom joined him soon after, as if he had been waiting for the sounds of stirring. Together they stepped out into the corridor where Melliflor was waiting.

Veitch had hoped the Queen would have come to see him off, but she was nowhere around. Instead, Melliflor led them to the armoury, a long, low-ceilinged chamber where the walls were covered with a variety of bizarre weapons and strangely shaped body armour. Veitch picked up one of the weapons which looked like an axe with a spiked ball hanging from it, but in his hands it felt a different shape completely to how it appeared and he replaced it quickly.

While Melliflor oversaw, three other members of the guard brought Veitch different pieces of armour. They strapped across his chest a breastplate which shone like silver, but which was covered with an intricate filigree. Shoulder plates were fastened on, and he was given a helmet which vaguely resembled a Roman centurion's, but was much more ornate. After mulling over the weapons for fifteen minutes he eschewed them all for his own sword and crossbow.

He had no idea of what the armour was constructed, but it was surprisingly lightweight; he could have walked for miles in it. He didn't have to, though, for as soon as he was ready Melliflor took him through to an adjoining stable which contained enough horses for a small army.

'Stolen from our world,' Tom muttered. 'It allows the lesser members of the Tuatha Dé Danann to travel quickly when they cross over.'

'This is no bleedin' good, I've never ridden before,' Veitch moaned.

'The steed will respond to your every movement. We have adapted it,' Melliflor said ominously.

Melliflor offered Veitch a handsome white charger, but he didn't feel comfortable with it. 'Too flash,' he grumbled. Instead he chose a nut-brown stallion indistinguishable from many of the others.

Once he had mounted the steed, Melliflor led it by its reins to a blank stone wall at one end of the stable. He made a strange hand gesture and the wall opened with a deep, rumbling judder. They were high up on a hillside with a vista over Loch Ness. Mist drifted across the water in the post-dawn light. From all around came the sweet aroma of pine trees. Everywhere was still and quiet.

Veitch turned to view the scene in the stables, but he couldn't think of anything to say to Tom. Instead, he merely waved; Tom nodded curtly in reply, but there was much hidden in the two gestures. Then Veitch spurred his horse and galloped off into the world.

The darkness licked at the foot of Mam Tor, an angry sea crashing on the rocks. From his vantage point beneath a burning sun and a brilliant blue sky, Church watched as hopelessness washed over him.

'They'll be coming up soon.' Laura's voice made him start.

'Best not to think about that.'

'Sure. Do you want me to help bury your head or can you do it yourself?'

Church managed a tight smile; he didn't have much humour left in him. With Ruth's condition worsening by the day, the strain of their isolation and the constant fear that their hiding place would be discovered at any moment, it was surprising he hadn't lapsed into permanent silence.

'No sign of the others yet?' Laura rested on his shoulder and peered out to the horizon. It was a running joke; she asked the same thing every day, knowing the answer.

'Not yet. Maybe tomorrow.' He tried, but he couldn't help believing that they wouldn't be coming back at all. He knew they had long distances to travel, with huge obstacles along the way, but they still seemed to have been gone a long time. Even if they did return, how would they be able to slip past the mass of Fomorii? He had been right the first time: best not to think about it.

'She's asking for you.' Laura continued to scan the horizon, as if by doing it everything in the foreground could be forgotten.

'How is she?'

'Not talking like she's pissed up for a change.' Ruth's lucid moments were increasingly few and far between; at times she ranted and raged in the throes of her delirium so much they thought they would have to restrain her. It always happened at night, in the small hours, snapping them out of sleep and filling them with fear that they were being attacked. Sometimes she would hold conversations with someone neither of them could see; on those occasions they didn't go to sleep again.

Church turned despondently to wander back to the house, but he hadn't gone more than a few steps when Laura grabbed him and gave him a long, romantic kiss. It was an astonishing show of emotion for someone who seemed ever more locked up with each passing day.

'What was that for?' he asked, pleasantly surprised.

'What's the matter? Can't I show you I love you?' She had turned and was walking away before he had a chance to grasp what she had said.

He mulled over it until he was in the house, but the moment he saw Ruth it was driven from his mind. Her skin was like snow, emphasised by the darkness of her hair, which was plastered with sweat to her head. There were purple rings under her eyes and her cheeks had grown increasingly hollow. Beneath the sleeping bag, her belly was hugely swollen. Her appearance was so shocking he had a horrible feeling she was going to die before Balor's rebirth. A part of himself that he never faced hoped that was the case; then he would be saved from having to make the awful decision to kill her.

Although he was creeping quietly, she looked up before he had crossed the threshold. 'Hi. You're starting to get a tan.' Her voice was just a rustle.

'You know how it is. Nothing to do apart from lie by the pool with a good book.' He knelt down next to her to brush a strand of hair from her forehead. When he rested his hand against her cheek, her skin felt like it was burning up.

She put her hand on top of his and gave it a squeeze. 'I'm glad you're here.'

'Sure. I'm doing so much—'

'I just feel better having you around.' He smiled; her eyes brightened briefly before she was forced to close them; a tear squeezed out and trickled down her cheek.

'I'm sorry you've had to go through all this,' he said gently. 'You've had the worst of all of us. One bad thing after another.'

'You know, bad things happen.' She pulled his hand round so she could softly kiss his fingers; her lips were too dry.

'You don't have any right to take it so well. You're giving us all too much to live up to. You git.'

They laughed together, and the sound of it in that dismal room made Church's own eyes burn. He blinked them dry. 'Sometimes I feel like I've known you for ever. I know it's only been a few months since that night under Albert Bridge, but it seems like a lifetime ago.'

'Maybe we have known each other for ever. Maybe it's that old Pendragon Spirit speaking. Telling you we've stood side by side across the centuries.'

'You're an old romantic.'

She tried to laugh again, but it broke up into a hacking cough. When the attack had subsided, her mood had grown forlorn. 'I just wish it wasn't happening here. This house feels bad, sour. I don't know what happened here, but sometimes I can hear voices whispering to me. The things they say . . . that Ryan's going to die . . . that other terrible things are going to happen—'

'Hush.'

'That writing on the wall . . . Sometimes words seem to leap out at me—'

He put two fingers on her lips to silence her. Gradually the delirium returned to her eyes as they started to roll upwards. After a moment or two she began to rave, occasionally speaking in tongues, thrashing from side to side. Church sat patiently beside her during the worst of it, then stroked her head until she eventually drifted off to sleep.

Sometimes Church thought he had never seen a night sky like the one above Mam Tor. Unencumbered by light pollution, benefiting in some indescribable way from the sheer height above sea level, they seemed to be enveloped by the sparkling heavens. If not for their circumstances, it would have been a sublime experience.

He stood with Laura in his arms, looking up at the celestial vault; for once she had removed her sunglasses. 'We've come a long way, despite everything. Pity if it had to end here.'

'No fat lady singing yet, boy.'

'No, not yet.' He watched a meteor burn up over their heads, wondering if it were some kind of sign. 'Sometimes it's hard to take a step back and appreciate exactly what we're doing here. You know, I look at myself, look at you and the others, and all I see is normal people with all the stupid kinds of problems everybody has. And that's who we are, but at the same time we're something else as well – the champions of a race, a planet. The living embodiment of the Pendragon Spirit, whatever that might be—'

'Maybe we're not special.'

'What do you mean?'

'Maybe this thing the old git calls the Pendragon Spirit is in everybody. Maybe it's the spirit of man, or some shit. Listen to me, I sound like some wet-brained New Age idiot. What I'm trying to say is, what if he's just calling us special to keep us on board. So we think sorting out this whole mess is just down to us.'

'Or so we dig deep to find the best in us to get the job done.'

'That too.' She rested her forehead on his shoulder. 'That would explain why we all seem like such a bunch of losers. We *are* a bunch of losers.'

'Doing the best we can. And doing a damn good job—'

'So far. But if we've not got any special dispensation, the chances of us fucking up are even greater. We've got through on a wing and a prayer and too much confidence. But sooner or later the blind, stupid luck is going to run out.'

Church thought about this while he continued to watch the stars. Then: 'I might have agreed with you a few weeks back, when we first met each other. But in all the shit we've waded through, everybody has shown a real goodness at the heart of them. There isn't anybody else I'd want around me at this time and there isn't anybody else I think could do a better job—'

'You don't know the thoughts in my head—'

'I can guess at them.'

'No, you can't. There are sick, twisted things crawling around up there. Take Little Miss Goody-Shoes back there. Sometimes I wish she'd hurry up and die so she wouldn't carry on getting between me and you. I know it's a nasty, evil little part of me and I hate myself for it. But I still do it.'

'She doesn't get between us.'

'You're too stupid to see it. She loves you and I think you love her, and if there wasn't a constant state of crisis you'd recognise that.'

Her words sparked rampant, brilliant bursts in his mind, but they were all too fleeting to get a handle on. He pulled back slightly so he could try to read her; she half-turned her head away. 'You're a good person, Laura.'

'You're a good liar.'

'You've got an answer for everything.'

'If I had, I wouldn't be feeling like my brains were leaking out of my ears. Too much thinking isn't good for anyone.'

'Look—'

She slammed her hand on his mouth. 'Don't say anything. It'll sort itself out one way or the other.' He didn't like the look that crossed her face when she said that.

He hated to think anything unpleasant of her, so instead he kissed her. At first she seemed to be resisting him, but then she gave in, and for the briefest instant everything seemed in perfect harmony.

But then an unseasonally cold wind came whipping across the tor and buffeted them. Church broke off the kiss, shivering. Away in the west, billowing clouds were sweeping towards them at an unnatural rate. Lightning flashed within them, illuminating the underside of the roiling mass; one bolt burst out in a jagged streak to the ground. But they were not storm clouds, and there was no thunder.

The wind grew stronger as the clouds neared until it was lashing their hair, then threatening to throw them to the ground.

'What's going on?' Laura said. 'Is this it?'

The clouds came down until they were rolling across the ground, and at that point Church realised there was a figure among them. At first it was just a silhouette almost lost beneath the shrouding mist, but then it came closer to the fore and Church realised who it was, and what was happening.

'Get back to the house.' The snap in his voice stifled any questions instantly. Laura took one more glance at the clouds, then ran for the cottage. Halfway across the turf she realised Church wasn't behind her, but when she looked back he waved frantically for her to continue.

Then the wind did knock him to his knees and as he tried to scramble to his feet again, it hit him with all the force of a rampaging bull. He rolled over and it kept him rolling, driving him towards the jagged cliff edge and the precipitous drop to the rocks far below. Desperately he tried to dig his fingers in the grass, but they were torn out immediately; his bones cracked on stones, his face was dragged across the rough ground until it burned and bled.

The cliff rushed towards him. He had a fleeting vision of his broken, bloody body smashed at the foot of the tor and then the wind eased off just as he was half-hanging over the edge. He sucked in a deep breath, shaking with shock, tried to scramble back using his heels for purchase, but another gust came and pinned him on the cusp between life and death.

He had to calm himself, order his thoughts; it was his only chance. The gulf beneath him tugged at his hair, made his head spin.

Niamh hovered in front of him a foot above the ground, wrapped in the clouds of her discontent. He barely recognised her. The beautiful face was lost; instead, it rippled and twisted, unable to settle in a vision his mind could comprehend; her fury and dismay had reduced her to her primal form.

'*Betrayal!*' The word seemed to come from all around them, not spoken by any human voice, filled with strange vibrations that reverberated in the pit of his stomach.

'I didn't—'

'*You gave me your word! You promised me your love solely! You lied! Untrustworthy, like all Frail Creatures!*' A gust pushed him another inch over the drop. His fingers ached from clinging on to the rock lip.

'I'm sorry!' He had to raise his voice to be heard above the wind that was rushing all around the tor.

'*No more lies!*' Her voice exploded with the fury of a breaking storm, but at the centre of it Church could hear her heartache.

'I'm sorry!' he shouted again. This time she seemed to hear him, for there was a faint lull. He seized the opportunity. 'I was stupid . . . confused—'

The wind hit him hard; he moved another inch. One more and he wouldn't be able to stop himself falling. His fingers felt like they were breaking from clutching on; the panic in his throat made it difficult to catch his breath.

'*Lies.*' Her voice sounded less frenzied, more openly emotional, more humanity creeping into it. Church forced his head up so he could see. Her face had settled back into the features he knew, but they were broken with hurt. At that moment his heart went out to her and he was consumed with guilt at how he had disregarded her feelings. 'We Golden Ones live our lives in the extremes of passion. We feel too strongly. You cannot even begin to understand the slightest working of our hearts and minds!'

The clouds continued to churn behind her, occasionally lifting her a few more inches higher before she settled down at the same level. Church wanted to say something to calm her, but he didn't have any grounds to defend himself and he was afraid he would only make it worse.

She floated closer to him, almost to the lip of the edge, so he could see her face without straining. Her pain had now turned to a cold, hard anger; he feared for his life once again. 'My people always said nothing good could ever come of an affair with a Fragile Creature, and it appears they were correct. I have watched you too long from afar, Jack Churchill, and I have allowed my judgement to be swayed by what I saw.'

The gale began to press on his chest; he could feel himself sliding. In that moment, thoughts went rushing through Church's head and he was surprised to realise he was less scared for himself than angry that he had once again allowed his emotions to ruin everything; if he died, every hope would die with him.

Before he could say anything the wind retracted and Niamh began to drift away, her face still cold and hard. 'Our agreement is broken.' Church followed her pointing finger towards the dark horizon; there, golden light flashed ominously. 'The Good Son will soon be paying you a visit.'

And with that, the clouds folded around her so she was completely lost to him, and the whole mass moved quickly back over the landscape until it disappeared beyond the summit of the tor.

Church scrambled back. When he was lying on solid ground, he gulped in mouthfuls of air and felt his pumping heart slowly return to normal. As he dragged himself to his feet, Laura ran from the house.

'You really know how to fuck women up, don't you?' she said breathlessly.

He could barely hear her. His attention was drawn to the occasional bursts of light in the distance and the engulfing darkness closer to home.

'I've done it again,' he said quietly.

'What?'

'Screwed everything up.' He couldn't even bring himself to tell her that a near-hopeless situation had suddenly become much worse. With his head bowed, he turned and trudged back to the house.

Veitch spent the first two days roaming through the heavily wooded slopes which enclosed the loch. It was a place like none he had experienced before, enveloped in its own strange, eerie atmosphere; purple hillsides cloaked in mist just beyond the tree boundary, outcroppings of orange, brown and black rocks, ancient trees, gnarled and twisted and scarred with green lichen that showed their great age, and over all the constant, soothing sound of the waves lapping against the pink shale and pebbles at the water's edge. The way the pines clustered so deeply to the shore on the south bank made him feel penned in, and there was an unshakeable sense that he was being watched from somewhere in their depths. But there was also a deep serenity, almost mystical in its intensity, with the birdsong hanging melodically in the air. At times the water was as still as glass, reflecting the verdant landscape and clear blue skies so perfectly he felt he could dive in and walk among the cool glades. At other times storms sprang from nowhere, sweeping up odd, eddying waves that crashed against the steep banks. Fog came and went among the trees, like ghosts, and at night, beneath a shimmering moon and diamond stars the valley was filled with the pregnant hush that came before a conversation.

He saw no traffic at all along the sinuous road that ran along the banks of the loch, and he didn't know if that was down to the Questing Beast or if everyone had simply fled to the cities. In Drumnadrochit, the quiet village that lay where Glen Urquhart intersected the Great Glen, the houses were still and locked, although a wisp of smoke rose from the occasional chimney. At the loch's southern tip, Fort Augustus was near-empty too, and the occasional resident who saw him coming quickly ran for cover.

He made camp on both nights in a tree-lined gorge not far from Fort Augustus. Without even the slightest sign of the Questing Beast, he had started to wonder if it was another of the Queen's incomprehensible machinations, perhaps to separate him from Tom.

On the third day, he realised his hunt was true. In the early morning, he travelled alongside the tumbling river at the bottom of Glen Urquhart. The valley was blanketed beneath the drifting white mist that seemed to come and go with a mind of its own, muffling and distorting the splashing of the water and the clipped echoes of the horse's hooves. In a lonely spot surrounded by acres of sheep-clipped grass he came across an old stone cairn. There was a fading majesty to it, and even he, who was usually insensitive to the blue fire, felt a hint of its power there. But among the standing stones beyond the cairn he came across the remains of a man, half-strung over a barbed-wire fence. From his clothes, he looked like a farmer or an agricultural labourer. He was partially disembowelled as if he had been gored by a bull or a boar, but he had been out there long enough for the carrion birds to have been at his eyes and genitals, so it was impossible to tell if the Beast had consumed any of him as well. Veitch inspected the corpse and the surrounding area for anything that might help him, but there was no spoor or other discernible sign. The only thing that troubled him was that the poor man's blood had splattered randomly on the ground in a shape that resembled a screaming face. After spending time with Shavi he had grown reasonably adept at reading meaning in things that appeared to have none, and that image began to eat away at his subconscious. As he moved away his mind's eye had already begun to paint a picture of the true appearance of the Questing Beast.

That night he made camp among the trees high up on the hillside where he had a clear view of the loch and the bleak southern slopes. The setting sun painted the water red and purple; it was once again so still the water gave the illusion of glass. The air was sweet with the aroma of pine and wild flowers, and an abiding peace lay over the landscape. Yet it was hard for him to rest knowing that the thing could come at him from any direction at any time; he had even started to think of it as invisible or as something that flew on silent wings. All he wanted was something solid to latch on to, something he could stab or shoot or hack at, and then he would be fine.

As he had done the other nights, he dined on chocolate, biscuits and crisps he'd taken from a mysteriously deserted garage in Fort Augustus; the sugar and the processed taste sickened him, but he would have felt ridiculous striding into a supermarket for something more sustaining in the armour bequeathed him by the Tuatha Dé Danann. He was almost too distracted to think of food. Whenever he rested, Ruth loomed heavy in his thoughts, her face, darkened by fear after her discovery of what she carried with her, a frequent, troubling image he never seemed able to shake. Spurred by Church's right-thinking motivations, he had set out to help in the fight, but he knew his own motivation had been a quest for redemption for his past crimes. The chance to become a better person still weighed on him, but now, more than anything, he was doing it for *her*; to find some solution to heal her in the short term, to save her in the long term, whatever the cost to himself. Being driven by love was a strange experience for him and he was surprised how much he liked it.

As darkness fell, he stoked up the campfire for warmth during the cold night ahead, before taking time to groom the horse of which he had grown increasingly fond. When he had asked Melliflor for its name, the reply had been something indecipherable, so he had secretly decided to call it

Thunder after the horse of some cowboy hero in an American comic he had read as a child. He would never tell the others something like that, but it gave him a deep, personal comfort. He got pleasure from treating it with affection, although he privately wished it were a little more responsive. It seemed unduly wary of him, almost as if it were scared, which he guessed must have come from whatever treatment had been meted out in the strange stables of the Court of the Yearning Heart. *I can't even get a horse to like me,* he thought as he stroked its flank; the notion was so ridiculous it made him laugh out loud.

It was Thunder who alerted him to danger as he settled down to sleep next to the fire under the fragrant canopy of a pine. It whinnied and stamped its hooves long before Veitch heard any sign, and he was up on his feet with the sword in his hands as the howl of fear came from somewhere near the road on his side of the loch. The cry was suddenly infused with pain, before being snapped off.

Veitch jumped on to Thunder and spurred him through the trees on the steep slopes down to the road. The horse was uneasy, but it responded to his heels and it didn't take him long to find the mangled remains of a motorbike. There was a pool of blood on the tarmac, but no sign of any body. He dismounted and examined the road surface. It was difficult to tell in the dark, but the splatters of blood appeared to point in the direction of the inlet overlooked by the ruins of Castle Urquhart. Briefly, he stopped and listened, but the night was as quiet as ever. He wondered how swiftly the Beast could move; perhaps it was already miles away. Cautiously he climbed back on Thunder and headed in the direction indicated by the blood.

The clatter of the hooves echoed loudly in the quiet. It still surprised him to be riding down the middle of a road without seeing any sign of headlights in the deep night that hung over the water.

Ten minutes later he passed the still ruins of Urquhart Castle. There was no anxiety within him, just a quiet, intense concentration that took over his mind and permeated his being. His instinct told him his quarry was somewhere in the vicinity; there was a constant resonance vibrating inside him that he had come to trust: a warning to be as alert as he could be.

Around the bend in the road that led to Drumnadrochit he came across a few shreds of bloodied clothing. He jumped down to investigate without once lessening the sharp focus of his attention. He could hear nothing, smell nothing. The Beast left no sign in its passing, but Thunder seemed to sense something; its eyes rolled and it stamped its hooves again.

From the shape of the clump of clothing he could at least discern the direction in which the Beast had been travelling when the remnants were dropped. It was moving towards the area where the road was darkest and the trees clustered claustrophobically close. Back on Thunder, he gently urged it on; slowly, slowly, eyes constantly searching the surroundings. He rounded the small bay; ahead, the road moved off towards Inverness.

From the corner of his eye he caught a sudden movement in the trees away to his left. It was a darkness deeper than the surrounding shadows, moving so quickly it disturbed him.

He spurred Thunder into the trees, his crossbow held over the crook of his arm, his finger poised on the trigger. At that point there was little opportunity to manoeuvre among the trees. The movement of the branches in the faint breeze made odd shifts in the ambient light that at times made him feel something was creeping up on him. His heart pounding, he kept glancing all around to reassure himself.

Another movement, again away to his left. Was it trying to circle him, come up from behind? He suddenly realised it was a mistake to be in such a constricted space and he quickly sent Thunder back on to the road. From somewhere came the sound which Tom had described as forty hounds baying. That didn't even begin to capture the bone-chilling noise which now drifted out across the deserted countryside: high-pitched and filled with an abiding hunger, it didn't sound like anything earthly at all.

Something shifted back up the road. This time he was ready. In an instant his mind weighed up all the evidence, projected the path of the Beast; he aimed the crossbow, loosed the bolt. It shot into the shadows, bringing what could have been a squeal of pain. His teeth went on edge. He spurred Thunder on while managing to use the crank to draw the crossbow for another shot.

There was no sign of the Beast at the point where he had hit it, but he hadn't expected to bring it down with just one bolt. But there were dark splatters on the tarmac which smelled like charred batteries. So it could bleed, he thought. It could be hurt. That was all he needed to know.

It was heading back towards the castle ruins which rose up like bleached bones in the cold moonlight. Once it got on to the rugged, irregular promontory jutting into the icy waters, he would have it cornered. Could he take it out with just a crossbow and a sword? His blood thundered with the thrill of the hunt. He thought he probably could.

The car park for the castle was lit for tourists who would probably never come again. Across the shadowed edge of it the deeper darkness moved. Veitch got another impression of something big and dangerous. He loosed another bolt. It rattled across the car park, slammed into the fleeing rear of the creature. Another squeal of pain. It was proving easier than he thought.

415

His horse trotted down the steep path from the car park that eventually ran across an open stretch of grassland up to the castle's defensive ditch. At the drawbridge he dismounted and left Thunder next to a light. He had more freedom to move and react quickly on foot.

The castle was ruined, but still robust enough to glimpse the majesty of the fortress that had looked out over the loch, in one form or another, since the Pictish kings ruled the land in the Dark Ages. The grey stone of the impenetrable walls stretched out on either side, while the still-standing tower loomed like a sentinel away to his left.

There was more ichor splashed across the path that ran under the gatehouse; it looked like the Beast had been seriously injured. Veitch reclaimed the two bolts that had been knocked loose and prepared for another shot.

He could hear movement within the castle compound. He entered through the gatehouse slowly, aware that the enclosed space, with its dips and hillocks and many ruined buildings, could be a dangerous maze. Cautiously he scanned the area. There were too many places in which the Beast could hide.

Another sound sent him sprinting up the steps across the grass to the Upper Bailey. From this vantage point he had a view across the castle and the loch beyond. Nothing moved. Sooner or later it would give itself away, especially if it was badly injured, he told himself; but it was possible, if he was clever enough, to herd it to the area around the tower where it would have no escape.

He spent a few minutes convincing himself it was nowhere in the Upper Bailey and then he advanced slowly towards the hulking ruins of the chapel, Great Hall and kitchens. A brief wind swept up from the black water, singing in his ears.

But as he crossed into the Nether Bailey a figure erupted out of the periphery of his vision. He had only the briefest instant to register what was happening and then he was flying through the air. The landing stunned him for a second, but his sense of self-preservation took over and he shook himself awake. He lay on the grass in the shadow of the North Lodge; nothing moved near him. There was a chill wetness across his chest. When he looked down he saw his jacket and shirt lay in ribbons and there were three deep gashes cut into his flesh. The blood was pumping out through his ruptured armour. Desperately he tried to staunch it with a torn-off piece of his shirt, but as he tended to himself there was another blur of movement. His head snapped round so sharply he thought his neck had broken. Stars flashed across his vision; then the pain came, thundering out in a wave across his temples. By the time he had caught himself, his eyes were filling with liquid. He wiped them clear with the back of his hand, glanced down, saw the dark smear, dripping on his trousers.

The blow had dazed him; everything seemed to be moving too slowly, fractured, as if a strobe had been activated. The terrible hunting cry rose up all around him, different this time, triumphant.

No, he thought. *I had it.*

A shimmer of activity, so quick he barely saw it. Somehow he managed to fire off a bolt. The Questing Beast avoided it with ease.

As it could have done before, he realised. How stupid was he? He searched for a path back to Thunder, the images coming in broken, stinging form; he had to get away, recover. But the blur of movement was going around too fast, circling, forcing him back. It had cut off all escape routes. He was trapped, his back coming up against a stone wall. Then he stumbled through the gap of the Water Gate and rolled over and over down a steep bank, coming up hard against more stone blocks beyond which was a small, pebbled beach and the dark, lapping water.

As his thoughts started to come free from his daze, he realised: the Questing Beast had shown a ferocious intelligence and cunning, recognising the danger from him, probably over the days he thought he had been stalking it. He had been treating it like a stupid beast; it had been waiting for the opportunity to neutralise him.

It lashed forward from the dark and retreated in the blink of an eye. A gout of blood erupted from his forearm.

The pain was lost in the wild reel of his thoughts. He tumbled over the stone blocks on to the beach; now there was only water at his back.

The Questing Beast knew he was wounded; fatally, he realised, the same time the word entered his head. He could feel his clothes heavy with blood. How much longer did he have? The fragility of his thoughts gave him an answer. He'd failed: himself, Ruth, all the others. His stupidity had come through as it always did.

The Beast no longer seemed to be hiding from him. Through the haze he could pick it out more clearly than he had before. Its shape was not fixed and did not settle down like the Tuatha Dé Danann did once his mind had formed an analog; it was as if it preceded form, shouting across the aeons from a time when there was only intelligence and emotion. He glimpsed writhing, serpentine coils, something hard and bony, something that moved like gelatin and lashed with the spike of a scorpion's tail; felt, in one terrible moment, the cold, hard fury of its mind, as if it could reach out physically and strike him. This was bigger than him, better than him.

And then he realised, with some primal instinct, that it was gearing up for the final blow. He had little sense left through the pain; most of it was leaking out with his life's blood. But he asked himself this question: how cunning was he?

How cunning?

Blackness formed a tunnel around the periphery of his vision. He dropped the crossbow, went down to his knees, blood pooling in his eyes; he only had his instinct to go on. He bowed his head, prepared himself for the final blow.

The Questing Beast came forward in a wave of night; it was as if the wind had teeth and was roaring at him.

Veitch threw himself down on his stomach. At the same time he somehow managed to pull the sword free and raised it above his head. He held it firm when he felt it bite deep, and even when the sheer force of the Questing Beast's attack threatened to knock it from his grasp, he dug in and angled. The stink of charred batteries filled the air. The liquid swamped him in one awful deluge. The Questing Beast's momentum carried it over his head, screaming so loudly his eardrums burst.

And then he was in a syrupy world of silence, didn't hear the splash as the creature plummeted into the water. He turned on his back, saw stars and the moon; knew, in a damp, sad way, it would be the last time he would see them. He'd lost feeling in every part of his body. There were just his thoughts now, bursting like fireworks, slowly winding down.

The play of light on the lapping water was hypnotic. It was a good sight to see as the last sight. But it wasn't the end, it wasn't the end. The Beast wasn't dead; not yet. The black shape was moving through the water like a stalking shark. Thoughts triggered, stumbled into each other and then ran away obliquely; and he wondered how many times in the past it had broken through before Otherworld sucked it back, slinking through the waves, creating ripples of mythology on flickering black and white frames.

And as he thought this, it suddenly spurred into life, sending a V-shaped ripple breaking out on either side as it hurtled towards him. He had only a second to force himself up on his elbows before it erupted out of the water in front of him. He had a brief impression of a blackness as deep as space, of sharp, clacking teeth, and things that could have been tendrils or tentacles or arms, and then he closed his eyes and waited for pain that never came.

Somehow his lids flickered open again, and this time he wondered if he was already dead, for the scene around him had changed dramatically. There was a flurry of activity. Melliflor was there with the rest of the Queen's guard, oddly twisted spears catching the moonlight, and nets that billowed like the sails of a ship. And there was Tom looming over him, looking like Veitch had never seen him before; not stern nor angry, but caring and frightened, and in that instant he knew he was dead; or dreaming; or both.

The tunnel around his vision closed in tightly. And as everything faded into oblivion, his mind flashed back to that brief contact with the alien mind of the Questing Beast. It was a moment of sublime mystery, but there were some human reference points he could grasp: loneliness, a terrible yearning for another of its kind, long, long gone, lost in those early days when the world was new. That was why it was questing. Pain and hurt as brittle as glass; not a beast at all.

How awful, he thought. To be hunting it in that way. For it to be imprisoned by the Tuatha Dé Danann in the stinking bowels of their court. How awful and stupid and meaningless.

'You'll be okay now.'

The voice: in his head, or somewhere outside? Then, like treacle flowing into his mind, the realisation that he was *hearing*; how could that be? When Veitch's eyes finally responded he saw through a haze the stables in the Court of the Yearning Heart. His blood stained the dirty straw. Thunder stood nearby, stamping its hooves.

With the return of consciousness, agony exploded throughout his body. He was slumped against the wall in the mangled remnants of his armour, now coloured browny-purple with his dried blood. The deep gash across his chest was still ragged, but it didn't look quite as deep; even so, Veitch couldn't understand how he was still alive. From the way he had started to shiver, his death still seemed a definite possibility. But he could hear again, although he knew his drums had burst at the lochside.

Tom hove into view, dropping down on to his haunches; it was his familiar Scottish brogue Veitch had heard earlier. 'What happened?' Veitch's voice a feeble croak.

'The Queen saw—'

'I saw your tremendous victory.' Tom stood up and walked over to the other side of the stables as the Queen knelt down next to Veitch. She was wearing flowing, diaphanous white robes that were startlingly out of place in the bloody grime of the stables. 'You proved yourself a great champion. My champion.' There was great pride in her voice. 'I had you brought here, for in my court nothing truly dies if I so wish it. Here your wounds will have time to heal. You will be well again, Ryan Veitch.' Melliflor laid a crystal bowl of water next to her. She took a white cloth from him, dipped it in the water and began to dab gently at his forehead, slowly wiping away the splatters of his blood.

'I can't believe it,' he muttered deliriously. 'A Queen . . . tending to me . . .'

'Even Queens must recognise great bravery. Your name will be exalted, even among the Tuatha Dé Danann. And that bravery was carried out in my name, a fitting tribute to the Queen of the Yearning Heart. The Questing Beast is back in its chamber—'

'It survived?'

'It exists, as always.'

Veitch had the sudden feeling the Beast had been released merely for him to hunt it down, a perverse sport for the Tuatha Dé Danann so they could see what depths existed within him; and on that front he had even surprised himself. 'Will you help Ruth?'

The Queen continued to dab at his forehead. Some of the water ran into his eyes and she wiped it away softly. A drop trickled down the bridge of his nose. 'I will be as good as my word, Ryan Veitch.' A smile he couldn't quite read.

Veitch could feel himself starting to black out again. The Queen's ministrations were so soothing, her touch so gentle; the coolness of her fingers seemed to ease his pain wherever they touched.

She wiped down his cheeks, brushed the drips from his chin. He had lost so much liquid his body felt like sand inside.

She dabbed at his brow, smiled enigmatically. Then she held the cloth before his face and squeezed tightly. A single droplet eked out of the bottom, hung for a second, then dropped. He stuck out the tip of his tongue.

'No!' Tom's voice, filled with the most indescribable anguish.

From the corner of his eye, he saw the Rhymer rushing forward. Melliflor and another guard restraining him harshly. The droplet hitting his tongue, so cool and refreshing, belying its size. Slowly seeing the Queen's expression change, from gentle care to something much darker, like a shadow falling across the face of the moon. Still not grasping what had happened. Hearing Tom shouting his pain to the heavens.

The Queen put the bowl to one side sharply, stood up and swirled her robes around her as she strode to the door; there she turned and flashed a smile that was both triumphant and proud, the expression of someone who always gets her way. Veitch, in his befuddled state, still tried to grasp why the ministrations had stopped. The break had been so harsh; he wanted to feel that cool touch of her fingers.

And hearing Tom's words for the first time and feeling instantly cold and hopeless: 'You took a drink, you fool! You took a drink and you're in her power now! She'll never you let go!'

Then she was gone, and Melliflor and the guards trailed out behind her, each of them smirking in turn at Veitch and Tom, knowing there was no longer any need to guard them.

Veitch's thoughts turned instantly to Ruth and the three days she had left. An awful emptiness opened up within him at the knowledge that he had failed her; he might as well have killed her himself. His part in everything was over. He was scum; when it all came down to it, that was all he was and all he could ever be.

'I can't leave you here,' Tom croaked. 'Not on your own. I'm going to stay with you.'

'The others need you.'

'You need me more.' Tom's face was filled with the all the terror and suffering that lay ahead for Veitch; that stretched out for years and decades and centuries.

Veitch looked through him, two thoughts turning over and over in his mind: that he wouldn't have the resilience that Tom had exhibited to survive the relentless tearing apart of his body and mind; and that he would never see the world, and Church, and Ruth, ever again.

Tom dropped to his knees and took Veitch in his arms. Veitch could feel vibration running through him, felt moisture splash on his face, and realised Tom was sobbing. And somehow that was more terrifying than everything, for all it said about what the future held for him there, in the Queen's incisive power.

chapter nineteen

gifts freely given

It was a perfect summer's day, echoing warm memories of half-remembered childhoods, infused with the scent of grass and trees and heated tarmac; and it was only two days before Lughnasadh. Church sat on his favourite rock with the sun hot on the back of his neck and thought of how he would kill his closest, dearest friend. He'd weighed up the problem, on and off, for three hours, between checks on Ruth's condition, and he could still barely comprehend it.

'You going to sit out here until you turn into a crispy piece of bacon?' Laura had come up behind him quietly and had spent almost a full minute watching him silently, wishing more than anything she could connect with him on a level deep enough to help.

When he looked up at her, her heart went out to him at the desolation that lay in his eyes. Her first reaction was some asinine comment just to get a cheap laugh, but the weight on him was too great. 'What's the big deal?' she said, pretending to look distracted.

He shook his head, barely able to bring himself to talk to her, but when he started it all came flooding out. 'How do people deal with these kinds of decisions? You know, the big-shots, the leaders of countries, the people who make the world turn? You reckon they've got some kind of equation to make everything square in their minds? Because otherwise how can they live with themselves? On paper it looks great. You sacrifice this nameless, faceless person here and save this many lives. Simple maths. Any kid can do it. But when it's someone you know and care for, it doesn't balance out the same any more. The rational side of your brain tells you one thing. The other side says this person is too valuable to sacrifice, whatever the outcome.' A long pause. 'And that's the truth, isn't it? *Everybody* is too valuable. Life is too important. This isn't a decision for people. It's for God.'

Her sunglasses stripped the emotion from her stare. 'So what are you going to do?'

He cursed loudly, looked round as if searching for something to lash out at. 'I'm going to kill her. Of course I am, and I'm going to damn myself for all eternity and I'm probably going to kill myself straight after.'

Laura snorted derisively. 'You know, I'm appalled you're even considering that.' She grasped for the words to express the unfocused dismay she was feeling.

'Can't you get real? We're talking the End of Everything. The life of one person—' he made an overstated weighing act with his hands '—it doesn't balance. Any idiot can see it doesn't balance.'

'I thought this New Age was supposed to be a good time for women more than anything else. Feminine values and all that shit after hundreds of years of testosterone stupidity. Look at her, in that house, what she's been through. You could at least have hoped it would be Veitch or the old git—'

'We've all suffered.' He knew he was only arguing as a distraction; it wasn't even relevant. 'I was tortured—'

'Yeah? How bad? That bad?'

'All right. What do *you* think we do? Wish upon a star? She's going to die anyway, when Balor comes through.'

'Oh, fuck off. I don't know. But I know she's one of the good guys and it shouldn't be her.' She walked off a few paces angrily, then turned and said, 'Don't ever, *ever* tell her I said that, even when she's acting like she's got a bug in her head.'

He had a sudden vision of when he and Ruth first met, when everything had seemed confounding, but the choices simpler. 'What the hell am I supposed to be doing?' he muttered.

'You're the leader, Church-dude. Why are you asking me?' She picked up a handful of stones and began to hurl them out into the void without a thought for where they might land. 'I'm just along for sarcastic comments and pithy asides. Go with your instinct or whatever you leaders do.'

She threw the last pebble then turned and sauntered back to the house as if she didn't have a care in the world.

The dawn of the final day broke through the ragged cottage window in pink and gold, but when Church went to get a little sun on his face he saw the sky was painted red along the horizon; the folklore warning of bad weather ahead wasn't wasted on him.

At least the faint warmth refreshed him after the dismal night. He hadn't slept at all. Ruth had spent the long, dark hours in the grip of a delusion that had left her screaming and clawing at her face and belly until blood flowed.

It had been almost unbearable to see, the cracking screech of her voice so dismaying he'd wanted to cover his ears and run from the place rather than listen to the magnitude of her pain or face the extent of her decline. But he'd stayed by her side for all that harrowing time, caring for her, doing his best to prevent her harming herself, and now he felt drained of every last emotion. Laura was huddled in a corner like a child, sleeping the sleep of the exhausted now that Ruth's ravings had subsided with the coming of the light. Several times during the night she'd had to leave the room, crying, unable to cope with what she was seeing. Church had pretended he hadn't noticed.

The faint breeze that came with the dawn stirred the stagnant air with a hint of freshness. He stretched the kinks out, then walked back to look over Ruth. Her sleeping face gave no signs of the terrible things he had seen during the night. Her chest rose and fell with an incongruous peace. She was beautiful, he thought, inside and out; it wasn't fair that she was suffering. For a moment he drank in that innocence and then a jarring thought crept into his mind: he could do it there and then. Smother her with the sleeping bag. Strangle her, gently at first so she didn't wake. It would be perfect; he wouldn't have to look into her eyes; he could remember her this way instead of twisted by the torments that were sure to come. It wouldn't really seem like murder at all, would it?

The thought hovered for a second and then he felt a twist in his gut so sharp he thought he was going to vomit. He couldn't do it now – he was too tired. But later, certainly; he had, at last, accepted it was an inevitability.

As he turned away so he wouldn't have to look at her, his eyes fell on the insane scribbling that covered the wall. From a distance the minute writing resembled some intricate pattern; swirls and waves like a Middle Eastern carpet. Only up close were the hidden messages revealed, incomprehensible, but with some sort of intelligence behind them. There was something in this observation which tugged at him, but he didn't have the energy to start getting philosophical. Instead he blanked his mind and allowed himself to be drawn in by the mesmerising scrawl, a Zen meditation where obvious meaning was discarded for an overall *sense*. He stayed in that state where all the words blurred into one mass for what must have been minutes, feeling the stresses of the night begin to slough off him, until he gradually realised he was becoming aware of certain words rising out of the morass. It was almost as if the wall was speaking to him. And what was it saying?

I love you.

A nice sentiment, he thought ironically. Perhaps Ruth had been wrong about something bad happening there. The house may have been a place where forbidden lovers trysted, or was that his stupid, sentimental, romantic side coming out? He thought he'd finally eradicated that on the hilltop overlooking Skye.

Church.

His breath stung the back of his throat, hung there, suspended. The word seemed to glow, then fade, so that he couldn't quite be sure it was his name he'd seen.

Marianne.

This time he felt sick. His head began to whirl and he thought he might pitch forward. Marianne, speaking to him. A tingle ran along his spine, warning him not to analyse what he was seeing too much or the spell might be broken. Just wait, he told himself. Be open to it.

For a moment or two he saw nothing else. His eyes started to burn from the effort of not concentrating on what was before him. He had that queasy feeling he always got when he looked at Magic Eye pictures.

Then: *Be brave.*

Be wary.

The end is

coming soon.

There was a cold sweat stinging the back of his neck. He wanted to ask questions, make some kind of direct contact, but he was afraid it would break the moment.

You have it

within

you, I always knew

that.

Don't fear for me. Don't

hold on to me.

Face the future.

Go forward.

Church wondered how long the words had been there, hidden in the garbled, idiot pattern, and he had never seen them till now; by accident. At the moment he needed them most. He knew what Tom would say: no accidents, no coincidences; there was meaning in every little thing. But if only he had seen it before, how much strength he might have drawn from it during the long, painful days they had waited there.

I

can see you even

when you

can't see me. We all

can.

There's a

reason
for everything, Church.
You just
have to see
it.

In that moment he wanted to break down and sob, all the repressed feelings of the years since she died, all the strangled emotions of the last few months, ready to burst out in one rush. But all he managed were a few, brief tears that burned his eyes and were easily blinked away.

I may be
trapped,
but they can't
hurt me.
And I'm happy now
they can't
use me to control
you.
Don't worry, Church.
I love you.

The message began to repeat like one of those tickertape electronic messages that run around buildings in New York. He stayed a few minutes longer, just to be sure, and then walked out into the pale sunlight, his cheeks still wet.

Her words had been few, but there was so much to take in; an entire worldview. He was overjoyed that she wasn't suffering, that the resilience he had admired was still there, but more than anything that she was still *around,* like an old friend, keeping an eye on him. And not just her; she had said.

We all can.

What did *we all* mean? He walked towards the edge and looked down at the flickering shadows moving across the landscape. For him, right there, at that particular moment, it meant the world. Never give up.

There's meaning in everything.

There's a reason for everything.

He only had to see it.

Church skidded over the grass and rock down the tor. He felt consumed by a renewed sense of purpose, almost courage, although he had never considered himself brave. Risking your life meant nothing when everything was meaningless; but now there was meaning. The clues had been around him from the start – even before – but he had never pieced them all together to accept the sublime patterns. Even the Fomorii, the antithesis of it, proved its existence. Tom had subtly attempted to guide him towards that illumination, Church realised, and now he had it, he realised why: the world looked different.

Now they couldn't afford to lose; not just for humanity, or life as they knew it, but for something so big it made even that seem insignificant. An awareness of that responsibility would have crushed most people; Church felt enlivened by a new sense of direction.

Halfway down the tor he paused at a huge boulder and slowly crawled out on top of it so he could survey the countryside beneath. To most eyes, the rolling fields would have looked a little darker than usual. Strange shadows flickered on the edge of vision, but beyond that everything appeared normal. Church's heightened perception, however, picked out the Fomorii's half-seen shapes for almost as far as the eye could see. It was as if an army had massed at the foot of the tor, ready for a siege on some mediaeval castle. For a moment he blanched at the prospect of what lay ahead; then he drove all thoughts from his mind and hurried down the tor.

His target was relatively easy to find in the stillness of the countryside where no cars moved, no birds sang. Waves of golden light washed upwards like some strange aurora borealis, gilding the surrounding trees; occasionally strange booming noises echoed among the hillsides as if a jet had passed over. Church kept beneath the level of the hedgerows as he progressed along the lanes towards the epicentre. He had judged rightly that there would be little or no Fomorii activity in that area. The fact that even they were scared should have given him pause, but he kept driving forward, working at the plan that had started to form in the back of his head. The risks were great – even being there was ridiculously dangerous – but at that stage bold action was the only thing that could work.

Close to the golden light the air was filled with an unpleasant charred taste. He dropped to his belly and wriggled forward until he could peer through a break in the hedge, every muscle tensed to flee in case he was seen.

Maponus roamed around the field, his path apparently random, but, on closer inspection, forming strange geometric shapes. A scattering of bloody bones radiated out from him in what looked like a blast zone. Church guessed when Niamh had plucked up the Good Son and deposited him here she had brought some of his victims in the backwash. Church watched intently. Sometimes Maponus dropped to his knees and scrabbled wildly at the turf. Other times he stopped to throw his head back and howl soundlessly. The chaotic rhythms of his madness were eerie to see: oblivious to the outside world, trapped in a repeating loop of thoughts. Occasionally they became so intense his face would dissolve into a swirl of wild activity in which Church saw snapping jaws, writhing things, razor-sharp blades glinting in the sunlight, then just a globule of unbearable light.

He looked away, suddenly queasy. Maponus' insanity was destabilising; it sucked at him, threatening to drag him in.

Cautiously he began to move around the perimeter of the field. How long would he have to search before he found what he was looking for? Could he have guessed wrongly?

He needn't have worried. Something hit him with the force of a wild animal, knocking him painfully across the road, pinning him beneath its weight. Stars flashed across his vision, but when he looked he felt a wave of relief. Yet the Bone Inspector's features spoke of a madness waiting to break out: he looked anxious, hunted, a man driven to the edge of survival.

Despite his age, his strength was almost superhuman. Church couldn't begin to wriggle out from beneath the wiry arms that held him tight. The Bone Inspector's eyes ranged crazily, his lips pulling back from his teeth in a feral grimace. For one moment, Church thought the custodian of the old places was going to dip down and tear out his throat.

'It's me!' Church gasped. 'A Brother of Dragons!'

The Bone Inspector's eyes cleared gradually. A long drool of spittle dripped on to Church's cheek. 'I know who you are, you bloody idiot!' he hissed. Cursing beneath his breath, he rolled off Church, instantly adopting the posture of a cornered animal, ready to fight or run. 'What are you doing here, you fool? Do you want to throw your life away?' His voice was strained with tension, but it barely rose above the sound of the wind rustling the leaves of the hedgerow.

He gave a sharp nod with his head, directing Church to a field on the other side of the lane. They scurried through an open gate and rested against a metal trough filled with stagnant water. The Bone Inspector closed his eyes for a moment, his lined face suddenly looking a hundred years old. His shirt was in tatters and a filthy, bloodstained rag had been tied roughly around his left hand. There were numerous gashes across his lithe, suntanned torso. A brief shiver ran through him and then his eyes filled with his old clarity. 'I've followed him up mountains and across rivers. I've waded through a swamp of blood, seen whole villages burning. I've lived on raw squirrel meat and drunk stagnant ditchwater. I've seen the kind of pain and suffering you can only imagine.' His voice was filled with a passion that bowed Church. 'And why? Because your idiot brethren dabbled with something they shouldn't! What did they think they were doing?'

'It had to be done—'

'Had to be done?' The Bone Inspector's eyes blazed furiously; Church

428

thought the old man was going to hit him. 'All that death and grief was a decent price to pay?'

'That's not what I meant.' His anger grew hard. He thought of Ruth and the decision he had to make, of the world he used to inhabit where there was a clear distinction between right and wrong, and then came a sudden rush and tumble of regrets and bitterness. 'You can't criticise me.'

The Bone Inspector seemed taken aback by what he saw in Church's face.

'We're all wading through shit trying to put this nightmare right. Nobody has the higher ground. Nobody,' Church said coldly.

The Bone Inspector looked away at the waves of golden light. 'Pretty, ain't it? I can't see how we're going to put it right. When he was first bound under Rosslyn there was a whole load of my people carrying out the ritual. There's no way I can do it myself. I thought it was all sorted when those golden bastards came for him—'

'What happened?'

'There were six of them. Some of the big-shots, all light and thunder and faces you couldn't see. You could tell they were desperate to get him back. "Finally," I thought, "they're going to start sorting out their own shit." They'd got him cornered up near Aberdeen in what was left of a village. I was down among the ruins, trying to pull out some kid, but the poor bastard was already dead. And he'd seen me, and he was coming for me.' The Bone Inspector looked down at his hands; they were trembling. 'They'd opened up some kind of doorway in the air and they were going to drive him through. And then that bitch came out of nowhere. Crazy. As mad as he is.' He jerked a thumb towards the wash of light. 'There was a big flash, felt like I'd been hit by a shovel, next thing I knew I'm here.'

Church felt a pang of guilt; he wondered if the Tuatha Dé Danann would punish Niamh for her actions.

The Bone Inspector looked up at him piercingly. 'So what are you doing here?'

'Looking for you.' The Bone Inspector's brow furrowed; Church smiled. 'Listen, this is what's going to happen.'

As Church moved speedily along the lanes back to the tor he was gripped with fear that in his absence the Fomorii would have swept up the mountain and taken Ruth and Laura. But as he neared he could see the slopes were still clear.

The hardest part of the return journey was a wide-open space at the foot of the tor and the lower reaches of the climb. Even though the power in the mountain kept them hidden from the Fomorii senses, plain sight was still a problem. He couldn't believe he had made it to the Bone Inspector and back without discovery; it left him wondering how powerful those Fomorii senses truly were. Perhaps they didn't need to hide on the mountain at all. Was it possible that they could creep away under cover of darkness and find another hiding place far away?

The blow came from somewhere behind him, lifting him high into the air. His body exploded in excruciating pain; there didn't seem to be any oxygen left in his lungs. He slammed down on to the grass verge and bounced into a barbed wire fence. The twisted talons snagged his flesh and tore. For a second he hung there suspended like a scarecrow, thought processes fragmented, aware only of the agony that fried through him. His awareness came back in jerking fragments. A deep, dark shadow was moving across the road. He looked up for the cloud, the low-flying plane.

It hit him so hard the barbed wire burst as it yanked out of his flesh. He skidded into a cornfield. The sharp stalks stabbed his back, the dust clouded round him. Next to his face on the ground a large black beetle scurried away from the disturbance.

Full realisation only came when he rolled on his back, trying to scrabble to his feet. The Fomorii warrior loomed over him. At first there was no sense of solidity, just an impression of an immense, sucking void about to enclose him. A perception shift came as if someone had grabbed his mind and twisted it through forty-five degrees. Suddenly there was bulk, the sound of armour plates clanking into place as if they were a part of it, that familiar, sickening zoo-cage smell. Still couldn't quite get a full fix on it. It was an enormous insect with dripping mandibles and multiple legs, something that was covered with fur, with glaring red eyes, talons poised. And at times chillingly human-shaped, though as big as a tank, with the blackest armour.

Church jumped to his feet, started to run. What could have been a powerful arm lashed out, catching him full in the stomach. The pain was so great it felt like his internal organs were rupturing. He came down hard again, deep in the swaying corn. He had been so arrogant, thinking he had escaped detection. It must have been stalking him, checking he was defenceless.

His thoughts fizzed out as he suddenly found the energy to roll and run. The beast thundered like a bull, missing him by an inch. And then he was away, leaping wildly through the corn, knowing that he couldn't outrun it for an instant. The vibrations from its pounding feet felt like a mini-earthquake beneath him, but at least it allowed him to tell when it was almost on him. He threw himself to the side, and it crashed past; its size and momentum prevented it turning easily.

Anxiously, he glanced up at Mam Tor. It was close enough for him to sprint towards it. The beast was so big he might be able to lose it on the slopes where a sure foot was more necessary than strength. But if the Fomorii hadn't already established where they had been hiding, he couldn't lead the creatures back to Ruth and Laura.

He leapt out of the way again. This time he cut it too fine and the beast clipped his foot, spinning him round like a top. Dazed, he glanced across the field. If he didn't go to the tor he didn't stand any chance at all. He only had a second to make up his mind; it was no choice. He headed for the centre of the field, accepting his sacrifice with an equanimity that surprised him, gloomy that his great plan would never come to fruition, afraid of what the future held for the others. But all this was wiped from his mind in an instant when the beast smashed into his back.

He went down, blacked out for the merest instant, and then came to with the sensation of being lifted into the air. The beast's grasp was biting into his flesh; he felt the skin around his waist burst and blood trickle down his legs.

Where's Ryan when you need him? he thought ridiculously.

And then a strange thing happened. It was suddenly as if he could look directly into the creature's mind, understand fleeting thoughts and emotions that were so alien they could barely be described as such. He knew as surely as he was aware of his own name that the creature hadn't alerted the other Fomorii, that it had no idea where Ruth and Laura were. The sensation both sickened him and fascinated him. But he knew what caused it: the reviving essence of the Tuatha Dé Danann and the corruption of the Fomorii mingling within him *had* made him something more, something closer to them.

The creature seemed to be surveying his face; perhaps it was reading his thoughts too. Slowly it raised what at that time seemed an enormous gauntleted fist and took his left hand. Then with a sudden flick of its wrist it snapped back all his fingers at right angles, a sign of strength to show how frail he was in comparison. The cracking vibrated through Church's body and he cried out in agony. It threw him to one side just as he blacked out again.

When he came round a few seconds later it was advancing towards him for what he knew would be the killing blow. It stopped a foot away and he waited, almost relieved that the pain that racked his body would finally be over.

At that moment there was a smell like burning oil. The creature threw its arms in the air and let out a howl that sounded like rending metal. Church covered his ears from the shockwave. Desperately he tried to understand. Was it some kind of bestial roar of triumph? It sounded like pain.

The Fomor's body was more insubstantial than those of its brethren, suggesting, he guessed, its particular power. But at that moment it seemed to harden into the armoured shape, now seen more clearly than he had done before. Its black helmet gleamed in the sun. In the eyelets, white staring orbs ranged with such an expression he was left in no doubt that it was in the throes of some terrible torment. Pustules erupted all over it, even on the armour, and began to burst and release a foul-smelling ichor that sizzled where it hit the ground. The warrior's hands went to the side of its head and for a second it stayed in that position, its eyes still rolling madly. And then, like an overinflated balloon, it burst open. Globules of black flesh streaming with ichor shot across the field in all directions; somehow most of them missed Church. He had a glimpse of a twisted skeleton that bore no relation to the creature's outward shape. Then the bones became like candle wax, melting and flowing until there were just indescribable heaps scattered across flattened patches of corn.

Church didn't have to guess what had happened. A few feet away, previously hidden by the warrior, a flock of birds whirled madly. Gradually they flew tighter and tighter, reclaiming their true pattern. They fluttered in a formation so concentrated it was unnatural that they didn't crash into one another. And finally they settled into something that resembled the shape of a man, still flying round wildly like a whirlpool of feathers, beaks and talons.

'Mollecht,' he muttered through the haze of his pain.

The powerful Fomorii tribal leader stood silently; Church didn't even know if he could speak. Whatever hideous experiment had transformed him into primal energy that could only be contained by the continuous ritual flightpaths of a murder of crows had pushed him even further beyond the boundaries of his already unknowable race. The Fomor had destroyed the warrior by opening it up to release his essence, the terrible power that seemed to mimic the effects of contagion. Church recalled their confrontation at Tintagel and his blood seeping through his pores; the only escape had been to plunge into the sea.

But why had Mollecht destroyed the warrior? They were of the same people; Mollecht had the same contempt for humanity as the rest of the Fomorii. The pain from his broken fingers was washing in waves up his arms. He leaned forward and vomited. All that had happened was that he'd swapped one form of death for another, and he guessed Mollecht would be infinitely more cruel than the brutish warrior. On the verge of blacking out again, he glanced around for other Fomorii coming to help capture him, but the surrounding fields were empty.

And when he looked back at Mollecht, the dark cloud of birds was already moving off through the corn. Where the creature had stood, a large, black sword stood embedded in the earth.

Church's head swam; he blinked away the tears of pain. Mollecht was setting him free? He limped forward to examine the sword, without actually touching it. It was definitely Fomorii; one edge featured the cruel serrated teeth that would inflict maximum damage in a fight. There was also an intricate pattern on the blade, scored so finely it was hard to make out unless the light was in the right place, but it appeared to be a pattern of magical symbols of some kind.

Mollecht was now just a black smudge following the hedge line. There was no doubt Church was being allowed to escape and that the sword had been left for his use. What did it mean? After the Kiss of Frost he was no longer so naïve that he would take an obvious Fomorii gift. But this time his instincts were telling him the sword was not a threat to him, although he had no idea what the ulterior motive was. A weapon would certainly be useful. He weighed up his options, and decided to go with his instincts after all. Tom would have been proud of him, he thought.

Fighting against encroaching unconsciousness, he tried to blot out the pain by using the sword as a staff to help him limp back towards the tor.

Shavi stood on the edge of the parkland that rolled up to Windsor Castle filled with a relief that pulled him back from the brink of exhaustion. For days he had played a cat-and-mouse game with the Fomorii, who knew he was in the vicinity, but hadn't quite been able to pinpoint him. It had meant advancing, retreating, doubling back, searching for each tiny break in their lines; on one day he had advanced a mile, only to find himself five miles back by evening. He had slept under hedges, curled in the branches of trees, once even dozed on a pile of Sunbrite at the back of a coal shed. There were times when he thought he would never reach his destination at all.

The Fomorii were everywhere, but only to his advanced perception. Most people seemed to be continuing with their lives, oblivious to the unusual shadows, the bushes and trees that were there one day, not the next, with only a vague feeling of unease to warn them things were different.

As Lughnasadh approached the Fomorii were growing more desperate. Shavi had noticed a light in the sky over Reading to the west which had the ruddy glow of an enormous conflagration. Strange, worrying sounds were occasionally carried on the wind, but they were too brief for him to recognise their source. But where were the army, the air force, the civil defences? He had seen no sign of any opposition. Perhaps they had already crumbled, or else there was a vaccuum at the top, the Government paralysed or fallen apart at its inability to confront anything so alien and powerful.

But finally he had seen the tower of Windsor Castle in the distance, the flag waving in the summer breeze, and he had skipped into the back of a lorry which had brought him directly to the park. Even so, time was short. Already the heat of the day was starting to fade. But if he acted quickly and Cernunnos could help, he could still commandeer a car that would get him back to the others before midnight.

Halfway across the parkland he was aware of a rejuvenating atmosphere that seemed profoundly magical. Clouds of butterflies danced across the grass and the air was clear of any stink of pollution, despite the proximity to the Capital; it smelled and tasted as fresh as a mountaintop. The sun had blazed from a clear blue sky all day, but there was no sign of parching on the ground, which was lush and verdant. A languid quality eased his troubled thoughts; he felt something wonderful could happen at any moment. He found himself smiling.

When he moved beneath the cool shade of the trees everything seemed to take on an emerald tinge. There was a fluttering among the branches high above his head which he at first thought were more butterflies, but when he looked up he caught sight of a group of gossamer-winged people, minute but perfectly formed, their skin dusted green and gold. They weaved backwards and forwards, sometimes merging with the leaves until they were completely invisible. One stopped to watch him curiously, then laughed silently before rushing away. He moved on, wishing the whole of the country was like this.

He had no idea where the Great Oak had been, but he was trusting his instinct to lead him there. Yet as he progressed he suddenly heard the sound of faint laughter and happy voices. He ducked down and moved through the undergrowth until he came to a sundrenched clearing. On one edge a teenage Asian woman lay in the arms of a young man with a skinhead haircut. From the disarray of their clothes it appeared that they had been making love. The woman rested her head on her boyfriend's chest and traced circles with a long nail on his bare, muscular stomach.

'No one can ever take this away from us,' she said.

He chuckled throatily. 'Who'da thought it, eh? You and me, no worries.'

'I can't believe we got out of Birmingham. Your dad—'

'He's not my dad.'

'You know what I mean.' She tapped him sharply on the chest. 'When that van came crashing into us on the motorway, I thought—'

'We had a guardian angel. I told you that.'

She rolled on her back and shielded her eyes from the sun, her fragile features framed by her long, black hair. 'I reckon things are going to get good from here on in.'

434

'There's a lot of strange stuff around.'

'Doesn't matter. This is about you and me. All that shit's behind us now.' She gave him a tight hug. 'There's no one to tell us what to do any more. We stand by each other, we can face up to anything. We've proved that.'

He started singing *Stand By Me* then burst out laughing at his feeble attempt. She gave him a short punch in the ribs for teasing. 'So,' he laughed, 'we going to get married?'

'Could do. Sooner or later. We've got plenty of time for that. We've got a lot to see, lots to do.'

She rolled over and kissed him passionately. Shavi felt suddenly like a voyeur and crept away quickly. But the tableau stayed with him. Strangely, it filled him with so much hope, and it wasn't just because they were at the start of their lives, on the cusp of the great adventure and a great love. After a moment's thought, he realised what it was. The woman had been right. The terrible upheaval, the failure of an entire way of life, none of it mattered. The truly important things were still continuing as they always had. Those things could never be beaten down. It was a simple thing, but at that time, in that magical place, it seemed like a great revelation to him and he was fired to tell the others when he got back to them.

For the next hour he searched among the woods. Every now and then he felt a strange sensation at the base of his spine, as if he were crossing some invisible electric barrier. Eventually he became sensitive enough to it to follow the waves which progressed in a spiral pattern, growing tighter and tighter, until he arrived at the epicentre.

He was in a grove among the wider wood. The trees rose up on either side to form an arched roof high above his head, and that deep, emerald light infused everything. A cathedral stillness lay all around. No wind touched that place, no blade of grass stirred. Even the calls of the birds sounded miles away, as if they had been muted by a dense wall. This was the Green Home, the place where the Great Oak altar had once stood, where men had worshipped the all-consuming power of nature for millennia. Unconsciously he bowed his head.

Almost by accident his eyes fell on a chipped, dirt-engrained horn lying in the grass; he was convinced it hadn't been there before. His palms were sweating with anticipation; he wiped them on his shirt before picking it up. It felt uncommonly light, too normal to be what he expected. He had at least anticipated some sense of great power or crackling energy that burned his fingers when he touched it.

He weighed it in his hands, knew it was only a delaying tactic, then slowly raised it to his lips. When he blew, the sound that emanated was strangely hopeful. It washed out through the woods in a cleansing wave.

For long minutes everything remained exactly as it was. Just as he was about to blow one more time, another horn answered, from far, far away. This one had a regal ring to it, but there was also something that sent a shiver through him. A few seconds later the wind began. It howled mournfully into the grove, forcing him to take a step back; it was chill, as if it had rushed hundreds of miles from a desolate mountaintop just to be there.

Shavi shuddered as he slowly turned, searching among the swaying trees, his hair lashing around his face. Something was coming; he could feel it deep in his chest; a heaviness. The branches moving back and forth, the noise; distracting. And then movement. Out of the corner of his eye, the merest flicker that could have been just a shadow. He turned sharply, but it was already gone. It was his other senses that picked up the true signs: the musky odour of horses on the wind, a muffled but unmistakable whinny, the thud of hooves on the wood floor. Dark shapes flitted in and out of the boles. They were drawing closer, circling him, but still not enough of the world to be easily seen.

Then they did break through. There was an effect like a heathaze over a road on a hot summer day; shapes shimmered, fell into relief, and suddenly he was aware of horses among the trees. The Wild Hunt had arrived.

He had been sure they could only materialise in that form at night, but in that place their power appeared much stronger. Another blast of the horn close at hand; all the hairs on his neck instantly stood to attention. Away beyond the horses in the deep shadows of the wood was the terrible baying of hounds yearning to be unleashed.

Shavi stood his ground as the horses came stamping and whinnying just beyond the edge of the grove, their eyes glowing fiery red. The riders still wore the furs and armour and carried the long poles topped with sickles he recalled from the grim pursuit across Dartmoor; he looked away from their shrouded faces. The ranks parted and a larger horse moved through, its nostrils steaming despite the heat. And on its back was the Erl-King and his face was not hidden; Shavi saw bare bone, scales like a lizard instead of skin, and eyes that glowed with an inner yellow light, the pupils just a serpent slit. His stomach tumbled in response.

As the Erl-King dismounted, he was already changing. His body grew bigger, hunched over like an animal prowling, an odd mix of fur and leaves spreading across his form. His eyes moved further apart, his nose wider, and then stags' antlers sprouted from his head. Finally Cernunnos stood revealed, the awe and terror of nature beating like a heart. He made a strange hand gesture and the other riders fell back into the trees.

'Who summons the Wild Hunt?' His voice was like the sound of the winds on a mountaintop, his presence radiating such power Shavi felt like bowing before him.

'I, Shavi, Brother of Dragons.' He lowered his head in deference.

'I know of you, Brother of Dragons.'

'I come on behalf of my sister, Ruth. Her situation is dire. Once, you said she could call to you in the harshest times. I am here before you now to ask for that assistance.'

Cernunnos hunched down over his massive thighs and scrabbled at the soft loam. Gently, he sniffed the breeze. 'A face of the Green lives within her, and she has carried out the Green's True Word to the best of her abilities, even at times of great trial. The Sister of Dragon's heart is strong.'

'Will you aid her?'

'I will.' He snorted; Shavi could smell his thick animal musk, even stronger than the horses'. 'What ails her?'

Slowly Shavi explained her capture by the Fomorii, the implanting of the black pearl, the suffering she was enduring as the medium for the rebirth of Balor; and as he spoke Shavi had the strangest feeling that Cernunnos already knew everything that was being said. After he had finished Cernunnos nodded slowly, grunting and snuffling. 'It was only to be expected that the Night Walkers would seek to bring the Heart of Shadows back to form, but the Sister of Dragons deserves better than to suffer their corruption.'

'What can be done?' Shavi asked. 'Other Golden Ones have refused to have anything to do with it. Some have said there is nothing that can be done.'

'Little can be done, it is true. The Heart of Shadows is a vile canker. Once established, it grows without respite. It is too hard in its corruption to be eradicated.'

'Then what?' Shavi stared deep into Cernunnos' gleaming eyes, trying to make sense of what he was saying. 'Is it hopeless?'

'Nothing is hopeless. We Golden Ones guard our secrets with pride, and this is mine: the Heart of Shadows can be removed without harming the Good Sister.' Shavi's mood brightened at once. 'The ritual must be carried out tonight, before the turn of the day when the moon is clear. And a sacrifice is called for.'

'Anything,' Shavi said without a moment's thought. 'I will do it.'

'Anything?'

Shavi nodded. 'She is a good person. She deserves more.'

'And you do not?'

'If there is anything I can do to help, I must.'

Cernunnos watched Shavi's face like an animal surveying something which could be prey or predator. Then he turned slowly, making strange, unnatural gestures with his left hand, and when he was facing Shavi again he was holding a small, smoky-coloured bottle with a wax stopper. 'Here is the radiance that will burn out the Heart of Shadows.'

He held out the bottle. Shavi took it gingerly. 'What will happen?'

Cernunnos' eyes narrowed until the light within them seemed like distant stars, but he said nothing.

The bottle felt odd in Shavi's hand, not like glass at all. He slipped it quickly into his pocket. 'On behalf of Ruth, I offer my great thanks for your aid. On behalf of all the Brothers and Sisters of Dragons.'

'Go with speed, Twilight Dancer. I have always entertained your forebears well.'

Shavi turned to leave, then paused, wondering if he dare give voice to what was lying heavy on his mind. 'When the Wild Hunt has been summoned, someone must die. Is that correct?'

Cernunnos said nothing; in the background the Hunt was growing restless.

'There are a young man and woman nearby. Do not take them.'

Cernunnos eyed him curiously for a moment, then nodded slowly in agreement. He looked towards the sun, now moving towards the horizon. 'When night comes, the Wild Hunt will ride.'

Though he had saved the young couple, Shavi felt the weight of his guilt: there would be yet another death on his conscience. Even the friendly powers that had colonised the world had no real respect for humanity; they agreed to whims with the gentle weariness of patrons who could turn suddenly if the mood took them. There would be no freedom until they were all driven out.

He bowed slightly, although it was a little curter than his greeting. Cernunnos made some strange animal noise, then moved back towards the riders, his shape slowly metamorphosing back into that of the Erl-King. After a few paces, he turned back towards Shavi, an enigmatic expression on his face. 'I hail your sacrifice, Twilight Dancer, and I wish you well in the Grey Lands.' And then he was gone, twisting and changing like sunlight on water. The horses moved away into the trees, the baying of the hounds more insistent; terrifying.

Shavi's shoulders sagged briefly, but then he pulled the bottle from his pocket. Here was confirmation that things were not all bad; that there were miracles among the nightmares. All he had to do was to reach Ruth before midnight. He checked the angle of the sun, then started to run across the parkland towards the nearest road. He would ride like the Devil was at his heels.

chapter twenty

VENCEREMOS

Church didn't know how he made it back to the house. The sword was his support over the rough ground, levering him up over rocks which were too much for his battered body to surmount. There was so much pain in every inch of him that he no longer focused on it; he simply floated in a cloud untouched by his senses. The most sensible thing would be to black out and rest where he fell, let his body heal a little. But night was not far away, and Lughnasadh was rising after that. Everything depended on the next few hours; a moment's weakness would doom them all.

Laura was waiting for him as he crested the last ridge, a look of such contempt on her face he thought she was going to punch him. 'Suicide boy,' she sneered. 'Looks like you got unlucky.' Then she saw the pain that was racking him. 'A close thing, though. Maybe next time, eh?'

He expected a supportive hand, but she marched back to the house, leaving him to make his own way.

By the time he reached the house he was feeling much better than when he had started his journey; the Pendragon Spirit was helping, coupled with whatever earth energies were focused within the tor, but he knew it would take many days to get back to full form; longer for his hand to heal properly. He had attempted to bind it with his handkerchief – the agony had almost made him black out. He would need Laura's help to fasten it up tightly enough for the bones to start to knit without any disfigurement.

But the moment he stepped into the house all thought of his own pain disappeared. Ruth was huddled in one corner, her belly distended and mottled grey, green and purple, as if it had been beaten with a stick. Her skin was drained of blood, the crescents under her eyes and the hollows of her cheeks so dark she looked as if she were close to death by starvation. There was no longer any ranting or delirium; her eyelids barely flickered and her breath was so shallow it was almost imperceptible. It was obvious the end was near.

Laura refused to look at her; she kept staring out of the windows or at the walls, as if there was something more interesting to see. 'So when are you going to put her out of her misery?' she said bitterly. 'I see you've found something for the execution.'

'There's still time,' he replied wearily; he didn't have the energy to deal with her baiting.

He knelt down and brushed the hair from Ruth's forehead; her skin was clammily unpleasant to the touch. Hesitantly he moved his hand down, hovering over her belly for an instant before he laid it on her skin. The instant he touched it something moved beneath. He snatched his hand away, stifling a cry of disgust. It had felt like a dog had snapped at him.

Laura must have seen something too, for there were tears in her eyes born of incomprehension and horror. 'How can that happen?' Her voice was a small child's. 'It can't really be inside her. Nothing's inside her, is it?'

Church rubbed a hand across his face, composed himself, then stood up and walked to the door. 'We'll give it till nearly midnight,' he said without looking at her. He had to find some place to rest so he could find the reserves he prayed were buried deep within him. 'We've got to have hope. There's still a chance one of the others could make it back.'

He felt her eyes heavy on his back, urging him to go back to her, comfort her. He paused briefly, then walked out into the afternoon sun, mentally preparing himself for what the night would bring.

The sun was uncomfortably close to the horizon when Shavi made it across the park to the nearest road. He was slick with sweat, his throat burned and his stomach was in knots, but none of it mattered; he knew instinctively he was the last hope for Ruth, for all of them. There was still time to make it back with Cernunnos' mysterious potion, just as long as he found a vehicle quickly.

Desperately he scanned the road in both directions. Normally there would have been a constant flow of traffic in both directions, but in the twilight of society's dissolution there was no sign of anything.

'Please,' he whispered. 'Whatever gods are listening—'

A white Renault Clio appeared from around the bend. Stifling a wave of exaltation, he took a step out into the road, furiously trying to think how he would convince the driver to hand over his vehicle, knowing he would take it by force if he had to.

As he neared he saw the troubled face of a white-haired old woman leaning over the wheel, peering ahead anxiously as if she expected a sudden rush of juggernauts. Suddenly she glanced in his direction and her expression froze in horror, her mouth a growing O.

What is wrong with her? Shavi thought.

He took another step into the road. She put a foot on the accelerator.

'No!' Shavi shouted. 'I need—!'

From somewhere nearby there came the strangest sound. It could have been the wind blowing across the park, but it sounded very much like howling. Sirens went off in his mind; there was something important he hadn't remembered. A second passed. And then he had it: the ritual in the woods with the travellers. The spirit construct hanging in the air, warning him, something about howling. Then he had it: *turn quickly.*

The pain in his back felt like a red-hot poker had been rammed through his skin. His thoughts fractured. He hung on to the image of the woman's face, her mouth growing wider and wider until he thought it was going to swallow her head; the car speeding up, rushing by, taking hope with it.

No, he tried to call, but his voice had gone with the car.

The howling, like a wolf.

And then suddenly he felt an arm round his chest, dragging him back, across the road, into the park, into the trees. He tried to fight, but in his shock his limbs felt like jelly, his thoughts in disarray.

Roughly he was thrust backwards, hitting the ground hard. His shirt felt wet near his shoulder blade. He could smell the meaty odour of the blood. Quickly his fingers slipped behind him. When he withdrew them, they were dark and wet.

The shock of the image kickstarted his thoughts into life and he threw himself on to his elbows, ready to drive up to his feet.

A boot cracked sharply on his right elbow and he fell back to the ground in pain. Before he could move again a figure was over him, brandishing a knife at his face. Shavi's immediate impression was of an enormous wolf and he knew at once that this was the creature that had stalked them from the Highlands. But gradually his perception fought back, struggling for the truth, and it was as if a mist was shifting from before his eyes.

The wolf began to grow smaller, the yellow eyes becoming less and less intense, until it coalesced into the shape of a man. At first, details were hazy, but as the veil was drawn back a feeling of revulsion slowly engulfed Shavi. The veins of his attacker stood out in deep black on his pale skin, as if they were filled with ink instead of blood. His eyes were lidless, the unchanging stare charged with a mix of insane fury and crazed despair. His teeth were rotting and blackened too, which made his mouth look like the gaping maw of an alien beast; although he couldn't possibly survive in that form, whatever the Fomorii had done to him kept him going.

It was almost impossible to consider him a man; yet in the straggly mane of silver hair and the shabby, dark suit, Shavi recognised him.

'Callow,' he hissed. Ice water washed through him at the thought of what monstrous things must have been perpetrated on the itinerant to transform him into such a thing.

But once the initial shock had dissipated, Shavi was overcome with a deep loathing. Normally he tried to maintain an equilibrium for all living things, but here was the man who had slashed Laura's face, sliced off Ruth's finger and delivered her into the hands of the Fomorii to be tortured; who had tried to sell humanity to the beasts for his own gain.

Shavi clapped his hand on his wound to staunch the blood flow; it didn't seem too bad. 'What have they done to you, Callow?' he asked, biding his time while he looked for a way out.

'What have they done?' Callow rolled his eyes insanely. 'Look at me! They've ruined me! Calatin's punishment for my involvement in the farrago which you and your pathetic colleagues brought about in the Lake District. Punishing me more for his own failures. The indescribable bastard!' He made a strange noise in the corner of his mouth which could have been a laugh or a curse; the insanity brought on by his suffering was writ large in every movement he made. 'And once he had tormented me, he didn't even keep me around. He threw me out into the world to make my own way.'

'You paid a terrible price—'

'Not fair!' He wiped his mouth feverishly with the back of his hand. 'It was your fault! All of you! You are the ones who should have suffered! That was why I sought you out. To make you pay.' He waggled his filthy fingers in front of Shavi's face. One was missing; the first severed finger they had found next to Loch Maree had been his own. 'Each one of you, a little pinkie!' He chuckled. 'The five fingers that held my fate in their grasp. I will sever each of you until I am free. And any other one who dares to hold me back.'

Cautiously, Shavi dug his heels in the ground and shifted his weight, ready to throw himself at his attacker if Callow dropped his guard. 'If all you wanted was revenge, why then did you deliver Ruth to the Fomorii?' Desperately he tried to keep the conversation going.

Callow's expression grew rueful. 'I thought she might buy my way back into the Midnight Court. She is the most powerful of all of you, you see. More powerful even than you. I explained to Calatin that this would make her the perfect vehicle for the return of their Dark Lord. The delicious irony! The champion of this world bringing about its demise! Calatin had no sense of irony, but he realised her strength would make her more likely to withstand the rigours of the pregnancy.' He chuckled crazily to himself. 'Pregnant! A virgin birth! They were going to use one of their own up to that point. So he took her, and then he threw me out again! But once I have eliminated the rest of you, he will take me back. I know he will.'

'Why do you *want* to return when they have done this to you?' Shavi could not keep the disgust out of his voice.

Callow did not seem to notice. 'He loves me. He shaped me with his own hands. I hate him and I love him too. There is nowhere else in this world for me now, unless it's by his side.'

In his words Shavi heard echoes of Tom's twisted relationship with the Tuatha Dé Danann. What was it in the psyche of humankind that made them complicit in the actions of their tormentors, he wondered?

Callow wiped his knife on Shavi's trousers, leaving a thin trail of blood. 'You have to give in to them, you see,' he continued, almost to himself. 'They're our gods. They control our lives.'

Shavi eyed the sinking sun nervously. He had to break free from Callow soon or all would be lost. 'We give in to no one. If humanity is to rise again, it will not come from kowtowing to any earthly power. We must seize control—'

Callow's painful laugh cut him short. 'You think they can be beaten?'

'Not easily. Not without a great struggle. But I believe it is man's destiny to rise, not to kneel in servitude.' The pain and the wetness in Shavi's back was starting to spread. The wound might not have been deep, but it still needed treatment or he'd bleed to death there, in conversation with a lunatic.

'You'll be the first to die. Then I'll take your finger. Or perhaps I'll take the finger first.' Callow watched him slyly with those permanently uncovered orbs like twin moons, glowing unnaturally white. He started to turn the knife slowly in his filthy fingers. Shavi watched his muscles tense, preparing to strike.

'We may be able to help you,' Shavi said with a comforting smile. 'The Tuatha Dé Danann have remarkable abilities and their opposition to the Fomorii may induce them to find a cure for you.'

'Really?' Callow's muscles untensed.

Shavi felt the relief creep into his chest. Now was the time to act. 'Yes. We can—'

Callow lunged forward like a cobra. The knife plunged into Shavi's chest with the force of a hammer, knocking him back on the ground. And again. And again. For an instant his thoughts flashed out and he was left in infinite darkness. When he came down he seemed to be buried deep in his head with only a tiny window to look out on to the world. There was an unbearable pain in his left hand, but he couldn't move to drag his arm away, couldn't even move to see what was happening. A receding part of him knew, but what remained of his conscious mind wouldn't accept the knowledge. It couldn't make sense of anything; there were just random impressions: the comforting feel of the grass against his cheek, the summery aroma of woodland, the feel of the heat slowly fading as the sun slipped down the sky, an overwhelming but fleeting grief that he had failed everybody, a snapshot of Ruth, Church, Laura, Veitch, Tom, Lee, his mother and father.

And then he heard Callow's voice as if from across a desolate pain: 'There is no cure. This is all there is – pain and suffering.'

The sounds of Callow shuffling away. Silence. Another face moving in towards him, familiar, but insubstantial; and it wasn't even dark. The guilt and regret. The voice that tormented him on a nightly basis, softly, so softly. '*You'll be with me soon, Shavi.*' Lee bending closer to tell him terrible things that would stay with him in the Grey Lands for ever.

And then there was nothing.

The sun was low on the horizon and long shadows ran across the Windsor parkland. Darkness had started to gather among the trees. From somewhere nearby came the forlorn baying of hounds. One shadow separated from the others and moved across the grass until it found Shavi lying in a pool of his blood. There was a brief snuffling around the recumbent form and then Cernunnos raised his antlered head and howled at the sky. It merged with the questing of the dogs into a sound that would have broken the heart of anyone who heard it.

Complete silence followed; no bird called, no insect chirruped; it was as if a blanket had been lain across the parkland, and that was somehow as unbearable as the noise that preceded it. Finally, Cernunnos groped inside Shavi's jacket and removed the smoky bottle he had handed over earlier. The god held it delicately for a moment, his head moving slowly from side to side, and then he loped back into the undergrowth.

Church sat on his favourite rock, watching the sunset. The sky had turned an angry red, almost apocalyptic in its intensity. His body felt like it belonged to someone else, a mass of aches and bruises highlighted by the throbbing in his hand, which had receded from its initial agony to a dull pain that made him feel sick. He had passed out briefly as Laura bound it tightly for him and she had chided him for that, although there wasn't much heart in her mockery.

445

The sword felt uncomfortable in his good hand, the strange, cold, metal more like the skin of a snake; sometimes he was even convinced it moved beneath his palm. The way he felt, though, he doubted if he would have the strength to use it.

He couldn't help continually checking his watch as he counted off the minutes until midnight. More than anything, he thought of Ruth. He recalled when they first met how he had the overwhelming feeling they were kindred spirits. Lying together beneath the sheets in her Salisbury hotel room when one of the Baobhan Sith was stalking only feet away. Sitting beside the campfire on Skye when she told him, 'We're not all going to come out of it alive.'

He bolstered himself with the thought that until Lughnasadh rose there was still a chance of the cavalry riding in to save all of them from damnation. Yet in his heart he knew a little piece of hope went with each glimmer of light that ebbed out of the sky.

Could he kill the woman he felt closer to than anyone, even though she was going to die anyway? Could he drive that last piece of life out of her, and watch as her face returned to innocence? For the first time in many years, he covered his eyes and prayed.

Laura sat in the corner of the room where Ruth slept, hugging her knees, watching the tremors that ran through the sleeping form. Seeing Ruth's suffering played out before her had been agonising, as much for what it made her think about herself as the effect it had on the woman she had professed to dislike. For so long she hadn't even been able to look at Ruth; now she could do little else. She didn't know if she was punishing herself, some subconscious reflex instilled by her parents' religious education, or if she was merely waiting for something to happen.

And she could sense they were on the cusp of something monumental. There was a feeling in the stale atmosphere of the room of unpleasant tension, as if a storm were about to break.

'Don't die,' she whispered. She told herself it wasn't a prayer, but then added, 'Bring Ryan or Shavi back with good news.'

She felt useless sitting around doing nothing, while heroic events were being played out around her. Was that why she'd been pulled into the whole damn mess – to act as little more than a cheerleader for others who had greater depths and more significant abilities? In fact, if she admitted it to herself, she had no skills, nothing to contribute at all; not even any homely wisdom to guide them out of a sticky situation. She'd been a coward, a fuck-up, jealous, divisive, manipulative, while secretly hoping some of the others' strengths would rub off on her. But all she'd got was

446

some hideous blood disorder that was doing God knows what to her insides.

Why *had* she been marked as a Sister of Dragons? What did she have to offer?

She covered her eyes, then regretted it when Church walked in because it made her look weak. He was too distracted to notice. His face was pale and drawn from the pain of the day; in the queasy, fading light he looked ten years older.

The deep currents of affection she felt for him began moving, as they always did when he was around, and her biggest regret was that she had never let him know how she really felt. Now it was too late. She could barely believe how, only a few weeks earlier, it had seemed perfect. She'd finally found someone she felt in tune with after a lifetime of searching; someone who was decent, hopeful, everything she wasn't. And, true to form, it had fallen apart almost the moment it had started.

''s up?' she said blandly.

His features grew dark and she knew the answer even before he spoke. 'I think it's starting.'

They crawled out on to the overhanging boulder and looked down at the pooling blackness far below. It took Laura a second or two to realise it was moving.

'They know where we are,' Church said. 'They're coming up.'

Laura shrugged. 'So, it's Alamo time. Well, it's not like it's a surprise or anything.'

Church looked at that fat, red sun hanging on the horizon. 'It's too soon.'

Laura followed his gaze, couldn't see anything. 'What do you mean?'

'I didn't expect them to make their move till after dark.' He gnawed on a knuckle, even more worried than he had been a few moments earlier. 'I've got to try to hold them off for a bit.'

Laura snorted with mocking laughter. 'Throw stones at them! That'll do some good.'

He rounded on her bitterly. 'I'm sick of your carping. Couldn't you say anything useful, even here at the end?'

'Sorry to be such an irritant, shithead.' She looked away so he couldn't see her face.

The black tide was rising quickly. Church was transfixed as it swallowed grass and stone, lapping ever upwards. At that distance Church couldn't make out any shapes within the greater mass, adding to the illusion of an ocean stretching out around the island of the tor; and with the sun so low it was impossible to guess how far it did reach, the night and the Fomorii merged into one. He guessed, from the average size of them, there must have been thousands gathered round the tor, ready to celebrate the rebirth of their own dark god and bear him back to whatever burrow they had made their own. And there he sat with a sword, nearly crippled by his injuries. If the situation wasn't so tragic it would be laughable.

The bitterness had drained out of him by the time he turned back to Laura. 'I want you to go back and sit with Ruth,' he said tenderly.

'Well, aren't you the big macho bastard. Send the womenfolk back to the homestead while you do men things.'

'It's not like that. Ruth deserves to have someone sitting with her, you know—'

'Up to the end?' She seemed to understand this. She stared back at the house impassively, and after a long pause, she said, 'You're not expecting me to do it, are you?'

'No. Don't do anything. That's my job.'

'But what happens if . . .' She struggled to find words that wouldn't hurt too much to say them.

'I'll find some way to get back in there to do what needs to be done before it's all over.'

She nodded slowly. 'This is it then. The fuck-ups fuck up big time.' Still nodding, she began to walk back to the house. She hadn't gone far when she turned and came striding back to him. The last rays of the sun highlighted the glimmering wetness in her eyes. She wiped them with the back of her hand, then threw her arms round his neck and hugged him tightly. 'I'd like to say it was fun, Church-dude. Bits of it even were. But I can say this – I'll never forget it until my dying day.' She kissed him passionately on the lips and then she was gone.

Church's thoughts turned to what lay ahead. He desperately tried to think of some delaying strategy to give him the added time he needed, but there were so many, whatever he did, they'd keep going right over the top of him towards the house. The building wasn't even protected enough for him to make any kind of stand. A pass in the mountains, that's where he needed to be, or at a bridge. Instead he was on a flattened ridge on a bleak mountaintop where they could come at him from every direction at once. Clever.

'Shavi. Tom. Ryan,' he said out loud. 'If you're going to make a move, now's the time to do it.' His words were picked up by the evening breeze and flung out over the countryside.

He sat on the boulder, his stomach muscles knotting, his heart beating faster and faster until he thought it would explode with anxiety. They were moving slowly, staying together in one tight corpus. It allowed him time to consider their nature. The times he had seen them en masse they had moved almost like one creature. He remembered the Lake District and how he felt like he was being borne along on a river of darkness. Perhaps that was the way to perceive them, as the embodiment of evil, one mind, one form, which could break itself down into smaller parts when called for. That line of thinking made his head spin. The Fomorii, and the Tuatha Dé Danann too, were so alien the only yardsticks he could apply to measure them were human ones which made no sense. There was a whole new set of rules and regulations out there which mapped the existence inhabited by those two races.

He wondered, with a note of dark humour, how the scientists were coping right then. Madly trying to apply their laboratory conditions to something which could not be measured or categorised? Going crazy trying to force all those square pegs into the round holes which comprised their intellectual life?

Yet, strangely, there were some parts of the Fomorii that were parallel to human experience, as if people had learned the baser part of their existence from the Night Walkers long ago. Or perhaps, he mused, everyone was cut from the same cloth. That thought was so depressing he wiped it from his mind immediately.

They certainly had a hierarchical structure, tribal in nature, with the different factions constantly rivalling. He guessed only the iron rule of Balor could keep them united, in fear and in the promise of ultimate victory over all existence. But while the Fomorii were like the barbarians in the outer darkness, the Tuatha Dé Danann reminded him of some emperor's court structure, but one that had passed its peak and was winding down into decadence and decay. How could they be gods when aspects of them were so human?

And so he waited. Halfway up the tor he began to hear those horrible animal cries and grunts that tormented his sleep. Then came the zoo smell, thick and stomach-turning. And then, finally, he could see them, no longer as one dark mass, but as swarming black insects, thousands upon thousands of bodies, scrambling upwards, clambering over each other, their shapes flickering in and out of his perception so that sometimes they seemed to have bony shells and wings, other times gleaming black armour, sometimes wielding twisted limbs with scorpion stings and lobster claws, other times brandishing cruelly deformed battle axes and those terrifying swords with the serrated edge along one side. It was too much. He had to withdraw from the edge as he felt the nausea rise to the point where he was almost blacking out.

He retreated until he was a few yards from the house door and then he took his stand again.

Laura watched the impending confrontation from the house with a mounting sense of desolation. All the suffering and heartache had come down to this: more failure. Behind her, Ruth had started to buck and writhe once more. *Getting ready to give birth*, Laura thought.

She wondered what it would be like to die, almost welcomed it in a way. But in contrast the thought of Church or Ruth passing filled her with an overwhelming sickness; it brought tears to her eyes.

As she blinked them away, she caught sight of a movement close to the house. Her stomach turned. The Fomorii had outflanked Church and were coming. It was an obvious ploy; they wouldn't leave their god in the hands of others for longer than they had to, she thought. She glanced round frantically for some kind of weapon. She'd go down fighting if she had to, protecting Ruth to the last. If only she could have had time to say sorry for all the terrible things she had done; for being so weak and pathetic and twisted when confronted by someone so unselfish.

Before the thought had barely formed, the door burst open and it was in there with her. Terror bloomed in her face and in that instant she knew it was over.

An age seemed to pass while the atmosphere grew charged with the overpowering force of an electrical storm; he tasted burnt metal in his mouth, felt disturbing vibrations run through the ground and into his legs. Although he tried to find that place deep within him where all his aspirations to heroism and bravery lay, when the Fomorii rose into view the cold fear that washed through him almost drove him to his knees.

The black tide came over the edge relentlessly. Images were caught briefly in his mind, disconnected: limbs that became tentacles before turning into articulated legs like a spider's, staring eyes that occasionally became multi-faceted like an insect's, body parts that looked like knives, wings that weren't, other shapes he couldn't decipher but which would haunt him for ever. There was one brief moment when everything just hung. Before him stretched the glistening blackness, the upper surface tinted deep red by the rays of the dying sun, swaddled in a stifling atmosphere of heat and tension. The acute impression of decay and corruption was almost beautiful in its intensity.

The sheer speed of their approach was terrifying; how pathetically naïve he'd been even to think he could do something to delay them. They swept across the turf and then rose up until they blocked out the sun. He waited for the black wave to crash down on him, pounding him into grains, but then it separated and flowed on either side until the serried ranks of the Fomorii formed a crescent around the house. And he was suddenly smothered in the stink of them, the sound of them.

Somehow he found the reserves to steady himself. He focused on some dim spot deep in his head so he didn't have to look at them, forced himself not to think about what the next minute would bring, hoped he didn't look like some weak, frightened *Fragile Creature*.

And then, in an instant, everything grew still. Wherever his eye flickered, nothing moved; the Fomorii may as well have been obsidian. The only sound was the plaintive whispering of the wind as it began to growing in intensity with the dying of the day.

What are they waiting for? he wondered.

And then he knew. A shiver of anticipation ran through the assembled throng and a second later the last glimmering of the sun winked out and darkness fell across the land. A sound rose up into the night like the rending of metal as the Fomorii gave voice to their feelings; Church gave an involuntary shudder. A second later silence fell once again, heavy with a different kind of anticipation.

Away near the edge Church noticed the darkness start to part, then reform, moving slowly towards him like a stingray slipping through the waves. He held his breath. The ripple broke at the front of the ranks and Calatin stepped out to face him. He was wearing a filthy white silk shift beneath unsettling black Fomorii armour and he was lightly holding the rusty sword that had killed Church at their last face-to-face confrontation.

'Here we are again, on the eve of another festival.' Calatin's fey voice was rich with contempt and triumph. 'Is one death not enough?'

Church said nothing, but his mind was whirling. The sun had set; perhaps there was still time.

'You chose well, Dragon Brother,' Calatin continued mockingly, 'hiding here in the blur of blue light rather than confronting us. Still betraying the tradition of the Pendragon Spirit. You recognise your abiding weakness in the face of a greater power—'

'We caused you enough problems in Edinburgh. Destroyed your base. Stole your . . .' Church paused for emphasis '. . . *prize*.'

A shadow crossed Calatin's face; his smile grew darker. 'And you discovered high-born Night Walkers are not easily despatched.' He limped forward a few paces, the sword almost too heavy for him to carry. The effort allowed him to compose himself after Church's gibe. He gestured up to the dark arc of the sky. 'This is a night filled with power and wonder. Soon, all of existence will align harmoniously, the cycles will turn further away from the light, and the Heart of Shadows will return once again to the centre of all there is. And you and your brethren will have played a part in that glory, Dragon Brother.' Another ripple ran through the Fomorii.

Church knew he would have to do anything to buy time. 'Why Ruth?' he asked.

'She is a powerful and resilient vessel, Dragon Brother. Stronger even than you.' Calatin smiled, as if this were the ultimate insult. 'The birthing cauldron must be able to contain the significant forces at play. She had that strength. It was not my initial belief, but when she was delivered to me the thought of a Sister of Dragons bringing about the return of the Heart of Shadows was so richly imbued with meaning, it had to be.'

Church tried not to let himself become angered by Calatin's words. 'You've been planning this—'

'This has always been our design. In the Far Lands, we were bereft – that was part of the pact agreed with the Golden Ones after the Sundering. But that could never have been our state in perpetuity. Without the Heart of Shadows, the Night Walkers are . . .' he made a strange floating movement with his hand '. . . insubstantial. And so we built the Wish-Hex to break the barriers and propel us out into this world once the cycles turned. And once here, we simply had to wait for the right alignment to set events in motion.' The light of someone seeking glory began to burn in Calatin's eyes. 'And it will always be remembered that I was the one who brought the Heart of Shadows back into existence. My tribe will hold the highest place. None of the others. Mine.'

'Balor isn't in your hands yet.'

Calatin stifled his tinkling laughter with the back of his hand before it broke into a hacking cough. Then he rested on the sword, one hand drooping over the handle, his chin almost hanging on top of it, while he surveyed Church with languid eyes. 'What goes through your mind now, Dragon Brother? Regret? Self-loathing at your inability to meet your responsibilities? What?'

'I'm not the person you met three months ago, Calatin. Now all my emotions are focused outwards. I feel contempt, for you and your kind, for all you outsiders who think you can come here and tell us how to live our lives. I feel a cold, focused anger for the pain you've inflicted on our lives. And for what you've done to Marianne—'

'Ah, yes!' Calatin made a flourishing gesture. 'Another failure on your behalf. I expected you to seek me out for vengeance, at the least. But you chose to abandon the one who occupied your heart while you entertained yourself with brief dalliances with others.' He punctuated his sneer with a sly smile.

Church knew it was designed to hurt, but it drove home nonetheless. 'Not *chose*, Calatin. I have learned to accept my responsibilities, whatever the cost to myself.'

Calatin laughed.

'You don't believe me?' He motioned towards the house. 'She's dead. I killed her earlier. And your god has died with her.'

A shiver ran through the breadth of the Fomorii, accompanied by a sound like knives being sharpened; there was a timbre to it that sent a corresponding shiver through Church. An incandescent fear alighted briefly on Calatin's face before he brought it under control. 'No! The resonance would have torn through us!' A tremor ran through his body; it looked like it wasn't going to stop. He couldn't prevent himself glancing towards the house. Then he half turned towards the wall of darkness at his back. 'If the Heart of Shadows was gone, we all would know.'

Now it was Church's turn to laugh.

Calatin rounded on him angrily. 'Besides, you do not have it within you. I have looked inside you, Dragon Brother, and you truly are too much of a Fragile Creature.'

'The only way you're going to find out is by going in there.'

The expression which rose on Calatin's face showed this was a prospect he relished; his smile froze cruelly. He raised one hand to bring the razored might of the Fomorii down on Church.

'What? You're not going to do this one-on-one again?' Church glanced towards the distant sky; still nothing.

'You remember—'

'Last time you'd hampered me with the Kiss of Frost. It wasn't a fair fight, it was a big cheat. You knew you'd win. Without that, I could beat you easily.'

Calatin's gaze wavered; Church could almost see every thought passing across his face: the reputation of the Brothers and Sisters of Dragons had sifted into Fomorii myth in the same way the Night Walkers and Golden Ones had entered human mythology; he couldn't quite be sure there wasn't some weight to it, that Church really could destroy him in an instant.

Church's palms were sweating as he gripped the handle of the sword. Things had reached a head. Every part of his rational mind told him it was time to throw in the cards, to run into the house and slay Ruth with one swing of his sword. But whenever he thought about it, his legs felt like lead.

And there was still time, he thought, still hope.

He raised his sword and prepared to face Calatin. And as he did, the strangest thing happened. Confusion, disbelief, then shock crossed

Calatin's face, he took a shaky step back. Another unnerving sound reverberated among the Fomorii, almost querulous this time.

'That sword . . .' Calatin pointed a tremulous finger.

Church eyed it curiously, then shrugged. 'Come on,' he said with a confidence that belied his thoughts. His hand was afire with pain and his body was racked with aches. 'Or are you going to back out now you know I'm ready to take you?'

Calatin raised his chin nobly, but his eyes flickered from side to side as if he were searching for a way out. There was an instant of brief despair that was so profound Church was taken aback, and then Calatin raised his own sword and advanced.

They circled each other warily; if either of them had expected an echo of their previous confrontation, they both soon realised the dynamic had changed. Calatin was cautious, his step unsure, afraid to come within Church's circle; that in turn gave Church confidence, although he couldn't grasp quite why things had altered.

Church knew his only hope was to eliminate all the negative impressions bearing down on him: the pain he felt from his many injuries, the physical and spiritual accumulation from weeks of striving, suffering and numerous set-backs. The upsetting wash of threat and evil that came off the Fomorii had to be put on one side, however much it felt like pins stabbing his flesh; but he had trouble shaking the rumbling paranoia that they were moving in to strike every time he turned his back to them. He fixed his attention on Calatin's face, a cauldron of conflicting emotions the Fomorii leader would have done better burying deep. In there, for the first time, Church saw hope.

The tension rose as they continued to move, feinting but never quite striking. And with each *faux* beginning to the battle Church could see Calatin's anxiety rising; he was *afraid* to attack, and just as afraid to continue dodging the battle for fear of losing face.

Eventually his twisting emotions proved too much for him. He lashed out, but even in his unfocused blow his remarkable skill came to the fore. All Church saw was the rusty, stained blade suddenly become a blur, whirling in circles before licking out. He ducked at the last minute, but the serrated edge still took a jagged slice out of the meat of his cheek; an instant's hesitation and he would have lost his head. He cried out in pain and a brief cruel smile leapt to Calatin's lips. The Fomor felt a surge of confidence from first blood, and pressed his attack with a rapid scything motion.

Church barely saw it, but his sword leapt up to block and Calatin's blade slid off with a bone-jarring clang. A coldness washed through Church's limbs; his sword had blocked it *of its own accord*. By rights he should be dead; in his pain-dulled state he hadn't seen enough of the attack to make any move himself.

He took his eye off Calatin to survey the grim, black sword. Calatin saw this opening and attacked again, lunging in an attempt to disembowel Church. The sword forced Church's arm to parry and then came up sharply, ready to attack if Church gave it the lead.

Church felt sick from the sensation; it was as if there was something alive in his hand. It no longer really felt like a sword at all; it was almost slimy and resilient in his grip.

When Calatin attacked again, this time swinging low in a bid to take off a kneecap or two, Church blocked it with ease. And at the same time he allowed the sword to guide him, putting his weight behind the attack. It passed through Calatin's defences easily and ripped open his forearm. Calatin howled wildly in pain. When it had passed Church saw the hesitancy of true fear in his flickering eyes. Church expected the ranks of Fomorii to show some sign of emotion at this weakness, but there was only utter silence; and that was more damning.

Church took a step back to inhale deeply; sweat was soaking through his clothes. He was ready for Calatin to seize the opportunity, but now his opponent was even more wary than when they had started.

Calatin moistened his dry lips, couldn't take his eyes off the sword. 'He gave it to you, did he not?'

Church ignored him, still breathing deeply. He was surprised to notice the perception of the blue fire Tom had taught him was now almost operating independently. Across the landscape he could see the thin azure lines growing brightly in the deep darkness. Some were broken, others intermittent; the land still needed to be truly awoken. But they were growing stronger. And there on the tor the earth force was strongest of all. He had a sense of being engulfed in a brilliant blue light shining up out of the ground; it was awesome and transcendent, and he could feel it seeping into every fibre of his being, refreshing him, starting to heal him. Above all, it gave him a deep sense of connectedness that added meaning to his existence, and from that he drew a deep, abiding strength. He was ready.

'I should have destroyed him,' Calatin said bitterly.

In desperation Calatin drove himself forward, hacking and slashing like a wild man. There was no sign of the decaying, fey persona he normally exhibited, just a driven, cruel ferocity.

But it was not enough. Infused with the blue fire, with the black sword dancing like a beast in his hands, Church moved sleekly to block every blow, returning each with a harder strike that drove Calatin back and back. A lunge came through and ripped open the Fomor's breastplate. Another sliced across the bridge of Calatin's nose; he howled again, flicking black droplets from the wound as he shook his head.

And still Church moved forward. A blow came down so hard that Calatin went to his knees to block it. He wriggled out and danced away as Church's next attack missed him by a whisker. But Calatin had nowhere to turn. The Fomorii forces were pressing too close, as if they were refusing to allow him to retreat; nor were they giving him any aid. And that was just how Church expected them to see it: in a race without any compassion, the weak should be allowed to perish so that the collective would grow stronger.

Although Calatin knew his end was coming, to his credit, he never gave in to his fear. It was only visible in his eyes, but to Church it shone out like a beacon.

Church bore down on him with the last reserves of his energy, all his joints aching from the explosive vibrations of sword on sword. A flurry of thrusting and slashing smashed through Calatin's defences, knocking his sword hand to one side. His chest was wide open for the killing strike, but Church knew there would be only a second before Calatin brought the sword back to block the blow. It was his moment of victory, yet he couldn't take it. Although Calatin was a god, there was too much humanity in his eyes.

Not a god at all, Church thought.

But the sword would not be deflected. With cruel efficiency it attacked, almost leaping from his fingers as it propelled itself into Calatin's chest, burrowing deeper like a worm in sand. There was too much black blood; Church had to cover his face with his free arm. Calatin bucked and writhed like there were thousands of volts going through him. As Church looked back he was struck by the expression on the Fomor's face: utter desolation that was almost painful to see. Calatin knew he was dying, finally and irrevocably, and for a being that thought he was an inexorable part of existence it was an ultimate terror that Church couldn't begin to grasp.

Sickeningly, the sword continued to vibrate in Calatin's chest, seeming to suck the life out of him, everything out of him. His cheeks grew hollow, his clothes and then his flesh began to fall in drapes on his bones, and then even the skeleton itself was pulled out of him. Church let go of the handle, but still the sword continued until there was nothing left of Calatin but a smear on the ground, and soon even that was gone.

But that wasn't the end of it. As the sword clattered on to the stone and turf, it began to change shape, growing smaller, sprouting legs like a scorpion, until it scurried off rapidly across the ground to disappear in the enclosing dark. And Church knew then that it was not a sword, but

Mollecht's own Caraprix, the strange, symbiotic creature that all the gods carried. But the vampiric qualities it had displayed in its final attack gave Church pause; he wondered whether the odd little creatures really did act at the behest of the gods, or if the gods were their puppets.

He didn't have time to consider the notion any more. The moment Calatin passed on, the Fomorii had begun to move warily, but now they had seen the Caraprix depart they were advancing on him menacingly. He wanted to fight them too, but all he could do was drop feebly to his knees, every last reserve of energy drained out of him.

This is it, he thought, more with weariness than despair. He'd done his best, more than he thought he ever could do. If he had failed, that was all he could truly ask of himself.

The Fomorii rose up in front of him, an enormous wall that must surely have been death. And up and up it went, his perception giving up as it tried to comprehend the eternal permutations of form. It hovered over him, like a tidal wave waiting to smash down on a coastal village, and he was cast in the coldest shadow he had ever experienced.

Church bowed his head, waiting for the strike. But the wave seemed to hang there interminably. In hesitant disbelief, he looked up just as it trembled, then twisted and finally broke apart in a wild thrashing. Dark, frantic motion erupted all around him, and he suddenly felt he had instead been sucked into a sable whirlpool. There was that strange rending metal noise he had heard earlier, faces that were alien, yet still filled with a recognisable fear, the rapid movement of fleeing forms.

And suddenly the whole night was lit in gold.

'Finally,' Church said, barely able to believe what was happening. 'The cavalry.'

The still-thrashing, dismembered body of a Fomor crashed into the ground in front of him, spraying foul gunk all around.

Another Fomor sent him flying several feet, and for a few seconds he blacked out. When he came round, chaos had erupted everywhere. The Fomorii were scrambling back and forth and the air was suffused with a high-pitched squealing like pigs in an abattoir. Church had to keep on the move to dodge the rampaging beasts, now oblivious to him. The ground had grown slick with the ichor that served as the creatures' blood and he was slipping and sliding, feeling his skin burn where it splashed up on him. Body parts rained from the sky, bouncing off him as he ran. In disarray and shock he had the awful impression he was looking at a vista from hell.

And then the blackness of the Fomorii parted and suddenly everywhere there was golden light, and before him was Maponus, moving through the scurrying forms like the righteous wrath of God, dealing out death and punishment on either side. Bodies burst into flames or just fell apart. Others were crushed by his powerful hands. His face was beautiful and serene, as if he were doling out salvation instead of carnage, but his clothes and his golden skin were covered in the black muck that sprayed out of his victims. As he advanced, his wide, innocent eyes staring out of a now-black dripping face, Church knew it truly was Hell. He fell to his knees in the face of such power, not strong enough to run any more. Maponus bore down on him relentlessly.

Before the Good Son reached him, a blur shot out of the corner of Church's vision, yanked at his shirt and dragged him across the grass out of the insane god's path. Church crashed, gasping, on to the ground and rolled over to look up into the face of the Bone Inspector.

'Nearly didn't make it.' The old man's eyes rolled with a hint of madness at the terrors he had experienced. 'Trying to drive him up here . . . get him to follow me . . .'

'You did good.' Church gripped the old man's forearm in gratitude. 'To be honest, I'd started to give up hope.'

'Never do that.' The Bone Inspector slumped down wearily, clutching his staff for support.

No longer able to talk, they both turned to watch the retreating darkness as the Fomorii swept down the tor like oil running off glass. Behind them the Good Son followed, wreaking his crazed vengeance for a spoiled existence; light flashed off him, wondrous and terrifying to see.

But when Maponus reached the foot of the tor, Church was surprised to see an odd effect in the sky, as if it were folding back on itself. And through it came riding members of the Tuatha Dé Danann, swathed in a diffuse golden light. At their head Church recognised Nuada Airgitlámh, who had helped bring him back from the dead on Skye. He was wielding the sword of power, Caledfwlch, which they had liberated from its hiding place. The five or six gods behind him were not known to Church, until he saw the final rider on a white horse with glaring red eyes. It was Niamh.

She couldn't shirk her responsibilities either, Church thought.

The Tuatha Dé Danann rounded on Maponus, herding him towards the rift in the air. At first he was reluctant, but then it seemed as if a small acorn of sanity in his mind recognised his brethren and he moved speedily and willingly towards the rift. A second later it closed behind them and the Golden Ones were gone.

Despite all the suffering he had caused, Church hoped the Tuatha Dé Danann would be able to find some kind of peace for Maponus after all his centuries in Purgatory. The Fomorii didn't appear to notice that their harrower had departed, or if they did, they were consumed with too much fear to give up their fleeing. The streams of shadows disappeared into the greater darkness of the night.

And then they were alone on the tor, a small island in a sea of carnage, as a sudden stillness descended over everything.

It was a moment that should have been savoured, but Church could no longer turn away from the horrors of his responsibility; there was nothing to distract him any more. He stood up, looking back and forth. Tears sprang from nowhere to brim his eyes.

'I wish I'd died,' he said honestly.

The Bone Inspector stared at him, uncomprehending. 'Where are you going?'

'To face up to my responsibilities.' Church looked along the bleak, million-mile walk to the house.

He flexed his fingers, wondering if he had it in him, knowing he had no choice. He sighed, brushed the tears from his eyes. He took the first step.

He was halfway across the distance, feeling his legs grow more leaden with each yard, when the door of the house swung open.

Oh God, not Laura now. He couldn't help a sweep of dismay at having to deal with her acid tone and cheap mockery.

But the figure that lurched out in a daze had a pale, beautiful face and long, dark hair. Church felt a swell in his chest that he thought would tear him apart.

And then he was running crazily, not knowing where the reserve of energy had come from, and he swept Ruth up in his arms and crushed her to him like some fool in a stupid romantic film. But it was honest, raw emotion: relief, and joy, and most of all, love. It filled every fibre of him to such a degree it was as if he were feeling the emotions for the first time.

He looked up into her face, afraid the features would change in some last, cruel blow, but it was definitely her. When he began to speak she silenced him with her fingers on his lips.

'No,' she cautioned. A panic seemed to be growing deep in her eyes. 'No. It's not like that. It's still bad.'

'What do you mean?'

She shook her head, unable to find the right words. Instead she made him put her down, then took his hand and led him back into the house. He looked round for Laura to join in the celebrations, but the place was empty.

'I'm so sorry,' Ruth said in a small voice.

459

chapter twenty-one

luGhnasaÐh

'It was like I was floating above myself. I could see and hear everything that was going on around me, and some things that were happening even further afield.' Ruth stared bleakly at the makeshift bed where she had lain for so long.

Church slumped in the corner, eyes fixed on the middle distance, too weary to attempt to rationalise anything. There was no sound apart from Ruth's voice and the occasional gust of wind battering against the aged walls.

'It was near the end . . . I know it was near the end because my consciousness was starting to break up like some radio station on the edge of its frequency. I could see what was happening to my . . . my shell.' She looked down at her belly, now returned to its normal size and shape. There was no sign of the disfiguring blemishes, and her skin had regained its usual colour. In fact, apart from the intense weariness that afflicted her spiritually as well as physically, there was no way of telling she had been through anything.

'You know, she wasn't as bad as we all thought,' she said, glancing up at Church.

'I never thought she was bad.'

'You didn't think she was good. I didn't. Especially me. And the worst thing was, she didn't even think it herself.'

Church let the exhaustion pull his head down. He could feel each breath going in and out of his lungs. 'What happened to her?'

'But she was good, you see. She deserved to be one of us.'

Church looked up sharply. 'What happened?'

'While you were out there facing up to the Fomorii there was a sound like an animal snuffling and scrabbling around the house. Laura got frightened by it. She looked round for anything that might make a weapon to defend

460

me. You know, she was pretty close to the edge by then, and not just because of what was going on outside.'

'You're pretty good with that perception.' It sounded a little more sour than he had intended.

Ruth ignored him. 'I think she was about to barricade the door when it suddenly burst in. It was Cernunnos.'

Church's brow furrowed. 'He came here? What about Shavi?'

Ruth shook her head. 'It wasn't his Wild Hunt persona. It was the pleasing side of him . . . the Green side. He had a bottle.' She was staring blankly at the wall of unintelligible writing as if the images were playing out like a movie. 'Small, smoky-coloured. He spoke to Laura—'

'What did he say?' Church snapped. His inability to understand her was grating on him; he could sense some mystery behind it all that he didn't want revealed.

'I didn't hear it all. But the bottle held some kind of . . . potion, I suppose . . . something that Shavi had been after—'

'And he didn't say anything about Shavi?'

'No, I told you. The potion was supposed to save me. It wouldn't destroy Balor. It would . . .' She struggled for the correct words.

'What?' Church said in exasperation.

Ruth took a deep breath to compose herself. 'He explained it all to Laura so she could make the right choice. He kept saying it was important she knew what she was doing. She didn't have to, there was no pressure, she could walk away – I remember him saying that, not quite in those words. But it was there if she wanted to use it. He wanted to help us, Church. He'd marked Laura and me—'

'A sacrifice. There always has to be a sacrifice.'

'With magic, yes.' She paused. 'I suppose there's a price to pay for everything.'

He put a hand over his eyes. 'What was it?'

'It wouldn't destroy Balor, but it could transfer him—'

'What?' He felt something cold and hard start to grow inside him.

'Cernunnos left the bottle on the floor and went. Laura stared at it for a while. I could see her face, all the emotions so raw on it . . . I wish I'd been nicer to her. I was a bitch.'

'She was a bitch. Don't start eulogising her.' What did he feel? Anger? Bitterness? He was surprised he felt anything.

'She took the bottle. I don't think she knew whether she was supposed to drink it or pour it on me or what. But when she pulled out the stopper this smoke licked up, and it moved like it had a life of its own. And suddenly I was in agony, I mean real pain, worse than anything the Fomorii did to me.

461

It was like wrenching, like . . .' She covered her eyes briefly. 'And the next thing I knew, Laura was face-down on the floor. Out of it. Completely. Mercifully. And Balor was inside her, or wherever he—'

'Christ!' Church chewed on a knuckle, staring at the floor, picturing the scene, wishing he couldn't.

'She transferred it from me to inside herself.'

'Christ.'

'She did it for me, Church. For all of us.'

'Christ.'

Ruth wandered over to the window. The Bone Inspector sat forlornly on the lip of the ridge, exhausted, but she didn't seem to see him.

Church looked round. 'Where is she, then?'

Ruth turned to him and her expression said it all. 'The Fomorii took her. While you were out there fighting Calatin, a few of them came in here. One of them was—'

'Mollecht.'

She nodded.

'He gave me what I needed to kill Calatin so he could seize control. And he took her?'

She nodded again. Then she came over and squatted next to him. He rested his head on her shoulder, acceptance crushing him down.

'So they have Balor. They've won.'

They drifted outside in silence. From their vantage point they could see civilisation lit clearly in sodium, the cities glowing orange in the distance, the village oases, the ribbons of lights connecting them, mapping out humanity's hegemony. Church checked his watch, waited. A moment later every light winked out as one.

'It's time,' he said bleakly.

From the south came a distant howling, growing louder. A wind tore across the countryside, bending the trees, ripping at the hedgerows, screaming up to them like lost souls en route to hell. The clouds tumbled before it, spreading out across the sky, obscuring the stars one by one until there wasn't even the light of the heavens to see by: only complete darkness, impenetrable, claustrophobic, too terrible for life. And in that awful howling wind Church could almost hear Laura's death-scream. It was all over. Balor had been reborn. The End of Everything had begun.

So this is the way the world ends, he thought.

Except it didn't. Things carried on the same, though sapped of hope, and everything he could pick out in the dark was dismally grey. There was the wind, quieter now, and Ruth beside him, unmoving. Or perhaps it was just an illusion, random flashes on his mind's eye. But it smelled the same, and it sounded the same, and that was worse than a sudden ending.

'I can't believe she's dead.' Church stared into the heart of the blazing fire, remembering Skye at Beltane when they thought they had suffered a terrible defeat; not really knowing what the word meant. Behind him, Mam Tor loomed up against the sky; he couldn't bear to stay on it any longer. But at least the initial shock and dissolution had finally subsided. Now there was only a sickening numbness as he tried to come to terms with what the future held.

'We all knew there was a chance we were going to get it at some point.' Ruth threw more wood on the blaze, enjoying the feel of the heat on her skin; despite everything, enjoying just being alive. 'I'm sorry, Church, that sounded really harsh and I didn't mean it like that—'

'I know, I know. We were all aware our lives were hanging by a thread. But however much you think about people dying, it never really prepares you.'

'It's a shock at the moment, more than anything because she was the last one you would have thought would have put her neck on the line. She never gave any sign—'

'That's because it was all going on inside.'

Ruth eyed him incisively. 'Did you know what she was really like?'

He shook his head. 'I knew she had depths, but I don't think anybody in the world really knew what was going on inside her head.'

'Did you love her?'

There was a long pause. 'I don't know. I don't think so. I *cared* for her. This sounds like some stupid sixth-form conversation!' He stood up and paced angrily around the perimeter of the firelight.

Ruth waited till he'd calmed a little before continuing, 'I wonder what's happened to the others.'

'I can't believe they're dead. I'm not even going to think it until I see the evidence in front of me.'

'You have changed, you know.'

He nodded. 'We both have. We've been to the lowest, darkest points of our lives and we've come out the other side. And I think we're both better for it.'

Ruth let his words sink in, then asked, 'Would you have killed me?'

He looked at her suspiciously across the fire, the dancing flames throwing curious shadows across his face. 'I don't know. I knew I ought to.'

'You were right. Of course you were. I would have done it to you. We have to think of the big picture—'

His look stopped her in her tracks; there was too much emotion in it, the backed-up excess of weeks of agonising deliberation. 'There is no big picture. The only one that counts is this one here.' He drew a small rectangle in the air in front of his eyes. 'Reality exists inside us, not out here.' He gestured towards the dark countryside. 'And sometimes one life is more important than millions.'

They stared at each other for a long moment, neither of them sure what to say next. They were saved from having to say anything in the too-charged atmosphere by the Bone Inspector, who strode out of the night with an armful of food. 'There are some houses down the ways. Nobody left alive in them.' He threw the provisions next to the fire and leaned on his staff for support; he looked hundreds of years old in the firelight.

'Are you sticking around?' Church asked him.

'No.'

'What are you going to do now?'

'None of your business.' He paused, then relented. 'There's a lot to do.'

'What's to do? We lost. It's over.'

The Bone Inspector snorted derisively. 'I was right. You are a pathetic little runt.' He was swaying backwards and forwards on his staff, obviously on the verge of collapse.

'What do you mean?' Ruth asked curiously. 'Balor's back. You saw the sky. You could feel it. At least I could, here, in the pit of my belly, like vibrations from a drill going off just under my feet.'

Church nodded. 'I felt it too, only for me it was a queasy feeling as if I'd eaten something rotten.'

'Everybody felt it, even the animals,' the Bone Inspector snapped. 'Something that big shakes the foundation of life.' He gave a hacking cough. 'Look around you,' he continued with watering eyes. 'Is it over? Has the world folded up and been put away? Are we dead and not realising it?' He dropped to his haunches, still holding the staff between his legs as if it were a rudder steering the world. 'Never give up hope. That's the message of life.'

Church noted how like Tom he sounded. He was surprised by how much he suddenly missed his old companion; he wanted the benefit of Tom's wisdom, and his incisive overview of any situation, however bad-tempered he always was.

'We could still do something,' Church suggested hopefully.

'You, not me. Of course you can still do something. That's what you're here for. *In England's darkest hour*—'

'I know, I know, *a hero shall arise.*'

'And if this isn't the darkest of all darkest hours, what is?'

464

Sighing, Church stared pensively into the fire. 'I wonder how long we've got before he starts wiping everything out.'

'He'll start straight away,' the Bone Inspector said. 'At least once he's recovered from getting dragged back into this God-forsaken world. He can't be in tip-top shape after being locked up on the other side of death for God knows how long. Then there's getting established in his new little nest,' he sneered, 'and motivating his troops, listening to all their whiny little pleas after all that time they've been separated from him.'

Church looked at him curiously.

'And of course he won't be at full strength till he's drained every last drop of power at the next festival, the big one on their calendar, when the gates really do open and all the worst nightmares in the universe come scurrying back to this place to be here for the end of it all.' The Bone Inspector fixed a cold eye on Church, almost daring him to continue.

Church glanced at Ruth. 'You're right, I have changed. Not so long ago I'd have rolled over and died at odds like that. But, you know—'

She nodded in agreement '—maybe there's a chance we *can* do something.'

'Don't get me wrong,' the Bone Inspector continued, 'the End of Everything *has* started. But it's still gathering pace. Maybe you can jam a stick in the spokes, maybe not.'

Church continued to look into Ruth's eyes and he was pleased at what he saw. 'Of all of us, I certainly don't think we were the most deserving. Veitch, maybe, Shavi, they were better than us in many ways. But we've learned a lot from all we've been through and maybe this is our chance to put it to good use.'

'Maybe we can finally prove our worth.'

'Rather you than me,' the Bone Inspector snorted; but Church glimpsed a faint smile before he wiped it away.

'This is our chance, then,' Church said. 'The last one. Rearguard action while the world's going to hell around us.'

Ruth pulled her knees up under her chin. 'It's amazing how brave you can feel when you've got nothing left to lose.'

Church realised she was right; surprisingly, he didn't feel any fear, nor any of the worries nor indecision that had dogged him before. There was a clarity to his emotions that gave him hope. 'What do we have to do?'

The Bone Inspector sucked in a weary breath of air. 'Are you expecting me to do it all for you?'

'I'm expecting you to use some of that knowledge that's been sitting around in your head gathering dust,' Church said sharply. 'We might not have got in this mess if you'd told us more before.'

'Don't get snippy with me. It's secret knowledge for a reason, you idiot. It's not there to be told to any little runt who comes asking—'

'Just give us some guidance,' Ruth pleaded. 'Where do we go from here? We've lost two-thirds of the people helping us – we don't know if they're alive or dead. We've got no idea what the next step is!'

The passion in her voice seemed to strike a chord with him. 'It's a good job you're here. I wouldn't have told that little bastard anything.' He pulled himself up on his staff and walked slowly to the twilight zone beyond the firelight; he appeared to be weighing up his responsibilities. 'All right,' he said eventually. 'But don't go asking me for anything else. The only way you're going to get anywhere is with the sword, the spear, the cauldron and the stone.'

'The Quadrillax,' Ruth said. 'But the Tuatha Dé Danann have them now.'

'And they're not going to help us while I've got the Fomorii taint in my system,' Church said despondently.

'Well you better do something about it, then, hadn't you?' the Bone Inspector said bluntly. 'Remember, it was the spear that killed the Great Beast last time. The sword, the spear, the cauldron and the stone are the only things in the whole of existence with enough power to do him in.'

Deep in thought, Church threw more wood on the fire so it roared away wildly. It seemed to him, at that moment, that the light was more important than anything and he had to do everything in his power to preserve it. 'When we came across two members of the Tuatha Dé Danann one night a few weeks back, I asked them how I could clear the Fomorii corruption out of my system. They said I should travel to the Western Isles to find something called the Pool of Wishes.'

The Bone Inspector shrugged. 'I wouldn't know about that. The Western Isles are somewhere in Otherworld, so the stories say. But I'll tell you this, there's another old story that says if you go down to Mousehole in Cornwall and stand at the quay and look across to Merlin's Rock, you can catch a fairy ship that will take you wherever you want to go.'

Church nodded thoughtfully. 'It isn't a lot, but we've gone a long way on much less.' The Bone Inspector dipped into his pocket and pulled out a half-bottle of whisky. 'Found it in one of the houses.' He took a long slug, then threw it to Church. 'You're at a turning point in your life. The mechanics of the mind are rituals. They tell that ancient bit at the back of your head to clear out the last cycle and prepare to move on to the next. This is your ritual, now – the best we can do under the circumstances. Make a toast.'

Church didn't have to think long. He held up the bottle and said, 'To absent friends. Let's hope they're all well. And to Laura, for being the best of all of us.' He took a drink and tossed the bottle to Ruth.

'I'll drink to that,' she said, 'and I'll say this. It's just the two of us now, like it was when we started. But that'll be enough. And we'll win.' There was so much fire and defiance in her voice Church almost believed her.

After that they sat drinking quietly, talking about their friends, trying to keep them alive with words; and at some point, they looked up from their discussion and found the Bone Inspector had gone, back to his age-old round of the sacred sites of their ancestors.

They moved as close to the fire as they could without burning themselves and kept it well-stoked against the oppression of the night. 'Do you really think we can do it?' Church asked above the crackling of the wood.

'Look what we've achieved so far.' Ruth slid next to him and rested her head on his shoulder; he put his arm around her. 'You killed Calatin—'

'With Mollecht's help.'

'But *you* killed him. And it was your planning that brought Maponus here to devastate the Fomorii forces. You pulled out a great victory when it didn't look like we had a chance.'

'There was a lot of luck—'

'And that's a quality a good leader needs.' She looked up into his dark eyes and smiled. 'But don't try lording it over me, all right?'

They rested silently, half-dozing, but too uneasy to sleep fully. Although they never discussed it with each other, they both knew the world had changed: a faint smell of cinders drifted in the chill wind and there was an unpleasant feeling of a great weight pressing in all around them. And though they waited and waited for the streetlights to come back on, they never did.

Somewhere away in the dark, the Heart of Shadows had started to pulse, a beat that was growing stronger with every passing minute; relentless, like the pounding of war drums signalling the End of Everything.

This story of the Age of Misrule
will be concluded in:

always forever

BIBLIOGRAPHY

Baigent, Michael, Leigh, Richard and Lincoln, Henry *The Messianic Legacy* (Corgi)

Brydon, Robert *Rosslyn – A History of the Guilds, the Masons and the Rosy Cross* (Rosslyn Chapel Trust)

Campbell, Harry *Supernatural Scotland* (HarperCollins)

Carr-Gomm, Philip *The Druid Way* (Element)

Earl of Rosslyn *Rosslyn Chapel* (Rosslyn Chapel Trust)

Hicks, Jim (ed.) *Earth Energies* (Time Life)

Hicks, Jim (ed.) *Witches and Witchcraft* (Time Life)

Knight, Christopher and Lomas, Robert *The Hiram Key* (Century)

Knight, Christopher and Lomas, Robert *The Second Messiah* (Arrow)

Lamont-Brown, Raymond *Scottish Superstitions* (Chambers)

Seafield, Lily *Scottish Ghosts* (Lomond Books)

Siefker, Phyllis *Santa Claus, Last of the Wild Men* (McFarland & Company, Inc)

Stewart, R.J. *Celtic Gods, Celtic Goddesses* (Blandford)

Tabraham, Chris (ed.) *Edinburgh Castle* (Historic Scotland)

Tabraham, Chris (ed.) *Urquhart Castle* (Historic Scotland)

Westhorp, Christopher (ed.) *Journeys Through Dreamtime* (Time Life)

Other books used were listed in *World's End, Book One of the Age of Misrule*